T0284817
I rose to my feet,
not as the true
PRIMAL OF LIFE,
but as a Primal of
devastating ruin and
WRATH.

BORN OF BLOOD AND ASH

ALSO FROM JENNIFER L. ARMENTROUT

Fall With Me
Dream of You (a 1001 Dark Nights Novel)
Forever With You
Fire in You

By J. Lynn
Wait for You
Trust in Me
Be with Me
Stay with Me

The Blood and Ash Series
From Blood and Ash
A Kingdom of Flesh and Fire
The Crown of Gilded Bones
The War of Two Queens
A Soul of Ash and Blood
Visions of Flesh and Blood: A Blood and Ash/Flesh and Fire Compendium

The Flesh and Fire Series
A Shadow in the Ember
A Light in the Flame
A Fire in the Flesh
Born of Blood and Ash

Fall of Ruin and Wrath Series
Fall of Ruin and Wrath

The Covenant Series
Half-Blood
Pure
Deity
Elixir
Apollyon
Sentinel

The Lux Series
Shadows
Obsidian
Onyx
Opal

Origin
Opposition
Oblivion

The Origin Series
The Darkest Star
The Burning Shadow
The Brightest Night

The Dark Elements
Bitter Sweet Love
White Hot Kiss
Stone Cold Touch
Every Last Breath

The Harbinger Series
Storm and Fury
Rage and Ruin
Grace and Glory

The Titan Series
The Return
The Power
The Struggle
The Prophecy

The Wicked Series
Wicked
Torn
Brave
The Prince (a 1001 Dark Nights Novella)
The King (a 1001 Dark Nights Novella)
The Queen (a 1001 Dark Nights Novella)

Gamble Brothers Series
Tempting the Best Man
Tempting the Player
Tempting the Bodyguard

A de Vincent Novel Series
Moonlight Sins
Moonlight Seduction
Moonlight Scandals

Standalone Novels

Obsession

Frigid

Scorched

Cursed

Don't Look Back

The Dead List

Till Death

The Problem with Forever

If There's No Tomorrow

Anthologies

Meet Cute

Life Inside My Mind

Fifty First Times

BORN OF BLOOD AND ASH

#1 *NEW YORK TIMES* BESTSELLING AUTHOR

JENNIFER L. ARMENTROUT

To see a full-size version of the map, visit
https://theblueboxpress.com/books/flesh-and-fire-map/

Born of Blood and Ash
A Flesh and Fire Novel
By Jennifer L. Armentrout

ISBN: 978-1-957568-78-2

Published by Blue Box Press, an imprint of Evil Eye Concepts, Incorporated

ACKNOWLEDGMENTS

Writing any book is hard, but the last book in a series? It's always the most difficult. You want it to be even more perfect. And getting it from my mind to your hands involves a whole team of people. Thank you, Hang Le, for your amazing cover design, and to Blue Box Press—Liz Berry, Jillian Stein, MJ Rose, Chelle Olson, Kim Guidroz, Jessica Saunders, Tanaka Kangara, the amazing editing and proofreading team, and Michael Perlman, along with the entire team at S&S for their hardcover distribution support and expertise. Also, my agents, Kevan Lyon and Taryn Fagerness; my assistant, Malissa Coy; shop manager Jen Fisher; and the hardworking team behind ApollyCon and more: Steph Brown, along with Vicky and Matt. Also, the JLAnders mods, Vonetta Young and Mona Awad, who help keep the group a safe and fun place for all.

I also need to thank those who've helped me procrastinate in one way or another—KA Tucker, Kristen Ashley, JR Ward, Sarah J. Maas, Steve Berry (for story times), Andrea Joan, Stacey Morgan, Margo Lipschultz, and so many more.

The biggest thank you to JLAnders for always creating a fun and often hilarious place to chill. You guys are the best! And to the ARC team for your honest reviews and support.

Most importantly, none of this would be possible without you, the reader. I hope you realize how much you mean to me. THANK YOU.

DEDICATION

For teachers and librarians—I don't know how you guys do it.
Each and every one of you is a true hero.

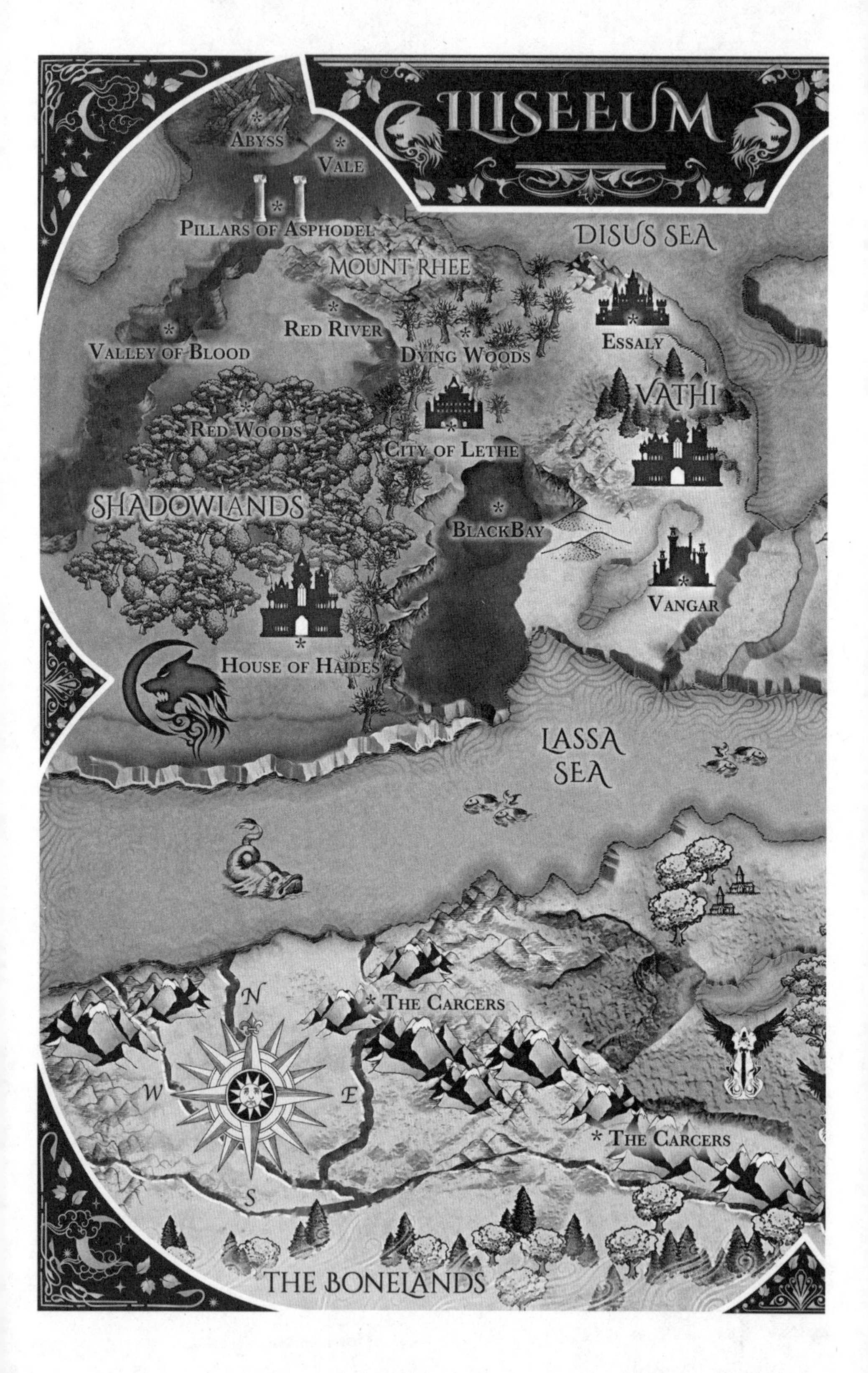

ILISEEUM
ABYSS
VALE
PILLARS OF ASPHODEL
MOUNT RHEE
DISUS SEA
RED RIVER
VALLEY OF BLOOD
DYING WOODS
ESSALY
VATHI
RED WOODS
CITY OF LETHE
SHADOWLANDS
BLACKBAY
VANGAR
HOUSE OF HAIDES
LASSA
SEA
N
THE CARCERS
W
E
THE CARCERS
S
THE BONELANDS

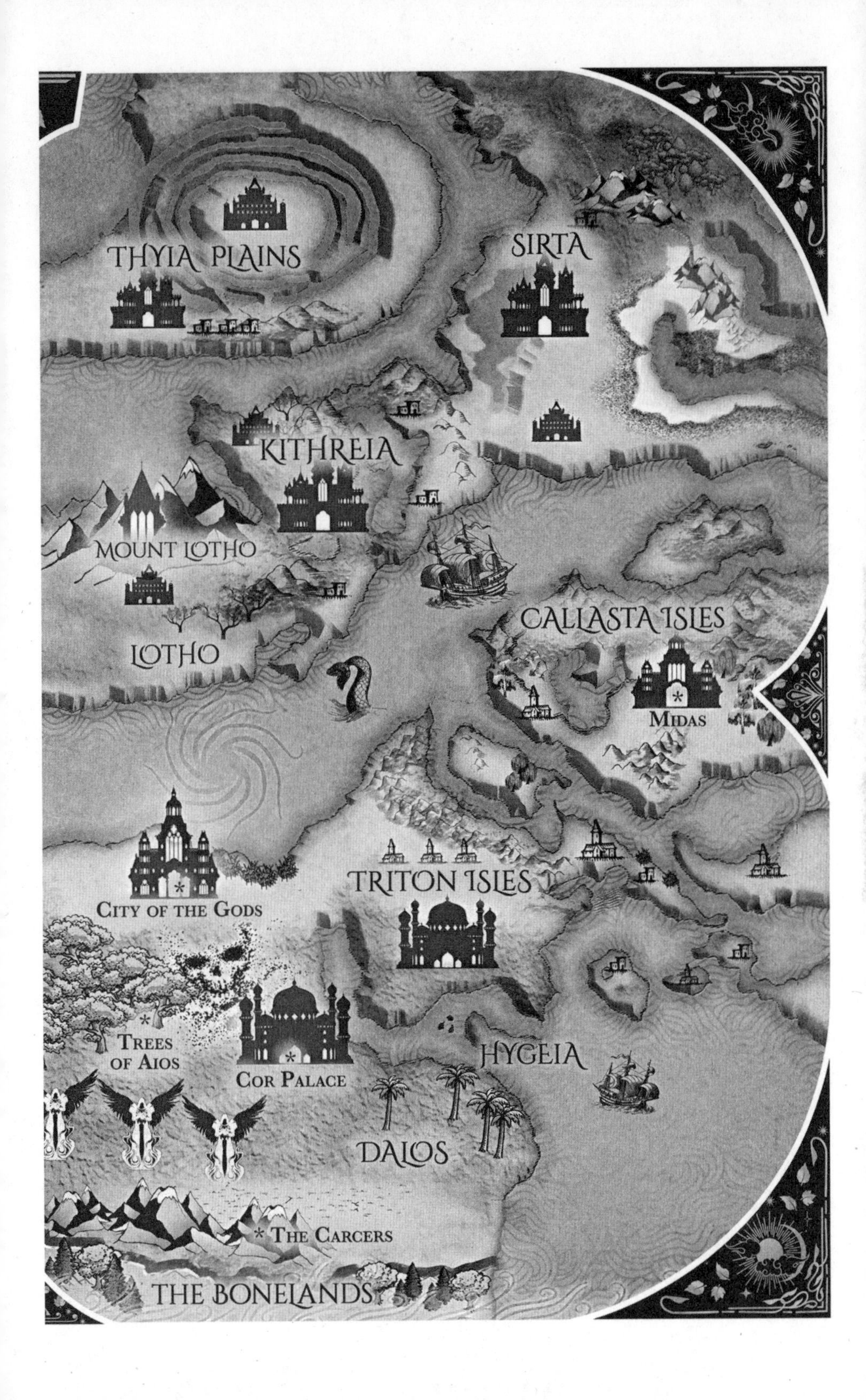
THYIA PLAINS
SIRTA
KITHREIA
MOUNT LOTHO
CALLASTA ISLES
LOTHO
MIDAS
TRITON ISLES
CITY OF THE GODS
TREES
OF AIOS
COR PALACE
HYGEIA
DALOS
* THE CARCERS
THE BONELANDS

PRONUNCIATION GUIDE

Characters

Aios – AYY-ohs
Andreia – ahn-DRAY-ah
Attes – AT-tayz
Aurelia – au-REL-ee-ah
Aydun - AYE-duhn
Baines – baynz
Bele – bell
Callum – KAL-um
Crolee – KROH-lee
Daniil – da-NEEL
Davina – dah-VEE-nuh
Diaval – dee-AH-vuhl
Dorcan – dohr-kan
Dyses – DEYE-seez
Eamon Icarion - AYE-mon IK-ayr-ee-on
Ector – EHK-tohr
Ehthawn – EE-thawn
Elias – el-IGH-us
Embris – EM-bris
Erlina – Er-LEE-nah
Ernald – ER-nald
Eythos – EE-thos
Ezmeria – ez-MARE-ee-ah
Gemma – jeh-muh
Halayna – hah-LAY-nah
Hanan – HAY-nan
Holland – HAA-luhnd
Hymeria - high-MAYR-ee-ah
Iason – IGH-son
Ione – EYE-on
Iridessa - EER-i-dess-ah
Jadis – JAY-dis
Jamison - JAYM-i-son
Kayleigh Balfour – KAY-lee BAL-fohr
Keella – KEE-lah

Kolis – KOH-lis
Kyn – kin
Lailah – LAY-lah
Lathan – LEY-THahN
Liam - LEE-um
Liora - Lee-OHR-ah
Loimus – loy-moos
Madis – mad-is
Mahiil – ma-HEEL
Maia – MY-ah
Marisol Faber – MARE-i-sohl FAY-berr
Mestra - MEH-strah
Mycella – MY-sell-AH
Naberius – nah-BEHR-ee-us
Nektas – NEK-tas
Nyktos – NIK-toes
Odetta – oh-DET-ah
Orphine – OR-feen
Pallas - PAHL-us
Peinea – pain-ee-yah
Penellaphe – pen-NELL-uh-fee
Phanos – FAN-ohs
Phena - FEE-nah
Polemus – pol-he-mus
Queen Calliphe – queen KAL-ih-fee
Reaver – REE-ver
Rhahar – RUH-har
Rhain – rain
Ronan Lesly – ROH-nahn LES-lee
Saion – SIGH-on
Sera – SEE-rah
Seraphena Mierel – SEE-rah-fee-nah MEER-ehl
Sotoria – soh-TOR-ee-ah
Taric – tay-rik
Tavius – TAY-vee-us
Thad – thad
Thierran - THEER-an
Theon – thEE-awn
Uros– OO-rohs
Varus - VAYR-us
Veses – VES-eez

Vikter Ward/Wardwell – VIK-ter WARD/WARD-well
Wil Tovar - WILL TOH-vahr

Places

Athanien Palace –ATH-ehn-ee-an pal-us
Callasta Isles – cah-LAS-tuh eyelz
Carcers [The] – KAR-serz
Carsodonia – kar-so-DON-uh
Cauldra Manor – kall-drah [manor]
Cor Palace – kohr pal-is
Creta - KREE-tah
Dalos – day-lohs
Elysium Peaks – ihl-LEES-ee-uhm peeks
Essaly – EHS-ah-lee
House of Haides – howz of HAY-deez
Hygeia – high-JEE-uh
Iliseeum – AH-lee-see-um
Kithreia – kith-REE-ah
Lasania – lah-SAHN-ee-uh
Lotho – LOH-thoh
Masadonia – mah-sah-DOHN-uh
Massene – mah-SEE-nuh
Oak Ambler – ohk AM-bler
Pillars of Asphodel – [pillars of] AS-foe-del
Skotos Mountains – SKOH-tohs MOWNT-ehnz
Sirta – SIR-ta
Thyia Plains – THIGH-ah playnz
Triton Isles – TRY-ton IGH-elz
Undying Hills – UN-dy-ing hillz
Vangar - VAN-gahr
Vathi – VAY-thee
Vita – VEE-tah
Vodina Isles – voh-DEE-nuh IGH-elz

Terms

Agna Adice - AYG-nah AY-dis
Agna Udex - AYG-nah OO-dex
Arae – air-ree
benada – ben-NAH-dah
ceeren – SEE-rehn
chora – KOH-rah

Cimmerian – sim-MARE-ee-in
dakkai – DAY-kigh
demis – dem-EEZ
eather – ee-thohr
eirini - ayr-EE-nee
eram - AYR-um
furie - FYOOR-ee
graeca – gray-kah
Gyrm – germ
imprimen – IM-prim-ehn
kardia – KAR-dee-ah
kiyou wolf/wolves – kee-yoo [wolf/wolves]
kynakos - KIGH-nah-kohs
lamaea – lahm-ee-ah
laruea – lah-ROO-ee-ah
lyrue – LIGH-roo
mayeeh Liessar – MAY-ah LEE-sahr
meyaah Liessa – MEE-yah LEE-sah
ni'mere - NIGH-meer
nota – NOH-tah
notam – NOH-tam
oneirou - AWN-eer-oh
por-na - POHR-nah
sekya – sek-yah
shrew – shroo
Sōl Eder - SOHL EE-der
so'lis – SOH-lis
sóls – sohlz
so'vit - SOH-veet
sparanea – SPARE-ah-nay-ah
stasi dato - STAH-see DAH-toh
stasi dato nori - STAH-see DAH-toh NOHR-ee
syhkik - SIGH-kick
te'lepe - TEL-ah-pee
tulpa – tool-PAH
unia - OO-nee-ah
vadentia - vah-DEN-chee-ah

NOTE TO THE READER

This book contains themes and/or discussions that some readers may find difficult to read. While there are no graphic scenes, there is mention of sexual assault, suicide, the death of children, and discussions of verbal, psychological, and physical abuse.

If you need to talk with someone about your experiences, there are people waiting to help.

Sexual Assault – General (RAINN) – 1-800-656-4673 or via their live chat
National Suicide Prevention Lifeline
(www.suicidepreventionlifeline.org) - 800-273-8255

The Asher

Nyktos, also known as the Asher, the One Who is Blessed, the Guardian of Souls, the Primal God of Common Men and Endings, the Primal of Death, and, currently, the God of Being Really Fucking Impatient, didn't want to be standing in the hall outside his bedchambers.

It was the last place Ash wanted to be when all he could think about was that his Queen—his mate of the heart, his wife, his entire world—was in their bed, waiting for him.

He'd only left her side a handful of minutes ago, but his flesh practically vibrated with the need to return to her. To look upon her. Touch her. Remind himself that she was safe, healthy, and alive. That her Ascension and the hours that'd followed hadn't been just a wonderful sort of dream.

Ash was desperate to remind himself that, despite everything he'd done to keep himself closed off from others, even going so far as to have his *kardia* removed, they'd still fallen together, cracking the thick shields they held close to their chests and shattering the barriers they'd erected to keep each other out. The sheer strength of Ash's will had defied fate. *They* had defied fate.

All because of what was most unpredictable.

The unknown and unwritten.

The only thing more powerful than the Fates…

True love of the heart and soul—*mates* of the heart.

But this conversation with Nektas was important. It needed to happen.

So, he would be patient.

Or, at the very least, tolerant of the interruption.

"The realm is quiet," Nektas shared, his voice low.

"For now."

"For now," the draken agreed, crimson-streaked black hair sliding over a shoulder. "The borders between the Shadowlands and Vathi are quiet. As well as the skies. There hasn't been any movement by Attes or Kyn, either."

Ash wasn't concerned about Attes—not that he didn't want to flay the skin from the bastard's bones. His hand fisted at his side. No. It was the Primal of Accord and War's brother that he planned to slowly, painfully eviscerate, starting by taking a strip of his flesh for every word he'd spoken to Ash while he'd been imprisoned—whether true or not.

"His Majesty was gracious enough to offer her to me once he tires of her." Kyn's eyes gleamed with a particular brand of sadistic joy as he got right up in Ash's face, thinking he was completely subdued. "Don't think she liked hearing that." He laughed. "Doubt she'll like feeling my cock in her ass either, but she'll come to enjoy it. Even beg for—" His words ended in a gurgle of blood and curses.

Ash had stretched the bone chains just enough to lift his arm and dig his fingers into the fucker's throat. Lost half the skin and a chunk of bone in the process, but he hadn't cared. He'd gladly do it again and again. That was how strong his fury was.

It was *still* that strong.

Just banked.

Eyes the color of polished sapphires locked onto Ash's. He was still unused to how the draken's eyes appeared now, but he recognized the look of understanding. Nektas knew where his mind had gone. He needed no bond for that. Not when the eldest draken was like a father *and* a brother to him.

Nektas's gaze slipped past Ash to the bedchamber doors. "Kolis remains hidden."

Shadows pressed against Ash's flesh, and the light from the wall sconces flickered wildly all along the hall. The mere mention of his uncle's name incited a rage so visceral it made what Ash felt toward Kyn seem…not so bad.

Because Ash *knew.*

Kolis had also liked to talk when he visited Ash. The difference was that he was smarter than Kyn and made sure to keep a safe distance from Ash as he spoke about Sera like she was his. Ash's jaw clenched, and the lights flared brightly.

"Ash," Nektas warned softly, stepping into the Primal's space. The blue of his eyes burned just as brightly as the lights on the wall.

"I'm level," Ash drawled, taking in a breath and forcing the violent, dark energy down.

An eyebrow rose. "You sure about that?"

He needed to be. "Yeah." He cleared his throat, and the lights dimmed around them. "How long do you think he'll be down for?"

"Hard to tell. A couple of days? A week?" Nektas's gaze flicked once more to the bedchamber doors. "I figure Sera is well?"

She was more than well. She was utter perfection. Still, he nodded. "She is."

"I'm relieved to hear that." Nektas paused. "Even if you did threaten my life the last time I knocked."

Ash felt warmth creeping into his face, clearly remembering telling Nektas that he would kill him if he didn't get the fuck away from the door. Then again, Ash *had* just eased his fingers from Sera's sweetness. "Yeah." He cleared his throat again. "Sorry about that."

Nektas chuckled. "No need to be. I remember what it's like…"

The light in the draken's eyes dulled, and man, Ash felt that in his chest harder and deeper than he had before. Because even with all the loss he'd experienced—his parents and those he cared for—it was nothing compared to losing one's other half. Their everything.

And Nektas had experienced that loss.

Kolis had made sure of it.

Ash clasped the draken's shoulder. "The oath I made to you before has not changed. Kolis will pay for what he has done to you and yours."

Nektas's nostrils flared on a deep inhale. "I know."

"Good." As Ash lowered his arm, the golden swirl of the marriage imprint along the top of his left hand glimmered. "I know the others want more than a brief update from me and wish to see Sera."

"They need to see her," Nektas responded, crossing his arms. "For themselves."

Ash understood that. The others needed to see that Sera was who they knew, confirm she hadn't lost her sense of self during the Ascension, and that she was exactly what they all felt.

The *true* Primal of Life.

But they would have to wait.

"I haven't gotten a chance to really talk with her," Ash began.

"Never would've guessed that," Nektas replied dryly.

A faint smirk appeared but then quickly disappeared from Ash's lips. "I need to talk with Sera before I'll be okay with the idea of *anyone* getting in front of her," he said. "I need to make sure she's okay."

Nektas nodded. "She's been through a lot."

"She has." He knew that, even though Sera hadn't shared much about her imprisonment.

But Ash *knew*.

Even if Kolis and Kyn hadn't run their mouths, Ash would never forget how desperate she was to know if he still looked at her the same way. And he knew *why* she would ask that, despite her claim that nothing had really happened to her. He knew exactly what could be done to someone to make them fear something like that. After all, he had firsthand experience in that fucked-up arena as both a witness and an unwilling participant.

A knot of sorrow and rage lodged in his throat, but he didn't let it choke him. If he did, it would choke her, too. "She'll need some time to get her bearings," he said. "I need you to make that happen."

"I can do that," Nektas assured without hesitation. "I'll make sure the others give you some space for the rest of the evening and night. I'll keep patrolling, just in case any idiots decide today is a good day to die."

A savage smile hit Ash's lips. He liked the sound of that last part. "May need more than a night."

"We'll cross that bridge if we get to it."

"I'll burn it if we get to it," Ash warned.

One side of the draken's lips curled, his attention shifting to the doors. "I doubt she'll even allow that bridge to be built."

Ash snorted. Nektas was probably spot-on with that assessment. "You're…" He trailed off as the sudden, tart taste of unease filled the back of his throat, an emotion he knew wasn't his. His spine went rigid. "I need to get back to her."

Nektas nodded. "She dreams." His gaze returned to Ash. "And they're full of unrest."

Surprise pierced the heaviness in Ash's chest. "You bonded with her already?"

"We bonded to her the moment she was born." Nektas's eyes shone a brilliant, luminous blue. "We just didn't know."

How could any of them have known? Only a few had known that his father, Eythos, had placed the last of his embers of life—and Ash's—in a mortal bloodline. And those in the know hadn't been any of them. Nor could they have expected a mortal to survive an Ascension and become a Primal. This was new territory for all of them.

Ash started to turn, then stopped. There was something else he needed to say. "Thank you."

Nektas's head tilted. "What for?"

A wry smile curled Ash's lips, and he clasped the nape of the draken's neck. "For your aid and loyalty all these years."

Nektas returned the gesture, and the weight of the draken's hand was grounding. "Our loyalty to you was forged in the sacrifices you made and from your strength of will, Ash. Our bond to you was earned and is no less powerful than a *notam*."

Ash lifted his chin in acknowledgment. "And Sera?"

A hint of approval filled Nektas's stare as he smiled. "She has earned it despite not having to." He squeezed Ash's shoulder and then dropped his hand. "Take care of her."

"Always," Ash swore, and it really was an oath—one he would spend an eternity fulfilling.

Leaving Nektas in the hall, Ash returned to Sera, slipping silently into the bedchamber. His gaze immediately found her, and it was as if time stopped.

She lay on her back, her silvery blond curls half-spread across the pillow and over one bare shoulder. He approached the bed, his eyes tracking those tresses down to where the rosy tip of her breast peeked through the strands, and then to the blanket he'd pulled over her before leaving the chamber.

The sight of her caused his gut to clench with need, but he checked his desire—something he probably should've done the moment she'd awakened. But damn it, he'd lost control. He didn't regret what they'd shared in the last handful of hours, and he knew she didn't either, but he also knew better.

As Nektas said, Sera's mind and body had been through a lot, and the evidence of one of those things was etched into her face now.

Her brows, a shade somewhere between dark blond and brown, were furrowed, creating a small crease between them. The freckles on her face—all thirty-six—stood out starkly against her paler-than-normal skin. Dark lashes spasmed against her cheeks.

She was dreaming. And it was full of unrest and unease.

Tension coursed through Ash as he pulled the blanket back and slid into bed beside her. Staring down at her, the sharp taste of lemon increased.

He wanted to know what she dreamed about, yet a weak part of him didn't.

Because he wasn't sure what he would do if he learned. Still, if he had to guess, it would probably be akin to what the vision—the one he had interpreted so fucking badly—had warned him about all those years ago. That he would set the realms on fire in his rage, leaving nothing but death and destruction behind.

And when he thought about Kolis, that was the kind of rage Ash felt. One reckless and wild enough that he would gladly see the realms crumble to dust if it meant he could witness Kolis's death. Because he didn't care how many souls his actions sent through the Pillars of Asphodel. He truly didn't. As long as Sera never had to worry about that bastard again.

However, his rage would inevitably harm Sera. Life could not exist without death. And vice versa. His rage would be the ruin of realms. Of *them*.

So, he needed to chill the fuck out.

Ash watched her, knowing she would likely punch him if she knew. His lips curled into a faint, brief grin. She seemed to have settled a bit, but he could still feel her unease. Hoping what plagued her would pass, he was reluctant to wake her. Sera had fallen asleep shortly after they'd made love, and she needed the rest. But after a few minutes of him keeping guard, her brows snapped together once more. Her hand twitched, and then her fingers curled into the blanket until her knuckles bleached white. Another emotion reached him.

Bitter and suffocating.

Fear.

Then she made a sound he'd rarely heard her make.

Sera *whimpered.*

Then screamed a word.

Just one.

No.

Ash's entire being split wide open.

Yeah, fuck. Lying there and doing nothing, even if it was just a nightmare, turned his insides to an icy mixture of anger and sorrow. A tremor ran through his arm as he lifted his hand.

Get your shit together, he instructed himself. She didn't need his anger right now. He closed his eyes and cleared his mind. What she needed was everything he'd denied himself after dealing with Kolis's punishments and that Primal bitch Veses' demands. Sera needed comfort and stability. Support. The tremor ceased. His chest loosened.

He checked his deadly anger. Lightly touching her face, his jaw hardened as she trembled in her sleep, a charge of energy passed through her to him, stroking the Primal essence.

Ash kissed her brow, easing the tension there. "Sera," he called, letting a little of his power seep into his voice. There was a chance it wouldn't work—compulsion couldn't be used against other Primals by anyone *but* the Primal of Life—but she'd just Ascended and wasn't anywhere near full power. He hoped it worked and then hated that he had that hope. Didn't like doing it at all. But he loathed her fear more. "Wake up, *liessa.*"

Ash's voice coaxed me from sleep. Feeling my pounding heartbeats slow, I forced a dry, almost painful swallow. My throat felt like I'd been screaming for days—years, even. But I hadn't screamed since the City of the Gods. Not since Dalos.

Cool lips brushed my cheek, and I immediately rolled toward the comfort of a long, hard body.. An arm lifted, giving me the space to nestle against his chest.

All the tension left me as I relaxed into him. That was his effect on me. I calmed. Every part of me.

Letting my hand rest against his side, I pressed my lips to the hollow of his throat. "I didn't mean to doze off."

Ash's lips brushed the top of my head. "It's okay, *liessa*."

Something *beautiful*.

Something *powerful*.

Every damn time he spoke that word, it washed over me like a gentle caress, filling my heart with an acute sense of belonging, of being wanted and cherished—two things I'd spent my whole life desperately wanting to feel.

"You were dreaming," he said quietly.

My stomach clenched. Had I shouted something? Was that why my throat felt scratchy? "I…I was?"

There was a pause. "You don't remember?"

"No," I lied, my skin prickling. "Was I, like, doing something weird?"

His lips coasted over my forehead once more. "No, *liessa*. You were just restless."

Oh, thank the gods.

I snuggled into him, trying to turn him into my personal cooling blanket. "How long was I asleep?"

"Not long at all." Ash folded his arm over my waist. "Less than thirty minutes."

Nuzzling the crook of his neck, I smiled. "Why do I have a feeling you're lying?"

"Because I am."

A raspy laugh left me, and his arm flexed, briefly tightening around me. "So, you were just trying to make me feel better about falling asleep after being in stasis for days?"

"The kind of sleep you experienced isn't necessarily restful," he explained with a level of patience I wasn't even remotely capable of. "Not when the body is going through such drastic changes." He paused. "And I haven't really allowed you to rest upon waking either."

Memories—some sweet and others downright scandalous—of the hours after I'd awakened from stasis rose and caused my toes to curl. "I'm not at all complaining about my lack of rest."

A darkly sensual chuckle teased the top of my head. "I didn't think you were." A hint of unadulterated male smugness had crept into his tone. "But the Ascension does take its toll. You need your rest."

"I don't feel like I need to be resting," I denied, speaking directly against the chest I was still plastered to.

"You should." He worked a knee between mine, managing to get even closer. "We have time. We have as much time as you need."

Time? What a funny concept. Sure, we had it, but how much? Not nearly enough. And we'd already spent quite a bit of it in bed, kissing, tasting, fucking, and making love while ignoring the realm beyond the bed.

Ignoring what awaited us.

And while I wanted nothing more than to remain in this place where nothing could touch us, unease bubbled beneath my skin. We had so much to deal with, and neither of us was prepared for most of it.

Starting with what I had become.

Ash's head turned slightly, and he pressed his lips against my bare shoulder, his fingers tangling in the curls there. "Have I told you how beautiful your hair is?" he asked.

My stomach suddenly twisted sharply.

That wasn't the first time he'd said that. Ash was as fascinated by my hair as I was by his smiles. He loved the pale shade. But I felt stagnant, heavy air. *Breathe in.* Smelled the suffocating scent of stale lilacs. And no matter how badly I didn't want to, I saw the true Primal of Death before me, his uneven smile fading. He looked at—no, he *scrutinized*—the color of my hair. I heard Kolis's voice—

"He hated my hair," I blurted, my heart thudding like a hammer against my ribs. I squeezed my eyes shut tighter, seeing bursts of white light.

Ash's fingers halted. "What?"

"Kolis," I whispered, realizing then that I was gripping his arm. I was with Ash, surrounded by his citrusy, fresh-air scent. It was *his* fingers in my hair. I was in the Shadowlands. Safe. Ascended and strong. Protected. But, most importantly, I was more than capable of defending myself. I forced my grip to relax. "He hated the color and brought it up often."

Tension poured into Ash's body, and his skin cooled even more.

Damn it.

I hadn't meant to take away his peace. Or maybe it wasn't me who had stolen it. Perhaps it was Kolis—who wasn't even here.

Ash's chest rose against mine as he took a deep breath. "Yet another example of how much of a fucking idiot Kolis is."

"Sotoria had red hair," I explained, picturing punching myself in the throat repeatedly. "I think that was the issue."

"I don't give a fuck *what* her hair looked like."

"It's not like it was her fault," I said, immediately defending the soul that, courtesy of Ash's father, had resided inside me until recently. Now, she—the only person who could truly kill Kolis—was in the Star diamond. But I felt protective of her.

I likely always would.

"I didn't say it was." His hand delved deeper into the mass of curls, and he gently guided my head back. "Sera?"

"What?"

"Look at me."

Was I *not* looking at him? Nope. Face burning, I opened my eyes. Only a few inches separated us, and all I could see were thick, black lashes framing irises the color of cooled iron streaked with white and lit by a glow of eather.

"I wanted you to be looking at me as I make you this promise." His voice was hard, as icy as the coldest, cruelest dungeon, and so at odds with how he handled me. "I know Kolis can't be killed. Not yet. But I *will* hurt him. Badly. I will make him wish he was dead. He will beg for it."

A shiver danced across my skin. I didn't doubt that oath. Not for one second. And while I wanted to be the one to cause the bastard unimaginable pain, Kolis had killed Ash's father and mother. And so many others. Kolis had caused Ash far more pain than I could comprehend.

"I have no problem with that," I said. "As long as I get a couple of minutes with him. With a very sharp object."

"Deal." His fingers curled around the strands of hair.

"I…" I trailed off, distracted. Having gained enough distance that the entirety of Ash's face came into view, I saw him—*really* saw him. All at once, the constant, almost chaotic stream of thoughts slowed. I scanned his features, and all thoughts of the realms disappeared. Wonder filled me.

It was like I was seeing him for the first time.

Everything about him appeared clearer to me. Details were apparent, vivid, and varied. His thick, wavy hair—even damp—was an array of browns, some dark and others light, mixed with hints of chestnut. One strand, already forming a loose wave as it dried, kissed the corner of lush lips a color somewhere between pinkish-red and brown. Another lay against the strong, cut line of his jaw. There was a shadow of stubble there I didn't think I would've been able to see before with my mortal eyes.

Good gods. How had I not noticed this the moment I came out of stasis?

Eyebrows that matched the darkest shades in his hair furrowed. "Sera? You okay?"

"Yeah." I dragged my gaze away from him and checked out the bedchamber, rising onto an elbow.

Only a small lamp by the bed had been left on. Normally, that wouldn't have been enough to make out any real details, but it was clear to me that Ash wasn't the only thing I could see better. The entrance to the bathing chamber had been left open, and I saw straight through to the other door that led to a private chamber used for meetings when Ash wanted to be near his personal quarters. I saw the vanity and could make out the faint strokes of gray in the marble. The marks left by a brush when the wood of the door had been stained were also visible to me. Even the glint of the shadowstone walls the lamplight didn't reach.

My stomach churned as I thought about what the false King of Gods had said about shadowstone. That it was slag: a combination of whatever had been melted by dragon fire—including things like *people*—and then cooled.

Gods, that still grossed me out.

His hand slipped from my hair and fell to my hip. "You don't seem okay."

"It's my vision. I can see things better. The chamber. You." I looked down at him. "How was I that unobservant to only notice this now?"

The release of the tension bracketing his expressive mouth was immediate. "You've been somewhat occupied since you woke from stasis."

"*That* occupied?"

One side of his lips kicked up. "It's also possible your senses are only beginning to heighten." Lashes lowered, shielding his gaze. "It's not always immediate, and it often happens in stages that can take a few hours. Even days."

I glanced around the bedchamber again. Heavy drapes shielded the balcony doors. "How long did it take for you?"

The cool tips of his fingers grazed the swell of my breast as he caught a curl and drew it back over my shoulder and behind my ear. "My vision was immediate."

I rolled my eyes. "Of course."

His grin kicked up a notch. "My hearing improved within several hours, but it took a couple of days for the rest."

"The rest?"

"Sensing the subtle shifts in those around me and the environment," he explained, causing my frown to deepen because I wasn't at all sure what that was supposed to mean. "And understanding the draken took a few days."

Surprise flickered through me. I stared at him, and then that strange sense of *knowing* kicked in. Ash really *could* understand the draken. All Ascended Primals could, as well as some of the oldest gods.

I'd thought he'd been joking or only sensed what they thought by knowing their emotions. But it was a combination of both. Sensing their general moods or needs and being able to hear their thoughts.

"It's called *te'lepe*," he continued. "A bond of sorts. A *notam* that allows the draken to transfer their thoughts to us. One can even form between them and gods, depending on how comfortable they feel with the god."

Notam? I frowned. Hadn't Attes mentioned that? I tried to imagine hearing the draken's voices in my mind and couldn't. "They can't hear us like that, can they?"

Ash shook his head. "I cannot, but I do believe my father could speak directly with them. So, you should be able to eventually."

I started to draw my lower lip between my teeth, catching the flesh on the tip of a fang before I could process what he said. "Gods," I hissed, wincing. "I'm not going to have a lip left at this rate."

He laughed roughly, the sound barely audible. Still, I heard the difference in the timbre. I loved his laughs because, like me, I knew he'd lived a long time without laughter. But now, there was a weightless quality to the sound. No restraint. A reminder that he no longer kept large portions of himself closed off from me.

Even though my lip stung, I dipped my head, bringing my mouth to his. The kiss started gentle, a soft proclamation of love, but a spark ignited, fanning the flames of desire coursing through our veins. His mouth molded to mine, catching the small droplets of blood I'd drawn. He parted my lips with his tongue, and he tasted like the oak and spice of the whiskey he'd drunk before I fell asleep.

And I knew that if I kept kissing him, we'd never leave this bed.

Reluctantly, I lifted my mouth from his and then collapsed onto my back with all the grace of a feral hog. "So…" I glanced over at Ash. His lips were still parted and slightly swollen, and the hue of his irises was a heated silver streaked with brilliant lines of eather—the Primal essence. The way he looked at me as if he wished to devour me… *Gods.* I quickly averted my gaze before I lost the rest of the restraint I was barely holding on to.

I cleared my throat. "I wonder how long it will take me to develop your special hearing. Hours? Days? Weeks?"

"It shouldn't take weeks." Ash settled onto his side, propping up his head with a fist.

"What if it does?" I questioned, twisting the ends of my hair between my fingers.

"It won't."

"You sound so confident." Meanwhile, I teetered on the edge of an anxiety spiral, even though I knew it was unnecessary. That was the messed-up thing about my mind that hadn't changed during the Ascension. Knowing there was no reason to worry didn't mean I wouldn't. It usually meant I worried *more.* "It's not like it's impossible. I *was* mortal. I wasn't supposed to Ascend. Something could've gone wrong. If it did, you'll need to, I don't know, exchange me for a…non-faulty Primal."

"Possibly."

My mouth dropped open, and my gaze slid to his.

Ash winked.

"Don't you be cute and wink," I ordered. "*Possibly?*"

He laughed, the sound still unshackled. "As if I would ever consider such a thing. Even if it were possible, which it's not." He caught my hand, pulling it away from my hair. "There's no one else for me but you. There never has been," he said, and my breath snagged, our gazes locking. "And there never will be."

"There is no one but you," I swore. "Ever."

"I know." His jaw hardened just a fraction, but his gaze was still soft and warm. "Which is why I'm still a little angry with you."

I frowned. "About what?"

"You wanted me to move on," he reminded me, gnawing at the words as if they left a bad taste in his mouth. "You wanted me to find a way to have my *kardia* restored and find someone to love. You actually said that to me, even though there is no way you, of all people, would've been okay with that."

"I said that because I was dying."

"Likely excuse."

"I think it's a very good excuse," I countered. "And what does *you of all people* mean? I spoke the truth when I said I wanted you to find love."

"That's bullshit, Sera."

"It's not."

His laugh was full of blades. "If I had somehow managed to restore my *kardia* and actually found someone else, you're telling me you wouldn't have found a way to haunt my ass?"

Crossing my arms below my breasts, I lifted my chin. "Absolutely not."

An eyebrow rose.

I held his stare.

He waited, then asked, "Really?"

"Yes."

Ash tipped his head down, stopping when only a few inches separated us. "I know who you are, Sera."

"I would hope so," I retorted.

"I know you are far more caring than you acknowledge. I know you're capable of unbelievable acts of kindness and sacrifice, which is only rivaled by your fierceness and stubbornness," he said, the glow of eather behind his pupils pulsing. "But you are not some holy, altruistic creature."

My lips pursed. "Well, I can't deny the last part."

"No, you cannot." Ash slid his hand over my folded arm, curling his fingers around one forearm. "Because, like me, you have a little bit of a monster in you. You're capable of cold, quick retribution. And I'd be lying if I said forgiveness pumps just as hotly in your blood as vengeance does."

I couldn't deny that I had far more monstrous tendencies than he did. He didn't attempt to wash away the stain of the blood he shed. He memorialized the lives he felt responsible for. My hands had never been stained. I didn't live with the lives I took. That would send most fleeing in the opposite direction.

Ash tugged my arms apart and brought his mouth to mine, nipping at my lower lip. "You give without thought, and you can take without hesitation. And, *liessa*, you're possessive."

"As if you're not," I said. "Did you forget how you basically promised to murder anyone I sought pleasure with? Or was that just…?" I smiled tightly. "More talk."

"Oh, I haven't forgotten. And I would've skinned the fucker alive, friend or foe." He kissed me, flicking his tongue over my fang. A sharp slice of pleasure cut through me, stealing my breath. "And you know what?"

"What?" I breathed.

"My promise to eviscerate whoever you used to satisfy your needs made you…" His lips brushed mine. "*Wet.*"

My chest rose on a sharp inhale. A mixture of embarrassment and desire scorched my cheeks. Well, it was mostly desire, with a tiny, barely-there dash of shame because he spoke the damn truth.

"And I know you would do the same. That part of me, right or wrong, recognizes that side of you. You love as fiercely as you hate." He lifted his head. "And just so we're clear, I believe you meant what you asked of me. It is the kindness in you that wanted me to find happiness. To live. But you wouldn't have rested peacefully knowing I was with another."

I opened my mouth but then shut it again. He started to grin. I *had* meant what I'd said. When I thought I was dying, I'd wanted Ash to finally and truly live. But *would* I have been at rest? Without him? Or would I have been one of those souls who refused to cross over? Deep down, I knew the answer. "Okay, I might've haunted you."

"No shit."

My eyes narrowed. "But I would've done it lovingly."

A laugh rumbled from his chest as he dropped his forehead to mine. "You are…adorable."

"Adorable?"

"Uh-huh." He brushed his lips over mine. "An adorably faulty Primal."

I moved to smack his chest, but he caught my hand and returned his cheek to his other hand.

He brought my palm to his mouth and dropped a kiss to the center. "Anyway, going back to the Primal changes." He lowered my hand to my stomach. "Have you noticed anything else yet, other than your heightened vision?"

I thought that over. "I don't think so—" I stopped myself, realizing there *was* something else. The intuition that was more a sense of *knowing*.

"I don't know if I mentioned it or not," I began, "but there's this uncanny sense of intuition I didn't have before. Answers—or knowledge—just form in my head at times. I experienced a little of it even before you Ascended me." I gave a small shake of my head. "It sounds ridiculous, but didn't your father have the ability of foresight? One he wasn't born with but developed upon his Ascension?"

"He did," Ash whispered, his eyes widening slightly. "*Vadentia.*"

"Foresight." Surprise flickered through me when I realized I understood the unfamiliar word spoken in a language I hadn't been fluent in before. "See! I don't know how I knew that, other than I just did."

"My father had the ability before Kolis stole the embers."

Curiosity sparked, fueled by the need to understand exactly what this ability was and its limitations. "Did he ever tell you about this…*vadentia*? Like how it worked?"

He shook his head. "If anyone would know the ins and outs of that ability, it would be Nektas. I'm sure he'll be around soon."

Making a note to ask the draken about it when I had a chance, I rolled onto my side to face him. "Is he not here?"

"I believe he's with his daughter and Reaver," he shared, skimming his fingertips down my side.

My heart squeezed as raw emotion twisted in my chest. I hadn't believed I would see the two young draken again. "I want to hug them," I blurted, feeling my cheeks warm. "Maybe just Jadis. I don't think Reaver would like it if I hugged him."

"He would." Ash pressed a kiss to my forehead, and I wondered if he had picked up on what I was feeling or if I had projected it. "You hungry?"

My stomach immediately woke up, grumbling rather loudly. I peeked up at him. "I might be a little hungry."

He chuckled. "There's fresh water in the bathing chamber," he told me. "Once you're finished in there, I'll get us something to eat."

"You don't have to wait on me," I told him.

"But I want to." He dragged his fingertip over my cheek and glanced down. "Plus, I get to continue enjoying the scenery."

Knowing that he was wary of leaving me alone no longer embarrassed me. Instead, his thoughtfulness and concern made my heart feel like it was doubling—maybe even tripling—in size. I leaned over and kissed him. "I would love for you to continue enjoying the scenery."

"Glad we're on the same page."

I grinned, letting my forehead rest against his. "But there are things we must do."

"There are." His fingers skated over my arm, leaving a wake of shivers behind.

"Important things," I said. "And I have a feeling the longer we stay in this bed, the less likely we'll be to get around to any of the important stuff."

"And *I* have a feeling," he said, his nose brushing mine, "that we fundamentally disagree on just how *important* the scenery is right now compared to those other things."

I laughed, relishing this playful, relaxed side of Ash that I'd only really gotten to see while still in the mortal realm before he brought me to the Shadowlands. That seemed like an eternity ago, and I hated to cut this short. "How am I being the responsible one right now? That's your job, not mine."

His lips curved. "I'm not sure I want that job anymore."

"If you retire from such a position, it will be pure chaos," I told him. "All day. All night."

"Good thing I like your brand of chaos." Ash's hand dropped to my hip, and he tipped his head back. His eyes, now a warm shade of steel, searched mine. "You sure you'll be fine?"

I nodded, and my heart filled to the point where it felt like it might burst.

"And you're telling me the truth?"

"I am." After everything with Kolis and almost dying, nearly being strangled to death in a bathing chamber no longer factored on the scale of things to be worried about. I didn't tell Ash that, though. Bringing up Kolis in that way or reminding him of what the godling, Hamid, had attempted wouldn't help.

"I'm good," I assured him. "You can go."

Ash hesitated but then nodded as if telling himself it was okay. I watched him rise from the bed and turn. My gaze immediately swept over the swirls of ink filling the length and width of his back as he retrieved a pair of pants. Those black blood drops were more pronounced against the warm, wheat-ish shade of his skin that held lustrous golden-brown undertones I hadn't been able to make out before.

The inked blood drops traveling over his back, along his sides, and down his inner hips represented those he'd lost. Lives he felt responsible for. And while the design was beautiful, it was also so very tragic.

There were far too many of them.

Hundreds.

He would never add another drop to his flesh. That was an oath I would not break.

Sitting up, I reached for the first piece of clothing, which turned out to be one of Ash's long-sleeved tunics. I pulled it on and rose to my knees, my gaze landing on the small wooden box with silver hinges sitting on the bedside table. There was a beautiful design carved into the wood, delicate vines that resembled the scrollwork I saw on the tunics of those in the Shadowlands and the throne room doors.

Ash had collected my hair ties, keeping them in that skillfully crafted box. It may seem like nothing to many, but it meant so much that he treasured something so simple merely because it belonged to me.

"By the way," he said as he pulled on loose-fitting linen pants. "The clothing Erlina made for you is hanging in the wardrobe." He faced me, showing off all *his* stunning scenery. And then he grinned. "Forget what I said about the clothing in the wardrobe. I want you like this. Always. It is the sexiest thing I've ever seen."

I raised a brow and glanced down at myself. The soft shirt was so long on me that it could double as a nightgown—a shapeless, baggy one. "Me wearing one of your shirts?"

"Yes," he said, the word a vibrating purr.

I looked up at him, and whatever I had been about to say vanished off the tip of my tongue when my gaze swept over Ash. He'd finished pulling his hair back into a low knot at the nape of his neck, showcasing the striking angles and planes of his face. There had always been an innate grace to how he moved, but now, even the fluidity seemed more apparent as he prowled toward the bed. It was like he was a part of the very environment around us.

My gaze lowered. The lines of his chest and the tightly packed muscles of his abdomen were more defined. I tracked the inked blood drops that appeared on either side of his waist and disappeared beneath his waistband.

"*Liessa*, you shouldn't look at me like that." The change in his tone drew my gaze to his. His voice had become richer, taking on a velvety resonance that caressed each word like a symphony of arousal.

I inhaled sharply, catching an increase in his citrusy scent. Was I imagining that? No, I *knew* I was really sensing his arousal. Not in the same way he could, by reading emotions, but there was no denying the newly discovered sense of awareness. I could *feel* his arousal in the echo of each heartbeat. This had to be one of those other developing senses Ash had mentioned. "Are you sure about that?"

"Unfortunately. Because you need to eat." He bent and curved his hand around my cheek. "I'll only be gone for a couple of minutes."

"Okay."

His eyes met mine as he tilted my head back. He moved closer, and when he next spoke, his lips brushed mine. "I love you."

My breath snagged on those three words. They should be impossible.

He tilted his head. The press of his cool lips was gentle at first but became fierce and hard.

My pulse was thrumming when he finally lifted his mouth from mine. "I—"

The balcony doors suddenly flung open, sending the thick curtains snapping toward the walls.

"What the…?" I trailed off. White mist rippled over the floor and began to rise. A strange scent reached me. Musky. Almost sweet. Eather throbbed intensely in the center of my chest, and every instinct in me told me this—whatever it was—had nothing to do with Kolis.

The change that came over Ash was swift. Shadows erupted beneath his flesh, swirling up his arms and across his chest as he whirled around.

Wisps of dark eather whipped out from his back, taking the shape of wings. I stared into the mist. Something was taking form. A guttural growl of warning rumbled from Ash, and he bared his fangs.

The skin along the nape of my neck tingled. I sensed something… "*Ancient.*"

I lurched from the bed and reached for Ash. My fingers grazed his skin as a charge of energy rolled through the chamber. "Ash!"

Darkness descended.

2

I woke on a hard, damp surface to a humming sound and a scent much like leather being tanned over a flame, but this smell was far too sweet and putrid. Way worse than the scent of stale lilacs. Where was…?

The white mist.

The darkness.

Ash.

I jerked upright, and my eyes flew open to a void of complete darkness.

"Ash!" I shouted, wincing as my voice echoed, mingling with what no longer sounded like humming but moans resembling a haunting chorus of hungry spirits.

A shiver tiptoed down my spine, causing tiny bumps to flood my skin, and that was all I felt. I pressed my palm to my chest, feeling the softness of Ash's linen shirt.

"Oh, damn," I whispered. There was no buzz of eather. No underlying thread of power just under my flesh.

I had to be dreaming.

Except…

Except the damp, cold stone beneath me felt too real, and that stench was so thick and rich I could practically *taste* it.

Suddenly, I remembered what I'd sensed before the darkness came. Something *ancient.*

My stomach churned, and I shifted onto my knees. Where was Ash? Panic knotted in my chest as I tried to make sense of what was happening. My throat constricted, making it even more difficult to breathe. I saw absolutely nothing around me as I started pushing to my feet. Just pitch-blackness.

Two pinpricks of silver light appeared. I halted in a crouch, my heart racing. The twin spheres seemed to double in size. Another set flickered into existence, and then a third, each growing as the one before them had. My lips parted, and I stared at the lights. I…I didn't think they were orbs.

They looked like eyes glowing with eather.

I slowly straightened, my already pounding heart speeding up. My fingers tingled with how fast the blood pumped through me. I may not be able to feel the essence inside me or that uncanny intuition, but all my other senses were firing. Sudden, icy dread seized me, turning my voice hoarse. I croaked, "Hello?"

The lights vanished.

A heartbeat passed. Other than the moaning, there was only silence. I took a step forward. A rush of charged air stopped me. Golden embers sparked in multiple places, igniting all around me. Flames erupted, casting a shining light onto the iron sconces. My gaze instinctively tracked the glow as it spread across dull, gray stone walls in some sort of cavern, bearing markings I'd seen in the Shadow Temples and on the Pillars of Asphodel—circles with vertical lines through them. The skin behind my left ear tickled. My Primal intuition kicked in then, and I continued following the light. Those marks were the symbol of Death. Of *true* Death—

I wasn't alone.

Every muscle tensed as my body flashed hot and then cold. Three figures sat before me on horseback, their heads bowed and cloaked, bodies hidden in robes of white that rippled. Three horses that were nothing but bones and tendons were also covered by pale shrouds.

I'd seen them before. At the Pillars. I remembered their names. I could even hear Nektas speaking them now.

Polemus. Peinea. Loimus.

War. Pestilence. Hunger.

They were the riders of the end of *everything*, only summonable by the true Primal of Life.

Every instinct I possessed, both the old and the new, screamed at me to run because these beings had never been mortal or god. They were primordial. Not Ancients, but created by them. That was why they felt like them.

But an innate knowledge warned me that if I ran, I would fail. I had no idea at what, so I held myself rigid.

The rider in the middle moved an arm, reaching inside the folds of its cloak. It withdrew a sword with a dull ivory hilt and a blade the color of blood.

"Prove yourself," a voice rasped through the air, rattling like old, dry bones.

My eyes widened when the rider turned the sword, holding it toward me, hilt first. I had a feeling this was Polemus. War.

Having no idea what the rider meant, I didn't dare move to take the sword. "W-where is Ash?"

Silence.

Maybe they didn't know him by that name? Seemed unlikely, but I cleared my throat anyway. "Where is Nyktos?"

"The Primal of Death is safe," the rider replied, its voice causing my skin to prickle. "Prove yourself."

"I want to see him."

"Prove yourself."

Chest thudding, I hopscotched between fear and anger. "I want to see him," I repeated. "Now."

"You must prove yourself, Primal."

The one to the left of the middle spoke, its voice brittle and aged. *Peinea*, I thought. Pestilence. "Prove yourself worthy."

"Prove myself worthy?" I stiffened even further, belly-flopping right into anger. "Of what and why?"

Words scratched their way from the third rider, who had to be Loimus. Hunger. "Prove yourself worthy of the crown and bearing the weight of Life."

"Yeah..." I scanned the space. There appeared to be no openings beyond some thin cracks and fissures, but there had to be. How else could I have gotten in here? "No offense, but I have no interest in proving that, nor do I have plans to summon the three of you anytime soon, so—" The stench of burning meat increased, threatening to choke me. "What is that godsforsaken smell?"

"Souls sentenced to the pits," Polemus answered.

My jaw went slack as the rider's words repeated in my head. The pits? That had to mean... "I'm in the Abyss?"

"Prove yourself," Polemus stated for what seemed like the hundredth time.

My hands curled into fists. "Look, I almost died, and that was *after* being held captive by an insane Primal. And now I've been taken into the Abyss against my will. So, thank you for that new trauma. I have no idea if my husband is safe or in the process of burning down the realm to find me—a realm I am supposed to lead, despite barely being able to finish a completed thought. And all I want is one nice night with my—" A horse whinnied, stopping my tirade. I forced myself to take a deep breath and calm down. These beings were as old as the Ancients. "Instead, I'm standing here in just a shirt, and I'm freaking hungry."

"Prove yourself," Loimus replied.

My head snapped in the rider's direction. "I swear to the gods if one of you says *prove yourself* one more time, I will—"

Polemus threw the sword at me. Literally chucked it without even a heads-up.

Cursing, I lurched to the side just in the nick of time. The weapon flew past me. "What in the actual—?" I gaped when the sword froze inches from striking the wall and remained there, hovering as if suspended by invisible strings.

"You must prove yourself," Polemus stated.

I closed my eyes and inhaled deeply. Immediately, I regretted doing the latter. The smell gagged me. Forcing my breathing to slow, I quickly thought over my options. I wasn't idiotic enough to challenge the riders, not when I knew they were something created by the Ancients, and I couldn't feel even a single bit of essence in me. And that earlier feeling? The intuition that warned me I would fail if I ran? It was still there, pressing down on me. I didn't really understand it, but apparently, I needed to do *something.*

I quickly came to the reluctant understanding that if I didn't do what they wanted, I would likely spend eternity here with the riders saying the same thing repeatedly.

Growling, I stalked toward the sword. The minute my flesh came into contact with the hilt, it warmed. I looked down, feeling the weight. It was almost as heavy as a broadsword. The weapon was some sort of crimson stone that reminded me of the sheer, vertical cliffs in the mountains of the Shadowlands.

My gaze shifted to the hilt. It didn't seem to be made of any type of common material. If I didn't know any better, I would've sworn it was made of bone. My lip curled in disgust. Yeah, it was best I not think about that.

"Fine," I barked, facing the riders. "Let's get this over with."

Polemus held up his right hand. I tensed, expecting them to charge me, but that didn't happen.

Flames roared, billowing toward the ceiling. Crimson light filled the markings etched into the stone. I took a step back, and the carvings all along the cavern suddenly appeared as if they were soaked in glowing blood.

"What…what's going on?" I asked.

There was no answer. Dust fell from the ceiling in a fine shower, drawing my gaze upward. A dark red glow filled the fissures there, the light becoming so radiant that it stung my eyes. My vision blurred as the light seeped from the cracks, spilling into the space between the riders and me.

With wide eyes, I watched the light pulse and grow, expanding until it took shape before me, becoming solid. *Terrifying.*

"You've got to be kidding me," I spat, and the golden flames calmed, casting dancing shadows across the cavern walls as I stared at the menacing green-and-blue-scaled creature looming over me.

I couldn't believe what I was seeing.

The beast was massive, at least twice as tall as I was, and had the body of a draken. Powerful legs and sharp claws that could not only clearly slice through flesh as if it were nothing but tissue paper but were also part of paws large enough to encircle the entirety of my waist. Its chest and torso were broad and muscular. The tail was thick and spiked, but that was where the similarities between it and the draken ended.

The thing had multiple heads.

Three, to be exact.

And its eyes, all three sets of them, were a brilliant shade of glowing silver, glinting with eather.

Possibly as bad as the three heads was its smell. It was rank. A stench somewhere between that of a rotting corpse and brimstone.

"Prove yourself," one of the riders ordered. "And slay the monster."

They expected me to fight this thing with nothing more than a sword? No armor? Not even a pair of boots or pants? And on an empty stomach?

"I feel like I'm extremely underprepared for this," I muttered, tensing.

Forked tongues hissing, the creature's left and right heads swayed in unison while the center remained still. It extended its long limbs, dragging wickedly sharp claws across the stone floor.

Breathe in. Reality or not, years of training with Holland had taught me that the first thing to do was to silence the mind. *Hold.* I couldn't think about Ash. What was happening outside the cavern, or what I faced after this—if I didn't get eaten by this thing. *Breathe out.* I couldn't even think about why this was happening. *Hold.* I had to shut it all down and focus only on the nightmare standing before me.

It wasn't like donning the veil of nothingness and becoming an empty vessel or a blank canvas. This was far more natural. There was no struggle or resistance when I silenced my thoughts and tensed my muscles. I became something I was far better suited for than being a Queen.

A fighter.

A warrior.

But that wasn't the only thing Holland had taught me. I firmed my grip on the sword. Sometimes, it wasn't best to strike first, especially when you weren't at a safe distance and were facing a new adversary. I had no idea what this beast was capable of, so I braced and waited.

I didn't have to wait long.

The middle head rose, coiling back in a fluid, serpentine manner that sent a chill of revulsion coursing through me. A heartbeat passed—

Striking as fast as the pit vipers found near the Cliffs of Sorrow, the left head shot toward me, its mouth stretching open to reveal fangs as long as my finger. I lurched to the side and then jumped back, expecting the right head to make a move. It did. The second head snapped toward me, leaving me only seconds to spin out of its reach.

Holding the sword level, I gritted my teeth and darted forward, my bare feet quick on the stone. I dipped under the sweep of the creature's claws and lunged, driving the sword into its chest. Or trying. The blade hit scales, and the impact jarred my arms.

Shock rippled through me, and I danced back. The scales were like some sort of armor.

Inching back farther, I caught sight of the shrouded riders and indicated with the sword. "You couldn't have given me something that actually works?"

"Prove—"

"Yeah," I cut Loimus off, focusing on the beast's scales. There were slivers of flesh between them, each maybe an inch or two long. "*Prove yourself.* You don't have to keep repeating it."

Like a mountain of muscle and scales, the beast charged, its claws digging into the stone. I spun to the right and dipped as it rose, thrusting up with the sword with more precision than before. I hit a spot between the scales, and there was little resistance this time. Flesh gave way. Cold, rancid blood spurted into the air, spraying my chest and face.

Gods.

The creature howled, rearing back as its tail scratched against stone and whipped toward me. Cursing, I jerked the blade free and jumped out of the way. I whirled, just as its right head struck. Lifting the heavy sword with a grunt, I spun and sliced down with the blade, aiming for the vulnerable spots between its armored neck scales.

My stomach churned as the blade sank through muscles and tendons. The creature shrieked, and the right head hit the floor, shattering into a puddle of foul blood.

Smirking, I leveled the sword once more and lifted my gaze. "So, which head—?" My mouth dropped open.

Before my eyes, red light streaked out from the stump as the beast thumped its tail. A brand-new head sprouted, mirroring the other two.

"What in the actual fuck?" I growled, frustration crashing into fury.

Anger pounded through me, and I lunged at the beast. It turned quickly, moving faster than I would've thought possible, and something Sir Holland had once said when he'd only been a mortal knight training me to fight registered.

"*Never let anger best you in battle. It is an act of a fool to use death's most favored weapon.*"

Gods, I was a fool.

Lurching back from at least two pairs of snapping jaws, I realized I'd taken my eyes off the rest of it.

An arm or leg—whatever—shot through the air. The beast seized me in a crushing grip. Bones ground together as it lifted me off my feet. Pain erupted, momentarily stunning me. My hands spasmed reflexively. The sword fell from my grip, clanging off the floor. With a ruthless jerk of its arm, it sent me hurtling through the air.

I slammed into the cavern wall, the contact knocking the air from my lungs. Agony shot down my spine. I hit the floor, rendered prone as a wave of torment crested.

A rider sighed. "Disappointing."

Sucking in a ragged breath, I rolled onto my side. "Comments are… unnecessary," I groaned, so done with this.

Shifting onto my knees, I rocked back. I caught sight of the sword lying a few feet in front of the beast. I needed to figure out how to take this thing down and do it quickly. Obviously, the space between the scales was vulnerable, but I'd pierced its chest. That had done nothing. And severing its head? It had simply grown another.

I lifted my gaze and peered through the strands of my hair. The two heads were swaying once more. The middle was still. Our gazes locked. Its eyes glimmered with more than just eather. There was hunger there, but also intelligence.

My gaze shifted to the other two heads. The glow of their eyes wasn't nearly as brilliant. Was it possible that those heads were more like limbs? If I took the middle one out, would it kill the beast?

I had no idea, but it was a plan—one that didn't involve getting thrown into walls again.

Rising to my feet, I was surprised to find that most of the pain had already subsided. The beast's gaze met mine once more.

One.

Two.

Three.

Four.

Five.

I rushed forward, dipping to grab the sword. The beast struck with the two side heads. My blade glanced off the scales of the left neck. Seeking to distract it, I spun and brought the blade down on that area. The stench of putrid blood increased. Sweat dotted my brow. Stone clashed against scales as I dodged the creature's relentless strikes and snapping jaws, dancing closer and closer until I saw spittle dripping from the middle head's fangs. *Breathe in.* Two of the heads drew back. *Hold.*

I lunged, blade arcing. With a swift slice, I cut through the air, the sword's tip striking the ground. Blood dripped from its length.

I'd found my mark.

The creature reared back, shuddering as it screeched. It stumbled, weaved toward the riders, and then moved away, its shrieks becoming quieter and less monstrous. Red light lit up the beast's body, following a scattered network of veins.

My breathing quick, I stepped back, torchlight gleaming off the bloodstained sword. The creature's legs went out from under it as the two remaining heads collapsed in a cascading, pulsing glow.

Lowering the sword, my lips started to curl up, but my smile quickly froze. Whatever triumph I'd begun to feel vanished.

Something was happening to the creature, and it wasn't death.

The beast was *changing*, its size shrinking and shifting under the flickering torchlight. Claws turned into hands and feet. Scales disappeared, replaced by flesh. Pants made of some sort of tattered burlap appeared, and…light brown hair. Suddenly, a male was on his hands and knees before me, trembling.

I knew. Dear gods, I *knew* before he even turned his head and I saw his features. Still, my heart stopped when my eyes locked with his—blue ones set in a face that had once been handsome but was now thin and filled with stark terror.

My stepbrother.

Tavius.

I went still, but my heart beat faster and faster. Unable to even look away, I stared at him, pressure clamping down on my chest.

He inhaled sharply, his entire body spasming. A guttural, wrenching sound came from his parched, cracked lips. His back bowed, body straining. His mouth contorted, stretching wide. Arms trembling, he gagged as something beneath the flesh and fragile bones of his throat *moved* upward, creating irregular bumps.

A fine tremor coursed through my arm as spittle ran down his chin. Strands of something several inches long that looked like slender, black ropes knotted at the ends fell from his wide mouth, spilling to the floor. He convulsed and continued to heave. His head kicked back, his jaw popped, and that cruel mouth of his gaped grotesquely around a thicker bundle of rope. Something oblong-shaped—solid and hard—pressed against his throat. His shoulders hunched violently as he gagged. His head bobbed—

Whatever it was worked itself free of his mouth, a handle attached to what I now knew were copper-twined leather strips.

A whip landed on the stone with a soft, reverberating thud.

The whip.

The one I could still *hear* hissing through the air. Still *feel* cracking against my skin. The one I had shoved down his throat.

Folding his arms across his chest and waist, Tavius rocked onto his knees. His entire body shook, and his head fell back. Saliva and blood-tinged mucus trailed from his mouth. Blood streaked his watery eyes. Our gazes met.

Time stopped.

It sped up.

"*Please*," he whimpered.

My reaction was immediate. I didn't think. I was past that point. I wasn't in the cavern before the riders. I was in Wayfair's Great Hall, bound to the stone feet of the Kolis statue as Tavius humiliated me. Hurt me because he harbored within him the same kind of relentless, rotten evil that Kolis had. Attempted to ruin me, not because he truly believed I was a threat to his claim to the throne of Lasania, but because he was a man, and he *could.*

Dropping the sword, I snapped forward and slammed the heel of my foot into his side. Bones cracked. I could still feel his weight crushing me… The bastard cried out as he fell onto his back, clutching his side, but all I heard was him demanding that I beg with *respect.* I kicked him again and again. I *stomped* him, hitting each and every one of those ribs and the shadows between them that were visible beneath his flesh.

That wasn't enough.

Neither was his death.

Or the revenge I'd already gotten. Falling to my knees over him, I gripped his hair and jerked his head back. I brought my fist down, over and over, cracking and shattering bone, seeing his sneer when he'd thrown that bowl of dates at my face. I saw only the cruel glee he took in tormenting Princess Kayleigh, not split skin and caved-in bone. I kept hitting him—

"Prove yourself." A rider spoke. "And slay the monster."

I sucked in a heady breath and jerked my arm back. My knuckles were smeared with blood. I stared at Tavius's unrecognizable features. Slay the monster? I could do that. Gladly.

Rising to my feet, I stepped over the trembling piece of shit and picked up the sword. I straightened and turned back to him, dragging the tip of the crimson blade over the stone as I walked back to Tavius.

The promise I'd made to him before whispered in the back of my mind, but this time, I wouldn't promise to see him burn.

That wasn't good enough.

I smiled as Tavius rolled onto his side, curling up as if he could make himself the small, insignificant man he'd been when he was alive. My grip firmed as he trembled and shook. The curve of my lips spread. "You will not return to the pits," I hissed, and this time, my voice was full of fire instead of smoke. "You will cease to exist in any form. Every part of you will be gone."

Tavius stilled, one swollen, half-open eye fixing on me.

"The physical body. Your consciousness. Gone. You will be no more," I promised. "I am going to end you."

That one eye closed.

I lifted the sword above my head, barely feeling its weight—

Do not allow this to leave a mark.

Ash… He had said that when he realized I wanted to deliver the final blow to Tavius. Ash, a Primal of Death, had granted my request.

I'd gotten my revenge, right or wrong. I had it. Reveled in it because Tavius was a bad man. He had it coming, and my hands had delivered it.

"Prove yourself," Polemus ordered. "And slay the monster."

My heart thundered. I'd already slain this particular monster.

"Prove yourself." Loimus's whisper was a stale wind against my skin. "And slay the monster."

I'd done as promised: I'd sliced the hands from his body. While I hadn't carved his heart from his chest or set him on fire as I'd wanted, I had done enough. I'd made him pay, and it had not marked me because…

I was a monster. Like Tavius, just of a different sort.

Panting, I held the sword tighter. If one of the riders spoke, I could no longer hear them over the rushing of my thoughts: Was this right? Did he deserve a final death? Could I even make that choice when it came to him?

Should I?

I blinked, my stomach churning. "I…"

"Prove yourself," Peinea urged.

"I can't," I said hoarsely. "It is not my place."

"You are the true Primal of Life," Polemus responded. "You may not rule the realm of the dead, but your will supersedes all."

My gaze cut to the shrouded riders.

"You are the *Agna Udex* and the *Agna Adice,"* Peinea said.

The Great Ruler.

The Great Condemner.

Robes stirred around Loimus. "It is your right, as you rule all. You hold within your hands the ability to reward and to condemn."

Dryness coated my mouth. My arm shook as my attention shifted back to Tavius.

"You did not hesitate before when you were in no position to take a life," Polemus said. "Why hesitate now when you bear the Crown of Crowns?"

That was a good question. It had been wrong then, and I'd done it without hesitation. I'd done it so many times, not really carrying any lasting guilt. Not even when I learned that by restoring the life of one mortal, I'd ended another's. Ash had said it was the influence of the Primal embers. Maybe he was right. Primals weren't meant to feel the way mortals do, not when it came to love and hate or life and death. Perhaps it was how I was raised—taught to become nothing. To feel nothing. It could've been the knowledge that I was nothing more than a sacrifice, a means to an end, that had sat side by side with me from the time I was old enough to understand my duty. Perhaps it was all those things that made me a monster of a different sort.

I didn't want to be that.

I never had.

But it was a choice. I knew that. Because Ash had carried that blood-soaked guilt deeper and longer than I had. Others were raised as I was, and some experienced worse conditions: being abused, neglected, or forgotten. Yet they were incapable of such terrible things.

I didn't want to be capable of such terrible things.

So, I made the choice not to be.

I would not be a monster.

"I will not condemn him." Staring at Tavius, I forced my grip to relax. The hilt slipped from my grasp, and the sword clanged against the floor. Murmurs came from the riders' direction, but something happened before I could look at them.

Tavius shuddered, and then he was…gone. There was nothing but empty space where he'd lain. The sword vanished in the next instant, and I stumbled back.

The horses each bent one bony knee, and all three of them lowered themselves. The riders' shrouded heads bowed, just as they had before on the road to the Vale.

"You have not slain the monster," Polemus said.

"But you have wounded it." This from Peinea.

"Because of that, you have been found worthy," Loimus added.

"Of us answering upon the time you summon us." Polemus's cloaked head lifted slightly, just enough for me to catch a glimmer of glowing, eather-lit eyes. "Until then."

Before I could say a word, their white-shrouded forms became transparent, like they were made of nothing more than smoke. Within seconds, I was alone in the torchlit cavern—alone with the knowledge that the monster I had been ordered to slay had been…

The one inside of me.

I stood in the center of the cavern for several moments, waiting to feel disturbed or, at the very least, shaken by the realization that the monster had been me. That the riders had somehow known what existed within me. A coldness that had always bothered and often horrified me.

Instead, I was *amused* by the symbolism of the multi-headed beast. That one could inflict as much damage as they wanted to the other heads, the parts of themselves that reacted to turmoil and conflict by inevitably causing more pain and heartache. One could continuously hack away at themselves, but it was the center head they had to face head-on. It was sort of like treating the symptoms but never the disease. And Tavius? I exhaled loudly, folding my arms over my chest. I doubted that had actually been the bastard. He was still somewhere in the Abyss, living his worst life. Either way, he'd obviously represented the part of me that could so easily be provoked and reacted violently to feelings of helplessness.

The part of me that could be horrific in its cold cruelty.

The monster inside of me.

And I got why they'd tested me. They wanted to know if I could control myself—my anger. That made sense since I'd have the ability to summon them, which, from what I could gather given what I'd been told and what my intuition confirmed, would bring about the end of everything. Clearly, they wouldn't want to serve someone who could get angry over something small and end the realms because of it.

My gaze flicked to the etchings in the stone. What left me unsettled was the fact that the riders had known I hadn't slain the monster.

I'd only wounded it. And did that by the skin of my teeth. Only because I didn't *want* to be the kind of person who made such choices.

But that *was* who I was.

The remaining question was why had they found me worthy when I hadn't succeeded? And even more importantly… "How am I supposed to get out of this damn cavern?"

The torches brightened in response, the golden fire rushing toward the ceiling once more. As the flames calmed, that crimson light reappeared in the markings, filling them in a wave that encircled the entire chamber. Stone groaned against stone. Half-afraid the cavern might fall on top of my head, I unfolded my arms. Dust and small rocks dropped in patches from the ceiling.

Before me, a glowing fissure appeared in the center of the wall, spreading toward both the ceiling and the floor. The crack increased in size, opening as rock ground against itself. It shuddered to a halt when the space became large enough for me to walk through.

"Um, thanks?" I said as if the cavern could somehow understand me. Maybe it could. What did I know?

Wanting to get back to Ash and make sure he was okay and hadn't, well, overreacted, I moved forward. The moment I entered the opening, the wall closed behind me.

Cold, inky darkness enveloped me, wrapping itself around each of my senses until all I could hear were those distant, haunting moans. I sucked in a sharp breath. "Damn it."

My steps slowed. I couldn't see anything as I forced one foot in front of the other, but I could feel a faint humming in the very core of my being. A spark of power—eather—ignited inside me.

"Thank the gods," I murmured, taking a deeper, longer breath.

Feeling a little better about the fact that I wasn't actually weaponless, I reached out blindly. My vision, as improved as it was, wasn't adjusting to the utter absence of light. Finally, I felt the cool slickness of a wall. Using it as a guide, I picked up my pace. Every couple of feet or so, I treaded across shallow puddles I absolutely refused to think about.

I followed the winding tunnel that twisted and coiled like a serpent, lost in the darkness until an orangey-red glow appeared in the distance. The scent of brimstone increased as I hurried toward the light, breaking into a run.

I burst out of the tunnel, and for a heartbeat, all I saw was fire—mountains of fire and winged creatures flying above the flames, shrieking as they carried thrashing bodies.

I knew what those creatures were. They were the ones Ash's friend believed had been visiting him at night and stealing his breath.

The *sekya.*

But I also knew their other names. Shrew. *Ni'mere.* Furie.

One of them dove, catching some helpless soul in its talons. Screams tore through the air—

Everything went dark.

I threw out my hands, coming into contact with smooth stone.

I jerked back, stumbling. My hip knocked into something hard. I looked down, recognizing the glossy shadowstone railing. The hem of my borrowed shirt snagged my attention. Confusion erupted. The material was worn but pristine, free of gore. Lifting my hands, I held them under the silvery glow of…*stars.* My knuckles weren't stained from blood or swollen as they should've been.

"What the…?" I spun around.

Open doors were in front of me. Open *balcony* doors. Heart thumping, I pushed off the railing and crossed the balcony. A sudden awareness pressed down on me, one that reminded me of the feeling I got when Primals were near, but this was different. The sensation didn't center only in my chest. It echoed throughout my body as I shoved the heavy drapes aside.

The bedchamber was dark, but I saw Ash asleep on the bed, his chest rising and falling with his steady breaths.

I had no idea how I'd ended up here from a tunnel in the Abyss, but in that moment, I didn't care. All that mattered was that Ash was safe. A shudder of relief went through me. I started forward.

A gust of air whipped across the balcony, sending strands of hair flying across my face. I caught a glimpse of a scaled underbelly. The largest draken and the first of his kind.

Shoving the hair from my face, I stepped back and looked at the roof of the palace just as Nektas landed with a shockingly quiet thud. Massive wings were spread wide, and the crown of horns along the top of his head glinted under the starlight as he dipped his broad nose to look down at me with vibrant blue eyes lit with the otherworldly glow of eather.

I gave him a rather jaunty, and definitely weird, wave.

The thin, vertical pupils constricted. Stretching his graceful neck, he tucked his wings back and then leapt from the edge of the rooftop.

Nektas shifted.

No matter how many times I saw a draken change from their true form to their god form, a breathtaking mix of awe and exhilaration consumed me. It was like he'd captured the stars from the sky and wrapped thousands of them around him. His body transformed as he fell, shrinking in mass while the shimmery spectacle faded. Arms appeared where wings had been. Fingers replaced talons.

My jaw unlocked as Nektas landed in a crouch on the railing, his long, crimson-streaked black hair slipping over coppery-toned flesh that was faintly ridged in the shape of scales.

Loose black pants appeared out of absolutely nowhere as he lifted his head. His eyes, their vertical pupils full of histories I couldn't even begin to comprehend, met mine. "*Meyaah Liessa*," he said in that rough, gravelly voice of his. "It is good to see you."

I started to cross the distance between us and embrace him, but I stopped myself. For starters, I didn't want to knock him off the railing. I'd also already offered an odd wave. I didn't need to add an awkward hug to the list.

But I wanted to.

Because there was a bond between us that I didn't even share with Ash, one forged on the trip to and from the Pools of Divanash. He'd heard the secret I'd whispered into the still, clear waters. That when I'd taken too much sleeping draft, it hadn't been an accident. I hadn't wanted to wake up. Nektas had heard that and hadn't judged me. He hadn't looked at me differently. All he had asked afterward was if I was okay. And then he'd said and done something I would never forget.

"*Not everyone can always be okay, and if you happen to find that you're not, you can talk to me. We'll make sure you're okay,*" he'd told me, and he'd done it while staring forward.

Giving me space while letting me know he'd noticed. Making sure I was comfortable so I could actually hear his words and know he cared.

It meant the world to me.

It always would.

I cleared my throat. "It is good to see you, too."

Eyes now the shade of polished sapphires flickered over my features. With everything that had gone on, I'd forgotten how their eyes had only turned the color of crimson after Kolis took the embers. "Are you all right?"

"Yes." I paused. "I think. I'm not entirely sure…" I glanced back at the bedchamber. "Something weird just happened. Or I *think* it did."

A breeze tossed strands of long hair across his chest. "You were tested."

"You know—?" I stopped myself, lowering my voice as I glanced back to the bedroom. "I don't want to wake Ash."

"You won't. He will sleep until the morning," Nektas explained, drawing my attention back to him. "All who inhabit the palace will. It was the same when Eythos completed the trial by blood."

"But Ash is fine, right? So is everyone else—wait." I frowned. "What did you just say about Eythos?"

"Yes, Ash is fine, as is everyone else. It is like…a spell. A harmless one."

I arched a brow. "A harmless spell?"

"Yes." A grin softened the hard lines of his face. "You were summoned by the riders, were you not?"

I nodded. "Yeah, they wanted me to prove myself worthy."

"The spell is to ensure that they're not prevented from testing the true Primal of Life," he said. "Eythos had to do the same."

I was a bit relieved to learn that I wasn't a special case. "It would've been nice of them to explain what they were doing instead of knocking me unconscious." I crossed my arms. "Because there's nothing like waking up in some dark cave in the middle of the Abyss."

"I doubt you were in the middle of the Abyss. You were likely on the outskirts," he said, as if that made a difference. "I would've warned Ash that this could occur, but it happened so long ago that it slipped my mind."

"You getting forgetful in your old age?"

Nektas chuckled. "I'm not considered old. More like…" He tilted his head. "Middle-aged."

My brows shot up. "Really?"

The wind swirled across the balcony again, carrying with it the scent of rich, damp soil. Chin tipping back, he closed his eyes. "It feels good to have the fresh wind against my flesh." He inhaled deeply, his lashes lifting. "All because of you."

"Me?" I squeaked. "I really didn't do anything."

"All because of you *and* him." He looked past me to the bedchamber. "This breeze I can feel? The life that has returned to the Shadowlands? My daughter touched a blade of grass today and will soon see clean water coursing through the lands." His vivid blue gaze, luminous with eather, returned to mine. "That is what your strength of will and his love has given my child. That would not be possible without the two of you. You survived. He persisted."

A knot clogged my throat. I turned my stare to the stars as I worked it free. "We didn't know it would work. All Ash wanted to do was save me."

"If either of you had faltered, if you were not as brave as you are or willing to love without condition or expectation? If he hadn't been so determined to save you or refused to believe that what he felt for you this whole time was love?" Nektas said. "You would've died, *Liessa*. And his pain would've turned the realms to ruin. That is not nothing. That is everything." He fell silent for a moment. "You didn't give up. Neither did he."

Swallowing around that tangle of emotion, I ignored the prick of pain as my fang scraped the inside of my lip. "I didn't want to die when he brought me to my lake. I…I stopped wanting that once I knew what it felt like to really live. Knowing that I'd finally be able to become something other than what my duty symbolized," I admitted, my voice hoarse. "It wasn't falling in love that changed that. It was that I could *feel* such an emotion when all I'd ever really felt was either anger or nothing at all. It was the realization that I could become *someone*—" The breath I exhaled was ragged. "Someone who mattered."

Nektas listened quietly as I continued, curling my fingers around my hair. "But I was prepared to die. I'd accepted it. I didn't give up. I gave in."

"So did Ash. You both gave in."

I thought about that. "I suppose that's one way of looking at it."

"It is the only way." Nektas watched me closely. "I don't think it's possible for anyone to be as uncomfortable when being praised as you are. Accept the praise. You have earned it."

I let out a short laugh. "Yes, sir." I peeked over at him. His bemused smile tugged at my lips, and it made me think of something. "Did you know? That Ash and I were heartmates?"

"There was no way for me to know that," he said, lowering himself from the railing in one fluid step. "But I knew he felt more than what he believed was possible when he had his *kardia* removed." Starlight glanced off his broad cheek. "I saw that in the way he spoke about you. How he cared for you. So, I began to suspect such, even with mates of the heart being so rare. Or perhaps I hoped for that since I didn't want to lose either of you."

It took me several moments to speak around the rising knot of emotion. "You know, you didn't even ask if I passed the riders' test."

"I don't need to ask." Angling his body toward mine, he propped his hip against the railing. "I know you did. You are worthy, *Liessa*."

"I'm beginning to think you're just trying to make me uncomfortable now," I muttered.

"I would never."

"Uh-huh." Something occurred to me. "Do you remember what Eythos's abilities of intuition were like?"

"I do." He turned toward me as the wind tossed his hair across his chest again. "I assume the ability is also developing in you?"

I nodded.

"What do you want to know?"

"Everything." I laughed, loosening my grip on the railing. "But mostly, I wanted to know if you knew how it works. Because it's like…one second, I feel this strange sensation and just know something. And the next, I have no idea, especially if it has anything to do with me."

"I don't know all the fine details." Nektas rubbed his chin. "But I do know that the *vadentia* became stronger as time passed. Eythos could look at a person and know nearly everything about them."

I frowned. "I don't think I can do that."

"It took Eythos several years before he could." The skin between Nektas's brows creased. "But the embers were already maturing in you long before your Ascension. It wasn't like that for Eythos. It may develop sooner in you."

I mulled that over. "Possibly. I mean, those embers had matured in Eythos and even in *Ash* to some extent before they were placed in my bloodline."

Nektas nodded. "But the intuition never worked regarding him either."

A measure of relief hit me. "So, it's not just me being broken or something?"

The furrow in the skin between Nektas's brows deepened. "No, I think it's more likely that it has something to do with balance."

"That's what Eythos believed?"

"Yes. It wouldn't be fair if one knew how every action and choice affected them, now would it?" Nektas offered up. "It would upset the balance."

"I guess." I wasn't sure what the Fates—the Ancients—had in mind when it came to restoring balance or if it actually helped. Their actions often seemed rather counterproductive.

"Ah, I just remembered something else." Nektas's brow smoothed out. "Usually, he had to think about what he wanted to know. Give himself time to, as he put it, listen to what the realm was telling him. That was hard for him."

I grinned, knowing exactly what he meant. Sometimes, I didn't allow a thought to finish before I spoke or another thought came.

"I know he was able to sense unrest within Iliseeum and eventually the mortal realm. I'm not sure if that was the *vadentia* or because he was the true Primal of Life, but he could feel the unrest in Iliseeum before sensing something happening in the mortal realm," he told me, the furrow between his brow deepening. "But there was something else. Sometimes, a feeling hit him—usually out of nowhere. It was like an urge, guiding him to either a place or a person. Even sometimes an object. When it came, he couldn't ignore it. It would drive him mad at times, especially when it hit in the middle of the night." Nektas brushed his hair back from his face. "And he didn't like not knowing where it was leading him or why."

That hadn't happened to me. Yet. "What were some of the reasons he was led to something?"

"It really varied." Nektas squinted, seemingly looking back through time. I wondered how he could remember all of this. "Sometimes, it was because he needed to see something. Other times, it led him to someone with something he needed to be told. I know there were even random items he came upon. Things that made no sense at the time but did later."

Curiosity rose. "Like what?"

"One I can think of off the top of my head was an old diamond necklace he was led to. Come to find out, it belonged to Keella and held some sort of personal value to her," Nektas shared. "She was always fond of Eythos before, but even more so afterward."

"Which probably made her even more willing to aid him when it came to Sotoria's soul," I surmised. "That's crazy."

He nodded. "There were other things. A sharpened edge of shadowstone. It was how he discovered its uses." He looked back at me. "I know I haven't told you much, but I hope it helped."

"It did. Thank you." I smiled, but it faded as my thoughts returned to the test. "I don't know why I passed the riders' test."

He folded his arms across his chest. "What do you mean?"

"I was supposed to slay the monster, and I did. Sort of." As I explained what had gone down, I pulled my hand from my hair and placed it on the railing. "They said I only wounded it. So, I'm not sure how I passed."

"You are not without flaw. Neither was Eythos. That did not make him unworthy. Nor does it make you unworthy."

I nodded slowly. "Yeah, but was Eythos's monster a cold, murderous part of him?"

"His monster was his ego. A trait shared with his brother and luckily not passed down to his son." Hair draped over the draken's shoulder as he cocked his head. "Eythos was not perfect. Ash may not have seen that side of his father. He was a different man by then, but he had an ego on him only rivaled by his joy in giving life. And doing that, creating and restoring life, fed that ego. It took him many lifetimes to tamp down the need to entice that monster." Nektas's exhale carried a faint rumble. "Unfortunately, the damage was already done by the time he mastered it."

Because when Eythos refused Kolis after granting so many requests, it kicked off all, well, all of *this*.

"But that wasn't his only monster," Nektas added. "Nor was it the one that killed him."

"His love for his brother?"

"His false belief that there is good in all living things, no matter how many times they show that all that is left inside them is rot. I don't think you will have that same problem, will you?" he said, the ridges thickening across the skin of his shoulders. "So, perhaps your monster will be your savior."

4

Even though I knew Nektas would never lie about Ash's well-being, I couldn't rest until I saw it with my own eyes. I sat beside him as he slept, waiting for the spell to lift. The hours stretched on for what felt like an eternity, but eventually, the sky beyond the balcony doors lightened, blushing with soft hues of pink and lavender. The light of dawn seeped in, slipping over the stone floor. Gradually, the golden beams kissed the foot of the bed.

It happened so fast.

A blast of energy rolled off Ash, sending me scooting toward the edge of the bed as it blew my hair back from my face. The temperature in the chamber dropped. His eyes flew open, his irises pure, crackling silver. Thick, swirling shadows appeared beneath his thinning flesh as he sat upright. Eather rose inside me as his lips peeled back over his fangs. A primitive, feral growl emanated from his throat.

"Ash." I scrambled onto my knees, reaching for him.

Our gazes locked as shadows raced across his chest. The look in his stare was wild, nearly feral. I wasn't even sure he saw me.

I clasped his cool cheeks, shivering. The snarling growl raised the hairs on the nape of my neck, making my heart race. Tendrils of dark eather snapped at the air around us.

"It's okay," I told him. He went completely still. "I'm right here."

A stuttered heartbeat passed, and then his mouth was on mine. The kiss was brutal, a clash of teeth and tongues. I could taste the panic and fury, feel the raw desperation in each agonized sweep of his tongue as his hands fisted my hair. He kissed me as if he sought to prove to himself that I was, indeed, with him. That I was okay.

I didn't know the exact moment the urgency became one of physical need or when the terror and anger turned to lust, but I felt him lose his grip on restraint and sensed the moment he *changed*. I felt it.

His flesh hardened and cooled even more. Energy rippled from him, buzzing over my skin and stroking my essence. A jolt ran through me as I fell back on my rear, the hem of his shirt gathering at my hips. Through strands of tangled hair, I saw that his skin had thinned even more. The shadows on his cheeks and chest deepened, joined.

My heart thudded as I stared at him, recognizing the hard line of his jaw, his wide, expressive mouth, and the cut of his high cheekbones. But like when I'd awakened from stasis, he was shadow and smoke turned to stone, his flesh the color of midnight streaked with churning moonlight.

Air caught in my lungs as wispy tendrils of mist lifted behind him, spreading out from his upper shoulders and thickening, forming shadowy wings made of pure energy.

Tiny bumps erupted over my skin as our eyes locked. There was nothing human about the way he looked, how his chest barely moved, or his piercing stare as shadow-laced eather slipped to the bed.

I felt no fear, even as the essence strained against my skin. I looked up at a Primal of Death: beautiful, terrifying, and *mine.*

Remembering the warning he'd given me the last time he'd lost his restraint, I shivered with anticipation and red-hot desire. My blood heated, becoming a fire that filled my veins. My nipples beaded beneath the shirt. A throbbing heaviness slid down to center itself between my thighs.

Ash's nostrils flared, and when I inhaled sharply, I caught the heightened citrusy scent of arousal.

There was no need for words. My breath was already coming out in short, shallow bursts as I leaned back and spread my thighs, offering myself to him. I shivered as the cool air kissed my heated, damp flesh.

Only a pinprick of his pupils was visible as his gaze lowered to what I offered. His stare was so heavy and intense that my breath caught once more, and my hips twitched.

Ash lifted his head, and a heartbeat passed before he struck with predatory grace. His weight pressed me to my back, and I caught a glimpse of his wings sweeping down and brushing the bed. A cry of pleasure tore from my lips as his cool length pressed into me. I stiffened, unaccustomed to his larger, Primal form as he filled and stretched me. The brief sting of pain faded as he seated himself deep inside me, causing my back to arch as I took him. Gods, he felt like he was everywhere. His presence inside me was almost overwhelming, nearly too much as I panted.

I slowly became aware of his stillness. His chest moved then, rising and falling rapidly against mine as he trembled.

Opening my eyes, I looked up at him. He tipped his chin down and stretched his neck from side to side. "Ash?" I whispered.

"I'm…" The hand by my head fisted, then his eather-filled wings flickered before collapsing in a shower of glittering sparks. "I just need a moment." He shuddered, causing my toes to curl at the sensation. "I…I don't want to hurt you."

"You won't."

Eather pulsed from his eyes before he slammed them shut. "You don't know that."

I did.

I was always safe with him.

I watched him battle himself, and that hidden, darkly sinful part of me didn't want him in control.

"Ash." I slipped my hands over the smooth, cold planes of his cheeks as I lifted my hips. He groaned, and I thought of the wicked words he'd said when he last lost control. A wave of wanton desire flooded me. "Will you fuck my pussy?"

"Fucking gods," he snarled, his hips jerking.

Then, he did.

And…gods. Ash *fucked* hard and fast, the force as savage as how his mouth moved over mine. I wrapped my legs around his hips, rising to meet him as my fingers tangled in the silky strands of his hair. We were frenzied as he drove into me, over and over, until I could no longer keep up with the wild rhythm. The sounds I made would surely turn my cheeks crimson later, but I couldn't stop myself as I trembled beneath him. He moved faster, harder, working an arm beneath my head. Either his fangs or mine nicked my lip, and he growled, drawing the little drop of blood into his mouth as he thrust into me all the way. With no space between us, he ground his hips. There was no steady build-up to release. I felt his cock begin to spasm, and that pushed me to the edge and right over it. A storm of pleasure, almost violent in nature, swept through me, kicking my head back against his arm as I cried out his name.

I didn't know how much time passed as we remained joined, our hearts slowing. But when Ash spoke, I knew he had complete control of himself.

"Sera?" he rasped.

"I'm here, and I'm okay." I tilted my head to the side, seeking. His lips found mine. The kiss was gentle and sweet but no less shattering than the ones that'd come before.

Ash eased himself from me, but his body didn't leave mine. Supporting his weight on one arm, he rested his forehead against mine. "Fates, Sera. I thought…"

He didn't need to finish the sentence. I knew what he thought, what must have preyed on his mind as he slept, kept under the spell and driven to lose his hold on his mortal form.

"It wasn't him," I whispered.

Ash's shudder of relief caused my heart to ache. Gods, I didn't think it was possible to hate Kolis more than I already did, but I was wrong. I knew this would always be a fear until Kolis was dealt with.

For both of us.

I cleared my throat. "It was the riders."

Ash lifted his head, and his brows rose. "What in the fuck?"

My lips twitched. "That about sums up my initial reaction."

His fingers coasted over my cheek. "Tell me what happened."

I did, sharing how I'd ended up in a cavern on the *outskirts* of the Abyss. Ash quietly listened as I explained how I'd had to prove myself worthy. His eyes narrowed as I described the three-headed beast. When I got to the Tavius portion, he went rigid.

"But it wasn't really him," I assured.

"No shit," he growled. I arched a brow. "He's a special case. I would know if he left where I last left him." He paused. "In pieces."

Pieces?

"How did—?" I stopped myself. "You know what? I don't think I want to know."

His smile was tight, toothless. "You sure about that?"

Actually? Yes. I ran my finger over the faint scar on his chin. "He was just a representation of me."

"How in the fuck is he supposed to be a representation of anything of you?" Ash demanded, the eather whipping through his eyes.

"The part of me that…reacts violently when I feel like I don't have control," I admitted. It was hard to share when his lips thinned, peeling back until the tips of his fangs became visible. "I didn't realize it wasn't really Tavius at first. I…I beat him."

"Good," Ash snarled, his eyes fierce. "What did I tell you before when it came to him?"

"Not to let him leave a mark."

"Exactly." He drew his thumb over my chin. "That hasn't changed, whether it was really him or not."

"I know." I smiled for him. "At first, I thought he was the monster I needed to slay next. I was about to kill him until I realized that if I did, it would be a final death. I would've…"

"You believed you would've destroyed his soul," Ash finished.

"I couldn't do it." My laugh was short and humorless. "It felt wrong. I dropped the sword, and he disappeared. That's when I realized I was supposed to slay the monstrous part of me. The cold bit."

His jaw flexed. "There is nothing cold about you."

"But there is," I insisted, my voice barely above a whisper. "I don't know if I was born this way, if the embers did it, or if it was how I was raised and the choices I made because of that. But I told you before, Ash. I don't feel things the same way you do."

"Sera—"

"I know you must sense it, that part of my soul. There's no way you haven't. And you don't have to lie. I don't want you to because, gods, the fact that you must have always sensed it yet still accepted me makes me love you even more." My gaze searched his. "I'm not like you. You carry those marks. Bear them. I don't. Not really."

"That's not true. It's not," he insisted, lowering his chin so we were at eye level when I opened my mouth to protest. "Kolis is someone who doesn't feel empathy or regret. Kyn doesn't. Veses is another. Are you like them?"

I was nothing like Kyn or Kolis, but Veses… What had she said after she told me she'd leveled half her Court when Kolis brought Sotoria back?

Our violent reactions regarding the ones we love is something we have in common.

We did have that in common.

But that was the only thing.

"No," I said. "I'm not like them."

"Thank fuck you said that," he replied. "You just carry those marks differently, Sera. The fact that we're even having this conversation proves that." His gaze found mine. "All of us, the good and the bad, are a little monstrous. I am no better than you."

A damn knot lodged in my throat, just as it had when he said this before we left to meet with Kolis to gain his approval for the coronation.

"But those parts?" Eather streaked across his irises. "They don't define you. They are not the sum of who you are. They never were."

"Do you believe that about yourself?" I asked, knowing he had far more good in him than I did in me. But he didn't see it that way. "And the monstrous things you've done?"

"I'm starting to," he admitted.

Surprise flickered through me. "What changed that?"

"You."

I rocked back. "Me?"

"Yes, you." His smile returned. "Because someone like you couldn't love me if I were the sum of the worst things I've done."

My breath caught as my emotions swelled. His features blurred. "I think I'm going to cry."

"That is not the response I was going for." Concern filled his tone as he rose slightly.

"It's because you're being sweet!" I exclaimed, blinking tears from my eyes. "And I don't know why I'm so damn emotional. I was never this way until I met you. It's annoying."

Ash chuckled, relief easing into his features. "It's cute."

"I completely disagree with that statement," I muttered, pulling myself together. "But back to the riders. They said I didn't slay the monster, but I did wound it."

A moment passed. "Did they find you worthy?"

"They did. So, I can now call on them if I want to end the realms." I rolled my eyes. "Or something."

"Well, that's a relief," he remarked, earning a sidelong glance from me. "But I'm not surprised. Because what I've sensed in you is not cruelty, Sera.

That is not what feeds this monster you speak of."

I almost asked him what did but stopped myself. What Ash sensed in me now was totally influenced by how he felt about me, and I didn't need my intuition to tell me that.

The truth was, Ash was right about some of the stuff he said. I wasn't evil. Kolis, Kyn, and even Veses *were*. None of them had started out that way, but they'd become evil. Me? I felt like I was somewhere in the middle of good and evil, teetering on a fine line. And I couldn't help but think that the true Primal of Life should be all good. Or, at the very least, mostly good.

Like Ash.

"What are you thinking?" he asked.

"I…I was just thinking about you," I said after a moment. "Like how your father wanted you to be the true Primal of Life. Everyone here wanted that."

But something went wrong when Eythos struck that deal with the desperate Roderick Mierel and placed the embers and Sotoria's soul in my bloodline. I wasn't reborn as Sotoria, and the embers became mine. Those two things were only the start of what had gone sideways with Eythos's plan.

"They were expecting me to Ascend to be the true Primal of Life, but I didn't," he said, propping his cheek up with a fist. "You did. There is no changing that, Sera."

"I get that. I'm just…" Words I shouldn't speak bubbled up. "I never desired to be a Queen or to rule anything or anyone." I sat up then, pulling my knees to my chest. Ash followed suit as I said, "I never wanted that kind of power, and I still don't. But I understand this cannot be changed. I just don't know how I'm supposed to be a Queen, let alone the Primal of Life."

Extending an arm, he brushed his fingers over the curve of my cheek. A faint charge of energy followed the contact. "Just be yourself."

I barked out a short laugh. "Really? Do you think that's good advice? Because being myself usually ends with me punching someone when they irritate me, and that doesn't sound like queenly behavior."

His lips twitched. "Depending on how irritating they are, I'm not sure I'd have a problem with that. But that's not all you are."

"Ah, yes. When I don't want to punch someone, I'm panicking and thinking I can't breathe," I said as he tucked a few strands of hair behind my ear. "And yes, I know I'm saying this stuff because I'm anxious. But knowing that doesn't mean I can stop myself from thinking it." I huffed out an aggravated breath. "You'd think Ascending into the true Primal of Life would mean I wouldn't have to deal with out-of-control anxiety anymore."

"This anxiety?" he said. "I told you before that Lathan experienced something similar."

My heart ached at the mention of the friend who'd been killed while watching over me in the mortal realm. Lathan used to experience the feeling of not being able to breathe before falling asleep as a child, leading him to believe it was the *sekya.* Obviously, that wasn't the case. It had been all the things that lingered in the back of his mind, catching up to him when his thoughts were finally quiet—something I had firsthand experience with. The godling hadn't grown out of it. He had simply learned to manage it. How? I wished I knew because not even my new ability of foresight spewed out the answer.

"It didn't make him weak or somehow less than," Ash continued. "As I told you before, he was as strong and recklessly brave as you are. The anxiety he had was just a part of him. Like it's only another part of you."

"There sure are a lot of parts to me," I mumbled.

"But the rest of who you are?" he continued, skipping over my comment. "The rest of you is brave and strong. Clever, loyal, and far kinder than you give yourself credit for. You were more than worthy of being a Consort to the Shadowlands, and you are more than worthy of being the true Primal of Life and the Queen of the Gods."

Giving his words time to sink in, I hoped they stuck. "Thank you."

"You don't need to thank me for speaking the truth," he said, slipping his fingers through the strands of my hair. "Nor should you *ever* feel like something is wrong with you—especially when it comes to this. Anyone would be nervous."

"Would you?"

"Yes."

The corners of my lips compressed as I shot him a sideways look.

"I would be, Sera. It's a lot of responsibility to carry." His fingers sifted through my hair some more. "It's a lot of power."

It *was* a lot of power. And authority that could be wielded in the worst ways. Kolis was proof of that. Still, anyone could fall prey to misuse. Common sense told me that my temperament would likely make me more vulnerable to such.

But it wasn't merely an abuse of power where things could go wrong. It was also the failure to use that authority and know when and how. Would my intuition kick in and guide me? Or would that also be something I had to figure out? I didn't know, and it all sort of terrified me.

"What are you thinking?" Ash asked quietly, curling strands of my hair around a finger.

"I…I don't know." My eyes closed. That was a lie. "I just don't want to disappoint anyone."

"You won't," he stated without a second of hesitation.

"I feel like you have to say that."

His forehead creased. "No, I don't."

"You're my husband," I pointed out. "So, yes, you do."

"I want to be supportive because I'm your husband. Not because I *have* to," he corrected, and I thought I melted a little right there. "And while I don't know much about relationships, I think I know enough to recognize that lying to you isn't being supportive."

I didn't know much about relationships either, but I thought he was right.

"I know they will not be disappointed in you, Sera." He tugged gently on the strand of hair he toyed with. "Ask me how I know."

"How do you know?"

"You have these knee-jerk reactions when it comes to your well-being," he said. "Reacting first and thinking about all the possible consequences afterward."

I started to frown because none of that really sounded like a good personality trait.

"But you don't when it concerns others," he said.

That wasn't always true.

"You thought about it," he continued, "taking what you felt and what the realms may need, and met it halfway. That is how you have earned respect and loyalty from the gods here, Sera. You've done so by fighting beside them to defend the Shadowlands more than once and risking yourself to keep them and their home safe."

"I only did what any halfway-decent person would do."

"Most people, be they god or mortal, say they would be the hero and ignore their instinct for self-preservation to rush in and defend others. Even good people believe that about themselves. But the truth is, their instinct for self-preservation is too great. What they say they would do is not what they *will* do. It's only what they have convinced themselves." He touched my cheek. "So, no. You didn't do what any half-decent person would do. You did far more despite the monstrous parts you may have. You always have."

I looked away, feeling my cheeks warm at his unwarranted praise. The way he saw me was a version of myself I wanted to live up to.

"I'm going to ask you what you asked me before," he said, pulling me from my thoughts. "What will you do about the Chosen?"

"Seriously?" I asked.

"Yes. Seriously. The Chosen were something you were clearly concerned about before. You are now in a position to change how things are done once Kolis is dealt with."

I opened my mouth to answer, but the realization that I *would* be able to do something about the Chosen struck me silent. He wasn't asking to hear my irrelevant, at-the-end-of-the-day opinion.

Gods, this felt far more real than being summoned to prove myself worthy to the riders.

I tightened my arms around my legs as my mind bounced all over the place. "I…I saw some of the Chosen while in Dalos. Some appeared to be in positions where they served the gods. They still wore white and remained veiled. Others didn't." I could still see Jacinta and the god, Evan, that Kolis had manipulated me into killing—*easily*. He'd manipulated me. I swallowed.

"Kolis said he gave the Chosen a choice: remain cloistered and be Ascended, or not. Those who chose not to act as servants could spend time with others. I didn't see any being forced to be intimate, but I also knew they weren't valued. I saw Callum kill one without hesitation. So, I know that just because I didn't see anyone being treated poorly, it doesn't mean it wasn't happening."

"I believe Kolis spoke the truth about giving them a choice," Ash said. "But I've seen the limitations of that choice with my own eyes."

I nodded. Too many had seen it for themselves. And then there was Gemma, one of the Chosen Ash had rescued. She had been so traumatized by what she'd experienced in Dalos that after spotting a god from there, she'd panicked and run into the Dying Woods, nearly losing her life. Actually, she *did* lose her life. I'd brought her back.

A lot of evil happened in Dalos that I hadn't been able to see.

"But it will not be that way under your rule," Ash pointed out. "If you choose to continue with the Rite."

I thought about it. "My immediate answer is to end it. As I said before, what the Chosen go through before they are brought to Iliseeum is bad enough. But you said it wasn't always that way." I lifted my gaze to him. "Right?"

"Right," he confirmed. "When my father ruled, the Chosen were not prevented from interacting with others, and they only went to the Temples the year of their Ascension, where they were taught the customs of Iliseeum."

Customs of Iliseeum? I hadn't really seen any of them, but I figured they were something else that went out the window during Kolis's reign. "You also said that the purpose of bringing in the Chosen and Ascending them to godhood was to ensure there were always gods serving in each Court that remembered what it was like to be mortal."

Ash nodded.

"And that is necessary." I folded an arm across my now-unsettled stomach. "So, I think I would continue with the Rite, but only if the third sons and daughters choose to be Ascended." A thread of excitement wove its way through me. "Like they would have until the year they would've entered the Temples under your father's rule to decide if that is what they want."

"Okay."

"And they could change their minds at any time," I added. "Well, up until the point they Ascend—wait." My eyes widened. "That means I would have to Ascend them."

"It does."

"Do you know how your father Ascended them?" I asked, wondering if what Kolis had said was true.

"The same way I Ascended you," he answered.

Another thing Kolis hadn't lied about.

"As for the Rite, that's how I thought you would answer," Ash said. "That is also why I know you will do right by Iliseeum and the mortal realm," he said. "I will not be the only one who sees this."

I nodded slowly, my heart thumping. Perhaps now that there was a true Primal of Life, the other Primals would be more likely to end their support of Kolis.

His gaze flickered over my face. "But you have to see it, too."

Gods. I wanted to believe that, as well as everything else he'd said, but it was hard. And I spent far too many years feeling like a disappointment to my family. It'd become what I expected. I wanted to have the kind of faith in myself that Ash had in me. I needed to try, though. If I didn't, I would mess up.

I would be that monster.

"*Liessa*," Ash called softly.

I turned my head toward him. "I know you said I shouldn't say this, but I'm going to anyway. Thank you."

Ash sighed.

I fought a grin as I tucked my chin against my knees, but I could feel his gaze on me. He was worried, likely sensing that I didn't carry the same level of faith in myself and wanted to push. It was time to change the subject. "This was an entirely too-serious conversation to have while naked. Good thing none of that matters. You know what does?" I latched onto the first non-related thing that popped into my mind.

"I have a feeling whatever you're about to say won't matter more than what I have to say," he replied.

"That's rude. And you're also wrong."

"Prove it."

"Your cock."

Ash leaned away, his mouth open, though he was clearly at a loss for how to respond.

"It's bigger when you're in your Primal form," I continued.

He blinked. "Is it? I never noticed."

"Really?" I replied dryly. "It's noticeably bigger, Ash. There's no need for modesty."

He chuckled, and I started to relax the moment I heard it. "Now I'm curious as to which cock you prefer."

"I don't know," I teased, unfurling my legs. "I'll have to think about that before I make up my mind."

"You can do that." Ash's hand landed on my side, then slid to my hip. His gaze followed. His grip firmed. "But I have a better idea."

"And what is that?"

Ash shifted onto his back and lifted me so I straddled him. "I can help you make up your mind."

I gasped, feeling him harden beneath me. And then he helped. Or at least he tried. There was no choosing between his two forms.

Both were perfect.

I stood alone, eyes closed, taking in the silence of the bathing chamber after cleaning myself in the water Ash had reheated.

As determined as I was to be responsible, I had failed gloriously. Ash and I had spent most of the day in bed once again, and the only things we'd accomplished were sleeping and sex. The sky had darkened before we finally decided to get it together.

Ash had left to find some food—thank the gods. I was starving. Not much time had passed, but he hadn't yet returned. I figured that whoever was currently present in the House of Haides wanted to know what had happened overnight and hear from Ash himself that I was not only awake but also fully aware of who I was.

Which was Seraphena Mierel, daughter of King Lamont and Queen Calliphe. A once-unnamed Princess and the savior of a kingdom that never knew I existed. A blank canvas—part assassin and part seductress. A figure of hope *and* of failure. But I couldn't be her any longer. Now, I just had to be *me.*

A wife.

The Queen.

And the *true* Primal of Life.

Kolis must be *infuriated.*

At the thought of the Primal of Death, red-hot anger pounded through me, mingling with the eather. Energy surged, crackling and hissing through my veins like lightning. The intensity of the power caused my breath to catch. I'd gotten used to the ebb and flow of eather, and even its intense force the handful of times I'd tapped into the essence of the Primals, but what I felt pulsing through me now was something else entirely. It was a storm of near-absolute power, hot and endless like the very sun itself. The air in the bathing chamber charged, causing my skin to hum. The rush of energy felt destructive, capable of creating true chaos if unleashed.

But I didn't think the Primal of Life was meant to be a being of chaos and destruction, so I drew in a deep breath and held it. I willed my heart to slow because far more dangerous, stifling emotions simmered beneath the fury.

"I'm not there," I reminded myself, gripping the edge of the vanity. "I'm not Kolis's willing prisoner any longer. I will never be that again."

And dwelling on my time with Kolis—my time in *Dalos*—served no purpose when I needed to focus on figuring out what to do about the Primal of Death. He couldn't be killed. Not without a god of his original Court to Ascend. And even though Ash carried embers of death, he didn't count.

In the quiet, I searched the library of knowledge erected in my mind during stasis. There was so much information there—almost too much. Like I now fully understood why Ash and the other Primals and gods often fought with weapons instead of the Primal essence. Using that raw energy against one another impacted the realms, usually manifesting as severe weather events. The impact wasn't always immediate, but whenever it was used against another, it would build and build until the realms could no longer contain the energy. The effect and consequences wouldn't be as severe as Primals using it against one another, but there was still a price to be paid in blood.

And that was good to know. Obviously. But randomly realizing such things made it harder for me to focus on single items.

However, even if I could focus better, it wouldn't matter. Nothing came to me. No weird feelings. No answers for how to stop Kolis without destroying the realms. Sudden knowledge didn't simply pop into my head. There was just a void of humming whiteness and questions that only led to more confusion.

There had to be more to Eythos's plan. He wouldn't have risked the destruction of the realms by creating—albeit failing at—the only weapon that could kill Kolis without knowing something could be done about the embers of death.

But even if we figured out a way, it required using Sotoria. Again. And, gods, she deserved to be at peace. Not forced to be reborn yet again, only to be used as a tool with no autonomy. I'd lived that life, and I didn't know if I could be a part of allowing another to do so. Especially someone who had already been forced to live far too many lives.

Kolis and what to do with Sotoria weren't the only things I needed to figure out, though. I also needed to learn how to, well, act like an actual Queen and be the true Primal of Life.

To find the faith Ash had in me, within myself. To be better. Less monstrous and…knee-jerky.

And not do what I desperately *wanted* to do, which was find Ash and demand that we seize Dalos and lay waste to any Primal who stood against us—especially Kyn for what he had done to Ector, Orphine, Aios, and so many others.

Eather thrummed beneath the surface as I closed my eyes. I could do it, too. I could Ascend gods in their Courts to replace those who fell, ensuring minimal impact to the mortal realm. I could take control, releasing the Chosen and any draken Kolis had forced into servitude.

But that was the part of me I hadn't slain talking.

Doing something like that would start a bloody war. Innocent gods and draken in the Shadowlands and throughout Iliseeum would die. It would spill over into the mortal realm, costing countless lives.

And as the true Primal of Life, none of that *should* feel as right as it did.

But as Ash had said, there was no changing this. And he was right. I didn't need intuition to tell me there would be no abdicating the throne. There would be no period of adjustment. This was my present and future, and there wasn't time to pretend that my entire existence and that of the realms hadn't changed—or freak out in a spiral of self-doubt.

So, I needed to be…well, less like the version of me who could lie as easily as I could kill. I couldn't continue being the temperamental, anxiety-ridden mess I was. Sure, Ash accepted all of that, even the part where I had attempted to kill him. He accepted *me*. But this was bigger than me—than us. I had the gods to think of now. The draken. Mortals. I needed to be better.

And standing in a bathing chamber with my eyes closed while giving myself the worst pep talk in history wasn't where I should have started.

Taking another deep breath, I opened my eyes. The first thing I saw was the golden swirl of the marriage imprint on the top of my right hand. The sight helped to calm me. I lifted my gaze to the mirror.

Oh, dear.

My hair was a nearly silver, pale-blond nightmare. Wet, tangled curls and waves fell past my shoulders, brushing the curve of my waist. I was so not looking forward to attempting to brush out the knots. My gaze shifted to my face. I looked the same as I had before: freckled, stubborn jaw, slightly pointy chin, arched brows. But the pallor and bruises I had while in Dalos were gone.

I lifted my upper lip to reveal two canines barely longer than before. Tentatively, I prodded at one of them with my tongue and immediately winced as I nicked it. They were definitely sharper, even if they were, at least according to Ash, small.

Nothing else had changed about me except for the fangs—

"Holy gods," I whispered, my lips parting in surprise.

The fangs *weren't* the only thing that was different about me. My eyes had changed, too. I leaned in closer to the mirror as if that would somehow change what I saw.

It didn't.

I looked past the glow behind my pupils. The aura had been there leading up to my Ascension, so that wasn't unexpected.

My eyes were still green—well, sort of. Streaks of silver now splintered the irises, giving them an almost shattered effect.

I blinked once and then several times, but the shimmery lines of silver remained. My heart rate kicked up, and the streaks and flecks *brightened.*

How had Ash and Nektas not mentioned this?

I pushed back from the vanity and forced a dry swallow. "Well. Okay, then." I nodded jerkily. "This…this is also who I am now. I can deal with it." My chin lifted. "I will deal."

And I would.

Because I had to.

The realms depended on it.

"So." I drew out the word as Ash placed a bowl of sugar-dusted strawberries on the table he'd moved closer to the couch. He'd done it so, as he'd put it, his Queen could be more comfortable while we ate. "When were you going to mention my eyes?"

"I did," he replied, placing several more covered platters down. "I told you earlier that they were beautiful."

"I just assumed you were being sweet." My stomach grumbled as the aroma of herbs and spices rose. Exactly when had I last eaten? I had no idea. "It didn't even cross my mind that you were saying it because they look broken."

His deep, melodic chuckle skated over my skin. "Your eyes don't look broken, *liessa.* They are as beautiful as they were before. Just slightly different now."

"But they're different than any other Primal's. Even Bele's eyes became silver after her Ascension."

"I'm not sure why that is, but I imagine it has to do with you once being mortal."

I watched him lift the lid from a plate of chicken, then another with beef. As he revealed another platter containing several helpings of different vegetables, my gaze lifted. I tracked each striking line of his face until I reached the curve of his jaw. "How did you get the scar on your chin?"

An eyebrow rose as he glanced over at me. "That was a random question."

"I know." My cheeks warmed. "It's just something I've always wondered, and I thought I might die without ever learning the answer."

Ash's hand froze with the knife poised over the chicken. Our eyes locked, and his chest rose with a sharp breath. The aura of essence brightened behind his pupils, seeping out.

Concern blossomed. I reached for him, hesitating for only a heartbeat before placing my hand on his arm. "Are you okay?"

"Yes." He cleared his throat. "It's just that, for a few moments, I forgot how close I came to losing you."

My heart stuttered as I squeezed his arm. "I'm sorry. I didn't mean—"

"Don't apologize. There's no reason to." He leaned over and placed a quick kiss on my forehead. "It happened when I was younger, a few years after my Ascension and before I was able to keep my temper in check while around Kolis."

My shoulders tensed. Of course, the scar was connected to the false King—also known as The Fucking Bastard.

"Kolis ordered me to sentence a god he'd recently killed to the Abyss. The god didn't deserve his death or the punishment. I refused, pissing off Kolis while being too close to one of his draken."

Gods, I *hated* Kolis.

"I thought the bastard was asleep," he went on, slicing the chicken. "I was wrong."

"Was it Naberius?" I asked, thinking of the large draken with the black scales tinged in red. "He was sleeping most of the time I saw him."

Ash smirked. "That would be him. Nab is nearly as old as Kolis."

Nab? *Nap* would've made a better nickname.

"He's also one of the crankiest sons of bitches you'll ever meet."

My attention shifted to the bare shadowstone wall above us. "I saw a couple of his draken. Diaval was one of them."

"You mean the blond-haired fucker?"

My lips quirked. "You mean the one with the prettiest hair I've ever seen? That fucker? Yes. When I tried to escape, he was with Elias when I got caught," I said, thinking about the guard who had been spying for Attes. "I hit Diaval with eather like I did to you in the Dying Woods. Knocked him back several feet. I think he was too shocked to really react to it."

A slow smile spread on his lips. "That's my girl."

My grin kicked up several notches. "There was another I never interacted with. I only saw him in passing, but something about him struck me as different than the others. He had light brown skin, and his hair was in braids."

"That's Sax," Ash told me. "He's the quietest of Kolis's draken."

"What do you mean by quietest?"

"I've never heard him speak. Not once." Ash looked over at me. "Diaval and Nab always belonged to Kolis. They were with him when he ruled the Shadowlands." He paused. "Sax was one of my father's draken."

Meaning he had been forced to bond with Kolis and was given no choice but to defend the Primal to the death. Gods, that sickened and angered me to the core. I fiddled with the edge of a napkin. It wasn't right. "What happened with Nab?"

"I was mouthing off to Kolis, and, like I said, I thought Nab was asleep. He wasn't, and when I stepped toward Kolis, the draken swiped out with his claws. He got me in my face—my chin and nose." Ash gestured with his knife at the fainter scar on the bridge of his nose. "And then my throat. Almost severed half my damn head."

"My gods," I whispered, my stomach clenching. "And all you have are those two little scars?"

"It's where his claws dug in. They did most of the damage. I looked a mess for a couple of days afterward."

I stared at his throat, stunned that the fingertip-width scar on his chin and the faint nick on his nose were all that remained of what must have been a nightmarish injury. And that he'd only looked a mess for a *few days*.

What Attes—the Primal of Accord and War—had said about the vulnerability of a newly Ascended Primal resurfaced. My new odd sense of knowing didn't spew any answers. "So," I said as Ash reached across the table and picked up a fork. My gaze flicked back to his face as he moved a chicken breast onto a plate. "I'm basically a baby Primal now."

"A what?" Ash's laugh tugged at my lips and heart. "A *baby* Primal?"

"Attes said that newly Ascended Primals are weaker than normal and used the word *fledgling* instead of baby, but that makes me think of birds for some reason." I saw his jaw tense at the mention of the Primal. "You're still mad at Attes."

Ash said nothing. He didn't need to.

"He swore to me that he would support you, no matter what. Besides that, your father trusted Attes enough to tell him what he planned to do with the embers and Sotoria's soul," I gently reminded him as I fiddled with the bottom of the charcoal-colored robe I'd donned. "At some point, you need to realize that Attes didn't betray us."

"I've realized that, *liessa*."

My lips pursed as he angrily diced the chicken breast into pieces small enough for a young child. "I feel like there's a *but* coming."

"But that doesn't mean I can forgive him for placing you in Kolis's hands."

"He did it to protect the Shadowlands, Ash."

A strand of hair slipped free, falling against his cheek. "You're really defending him?"

"I wouldn't say I'm *defending* him. I'm just pointing out that there were reasons behind what he did."

He stared at me. "How is that not defending him?"

"Because I, too, was ticked off at him." I picked up the glass of water. "Part of me still is. But his brother was about to lay waste to the entire Court, leaving only the Pillars of Asphodel and beyond. Attes did what he could at the time to stop Kyn."

"I get that." Ash placed the knife aside and scooped up a heaping helping of steamed cauliflower.

"Then you have to understand that he was only trying to prevent that."

"What I understand is that *I* would've prevented Kyn from destroying the Shadowlands." His eather-streaked gaze found mine. "And if not, the Shadowlands would've fallen, but you would've been safe. And *that* is all that matters."

My breath snagged as his gaze held mine. Even without foresight, I knew in my soul that he spoke the absolute truth. If it came down to the Court he'd spent the last two centuries guarding or my safety, he would choose me.

"That shouldn't surprise you, *liessa.* The dream or vision—whatever you want to call it—that I had the night you were born would've come to fruition." A charge of energy left Ash, causing the chandelier overhead to sway slightly. "I would've seen the realms burn if I lost you. You may not believe I would've allowed that to happen, just as you believe my decency extends beyond you, but it doesn't. I would've gladly seen it all burn." He flattened one palm on the table. "I'm sorry if that disturbs you. I truly am. But it's the truth."

My grip tightened on the glass. "I…I don't think you would've *gladly* seen it all burn, but I…" Heart thumping heavily, I took a drink and then set the glass down. "I would do the same for you." Eather stirred beneath my skin, reacting to the truth in what I'd said. I would do unspeakable things, stuff far worse than what I'd already done, to keep Ash alive. I was more than capable. "That's probably not good. Actually, it *isn't* good, considering the whole Primal-of-Life thing. But it doesn't disturb me."

Primal essence swirled in Ash's eyes. "Then, for the sake of the realms, we'd better ensure that both of us remain alive."

Holding his stare, I nodded. "Agreed."

Ash slid the plate toward me. "Please, eat."

I picked up my fork and, feeling his gaze on me, took a bite of the savory chicken. My stomach immediately thanked me.

"You are a fledgling," he continued after a moment. "Meaning you will tire more easily after repeatedly using the essence. But you will still be stronger than all the gods and likely many of the Primals." He speared a slab of grilled beef and moved it to his plate. "Looking back, you already were. A young god, let alone one in their Culling, wouldn't be able to do much with eather while surrounded by so much shadowstone."

I glanced at the ceiling's glossy surface. Shadowstone absorbed energy—the eather that could be found in all living things—from the environment, weakening the gods' and Primals' ability to tap into the essence. But I'd almost brought the entire palace down on our heads after finding the Primal Goddess of Rites and Prosperity feeding from Ash. Just thinking about Veses and how she'd taken advantage of Ash's need to protect me caused eather to thrum hotly within me. But I couldn't unsee her stricken features as Kolis handed her over to Kyn for punishment.

I shifted, feeling uncomfortable. How could I hate someone with every fiber of my being but still feel bad for them? I shoved several pieces of chicken into my mouth, refusing to think about her. Or feel all that bad for her.

"And newly Ascended Primal or not, you *can* kill another Primal. You're more dangerous now without the experience or control when it comes to the full extent of your powers, but you will have to replenish the spent eather more than you will as time passes. You can do it by resting, eating, or feeding." There was a second of silence. "I do hope you choose the third option."

Freezing with another piece of chicken halfway to my open mouth, I peeked over at him.

A shadowy grin appeared, and all kinds of parts of me coiled pleasantly. "Even if you don't use eather, you will need to feed more often in the beginning than you will later. Usually, once a week."

Oh…

"You will be more susceptible to injury than any other Primal. Wounds that would kill a god are normally nothing more than a splinter to a Primal, but for a newly Ascended one, it could take you down for several days. Even leave scars."

My stare dipped to the faint mark on his chin as I thought about weapons fashioned from the bones of the Ancients. I knew they could put a Primal into stasis, even kill a fledgling if left in them for too long, and it would utterly destroy a god or godling, leaving nothing behind for even me to bring back.

The tasty chicken lost some of its flavor with the knowledge that Kolis had most of the bones. "You don't have any weapons fashioned from the bones of the Ancients, right?"

Ash shook his head. "Kolis forbade it. Deeming me not entirely trustworthy."

I rolled my eyes.

"Neither does Keella. Though I'm not sure about Maia," he said, referencing the Primal Goddess of Rebirth, and the Primal Goddess of Love, Beauty, and Fertility.

I nodded absently. "I know the weakness can last several years."

"It can." Ash cut down the center of the beef and then began cutting half of it into smaller sections. "But the length of time varies between Primals. I'm in my second century and not at my full power."

Considering what I'd seen of him, that was hard to believe. "But you killed another Primal."

"Not sure Hanan counts," he remarked dryly.

I smirked at that. There were basically two ways to kill a Primal. One came at the hands of another Primal, which wasn't easy. And the other was…

well, death by the one they loved. I'd always believed the latter referenced only love between those not of the same blood, and it did, but Eythos's demise proved that wasn't always the case.

The skin behind my left ear tingled. Their weaknesses were different, as were Attes's and Kyn's. Their simultaneous creation from the same Ancient made it so their love could be a weapon wielded against each other. That was how Kolis had been able to kill his brother. And the fact that Eythos had placed what remained of the embers of life in my bloodline. It had all become the perfect storm.

A perfect, messed-up storm.

Because Kolis hadn't known that Eythos had passed on the rest of his embers, nor had he believed his brother still loved him.

Kolis hadn't meant to kill Eythos.

I glanced at Ash. He had a hard time believing that his father could still love his brother after everything. I couldn't fault him for that. There was a good chance he wouldn't readily accept the part about his mother having a fondness for Kolis either, and I wasn't even sure if that was something he *needed* to know.

I got my thoughts back on track. "Hanan did count, though. He was the Primal of the Hunt and Divine Justice," I said, trailing off. Bele was now the ruler of Sirta, the Court that had once belonged to Hanan. But was she a Primal? After the goddess Cressa fatally wounded Bele with a shadowstone dagger and I brought her back to life, no one knew exactly *what* she was. She felt like a Primal to the others but not. So…

The tingling behind my ear returned as I nodded to myself. Bele had Ascended when I brought her back, but she had *risen* into Primalhood with Hanan's death.

She was also a baby Primal.

I grinned.

"It has been eons since Hanan really had to fight anyone, and I was enraged," Ash continued. "That kind of anger can strengthen a Primal, even a fledgling, but it's temporary. If I was going up against someone like Phanos? The outcome likely would've been different if I had squared off with the Primal God of the Sky, Sea, Earth, and Wind."

I just loved how there was no cost to his ego to admit such a thing. He was strong and badass enough to know when he was outpowered, and that was a rare trait.

One I wasn't sure I possessed.

Okay. One I knew I *didn't* possess, which meant it was another thing I needed to work on.

"After taking out Hanan, I weakened damn near immediately," he said. "And that allowed Kolis to get the upper hand."

It wasn't just Kolis who had allowed that. My pitiful attempt to get them to stop fighting had only served to distract Ash. A wave of coldness swept down my spine as brief images of Kolis repeatedly shoving the shadowstone blade through Ash's chest flashed in my mind.

I gave my head a quick shake to scatter the memories.

Ash gathered up several pieces of the beef he had cut and transferred them to my plate. "But the heightening of your senses will occur long before you're considered to be at full power, and I imagine your intuition will also continue growing stronger."

I thought that over as he finally began helping himself to what was left of the meat and vegetables. "I have these memories of when I was in stasis. Not just of you talking to me, but of other things. It kind of felt like I was going in and out of consciousness."

He swallowed a bite of food. "Mine was similar to that. There was really no sense of time passing. I'd hear Nektas and then…nothing."

I nodded. "I think I even heard my nursemaid Odetta's voice at one point." My heart skipped as more of those memories became clear. "I saw how the realms began—how they really began. The Ancients were never Primals. They were something else entirely." I squinted, seeing in my mind what I had seen during stasis. "The essence comes from the stars—the Ancients themselves. They *were* stars."

Ash lowered his fork.

"Yeah." I twisted toward him, remembering what he'd told me. "You said that some of the Ancients were aware they were too powerful, so they created offspring from their own flesh—the Primals. Eventually, they transferred some of their essence to each one, establishing a balance of power. I saw that. Did you know they weren't Primals?"

Ash was quiet for a moment. "It was never stated explicitly that the Ancients were Primals. It was just something that I—well, that most of us—assumed. And my father only ever spoke of them when I was younger. When he did, what he said reminded me of fables shared with a child." His gaze searched mine. "Did you see more?"

"Yes." I took a bite of the seasoned beef, taking a few moments to make sense of the memories coming back to me. "I saw when they fell to this realm. When dragons ruled. I saw one of the Ancients burn beneath a dragon's flames and your father creating the first mortal. It took him so long," I murmured as my mind jumped back to the beginning of what I'd seen. "The Ancients? They fell to other lands far to the east and west, where cities were made of steel. Do you know of these other realms?" The answer came to me with my next breath. "You don't."

An eyebrow rose. "You would be correct."

"No one does but…your father. He knew the truth. So do Kolis and the Fates." My stomach pitched as I finally recalled what else I'd seen. "The Arae…"

Holy shit.

There was a reason the Arae were said to be everywhere and in everything. Why they didn't answer to Primals. It was because they were the Ancients—those who didn't go to ground or pass on when the Primals rose.

Which also meant *Holland* was an Ancient. And I'd kicked and punched him before. Cursed at him. I was also sure I'd probably threatened his life in a fit of anger at some point.

Ash watched me intently. "What about the Arae?"

I started to tell him what I had learned, but the words wouldn't come to my tongue. They came to my mind, though, along with a sense of bone-deep knowing.

I *couldn't* tell him.

My intuition didn't tell me why, but I knew there would be consequences if I did. Grave ones.

Hating that I had to keep this from Ash, I stabbed a piece of cauliflower and thought about the conversation I'd had with Nektas on the balcony. I was willing to bet that he knew exactly what the Fates were. "Just that they know about the other lands." I forced my thoughts there as the back of my neck prickled near my left ear. "They aren't separated by time, but by thick veils of eather our power cannot penetrate. They wanted things to be different there."

"Why?"

I bit down on the buttery cauliflower and searched my mind, finding nothing more on that topic. "I don't know, but there is more about the Ancients. I know there is. I just need a moment to think about it."

"And more cauliflower?"

"That, too," I murmured, forking more of the vegetable into my mouth as I squinted at the wardrobe. There was definitely something more about the Ancients. Something that had to do with balance. I stiffened as a chill whipped through my chest.

I twisted toward Ash. "There is more, though. When the Primals rose and defeated the Ancients, some entered Arcadia." Some became the Fates, but others… "There were Ancients who went to ground. They went into stasis, Ash. They are not gone. They are only asleep, and they can never wake up. They are why there must be true embers of life and death at all times. Why life must be created, and death must always come. It's not just because someone says there needs to be balance. The Ancients made sure of it."

Thoughts fired off rapidly as eather hummed beneath my skin. "It's why Kolis has been creating the beings he calls the Ascended. So far, it's kept the balance, but if that isn't maintained? Whatever the Arae did that linked the balance to the Ancients who went to ground will lift. They will awaken, and that *cannot* happen—" I gasped as the fork I held heated and trembled. My hand spasmed open—my *empty* hand.

The fork had evaporated.

My gaze shot to Ash. "I didn't mean to do that."

"It's okay." Ash stretched, picking up an unused fork. He halted, glancing from the utensil to my hand. "You good?"

"I think so."

Ash handed the fork over. "What exactly happens if these Ancients wake up?"

A chill went down my spine as I swallowed. "It's worse than what the Rot would've done. I saw them destroying entire lands. Killing nearly everything and everyone. And those in the ground? They are the ones the combined forces of Primal, draken, god, and mortal couldn't defeat. They could only be forced into stasis. I don't know how they did that, but what I do know is that no matter how long they remain in the ground, they are no longer the beginning of everything—the great creators and givers of life."

Ash had gone completely still, his gaze not leaving me as I spoke. I didn't even think he blinked.

"If they awaken," I said, Primal essence throbbing hotly through me, "they do so as *unia* and *eram*. The ruin and wrath of that once-great beginning."

"Fuck," Ash murmured.

Chilled to my very core, I exhaled slowly. "That was…dramatic-sounding." I laughed. "Wasn't it?"

"Yes, it was dramatic." Ash blinked several times. "*Unia* and *eram* are what many of the Ancients became before the end of their time, but any Primal can become it if their rage truly consumes them or if they go too long without feeding but manage not to go into stasis."

A shiver spider-walked down my spine. The idea of any Primal becoming that was terrifying.

Ash picked up a piece of beef with his fork. "You know, this begs one very important question—actually, more than one. But if the existence of the true embers of life and death keep the Ancients basically entombed underground, then why would a Fate train you to kill the true Primal of Death?"

"And why did your father, who had to know this, attempt to create a weapon that could?" I tacked on.

Chewing slowly, Ash raised his brows. "Another good question."

"Something isn't adding up." I brushed a curl back from my face, thinking about Holland and his kindness. I couldn't picture him as an infinite, unending being older than the realms. I just couldn't.

"Many things aren't adding up, starting with why this isn't more well-known. All Primals should be in possession of this knowledge," he said. "Why would only my father and Kolis know?"

"I…" I frowned as I studied my fork, seeing nothing in my mind except for a humming white wall. "I…I don't know." Frustration rose, but I cooled it before I obliterated another utensil. "But as long as there's balance, the Ancients won't be a problem." The tasty meat soured in my stomach. "You said that Kolis has been weakened due to my Ascension and that it has bought us time. I'm guessing not a whole lot of it."

Ash nodded, trailing the edge of his fork across his plate. "Exactly how much time cannot be answered, but there's a bit of chaos in all the Courts. I imagine most of the Primals are unsure how to react to your Ascension, which also gives us time."

Tension crept into my muscles as I stabbed another piece of delicious cauliflower. "Because they're using the time to decide whether to continue standing with Kolis or not."

Interest pinched his brow. "Is that what your foresight is telling you?"

"No. Just an assumption. But I can try to answer that." I frowned as I eyed the glass of water, trying to determine whether I was correct. Instead of being met with an explanation or silence, I hit what felt like another wall. "There's like a…a thick cloud of static in my head. I know you can't see static, but that's the best I can come up with."

"Sounds a lot like a mental shield." His fork hovered over the cauliflower. "It's what I see or feel when someone's blocking me from reading their emotions."

Sending him a wry glance, I thought that a shield was something I needed to work on. "It's the same thing when I try to think about something I want to know about myself." I forked up a piece of chicken. "Nektas said it was the same for Eythos when it came to anything having to do with him," I said. I'd told Ash about me running into Nektas between bouts of sleeping and sex.

Instead of reaching for the water, I willed it to move and continued. "And had to do with balance." I gasped as the glass shot across the table, smacking against my palm. Water sloshed over the sides, spilling onto the tabletop.

I winced, glancing at Ash. "Oops."

His lips were pressed together like he was trying not to laugh. "Careful," he murmured, picking up a napkin.

I grinned sheepishly. "I didn't realize the glass would move *that* fast."

Dabbing at the table, he arched a brow. "Perhaps you should practice with something you don't need to eat or are trying to consume."

"Good idea." I took a careful sip of water.

Ash tossed the napkin aside. "Anyway, about the *vadentia.* It reminds me of how the Arae can't see the fate of risen Primals."

"Seems rather convenient," I muttered.

"And unhelpful."

My grin faded as my mind raced back to what he'd said about Hanan. Something about that nagged at me as I poked at what was left on my plate. Ash had said his anger and Hanan being out of practice had helped him defeat the other Primal, but…

"By the way, when you spoke about the Ancients Awakening?" Ash said, drawing me from my thoughts. "You sounded like the true Primal of Life."

Curiosity rose as I sat back. "How does the true Primal of Life sound?"

"Powerful."

The corners of my lips turned up. I liked that. Probably too much. "And how do I normally sound?"

"Beautiful."

Rolling my eyes, I laughed. "I know I normally sound like a rambling, half-intoxicated mess."

"I like the way you sound—how you normally talk." His head kicked back as he eyed me. "I wouldn't describe it as sounding like a half-intoxicated mess, though."

"But you would describe it as being rambling?"

A half-grin appeared. "I would say entertaining."

"Uh-huh." I smiled at his chuckle. "By the way, have you seen Nektas since you threatened his life, and did you apologize?"

A faint flush stained Ash's cheeks, bringing a grin to my face. "Actually, I did." He cleared his throat. "He let me know that things were quiet."

"That's good."

"It is."

Thoughts dwelling on *why* things were quiet, I ate a piece of chicken. If we were lucky, Kolis was still in stasis, but that seemed doubtful. "It won't stay that way for long."

"No, it won't." He paused. "Soon, there will be a city full of people wanting to see you."

My chest spasmed as I lowered the fork. "Who and why?"

"Some will be from Lethe," he said, speaking of the city within the Shadowlands. "Others will be from other Courts, coming to pay homage to their new Queen."

My stomach plopped to the general vicinity of the floor. "They don't need to do that."

His lopsided grin returned. "They do it because they want to, *liessa.* Not because they have to."

My throat constricted. "Is there a way to make them, I don't know, *not* want to?"

"It's been centuries since there has been a true Primal of Life, Sera." His silvery gaze met mine. "I imagine they are excited and hopeful for stability and safety."

My panic receded for a moment as I was struck silent by the deep warmth in his eyes and voice. *Love.* I'd seen it before when his features softened as he looked or talked to me, but I just hadn't recognized it for what it was. How could I when it should be impossible? But I saw and felt his love, and that mattered so damn much. My very being swelled with so much joy I felt as if I could float right to the ceiling.

His head tilted, sending one of those stray locks of hair against his jaw. "What are you thinking about?"

"Are you reading my emotions again?"

"It's kind of hard not to when you're projecting."

I sighed. "I really need to work on that shield."

"It won't help if you're projecting," he reminded me and lifted his hand. The bowl of fruit slid smoothly across the table, coming to a stop at his fingertips.

I narrowed my eyes. "Show-off."

He grinned. "I could taste your nervousness and unease when you were talking about the gods coming to Lethe. It was thick and tart, and then it changed to something…sweet." His brows knitted as he studied the fruit in the bowl. He nudged several pieces aside before picking up a glistening, vivid red strawberry. "Like this but dipped in chocolate."

Warmth lit up my chest as I twisted toward him, drawing one leg up. "Is that what love tastes like to you?"

His eyes returned to mine as he offered me the strawberry. "Was that what you were feeling?"

I took the fruit. "Yes."

"Then that is what it tastes like to me." He picked up another berry without looking at it and popped it into his mouth. A tiny drop of juice clung to his lip, drawing far too much of my attention. "Decadent and lush."

Muscles low in my stomach curled, and I had to force myself to look away before I did something rather inappropriate. Like climb all over him midsentence.

"You know," he said, "if there was a way to prevent the others from realizing you Ascended and give you more time to adapt, I would do it."

"I know." I took a small bite of the fruit, which was difficult to swallow. The rise in anxiety was *so* not me having faith in myself. "I'm just being ridiculous."

"No, you're not." He set the bowl aside as I finished off the berry. "You weren't prepared for this, Sera. And even if you had been raised from birth to expect such, you've gone through a lot in a very short period of time."

Not wanting to think about the *a lot* I'd gone through, I nodded and wiped stickiness from my fingers.

"But you won't be facing any gods or Primals alone," he stated softly. "I will be right beside you, as will those who serve the Shadowlands."

I glanced at him, finding another sugar-dusted strawberry between his fingers. I took the tasty fruit and bit into it.

One of those rare, wide smiles appeared, exposing the straight line of his teeth. As I stared at him, I was mesmerized by how it softened the harsh beauty of his features. There was also a naturalness to this kind of smile, like his lips were always meant to be curved in such a way. And I thought that if he had lived a different life, that smile would be the first thing seen by many.

Wondering how I got so damn lucky, I pressed my forehead to his. "I love you," I whispered. "I love you so very much."

Ash clasped the back of my head, his fingers curling around the strands of my hair. His lips found mine, and the kiss conveyed those three words with just as much power as if they had been spoken.

"Finish eating," he said against my lips, and I felt his mouth curve into a smile. "Please."

My lips twitched as I picked up my fork. In the silence, my mind went back to what we had been talking about before all of that. I pushed another chunk of chicken around my plate, wondering how long the realm would remain quiet. My intuition told me nothing, and without eyes in Dalos, we had no way of knowing.

I suddenly thought about Elias, one of Kolis's close guards who had been spying for Attes. "Do you think Attes has any other spies in Dalos?"

"I'm sure he does." Ash speared a sliver of meat. "He came by when you were in stasis, but I didn't speak with him. Nektas did."

"Did Nektas say if Attes knew whether Kolis was still in stasis or not?"

"The only thing the Primal mentioned was that Kolis had not been seen in Dalos."

That could mean anything.

"But I'm sure he'll be back." Ash paused. "Unfortunately."

Ignoring that last part, I hoped Attes returned soon. I wanted to make sure he had the Star diamond somewhere where Kolis nor anyone else could get their hands on it—

I nearly dropped my fork. "That golden, mask-wearing motherfucker."

"What?" coughed Ash, swallowing.

"*Callum.*" I pitched forward, rattling the table. "The blond-haired Revenant who is always with Kolis."

Ash reached for his glass. "What about him?"

"You know how Kolis favors Callum?" When he nodded, I continued. "I couldn't figure it out at first—why Callum was the only one who was allowed to be alone with me or how he clearly had more leeway with Kolis than anyone else. There were times he would actually disagree with Kolis."

Ash halted. "If you're about to tell me that Callum is Kolis's child…"

"Uh, no." My lip curled when I thought about how Kolis hadn't been with anyone since he'd held Sotoria captive. It wasn't his celibacy that disgusted me. It was the reason behind it. "Callum never believed I was Sotoria. He was adamant that I wasn't, even after Kolis summoned a goddess from the Thyia Plains," I said, referencing the Primal Goddess of Rebirth's Court. "He wanted her to confirm whether what I claimed about being Sotoria was true. She can read memories like Taric could. Her name is Ione. Do you know her?"

The skin between his brows creased. "I know *of* her. She often accompanies Keella. I didn't know she had the ability to scour the mind." His jaw clenched. "Did she look into yours?"

"She did, but she made it as painless as possible," I quickly told him.

"And she lied for me, Ash. She saw the truth and lied." Worry for the goddess surfaced. "Kolis has to know that now. I hope she's okay."

"If she lied to Kolis, she knew what she was doing, and she will likely be smart enough to make herself scarce," Ash stated. "Callum didn't believe you were Sotoria, even after that?"

"No, and the reason he didn't is the same as why he's so close to Kolis," I told him. "Callum is Sotoria's brother."

Ash choked on his water. "You have got to be joking."

"I wish I were." Gods, did I ever. "If you thought things were messed up before? Wait until you hear this."

"Great," Ash muttered.

"The day Kolis saw Sotoria on the cliffs and scared her? She was picking flowers for her sister, Anthea. Callum was supposed to be with her but was messing around with someone instead. He felt responsible for her death." I held up a hand. "Look, I don't like Callum at all, but he wasn't responsible for his sister's death. Kolis was."

"Agreed."

"So, Kolis, being possibly the least self-aware being in all the realms, went to Sotoria's parents to let them know that he'd petitioned Eythos to restore Sotoria's life." I watched as Ash captured my hand and brought it to his lips. He pressed a kiss to my palm, then lowered it to my lap as I told him how Callum had asked to be taken to Sotoria so he could apologize, and how that had ended for him when Kolis explained that he couldn't. "Callum slit his own throat."

"Fuck." He exhaled roughly.

"Yeah, and Kolis…" I shook my head. "Gods, I could hear the anguish in his voice when he spoke of holding Sotoria as she died and then did the same with her brother."

"You sound bothered by that."

"I was. I *am*," I admitted. "What happened to Sotoria and Callum is a tragedy. And back then, Kolis wasn't who we know today. I'm not saying he was good then," I tacked on. "Clearly, he had obsessive tendencies and really poor peopling skills." My cheeks puffed with the breath I blew out. "But I don't think he was pure evil."

Ash said nothing to that.

It was understandable. Ash would never see Kolis as anything but who he knew. "Kolis couldn't allow Callum to die, and he knew Eythos wouldn't intervene. So, he did what was forbidden."

Ash inhaled sharply. "He gave life?"

"He used his blood to Ascend Callum, but he's not a demis," I said, speaking of the Ascended mortals who don't carry enough eather in their blood—not like the third sons and daughters. "And he's not one of the Ascended. He's not even like the other Revenants. He's who he was before his death. But the other Revenants? They have no desires—not for blood, food, sleep, or companionship. They are driven only by the need to serve their creator. Kolis. And that is all."

"That is why death cannot give life. Doing so is a mockery of such—just soulless, reanimated flesh and bone." Anger tightened the corners of his mouth. "These Revenants sound like a type of Gyrm," he said, and my lip curled at the mention of the once-mortals who had either willingly entered into eternal servitude upon death to atone for past sins or had given their souls to a god or Primal upon death in exchange for a favor. "But a more improved version."

"Yeah, I don't think they're filled with serpents," I murmured, shuddering. "Anyway, Kolis sees nothing wrong with it. He thinks being incapable of wanting or feeling anything is freeing." I turned my head to Ash. "If I hadn't had embers of life in me, could that have happened when you Ascended me?"

"No. I am a Primal of Death, but I am not true Death. My blood likely would've done the same as any other Primal's," he said. I didn't know why that relieved me because it was moot at this point. "Did Kolis ever explain why Callum is different?"

"He said that Eythos once told him that whatever the creator felt at the time shaped the creation." I rubbed the skin behind my ear. "And he was right. It's what the creator truly feels—what is real and cannot be forced. And everything Kolis felt when bringing Callum back to life was real—desperation and bitterness."

My stomach soured. "He even felt joy. But he only felt duty with the others. The only magic involved was that Callum retained something akin to a soul." My brows knitted. "But creation is a reflection of who and what we are. A mirror of all our best and worst traits. Callum is an echo of who he and Kolis once were. But the other Revenants?"

"They're an echo of who Kolis is today," Ash surmised, a muscle along his jaw ticking. "And basically indestructible. But what about Callum? Shouldn't he be easier to kill if he has something akin to a soul?"

"You'd think, but considering how often I've seen him die only to return to life? Even after I did a real number on him?" The satisfaction that came with wiping that smug look from Callum's face was brief. "I'd say no."

Ash looked away as he reached across the table to pick up a bottle of wine. He pulled the cork and poured himself a glass and then turned an empty glass upright to pour another. "I want to ask you something."

"Okay."

He placed the wineglass near my plate. "When I was being held in the Carcers," he began, speaking of the mountains west of Dalos, "I was in and out of consciousness. Kolis always managed to be there when I was awake." He shifted his gaze to the glass he held. "He liked to talk."

My throat dried.

"He said you tried to escape."

Dropping my hands to my lap, I nodded. "I did. That's…that's when I messed up Callum."

"How did Kolis handle that?"

"Surprisingly well," I said. "He actually didn't seem all that mad."

Ash's head slowly turned to me.

"I know. It sounds unbelievable, but he…he wanted so badly to believe I was Sotoria." I let my head fall back. The lamplight from the chandelier glowed softly as I stared up at it. "I think that kept his temper in check."

"Most of the time."

I tensed, briefly closing my eyes. Ash was likely talking about the bruises he'd seen when we walked in each other's dreams, but my mind went to Kolis's punishment for when I attempted to intervene on Veses' behalf.

For the briefest second, I could almost feel the muscles in my arms stretched unbearably.

I opened my eyes. "The bruises you saw when we dreamwalked happened after he took me to Hygeia and summoned Phanos—" I drew in a ragged breath as I saw the reluctance in the Primal God of the Sky, Seas, Earth, and Wind's eyes flash before me. My throat thickened. "And after the ceeren transferred their essence to me. I saw my chance to kill Kolis—or what I thought was my chance. I grabbed a shadowstone blade and stabbed him."

"Gods." Ash drew his other hand over his chin.

"It wasn't a very well-thought-out plan. His reaction was immediate. I don't think he even meant to hit me—

"You stabbed *me*, and I did not strike you, Sera."

"I know." I looked him straight on, thinking I likely wouldn't have faulted Ash if he had reacted in some way to defend himself. After all, I *had* stabbed him in the chest. Literally. I would've done way worse if it had been me…and I'd survived. "I'm not excusing it. I'm just explaining that he has better control of his temper than what is made of him."

"He had that control because of what you mean to him," Ash bit out. "You saw a side of him that no one else has seen, at least not in my lifetime."

I swallowed as nausea crept up my throat. Between my stomach and the dark energy seeping out of Ash and charging the air around me, I really needed to get to the point of why I'd brought this up before I vomited on myself and the table. "All I'm saying is that's what caused the bruises. And even then, that was it." But it really wasn't. He had used compulsion, ensuring that I *behaved* and could only stand there while—

Nope.

Wasn't going there.

Feeling Ash's gaze on me, I forced my thoughts past that. "It didn't happen when I tried to escape after he brought me back to Dalos. All he did was lecture me. And now, I think it was because my actions reminded him of Sotoria. The whole attempting-to-escape-him thing. How fucked up is that?"

"There are no words to capture how fucked up that is."

He was so right. "When we were on the beach in Hygeia, I saw what he really looked like—his Primal form." Tiny goose bumps formed as the dull gleam of Kolis's bony face appeared in my mind. "I saw true Death."

Ash had gone completely still, his expression devoid of any emotion. I counted. It took six seconds before he spoke again. "When we were talking before, you said he made you wear revealing clothing?"

"Yeah."

Those enviable lashes swept down and then lifted. The eather streaking his irises brightened. "What else did he make you do?"

It felt like all the air had been sucked out of the chamber. My lips parted as my mind began racing, but the stench of stale lilacs returned, choking me and not allowing any words. What else? *What else?*

Nothing.

That was what I needed to say. Nothing else really happened.

But I could still feel the scrape of Kolis's fangs against my throat. A shudder slithered its way down my spine, and I jerked my hand away. I took a deep breath and held it, utilizing the breathing techniques Holland had taught me. All I had to do was look around to see that I wasn't being held captive. I wasn't in a cage—a *gilded* cage that no longer even existed. *I'd* destroyed it. *I'd* taken Kolis out—if only momentarily. *I'd* freed Ash from his prison.

Breathe out.

That had been *me* and *my* strength—strength fueled by pure rage, terror, and agony.

I knew that, but it felt like a part of me was still locked away where all my rights and freedoms had been stripped away, taking my identity and voice with them. The desperation and helplessness I never wanted to feel again crept in, threatening to soak my skin like rancid water. The rot of those emotions pressed in on me, and in the deafening silence of the chamber, I felt I would drown in them if I wasn't careful. I wanted to shed those feelings like a serpent discarded its skin, but they lingered like a bad omen.

I'm not there.

I didn't even understand why I was so affected. I should be able to handle this better. Whether Ash or Kolis, becoming the Primal of Death's weakness and ending him had been my duty since birth. I'd been trained to fight from the moment I could lift a sword. Groomed to seduce as soon as I became old enough to learn how flesh could become a weapon. I lived the entirety of my life knowing what was expected of me, yet I hadn't been prepared for Kolis's volatile mood shifts and twisted sense of honor. His cruelty and manipulation. His obsession. And even his moments of tainted kindness.

I hadn't been prepared for when he threatened to give me to Kyn, the Primal of Peace and Vengeance, who was nearly as messed up as Kolis was.

What else did he make you do?

I hadn't been ready to stand by as he turned a Chosen into something neither mortal nor god, but rather a being that hungered for blood. No amount of training had prepared me to pretend to not only be willing to spend time with him but also enjoy it. *Breathe in.* To see his fake, well-practiced smiles, and worse yet, the real ones whenever I made him happy or he spoke about Sotoria. *Hold.* Witnessing how he came alive then, finally showing he was capable of feeling something other than malice and self-persecution.

What else did he make you do?

To allow him to sleep beside me. Hold me. Remain still as he fed from me and found pleasure—

"*Liessa*," Ash whispered.

The sound of his voice jerked my head back, snapping me out of my thoughts. My gaze flew to his. I had no idea how long I'd been sitting there. Definitely more than a handful of seconds. Had it been minutes? My heart was still pounding.

Reaching between us, Ash gently folded his hand around my wrist and pulled my fingers from my throat.

Dozens of tiny balls of unease settled in my stomach.

There is more.

I knew that.

Ash knew that.

"Talk to me," he said, so quietly I could almost pretend he hadn't spoken.

I wanted to run for the balcony doors. A better option was to change the subject *slightly*, and I knew exactly what to bring up. It was possibly the most important thing we needed to discuss and hadn't yet.

"There isn't much to say about any of that." I cleared my throat as I slipped my hand free of his. "But we do need to talk about Kolis. What are we going to do about him?"

That muscle flexed along Ash's jaw again as he reached for his glass and drank while I did everything in my power not to squirm.

Did he realize I'd changed the topic on purpose? Of course, he had. But had it angered him? Disappointed him? I didn't want that. I just *couldn't* talk to him about that. Not now. Not when I didn't even know what to think about it.

After what felt like a small eternity, Ash said, "Discussing how we're going to remove him from power is something we need to talk about with

Lailah and Theon. Even Attes," he said, surprising me a little that he thought to include the other Primal in, well, anything. "But we do need to be on the same page regarding what to do with Kolis."

"Agreed." I relaxed a little. "We know we can't kill him."

"Unfortunately, not at this point."

My thoughts flashed to Sotoria, and my stomach soured. "Nor can we allow him to continue as the false King or the true Primal of Death. So, what does that leave us with?"

"Only one thing."

My mind immediately went to the Ancients. "We need to entomb him."

Ash nodded.

I prodded at my fang, thinking that over. "That won't be easy. Kolis is old. He's powerful. Capable of healing any wound."

"*Almost* any wound," Ash corrected.

I started to frown, and then it hit me. "Ancient bone—wait. The true Primal of Life and the true Primal of Death can break through those."

"Yes, but if such a weapon is left in a Primal, it severely weakens them," he reminded me. "Whatever injuries they incur will not heal while the bone remains in place."

A chill skated down my spine. "Isn't that what Attes planned to do when he took Kolis?" When Ash nodded, I continued. "Has that been done before?"

"It has."

Part of me thought I already knew when and with whom, but I had to ask. "Has he done it to you?"

"Once," Ash answered flatly. "A few decades ago."

"Fuck," I rasped, pressing my hand to the table as eather thrummed hotly inside me. "I want to make Kolis bleed and then dance in his blood."

Ash's gaze flicked to mine. "I would love to see that, so let's ensure it happens."

I checked my anger before I started destroying more silverware. It wasn't easy. "We will also need chains made of the bones of the Ancients, won't we? And I assume there's not much just lying around."

"I know Attes has a small stash, but not nearly enough to make chains," he said. "And there are limitations for using Ancient bones against a Primal. Even leaving it inside them. The ground will seek to restore them, pushing any bone blades from the flesh like a splinter. And roots will eventually crush the bone chains."

Gods, I hadn't even thought about how the roots had come out of the ground when I almost pushed myself into an early Ascension. "How long does it take for that to happen?"

"For you or me?" He leaned forward. "Hundreds of years. For a Primal of Kolis's age? A handful of years. A decade if we're lucky."

"Gods." I sat back, fingers finding their way to my hair. "What about the tombs here?"

"They won't hold a Primal," Ash said, watching me. "And there would be a whole other issue with that."

"What…?" I trailed off as the answer pieced itself together for me. "You still rule the Shadowlands, meaning you receive the summonses at the Pillars and beyond. But if Kolis steps foot in the Shadowlands, he will gain control of the Abyss, the Vale, and all those who serve the Shadowlands, including the draken."

"Because he's the true Primal of Death," he said. "Yes."

I faced him.

"But he'll be reluctant to do that. If he comes here, that would leave Dalos vulnerable and open for you to do the same there. As of now, that is the seat of power."

That was good news. Kind of. "So, we need to figure out how to entomb him and keep him there for longer than a decade." Or keep him there indefinitely so Sotoria wasn't needed. That would be the best possible outcome.

There had to be a way to keep him entombed because the— "The Ancients." I whipped toward Ash. "They've been entombed for thousands and thousands of years and are more powerful than a Primal. How are they entombed?"

Ash lowered his glass. "That's a damn good question. One I'm guessing the *vadentia* isn't helping with."

He was right. My intuition was silent. "But I know who holds that knowledge. The Fates. I also know the likelihood of them telling us is slim to none."

"But that means the knowledge is out there," he said. "We just need to find it."

"Yeah, that's all." I laughed. "Should be easy—" I halted again, almost not wanting to suggest what I was about to. "What about the Pools of Divanash?"

"They can only show a person or an object," he answered. "And if there *is* an object out there that helped entomb the Ancients, and only the Fates know what it is, it likely won't reveal that."

Frustration grew as I twisted my hair around my finger. It shouldn't be this difficult. And in reality, the Ancients should be helping us.

"There is only one Primal almost as old as Kolis who may know and would have taken an active role in entombing the Ancients, while the others likely weren't old enough to fight," he said. "Keella."

I twisted my hair tighter, hope sparking. There was no guarantee that Keella would have the information, but it was something. "Can we go now? To the Thyia Plains?"

"We can, but I think we should meet with the others first," he suggested.

"You're right."

"Always," he replied, and I shot him a look. He grinned as he reached between us and pulled my fingers free of my hair. "So, the game plan is to find a way to entomb Kolis. Once we have that information—"

"We have to go after Kolis, which will start a war."

"I'm afraid that is inevitable," he stated, refilling our glasses.

So inevitable, it seemed, that Ash had started planning for it by growing and training his armies long before I came to the Shadowlands.

"And how damaging that war is, how costly it becomes, will depend on how big it is. Because it won't just be us against Kolis," Ash continued. "It will be us against whoever stands with him, and he will have his loyalists among the gods and Primals."

"I just don't get how any Primal could stand with him before and continue to do so now that there is a true Primal of Life." I shook my head, frustration growing because I *did* understand how on some level. "But they don't know me. However, they *do* know what Kolis is capable of."

He nodded as my gaze fell to the golden swirl on his left hand. Something occurred to me. "We won't rule as Kolis has. Obviously. But when your father ruled, did any of the other Primals take part in the decisions that were made?"

"As far as I know, mostly not," he answered.

"And this included decisions involving other Courts? And the mortal realm?"

"I believe so." Curiosity filled his expression. "Why are you asking?"

"I don't know. I'm just thinking. Like, I know things will be different with you being King instead of Consort, but why shouldn't all the Primals be involved in making major decisions?" I said. "Like officially involved."

Ash's head cocked. "Why would you want that?"

"Because no two people, Primal or mortal, should decide everything, especially when it comes to things they have no experience with and others do," I pointed out. "Power should be shared. That's what the Ancients did, right? The Ancients shared their power by creating the Primals."

"Yes," he said. "Inevitably, it didn't stop what was to come, but if they hadn't done what they did, none of us would even be here."

That was a scary thought.

Ash was quiet for several moments. "There was a kingdom that existed when my father was alive. It was in the west, where Terra exists today, and was ruled by a council of elected officials. I believe it was called the kingdom of Creta."

"I haven't heard of that kingdom," I said.

"Probably because it was a young one full of ideals and people who also believed they should not be ruled by a King and Queen," he said. "They inevitably collapsed into infighting when no one could agree on anything from common laws to how rent should be collected."

"Well, that's disappointing to hear," I muttered.

"But one failure doesn't mean it shouldn't be attempted again."

I glanced over at him.

"I think the other Primals should be involved in the decisions. It would make them more invested in what occurs outside their Courts and Temples," Ash continued. "But it won't be easy."

"Oh, trust me, I know. My brief interaction with some of the Primals tells me that. But…there could be safeguards in place, you know? If the majority decides something terrible—which, again, based on my interaction with some of them, could happen—a veto power or even a non-Primal could also step in. Actually, why should it just be the Primals? Shouldn't the draken be involved in decisions?" Excitement grew. "Like Nektas."

"I doubt he'd sign up for that," Ash stated.

"Or any draken," I said, silently adding that it would totally be Nektas. "There are so many better ways to do it."

"There are." He paused. "What made you think of that?"

I lifted a shoulder in a shrug. It wasn't the first time it had crossed my mind. "I just don't think one or two people should ever rule. And perhaps some of what has happened here wouldn't have occurred if the other Primals were more invested in the decision-making."

A faint smile appeared on his lips. "And you think you wouldn't make a good Queen."

"Shut up," I mumbled, my face warming because I could clearly hear the pride in his voice. "Anyway, I brought this up because, as we said, the other Primals don't know what it will be like if we rule. They don't know that it can be better. So, why don't we convince them?"

His gaze sharpened. "You're talking about summoning the Primals."

It was a bold move. One that could pay off or end in disaster, and my mind immediately wanted to travel down the darker road, telling me that it would be impossible to convince most of the Primals that we would be a better option than the false King. Because some would only see me and choose to remain loyal to Kolis, simply because I was once mortal. Because I am a woman. Because the last time some of them saw me, I was dressed in transparent gowns and seated at Kolis's feet. Because—

Stop.

I took a deep breath to ease the tightening in my chest and nodded. "But not Veses or Kyn. I have no interest in convincing them of anything."

"Neither do I." Ash reached over and brushed a stray curl back. "I think we need to go over this with the Shadowlands gods, but if we can get the other Primals to side with us, taking Kolis down will be far easier." He fell quiet for a moment, eyeing me. "I must admit, I'm surprised."

"By what?"

"You." He reached for the bottle of wine and refilled his glass. "I didn't expect your response for how to handle Kolis to be so…measured."

"Me neither," I said. "It feels weird to be the practical one in a situation.

Honestly, I don't like it."

Ash let out a low laugh. "Welcome to my world."

I cracked a grin. "Is it a bad thing? To be measured?"

"No." His head tilted. "It's just that I expected you to be more of the attack-first-and-*then*-think-about-it type."

"Well, that is my initial instinct," I admitted, thinking back to when I'd stood in the bathing chamber. "To go straight to Dalos and take out anyone who stands in our way."

"And *why* aren't we doing that?"

"Because that would be rash and impulsive. It's not really a plan. And…" I set my glass down, unsure how to put what I was thinking into words. "And it just seems like it would be a monstrous act."

"I see," he said, leaning back. "What happened with the riders has really gotten under your skin."

There was no point in denying that. "I haven't forgotten what we spoke about this morning."

"You just don't believe what I said to you about being a monster."

"No, that's not it," I was quick to say. "I do believe it. I know I'm not like Kolis or Kyn, and I get that we are all a little monstrous." I twisted toward him, dropping my hands to the robe's velvety skirt. "I do. But I also know that I am more…prone to giving in to that side of me and I am trying to make a conscious effort not to do that." I searched his gaze as my fingers curled against the soft material. "Is that wrong?"

"No, *liessa*." He reached between us, straightening the collar of my robe. "It's actually very wise."

"Good," I said. "Because I think approaching this cautiously will benefit us. Kolis doesn't want—" I frowned as a sudden awareness pressed down on me.

"Kolis doesn't want what?"

"War," I whispered, concentrating on the feeling. It reminded me of what I felt when Primals were near, but this was different. The sensation didn't center only in my chest. "Someone is coming."

Ash tensed. "I don't feel anything—" His head whipped toward the doors. "You felt them before I did." He faced me, a faint grin on his face. "Your senses are progressing fast."

A noise came no more than a heartbeat after he spoke. It was light, barely audible. The sound of scratching. My gaze darted to the doors.

"We have visitors." Dipping his head, Ash kissed my forehead. "Welcome ones."

I tipped forward as Ash rose. He took one last drink of wine and then moved the table back a few feet with a wave of his hand. Scooting to the edge of the couch, I tried to see around him as he cracked open the door. A new smell wafted into the chambers—a wild, earthy aroma mixed with something sweet.

I knew that scent, even though I'd never noticed it before. It belonged to the draken, as did the sense of awareness. I stood.

"Sorry." The far-too-serious voice for one so young confirmed what I felt. "Nek is doing patrols. I've been trying to distract her, but she got away from me."

Before either Ash or I could respond, a small, greenish-brown blur of scales and thin, leathery wings darted around Ash's legs. The small draken launched herself a good four or five feet into the air—

Panic exploded. She was only four years old and unable to fly. Not that it stopped Nektas's daughter from trying. Repeatedly. I shot forward, catching her around the waist just as she started to plummet back to the hard stone floor. One wing whipped around, catching me in the side of the face. The slap stung, but how she clung to me made up for it. Her embrace was strong and at odds with her slight weight, but gods, it was one of the best hugs I'd ever received.

"Jadis." I laughed, jerking my head back from her flailing wings.

"I think someone missed you," Ash remarked, his voice warm.

Jadis gave a muffled chirp as she grasped onto my hair with her tiny, clawed fists. The tug sent a fiery wave of tingles across my scalp, but I honestly didn't care as I held on to her. She wasn't trying to hurt me. Plus, Nektas had said that my hair likely reminded Jadis of her mother. She'd only been two when Halayna was killed. Not nearly old enough to build a wealth of memories to look back on when she missed her momma. I held her tighter.

"And I also think this one may not have tried all that hard to stop her," Ash added, his arms folded over his chest as he looked down at Reaver.

The shaggy-blond-haired draken's cheeks pinked as he stared at the floor. He wore loose pants and a sleeveless tunic the color of cream. At the moment, Reaver looked like any mortal child, except for the vertical pupils and the somber seriousness of the old soul he carried.

Life had not been easy for either of them.

While Jadis had lost one parent to Kolis, Reaver had lost both of his before he was even old enough to hold on to his mortal form. They'd died defending the Shadowlands after Kolis grew angry with Ash for not responding to his summons quickly enough. Did Reaver have any memories of his parents? If not, I knew what kind of aching emptiness that left behind. I had none of my father.

I drew my hand down Jadis's back, her scales dry and smooth against my palm. I couldn't help but think of how they continued to experience loss. Ector. Davina. Orphine. Both she and Reaver had likely been close to them. Perhaps even thought of them as family. A wealth of emotion swelled in my chest. They had already suffered far too much senseless cruelty and loss.

I glanced at Ash, finding him watching me with a gentle look. Figuring I'd been projecting again, I cleared my throat. "Hi, Reaver."

"Hello." He dragged a bare foot across the stone floor in front of him. "How are you feeling, *meyaah Liessa*?"

"You don't have to call me that. I'm Sera to you." I patted Jadis's back as she wiggled as wildly as tree bears were rumored to do. "And I feel fine."

"I told Jadis that she'd be able to see you in the morning." His fingers were curled around the hem of his tunic so tightly that his knuckles had bleached white. "We felt you when you woke up. Nek told us to give you guys some time, but Jadis has been scared. She didn't know where you went," he said, his voice carrying hints of frustration and fear. "No one would tell us where either of you went or let us see you when you returned."

I lowered my chin to the top of Jadis's head, my heart aching at the fine tremor in Reaver's voice. "They didn't want you to worry."

"But we did worry." Reaver's head lifted then, his cheeks even redder, and his eyes, now as blue as Jadis's, glistening. "And even though no one would say it, I know it was *him*." His hands balled into fists as he looked up at Ash. "I know he took her, and then he took you."

Jadis squirmed, twisting her long, slender neck toward Reaver.

"And we didn't know if we would ever see either of you again." Reaver's voice trembled and cracked. "If you'd leave us like—" He cut himself off, his pointy chin jutting out as he clamped his jaw shut.

"We're not leaving you." Ash crouched before him so they were as close to eye level as possible. "Hear me? We will never leave you."

Reaver gave a quick, jerky nod while Jadis planted her hands on my shoulders and pushed. She squawked—

My head whipped toward hers in surprise. She had made a sound that was nothing like any language I'd ever heard, but I swore I understood her clearly. She'd said, "*down*" in that sweet, high-pitched voice of hers.

I stared at her. There was no way I'd heard that. Ash had said it took him days to understand the draken.

"Sera and I are okay," Ash said to Reaver. "You feel that, right?" He pressed his palm against Reaver, the width of his hand nearly that of the draken's chest. "You can feel her right there."

Reaver nodded.

I straightened, still holding on to Jadis. The draken wasn't a fan of me holding her the way I was. Straining, she pushed harder against my shoulders.

"She's not going to leave you," Ash told him, keeping his voice low. "Neither will I."

Reaver's head jerked up and down, but that red flush now stained his throat, and his entire body trembled. He folded his arms tightly across his chest and hunched his shoulders.

Clasping the back of Reaver's neck, Ash tilted his head. "I hate that either of you had to go through that. You shouldn't have had to, but it's okay to be upset. Understand? You can be angry, and you can be sad. You can even be afraid. There's nothing wrong with that."

Sorrow filled me as Reaver's face crumpled. He *could* be angry, sad, and scared, but damn it, he shouldn't have to be *any* of those things.

Without saying a word, Ash gathered the young draken into his arms, lifting Reaver as he rose. A muffled, hoarse sob came from the child as Ash turned so Reaver remained hidden by his frame. Cradling the back of Reaver's head, Ash spoke quietly as the youngling clung to his shoulders, the knuckles of his small hands bleached white from how tightly he held on.

Gods. Ash was…he was so damn good with Reaver.

Sensing that Reaver likely wanted some time to himself, I turned the wiggling Jadis to the table. I swallowed the knot in my throat and decided to go with the only thing I felt would distract her. "Jadis, baby? Would you like a strawberry?"

Jadis's attention was still on Reaver, but her fully extended arms ceased their relentless pressure.

Tears filled my eyes as I smiled. "They're very sweet and tasty." I went around the table and sat on the couch. "I think you'll like them."

Jadis pulled her diamond-shaped head back, her incredibly big, blue eyes moving from me to the bowl and then to Reaver.

"They're one of my favorite fruits." I picked up a fork and sliced the strawberry in two. "Do you remember when I had you eat from a fork before?"

Jadis hesitated, then nodded as her hands returned to my hair, grabbing fistfuls.

Figuring that was a good sign, I picked up one of the halves. "Just in case you've forgotten, watch me."

She didn't take her eyes off me or the fork as I took an incredibly slow bite. She chirped twice.

"Me, me."

"Me." I whispered what I'd heard in my mind, utterly dumbfounded. Was I really hearing her? Getting the other strawberry half onto the fork, I glanced over at Ash and Reaver. The space where they had been was empty, and I wondered if they'd gone through the door in the bathing chamber that led to the adjoining meeting space.

Like before, Jadis stared at the utensil for several moments, her eyes narrowed. Her claws snagged in my hair as one hand let go and dropped to my arm. She tugged.

I smiled at her. "Ready?"

She snapped forward, closing her mouth around the fork. Her teeth clanged off the silver, but she did get the strawberry off without me losing the utensil or her losing a tooth.

"Good job. Want more?" I asked, not worried about feeding her strawberries since Ash gave her all the food under the roof when he thought Nektas wasn't paying attention.

Jadis nodded. She watched avidly as I cut several more strawberries in half, holding on to my arm and humming. It still took a couple of seconds for her to remember what to do and trust the utensil, but by the time we got to the last strawberry, she was no longer hesitant, and I felt Ash's and Reaver's presence again.

"Jadis," Ash called as he strode toward the table and couch. "You haven't even acknowledged me yet."

Jadis squawked excitedly, then threw herself against the arm I was using to brace her and keep her upright.

Feeling like second best, I grinned as I let her go. She scampered across the couch and then stood on her hind legs, stretching her arms up.

"I'm still your favorite." Ash gave me a wink as he picked Jadis up, holding her to his chest. "Knew it."

Jadis pressed the top of her head to his cheek, her eyes squeezed shut.

Reaver quietly approached. His skin was no longer ruddy, but his eyes were puffy as he peeked up at me through dusky lashes. "Hi."

"Hello," I replied, and then we…

We just stared at each other.

I honestly had no idea what to do with children, especially upset ones, other than distract them with food. I didn't think that would work with Reaver, but when I looked at him, I was reminded of how close he'd come to dying due to Veses. He'd been keeping me company when she arrived and had gone after her in an attempt to defend me—something draken weren't supposed to do. She'd attacked him viciously enough to deliver a near-fatal blow, and I could still feel the panic of seeing him lying there in his mortal form, unmoving.

So, I got over my awkwardness and patted the seat next to me. "Sit with me?"

Reaver nodded and hopped onto the couch beside me. He kept his chin lowered and his hands clasped in his lap.

"Hungry?" I asked.

He shook his head.

"Damn." I sighed. "I was hoping I would get to teach you how to use a fork."

"I know how to use a fork."

"You sure?" I grinned as he glanced over at me, and I could see through the strands of his blond hair that his brows were furrowed. "I'm exceptionally skilled at teaching one how to use utensils."

Those serious, now-jewel-blue eyes met mine. "I can pretend I don't know how if you'd like."

I laughed. "That won't be necessary."

"Good," he said, shifting his stare to his hands and then back to me. "I really didn't mean to interrupt you two."

"It's okay. I'm glad you did. I missed you all—" My chest hitched as I remembered standing in the Bonelands, thinking I might die before I got to see them again.

Reaver wiggled closer. "Are you okay?"

"Yes." Clearing my throat, I glanced at Ash. He was filling a glass of water as Jadis, now draped over his shoulder, chattered in his ear about something to do with… "Grass—green grass."

"You can understand her now?" Curiosity filled Reaver's voice.

"I…I think I can. I swore I heard her earlier, and this time, I just kind of have a feeling about what she's saying." I sent Ash a smug look. "Either that or I'm hallucinating."

"Likely the latter," Ash teased.

I snorted. "Someone sounds jealous." Wanting to distract Reaver and brag, I said, "Did you know that it took Ash actual *days* before he could understand the draken?"

Reaver looked between us while Ash raised a brow. "I didn't."

"Apparently, it's not taking me that long," I boasted.

"You're such a quick learner," Ash stated dryly.

I grinned. "I actually thought Ash was lying when he said he could understand you all."

"He never lies," Reaver replied solemnly, and Ash's grin spread. "She's really excited about the grass. She's never seen it green before."

I focused on Reaver. "You haven't either, have you?"

Reaver shook his head. "It's different." He sat back a little. A moment passed as he looked between Ash and me. "Did you really miss us?"

"Very much so." I pushed the now-even-more-tangled hair back from my face. "And I was worried about both you and Jadis. I…" I swallowed, dropping my hands to my lap as I whispered, "I was also afraid."

Mashing his lips together, he blinked damp lashes. Chest squeezing, I extended an arm. After a second, Reaver closed the distance between us and pressed himself against my side.

Folding my hand under the soft strands of hair at the back of his head, I closed my eyes. "But like Ash said, we're safe. We're good. All of us. And we're going to stay that way."

"Promise?" Reaver asked in a rough whisper.

"Promise," I swore, kissing the top of his head.

Tension eased from Reaver's thin body as he relaxed against me and quieted as I idly ran my fingers through the soft strands of his hair. Some time passed, and the release of all the emotion that had been building up in Reaver must've exhausted him. He fell asleep and ended up using my leg as a pillow.

I kept threading my fingers through his hair, worried that he'd wake up if I stopped. Sleep was always best after a good cry.

My mind wandered over everything it would take to make the promise Ash had made to Reaver happen as I listened to Ash's footsteps and Jadis's waning chatter. Even without the prickly sense of knowing, I feared I knew where this was headed.

And yes, it was a real, cold, cutting fear. Because no matter how many gods or Primals decided to stand with us, I knew lives would be lost.

I did what I didn't want to. I thought about Kolis. There were moments when he was like how he must've been before bitterness and envy rotted him from the inside. Before that fateful day on the Cliffs of Sorrow when he saw Sotoria. But whoever he had been that allowed Eythos to continue loving him so irrevocably was long gone. His rot had decayed him so thoroughly that it ruined even his best intentions.

He was truly a monster now.

Kolis wouldn't bow out. He thrived on ultimate power and authority. Got off on it. Without it, what did he have? Bitter truths and tainted memories?

But I knew Kolis wanted to avoid war. That was what I'd been about to tell Ash before the young draken arrived. Kolis wasn't completely irrational. He knew what was at stake. He also didn't want to fight in a war he believed he could lose.

And if we got the majority of the Primals to back us? Would he back down then? Maybe a little. Perhaps just enough to give us a chance to take him down.

Ash's shoulder brushed mine as he sat beside me. Jadis was passed out against his chest, one of her scaled cheeks resting just above his heart. I lifted a brow as I saw that the little draken was all but swaddled in what appeared to be one of Ash's sweaters.

"Just in case she decides to shift into her mortal form. It's been happening less and less, but I don't think she's quite grown out of it," Ash said, his voice low as Jadis wiggled in her sleep, managing to poke one clawed foot free of Ash's sweater as he glanced down at Reaver. "How he was earlier? I haven't seen him like that since his parents died."

My attention shifted back to Reaver's sharp features and the slight parting of his lips. "I promised him we would all remain safe," I admitted.

"We will."

I nodded as I smoothed my hand over the crown of Reaver's head, but I knew I shouldn't have made any promises.

There would be a fight.

Would it only be between us and Kolis, or would it become the war Attes spoke of and Kolis swore he wanted to avoid?

Either way, lives would be lost.

And we wouldn't be able to keep everyone safe.

"You just missed Ash," I said, holding the bedchamber door open for Nektas. "He took Jadis and Reaver to the chamber they normally sleep in."

"Ah," he murmured, glancing down the hall. "I'm guessing they were still asleep?"

"They were when they left, which kind of surprised me," I admitted, having figured one of them would've woken when Ash draped them over his shoulders.

His head tilted. "Younglings are deep sleepers. Once they fall asleep, they're out until morning."

"Huh." From what I knew, that was the complete opposite of mortal children.

His attention shifted back to me. "I hope you got some rest after your eventful night."

My thoughts flashed to the hours spent in bed with Ash. There had been some rest involved. "I did."

"That's good to hear," he said. "You may feel stronger than ever."

"But I'm a baby Primal and, therefore, need lots of nap time," I said, eyeing him. "Why do I suspect that you knew exactly where your daughter and Reaver were?"

A faint smile tugged at Nektas's lips. "Am I that transparent?"

"Yes." I stepped aside. "Would you like to come in?"

His chuckle was low and raspy as he walked in. "This is unexpected."

"What is?" I asked as I closed the door.

"This," he answered with a sweep of his arm.

I scanned the chamber and winced at the bed in complete disarray and the leftover food and clothing scattered about. "The place is a bit of a mess, isn't it? We had just finished dinner when Reaver and Jadis came by."

"A mess?" Nektas surveyed the space. "It actually looks lived in." He bent, picking up a napkin that had fallen to the floor. "You remember what it looked like before."

Cold. Neat. Almost empty and devoid of…life.

"It is actually a relief to see such a mess." He placed the napkin on the table. "There is a warmth to it."

A mix of emotions surfaced as I fiddled with one of the buttons on my robe. I was at once glad that there was life here and sad that there hadn't been before.

That Ash hadn't been able to allow that.

"I hate Kolis," I whispered as a surge of essence rippled through me.

Nektas turned his head to me. "For what he has done to Ash and to you."

My breath snagged. What he'd said hadn't been posed as a question. It was a statement of fact. "Yeah." I swallowed thickly. "By the way, I heard Jadis tonight through the *te'lepe*."

Crossing his arms, he faced me. "I believe we were right in our assumptions regarding the maturity of the embers."

I nodded.

"I did come here for a reason," he said after a moment. "I wanted to apologize for tonight's interruption. Both Jadis and Reaver were told to give you and Ash space."

"Oh, gods. Please don't apologize. I was glad to see them. I missed them, and I think they needed to see us to know we're okay. Especially Reaver. And I needed to see *them*. There was a time I didn't think I would see them again." Avoiding Nektas's gaze, I cleared my throat and then did what I had already done more than once this evening. I changed the subject. "Ash and I discussed Kolis," I said, giving him a brief rundown of what we'd planned.

"All of that sounds good," he replied. "Though I have no interest in speaking for the draken."

My lips pursed. Who would be better? "But you really do think it's a good idea?"

"It's a change." He scratched his chin. "But change is good, especially when it's needed."

Exhaling slowly, I nodded. "There's something else. Something I realized after speaking with you."

He picked up an untouched strawberry. "What is that?"

"The riders. Do you know what they are?"

He finished off the sugar-dusted fruit. "What do you think?"

"I…I think you know more than you've shared with Ash," I said after a moment.

Picking up another berry, he went quiet for a moment. "I was still of only one form when the riders came into existence, created to bring about the end."

"Gods, you are so old," I mumbled. He shot me a narrowed-eye look, and I flashed him a quick, bright smile. But he *was* old, and I knew what that meant.

"Why do you ask?" he questioned.

"It wasn't until I was having dinner with Ash that I remembered all the stuff I'd seen during my Ascension," I explained. "You know who the Fates are, don't you?"

He nodded, looking out over the courtyard. "I remember the Ancients more clearly than the eldest of the Primals. I know what some became."

"And you never said anything to Ash?"

Nektas shook his head as he wiped his fingers on the napkin he'd picked up.

"I didn't either. I almost did, but I had a feeling I shouldn't. That there would be consequences if I did," I told him. "But I don't know why. I was wondering if you did."

"Power. Ancestry," he stated. "Some gods and mortals would seek to follow them instead of the Primals—those who would always align themselves with those they believed were the strongest—who they descended from in one way or another. We are lucky the Arae know the truth."

"What truth?"

"That beings who wield control over life and death, the lands and the elements, those who hold within them such unyielding power, can never be in a position to rule," he said, eather flashing in his pupils. "For they are blood and bone."

"The ruin and wrath of a once-great beginning," I whispered. A fine shiver curled its way down my spine at the same moment cold fingers of dread pressed into the skin behind my left ear. I thought about what Kolis had sought to become.

A Primal of Blood and Bone.

Of Life *and* Death.

"The Ancients," I said. "They held power over all, right? Before they split their powers and went into Arcadia or became the Fates."

"Before then, a single Ancient could influence gods and mortals to go to war or make peace. They could inspire invention and love, or slothfulness and envy, and ensure that the lands were as fruitful as a union between the two," he said. "One could turn an entire village propitious or curse every inhabitant with misfortune." His gaze met mine. "It is because they wielded control over all forms of life and death."

A chill went down my spine as I crossed the chamber, stopping at the balcony doors. "The part about them being able to create new realms wasn't hyperbole."

"I never saw them do it, but it was said they could," he said as I pulled a curtain aside. "But they could also undo the realms. They could topple the mountains and flood the lands. That is what some wanted to do. Not complete destruction, not a complete undoing of the realm, but they *had* done it before. In different lands."

"Lands to the east and west, separated by unending seas and mist," I murmured, thinking about the mountains I'd seen erupting into flames, and the steel buildings that had fallen. Had they already done what I'd seen? Was that why we couldn't pass beyond the veil of eather?

Or was that what was to come?

"But you know what the Ancients were capable of and what the ones who went to ground still are," he said.

"I know. I was just thinking about why there has never been a Primal of Life and Death." My fingers tightened on the curtain. "It's because they would be…"

"Not just mightier than any Primal," he finished, "but a Primal of Life and Death. Therefore, as powerful as an Ancient once their essence reached maturity."

I stared at the dark skies beyond the glass. "If Kolis drained his brother and took the embers that way, he…" I rubbed the nape of my neck. "He would've taken all of them." The prophecy whispered through my thoughts. "*For finally, the Primal rises…*" It spoke of the Primal of Blood and Ash. Blood and Ash stood for Life and Death. Blood and Bone. "He would've become the Primal of Blood and Bone." I forced in a slow, even breath. "He could still become that."

"Will you allow it?"

My gaze flew to him. "Fuck, no."

"Will Ash?"

"Absolutely fucking not."

Nektas smiled. "I didn't think so," he said. "Once Kolis is dealt with, such a being will not be a concern."

Unease stirred as I stood there, leaving me a little—or a lot—confused. I didn't think it had anything to do with Kolis, despite the fact he was a threat in more ways than…five hundred. It was the idea that such a being as a Primal of Life and Death was impossible. But I wasn't sure why. My intuition was quiet again.

Except for one thing.

Even when Kolis was dealt with, a being of such power was *not* impossible.

Gold spun before me.

Gilded bones.

Gold chests.

Chains.

And I felt *him* behind me, beneath me, his body too hot. Too still. Weight crushed my chest.

Crushed me.

"I cannot believe you would bring him up as I hold you," Kolis hissed in my ear.

I twisted in his grip and saw him, his flesh thinning until the dull gleam of bone was visible.

No, this isn't real.

"That you would even speak his name."

I couldn't get air into my lungs as I stared into pools of gold-flecked eather.

This isn't real.

I'd escaped.

I'd freed myself.

His lips peeled back, baring elongated fangs.

No. No. No—

"Sera."

Upon the sound of my name—the sound of *his* voice—I could breathe again. Air poured into my lungs. The stale scent of lilacs got washed away by fresh air and citrus. Kolis faded away, dissipating like smoke. The gilded cage collapsed, crumbling into nothing.

The nightmare disappeared into a gray, tranquil void, and this time, I thought I felt the cool touch of Ash's lips against my brow. As I slipped further into the void of sleep, I thought I heard Ash's voice again, telling me that it was only a dream. That I was safe, now and always. That he was there and would watch over me. Keeping the nightmares at bay.

8

Standing in the center of the bedchamber, I smoothed my hands over the fitted black vest and simple, quarter-sleeve shirt of the same color I'd found in the pile of clothing by the wardrobe. After being forced to wear transparent gowns for weeks, I had immediately grabbed a pair of leggings. There were other tops in my size, too, one that reminded me of the style Ash and his guards wore, but it seemed too…fancy for right now.

A curl toppled forward as I looked down at myself. Gods, I was so happy to be wearing clothing of my choosing again. But as I stood there, it suddenly struck me why I hated the gowns Kolis forced me to wear.

Not having a real choice was a huge part of it, but it was also that they reminded me of my failed presentation as the Consort—the gown I'd been forced to wear when I was first taken to the Shadow Temple. It, too, had hidden absolutely nothing and put me and nearly every inch of my body on display.

How I hadn't made the connection until now was beyond me.

My stomach roiled so suddenly and sharply that I smacked my hand over my mouth out of fear that the breakfast Ash had scrounged up for us might come right back up. Closing my eyes, I waited for the wave of nausea to pass, half-afraid that it wouldn't. But it did after a couple of minutes.

Gods. I needed to get a grip.

I blew out a long breath as I glanced over the bare walls and the scant pieces of furniture, still a little rattled by how vivid everything was. The space contained only the necessities: a long, tall wardrobe and several chests, the small, round table by the couch, and the new charcoal-gray armchair sitting near the bed. I'd heard Nektas's voice when I was in stasis.

Was that where he'd sat?

Nektas was right last night, I thought as I took in the rumpled blankets, discarded clothing, and used dinnerware on the table. The chambers did looked lived in. There was life here now. Not much, but enough that it had started to chip away at the kind of existence Ash had had for a little over two centuries due to Kolis's far-reaching and toxic influence. One that allowed for no warmth and no time or desire to form attachments, bonds, or even interests.

But that was changing. And it would *continue* to change.

I turned to the doors. After eating, Ash went back downstairs to check on things. When he returned, it would be time to meet with the others and go over what Ash and I had discussed last night.

I swallowed, shifting from one foot to the other. I knew I didn't have to wait for him to return. I could go downstairs now. I could go anywhere I wanted. Well, mostly. But given how my heart pounded, you would've thought a pit of forked-tongue vipers waited just beyond.

Feeling foolish—and not in a good way—I let my head fall back. I couldn't believe that I was hiding in my bedchamber because the idea of facing anyone without Ash stressed me out. Especially not after everything I'd been through—all I'd done.

That didn't mean Ash's pep talk had gone into one ear and out the other. I just wasn't getting a grip yet. I would before we met with the Shadowlands gods.

Thinking about that caused a small spike of anxiety as I turned. A thin line of light between the balcony door's curtains caught my attention. I started toward them as I sensed the presence of another drawing near. A god but not…

A series of quiet knocks jerked my head toward the chamber doors. Knowing Ash wasn't who I'd felt and that he wouldn't do that when entering his own chambers, I hesitated as I wrapped my hand around the door handle.

"Sera?" A soft, muffled voice came from the hallway. "It's Aios."

Now, I understood what I had felt. Aios wasn't just a goddess, nor was she a risen Primal. She was somewhere in between since I'd brought her back.

I yanked the door open, half-surprised that I didn't tear it right off its hinges. Whatever I had been about to say vanished as I came face-to-face with the fiery, red-haired goddess. For a moment, I was struck speechless. The last time I'd seen her, she'd been so terribly wounded, drenched in blood, dead. And then…not dead. I knew she lived, but seeing her standing here, healthy and whole, sent a shudder of relief through me.

"Your eyes," Aios rasped, her once-citrine and now pearly silver eyes widening as she stared at me. A hand flew to her throat—to the delicate silver chain Rhain had returned to her.

Swallowing, I tore my gaze from the necklace before everything that involved the piece of jewelry took center stage. "I assume they're still silver and green?"

Aios blinked. "They…most definitely are." Her stare lingered on mine for a fraction longer, and then she crossed the threshold, throwing her arms around me.

Unused to such a physical expression from anyone outside of Ash, I returned the embrace with stiff, awkward arms.

Gods, why did I have to be so damn weird?

"I'm sorry," she said, her arms tightening around me. "I know I should greet you a certain way now, and I have this impression that you're as fond of hugs as Bele, but I couldn't help myself."

"I can't picture Bele hugging anything." Inhaling the vanilla scent clinging to Aios's hair, my arms finally relaxed. "Not even a cute, cuddly kitten."

Her laugh was shaky as I closed my eyes and let myself soak in her embrace. Besides Nektas—and gods, *Ector*—Aios had been one of the few to warm up to me when I first arrived in the Shadowlands. I'd thought we might actually become friends, but when she learned that I'd originally believed I had to kill Ash to save my kingdom, she hadn't been angry. No, it was worse. She had been saddened and disappointed. And, gods, I'd rather be on the receiving end of her anger than that. Her disappointment cut far deeper. So, this hug? It made all the awkwardness more than worth it.

"You saved my life," Aios whispered hoarsely. "I wish there was something better than these two words, but…thank you."

"Those two words aren't even necessary." My throat thickened as I thought about what I'd done. "I should be apologizing—"

"What?" Aios drew back, sliding her hands to mine. "Why would you think that?"

"When I brought you back, I did it without considering whether you wanted that. I don't regret doing it," I quickly added. "But I should've stopped and thought about it."

"You did the right thing. Just like you did for Bele."

"That was different. She died right before our eyes." Not that Aios needed the reminder. "But you were…" I trailed off. I had no idea how much time had passed for Aios by the time I brought her back, and the idea that I could've ripped her away from peace had haunted the back of my mind ever since. "I didn't know if your soul had passed on or not."

"If it did, I don't remember it," she said. "And that doesn't matter. I wasn't ready to die. And I wouldn't be here if it weren't for you, so yes, you did the right thing. And a thank you *is* necessary." She squeezed my hands before letting go. "Okay?"

I couldn't shake the feeling that her soul had crossed over to Arcadia, a realm of peace very much like the Vale, or had been in the process of doing so. But hearing her say what she had lessened that concern for me. Letting out a ragged breath, I nodded.

"Good." Her glistening lashes fluttered as she cleared her throat. "I ran into Nyktos downstairs. He got sidetracked by Theon. He just returned from the Bonelands."

The Bonelands was a stretch of uninhabited land between the mountainous Carcers and the Skotos Mountains where the mortals had fought alongside the gods and Primals against the Ancients. The draken believed it was sacred given the bones of the fallen that remained unseen but were still there. Theon had been stationed there with several ships and soldiers.

"Is everything okay?" I asked.

"Yes. Theon is only updating Nyktos. He'd been waiting, wanting to give you two some space and time," she explained, clasping her hands at the waist of her deep forest-green gown. "I told Nyktos I would let you know, and he asked me to tell you he would be in his office for a bit."

He was likely writing the names of the recently deceased—in blood—in the Book of the Dead.

And yeah, that still creeped me out.

"Are you up for company until he returns?" Aios asked.

"Of course. I'm glad you came by," I said, and Aios's smile widened. "I've been so worried about everyone. How you were after what happened, and with…" My breath caught, causing the essence to hum through me. "And with Orphine and Ector."

"You'd think one would become used to such deaths after a while, especially being where we are." Aios sat on the edge of the couch. "But it doesn't get easier. Not even when we know, without a doubt, that it's not like they cease to exist. We know they are at peace."

"You're right. It doesn't make it easier." Walking to the couch, I sat beside her. "I wish I could've gotten to Ector sooner and been there for Orphine, but…"

Aios's heart-shaped face tilted to the side as she eyed me. "But what?"

But the list of those I'd brought back to life was adding up, starting with Marisol and ending with Aios. There was even a draken on that list.

Should I have brought any of them back?

Would I have done so with Ector and Orphine if given the chance? My immediate response was yes, but I knew that it wasn't as simple as what I wanted. And it wasn't my new, uncanny sense of knowing that told me that.

"Sera?" Concern filled Aios's voice.

"Sorry. I got a little lost in my thoughts." I clasped my knees. "I was thinking about those I've restored life to and balance. How when there is life, there must be death. Like an exchange."

Aios's brows rose and then furrowed. "Are you saying that when you bring someone back to life…"

"Another dies," I finished for her, thinking about my stepfather. When I'd brought Marisol back, the former King of Lasania had paid for it with his life.

Her face drained of blood. "Did someone else take my place?"

My eyes widened. "No. Gods, I'm sorry. I should've clarified. It only happens with mortals, not gods or draken."

"Oh, thank the Fates." Aios blinked rapidly as she looked away, her throat working on a swallow. "I wouldn't know what to think if that were the case." Her gaze found mine. "When you brought Gemma back, do you know who…?"

"Who paid for her life with theirs?" I continued. "I don't. And I don't want Gemma learning about this."

Aios nodded slowly. "Agreed. She would likely blame herself."

Marisol would, too, if she ever learned what'd happened. And, gods, that would be super complicated, considering it had been her wife's father who had ended up in death's grip.

"There was another before Gemma," I said, telling Aios about Marisol. "I didn't know what would happen then. Honestly, I didn't even think I would be able to bring her back to life. She was my first mortal."

"Would knowing that another life had to be forfeited have changed what you did?"

A wry grin tugged at my lips. "You asked something similar of me before. And by the way, you were right that day when you said that creating life out of death was in my nature."

Her silver eyes lightened. "I was, but I don't think either of us knew just how right."

"No doubt." I laughed, sliding my palms over my thighs. The last time she'd asked this, it had been about Bele and whether I would've still brought her back if I had known that her Ascension would draw the attention of the other Primals. This time, I put it into words. "I would've still done it to save my stepsister the heartbreak of losing someone she loved." The irony that the act had taken another she loved was cruel. "And if I had gotten to Ector in time or had a chance to save Orphine, I would've. But—" I cut myself off, shaking my head. "Never mind. You don't need to hear any of this."

"No. It's okay." The hem of her gown swayed across the stone floor as she angled her body toward mine. "Please, continue. I find this topic… interesting." Her nose wrinkled. "I feel like that may have been inappropriate to admit."

I raised a brow. "I'm the last person you need to worry about being inappropriate with."

"Actually, you're technically the *only* person I should worry about my behavior around," she corrected. "You are the Queen."

My heart skipped several beats. Somehow, that fact kept slipping my mind.

"Many of us either weren't born when there was a true Primal of Life or weren't close enough to Eythos to ever hear him speak of what it was like."

"I'm not sure I even know what it's like," I admitted. "But I was just…I was just thinking about knowing when to use the ability to restore life and when not to. Like I can't bring everyone back, but if it really is in my nature, how do I stop it? How do I decide—and I hate using this word—but how do

I decide who deserves it and who doesn't?"

You don't.

I stiffened. The voice that whispered in my thoughts was mine, and the knowledge came from my Ascension. "It's not the Primal of Life's place to intervene in the natural order of things," I whispered, but…that was *bullshit.* "What was natural about how Ector and Orphine died?" I turned to Aios. "Or you. There was nothing natural about what Kyn did when he attacked the Shadowlands. That *can't* be a part of the natural order of things."

"There was nothing natural about any of that. What Kyn did was unnecessarily cruel," she said, and knowing what I did about the Primal, I didn't doubt that for a moment. "I should've stayed inside." Tears built in her eyes, clouding the pulse of eather. "I don't know what I was thinking when I went out there. I'm not trained to fight like you and Bele, but I thought I could at least help the wounded get inside."

"You're not trained, but you had to do something," I said, choosing my words carefully. "Wanting to help is understandable."

She pressed her lips together. "I know, but…Kyn saw me when he entered the courtyard. He came right for me. And, Fates, I still don't understand why. He knows I'm not a fighter—that I was no threat to him—but he grabbed me and dragged me toward the pikes where the dakkais were feeding on some of the restrained who were still alive." She sucked in a sharp breath. Closing her eyes, she shook her head. I waited in silence until she could speak again, knowing she was seeing in her mind what I was. The lives lost on those pikes, their bodies brutalized in unimaginable ways. Except she'd been there when it happened. "In all the years I've lived, I've never witnessed anything like that. Not even in Dalos. Not even from Kolis."

There was a good chance I stopped breathing. I was betting that Kyn had gone for her because of her time spent held against her will by Kolis. And I also wouldn't be surprised to learn that Kolis had offered Aios to Kyn at some point.

Her fingers twisted the chain at her throat. "Ector saw it happening and tried to stop Kyn, even though he knew he shouldn't. Ector got Kyn good, though. Nearly took his arm off." She hastily wiped her palm over her cheek. "Ector's death was quick. At least, there was that."

Hearing that did bring me some peace, but it didn't dampen my building fury.

Aios cleared her throat. "Kyn may have been following orders to attack the Shadowlands, but he enjoyed it. He likes the pain and fear he inflicts."

Anger rushed to the surface, and I was suddenly standing before I even realized it. The corners of my vision turned a silvery white. "Tell me I can't go to Vathi and rip out Kyn's innards."

"You probably shouldn't do that."

Energy throbbed through me, charging the air. My skin heated. The chandelier began to swing as eather crackled along my skin. "Probably?" That one word dropped from my lips like a clap of thunder, causing Aios to jolt.

"Okay." She drew out the word. "You definitely shouldn't."

"I shouldn't," I hissed. My hands closed into fists as I closed my eyes, counting just as I had in the gilded cage while I sat in that bath. Just as I had when I drove the Ancient bone into Kolis. And as I counted, I willed the essence to calm. *One. Two. Three. Four. Five.* I opened my eyes. The chandelier no longer swayed. "It would be very un-Primal of Life-like behavior if I did."

"Uh-huh." Aios watched me sit back down. "By the way, your eyes sort of changed color there for a few moments."

"Really?"

She nodded. "The green turned gold. Your eyes were gold and silver."

I opened my mouth, but all I could say was, "Oh."

"They're back to green and silver now." Aios paused. "Your voice also did something different. You spoke out loud, but it was a breathy, hot sound. I know that sounds weird, but that's how it felt. And I also—"

"There's more?"

She nodded tentatively. "I heard your voice inside my head."

My chest clenched. "I don't know how or why that happened."

"I think you might've been going full Primal of Life."

"Did I physically change in appearance?" I asked, thinking about how Ash looked when he did. Then I thought about Kolis in his full Primal form. "Please, tell me I didn't turn into a skeleton."

"What?" Her brows snapped together. "No, your appearance didn't really change."

"Oh, thank the gods—wait." I twisted toward her. "What do you mean by *really* change?"

"Your skin sort of took on a golden hue," she said. "It was actually very pretty."

I stared at her.

"Truly." Aios smiled so widely it looked painful. "But that was all."

That was all? I almost laughed as I sat back, now wondering what I would look like when I *did* go full Primal. I'd only seen Ash and Kolis do that.

Giving a shake of my head, I looked at Aios. "I hope I didn't scare you."

"You didn't," she quickly assured.

"Okay. Good." I placed my hands on my legs. "I hate that you had to experience any of what you did, that pain and fear were your last thoughts. That it could've been the last thing Ector or any of the others felt. I'm sorry."

"I know," she whispered.

"And I will make sure Kyn pays for what he did," I promised. "No matter what happens from here with Kolis, Kyn *will* be punished." Energy hummed through me as I held her gaze, and as I spoke, the words became an oath inked into my very bones. "That, I swear to you, Aios."

Eather pulsed in her eyes, and they widened. She stiffened. "Sera, you made an oath—"

"I know." I exhaled, lifting my chin. "And I also know that an oath made by a Primal cannot be broken. He will pay, Aios."

A fierceness I'd never seen before settled into her features. The corners of her lips tightened, and her eyes, normally so full of warmth, filled with the icy flames of vengeance. "I accept your oath."

I smiled. I probably shouldn't have, but I did. "Good."

Aios sat back, running her fingers over the necklace. She cleared her throat, then went on like my first act as Queen wasn't to make an oath to take out another Primal. "Do you think that a natural death versus one that isn't makes a difference? When it comes to mortals, at least?"

"I…I don't know." No feelings or certain knowledge came, but it made me wonder if it did matter. Was there another way to restore the balance? I blew out a breath. "Even if it did, I feel like I'd probably be traveling down the same path Eythos did."

"True." Her lashes lowered, then swept up. "Attes told us about Sotoria and how her soul was in you but you weren't her," she shared. "You were right when you insisted that you weren't the same person."

I shifted, so damn uncomfortable whenever I thought about Sotoria's soul now stuck in a damn diamond. At least I knew Attes would keep her safe.

"Anyway, you're fine, right?" she asked. "The only thing that has changed is your eyes?"

"I was tired upon waking. Slept a lot like Bele did," I shared. "But I feel as I did before."

Something else popped into my head then, bringing a smile to my lips. "So." I drew out the word. "Bele?"

Her forehead creased. "Yes?"

"And you? Together?"

A pretty pink flush stained her cheeks. "We are."

The curve of my lips spread as I pictured them. There likely couldn't be a more beautiful couple. "Is it new, or…?"

"Yes, and no." Her blush deepened as she laughed. "We've been friends for many years, and we were together once before, about—oh, let's see…" The groove between her brows deepened. "Eighteen years ago? Almost nineteen."

I choked on my breath. "I'm sorry. You two were together almost two decades ago?"

"Yes." A small grin appeared. "Why do you look so confounded?"

"Because you speak of two decades like it's two months," I sputtered.

"Compared to the span of a mortal life, it feels like an equivalent comparison." The glow of eather pulsed behind her pupils. "Eventually, two decades will feel like two months to you, too."

Once more, my heart leapt. "I can't even imagine that," I admitted. "Feeling that way. Looking as I do today, two decades or centuries from now.

Like…my mind cannot process that."

"It will likely take nearly that length of time for you to do so."

"Probably." A breeze drifted into the chamber, stirring the curtains. "By the way, have you heard from Maia?" I asked. The Primal Goddess of Love, Beauty, and Fertility would've felt Aios's Ascension. "Or do you have any idea how she's handling this?"

"I haven't heard anything, and she hasn't summoned me," she answered. "But we've always been on good terms."

"So, you don't expect her to handle this like Hanan did?" Fearing that Bele would challenge his position after she Ascended, the former Primal God of the Hunt and Divine Justice had put a bounty out on her head.

Aios laughed softly. "No. While Maia may enjoy witnessing conflict and drama from time to time, she does so from afar. She doesn't like to be involved in it herself." She brushed a lock of thick, red hair back. "Maia also knows that I have no interest in ruling Kithreia. She won't be threatened by me."

I hoped it remained that way. I knew very little about Maia, having not met her outside of my coronation, but Ash must've felt some level of trust to go to her to have his *kardia* removed.

Aios tipped her knees toward me. "By the way, how are you handling everything?"

"Other than not coming to terms with what I am?"

Aios laughed lightly. "Yes. Other than that."

"I'm fine. Perfect, really." I dropped my hand to the arm of the couch. "And regarding the whole Ascending-as-the-true-Primal-of-Life part, I really haven't had much time to think about that. But I'm good."

"I'm relieved to hear that." She drew her lower lip between her teeth. "I didn't expect you to Ascend as the true Primal of Life."

"Yeah, well, neither did I since it should have been impossible."

"Apparently, it wasn't," she remarked dryly.

I cracked a grin. "You know the plan was for him to take the embers and Ascend, but the embers had sorta melded with me—became a part of me. I wouldn't have survived them being removed. Ash knew that and refused to take the embers." My voice thickened, and I swallowed. "He didn't know what would happen if he Ascended me. All he knew was that he couldn't let me die, no matter the risks. It wasn't until afterward that we realized we were heartmates."

"That is almost more shocking than your Ascension." Awe filled Aios's voice. "Such a union of hearts and souls is so rare that I suspect even Maia would be stunned."

I nodded, thinking about my parents. "You know, I always wondered if my mother and father were heartmates. Even as a child, when I wasn't entirely sure such a thing was real. Because my mother never seemed to get over my father's death, even though she remarried. She was always sad, even when she was happy."

"They do say that mates of the heart are linked to create something new or usher in a great change." Aios crossed her ankles. "They could've been destined to bring you into the world, and you…you are the definition of a great change."

But wouldn't that have meant the Fates—the Ancients—had seen everything? The intuition didn't kick in, but I did remember the unexpected thread of fate Holland had spoken of. The one that had broken off while all the others ended in my death.

"Sera?" Aios said softly.

Pulling myself from my thoughts, I focused on her. Aios's smile remained but it had changed. The curve of her lips was now forced. Almost brittle.

"When I asked how you were doing," she said, her gaze flickering over my features, "I wasn't just asking about how you were handling the Ascension."

Every muscle in my body tensed.

A too-long moment passed. "Is it true that…that Kolis believed you to be Sotoria for some time?"

My insides chilled. "How did you know that?" The answer came to me. "Attes."

She gave me a somewhat sheepish nod. "When he came by, we…well, to be honest, we bombarded him with questions. He didn't give us a lot of detail," she added quickly. "When Nyktos returned with you, and you were in stasis, there wasn't a chance to ask him anything. Not that anyone tried. We knew he wouldn't leave your side." She took a breath. "But no one knew what had happened. Only what we'd heard."

Blood pounded in my ears. "Like what?"

"It was said that you were seen sitting beside Kolis at court," she said. "But when Rhain and others saw you, you were…" She briefly closed her eyes. "You were not free to move about."

I'd been caged. Just as she had. "I was never free to move about. Kolis brought me to court and put me on display," I stated flatly. "Part of the reason was that he knew it would get back to others."

"None of us believed you wanted to be there. None of us," she insisted. "It just made us worry more."

I was holding myself completely still. "What else did you hear?"

"There were whispers that you'd attempted to escape, and we heard that Kolis claimed he hadn't given you and Nyktos permission for the coronation."

Kolis had lied. So had Kyn, who'd witnessed him giving us permission.

"Then only what Rhain said," she continued, and my stomach twisted sharply.

Rhain hadn't told anyone that I'd struck a deal with Kolis in exchange for his freedom. And while he'd been unconscious for the details of the deal, it took no leap of logic to guess what he believed I'd offered.

And I *had* offered anything Kolis wanted for Rhain's life. Kolis's voice intruded as pressure clamped down on my chest. *Then, tonight, we will share the same bed.*

What if Rhain's silence had changed?

"And what did he say?" I heard myself ask.

"He said that you convinced Kolis that freeing him was the best way to handle the situation." Her fingers went to the chain again—the very same necklace Rhain had used as a token to communicate with Aios. I'd pretended it was mine. "But I…"

"What?"

She was quiet for several moments. "I just know that your time in Dalos couldn't have been easy."

Feeling my chest tighten, I focused on the mess of clothing as I breathed in. I really didn't see the clothes, though. I saw jeweled, gold-plated chests. Pressing my lips together, I ignored the sting of my fangs scraping the inside of my lips. *Hold.*

"*I know,*" she repeated.

Gods, she did. Unfortunately, she had ended up as one of Kolis's favorites. I knew now, without a doubt, that her suspicion that it had been because of her hair color was correct. *Breathe out.*

"And I just wanted to say that I don't need to know what may have occurred to know that I'm so sorry for whatever you experienced."

"Thank you." *Breathe in.* My fingers dug into the arm of the couch as I made myself meet her gaze. *Hold.* "With some help, I was able to convince Kolis that I was Sotoria. Because of that, I…I got lucky."

"Lucky?" she repeated. "Compared to who?"

My ribs felt like they were too small. "To all those not sitting here who are free of Kolis."

Aios's mouth opened and then closed. "Very true." Her fingers continued dancing over the chain. "But I know the whole time I was held and made to listen to him, he only ever spoke about her."

Her.

Sotoria.

Fucking obsessive creep.

My breathing exercises belly-flopped out the window.

"So, I also know that my luck traveled further."

Kolis had never touched any of his past favorites. That wasn't the case for me. My chest shrank until it felt as small as a thimble.

Aios fixed another pained smile on her face. "I just wanted to let you know that if you ever need to talk, I'm here. Okay?"

"Okay," I said, knowing my smile was as wrong as hers. "I appreciate that. I do. But what happened when I was there? It was nothing."

Aios was speaking. Her lips were moving, but all I heard was "*it was nothing*" echoing over and over. But it was in Veses' voice. The Primal bitch of Rites and Prosperity had said the same thing in response to what Kolis had done to her. And as much as I hated her for what she'd done to Ash, it hadn't been *nothing*. What had been done to me wasn't—

Panic blossomed, and while it didn't stir the embers, it did loosen my tongue. "When you were held?" I cut Aios off. "Were there chests in the cage he kept you in?"

Aios went quiet.

I turned my head toward her, knowing her silence was my answer. "I saw what was in them. I know what he had his favorites do with them. So, I don't think your luck could've traveled much further than mine."

Aios blanched, sucking in a sharp breath.

Guilt seized me immediately. "I shouldn't have brought that up. I'm—"

"Don't apologize," she interrupted, eather pulsing brightly in her eyes.

"But I think I need to."

"No, you do not." She leaned in until our faces were inches apart. "I get it, Sera. More than anyone here. Maybe more than even Nyktos. I get it. The anger. The fear. The fucking awkwardness," she said. At any other time, I would've giggled at hearing her curse, but not now. Never now. "The helplessness and the godsdamn choking shame. I know how all that feels. How all those feelings become something worse than any act committed against you." Streaks of eather darted across her irises. "Because that anger, the fear and awkwardness, the helplessness and shame, they get into you. Into your very marrow. And it's hard to claw them back out."

I choked then, dying a hundred times without my heart ever stopping.

"You will say and do anything to avoid feeling or thinking about it, but eventually, you have to." Aios straightened, her features stark. "Because no matter what, Sera, it wasn't *nothing*."

The late-morning sun warmed my face as I stood at the balcony railing. I was never much of a fan of the sun, preferring cloudy, overcast days. It probably had a lot to do with the unbearable heat that plagued Lasania. But now, I wanted to soak it up until I disappeared into its warmth.

I was so unbearably cold inside.

Aios had left only minutes ago, but her voice was in my head as my hands curled tightly around the railing.

It wasn't nothing.

She had meant well, but she was wrong. What I'd experienced in Dalos was nothing like what those who had come before me had to deal with. I hadn't been forced to use the toys I'd found in that chest. I hadn't been tossed aside and given to gods who behaved like a pack of rabid dogs. I was lucky.

But why didn't it feel that way?

Chest shrinking, I felt the wind pick up, tossing long curls across my face. I needed to get myself under control before Ash returned because I was sure I was hurling emotions in every direction.

Holding my breath this time, I used the technique Ash taught me. Pressing my tongue to the back of my teeth, I straightened my spine and counted, repeating it until the sensation of fists clenching my lungs eased.

I slowly opened my eyes. My pulse was calm. So were my thoughts. I was…level.

My gaze flicked down. Sunlight glittered off the shadowstone railing that Nektas had been perched upon last night. I lifted my gaze to the sky and saw something I'd never seen in the Shadowlands before. Clouds—thick, fluffy clouds. And between those puffs, stars glimmering vividly. It was an unreal and beautiful sight.

Tipping my head back to the sun, I closed my eyes and inhaled deeply.

The stagnant scent from before was gone. The air was pleasant, if a little on the cool side, reminding me of the autumns from my childhood memories before the days and nights became overbearingly hot and humid.

I looked out over the courtyard. Thin tufts of green broke up the barren brown land.

Was that what was happening in Lasania, too? Was the soil already beginning to repair itself and sprouting new life? Better yet, what did my stepsister Ezra think?

"What is my mother thinking?" I asked aloud and then let out a short, shaky laugh.

Honestly, they probably weren't thinking about much beyond being so damn relieved. With the end of the Rot, more than just the decaying land would change. The weather would, too—the stifling heat and long droughts ended only by torrential downpours that did more harm than good. More fields could now be plowed. Crops planted. The people of Lasania had more than just a future. *Queen* Ezmeria and her Lady Consort Marisol could plan for a future, and that of coming generations. There was hope.

And I supposed once the shock lifted, they'd begin to think about how this was all possible. They'd probably assume I was dead. What else would they think? They both knew I couldn't survive what we'd believed my duty to be—a fact that had always bothered Ezra.

And something my mother had accepted.

Though everything was different now. I doubted I would be such an utter disappointment to her when she realized I was Queen of the Gods and *the* Primal of Life. Maybe she'd be interested in actually being a mother to me.

I pressed my lips together as an uncomfortable mass of guilt frothed to life. Was it fair to think of my mother that way? I wasn't so sure anymore, as I thought about her in the Wayfair gardens.

She'd found me sitting in front of beautifully scented flowers with purplish-blue spikes. She'd said that my father also enjoyed them. It had been one of the rare times she'd spoken of him. She'd been crying that night, and I didn't think it had much to do with the ache in her head that often plagued her. Those tears had everything to do with my father. Her feelings were wrapped up in a whole lot of grief because when she looked upon me, she saw my father and felt nothing but heartache.

Still, I was her child. It wasn't my fault that King Roderick had made that deal all those years ago, setting everything in motion and inevitably leading to my father's death.

A biting ache I thought should've vanished by now sliced through my chest. Everything with my mother still cut deep, even after all these years—even as I grew to have a better understanding of her. And maybe that would never go away, only lessen with time.

But I wanted to see Lasania for myself. I wanted to see Ezra, Marisol, and even…gods, even my mother. But I knew that would have to wait.

I leaned out, stretching until I saw the Red Woods. "Good gods."

The large swath of crimson leaves was afire in the sunlight, a sight just as beautiful as the sky despite the blood of the gods entombed beneath them that gave the leaves their vibrant color.

Gods that were as cruel as Kyn.

The skin along my neck tingled as I took in the shocking, almost twisted beauty of the Red Woods. Many of those gods had been entombed by Eythos himself. Not all. Quite a few had been placed there by Ash, but I *knew* those beneath the trees were the worst sort. Some were power-hungry. Others were lost to bloodlust. Many were abusers. Rapists. Most saw mortals as beneath them and only suited for worship and servitude.

I also knew they were loyal to Kolis—or would be if ever freed.

While Kolis hadn't gone into that much detail with his plans for exactly how he intended to *humble* mortals if he Ascended as the Primal of Life and Death or continued on as he was now, I knew he sought a more active role among the mortals.

Those entombed gods would support such endeavors.

Essence thrummed hotly through my veins. I doubted that any of them would have a change of heart upon Awakening. Why risk the chance of another Primal attempting to free them, but for vastly different reasons than causing a distraction this time?

All were users of some sort, destined for an eternity in the Abyss. So, why delay it?

Power gathered in me, pooling in my chest. The eather throbbed there as my grip tightened on the railing. I could end them before they had a chance to become a threat.

And I should.

Not because I wanted to but because it made sense tactically. I knew it did because, out of all the racing, scattered pieces of knowledge, there was one rapid, fleeting line of thought that warned me that Kolis *could* summon those loyal to him just as I *could* call upon the riders. Perhaps his pull would be strong enough to free those entombed.

That was something I would not allow.

Eather pressed against my skin. The corners of my vision turned silver. My muscles tensed—

I jerked myself back with a gasp. "My gods…"

Blinking, I pressed my palms to my stomach. Had I been seconds away from freeing the entombed gods just to kill them?

Yes. The answer was yes.

I shook my head, irritated with how quickly I'd proven that I'd only wounded that wild, reckless part of me. Gods, that was really concerning.

Okay. Maybe only slightly concerning because I needed to get real. It wasn't like anyone would be all that mad about ending those gods, but was that really how I wanted to start my reign? With what felt like an abuse of power?

Something *monstrous*?

Something Kolis would do?

Frustrated with myself, I let out a heavy breath as my gaze settled on a guard patrolling the Rise surrounding the House of Haides. While I watched him walk the wall, something…bizarre happened.

I heard a name.

Eamon.

Eamon Icarion.

And I heard more than just a name. Details whispered among my thoughts. Eamon was a god who'd seen three centuries. I knew he'd been in the courtyard when I challenged Ash to train with me, even though the sandy-skinned man was too far away for my improved vision to recognize any of his features. I also knew he was born in Lotho, the Court belonging to Embris, the Primal God of Wisdom, Loyalty, and Duty, and the mountainous home of the so-called Fates. Instinct prodded to me to push, and then push harder to follow the invisible thread connecting us. He'd been in the Shadowlands since Ash began his rule, having lost his family when they expressed dismay over Eythos's murder. He loved a godling he'd met in Lethe, and I felt—no, I *knew*—that Eamon was a good man, with the blood he'd spilled marking his *soul.*

I sucked in a sharp breath as awareness coursed through me. I turned to the bedchamber, sensing a draken, but I also felt the dual throbbing awareness of a Primal. And then another. It was strange because I knew the first was Ash because he felt different. Some innate part of me recognized that he was closer now. Was it because we were heartmates? I had to think so as I heard the interior chamber doors open.

Ash walked out, dressed as he'd been when he left this morning, having donned an ivory shirt. He'd left the collar laces undone, and had the sleeves rolled halfway up his forearms.

I would fight anyone who disagreed that no one else looked as good as he did with or without a shirt.

As he stepped to the side, a purplish-black-scaled draken flew out from the open doors, gliding smoothly through the air.

Reaver landed on the railing, but unlike with Nektas, my heart dropped. We were several stories up. If he fell… "Is there not a better place for you to sit?"

Tucking his wings close to his sides, his head tilted. He let out a series of low chirps that I understood—not so much heard but sensed. It was strange.

"I know you can fly, Reaver-butt," I responded. "But that doesn't mean there aren't other, more suitable resting places." I gestured around the balcony. "Literally any place else that doesn't make me feel like I'm about to have a heart attack."

He nudged my arm with his head and then hopped off, landing on the balcony. He sat at my side, his head just above my knee. "There is a daybed, like…right there."

Reaver leaned against my leg in response.

"He wants to be close to you," Ash explained as he stopped by the doors. "Jadis, on the other hand, is currently terrorizing Bele."

I glanced up with a grin and then looked closer at Reaver. "Have you gotten bigger?" I asked. Nubs of what I suspected would one day become horns had sprouted from the middle of the flattened bridge of his nose to run up the center of his diamond-shaped head where they split into a vee-shape.

"He has grown about two inches in the last couple of weeks." Ash loosely crossed his arms. "He's at the age where he'll hit his first growth spurt. In a few months, he'll be almost twice the size he is now."

My eyes widened. "I'm not sure I can still call you Reaver-butt when you're nearly as tall as me."

Reaver ducked his head and pressed it against my leg. Figuring that meant he wanted attention, I reached down and ran my hand between the bumps. He purred, stretching his neck.

"When will he have another growth spurt?" I asked.

"Another will occur in a few years. He'll be larger than Odin by then," he said, speaking of the warhorse that often resided within the cuff Ash wore on his upper arm.

Which made me think about the fact that neither Bele nor I had one yet. Apparently, ours would appear out of thin air when we were *ready*.

Whatever.

"Did Aios come by?" he asked, coming to stand on the other side of Reaver.

"She did." Leaning against the railing, I crossed my arms. "She said Theon needed to speak with you."

"He did." One of the shorter strands of hair slipped from the knot at the nape of his neck to kiss his jaw. "No ships have been spotted beyond ours. If another Court outside Vathi was planning to launch a sizable attack against the Shadowlands, bringing with them gods that are unable to shadowstep from Court to Court, we'd be able to see them from the cliffs in the Bonelands."

Vathi, the Court jointly ruled by Attes and Kyn, was across the Black Bay. If Kyn wanted to move his armies toward the Shadowlands as he had before, he wouldn't have to go into the open seas. He'd simply need to cross the bay.

"The Shadowlands is uniquely positioned, even more so than Vathi. To cross the Lassa Sea, traveling from the Shadowlands to the Bonelands is only a day trip by ship, and the Primal mist that prevents mortals from traveling too far east also cloaks our movements. The same cannot be said for Vathi," Ash said.

The mist would kill any mortal, so I guessed it was a good thing no mortals called the Bonelands home. "But doesn't Lotho share the same land mass as both the Shadowlands and Vathi? They could travel by foot."

"The canyon between Vathi and Lotho makes it difficult but not impossible," Ash said. "Several Courts share the same land. Kithreia—Maia's Court—is joined, and a narrow land bridge connects it to the Court of Sirta, but moving forces this way would be unlikely at the moment."

"Why?" I asked, genuinely curious. Considering that I was the Queen, I needed to get familiar with Iliseeum's layout.

"Besides the fact that it would take longer to travel by land than it does by ship, none of the Courts will want another's army moving through their lands. Doing so would be considered a political move," Ash explained. "Permission must be granted. So, Embris would have to approve Maia's forces traveling through Lotho, just as Maia would have to give permission for Bele to move Sirta's armies through Maia's Court."

"Is Sirta still a mess?" I asked.

"Yes, but that's no different than when Hanan ruled. Very few who call Sirta home actually served him. His Court had mostly become a haven for thieves and raiders."

I laughed. "I'm sorry. None of that is funny. It's just ironic that the Court of the Hunt and Divine Justice has become an asylum for injustice."

"Not that I want to make it seem like Hanan wasn't responsible for his actions, but it's partly due to Kolis. The moment he stole those embers from my father, a different kind of rot invaded the Courts," he reminded me. "Twisting what us Primals were meant to stand for."

Us.

Hearing that gave me a start. I didn't think it would ever *not* do that. I reached down to pet Reaver. "Speaking of other Primals, I made an oath to Aios."

"You did?"

"You might be mad."

Interest sparked in his eyes as he rose. Not judgment or anger. "I doubt that."

"Well…" My lips pursed. "It was kind of reckless."

"Did you forget?" Sunlight slid over his cheekbone. "I enjoy the reckless side of your nature."

My lips twitched. "I haven't forgotten, but I also know that doesn't hold true all the time." I clasped the railing. "I promised her that Kyn would be punished for what he did to her and Ector. To the Shadowlands."

He tilted his head. "Why would I be mad about that?"

I lifted a shoulder. "Because the first thing I did as Queen was to make an oath to potentially kill another Primal. One who is the twin of another, who is our ally. And I did it without conferring with you first."

Ash stared at me as if I'd sprouted an extra mouth. Then he chuckled.

"What?" I turned sideways to him. "What's so funny?"

"*Liessa*," he all but purred. "While I would appreciate you discussing such things as this with me first, I also expect that your temperament will prevent that on occasion."

I eyed him as if he were growing another set of lips. "Expecting that doesn't make it okay."

"It does when I have no problem with it," he remarked. "And I also know that when it's something you think I may not agree with, you will consult with me first."

He was right, but still. My eyes narrowed on him. "Are you being so understanding because I should be dead instead of alive and standing before you, making reckless oaths?"

"Making *exquisitely* reckless oaths," he corrected, brushing strands of hair back from his face. "And perhaps that has played a role in my understanding."

I huffed out a short laugh as I turned back to the Rise. One of the guards shouted to another, reminding me of what had just occurred. "By the way, something different happened a couple of moments ago. You see that guard there?" I straightened, pointing at Eamon. "I looked at him and knew his name—knew more than that. Like I knew his life." My head swung back to Ash. "His soul."

"Godsdamn," Ash murmured, his jaw loosening. "My father could do that, even after Kolis took the embers. It was the only ability of the true Primal of Life that remained."

"I think it's a part of the *vadentia* growing stronger." At least, that's what I thought based on what Nektas had shared with me. "I'm kind of surprised it's happening already."

"I'm not." Ash picked up a strand of my hair, eyeing it quite seriously in the sunlight. "Is that what you were thinking about when I arrived? I could sense your unease."

I tensed. *You're safe, now and always.* I sucked in a short breath at the memory of the nightmare. My gaze flew to his. I'd dreamed of hearing his voice last night. Hadn't I? It hadn't been real. At least, I prayed it wasn't and that I hadn't woken him.

I cleared my throat. "I'm really getting annoyed with that talent of yours."

"I know."

That was all he said. He waited, and I had a pretty good idea what he was talking about.

It wasn't nothing.

Feeling my stomach twist sharply, I looked away, searching my mind for a reason. My gaze landed on the crimson leaves of the Red Woods. Seizing on that, I said, "No. Something else happened," I lied far too smoothly. "I was looking at the Red Woods and thinking about the entombed gods. That intuition thing kicked in," I told him, sharing what I'd felt. "I was seconds from waking them and…"

His fingers slid down the strand of hair. "And what?"

"And killing them before Kolis could, like…summon them," I admitted.

"Why didn't you?"

My head cut toward him. "Is that a serious question?"

He raised a brow. "It is. As the true Primal of Life, you could've done it. And you would be within your rights to do so, whether any of those gods have changed or not."

I gaped at him. "If I'd done that, it would've been an entirely different kind of recklessness."

"Not to sound repetitive, but whether or not it was reckless wouldn't matter. You are the Queen. If you wish to wake all the entombed gods, that is your prerogative."

"Just as whatever Kolis decided to do was his?" I countered. "He was within his rights to do a lot of shitty things just because he was King."

Ash curled my hair around his finger as he said, "And because he was King, did it make what he did right?"

"Obviously not."

He stared at me, waiting…

"What? Why are you—?" Then it hit me. Rolling my eyes, I sighed. Considering what I'd gone through with the riders, I should've figured it out a lot sooner. "I didn't do it because I knew it wasn't right, even though it really felt like it was."

"Glad you figured that out." He tugged on the strand. "I was starting to get worried."

"Shut up." My glare dipped to Reaver as he made a low huffing sound. "Your laughter only encourages his nonsense."

Reaver plopped his head against my leg.

"I get the point you were making," I said. "But I think you also keep forgetting something."

An eyebrow rose. "Is that so?"

"You are my King—*the* King. I decreed it. That means it's not just me making decisions. I don't have supreme power or whatever."

"That is right." His silver eyes glimmered.

"I'm beginning to think you didn't forget that and just wanted to hear me say you're my King."

One side of his lips tipped up. "Maybe."

"You're ridiculous."

"Ridiculously in love with you."

My heart felt like it tripled in size, and I wanted so badly to show him, with words, my body, and even my tongue, just how much I loved him. The desire to do just that was strong, but I had to be stronger. Responsible. I also didn't want to traumatize poor Reaver.

"Do you think that some of the entombed gods have had a change of heart? Or were you just trying to make a point?" I asked.

"Not all the entombed gods committed unforgivable crimes, Sera. Some made bad choices. Some acted upon Kolis's orders because they were given little choice." Eather glowed faintly in his eyes, and I was reminded of Attes stating nearly the same thing. "A few were likely far less guilty than I am given the crimes I've committed."

My heart twisted as I whispered, "Like what?"

His fingers stilled. "Kolis didn't tell you?"

I shook my head. "He didn't tell me anything about you, and that is the truth."

Ash was quiet for a few moments, then dropped my hair. I wasn't surprised he hadn't elaborated, but I was disappointed. He never went into detail about the things he'd done. All I knew had been learned from others. But how could I hold it against him when I wasn't sharing everything with him either?

I couldn't.

"I can't believe how different the Shadowlands already looks," Ash noted, coming to the railing. "It's a miracle."

It did feel that way. "How long do you think it will take before all the grass comes back?"

"Not sure. Could be days. Maybe even weeks," he said. "If the rivers return, it would be faster."

"I imagine quite a significant rainfall would be needed for that to occur." With more and more gods arriving in Lethe, I wasn't sure we had the time to allow nature to run its course. A rush of something akin to restlessness surged through me. "Several rainfalls."

Ash made a sound of agreement.

"And who knows when that will happen? Unless the Shadowlands once had a rainy time of year, and we are about to enter it."

"We had one, but that season is months away," he said as he briefly looked over his shoulder. "We'll be encroaching upon winter."

Stroking Reaver's head, I remembered what he'd said about how the winters had once been full of snow, and while that would help fill the dried riverbeds, I doubted it would be enough. Plus, the grass would likely die again by then, this time naturally. Which meant we were months from seeing the Shadowlands truly come alive.

Disappointment filled me, even though there were far more important things to be concerned about. But seeing life return to the Shadowlands felt equally important. So much could happen between now and then. There was no guarantee that any of us would be in the right state of mind to enjoy the miracle of life returning. My chest tightened. Gods, there was no guarantee that any of those residing in the Shadowlands would even be here then.

Throat thickening, I looked at Ash, tracking the striking lines of his face. I wanted the residents of the Shadowlands to have that experience now. I wanted *him* to enjoy that beauty. But it felt like…more than that. As if there was another reason it was so important, but one I didn't know.

Pressure immediately clamped down harder on my chest. The response was silly, but other than Aios, I hadn't seen any of the other Shadowlands gods, and despite the honor they had shown me when they believed I was dying, I had no idea where I stood with most of them now. I hadn't made the greatest first, second…or *tenth* impression with them. They would support me, but I was sure it was mostly because of their loyalty to Ash.

And it was more than just how they responded to me. I knew I was the Queen. I accepted that. But was I ready to behave as one?

"We don't have to meet with them right now," Ash offered, angling his body toward mine. "We can do it later tonight."

A tiny part of me wanted to take him up on the offer, but that was cowardly. "I'm ready."

Ash didn't budge, so I pushed off the railing and went toward the doors on strangely weak legs. "I just need to find a comb and do something with this hair."

Ash and Reaver followed. "They can come back later tonight or even tomorrow morning."

"Just give me a moment to—" I squeaked in surprise as Ash appeared in front of me. "I'm so going to do that to you every chance I get," I warned, trying to sidestep him.

"Looking forward to it," he replied dryly. "We don't have to meet with anyone right now."

"I know." I crossed my arms. "But I want to."

Ash arched a brow.

"What?" I challenged as Reaver landed on the arm of the couch.

"I don't think you realize how much you project." He ignored the glare I shot him. "Your anxiety spiked."

"My anxiety is always spiking."

"It doesn't need to be right now." His eyes searched mine. "And you don't need to be bothered right now."

"It's not a bother, Ash."

Eather pulsed in his eyes. "We will have to disagree on that."

"This is a responsibility."

"One that can wait," he argued.

"Ash." I wrapped my hands around his arms. "I appreciate what you're doing right now. I do. It's sweet." I stretched onto my tiptoes and kissed him. When I settled back on my feet, I saw that his eyes were now like pools of warm silver. "Not only am I ready to do this, I feel fine. But if I start to feel like I'm hiding, I won't feel fine."

"You're not hiding." His fingers trailed over my cheek. "I'm hiding you."

"You're hiding me because you don't want me to get overwhelmed."

"Damn straight." His jaw hardened. "You've been through a lot, Sera. They can fucking wait."

I stared at him for a moment, my heart feeling like it was turning to goo. "Gods, I love you. And honestly, if we didn't have this meeting, I would throw myself at you."

The streaks of eather whirled. "Meeting is canceled."

"Reaver is right behind me," I reminded him.

He dragged his teeth over his lower lip as his gaze dropped to my mouth. "He can join Jadis in terrorizing Bele."

I laughed. "We're going to have this meeting. We need to. Kolis may be holed up in his Court recovering, but he won't stay that way for much longer. We can't waste any time."

Ash held my stare. "Fuck," he muttered, his lashes lowering.

Knowing I had won, I smiled. "I just need to do something with my hair." I waved in the general vicinity of my head. "I'm sure I look like a madwoman."

Reaver made another low chuffing sound. Little brat.

"You look beautiful," Ash replied. "But I'll grab a brush."

Before I could say anything, Ash disappeared into the bathing chamber and returned quickly, comb in hand. He gestured to one of the chairs. "Sit."

"Are you sure you want to do this?" I asked as I went to one of the dining chairs and sat. Reaver followed, taking up position once more by my legs. "It's a real pain to untangle."

As Ash carefully worked the comb through the curls and waves, holding the strands above the comb so my head didn't jerk, I felt Reaver rest his head on my knee. I reached down and gave the back of his neck a scratch. A soft purring sound radiated from him. "You like that, Reaver-butt?"

His vivid blue eyes closed, and he let out a happy little trilling sound. I smiled at his reaction to his nickname, relieved to see him in a better headspace than last night.

My eyes drifted shut as Ash quickly and painlessly freed the tangles. He was far gentler than I was with my hair, and there was something incredibly soothing about him combing it. I practically tore the thing through the strands, impatient and annoyed with how easily it tangled.

"You know," I said, opening my eyes, "for a Primal of Death, you're really good at getting the knots out of my hair."

"It's another of my hidden talents." Tossing the comb onto the table, he divided the strands into sections and quickly braided the length, tying it off with one of the remaining hair bands. "As is braiding hair."

"I like your diverse skill set."

Chuckling, he pulled on the braid, tugging my head back, then bent to drop a kiss on my lips. "Ready?"

I stood, glancing in the direction of the adjoining chamber. Tiny balls of anxiety started bouncing in my stomach, but I squashed them before Ash absolutely refused to hold the meeting.

Reaver sank back onto his haunches and then pushed into the air, rapidly moving his wings until he rose and was at my shoulder. It still blew my mind how the draken switched forms, changing their entire body shape. What did it feel like when Ash shifted into the silver wolf? I hadn't asked him—

I jerked to a stop. "Cave cat."

"What?" Ash halted in the arched doorway, turning to face me.

"I had a dream while in stasis." I pressed a hand to my chest as I stared up at him. "It was right before I woke up. I was at my lake, and I saw a cave cat standing on the shore—a silver cave cat." I'd seen something else but couldn't focus on the memory long enough to remember what. My heart thundered. "All Primals have…what is it called? A *nota*? An animal they can transform into. Right?"

Ash squinted. "Yes."

"Okay, so when I saw the cave cat, she felt like *me*," I told him. "Like I was looking at myself. Could that mean I can…?" It was almost too impossible to say. "Can I shift into a cave cat?"

"I don't remember seeing anything like that during stasis, but it could mean that," he said. "It usually takes time for a Primal's first shift into their *nota*. Took me about a year or so before I could. You will likely be different, though."

So many things ran through my mind as Reaver circled me, and I blurted out what had to be the weirdest and possibly the most idiotic one, "Hopefully, we'll still get along in our *nota* forms."

His dark brows pulled together as Reaver's head swung toward me. "Come again?"

"I mean, with you being a wolf and me being a very large cave cat," I explained. "It's like cats and dogs, right? And I know a wolf isn't a dog, but still."

Ash's lips parted into a faint grin as his silver gaze gleamed. "The things that go through your mind must be a constant source of entertainment."

My eyes became thin slits as I fixed a piercing stare on him. "Then I assume I'll be just as irritated with you in that form as I am in this one."

That grin kicked up a notch, revealing a hint of fang. "Yes."

"Whatever," I muttered as that low chuffing sound came from Reaver again. "How do I shift?"

"You just will it to happen and—" Ash shot forward, cupping the nape of my neck. "Fates, Sera, do not will it to happen right now. For one thing, I don't know if you'll be able to, but on the off chance you can, it wouldn't be wise for you to do so now if you plan to meet with the others."

My lips pursed. "I wasn't going to will it to happen."

Ash arched a brow. "*Liessa…*"

"Okay." I sighed, rolling my eyes. "Maybe I was going to. I would've switched right back, though."

"Yeah, it doesn't always work that way the first time." He swiped his thumb across my bottom lip, sending a charge of energy through me. "The transformation can be…overpowering."

"And exactly what does that mean?" I asked. "Does it hurt?"

"The first time your body changes shape and form can be uncomfortable."

My heart tripped over itself. "Well, that's the first thing I've heard about shifting forms that actually makes sense."

"That's not all," he said softly. "The *nota* is strong, and it will want to take over. When you first do it, it can be difficult to pull yourself out of it."

I swallowed. "That sounds ominous."

"It's really not. You won't get stuck in that form," he assured me, dropping his hand, "you just need time to go through the motions."

"And we don't have that time right now."

"Clearly," he remarked dryly.

"Smart-ass." I gave him a light shove.

He chuckled and said to Reaver. "I remember a time when you would've attempted to light someone on fire for even thinking of offending me."

"Sorry," I said, smiling broadly as the draken lifted his wings, keeping himself in the air. "He's my Reaver-butt now."

Reaver chirped his agreement.

"That's okay." Ash smiled. "My fangs are still substantially more impressive than yours."

"I'm debating kicking you, just so you know," I warned him, even though I thoroughly enjoyed his teasing.

Because, gods, I hadn't realized how badly I'd missed the side of him I'd seen in the mortal realm when he was just Ash, and I was—

No. The Ash in the mortal realm, where he'd been able to shed the weight of responsibility and forget the cause of those blood drops inked onto his flesh for a little while, *was* who he was. And he was once more that Ash.

He took my hand and kissed my palm. He then nodded toward the antechamber. "You ready now? For real this time?"

I nodded.

His gaze lifted to mine. "Just remember, when you walk through that door, you will not do so as the Consort. You will be doing so as the Queen."

"And you as their King."

Ash nodded, cupping my cheek with his other hand. "Together."

I turned my head and kissed his palm. "Always."

The moment we exited the short, dimly lit hall on the other side of the bathing chamber, conversation ground to an utter halt in the antechamber.

Everyone froze as Reaver flew in behind me and soared upward, landing atop the gleaming cherrybark oak credenza, precariously balanced on its thin top. Well, everyone except Jadis.

The little draken scrambled across the chamber, darting past the oval table on a raised dais framed by two shadowstone pillars. She ran straight for where Reaver had perched himself, arms outstretched toward him, her small wings fluttering wildly and lifting her a few inches off the floor.

Ash swooped down and picked her up before she started scaling the credenza. She responded with an unhappy shriek. "Here," he said, giving the underside of her chin a rub. "You can see him better up here."

Reaver huffed as my gaze bounced over familiar features, seeking out a vibrant redheaded goddess. Everyone was there except Aios. Things had gotten strained toward the end of our conversation, but I didn't think she was angry or upset when she left. Where was—?

All at once, those seated stood, their faces becoming blurs as they lowered to one knee, folded their right palms over their chests, and flattened their other hands against the floor. Heads bowed, one after another in a wave. Every single one of them.

Heart stuttering, I jerked back. "What is everyone doing?"

"We are bowing," Rhahar answered, "to you, *meyaah Liessa*."

"You don't need to do that." Warmth crept into my cheeks. "Or call me that."

Beside him, his cousin's head tilted slightly, revealing a hint of one rich, deep-brown cheek raised in a grin.

"It's tradition to greet the Primal of Life in such a manner," Ash explained, and my gaze swung to him. He kept a hand on Jadis's back as she all but teetered on his shoulder.

"Gods are supposed to bow to any Primal, which none of them do for you," I pointed out.

A clawed hand fisted in Ash's hair, tugging strands out of the knot at his nape as he said, "That's because I don't require it of them."

"I don't either."

"You're different, *liessa*." He reached up and gently pulled Jadis's claws free of his hair. "You're the true Primal of Life. This is how they honor you whenever you enter the same space as them."

"I'm not different." I threw up my hands in frustration and turned to them. "You don't have to do this—wait." I spun back to Ash. "Are they supposed to do this every time I enter a space?"

Jadis let out an angry screech.

"Yes," Ash stated, catching Jadis's hand as she made to go for his hair again.

"Oh, no. Nope. We are not doing this every time I enter a chamber," I told them, horrified. "I will lose my mind."

"Please, don't do that," Saion said. "We've already dealt with one supreme ruler who wasn't quite right in the head."

Someone who sounded an awful lot like Bele chuckled under her breath. My narrowed gaze swung toward the dark-haired Primal goddess.

"You know," Ash drawled from behind me, "all you have to do is command that they don't."

I opened my mouth.

"But perhaps you should give them permission to rise first," he tacked on.

I slowly turned my head to him. "You couldn't have reminded me of that at the beginning?"

"Perhaps." He once more tugged Jadis's hand free of his hair.

"I hope she pulls out every single strand," I hissed.

"Godsdamnit," Rhahar groused.

"You know what I always say," Saion replied, each word rolling off his tongue with an unmistakable undertone of amusement. "A wise man never makes the same bad wager twice."

My mouth dropped open. "You two bet *again* on how long it would take before Ash and I started arguing?"

"More like Saion is stealing money from his cousin again," Bele retorted.

"Oh, my gods." I pinched my brow, briefly closing my eyes. "Why are you all still bowing?"

"You haven't given them permission to rise," Ash commented.

"For fuck's sake," I snapped.

"Language," Ash whispered as he passed me, stepping onto the dais. He placed Jadis in one of the chairs at the table. "There are younglings present."

"How about you go—?" I cut myself off as two wide, sapphire-blue eyes appeared above the back of the chair.

Clutching the sides of the chair with incredibly small, clawed hands, Jadis chirped, and I heard something that sounded like…*wee.*

"Can the true Primal of Life get tension headaches?" I asked of no one in particular as Ash motioned for Reaver to get down. "Because I really think I'm getting one."

"It's not likely," Bele answered, her voice trembling with restrained laughter as Reaver pushed off the credenza, extending his wings to slow his descent. "But not impossible."

"Can we rise yet?" Theon asked from where he remained, kneeling beside his twin sister.

I sighed heavily. "Yes. Please. You all may rise."

"Thank the Fates," Saion muttered.

My lips pursed. "And I command that none of you bow to me just because I enter a chamber."

Tightly braided hair fell back as Lailah lifted her head. Grinning, she rose as I remembered the somewhat flirty argument I'd witnessed between her and Attes. I so badly wanted to ask her what was up between them, but it was likely none of my business and not really important at the moment. Still, I was nosy. "Your command is our will," she said.

"*Meyaah Liessa*," Bele tacked on.

"Now you're just trying to annoy me." I folded my arms.

Adjusting the sheaths on her forearms, Bele lifted her head. "I would never—holy shit, your eyes."

"Are beautiful," Ash said—or warned—from where he was pouring whiskey into two short glasses, his voice lowering the temperature in the chamber by several degrees.

Essence throbbed throughout my body. "If that was supposed to be a compliment," I told him, "it sounded more like a threat."

"Yeah, it did." Bele leaned against the table.

Ash arched a brow, not denying it.

"But they are really…" Bele trailed off as Ash's icy stare shifted to her. "Amazing. They are so amazing."

I stared at her.

Saion approached, brows pinching with curiosity as Reaver watched with keen alertness. "I've never seen eyes like that." He glanced at Rhain. "Have you?"

The auburn-haired god shook his head. "I have not."

Everyone was staring at me, and I, well, felt like throwing myself onto the floor and pretending I was still in stasis. "Ash thinks it's because I was mortal. But yes, they are super unique and weird—"

"And beautiful," Ash repeated.

"And," I stressed, "we are going to stop talking about my eyes now."

Saion opened his mouth as he lifted a hand. Rhahar dropped coins into his palm. "Never mind." Grinning, Saion tucked the coins into the inside of his tunic. "In all seriousness, we are so damn glad to be getting on your nerves."

"And you have no idea how happy I am to be making really bad bets," Rhahar added.

I laughed. "I'm only partly sorry to be the cause of you losing money."

"I'm not at all," Saion called as he moved to stand behind a chair.

Rhahar flipped him off.

"We are glad you have returned to us," Theon said, and then his gaze darted to Ash. "And to him."

My breath snagged, and all I could do was nod.

"Not to sound repetitive," Lailah said, "but I, too, am glad you returned to us."

I smiled and felt a knot of emotion clogging my throat as Ash watched quietly from where he stood a few feet back, not interrupting but also not straying too far. "Thank you."

"I'm glad you're alive and shit," Bele shared. "Just thought I'd say that since everyone else is."

I gave her a thumbs-up as Lailah stepped onto the dais. The goddess paused to give Jadis a quick pet where the draken still watched from behind the back of the chair. "Where is Aios?"

"She planned to be here, but Kye, the Healer, asked that she join him in Lethe," Bele answered. "He wanted her to assist with a birth."

Concern rose. "Is there something wrong?"

"Other than how disturbing it is that one is expected to push a nine-pound-plus babe out of an area nowhere—"

"Please, don't go into any more detail." Theon held up a hand, and Rhain grimaced.

Bele smirked. "Anyway, being a goddess of fertility and such, Kye likes to have her around. Makes his life easier."

That was a relief. I guessed.

"I, too, am glad," a quiet voice came.

The muscles on the back of my neck tensed as I turned to Rhain. The reaction had nothing to do with how things had started with us. From day one, Rhain had been wary of my presence, but when he'd learned about my original plans, his distrust—and dislike—had been all too apparent. I didn't hold any of that against him. If I had been in his shoes, I would have felt the same way. But the way he looked at me now made me want to make a quick exit out the balcony doors. It was the warmth in his hazel eyes that had nothing to do with the aura of eather behind his pupils or the reason behind Rhain's change of attitude toward me as he extended his hand.

My chest spasmed when my gaze met his. *Breathe in.* I stopped myself before I let that dread spark into something bigger and nastier, forcing myself to hold my breath as Rhain clasped my forearm. Now was not the time for any of that. "Thank you," I managed, fixing what I hoped was a normal smile on my face as I grasped his forearm in return.

"Whoa." He blinked several times. "Got a nice little charge with that."

"Sorry?"

"Don't be. Weirdly felt kind of good." Rhain's gaze held mine and then darted away as he bowed curtly. Pivoting, he joined the others.

Ash lifted Jadis from the chair and placed her on the floor. Crouching, she eyed Reaver with narrowed eyes as her tail swished back and forth like an irritated feline.

A heartbeat later, she launched herself off the dais and crashed into him. The older draken squawked, but all Jadis did was press her little head against his and then scramble back onto the raised floor.

"Okay, then," I murmured, glancing up.

It took a moment for me to realize that all of them were waiting for me. Blinking, I got my feet moving and went to where Ash had pulled out a chair at the head of the table.

Molten, dove-gray eyes met mine. "Your seat, *liessa*."

"Thank you," I whispered as Reaver followed, this time brushing his head over Jadis's.

"Why does he get to call you that?" Bele asked, adjusting her forearm sheaths. "And we don't?"

Ash glanced up. "Because she enjoys it when I call her that."

As Bele's brows lifted, my cheeks caught fire. I plopped into the chair with the grace of a tree bear, and then everyone else sat. Ash moved to my right, taking his seat there. The subtle shift in positioning—in power—didn't pass me by.

Once again, the shock of how real this was hit me as Ash placed a glass of whiskey on the table for me. It felt like a cloth had been shoved into my throat. My hands tightened around the arms of the chair as my mind sort of emptied. Or maybe there was just so much going on in my head that it felt like there was nothing.

Rhain cleared his throat. "I'm not sure who is aware of what, but many gods have been arriving in the Shadowlands the last several days, coming from many Courts."

The cloth doubled in size as I spoke around it. "Nyktos mentioned something."

"They are being vetted to the best of our abilities and then temporarily placed in our insulas—" He stopped himself, noting the confusion surely creeping into my expression. "You haven't been to Lethe other than the night of your coronation. Right." A faint pink stained his cheeks. "Insulas are homes several stories tall that house many people—up to forty or so. When you see the lights of Lethe, you're likely seeing those buildings. I believe mortals would call them tenements, but they're not as…"

"Poorly outfitted?" I suggested. The tenements in Croft's Cross, the poorest district of Lasania, had these so-called apartments. They were dark, cramped dwellings not even suitable for rodents. Ezra would change what our parents should have done ages ago. "Are we providing housing because they are planning to stay?"

"Probably, since many of them will have no Court to return to," Rhain said.

"Not all the Primals allow their subjects to leave their Courts without permission, and I doubt most would've sought that," Bele spoke up. "When I left Hanan's, it was considered treasonous. They could be imprisoned or killed upon their return."

"Gods," I breathed. "How many have arrived?"

"Hundreds," Rhain answered. "Dozens more with each passing hour."

My stomach dipped. "And we have enough housing for them?"

"For now," Ash said. "We do."

But would we later, if more and more continued to come? Obviously, not. I didn't know the details of how food had been provided all these many centuries, but it took no leap of logic to assume that the goods had been imported. "What about food—?" I cut myself off. "Crops can grow here now."

"Yes," Saion confirmed. "And once we get some really good rainfall and the rivers return, we'll be able to use them as a source of irrigation, allowing us to plant more. I've already begun to survey which areas would be best suited for such."

"That's a relief to hear," I said, ceasing my wiggling in my chair. "I want everyone who comes here to have a home, whether it be temporary or long-term, and for there to be food on their plates. But it's going to be rough until the crops can grow." My head cocked. Could I assist with that? I was the true Primal of Life. Did that not extend to plant life? I believed so, but… "There will still be a length of time before we can comfortably provide for everyone." Worry grew. As someone who had lived a life of limited basic essentials with an ever-increasing populace, I knew how quickly that could take its toll.

"That's tomorrow's problem," Ash spoke softly, snapping me from what was sure to become a spiral of worst-case what-ifs. "One we're already working on fixing. But we have to get to tomorrow."

I nodded slowly, getting what he was saying. None of us would go the route of my mother and the former King of Lasania by putting off dealing with dwindling supplies. The Shadowlands wouldn't do that. But we also had to get to the point where it could be a problem.

Meaning Lethe had to survive until then.

As silence fell around me once more, my tongue felt heavy and unusable. I truly wasn't suited to leading meetings. Weight pressed down upon my shoulders and chest as seconds ticked by, becoming what felt like hours. My panicked gaze swiveled toward Ash—

"We all know why we're here," Ash said, picking up Jadis and placing her on his lap. "To talk about Kolis and what we're going to do."

"I already have a suggestion," Bele said, sliding a slim shadowstone dagger free from its sheath. "Hunt him down."

Rhahar nodded. "I second that."

"That's *part* of the plan," Ash replied as Bele tossed the dagger into the air. "But we have to get to that part first."

As I glanced around the table, no one seemed to care that it had been Ash who'd started the meeting. Or maybe they hadn't even noticed my inability to speak because it hadn't actually been minutes or hours that had passed in awkward silence.

Letting out a long, slow breath, the pressure started to lift. I loosened my grip on the arms of the chair and picked up my glass of whiskey.

"And we can't skip to that part?" Bele asked, throwing the dagger up again. This time, Jadis's head followed the movement. "Because I know what Kolis will do once he's done licking his wounds."

"And what is that?" I asked, finding my voice as I sat back, glass in hand. The moment the whiskey hit my tongue, my stomach churned. I had to force myself to swallow like I was drinking the utter trash often served at some of the gambling dens in Lower Town, a district in Lasania, which made no sense. The Shadowlands had the finest whiskey I'd ever tasted. Weird. I placed the glass on the table.

Ash glanced at my glass, a slight frown appearing. He picked up Jadis and handed her off to Lailah. The youngling immediately went for the goddess's braids.

"Gather his loyalists and hunt us down," Bele stated, catching the dagger by the hilt. Eather pulsed behind her pupils as her gaze locked with mine. "And attack."

"I hate always being the cautious one in the room," Lailah said as Ash rose. "It's boring. I know." She shot Bele a look, and the Primal goddess snapped her mouth shut. "But hunting Kolis down and attacking is not a plan. We know we cannot…" She glanced down at Jadis as the draken whipped her braids from side to side. "Remove him permanently," she said, her choice of words bringing a wry grin to my lips. "We need to plan for how we'll handle him."

"I agree," Theon chimed in as Jadis wiggled free of Lailah's hold and climbed onto the table. "We cannot plan for what we do not know."

"Very true," Rhain remarked as the little draken crept toward Bele, her belly low to the tabletop as if she were in stealth mode. Beside me, Reaver sat up to watch her with a wary eye.

"I get that, but I think it's safe to assume that Kolis will not disappear quietly into the night," Bele argued, glancing to where Jadis had placed herself directly in front of her. She frowned. "He knows what her Ascension means to him and Iliseeum. It is not like he's going to pretend that a true Primal of Life hasn't Ascended. Nor will any other Primal."

"I think he will," I said, remembering how Kolis had nearly glowed as he sat on the throne that belonged to the true Primal of Life—to *me*. I glanced at Ash. He was at the credenza, picking up a stone pitcher and another glass. "At least for a little while. He will need to remind himself that he's in charge. He'll hold court."

Bele gave the dagger another toss. "Yeah, but he's only playing King while everyone knows a Queen rules."

"A King also rules now," I corrected her as Jadis eyed Bele's dagger, her thin tail swishing back and forth.

Ash returned to the table, placing a pitcher and a glass of what appeared to be water before me. If there was anything I missed from Dalos, it was the fruity, bubbly water. I made a mental note to ask Ash about it later since his father had apparently created the drink.

"Thank you," I said, and he smiled in return. "Nyktos is no Consort. He is my equal, so if I'm Queen, then he's King."

Surprise flickered across the others' faces. "There has never been a Queen and a King of the Gods," Rhahar murmured, sitting straighter. "Then again, there's never been a Queen at all."

I reached down to where Reaver sat, scratching him under the chin. He hadn't taken his eyes off Jadis. He was likely waiting for the same thing I was—for her to make a grab for the dagger. Then again, she also looked like she was close to falling asleep. I was hoping for the second option. "Well, it's my choice that Nyktos be King, and I'm under the impression that what I say goes."

"You'll get no argument from any of us." Saion grinned as he looked across the table at Ash. "And it makes sense."

"I really didn't think any of you would have a problem with it," Ash replied dryly. "But back to Kolis. He'll attempt to control the narrative and the situation by labeling Sera a usurper and a false Queen, exploiting that she was once mortal, that most do not know her, and that she is now a baby Primal."

"A baby Primal?" Rhain murmured, his nose scrunching. He shook his head. "Anyway, I expect Kolis will seek to remind all of them exactly who he is in case any are thinking of defecting."

Bele's nostrils flared. "Yeah, and by *reminding* them, you mean by committing some violent, heinous act upon those likely undeserving of it."

Lailah nodded, her features drawn. "Unfortunately."

I leaned back, thinking that over. What she said made sense, but… "I think you're right, but he'll be careful about who he decides to make an example of."

"Careful?" Ash raised a brow. "I think we have two different understandings of the word."

"He's not some chaotic villain with no control over his actions," I countered. "Well, most of the time, he's not. He's far more calculated." My thoughts flashed to when Kolis had discussed the Shadowlands' forces possibly invading Dalos. "And I think he's aware of just how tenuous his hold on the realm is."

"Why would you believe that?" Ash asked.

It was hard to answer that when I wasn't even sure what I believed when it came to Kolis. "The Kolis I met when I was first brought to Dalos was almost completely different than who he was after. Even before he believed I was Sotoria. He went from wanting to see all the Primals burn to claiming that he didn't want war among them."

Ash picked up the pitcher, topping off my glass. "I can tell you what claim I believe."

"You believe he's the burn-it-all-down version."

Ash arched a brow as he picked up his glass and sat back. "Exactly."

"I think we can all agree with Nyktos," Rhahar commented. "We've all seen that side of Kolis more times than we care to think about."

There were murmurs of agreement from all except Rhain, who then spoke up. "But what do you think, Seraphena?"

I ran my thumb along the delicate rim of the glass as the bob of Jadis's head slowed, and the time between each blink grew longer. "I think…I think he's both. He wanted the embers so he could Ascend as the Primal of Life and Death."

Someone cursed.

"And that is when he spoke of killing all those who wouldn't bow to him, correct?" Ash stated, and I nodded. "Then he changed his mind when he believed you were Sotoria. Because he knew that, no matter what, removing those embers from you and then Ascending you would come at a risk. This other side of him only showed itself when he believed you were Sotoria."

"He did things that didn't align with his seeing-all-the-Primals-burn ideology before he was convinced I was Sotoria," I insisted.

Ash eyed me over the rim of his glass. "For example?"

"For example, he stated clearly that he didn't want a war. That was why he didn't attack the Shadowlands' forces. He knew that doing so would escalate the situation."

"And you believed him?" Saion demanded, all amusement gone from his tone.

"I didn't. Not at first. But when Kyn wanted to level the Shadowlands to make an example out of this Court, Kolis denied him." I looked around the table. "And again, that was before he believed I was Sotoria. He had no reason not to allow Kyn to do as he pleased other than knowing what would come of it."

"And he had no reason not to kill me, let alone release me," Rhain stated, and my heart felt like it hit the floor. "But she was able to convince him that killing me—someone loyal to the Primal they served—wouldn't inspire loyalty to him in others. It was a straw-man argument, but one Kolis was willing to accept."

I relaxed. A little.

"I'm still not over the fact that Kolis released you." Saion looked at Rhain. "Don't get me wrong, we all thought you were gone, and we're fucking ecstatic that we were wrong, but none of us expected that."

Rhahar nodded. "I have to hear this straw-man argument of yours."

My relief vanished as Ash's jaw flexed. His stare was on the open doors as he took a drink, his lips peeling back.

Did he…did he know? About the deal? What Kolis had asked for? If so, he would think it meant more—

I couldn't think about that right now. Drawing my gaze from Ash, I cleared my throat. "I don't think it was such a straw-man argument. He agreed because he knew killing Rhain would further escalate tensions," I lied smoothly. "And when I challenged him about what he said before regarding killing the other Primals, Kolis admitted that he wouldn't start a war he couldn't win or one that would leave the realms a mess. But he still planned to rise as the Primal of Life and Death. Who would really refuse to bow to him then? His rising to such a powerful being would prevent a war." I met Ash's stare as his attention returned to me. "And here's the thing. He's not going to get his hands on me again."

"No," Ash growled, streaks of eather piercing his eyes. "He will not."

"And that means he's not going to Ascend to that."

"I see what you're saying about Kolis," Ash said, "but I think we see different end results."

"How so?"

"You see him being more cautious, possibly more reserved in his actions. And perhaps even reasonable since he seemed to understand that he couldn't win a war without rising as the Primal of Life and Death." His fingers returned to their soft tapping, drawing a sleepy Jadis's attention. "But I see a far more unpredictable Kolis. One who is on the verge of losing what power he has and won't be as careful about when and where he strikes."

My gaze shifted to the doors behind the twins. What Ash saw was a far scarier outcome and could be the likelier one. I'd known Kolis for a far shorter time than everyone else in the chamber. And I did understand that my experience was heavily prejudiced by who he thought I was and how he behaved because of that. Even before Ione confirmed it, he was desperate to believe I was Sotoria. Now, he had to realize he'd been lied to. That I wasn't Sotoria. And he would likely revert to the Kolis who would only accept fealty or death.

"Whether Kolis is more cautious or not, we're still in the same position," Theon stated.

"And we cannot sit by and do nothing while we wait to see how Kolis will respond," his twin finished.

"I agree with that." My gaze met Ash's. I took a deep breath and then looked at those sitting at the table with us. "I wasn't ready for this—being Queen, let alone planning a war. I'm not a strategist, and I'm far better suited to fighting than this." Anxiety rose, but I focused on what Ash had said yesterday. I wasn't alone in this. "So, I'm going to be honest here. I don't know the correct answer, nor will I pretend I do. I'm sure that's not very reassuring, but it's the truth."

"That is reassuring," Theon said, relaxing into his chair.

"Really?"

Lailah nodded. "Yes. I'd rather have someone acknowledge a lack of experience than pretend, thus needlessly risking lives in the process."

"Knowing when to rely on others is a strength," Rhain added. "One that inspires confidence instead of worry."

"There's just one thing I have to say." Bele started to toss her dagger once more but stopped as she finally noticed how close Jadis was. "I'm somewhat disturbed that you, of all people, are being logical." Bele sheathed the dagger, sending Jadis a playful scowl as the youngling reached for the blade. "I expected better from you."

"Sorry to fail you," I replied dryly, glancing at Ash. He nodded for me to continue. "Nyktos and I have spoken about the importance of showing the others that we will be significantly better rulers than Kolis."

"I would be a significantly better ruler than Kolis," Bele chimed in. "And that isn't saying much."

"A dakkai would probably be better," Saion suggested, his elbow resting on the arm of his chair.

Lailah sighed and ran a hand across her brow. My lip curled. A picture of the beasts the size of horses with featureless faces except for gaping mouths full of jagged teeth filled my mind. I still couldn't believe one had sat on the dais at Kolis's feet, snacking on what I really believed was someone's leg bone.

I shook the image from my mind. "We want to summon the Primals, excluding Veses and Kyn. They can fuck right off."

That brought a savage smile to Bele's face.

"To the Shadowlands?" Saion clarified, and I nodded. "That's a huge risk."

"We know." My heart kicked against my ribs as I noted the unease on several of their faces. "Those who answer the summons will likely support our claim to the throne of Iliseeum."

"But those who may not support us could send spies in their place—gods of their Court," Theon warned.

Ash shook his head. "We won't allow any god to show in their Primal's place."

Theon nodded, his expression turning thoughtful. "I doubt Kolis loyalists would risk angering him by responding, even if to spy."

"That is not all," I said, glancing toward Ash. His smile was small but filled with so much warmth and pride. A little more of the pressure lifted from my shoulders. "Speaking to them won't prove anything."

"Correct," Bele murmured.

"That's why we discussed changing how things have been done," I continued. "Instead of one or two making all the decisions, each Primal will have a vote in what is decided. So, basically, we would form a council."

All of them stared at me.

I swallowed and forced myself not to start second-guessing my decisions. "The draken would also have a vote. Not only would that create checks and balances of sorts, but we would all have more of a vested interest in whatever is decided, and it stops any of us from having too much authority." I paused and took a long, slow breath. "Of course, we want your support first."

There were several exchanged glances. Lailah was the first to break the silence. "I think summoning the Primals is smart. We need to know who is on our side before we decide anything."

Rhain nodded. "And this council you speak of? Nothing like it has been tried in Iliseeum. That is something new. And it should be very appealing."

"And if the Primal of a Court is on board with real change, it will make getting their Court under control far easier," Lailah noted.

That piqued my curiosity. "Other than a few things shared here and there, and what I've picked up myself, I don't know much about the other Courts or how they're ruled." I paused. "Or *not* ruled. But they can't all be bad."

Bele snorted.

"At least, I hope not," I muttered.

"Not all of them are bad, and even Courts like Kyn's have pockets of communities whose values and beliefs align with the common good," Rhahar said, his brow pinching. "The Shadowlands is the only Court with one city."

"But that can now change with life returning to all the land except for the Dying Woods," Ash interjected.

Rhahar nodded. "But when it comes to the other Courts, they each have a capital—the largest city within the Court—where the Primal usually takes up residency. For example, the island of Hygeia is the most populated of the Triton Isles and that is where Phanos lives. But the other islands are also populated and either ruled by a trusted god, one who has curried favor, or someone who took out their competition."

My brows rose.

"It's a coveted spot in many of the Courts. The gods overseeing the smaller cities or islands often turn them into mini fiefdoms. Some are ruled justly and others cruelly," Saion explained. "It's been a while since I was in Phanos's Court," he continued, glancing at Rhahar. "I personally don't have an issue with the smaller cities of the Triton Isles, but from what I've heard, Phanos has taken more of a laissez-faire approach."

"As long as the other islands don't stir Kolis's ire and, therefore, cause Phanos to pay a blood tithe," Rhahar added.

Frowning, I turned to Ash. He nodded as he said, "You must not have seen that occur while you were there." He leaned over and picked up the pitcher. "In the mortal realm, when a citizen overseen by a noble displeases the crown, the crown often seeks a monetary tithe if the offense was not a significant crime. Not Kolis. He has no need of coin."

"I get it." Anger stirred, and Reaver nudged my hand again. I rubbed him under his chin. "What of the other Courts?"

"Embris definitely doesn't take a hands-off approach," Theon stated. "He rules the entirety of his Court with a strict hand."

"Why do I have a feeling that's not a good thing?" I said, my thoughts flashing to Penellaphe.

Ash topped off my glass. "Embris is what one would call a traditionalist."

My brows shot up. "A traditionalist? Wouldn't that mean he should have stood against Kolis?"

"He did at first," Ash said. "Or he tried to. It did not end well for him."

Gods.

"You say traditionalist," Lailah commented. "I was thinking of a different word that starts with the same letter. Tyrant. He or one of his trusted gods oversees everything from when his subjects awaken to when they go to sleep."

"The only place his rule does not reach is Lotho—the highest peak of Mount Lotho to be exact," Rhain said. "That is where the Fates and the *oneirou* are." He frowned. "Or what is left of the *oneirou*."

"A God…of Dreams," Startled, I glanced at Ash. "Odetta, my nursemaid, used to speak of them—well, she used to say that if I misbehaved, the *oneirou* would find me in my dreams."

"Wow," Saion murmured, his brows raised. "That's a bit much to tell a child."

"No shit." Theon chuckled roughly.

"*Odetta* was a bit much," I replied dryly. "But no one else really spoke about the Gods of Dreams. I figured they were extinct or something."

"Very few would remember them. Like with the Gods of Divination, most were killed when Kolis stole the embers," Ash explained. "There aren't many left."

Gods, Embris's Court really had taken the brunt of Kolis's actions, which likely explained why the Primal was so tyrannical. Traditionalist or not, there was no way he would want to continue supporting Kolis.

"But the ones who are still around are powerful. They can move seamlessly in and out of dreams. Controlling them. Causing either pleasant dreams or nightmares while working out whatever information they want from you. They make for good spies that way," Ash continued.

"The good news is that there are little to no outbreaks of violence like there are within Kyn's side of Vathi or in Veses' Court."

"The bad news is that when one steps out of line—and by stepping out of line, I mean being out past curfew—the punishment is severe," Theon tacked on.

My jaw clenched. "Great."

"His Court rarely incites Kolis's wrath," Ash shared.

"So, Veses' Court is a cesspool." I glanced at Rhain. "No offense."

"None taken." He held up his hands. "I claim no ties to that Court."

"I assume Keella rules fairly?" I said. "As does Attes."

"Yes," Lailah confirmed.

Theon opened his mouth like he wanted to say something, but Lailah shot her brother a look. "Both have had their rough patches, but they have overcome them and rule fairly while entrusting the oversight of the smaller cities to those who will honor their values."

"And Maia?" I asked.

"Well," Bele drawled, and I wanted to bang my head on the table. "She's not necessarily bad, having spent the last several hundred years more focused on entertaining herself than governing. Some of her cities are rather calm. Others are pretty much a giant org—" She stopped herself as Reaver peered over the top of the table at her. "They are like giant adult parties. Not bad, but not really productive or useful, you know? So, sometimes things get a little heated, and not in a good way. There are lots of jealousy-fueled murders, and they sometimes fail to harvest crops or search for children who wander into the forest." She squinted. "Or even realize they're missing."

"Oh, my gods," I murmured, rubbing my brow.

"Hey, cheer up!" Bele exclaimed with one of her too-wide smiles. "I've heard Maia has gotten better. For example, there are fewer…adult parties."

Ash laughed as he took a drink.

"Wow." And here I thought my mother was a bad Queen. "Do I even want to know *how* bad the cesspool that is Veses' Court is?"

"Veses rules like Embris one day and Phanos the next," Ash said. "Her Court is as bad as Hanan's was."

Bele sighed.

"No pockets of…goodness?" I asked. "How is that possible?"

"All who had an ounce of morality in them are here." Rhain shook his head. "The same with Kyn's Court. Those who disagreed either joined Attes or came here."

"So, you're telling me that all those who remain in Veses' and Kyn's Courts are…what? A lost cause?" I took in the somber expressions. "Seriously?"

"I wouldn't say they are a complete loss," Ash stated. "Perhaps some can be reached, but when Kolis first took the embers, switching places with my father, it disturbed the balance. Death ruled over life, and life ruled over death. All Primal power has a good and a bad side to it. And with all the Primals being weakened, it made it far easier for them to succumb to the poisonous sides of their natures," he reminded me. "And then that poison spread to those who served them and the mortals they interacted with. Most of them are not who they once were or were born into a society that embraces that toxicity."

"I get that. I do. It's not really their fault, and blah, blah bullshit. Whatever." Frustration joined the anger as Bele widened her eyes. "We basically only have two Courts that appear to have any sense of a greater good. Then we have one Primal who really doesn't seem to care about his Court, as long as it doesn't cause him trouble. Another who rules so strictly the entire Court has a bedtime and punishment for not adhering to such is—"

"Sometimes death," Rhahar filled in.

Good fucking gods. "Another Court is pretty much a giant *adult* party with a dash of murderous tendencies, and two more are just complete garbage fires—"

"Don't forget my Court," Bele interrupted. "I have about a hundred good ones in Sirta."

"My apologies."

Bele smiled and flicked her wrist. "Accepted."

"So, we have two decent Courts and one *really* underperforming Court," I corrected. Bele's eyes narrowed as I turned to Ash. "That leaves me with just one question."

"I truly cannot wait to hear what it will be," Ash murmured as he eyed me over the rim of his glass.

"Why are we even bothering with these Courts and not just seizing them?"

"Now, *that* is the Sera I was expecting," Bele said, and Saion nodded in agreement.

"After seizing them, what would we do?" Ash countered, lowering his glass.

"Put someone else in charge? Like one of them," I suggested, gesturing at those around the table.

"Uh," Lailah started.

Ash held up a hand. "I don't think the Primals who rule over those Courts would take too kindly to that. They would fight back. We might have to kill them."

"Then I could Ascend another god to take their place," I countered.

Rhain's gaze sharpened on me. "Or you could take the Court as your own. The Primal of Life can take a Court. And with the energy going to you, it would lessen the impact of there being no Primal to rule."

I started to ask how that was even done, but with a tingle in the skin behind my ear, the knowledge came in a flash of images. I frowned slightly. Taking another Court required no ceremonies or words. All I had to do after draining the Primal was take their eather into me before it released. Not that I was complaining. It was just…the process was frighteningly *simple.*

"But not even Kolis did that," Rhain added after a moment.

Ash looked over at him.

"Technically," he corrected. "But having a Primal of Life that just takes on the Primal influence of other Courts doesn't sound like something you would want to do."

It wasn't.

"Not only that, but it is unlikely we could defeat those Courts and Kolis with Attes, Keella, and one really underperforming Court," Ash pointed out. "Not only do we need as much support as we can get, but you also want things to be different. Would that be any different?"

"No." I sighed. "I wasn't being serious."

Ash's head tilted as he took a drink.

"Okay." I rolled my eyes. "I was only being fifty percent serious."

His lips twitched as he placed his glass on the table. "So, are we in agreement? Summon the Primals?"

Murmurs of approval rose around the table, and I nearly slumped in my chair with relief.

"Then what comes next?" Bele asked.

"I think you will enjoy this answer." I met Bele's stare. "We remove Kolis from the throne."

"Violently?"

"Is there any other option?" Ash replied.

"No." Bele smiled in a way I should've found disturbing but didn't.

"Exactly how will that be done?" Theon followed up.

"We entomb him," Ash said.

"That won't be easy," Rhain stated.

"We know." I idly petted Reaver's head. "But there has to be a way. After all, the Ancients have been entombed for thousands of years."

Rhahar choked on what he was drinking. "Come again?"

Well, apparently that was something else they weren't aware of. "Not all the Ancients entered Arcadia or were killed. Some could only be put into the ground. That is why there must be balance—why there must always be life and death." I then explained what Kolis had been doing with the Chosen—turning them into the Ascended. "That has been working, but I know that at least Kyn was worried it wouldn't continue to do so. And if balance is not kept, the Ancients will wake."

Blood drained from Rhain's face as he sat—or collapsed—back into his chair.

"Do I want to know what would happen then?" Bele said.

"They would finish what they started when the Primals rose against them. Kolis would be the least of everyone's worries," I said, keeping my hand on the curve of Reaver's neck. "Either way, we need to discover how the Ancients were entombed. What worked for them will work on Kolis."

"Keella is the eldest Primal after Kolis." Ash drew his fingers over his chin. "We plan to speak with her."

"So, we entomb Kolis. For what? Thousands of years?" Rhain asked.

"That will ensure the balance is kept," I said. It finally hit me that could mean we didn't need to use Sotoria's soul. Hope sparked. "Nyktos will continue as a Primal of Death, and I as the Primal of Life."

A crease formed between Ash's brows. "Or until Sotoria can be used. Her soul could be released once Kolis is safely entombed. And then once she is old enough..." Ash sent those around the table an icy smile. "Then Kolis will be no more."

Theon smiled tightly. "Now *that* I like the sound of."

My gaze lowered to Reaver's as several cheers of agreement rose. I couldn't blame them for wanting a future that included a dead Kolis. None of them knew Sotoria. They didn't know what she had already been through. I looked up, finding Rhain's gaze on me.

I shifted in my chair and refocused, returning to stroking Reaver's neck.

"So, how do we go about summoning the Primals?" I asked. "I assume it isn't as easy as sending them a missive."

"No, it is not." Ash refilled my glass. "You, as the true Primal of Life, can issue the summons simply by willing it."

My lips parted at the memory of the painful, reddish-black symbol that had appeared on Ash's palm when Kolis had summoned us. "I don't think hurting them is a wise way to start off."

"It doesn't have to be painful. What Kolis did was an ability provided by the true embers of death. It's a death mark," Ash explained. "But I agree. Forcing them to answer is something Kolis would do. Luckily, there is Attes."

I raised a brow at that. "*Luckily*, you say?"

Ash smirked. "Yes. Just this once. He could prove useful and contact the other Primals."

Attes had already proven himself useful, but I wisely kept that to myself.

Jadis had seemed to grow bored with Bele once the Primal ceased throwing her dagger. She rose now, stretching with a little squeak of a yawn.

Either sharing in Ash's dislike of the Primal or still harboring distrust toward him, Rhain's tone was cold as he asked, "And if Attes decides that he'd rather not be useful?"

Ash leaned back, resting the ankle of one long leg on the knee of the other as Jadis's claws scraped against the table when she crawled forward. "I will convince him that it would be in his best interest to be very useful."

"Wait." My hand halted on the back of Reaver's neck. "As in you'll go speak with Attes?"

A lock of hair lay against his jaw as he tilted his head. "That would be the plan."

"I don't know if that's wise," I pointed out, leaning forward to catch Jadis before she fell right off the table.

Reaver lifted his head, eyeing the little one as she mewled, wanting to be on the floor. For his benefit, I placed her on my other side.

"That is exactly why I'm best suited to speak with him," Ash countered as Jadis immediately scrambled under my chair, causing Reaver to shuffle back. "I'm the last person he wants to piss off."

I wasn't so sure about the plan as I tried to keep an eye on the two draken. Jadis had grabbed one of Reaver's legs—thankfully with a hand and not her mouth. "The last thing we need is you hauling off and punching him."

"I think that is the very first thing needed." Ash gave a shadowy smile that frosted his eyes. "Besides, he has it coming and knows it."

"That isn't going to help us," I said, relieved to see Jadis plop down beside Reaver…or half on top of him. She managed to get her head on his back, causing him to peer up at me with resigned exasperation. Poor guy.

"She's being logical again," Bele stated. "I'm not sure how I feel about it."

I shot her an arch look, feeling the awareness of…another draken. But it was different this time. Stronger. In my mind, I saw Nektas. I shook my head, refocusing. "You sound like I normally run around being illogical."

"Well," she drawled, her silver eyes dancing with amusement as a large shadow fell over the balcony.

Sending Bele one more look of warning, I focused on Ash. "Then I will go with you."

"Now, that *wouldn't* be wise," Ash replied, sipping from his glass. "You will remain here."

His tone and demand stoked my temper like it always did. "You want to know what's not wise?"

"I'm sure I can guess." His gaze flicked to me. "You were about to say me making demands of you is unwise."

"Since you know that, why do you think it's *more* unwise for me to go to Attes than you—who wants to skin him alive?"

Bele's lip curled up on one side. "Thank the Fates, I feel like something very illogical is about to occur—"

"Something illogical always occurs around you, Bele." Nektas entered through the balcony doors, his long hair resting against his bare shoulders.

Huh.

I had been right about it being him. Had I actually sensed it, or was his presence just a logical conclusion? No. Instinct told me I had sensed it was Nektas.

Eyes that shimmered with ethereal brilliance swept across the table, finding mine. His broad jaw softened with a smile. Stopping behind Theon and Lailah, Nektas placed a fist over his chest and bowed his head and upper body. He spoke in that raspy voice of his. "*Meyaah Liessa*."

"She doesn't like to be called that," Saion advised.

"I know, but she will allow it of me." Nektas straightened.

"I will."

Bele's lips pursed. "Rude."

Nektas inclined his head toward Ash and strode around the table. His steps slowed as he spotted his daughter asleep half on top of Reaver. "I hope Jadis hasn't been too much of a handful?"

I took a drink, raising my brows as several others averted their gazes. Images of Jadis tearing at Ash's hair and tugging on Lailah's braids danced in my mind.

"Oh, yeah. She's been a real peach." Bele's tone was as dry as the desert lands near Massene.

"Of course, she has," Nektas replied with all the confidence of a parent whose child was the apple of their eye. He reached down and scooped up his daughter. She let out a little murmur and wiggled before flopping over his shoulder. He gave her scaled back a tender pat and said, "I feel like I may have walked into the middle of an argument."

"I would say it's more of a…heated exchange," Saion replied.

Raising a brow, Nektas sat on Ash's other side and leaned back, propping one foot on the table. "About?"

"Sera and I," Ash said, lifting an arm. A second later, a small ivory blanket shot between Rhain and Saion, coming from somewhere in the chamber. It landed in his hand. "Are not in agreement."

"As unsurprising as that is," Nektas began, taking the blanket from Ash and laying it over Jadis, gently tucking it around her wings, "whose side am I supposed to be on?"

"Mine," Ash and I answered at the same time.

Nektas smirked.

"Ash has suggested using Attes to issue the summons and thinks it's appropriate for him to speak with Attes, even though he wants to rearrange the Primal's internal organs," I explained. "Meanwhile, he thinks I should remain at the palace, polishing the swords or something."

Rhahar coughed and then took a long swallow of his drink.

"That is not what I expect you to do." Ash dragged his teeth over his lower lip, sending me a sidelong glance. "I feel rather confident assuming the only thing you would do with a sword is use it."

"Want to find out?" I suggested with syrupy sweetness.

"Later, when younglings aren't present," he replied with a smoky, midnight smile. "I'd love to."

"Oh, dear," murmured Bele.

I shot Ash a glare.

He winked.

He actually *winked* at me before turning his attention back to Nektas. "But I haven't gotten to the point yet where I explain why it would be wise for her to remain behind."

"Because she's newly awakened," Nektas suggested, jerking his head to the side as Jadis worked a wing free. "And the moment she enters Vathi, her presence would be sensed."

I opened my mouth.

"Exactly," Ash confirmed. His teasing smile was gone now. "Kyn will know you are there."

Hot, prickly anger swept through me, whipping up the essence. "That's fine by me," I said as Reaver lifted his head from my leg. "I would love to *speak* with him."

Eather lashed through Ash's eyes as our gazes connected. "As would I, *liessa*, but as much as it would please me to rearrange *his* internal organs, we just discussed making no moves until we know who our potential allies may be."

"We know Kyn isn't one," I stated.

"Agreed. But should your first act as Queen be one of violence?" Ash asked.

When it came to Kyn? Yes. But as I tore my gaze from his and focused on the sunlight beyond the balcony doors, I thought about the conversation regarding the entombed gods. Kyn was a different story. But would the other Primals understand that? Or would they view me as just another violent, monstrous ruler?

"Gods, now I'm going to be logical," Bele said as if it were something contagious. "You are a fledgling Primal, just like me. And you know how much I hated having to lay low, but I did it. I'm still doing it, until there's no other choice but to take the risk." Her gaze met mine. "I want nothing more than to take my revenge on Kyn in any way I can, but I know doing so right now is too risky." She exhaled heavily. "And yeah, I hate having to be logical about it. You may be stronger and stuff, and able to take on Kyn even now, but why risk it over that piece of trash?"

My lips pinched as I sat back. She'd made her point. "Okay. I get it." I turned to Ash. "But I don't think you should go alone."

"I can go with Nyktos," Lailah offered, drawing a look of ire from her brother and my rabid curiosity. "And make sure they both—"

"Behave?" I suggested. "Like two misbehaving toddlers?"

Now, it was Ash's eyes that narrowed.

"I wasn't going to use those exact words." Lailah rested her clasped hands on the table. "But Attes will be reluctant to allow things to escalate with me there."

"You have far too much faith in him," Theon snapped and fisted his hand on the table.

"I can agree with that," Ash murmured.

"And you never had enough faith in him," Lailah shot back at Theon. "He's not like his brother."

"I can agree with the last part." I tossed in my two cents, because why not when it felt like the meeting was about ten seconds from descending into chaos?

"Sure, he's not like Kyn—thank the Fates." The essence brightened in Theon's golden eyes. "But he's no benevolent being. Every time he's near you, he spends each moment attempting to seduce you."

I opened my mouth then closed it while Bele and the cousins watched with avid interest. Rhain, however, appeared as if he wished to sink through his chair and maybe even the floor.

"That's not true," Lailah hissed, her eyes turning luminous. "And do we really think this is an appropriate conversation to be having right now? On second thought…ever?"

"We have no problem with it," Saion remarked. "Please, continue."

Propping his elbow on the arm of his chair, Rhain drew his fingers over his brow with a sigh.

"Lailah is welcome to join me if she wishes," Ash cut in. "And while she makes sure I behave, I will do the same when it comes to Attes."

My head just about spun off my shoulders as I turned to him. "You will only do that if that is what Lailah wants."

"Of course. *If* that is what she wants," Ash amended. "Which I imagine she would, considering how levelheaded she normally is."

Sitting back, Theon huffed as he crossed his arms. "Yeah, real levelheaded when it comes—"

"I swear to the Fates, if you finish that statement," Lailah warned, "I will knock you from that very chair and into the Abyss."

Theon's jaw clamped shut so tightly I almost expected him to snap his fangs in half.

"So, it's decided?" Rhain dropped his hand onto the table. "Ash will speak with Attes to summon the other Primals."

Those at the table nodded in agreement. Even Reaver.

"We'll want to ensure Attes is in Essaly first," Rhain suggested.

"Essaly?" I questioned.

"It's a city in the northernmost portion of Vathi. Where Attes resides. You were there briefly," he reminded me.

At once, my mind conjured up the memory of rolling hills covered with lush pines, snowcapped mountains, and an ivory-hued Rise. I had been there when I'd brought Thad, the young draken Kolis had forced me to kill, back to life.

"He's likely at his residence." Nektas smoothed a hand over Jadis's back. "But we can have Ehthawn check first."

"I want him to wait until nightfall," Ash said. "In case any of Kyn's draken are in the sky. If Attes is home, I'll leave in the morning."

I felt my stomach drop a little. I knew that Kyn wouldn't sense Ash unless he was in his lands, but I still worried for Ash and Lailah. "What if Kyn learns of your arrival?"

"I will not engage." His fingers drummed on the arm of the chair.

"That's not what I'm worried about." I forced my voice to level. "What if *Kyn* wants to engage?"

"I'll back Ash and Lailah up," Nektas decided. "With me and the draken loyal to Attes, he won't be idiotic enough to come near Essaly."

Hearing that was a relief, but I wasn't sure about Kyn not being idiotic enough.

"There's one more thing I didn't get to," Rhain added. "What you said about wanting those who have come to Lethe to have shelter?" He glanced between Ash and me, and then his chest rose with a deep breath. "I think it's important that they hear that from you—both of you."

"You mean like doing a public address?" I asked, my heart kicking against my ribs.

Rhain nodded.

My stomach twisted sharply at the mere thought of going before so many people. Walking the aisle during my coronation had been hard enough, knowing that everyone saw me.

"I can handle that," Ash said, drawing my gaze.

"You can, of course." Rhain paused. "But those who have come here have done so to see her. And they have done so at great risk."

"And we are honored that they took that risk." Ash's tone had cooled. "I can convey that—"

"No," I interrupted. My chest tightened even as my heart filled with warmth. I knew what Ash was doing. He'd likely picked up on my rising anxiety. He was protecting me. Seeking to ensure I didn't get overwhelmed. While I was not the kind of person who gave speeches, and just thinking about it made me break into a too-hot sweat, I needed to get over myself. "*We* can convey that."

"It's not necessary for you to do this," Ash insisted.

"But it is," I said. "The people risked their lives to come here for us—"

"For you," Nektas interjected, shifting Jadis higher on his chest. "No offense," he said, directed at Ash.

"None taken," Ash replied dryly.

"But sooner or later, they'll start showing up here to see her," Nektas continued.

Ash didn't look thrilled with the prospect.

"Going before them and letting them know is the very least I can do, and I *need* to do this," I added quickly, seeing his jaw harden. "Look, speaking and being all queenly in front of an entire city makes me want to barf."

"Ew," Bele muttered.

I ignored her. "But they need to see and hear me. If I can't do that?" My face began to warm. "How will I be able to convince the Primals to support us or handle the ones that don't?"

A muscle started ticking along Ash's jaw as he held my gaze.

"She has a point," Rhahar said.

Another moment passed with Ash's gaze holding mine. "Are you sure?"

"I am."

He exhaled heavily and then nodded. "Okay."

I smiled at him. "Thank you."

He gave me a small shake of his head, and I could tell that he was still concerned about me getting overwhelmed.

"When do you suggest we address the people?" I asked Rhain.

"I would say as soon as possible," he said, looking between Ash and me.

Concern blossomed. "Are people worried they're not welcome?"

"No," Rhain was quick to assure me. "There is just some general nervousness. Many have been through a lot, and even those who were aware of you don't entirely know what to expect."

I nodded slowly, thinking it over. "Summoning the Primals is important, but I think assuring the people that they are safe and welcome here is a priority. It's something I doubt Kolis would do."

"You can count on that being correct," Bele commented.

Ash shifted in his chair. "How long would it take for the City Hall to be secured and prepared for such an address?"

Theon looked at his sister. "What do you think? I'll be in the Bonelands."

After a moment, she said, "Tomorrow afternoon would be the earliest. It would be tight, but doable."

I looked at Ash. "Can we postpone going to Vathi until the day after?"

"We can."

My stomach twisted and dropped but I pushed past it. "Then we'll address the people of Lethe tomorrow and then speak with Attes."

"Sounds like we have a plan," Ash said, glancing across the table at Rhain. "See to it."

Exhaling slowly, I nodded as I looked around the table, hoping we—I—were making all the right decisions. I felt it was right when it came to prioritizing speaking with the people of Lethe, but everything else? Despite my instinct being more aligned with Bele's strike-first mentality, I did believe that being cautious was the way to go.

But if I was wrong?

Blood would flow.

"It's called the Valley of Blood," Ash said. "The Red River used to run through here and, according to my father, was once as wide as an ocean. But long before I was even born, it began to thin out. What you're seeing is the old riverbed."

Seated astride Odin, my hand tightened around Ash's arm. I could easily see where the valley, nestled between the city of Lethe and another sweeping wall of shadowstone, had gotten its name. The land, all but what appeared to be large, jagged outcroppings of shadowstone, was stained red. While that alone was shocking, it wasn't what caused my lips to part. Nor was it the snowcapped mountains of Vathi that I could see in the distance. It was what occupied the crimson valley below.

After the meeting, I'd asked about the Shadowlands' forces—how many we had, how they were trained…

Instead of giving a vague answer as Ash had done in the past, he'd offered to show me. There was no wild dash through the Dying Woods like the last time I'd been this close to Lethe. We'd left through the Rise gates, joined by Rhain and Lailah, and I saw that the once-bent, crooked trees that crowded the shadowstone wall had sprouted buds and even small, glossy leaves. As we traveled, I spotted tiny white flowers in some of the burgeoning meadows. There was green everywhere I looked—so much more than just a day before.

That was until we neared the Dying Woods. They had remained as such, heavily shadowed and even more somber. My skin crawled as we skirted them, traveling a narrow path along the bluffs. I'd seen the gray, shadowy forms of the Shades moving in and out of the dead trees several times. Eather had pressed against my skin upon seeing the souls who refused to pass through the Pillars of Asphodel out of fear of judgment for their sins while alive. It was almost as if they were tracking us.

Tracking me.

I'd exhaled the moment we cleared the Dying Woods, and the Black Bay, along with the tall Rise surrounding Lethe, appeared. I wasn't looking forward to passing them again, and I wasn't exactly sure why, beyond the fact that the Shades were incredibly creepy. But thoughts of Shades fell to the wayside as the path we traveled diverged from the fortified city, followed the widening contour of the bluff, and opened to the valley.

Rows of squat, one-story buildings faced the Black Bay, built in a semi-circle. There had to be hundreds of what looked to be dormitories. Towers flanked them, taller than the Rise, and clearly used to keep an eye on what lay to the south and the east. My gaze shifted northward to where an utter sea of soldiers dressed in black and red trained. It would be hard to pick them out from the environment from a distance, but I saw them. All of them.

"How many are there?" I asked.

"Approximately forty-two thousand," Ash answered.

"Forty-two thousand?" I whispered.

"I know that sounds like a lot." Ash's thumb traced an idle circle on the flare of my hip.

"It's not?" I glanced over my shoulder at him. "Lasania only had about half that."

"And Vathi has three times that number, equally spread between Attes and Kyn," Rhain commented, his head tilting. In the sunlight, his hair was a burnished auburn.

"Oh." I swallowed as I watched what appeared to be archery training.

"And they have far more gods than we do," Lailah chimed in.

I looked to where she sat upon a deep chestnut horse. "How many do we have?"

"About forty percent of our army are gods," she said, shifting on her saddle. "The remaining numbers consist of godlings and mortals."

Mortals.

My gaze shifted back to the valley. Several of those who had been working with swords had stopped and clustered together. They had clearly noticed us.

"They volunteered," Ash stated. "And they know the risks."

"They are the bravest among them," Lailah added, pride filling her voice. "But they are far easier to wound and kill, which I'm sure you're thinking about. Because of that, most are auxiliary units of longbowmen, trained on foot and horseback."

Archers. "Makes sense." I toyed with the edge of a fang with the tip of my tongue, thinking about what I'd seen when Kolis had brought me to the rooftop of the Sanctuary. "I never saw any soldiers while I was in Dalos, unless the guards pull double duty."

"For some of the Courts, the guards and soldiers are one and the same, but you wouldn't have seen soldiers like these there," Ash said. "Dalos does not have its own army."

"What?" I exclaimed, surprised as Ash looked down at me. Then I got it. "Because the Primal of Life has the armies of all the Courts."

"Supposed to." His gaze shifted to the soldiers below. "That is how it has been since my father. Not even Kolis openly defies that rule."

"But that doesn't mean he follows it."

Ash nodded. "I imagine his creations make up a portion of his defenses."

I thought that over. "I'm sure his creations serve a dual purpose—continuation of the balance and as defense. But the ones he calls the Ascended? They can move about during the day—I saw them in the atrium of Cor Palace—but they cannot go out in the sunlight. That's a weakness. But the Revenants?"

"They will be a problem," Ash stated.

"Revenants can be momentarily killed, and based on what I saw, the type of wound determines exactly how long they stay down," I shared. "But it's not that long. I got Callum under the chin, and within fifteen minutes or so, he was back on his feet."

"Most wounds inflicted in battle are to the head or chest." Lailah's forehead creased. "Quick strikes. Not to say there aren't ones that do more bodily damage."

"But on the whole, those are injuries a Revenant would quickly recover from." My gaze shifted to the snowcapped mountains. "What about the other Courts?" I asked, my attention snagged by those training on horseback. They, too, had slowed or stopped.

"Hard to tell for sure," she said. "Many of the Primals keep their true numbers hidden."

"But you have guesses?"

"We do." She sent me a quick grin. "But first, I think you're about to experience something I have a feeling will make you uncomfortable."

Bewilderment surged. "What do you mean?"

"Look down into the valley," Ash urged.

I did as he instructed and locked up.

On the field below, all the soldiers had stopped, and those on horseback had dismounted. They stood in endless rows, facing us.

"What…what is happening?" I asked.

"They're about to do your new favorite thing," Ash said, his voice heavy with amusement.

My eyes went wide. "They don't—"

The soldiers kneeled, row after row of them in a wave that stretched the valley, one hand on their chests, and the other on the ground. My lips parted as I took them in.

I jumped when a loud thump echoed through the valley. The soldiers were slamming their palms against the packed ground, over and over, until the valley was filled with the sound.

"This is different," Ash said, speaking into my ear. "They are not just paying homage to their Queen. They are telling you that they are yours, and that, if it comes down to it, they will go to war for you."

My breath caught. "For us."

His lips brushed my cheek. "For us."

Then the pounding stilled, and silence came. Their heads lifted. They waited.

"I…I don't know what to do," I admitted, my cheeks warming. "Yelling to them that they may rise doesn't seem fitting."

Ash chuckled. "You can just lift a hand."

"Oh." That was far easier. I raised my hand and then gave a little wave because holding it still felt awkward.

It worked, though.

The soldiers rose, and after a few moments, they returned to their training. Seeing thousands of people I'd never spoken to, had likely never even crossed paths with, willing to go to war for me—for us? It rattled me.

"So, about the armies," Lailah said as Ash gently took hold of my still-raised hand and lowered it. "Phanos has the second-largest army. Around forty-five thousand."

All thoughts of awkward displays of loyalty fell away. My stomach dipped. "And what type of soldiers does he have?"

"Mostly those on two feet," Ash answered, gently squeezing my hip. "But he rules the seas with the ceeren."

I felt my heart clench at thoughts of more ceeren dying.

"Among other things," Rhain muttered under his breath but continued before I could question that. "Embris has slightly less than we do. About forty thousand."

Lailah straightened the strap of her baldric. "With the exception of Bele's, the rest of the Courts have about five thousand."

I nodded, running my hand over Odin's glossy mane. "Do we have any idea how many Cimmerian Kyn has?"

"No more than a thousand," Rhain answered. "And that likely includes those who returned to Vathi after Bele's Ascension."

That surprised me. "I would've thought there'd be more."

"Lucky for us," Ash drawled, "the Cimmerian's love of fighting equals a very short lifespan."

I snorted at his comment. A thousand senturion warriors that could summon the night to cloak themselves in battle was still a problem.

"Any Court that wants to move their armies against us would have to do so by foot," Lailah shared. "And none of the Courts are likely to give such permission because it could be perceived as a pronouncement of their loyalties."

I considered that. "So, any Court outside Vathi will have to travel the Lassa Sea, which is good news since we would see them."

"Except for the Thyia Plains," Rhain interjected. "But they cannot cross the Disus—the sea between our Courts and to our north. The waters there are part of the Vale, and as such, protected. Not even Kolis would dare travel those. That leaves the Bonelands."

"The gods could shadowstep from their ships to land," Ash said, "but they risk destroying their vessels in the process."

"True." Rhain's lips pursed. "And they would also have to travel the length of the Bonelands with no cleared lands and no roads. If any come, they will do so by the Lassa."

For now, went unsaid.

"This could all change if a number of Courts decide to support Kolis." I stated the obvious.

"Yes." Ash gently squeezed my hip. "It would all change then."

"If that happens, they will come for us by land, sea, and air," Lailah said, her brow furrowed. "Fighting a battle on two fronts is not something anyone wants to do—let alone three."

A sudden awareness echoed through me. I looked at the sky, squinting until I could make out the distant shape of a draken.

"That's one of ours," Rhain said, noting where my attention had gone. "They're patrolling."

As I watched the draken glide closer, I knew it wasn't Nektas. It wasn't as large as him, and the draken didn't…*feel* like him. I thought—or perhaps *felt*—that it was a draken I wasn't familiar with, which made me think of something. Draken would only attack if the Primal they served was in danger, but instinct told me the rule didn't necessarily apply to wartime. "What's the draken situation with the other Courts?"

"Good and bad," Lailah said. "Which one would you like to hear first?"

"The bad."

A wry grin appeared. "Kolis has a legion of a dozen," she said. "Kyn has about ten, as does Embris. The other Courts have five or fewer."

I frowned. "Those numbers are lower than I expected."

"The draken go through cycles that last about a century and can only conceive for a few weeks during that time," Rhain explained, watching the soldiers on the field. "And from what I can gather, many of the draken have taken active steps to prevent conception since Kolis's reign began."

A knot of sadness gathered in my chest because I could understand why they wouldn't want to bring a youngling into the realm under Kolis's rule. Look at what he had done to Thad—the young draken who had served Kyn—Nektas's mate, Halayna; Reaver's parents…and only the gods knew how many others.

Ash's chin grazed the top of my head. "Ready for the good news?"

"Yes. Please."

"We have the most." Ash dragged his thumb along the crease between my thigh and hip. "Fifteen, not including the younglings. And we have Nektas."

The skin beneath my ear shivered. "Because…he's the first."

"Exactly. Most are not like Davon," Ash confirmed, referencing Nektas's now-deceased distant relative. "Or the draken who have always served Kolis. If the others come up against Nektas, they will back down."

That was good news.

But not nearly enough.

We had Attes, and I was confident that Keella would join us. Maia, as well as Phanos and Embris, were up in the air. Kyn would obviously side with the false King. So would Veses. And if either Phanos or Embris stood with him? Or, worse yet, both?

We would be outnumbered.

12

"I agree with what Ash said about keeping the address short and to the point," Rhain said, referencing the discussion we'd had on the way back from the Valley of Blood. "That would limit the probability of something being said that shouldn't be."

My brows pulled together as I glanced over Reaver to where Rhain sat on the antechamber couch. Exactly what did he think I would say that I shouldn't?

"And it also lessens the risks involved with going before so many people," he continued, looking down at the bound parchment resting in his lap. Jadis had torn off and almost consumed half the pages before Nektas took the little draken outside to play and work off some of her energy before supper.

With the way my knee was bouncing, it should be me out there working off unspent energy.

Reaver lifted his head from the cushion and placed it on my knee, peering up at me as if he had read my mind. I grinned down at him.

"I also think sharing what you did during our meeting would be wise. That it is your decision and choice for the realms not to be ruled by one individual," he said, drawing my attention to him. "I know we touched on that on the way back here but telling the people that it was your choice is important."

I nodded, my mind flipping over our prior discussion. Ash and I had decided that we would first assure the people they were welcome and we were doing everything in our power to provide for them, then move on to the whole Queen and King business. We'd decided to tackle that part together during the speech.

"Will I have to walk the aisle again?" I asked.

Rhain looked at me as if he couldn't believe that was a concern given everything we were discussing, but it was one long-ass aisle. "Do you not want to do that?"

"Not particularly."

"Okay." He scribbled something down. "I will announce you and then Ash. Once that is finished, you two can shadowstep onto the dais."

"Wait. Why would I be announced first? Where I'm from, it's always the King."

"That's because mortals operate in a very patriarchal society."

"As if this one is any different?" I retorted.

His lips pursed. "You have a good point there, but in this case, it has nothing to do with gender and everything to do with your Primalhood. You are the true Primal of Life, and even when ruling jointly, your Primalhood asserts supremacy. You will be announced first."

"Well, that doesn't sound very equal." I looked down at Reaver. "Does it?"

He chirped, and gods, it was still bizarre to hear his voice in my head. Even if it was one word, which was *no.*

"Moving on," Rhain said, sighing. "You two will then take your seats on the thrones."

I opened my mouth.

"And because I know you're going to ask why," he went on, "it is simply tradition."

"I wasn't going to ask."

Rhain sent me a bland look.

"Whatever," I muttered as Reaver huffed out a laugh.

"During this time, the people will have bowed. You will tell them to rise—and yes, it will be you."

I was so bored with this conversation I didn't ask why it had to be me. "Ash mentioned having wine provided for them. Will that be possible?"

"Yes." Rhain checked off what I could only imagine was *annoy Sera* from his list. "We have many barrels that can be used for such. Unfortunately, there isn't enough time to have food prepared."

"What about this?" Aios's voice floated out from the narrow hall adjoining the chambers. Gods, she had been going through the wardrobe for so long I'd forgotten she was even here. She appeared, holding a crimson gown draped from a hanger. "It's really gorgeous, isn't it?"

My gaze flicked over the dress as I idly stroked the top of Reaver's head. The gown was beautiful, and the crushed velvet looked soft, but for some reason, the color was a turn-off for me. "It is, but it doesn't feel right."

Aios lowered her arm until half the gown pooled on the floor. "This is the fourth gown that doesn't feel right. You don't have many more options."

"I know." I winced, feeling like I was wasting her time. Which I was, especially considering she had spent the better part of the day assisting with the birth Kye had summoned her for. When she offered to help me find something to wear, I should've told her to rest, but I was glad she wanted to help after how our conversation had ended this morning.

Aios eyed me for a moment and then nodded. "I think I know what the problem is. I will be right back."

I watched her spin on her heel and disappear back down the hall.

"I doubt she will be right back," Rhain commented as Reaver lifted his head and stretched.

"True." I leaned back. "Why can't I just wear what I'm wearing now?"

Rhain appeared positively aghast. "You should dress for the role."

My lips thinned. "And how should I be dressed?"

He gave me the most unsexual once-over I had ever received in my life. "Not like that."

"What's wrong with this?" I glanced down at my vest and black leggings. "Ash has no problem with it."

"I'm sure he doesn't," Rhain replied dryly, earning a confused head tilt from Reaver. "But it's not appropriate."

Aios reappeared, holding a dark gray tunic with silver embroidering that matched the design on the throne doors. Immediately drawn to it, I rose and went to her, passing the pillared dais.

Rhain sighed for what had to be the hundredth time. "That's a tunic."

"Never would've guessed that," I murmured as I took the lightweight garment from Aios.

"You should wear a gown," Rhain insisted.

My gaze cut to him as a wave of prickly heat swept over the back of my neck. I knew this was in no way the same as my time in Dalos, and none of the gowns Aios had brought out were even remotely transparent, but my skin still felt itchy and too tight. "A gown is not me," I said as Reaver launched himself off the couch and came to my side. "This,"—I thrust the tunic out—"is me."

"Is that you as a Queen?" he countered.

"I don't see why it can't be."

His chest rose with a deep breath, and I suspected another sigh was coming. "Let me ask this… Do Queens in the mortal realm dress as you are now?"

The tunic featured a stiff collar, giving it a more formal appearance. I liked the elbow-length sleeves. "I don't know every Queen in the mortal realm, but from what I saw, no. You know what I also saw?"

"Hmm?" he asked.

"A Queen who wore pretty silk gowns and glittering jewels." The image of my mother took form. "And, at the end of the day, she was a terrible Queen."

"I interact with the people of Lethe often," Aios said. "I don't think they will care if she wears a gown or breeches. And to be frank, I think less finery would also serve to show those who do not know her that she is not invested in fancy trappings like some Primals are."

The sigh came then.

"Plus," Aios continued, taking the tunic from me and holding it to my shoulders. One side of the garment ended up draped over Reaver's head, but the back of the top appeared as if it would reach just above my ankles. The front curved elegantly into a V-shape, coming together at the navel to create a flowing and elongated silhouette. "It is nearly as long as a gown and could easily be seen as such."

"I don't think anyone would mistake that for a gown."

Did he not remember what he'd seen me wearing while in Dalos? This was more of a gown than I'd worn there.

"Disagree," Aios stated, letting me take the tunic again and crossing her arms.

He was quiet for a moment and then stated flatly, "I do hope pants are involved in this attire you must wear."

"No, I was planning to wear just this." I raised a brow as I saw his lips twitch. "Was that an actual joke?"

"I would never." He lowered his gaze, closing the leather folio over the bound parchment. "Anyway, I see the point you're making—the point *both* of you are making."

I sent Aios a grateful look. She gave me a barely noticeable nod, leaving me to wonder if she knew why I didn't want to wear a gown. She probably did.

"But when it comes to the meeting with the Primals," Rhain said, "I suggest you consider something different. Those like Embris will expect you to present yourself in a certain way."

I couldn't give a barrat's ass about how Embris expected me to present myself, but Rhain wouldn't be happy with that answer. "I'll consider it."

Rhain eyed me as if he didn't believe for one second that I would, but I suddenly felt Ash drawing close. The sensation of a dozen birds taking flight filled my chest.

The doors opened moments later, and he entered. His gaze immediately found mine. "I would like some time..." His head tilted as a slight frown appeared. "Is that Reaver under the dress?"

"Ha!" I exclaimed. "Even he thinks it's a dress."

Rhain rolled his eyes.

"And yes, it's Reaver," I said, and the youngling popped his head out from under the garment. "He's helping."

Reaver nodded.

"Well, I hope he's done helping," Ash replied. "I would like to speak with my wife before supper."

My wife.

Those birds turned into giant, carnivorous-but-happy hawks.

"We were just finishing in here." Rhain rose, and Reaver looked up at me. I nodded, and he lifted into the air.

"Oh! I almost forgot," Aios said. "I ran into Erlina earlier. She wanted to come see you, but with everything going on, I told her you may be a little busy."

A bit surprised that the seamstress wanted to see me, a warm glow filled my chest. "The next time she comes by, I would like to see her."

Aios nodded. "Until tomorrow, then."

"Wait," I called as Aios passed Ash. "Will you all be having supper in the dining hall?"

"We normally do," Rhain answered.

"Since it's later, Bele and I will likely have our supper here," Aios said as Reaver hovered by them.

"Can we have supper in the dining hall?" I asked Ash.

"If that is what you'd like," he said.

"I would."

Ash turned to Rhain, whose eyes were slightly wide. "When will dinner be ready in the hall?"

He blinked. "In about an hour."

"We will see you three there then." Ash turned back to me.

Rhain was still standing there as if stunned. "Let's go." Grinning, Aios gave Rhain a light shove. "We need to make sure there are enough chairs in the dining hall."

"There are more than enough chairs," Rhain argued as Aios opened the door.

"Let's double-check," she suggested, following Reaver out.

"Was it just me, or did Rhain seem really surprised by that request?" I asked after the doors had closed.

"We haven't joined the others for many suppers," he said. "And before you, I didn't do so often."

Sadly, the last part didn't surprise me.

Ash plucked the hanger from my grasp and tossed the tunic onto the couch.

"I really don't need that wrinkled." I started toward it but didn't make it very far. Ash snagged me by the waist and turned me back to him. "Rhain will be very displeased if that ends up wrinkled—"

"He'll get over it." He tugged me to his chest.

"I'm not so sure about that," I protested, my gaze lifting to his. The heat in his molten-steel eyes sent fine tremors radiating through my limbs. I immediately stopped thinking about Rhain and the state of the tunic.

Clasping the back of my neck, Ash brought his mouth to mine. I was at once completely enraptured by how he kissed like a man starved and wasn't aware of what he was up to until he lifted me. His tongue delved deep as he stepped onto the dais and carried me toward the table, setting me down on the edge. I tasted whiskey on his tongue as he deepened the kiss. His fingers traced the outline of my collarbone before moving slowly downward. His touch was electric, sending jolts of pleasure throughout my body.

He nipped my lower lip, then lifted his head from mine. "Why were you surprised that Erlina wanted to see you?"

I sighed. "Was I surprised enough that I projected?"

"You did." He kissed the corner of my mouth. "Why?"

I shrugged. "I don't know. I guess I'm just not used to people wanting to see me," I admitted, my cheeks flushing with embarrassment. "That sounds kind of pathetic, doesn't it?"

"No, *liessa*, it doesn't. You grew up not being known by many. Being surprised is understandable." He drew his fingers down my cheek. "But you should probably start getting used to people wanting to see you."

I honestly didn't think I ever would, but I still said, "Yes, sir."

Chuckling, he planted his hands on either side of my legs. "I noticed something today. You grew incredibly anxious as we rode past the Dying Woods. Did you feel something?"

It took me a moment to think back. I had been nervous, and I hadn't been that affected before. I wasn't sure why. Well, that wasn't necessarily true.

I'd had a *feeling*.

One that made me think of the Shade I'd touched during my poorly thought-out plan to end Kolis. The creature had been nothing more than smoke and bone, but after a single touch, I'd seen organs and muscles form, almost as if I'd been restoring life to it.

Ash's chin brushed the curve of my jaw. "Sera?"

"Sorry." I started to tell him that nothing had disturbed me but stopped myself. Sharing thoughts was important, even the incoherent ones. "I was just thinking about that Shade I touched back when I was in the Dying Woods."

"Back when you last held a dagger to my throat?"

"Was that the last time?" I asked wryly.

He chuckled. "You're talking about the one that seemed to regenerate?"

"Yes." I ran my fingers along his. "I was thinking about how powerful my touch was that it could bring back a Shade, even then. Who knows how long it had been dead?"

"Based on the state of it, I'd say quite some time." He kissed my jaw. "Likely several decades, if not longer."

"That's…kind of creepy."

"Just be careful when touching dead things."

A grin tugged at my lips. "That's possibly the strangest advice ever spoken."

"Possibly." Dipping his head, he kissed my cheek. "Is that what made you nervous when we rode past?"

Again, my immediate response was to shrug it off, so I took a moment to put my thoughts into words. "I could feel the essence swelling inside me as we rode past and thought I could see them following us through the trees. I think they may have felt my presence, and I was glad we weren't going into the woods." I tipped my head back against his chest. "Because I feared I…I worried I may do something I shouldn't."

"Like return life to them?"

Pressing my lips together, I nodded. "What if I still can't control that?"

"But you have, *liessa.* More than once."

"I know, but there have been times when I haven't." I thought about what Aios and I had discussed. "Do you know how often your father brought people back?"

Ash was silent for a few moments. "I know my father struggled with that. I also know he used the ability far more in the beginning than he did toward the end," he said. "When people came to one of his Temples to plead for the return of their loved ones, it was hard for him to ignore it. Especially if the deceased was young and the death unexpected. He would almost always grant those requests."

"Even knowing that if he granted life—"

"Death is never cheated?" Ash finished. "Yes." A moment or two passed. "As I've said, my father wasn't perfect. Wanting to ease the pain of those suffering was only part of the reason. The act of granting life may have come from an altruistic place, but there were…personal benefits gained from such."

"He enjoyed the worship it brought him?"

"Yes." His lips grazed the corner of mine. "Once my father realized that he could not continue granting life as he was, he knew he couldn't personally answer the summonses. That's when gods began acting as the middle people between the summoners and the Primals. It started first with Eythos, and then the rest of the Primals followed suit."

My brows knitted. "But you can still feel the summonses, right? Eythos had with King Roderick. And I know Kolis did." I swallowed. "He heard my father's summons."

Ash slipped his hand from under mine and straightened in front of me. "What do you mean?"

I realized just then that I hadn't told him about this. There hadn't been much time to share things with him after we were finally free of Dalos. "The night I was born, my father knew what it would mean. He summoned Kolis, having no idea that Eythos had answered Roderick in the past."

"Why did he…?" Ash cursed. "He wanted the deal undone."

I nodded, my heart twisting for the man I'd never met. "He didn't want that kind of future for his daughter."

"What father would?" Ash stated, the respect evident in his voice. "If I were to have a child, I wouldn't want them to live a life of no choice, one where their future was already determined for them."

My stomach dipped again, this time solely due to the idea of Ash as a father. "You know what that means, right?"

"That Kolis always knew about you?" When I nodded, he sighed. "Yeah, I'm figuring that out."

I squeezed my eyes shut. "I'm sorry."

"Why are you apologizing?"

"Because of everything you did to prevent Kolis from discovering me. What you've sacrificed." Anger boiled, stoking the embers as I drew in a deep, calming breath. "It was for—"

"It wasn't for nothing, Sera. I don't regret a damn thing I did to keep you safe," he said. "And it's not something you ever need to apologize for."

The calming breath did not help.

I placed my hands on the table. "How can you not be mad? You kept yourself away from me out of concern for Kolis taking notice of me. You had people watching me. Lathan died doing so."

"I haven't forgotten any of that."

Eather pulsed hotly through me as I rocked back. "You made a deal with Veses to keep her from telling Kolis about me, and there was no reason for you to do so."

Ash's gaze locked with mine. "Nor have I forgotten what I've done, Sera."

"Then why aren't you furious?" My fingers pressed into the tabletop, and power vibrated along my skin. What I had experienced was *nothing* compared to what he'd had to go through with Veses. Essence crept into the corners of my vision, the violent energy seeping out. The chandelier creaked as it began to sway. "I am."

"I never would've guessed that," he replied dryly. "You should calm down."

My chin dipped. "Hearing that makes me want to do the exact opposite."

"My apologies," he drawled, the essence flaring brightly behind his pupils.

I inhaled sharply, my eyes narrowing. "I'm choosing to ignore the lack of sincerity in your tone."

"And I'm choosing not to let anger over something I cannot change consume me."

My fingers lifted from the table as a scorching, pulsating energy coursed through them. A hot, stinging power throbbed, and the very air itself seemed to cling to my skin and then contract as I stared down at Ash. "Then I *choose* to be angry for the both of us."

"How about you *choose* not to levitate?"

"How about—*what*?"

"You're levitating." Full lips twitched. "As in, you're rising into the air—"

"I know what levitating means." I glanced down, and…yep, I was definitely doing that. My ass was no longer on the table. Like, not even remotely. My legs were straight, and I was several feet above Ash. The shock of seeing that dampened my anger, and I immediately started to drop with a yelp.

Ash caught my arms and lowered me to the table. "Steady."

Looking up through strands of hair, I cursed. "I didn't even realize I was doing that."

"It happens," he said, like floating into the air wasn't a big deal. He curled his hand around the nape of my neck, bringing our faces together so we were only inches apart. "I don't want you to be angry for both of us, Sera."

"But Veses—"

"She's not worth it." His gaze caught and held mine. "Neither of us can change the past—undo the decisions we've made. I'm not saying it isn't fucked up. It is," he said, smoothing the hair back from my face. "But I refuse to allow anger over what is already done and over with to rot inside me." His gaze searched mine. "The deal I made doesn't matter."

We'd have to disagree on that.

"Please tell me you understand," he said.

I did…and I didn't, because his lack of regret didn't change the fact that he had forfeited his autonomy to keep me hidden from Kolis. Still, I nodded.

But what he'd said struck something in me. If he could move past what Veses had done to him, then why not do the same with Kolis?

As soon as that thought formed, I realized how shortsighted it was. Veses' actions paled in comparison to Kolis's.

Either way, Veses would pay for her role. *That* was another vow I made to myself.

"Anyway," I said, quickly kissing him, "these summonses can be felt?"

Ash was quiet for a few heartbeats. "Not like before. Only the strongest and truest pleas reach us now."

I frowned. "What does that even mean?"

"Pleas made while feeling extreme emotion," he explained, running his fingers up under the sleeve of the blouse I wore under my vest. "Those reach us."

"How does it feel?"

"It's hard to put into words." His thumb swept over my elbow. "It feels like a calling—a pull that demands your attention. You feel it here." He placed the palm of his other hand between my breasts. "The tugging sensation is very similar to what I feel when I am summoned to the Pillars. I imagine it's sort of like your foresight demanding you do something."

I drew a wavy line across his arm. "And what…what do you do then?"

"It is up to you."

"Well, that's not a helpful answer."

He chuckled. "It's the truth. You can…*choose*," he said, and I rolled my eyes, "to answer or not."

I turned my head to the side. "You do."

A tight, icy smile appeared. "Only because anyone who summons a Primal of Death does so at their own risk."

I remembered him telling me that before. Anyone summoning a Primal of Death usually wanted something terrible.

"There is no wrong or right way to handle it. Only what you're comfortable with," he added as my gaze lowered. "And you can change your mind at any time. You will, however, need to assign gods you trust to act on your behalf."

I nodded, thinking things over. Obviously, the smartest thing to do would be to not answer the summons in person. That way, I could be more objective and…responsible.

And possibly prevent a Kolis-type situation down the road.

"It is rare for the summonses to reach us," Ash added. "It does take the type of desperation most are lucky not to feel." He looped his other arm around me. "I imagine you don't have the highest opinion of my father after hearing that."

"No, that's not the case. I mean, I honestly don't know what to think of any of that," I admitted as I traced a circle on his forearm. "I can't exactly judge him. It would be difficult to ignore the pleas of the mourning when you could do something to ease their pain." Once more, I thought about my conversation with Aios. "And I was thinking earlier about how one decides when to grant life and when not to—like, obviously, the ability would not have been shared if the Ancients hadn't wanted it to be used. And that can never be an easy decision to make." I tipped my head back. "It was one I never wanted to be in charge of making."

He kissed my brow. "Most would not want that responsibility."

"I was also thinking that maybe how someone dies plays a role," I told him. "Like if the death is unnatural or…unjust."

"I don't think my father ever figured out for sure when it was and wasn't right to do so, but I don't think you'll struggle as much as he did."

"Why is that?"

"Because you don't have his ego."

I snorted. "Really?"

"Let me rephrase that," he said. "You don't want to be worshipped."

"You're right about that, and also wrong."

"You don't want to be worshipped by anyone but me."

"Exactly."

He kissed my temple and then settled beside me. "Are you sure you're ready to go in front of the people tomorrow?"

"I am." My stomach tumbled a bit. "I mean, I'm nervous about it. I've never done anything like it. But I am ready."

"Okay." His fingers slid back down my arm. "I just don't want you to feel overwhelmed."

"I know." His consideration reminded me of something. "I didn't get a chance to thank you."

"For what?"

I smiled. "For starting the meeting when I couldn't."

"You don't need to thank me for that."

"Yes, I do," I insisted. "You stopped me from looking more unprepared than necessary."

"*Liessa*," Ash began.

"I'm being serious." I placed my hands on his chest, feeling his cold skin beneath his shirt. "Look, I'm not being too hard on myself. I panicked a little, which I'm sure you picked up on."

Ash raised a brow.

"You jumped in without making it a big deal," I continued. "And that gave me time to find my footing."

"I get what you're saying, but I only did what I needed to do for you," he replied, tucking the hair that had fallen forward behind my ear. "I only did what I should do. That is never something you need to thank me for."

My lips pursed. "I'm still going to thank you when you do things you '*should*' have done."

"Figured," he stated blandly.

"Perhaps instead of vocalizing my thanks, I could show you?" I suggested.

Eather brightened in his eyes. "As long as you're still using your mouth, I'll have no complaints."

A small, shocked giggle snuck free. "Pervert."

"Been called worse."

Laughing, I clasped his cheeks and kissed him. His cool breath mingled with mine, creating an intoxicating blend. A rush of desire surged, sending a current of pulsing pleasure through me that seemed to travel from my mouth to every inch of my body.

"How much time do you think we have before supper?" I asked.

"Not nearly long enough to do what I want." The smoky arousal in his voice caused muscles low in my stomach to curl. "Which is to strip you down and fuck you on this table."

My entire body flushed at the prospect. "That's too bad."

"Yes." His lips coasted over mine.

"But I do think we have time for an appetizer."

Ash drew back, his brows furrowing as I slid off the table and lowered myself to my knees in front of him. "I'm not sure what you on your knees has to do with an appetizer."

One side of my lips curled up as my innuendo failed to land. It was easy to forget his lack of experience when he was such a quick, adept learner.

"You'll see," I said, sliding my hands up the front of his thighs and then inward.

He sucked in a ragged breath as my palm dragged over his rigid length.

"I think I'm starting to understand."

"Good." I undid the flap of leather and then shoved his pants down, baring him to me. I took in the sight of him—thick, hard, and straining. I licked my lips. "Yum."

"Fuck," he groaned.

Grinning, I encircled him with my fingers, awed by how his entire body reacted, and then I took him into my mouth.

I carried through on what I'd said. I showed him my thanks with my mouth and tongue.

And there were no complaints.

I sat in the middle of the mattress, staring at the small wooden box as Ash readied himself for bed. I could hear the splashing of the fresh water that had been brought up after supper.

I was restless.

Again.

Every couple of moments, my muscles tensed as if I were about to leap to my feet and…do something. What? I had no idea.

I drew my legs to my chest, my gaze tracking the delicate carvings along the lid of the box. It felt like a sense of urgency, but I didn't know what for.

I poked at a fang with my tongue, my brows furrowing. I thought I recognized the feeling. It was the same as the year I'd forgotten Ezra's birthday. On and off throughout the day, I'd kept feeling like I was forgetting something, but the *what* had danced just out of my reach. This restless urgency was similar to that. There was something I needed to do or remember. Something important. And this wasn't the first time I'd felt this since waking from stasis after my Ascension. It had steadily increased as the day passed, though.

Resting my chin on my knees, I closed my eyes. The only time I hadn't felt the restlessness had been during our utterly *perfect* supper. I hadn't said much during it. I'd just sat back and listened to the conversations around me. Honestly, doing something as simple as sharing dinner with Ash and the people I was beginning to consider family had been something I'd only dreamed of as a child.

But as soon as the meal and conversation ended and my mind quieted, restlessness surged through me. Exactly like when I'd been with Rhain and Aios earlier. It had nothing to do with Kolis. I didn't think it had anything to do with tomorrow's speech or Ash's upcoming trip to Vathi. Or our plans to go to Keella. It wasn't about us. Not really. Maybe it had something to do with Lethe or the Shadowlands in general. Perhaps it had to do with all the new arrivals to Lethe and how long it would be until crops—

Wait.

My eyes went wide as I lifted my head. When Saion had spoken during the meeting about surveying the land for crops, I'd been thinking about how I should be able to help speed that process along.

Not should…

The bathing chamber darkened as Ash strolled out. The sight of him was a distraction. My gaze eagerly tracked the drops of water coursing down the sculpted lines of his chest, and the nape of my neck tingled. A sudden sense of knowing seized me. Eather throbbed from deep within me as if it were waking up.

I *could* do something.

I shot to my knees, sending my hair falling over my shoulders. "I'm the true Primal of Life."

Ash stopped at the side of the bed, his brow beginning to furrow and then smooth out as his gaze dropped. "I do hope you're not just realizing that now. If so, I don't think summoning the Primals tomorrow is a good idea."

"Why would I just now be—?" I pressed my lips together. He was teasing. I squinted. "*Anyway*. I can restore life, and while water isn't really something alive, it's—" My thoughts were racing so fast I could barely make sense of them. I shook my head. "There *is* life to water and to everything." My nose scrunched as I tried to grasp that piece of knowledge because I knew it was important and would lead to something even more so. But I shook my head, refocusing. "I was able to restore life with eather before. I was able to heal—are you even paying attention?"

Ash dragged his teeth over his lower lip and nodded. "Of course."

"You are definitely not." Leaning forward, I grasped his chin, guiding his attention away from my sheer nightgown. "You're staring at my breasts."

"You're right. I am." He pulled back, kissing the tip of my finger. "They're beautiful." His gaze dropped again. "But like this, with the gown and your hair spread across them?" The featherlight touch of his fingers between the strands of hair drew a shiver from me. "I cannot help myself, *liessa*. I'm eager for dessert."

"I'm flattered."

His gaze returned to mine, and he lifted a brow.

Sighing, I rolled my eyes. "Okay, I'm really flattered. Thank you. And you can show me how beautiful you find them later."

The tips of his fangs appeared. "Oh, I very much plan to do so." His head dipped, and his lips glided over my cheek. "You had an appetizer earlier, but I haven't had dessert yet."

Muscles low in my stomach tightened, and it took a lot for me to ignore that, but I *had* to. "Ash."

"*Liessa*?"

"We don't have to wait for it to rain or for the snow to fall and then melt," I told him. "I can restore the rivers and lakes in the Shadowlands."

That got his attention.

He was no longer checking out my breasts. "Are you sure?"

"Yes." Or at least I thought so. "I can do it." Resolve filled me, and Ash either saw it in my stare or sensed it, because the line of his shoulders became rigid. "I can do it *now*."

Ash and I rode through the Rise gates, leaving the guards there in stunned speculation. We both wore cloaks concealing our identities, but there was no way they hadn't recognized the massive, sable-coated warhorse. No others were as large or handsome as Odin.

And the glimpse of my bare calf as Odin's pace picked up, causing the cloaks to flutter around our legs, was likely also a dead giveaway.

Ash and I were fully dressed—at least, mostly—yet neither of us was in what one would consider appropriate attire beneath our cloaks. He wore pants. I wore my translucent nightgown. I'd been *that* eager to test out the feeling telling me I could do something. I didn't know if Ash believed me or was simply humoring me, but he hadn't even insisted we take a few moments to think things over.

Glancing back, I could still see the guards standing at the towers by the gate as if frozen. "I think they knew it was us."

"There's a good chance they did."

"Do you think they'll alert anyone?" I asked, petting Odin's mane as the eather hummed beneath my skin, almost as if ramping up and preparing itself. "I really hope not. In case I'm wrong."

"They won't."

An echo of awareness shuttled through me as I looked up to the star-strewn sky and spotted a draken in the distance. It didn't feel like Nektas.

"It's Ehthawn, isn't it?" I asked.

"It is." There was a pause. "He is still too far out for you to see which draken it is. You sensed who it was."

"I did. Or at least I *think* I did. It feels like an echo or imprint of who they are." I squinted, seeing another draken in the distance. "Is that what you feel?"

"I guess I would describe it as an echo that is felt instead of heard," he said.

My heart clenched as I lowered my gaze to the unlit torches lining the road. "How is Ehthawn doing?" I wanted to smack myself the moment I stopped speaking. "That's a foolish question. He's obviously not doing well, having lost his sister."

"It's not a foolish question, *liessa*." Ash's arm tightened around my waist. "He mourns, but he's not alone. Ehthawn still has family—his cousin and those not by blood."

I nodded, my chest heavy as the last of the torches appeared on the small hill ahead. I didn't think Orphine had considered me a friend, but I believed we'd been on the road to becoming that. And her quick, sharp-tongued responses amused me. "I…I'm going to miss Orphine."

"As will I." Ash shifted behind me. Farther out, another winged creature became visible in the sky. "Crolee flies with him."

I'd briefly seen Ehthawn and Orphine's cousin when we were in the Bonelands. Crolee had also been on this very road when Ash first brought me into the Shadowlands. I'd thought he and the other draken were hills, but I'd known very little about the draken then.

As we crested the hill, I forced a deep, even breath and focused on the land. At night, the skeletons of the bare, twisted trees beyond the dried-up river channels on either side of the road couldn't look creepier, even with their budding leaves. I scanned the ground as Odin slowed. My improved vision allowed me to see the wide swaths of grass among the washed-out Rot. Not a lot, but still striking to see in a land that had once *only* been shades of gray.

"I think here will be fine," I decided.

Ash guided Odin off to our right onto what I thought was once the banks of the river. We came to a stop, and Ash swung himself off Odin with enviable grace. I turned to where he now stood, his hood down. Silently, he lifted his hands to my hips. Grasping his arms, my stomach was a jumble of nerves as he helped me down.

Scanning the landscape, his hold lingered for a few heartbeats before he stepped back. "Do you know what needs to be done?"

I swallowed, looking around. "Would you believe me if I lied and said yes?"

"Not when you just admitted you'd be lying." The faint curve to his mouth warmed the harsh, cold beauty of his face.

I snorted as I tugged the back of my hood down. "Then you know the answer. I'm really not sure." Lips pursing, I turned back to the parched earth. Doubt began creeping in. "What if I was experiencing delusions of grandeur?"

His rich, smoky chuckle danced in the rapidly darkening sky. "I don't think that's the case."

I probably should've stopped and thought about this, but I hadn't been able to. Literally. Uneasy, my hands opened and closed as I walked forward.

Dead grass crunched under the thin soles of my slippers. I stopped by a patch of green and knelt, running my fingers over the fragile blades. My brows knitted as I noticed something I hadn't before. I lifted my head. "There's no smell." I rose, inhaling deeply. "I don't smell the stale lilac scent of the Rot at all."

"I haven't smelled it since you Ascended." Crossing his arms, he surveyed the ground. "The rest of the grass will come back without any intervention."

I knew that, but water would obviously aid it along. Messing with one of my fangs with my tongue, I made my way to the edge of the riverbed. Should I instead attempt to bring back the grass? Regenerate new soil? No. We would have to spend the gods only knew how long traveling around the Shadowlands for me to place my hands on the ground, and I couldn't wait for that.

We couldn't wait.

Unnerved by the intrusive thought, I eyed the land. Either Ash had mentioned this before or my intuition had told me that these two riverbeds were fed by headwaters located in Mount Rhee, the place the draken called home. These waters didn't connect to the Black Bay or the Red River, which started in the Abyss. Should we have gone to Mount Rhee instead? "There were animals here, right?"

"There were."

Fresh, running water would bring them back. Eventually. "What kind?"

"Some were what you'd find in the mortal realm—deer, livestock, wolves, tree bears. All manner of birds." He paused. "Serpents."

My lip curled. "You didn't need to tell me that."

"Has it changed your mind?"

"No."

"Didn't think so," he replied. "There were also animals never seen by most mortals. Beasts both large and small."

Curiosity rose as I rubbed my damp palms on my cloak. "Like what?"

"Too many to name. But the Shadowlands was once home to the *lyrue*."

"The *lyrue*?" I repeated, the name tugging at the edges of my memory, but I wasn't sure I'd ever actually heard the term before.

"They were one of my father's lesser-known creations. Some would say they were a mistake," he explained, and I glanced over at him. His features were highlighted under the brightening starlight. "They were originally mortal, and legend says that my father believed he could give mortals a dual life like he did for the draken. But this was different. For what he created were beings mortal by day that took the form of beasts similar to wolves but on two legs at night."

My forehead creased. "I assume they were considered a mistake because…?"

"Because they had no control over their forms once night fell."

Why would that be such a big deal when other creatures in Iliseeum weren't exactly normal to look upon?

Ash cleared that up a moment later. "And because they would then dine on the flesh of others, from cattle to gods and everything in between."

My mouth dropped open. "Them *eating* people should've been the first thing out of your mouth."

A wry grin appeared as his head tilted. "You have a point there."

"Yeah, just a small one," I replied. "They ate people?" I shook my head. "And they couldn't be asked to, like, not do that?"

"You could ask them all you wanted, but the moment the sun set, they became nothing but insatiable hunger." Flat, silver eyes met mine. "It didn't matter who they were when the sun was high or who they loved. Nor did their horror upon discovering what they'd done in the darkest hours of night when they became the most brutal, primitive versions of the wolf. They'd feast on their babes if left alone with them once the sun faded."

My stomach hollowed. Eating people was bad enough, but chomping down on one's own children? That was next level. "They're gone now?"

Ash nodded.

I started to ask how, but the answer occurred to me. A new horror took root in my chest. "With it not being a true day or night in the Shadowlands…"

"The *lyrue* remained in their beast forms," he answered, his jaw hardening. "They had to be hunted into extinction, and for most of them, it was a relief—a release from a life that had become a curse and one they never would've chosen for themselves."

Good gods.

Wondering what could've gone so drastically wrong, I turned my attention back to the riverbed, unable to understand the difference between giving a creature a dual life and creating one from a mortal. But the line between them was thin. Eythos had given the dragons a dual life, creating the draken. Why had—?

I stiffened, my skin tingling. "He…he didn't give them a choice."

Ash's head snapped in my direction. "How did you—?" He inhaled deeply, his chin lifting. "Foresight."

Nodding, I swallowed hard. "Why didn't he give them a choice?"

Ash held my stare for a moment before his gaze slid away. "I don't know. All of that happened long before I was born, but my father wasn't without flaws."

A knot lodged in my chest. No, he was not. "Kolis believes that everyone saw his brother as flawless."

"And Kolis is a fucking idiot," he snarled, shadows appearing beneath his thinning flesh. "There were likely those who did believe that, but no one who knew my father could've possibly continued doing so. He made mistakes."

"Like with Sotoria?" I blurted out.

His gaze swung back to mine. "You're talking about what he did with her soul—the deal he made with your ancestor?"

Now, it was I who looked away. I nodded, but I wasn't thinking about Eythos's deal with King Roderick Mierel and how he'd placed Sotoria's soul along with the embers of life in my bloodline. It was what Kolis had claimed Eythos had done to Sotoria. What I knew was true.

Eythos had been the one to end Sotoria's second life.

"Even though whatever he planned didn't work as intended, what he did can't be a mistake," Ash said quietly, but he was closer. I could feel him. "If he hadn't done that, our paths may not have crossed."

Slowly, I turned to him. The shadows had receded from his flesh, but the eather pulsed brightly in his eyes. I started to tell him that wasn't what I'd meant, but that would open a door, and it wasn't a good time to walk through it because that conversation would lead to another truth Kolis had spoken—albeit a partial one. The one about Ash's mother.

So, I did what Ash normally did.

I got the subject back on track. "I know you said you don't know why your father didn't give them a choice, but do you have any guesses? Because it seems so out of character for him."

Eyeing me for a moment, he shook his head. "If I had to guess? Ego. He thought he knew best."

"And he learned quickly that he didn't?" Sighing, I turned back to the riverbed. "I should probably stop delaying this."

"You know, you don't have to try this," Ash countered as a shadow of one of the draken fell over us. "Since the Rot has lifted, it will eventually rain. Even with winter on the way."

I nodded. "I know."

A moment passed. "And neither of us has any idea how much energy something like this will take. There's no reason to tax yourself."

But there was.

Parts of the Shadowlands had already fallen to the Rot by the time Ash had been born, but he'd said much of it resembled the Dark Elms of Lasania. Wild and lush. It hadn't become this even when his father died.

Nearly twenty-one years ago, all the trees lost their leaves, and all the bodies of water, except for the Black Bay, dried up.

That had happened the night of my birth, signaling the start of the slow death of the embers.

Even though I knew it wasn't my fault, I felt responsible for the final thing stolen from Ash and all those who resided in the Shadowlands.

I wanted to give it back to them. Now. Not later.

But again, it was more than that. Life needed to return to the Shadowlands. "I…I don't know how to explain it, but I just have this feeling. Here." I pressed my hand to my upper abdomen. "Like I have to do this. It's an urge, and…" I glanced at him. "I don't know if I can't *not* try. I need to."

Ash frowned. "Like you're unable to stop yourself?"

I thought that over. "Not in the same sense as the *lyrue* being unable to stop themselves from eating people."

"Well, that's a relief to hear," he said dryly.

I smiled. "But I don't think I would be able to rest if I didn't try. Like, I already feel a restlessness and an inexplicable sense of urgency."

"Nektas mentioned something like this to you, didn't he? When you asked him about my father's abilities."

I nodded. "I think this is like that."

The draken dipped low then, blotting out the remaining rays of sun and starlight. The wind whipped, catching strands of my hair and tossing them across my face. Extending their wings, the draken slowed, landing on their forelegs first.

Odin snorted, shaking his mane and stomping his front hoof as he eyed the black-and-brown-scaled Crolee.

"You're fine, Odin." Ash sighed. "They're nowhere near you."

I grinned as Crolee turned his large head toward the warhorse and let out a huffing laugh as Odin slammed his hoof down again.

"What's his problem?" I asked.

Ash looked over at me, his hair more of a deep brown in the starlight. "He feels upstaged."

I laughed as I glanced at the other onyx-hued draken. Ehthawn was slightly larger than his cousin, and his horns were thicker but not as numerous as those on Nektas. He watched me curiously as if wondering what in the world I was doing.

Poking at my other fang, I refocused. The feeling I had probably wasn't delusions of grandeur. It was foresight. The heightened intuition that told me life didn't just exist in mortals and gods. Life was all around us, in the trees and the ground. I studied my hands, thinking about how I'd healed the wounded hawk in the Red Woods—the *chora*, an extension of a Primal that takes the form of their Primal *notam*. Unbeknownst to me, the hawk had belonged to Attes.

There had also been Gemma.

The embers had healed the wounded. Was the land here not wounded? While I'd tried to use my touch before against the Rot and failed, it was different now. The Rot was gone, and I was no longer a vessel for the embers. I *was* the embers.

"It might work the same way as it does when I heal someone," I said, lifting my gaze from my hands as that tingling sensation returned. "It's worth a try."

A moment passed. "You really feel like you have to do this?"

"I do."

Ash opened his mouth but then closed it. He nodded, and I had a feeling he wanted to talk me out of this.

"I'll be fine," I assured him.

Ash inclined his chin, but the tic in the muscles of his jaw said he saw right through that assurance.

Hopefully, I would be okay. Healing hadn't really taken that much of a toll on me before, but this was obviously different. And it was a risk, and possibly a foolish one.

But it was also a *gift*.

Lowering myself to my knees, I placed my palms against the dry earth of the bank. Soil crumbled at my touch, slipping between my fingers. Feeling Ash getting closer, I closed my eyes and did what I'd done before.

The essence throbbed within me, heating my skin. I opened one eye just as an aura of gold-streaked silver eather pulsed from my palms, spilling onto the dirt.

I waited.

And waited a few more moments.

"Nothing's happening, is it?" I said.

"Not yet." Ash knelt behind me. "Maybe it takes some time."

"Or maybe I have no idea what I'm doing."

"There is that."

I slowly turned my head to him.

His silver eyes were the color of the stars above as they met mine. "What are you thinking when you try this?"

"What I've done before," I answered. "I'm wishing for water to return."

A dark eyebrow rose. "And that is what you did before? You simply wished to heal wounds and give life?"

"I know it doesn't sound exciting, but yes, that's what I did."

"What about when you used the embers to fight?" he asked. "When you freed me?"

"I did the same."

A lock of hair fell against his cheek when he cocked his head. "I don't think that's all you did."

"Well, if you know what I did, then why don't you tell me—?" I snapped my mouth shut as it suddenly occurred to me. "It was different as the embers grew stronger. I didn't wish. I *willed* it."

Holding my gaze, Ash nodded. "Remember what I said earlier? The essence is tied to your will. Not your wishes. That is what it responds to." He paused. "Then again, maybe you're not capable of bringing water to life."

My eyes narrowed.

Ash grinned.

"Shut up," I muttered halfheartedly as I turned to the river channel.

Taking another deep breath, I once more flattened my hands against the arid soil. I didn't close my eyes this time. I stared at my fingers and the golden swirl on my right hand. Focusing on the pulse of eather inside me, I held on to it, coaxing it to the surface. My skin grew even warmer. A faint golden glow appeared beneath the skin of my hands, slowly traveling up my arms. I felt it flowing across the skin hidden beneath my cloak as I lifted my gaze to the river channel.

In my mind, I pictured fresh, clear water filling the waterway, rolling over the parched earth and soothing its cracks and scars. I *willed* it. Holding the image in my mind, I demanded it. Water *would* come. It *would.* Water *would* come.

The glow around my hands intensified, flaring with brighter pulses. Water *would* come. It *would* rush through this channel, healing this land. Bring life back to it. Water *would.* I *would* restore life—

Energy swelled, pressing against my skin. I'd gotten used to the ebb and flow of eather I used to only feel in the center of my chest, and even its intense force the handful of times I'd tapped into the essence of the Primals, but what I felt pulsing through me now was something else entirely.

A low trilling sound came from Ehthawn. Eather pulsed from my palms, rippling out in dozens—no, hundreds—of fine streaks. Arcs of eather went in every direction, covering the riverbed in a network of silvery-gold radiance that beat back the encroaching night. The spiderweb of luminous brilliance throbbed rapidly. One. Two. Three. Then slapped into the dry earth with a shocking, thunderous clap.

Sucking in a startled breath, I jerked back. Ash caught me by the arms, stopping me from toppling over.

"Sera?" Concern filled his voice as he cupped my cheek. He started to turn my head to his.

The ground trembled beneath us. All around us. Dirt beaded and clumped, rolling down the sides of the riverbank.

"Shit." Ash stood, lifting me as Odin whinnied nervously. He urged me back a step.

Crolee lifted his head, letting out a low-pitched, staggered cry as the riverbed *shuddered.*

My stomach dipped. "Is it possible that I created an earthquake?"

"I'm beginning to wonder that myself. We should probably move—" he cut himself off with a sharp inhale. "Fates."

"What?" I scanned the land, not seeing what had caused him to stiffen.

"Look," he whispered hoarsely.

"I'm looking." Panic and frustration crashed together. "Where?"

Ash curved his fingers around my chin and guided my gaze down to the center of the channel, where he pointed with his other hand. "*There.*"

I didn't see what he was talking about at first. It was just the ground vibrating hard enough to cause the pebbles to bounce. But that…

"That's not pebbles," I gasped.

A short laugh burst from him. "No, *liessa*, it is not."

Slipping free of his grasp, I went to the edge and bent slightly to get a better look. What I thought had been pebbles dancing in the vibrations were thousands of waterdrops. I looked down the riverbed a ways, stunned to see small puddles forming.

"It's like it's raining from the ground." I laughed. "Gods, that sounds silly."

Ash was right behind me. "But that's what it looks like."

Clasping my hands together, I tried to fight a smile but lost as I looked back at the palace. "This is…wow." I glanced up at Ash. "It's going to take forever this way, but this—"

I jumped back as a geyser of water erupted from the center of the riverbed, spraying the air with dirt and cold liquid. Ash caught me with an arm around my waist as the water expanded and grew, forming *wings*.

He all but picked me up and dragged me back to where Odin and the draken waited as another funnel of water broke through the ground, stretching high into the sky and sprouting water wings. Then another and another—

"I feel like the eather heard your complaint," Ash stated dryly.

"I didn't mean to complain." Wide-eyed, my focus remained on the riverbed. The winged geysers curved forward, crashing back into the bed. "I was just pointing out how long it would take."

He brushed dirt from my cheeks. "But not any longer."

"No," I whispered. "Not any longer."

Fresh, white-tipped water covered the ground now, flowing down the deeper grooves in the earth as it rushed toward the riverbank, lapping against the sides.

Crolee shifted closer, his head tracking the spouts. Ehthawn reared, lifting his head to the sky. The low trilling sound came once more.

"Am I seeing things, or does the water look like it—?"

The air all around us charged. The essence in me pulsed as the draken lowered themselves until they were almost on their bellies. Energy built and built, constricting—

Ash spun toward his horse and ran his fingers along the silver cuff on his upper arm. "Odin, return to me."

The horse's form rippled as I stepped back. Odin turned to smoke, crossing the distance between us and returning to the cuff.

Ash's hand found mine as a jet of water erupted again, this time behind us. All of us looked at the other side of the road. Fountains of water gushed into the air like moving, winged pillars. They arced, slamming into the riverbed.

"What the…?" Ash hauled me against his chest.

Tiny silvery lights appeared in the empty air before us, then over the riverbanks, the road, and then *everywhere.* I sucked in a startled breath. It looked like the stars had descended to the land, and in a way, they had.

"It's the essence," Ash rasped, shuddering. "It's the eather of the realms—of the air and the land."

The lights flickered, becoming gold. Pure, Primal energy flashed from all the stars above and around us, casting the entire Court—the entire realm of Iliseeum—in bright, golden light streaked with silver.

The eather hummed inside me as the very realm itself seemed to hold its breath.

Then it exhaled. Energy rolled out in every direction, the force of it more powerful than any wind I'd felt. Ash dug in, his arms tightening around me as he slid back a foot or so. The pressure even moved the draken as the ground began to tremble once more.

As the eather rippled out, kissing the land in its golden-silver glow, the dull grayness of what was left of the Rot vanished.

"Oh my gods," I whispered. "*Ash.*"

"I see it." His eyes were luminous pools in the gold-and-silver glow of the realm.

Along the road, blades of grass broke free of the top layers of soil and spread out, reaching the river and beyond. Fragile stems sprouted, stretching upward as leaves unfurled, and red buds formed.

"Poppies," Ash breathed.

They grew along the road in clumps as the twisted trees shook out their gnarled limbs and straightened. Deep, violet leaves burst forth, filling the once-bare branches.

The glow of eather began to fade, and the energy left the air. Night fell once more. Starlight returned, and none of us moved as we stood there, listening to the hum of rushing water and the wind shaking the leaves.

My gaze fell on the poppies. They opened, slowly revealing their crimson petals to the stars.

"I hope the poppies are in a good mood," I said. "And don't poison us."

Ash didn't answer.

Heart thumping, I tore my gaze from the flowers.

Ash was staring at me with eyes wide and full of swirling streaks of eather, lips parted enough that I could see the tips of his fangs.

I touched his chest. "Ash?"

His throat worked on a swallow. "How are you feeling?"

"Normal. Fine." I searched his features. He looked a little pale. "How are *you* feeling?"

He shook his head silently as he lowered himself to one knee before me, my hand still held in his.

A jolt ran through me. This wasn't the first time he'd done this. I'd never forget how, upon learning that I carried the true embers of the Primal of Life, he'd knelt before me. It still shocked me.

Crolee rocked back then, lifting his head to the night sky. His call echoed Ehthawn's—one I heard in my bones and understood as Ash's lashes lifted. Molten silver eyes pierced the night.

"Awed," he rasped. "I'm in fucking awe of you." He bowed his head, pressing his lips to my palm and the golden swirl of our marriage imprint. A faint tremble radiated from his hand to mine. "My Queen."

I woke to find myself half-sprawled across Ash's chest and feeling…strange.

And nauseous.

I lifted my head, glancing toward the balcony doors. The world outside still carried the darkness of night. Gods, I couldn't have slept that long after returning to our chambers.

I started to lay back down when the inside of my mouth filled with saliva, forcing me to quickly swallow. My eyes widened at the acidic taste in my mouth.

Oh, gods, I wouldn't vomit on Ash as he slept. Or anytime.

Carefully, I eased out of his lax embrace, not wanting to wake him.

I failed.

Before my foot even hit the floor, Ash stirred. "*Liessa…*"

"It's okay," I assured him, wincing at the churning in my stomach. "I'm just getting something to drink and going to the bathing chamber. I'll be right back."

"Hurry."

I smiled despite the nausea and quickly rose. Padding barefoot across the floor, I stopped at the small table and poured myself a glass of water. Taking a few quick sips, I glanced at the bed and made my way to the bathing chamber. Ash remained on his back, one arm curved against the pillow beside him and the other hand resting on the blanket gathered at his lean hips. Despite feeling queasy, heat pooled low in my core. As weird as it sounded, there was something decadently sensual about a sleeping man. I'd never noticed before.

Gods, I wanted to rip that blanket aside and straddle him.

A sleepy growl rumbled from Ash's chest, causing tight, fine shivers to race down my spine.

"*Liessa*," he murmured, his voice thick with sleep and… I inhaled deeply, catching the scent of his arousal. "I can taste your slickness on my tongue."

My lips parted at the sharp pang of desire his words elicited.

The deep growl came again. "You should come back to bed now."

I was half-tempted to do just that, but until I was sure I wouldn't throw up, I figured it would be a bad idea. "I'll be right back."

His snarl of disapproval brought another smile to my face as I tore my gaze from him and entered the chamber. I drank as much water as I could, erasing the taste in my mouth before placing the glass on the vanity. Luckily, as I took care of personal needs, the nausea subsided. I felt completely normal.

Actually, that wasn't entirely true. I still felt strange. My skin prickled on and off. I figured it must have something to do with me using the essence earlier to restore the river.

I picked up the glass of water, drinking what was left—

I gasped, nearly dropping the glass as Ash appeared behind me in the mirror. He wordlessly reached around me, plucked the glass from my grasp, and placed it on the vanity. "Did you just shadowstep from the bed to the bathing chamber?"

"Maybe," he said, burying his face in the crook of my neck as he folded an arm around my waist and pulled me against his chest. His right hand rested on my belly, just above my navel. Even in the dim light of the bathing chamber, the contrast between my paler skin and his rich tones was stark. "I grew impatient."

He'd also grown hard.

My skin flushed at the feel of his thick length against my back. "I wasn't gone that long."

"We will have to disagree on that," he said, and I saw his hand sliding down in the reflection. I widened my stance, giving that wandering hand of his permission.

My heart thudded as I watched his other hand curl around my right breast. My already pebbled nipples hardened as he drew his finger across the peak. The breath I took caught as his lips coasted up the side of my neck, drawing forth blade-sharp anticipation of feeling his fangs against my skin *and*...an emotion I refused to focus on.

I bit my lip as he rolled the nipple between his forefinger and thumb. A tremor went through me. "Should we return to the bedchamber?"

"I'm too impatient to do so." He nipped at my ear as his hand delved between my thighs. One long, cool finger slipped inside, drawing a ragged moan from me. "And you know what you are?"

I watched the tendons of his hand flex as his finger—*fingers*—moved inside me. "What?"

"You're just as slick and wet as I tasted earlier."

Oh, gods.

A shudder of heat and desire went through me as my hips twitched against his hand. His fang scraped my earlobe once more as he withdrew his hand from my thighs and dragged his palm up my stomach, leaving a glistening trail in its wake.

"So very wet," he purred.

My skin was burning, but it had little to do with how blatant my arousal was. His fingers dragged over my left breast as his lips brushed my temple—

Something cool and soft slipped over my calf, causing my body to jerk. I started to look down, but Ash folded his hand over the front of my throat. He tipped my head back, and I caught a brief glimpse of the silvery orbs of his eyes before he claimed my mouth with his.

The kiss was fierce, parting my lips with one sweep of his tongue as that cool, swirling mass of energy reached my knee. My pulse pounded as his tongue swept over my fangs. The rich, smoky taste of his blood hit my tongue as cool air kissed the area between my thighs. A shudder racked me as I felt another tendril curl itself around my upper leg, lifting it and spreading me open. Ash chuckled against my lips and then deepened the kiss, his tongue thrusting just as the essence did the same. I cried out, my back arching as his Primal essence filled me. His mouth left mine, but his hand stayed at my throat as my gaze flicked back to the mirror.

I was transfixed by what I saw, unable to look away as the thick, shadowy tendril wrapped around my right leg moved deep inside me.

"You're even wetter now." Ash's rough voice vibrated through the bathing chamber as he, too, was fixated on our reflection. "Even more soft and hot."

Gods, he was…

Ash was *wicked.*

I trembled as I felt crackling air spin itself along my right leg, the buzz of energy teasing and humming as it climbed. My breath stuttered as I felt his essence beneath my rear, lifting me until neither foot touched the floor.

"That's my pretty, wet pussy," he whispered in my ear. I moaned as the hold around my waist tightened. "I need to feel it on my cock."

"Yes, please."

His laugh was short and rough. The essence retreated, but before I could mourn its loss, Ash's cock was buried deep inside me.

"Oh, gods," I cried out, feeling all my tiny muscles clench around him.

Ash wasn't in the mood for sweet, tender lovemaking. Obviously. He fucked, and with the way he and his essence held me, how the pulsating strands of eather moved me back against him as he thrust into me, he had complete control. And that heightened my lust to the point where it was almost painful.

"You're so beautiful," he rasped. "So perfect."

My head fell back against his chest as he rocked against me—

A thin tendril danced over the curve of my ass cheek. My eyes flew open.

Ash's movements stilled. His gaze in the reflection snared mine. The wisp of energy slipped over where we were joined, teasing the empty, sensitive opening. "What do you want, *meyaah Liessa*?"

I immediately knew what he wanted to hear me say. "Fuck me," I whispered. "Fuck my pussy and my ass, my King."

His chuckle was darkly sensual. The current of eather pulsed and then eased itself into me. The sound I made scorched my cheeks as the pressure filled me to the point where I felt like I would lose all sense. Tension curled so tightly there was a good chance I would come if he so much as twitched.

But he didn't. Ash was utterly still behind and in me.

"You forgot something," he chided.

"What…?" My eyes narrowed as I realized what he meant. "How about, fuck me now?"

"That's not it."

"I know."

The tendril expanded slightly, drawing out a ragged curse. "What do you want, *meyaah Liessa*?" he asked again.

I could refuse, and if I did, I knew he'd still give me what I wanted, but he also knew it wasn't what I needed.

I turned my head toward his. "Fuck me." Our lips brushed. "Fuck me in my ass and pussy, *Ash*."

He groaned. "As you wish."

And that is what he did. His hips and essence moved in perfect rhythm. The pleasure was all-consuming, almost too much, and I strained and twisted in his hold as the curls of tension built quickly. Ash thrust deep and hard, holding me tightly as I ground on him. The coil deep inside me spun and spun until I didn't think I could take much more. My entire body was too sensitive. I was too full.

The hand at my throat tipped my head back. "I love you," Ash whispered against my lips, kissing me.

Those three words sent me over the edge. The climax took me hard, rushing through me in pounding waves of ecstasy. My cries were lost in Ash's groan as he found his release.

I didn't know how long we stayed that way as sweet aftershocks fluttered through both of us, but my knees were still a little weak by the time he eased himself from me and placed me on my feet.

He kissed my temple. "Stay right there."

"Yes, sir," I murmured.

He shot me a quick grin, then found a washcloth that he dampened. Returning to stand behind me, he kissed the corner of my lips as he gently swept the washcloth between my thighs. The act of him cleaning me up was so sweet I thought I might cry. Like seriously. Tears clogged my throat, and I rolled my eyes at myself. I had no idea why I was so emotional. I was going to blame post-orgasmic bliss.

"Coming back to bed?" Ash asked, tossing the washcloth into a hamper.

I nodded. "In a minute."

"Don't take too long." His lips brushed my forehead. "You've kept me up long enough."

"Me?" I laughed as he stepped away. "I was minding my own business in here, thank you very much."

"Yes, you were minding your own business walking around naked." He opened the door as he looked over his shoulder at me. A lock of hair fell across his face. "While being as wet as sin."

My mouth dropped open.

"What else was I to do?" he questioned, one side of his lips curving up.

I snapped my mouth shut as my eyes narrowed. He chuckled, turning away. "You know," I said, "it's inappropriate to point out things like that."

"One would also think having such a hungry pussy is also inappropriate," he replied.

A shocked giggle burst from my lips. "Naughty Ash."

"Naughty pussy, more like."

"Oh, my gods." I smacked my hands over my face. "I think we can stop saying pussy now."

Ash chuckled. "I'll be waiting for you."

I shook my head as he closed the door, even though I absolutely loved this dirty side of him. I thought back to what we'd just done. I *really* loved the dirtier side of him.

Figuring it would be best if I stopped thinking about that before I found myself once more in Ash's arms, I bent over the vanity and splashed cool water on my way-too-hot face. I plucked up the nearest clean towel to dry myself as my gaze drifted to the mirror.

Even in the dim glow of the lamplight, seeing my eyes still came as a shock, despite looking like my freckled self.

Well, not *completely* like myself. There was a slight golden glow to my skin that hadn't been there before I rose as a Primal. I lifted my upper lip until the tips of the two small fangs appeared.

What would Ezra think upon seeing them? Gods, she would have so many questions, and I…I wanted to answer them. My eyes closed as a pang of yearning ran through me. I wanted to see her and Marisol. Perhaps even my mother—

The sudden sensation of pins and needles erupted as the eather pulsed in the center of my chest and formed what felt like a cord. A *connection.* That link surged through me, pulling taut as it stretched beyond the palace and the Shadowlands. Essence swelled, flooding my veins. Behind my closed eyelids, I saw gold and silver. The intensity snagged the breath I took. I pressed my hand to my stomach as the rise of power crested and then steadied, leveling out.

It balanced.

Black washed over the silver-laced gold light. Black streaked with crimson.

Sucking in a sharp breath, my eyes flew open—

My heart lurched.

What I saw was brief and only lasted a heartbeat, if that, but I *saw*.

And it wasn't my eyes that met mine. It wasn't my reflection that stared back at me.

It was silver eyes streaked with red. It was the face I saw in my nightmares.

Kolis.

Ash once more shadowstepped into the bathing chamber. "What's wrong?"

I staggered forward, my mouth dry. What I saw now was my reflection. The same as before, except the freckles stood out more starkly. But I had seen him.

"Sera?" Ash was at my side, placing a hand on my lower back. "Talk to me."

"I'm okay," I said hoarsely. My heart pounded as I gripped the vanity, willing myself to calm. "I…I just need a moment."

He ran his hand up and down my back. "Take as many as you need."

The calming sweep of his palm helped push away the panic and confusion, clearing my thoughts enough for me to focus on what'd just happened. I knew Kolis hadn't really been here, but I also knew what that cord-like sensation meant. What it was telling me. It was either the *vadentia* or all the information I'd gained during the Ascension.

That link—that *connection*—had always existed between the true Primal of Life and the true Primal of Death. After all, Life could not exist without Death. They walked the realms side by side, and all that link meant was that Death had awakened. Had become conscious. Aware. That was why I hadn't felt it before, and I would also bet that it was the source of what had awakened me and left me feeling nauseous. Shockingly, Kolis had still been in stasis up until this very moment.

"Fuck," I whispered, and Ash's hand momentarily halted before continuing. Opening my eyes, I faced Ash. "It's Kolis."

The tendrils of eather stilled in his eyes as he curved one of his hands around mine. "Talk to me," he said.

"I sensed Kolis."

Those wisps of eather brightened as intensely as stars. "I'm going to need more details."

As I told him what happened, his jaw clenched and became as hard as the shadowstone around us. "It was weird, but I *know* he's been in a stasis until now."

"Do you still feel him?"

"No." I frowned as I thought twice. "I mean, I don't technically feel him."

Frigid air blew off Ash. "What does that mean, Sera? Do you hear him? Feel anything?" His flesh thinned as his head dipped until we were at eye level. "Please, do not lie to me about this. I beg of you."

"It's more an awareness of him, of him being conscious," I quickly clarified. "And that is all." I squeezed his hand. "I swear."

His chest rose with a heavy breath. "I didn't know that was possible."

"I didn't either. Well, I did but didn't realize I knew," I said, knowing that made little sense. "There's a lot of stuff in my head. Too much, really. But it's quite possible that no one else knew about that, not even Nektas."

Ash nodded, his flesh gradually thickening. "If he did, he would've said something." His jaw loosened. "Well, now we know why he has been so silent. Stasis was the true cause of his absence and lack of action."

I wanted to deny it, but it would be foolish to do so.

"This doesn't change our plans." He cupped my cheek.

"I know."

"You done in here?"

I nodded, and worry started to fester as Ash led me from the bathing chamber. I took a deep breath, reminding myself that nothing had changed. We'd been operating as if Kolis had been awake this entire time anyway.

But even I knew that was a whole lot of bullshit because Kolis was awake, and that changed *everything*.

The following morning, I knew I should be with Ash as the security for today's speech was discussed, but instead, I was on the Rise, walking toward the wall facing Lethe. It was the easiest way for me to see the Dying Woods. Something had occurred to me.

The Shades.

The slight heels of my leather boots clapped softly on the stone as I glanced down, seeing lush grass filling the courtyard and Rhahar's lurking figure just beneath me. He wasn't alone. Kars, the fair-haired and muscular guard who had once offered to train me, was with him. They had been following me since the moment Ash left.

Something odd had happened when I'd spotted Kars as I climbed the Rise. I'd never been able to tell before if he was a god or a godling—the child of a mortal and a god—but I'd known right then that he was one of the rare godlings who entered the Culling and survived. It was similar to what had happened when I saw the guard on the Rise yesterday.

The *vadentia* sure was strengthening quickly.

However, the embers inside me since birth had already matured to an extent, which likely explained why things were happening faster for me.

But that rapidly developing ability wasn't why I was on the Rise.

When I used the essence to fill the riverbed, I'd been focused on bringing water back to the Shadowlands. But I'd restored a lot more than that.

The Shadowlands were virtually unrecognizable.

A pleasant breeze swirled along the Rise, lifting a stray curl as I continued on. I thought I had a good idea how this had happened. When I tapped into the essence, I had also willed life to return to the Shadowlands. That was how the fields of poppies and grass had appeared. How the trees along the road into the Shadowlands straightened and sprouted glossy violet and green leaves. It was why the soil was a rich, dark brown. I did more than I had intended to. That wasn't necessarily a bad thing, except that there were dead things moving about in the Shadowlands.

The Shades.

Had my will impacted them?

The eather stirred restlessly as my steps slowed. The sea of vibrant crimson thinned, and the twisted, bare, ashen trees appeared, scattered at first and then becoming more crowded as the woods thickened.

I stopped at a parapet to scan the Dying Woods. A gloom clung to the trees where the forest was the thickest, obscuring everything below the tops of the thin, gnarled branches. My gaze traveled to the thinnest part of the Dying Woods. I could see the dull, lifeless ground through the stagnant fog gathered midway down the trees.

The Dying Woods hadn't changed.

Movement drew my attention toward the heavier parts. The gloom there had thickened, and it *moved.* Eather throbbed, pressing against my skin.

Shades.

I sucked in a sharp breath and took a step back. My hands spasmed and then fisted. Wispy gray forms slunk around tree trunks, creeping toward the edges of the Dying Woods. I closed my eyes, pushing down the swell of eather as my fingers tingled. The Dying Woods remained as it had always been. That was good news. A part of me had been half-afraid that I'd brought all the Shades back to life.

And I was a little sad.

Not all the Shades were evil—well, now they were, but they hadn't all started out that way. Some had just been afraid when they came upon the Pillars of Asphodel, terrified that they would be sentenced to the Abyss for stealing, telling lies, forgery, or adultery. Bad things, but sometimes necessary. Mistakes. Actions that hadn't damned them.

Until now.

Now, they were lost.

And I knew why that bothered me. I'd spent the better part of my life fearing where I would end up after my death. Even after Ash, I had been afraid. I didn't know if the Fates would intervene, preventing Ash from judging me kindly. The worst part was that I knew where I deserved to go. It wasn't the Vale, yet I was the *Agna Adice.*

The Great Condemner.

And how messed up was that?

A lot. The answer was a lot.

But why hadn't my will affected the Shades and the Dying Woods? Opening my eyes, I saw that the Shades were closer, gathering near the edge of the trees. The sensation of fingertips along the nape of my neck hit me as the answer to my question formed.

The Dying Woods belonged to Death, as did the Shades. Just like they were mostly prevented from leaving the Dying Woods, I was blocked from bringing life to that stretch of land. But…

I frowned. But neither life nor death was absolute. My thoughts raced. There was something about that. The wards that trapped the lost souls in the woods sometimes weakened, and I had almost brought one back. I had been in the Dying Woods then, touching the Shade. That was the difference.

Death couldn't break the bond of Life's touch. That kind of power? It was the same as I'd displayed last night.

I turned away from the Shades and knew that what I had done last night had awakened Kolis.

After spending an ungodly amount of time trying to decide whether to wear my hair loose or in a braid, I finally decided to leave the curls free. Ash liked it that way, and I loved that he did.

I stepped back so I could see myself in the mirror attached to the wardrobe door. The tunic Aios had picked out was fitted at the breasts, almost too tightly, like the measurements might have been off just a little bit, but the cut was flattering, and the stitching Erlina had done was beyond beautiful. I couldn't remember if I had thanked her for her hard work, and even if I had, I wanted to do so again.

I'd followed Aios's suggestion and paired the tunic with black leggings, and I didn't think Rhain would have any reason to complain.

I took a deep breath, nodded at myself, and then walked through the bathing chamber. Tiny knots of anxiety bounced around in my stomach as I headed down the narrow hall to the antechamber. There, I found Reaver in his mortal form, seated on the couch with a pad of parchment.

He looked up as I entered. "You look nice," he said, and a hint of pink appeared on the cheeks I could actually see through his hair.

"Thank you." I approached. "Hopefully, Rhain agrees."

A grin appeared, but it quickly disappeared. "Are you feeling okay?"

"I'm just anxious. That's all." I smiled, hoping it eased his concerns as I glanced at the paper in his lap. "Are you drawing something?"

Pale hair flopped over his forehead as he looked down. One shoulder lifted. "I'm supposed to be working on my letters."

My lips twitched. "And you're not?"

Wordlessly, he lifted the parchment and showed me. There *were* letters written in surprisingly fine, sophisticated lines. About half as many as there should be. The rest of the page was filled with swirling ink strokes I quickly recognized. "You're drawing the design on the throne doors."

"Trying to," he mumbled, kicking feet that didn't reach the floor.

I peered down at the paper. He'd captured the leaves on the ivy-like vines that adorned the throne room doors and decorated my tunic. "I think you're doing a good job."

"Thanks." Another splash of pink traveled across his cheeks. "I don't think Liora will be happy, though."

"Liora?" I sat beside him.

"She's like me," he said, shading a tiny leaf. "But older. She doesn't leave Mount Rhee much, but she did come by while you were asleep. All the draken did." He frowned, appearing to search for a word. "We all felt you rise as the true Primal of Life," he said, speaking as if that were something entirely normal.

And I guessed it was since I had basically felt Kolis do the same.

I clasped my knees. "Is Liora who watches you and Jadis sometimes?"

He nodded.

"Maybe you should finish the rest of your letters for her," I suggested. "You're almost halfway done."

"I will." Dragging his lip between his teeth, he glanced over at me. "Do you want to draw? It helps me when I'm anxious."

"Drawing makes me anxious," I joked. "But thank you." My gaze flickered over him. "Why are you anxious?"

"I'm not."

I raised my brows. "You just admitted to drawing when you're anxious," I pointed out. "So, why are you anxious?"

His little nose pinched as he looked away. "I'm anxious because you are."

I drew back. "What?"

"You're *meyaah Liessa.* I…I can sense it," he said.

"Oh, gods. I didn't know that." Uncomfortable, I shifted in my seat. Actually, I *did* know that. It was just lost in all the other stuff I suddenly knew. "The *notam.*"

Reaver nodded.

It was the bond all draken had with the true Primal of Life. "So, all the draken can feel when I'm anxious?"

Swinging his feet, he nodded. "The older ones know how to block it out. I just haven't learned how to do that yet."

"What about Jadis?"

"I don't think she can feel anything yet," he answered. "She's too young."

That was kind of a relief, but not really. I didn't want my almost constant state of anxiety affecting Reaver. "I'm sorry."

"It's okay." He tilted his pointy chin up. "It's not real bad."

I wasn't sure I believed that, which meant I needed to get my anxiety under control.

"I think you'll do fine today, by the way. The people already like you, and after what they saw this morning? They have to love you. So, you have no reason to be anxious," he said earnestly and with a seriousness far beyond his age.

"Thank you." I ran my hands over my knees. My anxiety at the moment had little to do with the speech, but I was sure that would rear its head sooner or later.

Once Reaver finished his letters, we moved out to the daybed on the balcony. He was telling me about Mount Rhee and some of the draken I hadn't yet fully interacted with when I *felt* Ash near the bedchamber.

He joined Reaver and me, striding out onto the balcony, the hair at his temples damp.

"You two kind of match," Reaver said, kicking his feet off the base of the daybed.

We did.

Ash wore a sleeveless, black tunic trimmed in the same silver brocade. It stretched across his broad shoulders and was perfectly tailored to his tapered waist. He looked magnificent.

"Great minds think alike," he murmured, bending to kiss me.

Reaver groaned. "You two do that a lot."

Ash chuckled as he straightened. "One day, you will understand why."

"Nuh-uh," Reaver denied, his lip curling in disgust.

"I'll be sure to remind you of that when the day comes." Ash reached over, the silver band on his upper arm glinting in the sunlight as he ruffled Reaver's mop of blond hair. "Mestra will be here shortly to take you back to Mount Rhee."

Reaver had briefly mentioned the other draken I had yet to meet. Besides Jadis and Reaver, she was the youngest of the draken, a little over a century old.

"I'd rather go with you all," Reaver said.

"I know," I told him. Reaver had mentioned wanting to go with us no less than two dozen times since we decided to talk to the people. "When you're older, I'm sure it will be fine for you to be with us."

He wrinkled his nose. "Why am I not old enough now? You two are just giving a speech."

"Yes, we're only giving a speech, and nothing should happen," Ash said, his tone gentle. "But you are too important to take that risk. Understand?"

Reaver nodded, clearly unhappy, and I felt for the little guy. Considering what he'd been through, it was no wonder he wanted to stick close to our sides.

"Rhain wanted to show us something." Ash offered me his hand. "He's waiting for us downstairs."

"Hopefully, it's not an example of appropriate attire," I muttered, taking Ash's hand.

Reaver snickered.

"What?" Ash's brows knitted.

"Nothing." I shot the draken a look as Ash pulled me to my feet. "Did he say what he wanted to show us?"

He shook his head. "Only that it was important."

"Probably has to do with gowns," Reaver commented.

Ash's head tilted as he tugged me to his side. "I feel like I'm missing something."

"You are," I confirmed. "But it's nothing interesting."

"I'll have to take your word for that." He looked back at Reaver. "You're walking us down, right?"

The smile that came across Reaver's face was brief but beautiful before he ducked his head and the sheet of golden hair obscured his face.

"Lead the way," Ash instructed Reaver, keeping his hand wrapped firmly around mine.

I grinned as Reaver took Ash's request very seriously, skirting us. "Can you give Ash and me a moment, though?"

Reaver stopped in the doorway, crossing his arms over his chest. "You guys are going to have a serious conversation you don't want me to hear."

"Now, why would you think that?" Ash questioned.

"Because every time something serious needs to be said that no one wants me to hear, I'm either sent from the room, tasked to look after Jadis, or others speak in a weird way like they're leaving out words and stuff."

Note to self: Reaver is far too observant. "We weren't going to talk," I told him. "I was planning to do more kissing."

There was no hesitation. Not even a second. "I'll wait in the hall." Reaver pivoted and disappeared in a heartbeat.

"Wow," I murmured. "I didn't think it would be *that* effective."

"Well, I, for one, am not disturbed by the idea of more kissing."

"I hate to disappoint you," I said, "because Reaver was right. It's something I didn't want him to hear."

"What is it?"

"Something I realized this morning," I said. "I think I figured out what woke Kolis—no, I know. It was me."

Ash's eyes searched mine. "I'm sure you had nothing—"

"I didn't do it on purpose," I cut in. "It's what I did last night when I brought the river back and, well, everything else. That power? It was a lot."

"Yeah," he said, straightening the collar of my tunic. "It was."

"And I'm sure it was felt all across Iliseeum. That's what woke him from stasis. He felt it."

Ash appeared to think about that for a moment. "If that is the case, do you regret what you did?"

"No," I said without hesitation.

"Then it is what it is," he said softly. "It's not your fault he woke."

"I don't…" I fell silent upon his knowing look. "I don't regret it, but I do feel a tiny bit responsible."

"I get it," he said. "But you know he would've woken eventually."

"Would've been nice if he still remained in stasis, though."

"Maybe." He tucked a curl back behind my ear. "But I personally enjoy knowing that it was you being a powerful Primal that possibly woke him sooner than he would've naturally."

My brows lifted. "I hadn't thought of it that way."

"Now, you have," He dipped his head and kissed me.

"We should join Reaver before he becomes traumatized by something we're not even doing."

That brought a faint grin to his lips, and by the time we joined the youngling, he appeared calmer.

"How are you feeling about the speech?" Ash asked as we entered the hall with Reaver several feet in front of us.

"I'm good." I paused and then admitted, "And a little nervous."

"You'll do perfectly," Ash assured, dipping down to press a kiss to the top of my head.

"That's what I told her," Reaver called from the top of the staircase, where he waited.

"She should start listening to you, then," Ash responded and then glanced down at me. "You look beautiful, by the way."

"Thank you." I smiled up at him. "You don't look too bad yourself."

Ash chuckled. "I believe you're underplaying how extraordinarily handsome you find me right now."

"Perhaps."

I could see Rhain waiting for us beneath the crystal chandelier as we reached the second floor of the grand staircase, and then Reaver shocked the hell out of me by doing the most childlike thing I'd ever seen him do. He hopped from the next to last step to the floor. When we followed suit, minus the hopping, I caught sight of Rhahar waiting near the vacant marble pedestal with Kars.

I frowned at that damn pedestal. I really needed to find something to put on it.

"You said there was something you wanted to show us?" Ash asked, drawing my attention back to the god.

Rhain nodded, and this time, there was no stopping the concern from taking root at the sudden tension hardening his features. "It's the crowns."

Reaver and I followed Ash and Rhain as we passed the throne room, Rhahar and Kars keeping pace behind us. I had no idea where the crowns were kept. If I *had* been told, I'd definitely forgotten. At first, I thought we were heading toward the war room, but it was an antechamber of it, accessed through a door that led to a narrow hall. "I was going to have them polished and made the discovery," Rhain told us, holding the door.

The chamber was small, and everything was white—the marble floor, painted walls, the ceiling, and the two pedestals in the center. The crown was the only thing that wasn't white.

Wait.

A crown.

Ash halted as I turned halfway, thinking I'd missed something, but there was nothing else in the space.

"What the…?" Rhahar exclaimed from behind us, his eyes going wide and filling with essence as Ash approached the pedestal.

"Where is your crown?" Reaver asked as he peered up at a pedestal as empty as the one in the foyer.

"I was asking the same thing." Rhain moved to stand behind the pedestals.

"Shit," Ash murmured, placing his palm on the flat surface. "Kolis." He turned to me, his eyes brightly lit. "Touch your crown."

"What?" I glanced at the beautiful crown I'd only worn once, taking in its shadowstone spires and glittering crescent moons.

"Just touch it," he insisted.

"I'm glad I understand the context of this conversation for once," Kars commented under his breath.

Rhahar turned to the godling. "Seriously?"

Kars shrugged.

"Wait." Ash stopped me. "Better yet, stand still."

I did as he asked. Reaver watched avidly. "I'm standing still, so will you tell me what your missing crown has to do with…?" I trailed off as the knowledge started to come to me. My eyes went wide.

Ash nodded.

Heart thundering, I watched Ash lift the crown and turn to me. Silently, he placed the crown on my head, and before I could even register its weight, the crown *shuddered.* The room was suddenly awash in bright, golden light.

Rhahar's hand fell from the hilt of his sword. "Holy—"

"Shit," Kar whispered as Rhain staggered back a step.

The fading golden glow warmed Ash's face as he reached for the crown again. His broad hands carefully lifted it from my head, and even though I knew what I was about to see, I couldn't believe it.

"Whoa," Reaver murmured.

Ash held the crown I'd last seen upon Kolis's head. "The Primal crowns are almost like a *chora*," he said, referencing the type of animal that used to be formed from a Primal. "An extension of the Primal that can be summoned to them at will but only called to the true bearer of that crown."

I stared at the nine shining golden swords and the sun rising from the middle one, glittering with diamonds. As if seeking to confirm it was real, I touched the center sword. The gold turned luminous, casting soft light across the walls.

"Kolis must've tried to summon the crown," Ash said. "And what he got was likely not what he wanted to see."

Pulling my hand back, I looked up at him. "Your crown is now his," I whispered.

"And your head will bear the true crown of the Primal of Life," he replied.

"But yours—"

"It returned to its rightful owner," he cut in.

I didn't like that. Not for one second. "At least for now."

Ash's gaze met mine. "For now."

Much to Rhain's displeasure, I didn't wear the crown as Ash and I left the House of Haides. It just didn't feel right with Ash missing his.

Besides, I didn't believe a crown—no matter how glittery—made a Queen or King.

But all thoughts of crowns quickly fell to the wayside when the sweeping colonnade and endless archways of the City Hall came into view.

It seemed like it had only taken minutes, even though Ash had summoned the warhorse Odin from the silver band around his biceps instead of shadowstepping. That method would've been quicker. We wouldn't have needed nearly every guard on duty to surround us or the three draken that flew above us. But the moment it came time to leave, my stomach began dipping and lurching. My thoughts raced, telling me I would sound completely idiotic when I addressed the people. I knew without a doubt that Ash had picked up on my anxiety and had chosen to travel this way to give me time to, well, find my footing again.

He was too damn perfect because, even though I was still nervous, I was far calmer than I thought myself capable of.

Odin slowed as the draken glided toward the open coliseum, extending their wings to slow their descent. I watched as Ehthawn and his cousin Crolee landed on the colonnade. Pallas, a large, striking gray-and-black draken, followed, landing on the other side of the colonnade. I was pretty sure he was the one I'd spotted when I surveyed the armies.

But several more draken of various sizes were already perched on the columns. I quickly counted them. Ten. Nektas wasn't here yet, and I knew Mestra had taken Reaver back to Mount Rhee. I bet Liora was with them, along with two more draken, who would likely remain at Mount Rhee to watch over the younglings. I swallowed, having never seen so many draken in one location before.

As Odin came to a stop, I picked up on the hum of conversation coming from within the City Hall. I dragged in a deep breath of fresh air. There was no scent of burning oil as my gaze lowered and swept over the rows of armored soldiers. I didn't remember seeing the headpieces the last time I'd seen them standing before the City Hall. The steel-and-shadowstone helmets weren't something easily forgotten.

Instead of a decorative ridge of dyed horsehair, the steel and shadowstone had been shaped into a crown of horns that bore a resemblance to Nektas's. The cheek pieces swept out and up into draken wings. The helmets were as fierce as they were beautiful and were surely a fearsome sight in battle.

Rhahar and Kars had already gotten down from their horses and were waiting for us, along with Rhain. I knew Saion, Bele, and the twins were already inside the City Hall.

Along with likely everyone who called Lethe home.

Ash dismounted with a swift and graceful motion, landing lightly on his feet. His eyes caught mine as he reached up. Heart thudding, I took his hands, and he helped me down without pointing out how hard I was gripping his fingers.

He lowered his head to mine and whispered, "Breathe, *liessa*."

I hadn't realized I had been holding my breath for over five seconds. It seemed I wasn't as calm as I thought I was. I sucked in a long, deep breath, drawing in his fresh, citrusy scent. Neither of us moved for a few moments. Could've been minutes. I stood there, shielded by his body and Odin's. He didn't move until my breathing steadied. Then he pressed his cool lips to my forehead.

He stepped back, and I gave Odin's glossy black mane one last pat, thankful that he didn't attempt to nip at my hand today. He hadn't last night either.

Apparently, he'd gotten over the whole me-trying-to-kill-Ash thing.

With my hand folded firmly in Ash's, we turned to the entry house as the three guards stepped to our sides.

Every soldier moved in perfect harmony, kneeling as they thumped their fists off their armor while two rows of about three dozen more faced one another, unsheathing shadowstone swords. They raised them high, creating a walkway.

"Wow," I murmured, my eyes wide as I realized the echo of their fists had silenced the chatter coming from within the City Hall.

One side of Ash's lips curved up as his thumb moved back and forth over mine. "You liked that?"

"It was rather impressive," I said as we walked forward.

I could hear the hiss of swords slicing through the air, lowering behind Rhahar, Kars, and Rhain as they followed us. That was how quiet the City Hall had become.

We passed through the doors of the entry house, and my gaze immediately flicked to the rounded archway leading to the City Hall's main floor. I remembered exactly how long the walk was from that doorway to the dais.

It felt like it took ten years.

"I'm going to head out," Rhain said, glancing between us as the doors of the entry house closed. "And announce your arrival."

"I wish we could just enter without it being a big deal," I admitted as Ash's thumb continued to sweep over my hand.

Rhain arched a brow. "It's tradition, Seraphena."

"Sera," I murmured, eyeing the archway.

"And Rhain also likes to make the announcement," Rhahar commented, his shoulder brushing Rhain's as he moved to a narrow table along the opposite wall. "Because he's good at it."

The auburn-haired god's cheeks turned pink. "I'm excellent at it," Rhain corrected.

Rhahar snorted as he picked up a pitcher and then came to our side with two bronze chalices. "I believe it's mulled wine."

"Thank you." I accepted the chalice and took a hasty gulp. I barely tasted the spice.

Ash took a far more sedate drink as Lailah appeared in the archway, her braids swept back into a knot at the nape of her neck. "Everything should be ready in a few minutes."

Only a few minutes?

I took another drink, this time only a sip. "How many people are here?"

Lailah glanced back over her shoulder. "Everyone."

"Everyone?" I squeaked. That was *a hundred thousand.* My grip tightened on the chalice. Well, it would be more than that, actually, if one counted the new arrivals.

Holy shit.

"Go ahead and make your way out there," Ash said. "Just give us a couple of minutes before you make the announcement."

Rhain nodded, glancing briefly at me. He started to turn but stopped and spoke in a low voice, "You will do fine, Sera."

"Thank you," I whispered.

"Us, too?" Rhahar asked as Rhain passed him and entered the main floor.

"If you would," Ash requested.

Rhahar turned as Kars bowed curtly. "We will see you out there," the godling said.

I gave them an awkward wave that earned another grin from Kars.

Then, it was just Ash and me.

Ash set his chalice on a nearby pedestal. "Do you remember the last time we were here?"

"Of course." My heart skipped, but for a far different reason this time. "It was when I realized I was in love with you."

His lips parted. "Is that what you wanted to say when you told me you wanted this union between us?"

"Yes, but I was too afraid and thought—"

Ash kissed me.

And gods, it was a wrecking kiss that was beautiful and raw, yet somehow infinitely tender. It was another of his kisses that spoke so much love.

He was breathing heavily as he rested his forehead against mine. "When we were here last, I told you that your beauty captured my breath," he said, cupping my cheek. "That remains true, is even more so now, but it is your strength and your courage that have truly ensnared me."

A rush of emotion swelled, stirring the eather.

"And it's okay to be nervous right now," he said, his eyes searching mine. "But do not forget how strong and brave you are and what you have faced and conquered. You've got this. I have faith in that." His thumbs swept over my cheeks. "In you."

A tremor went through me as I nodded. I didn't think he could ever know how much his words meant to me because the next breath was lighter and easier.

Ash had faith in me.

And it was time I started to have some in myself.

"I've got this," I said.

Ash smiled. "Without a doubt."

"Bow." Rhain's voice suddenly boomed from the City Hall. "For the One who is born of Blood and Ash, *the* Light and the Fire, and *the* Brightest Moon, the *true* Primal of Life, and the *Queen* of the Gods and Common Man."

"That's a really long title," I whispered to Ash in the silence.

He grinned as he took the chalice from my hand and placed it beside his.

"Bow." Rhain's voice came again. "For the Asher, the One who is Blessed, the Guardian of Souls, and the Primal God of Common Men and Endings."

"Ready?" Ash asked as the silence continued from within the City Hall.

My heart thudded. "Yes."

Dipping his head, he kissed me once more and gently squeezed my hand, then we shadowstepped onto the dais.

The sound of a collective gasp reverberated through the crowd as the Primal mist receded from around us. I started to look past Rhain, but my gaze flew back to him. He had knelt. So had Saion and Rhahar. I briefly saw Bele, who knelt to our right, along with Lailah, and I felt Nektas drawing closer.

Everyone but Ash and I was down on one knee, their palms pressed to the floor and to their chests. Even the smallest in the crowd knelt, as did the soldiers lining the colonnade, their backs to the iron-gray banners that bore two crescent moons facing one another above the head of a wolf.

Ash had explained this morning what would come next. Briefly meeting his eyes, we turned. Two thrones made of shadowstone stood adorned with intricately carved wings on their backs, much like the soldiers' helmets, their graceful arches meeting. The banners hanging behind them rippled in the breeze as we approached.

My throat was incredibly dry as we stepped up to the slightly raised thrones, causing me to wish I had drunk more. At least my neck didn't feel tight as Ash gave my hand one last squeeze and then let go. We turned back to the coliseum floor then sat. I could've sworn the sun-warmed shadowstone pulsated with energy as I flattened my palms on the arms of the throne.

A burst of intense, silvery fire rolled across the sky above the Hall. I sucked in a sharp breath as the draken lining the columns of the colonnade lifted their heads, letting out staggering, high-pitched calls. A thick shadow fell over the crowd, blotting out the sunlight. A gust of wind swept over the floor of the Hall, stirring the strings of lights that crisscrossed the entire length of the massive circular structure and lifted the tendrils of my hair as I looked up.

With a graceful sweep of his black-and-gray wings, Nektas descended from above, landing in front of the thrones just as he had during our coronation.

This time, I was prepared for when he swept his wings back over our heads, and his front talons slammed down on the edge of the dais. The thick frills around his head vibrated as a sound like thunder rolled from him. He prowled forward, narrowly avoiding Bele and the twins as his tail whipped across the dais to curl at the foot of the thrones.

Nektas surveyed the crowd as he lowered himself onto his belly, his horned head resting on the dais's edge.

The draken sure did love his impressive arrivals.

I looked up from where Nektas remained. The draken along the colonnade lowered their wings and waited as those below lifted their heads. Their faces were a blur to me, and the next breath I took was a little thinner but not too bad.

Following Ash's instructions from this morning, I cleared my throat. Eather throbbed throughout my body, and when I spoke, I felt the raw energy in my voice. "You may rise."

I watched as they rose in silence all across the coliseum floor. My gaze landed on a woman and man near the front. A young boy, maybe ten or eleven years old, stood between them. The adults' faces were guarded, maybe even nervous, and they each had a hand on one of the boy's shoulders. But he…

He trembled as he stared up at the thrones, his amber eyes wide. However, he didn't look afraid. My breath caught as I recognized the emotion on his face.

Part of me had expected to see uncertainty and unease, and I wouldn't have blamed them if they felt that way. Only those who had called Lethe home knew about me, but none of them expected me to rise as the true Primal of Life. And those who'd just come to the Shadowlands had no idea what to expect from me. They didn't know if I would be any different. Better. Or worse.

But there was none of that in the expressions of those below.

Many of the faces showed various degrees of wonder and maybe even a little disbelief, echoing the awe I saw in the boy's expression. The *acceptance.* The *devotion.* Seeing that stunned me because, gods, I didn't feel like I'd done much to earn it.

But I could change that.

We would show them.

But, I couldn't do it like this. I twisted to Ash, and his eyes immediately met mine. "I don't want to do this while sitting on a throne," I whispered.

"We don't have to," he answered, a faint curve in his lips appearing. "How do you want to do this?"

"I…I want to be closer to them."

"Then that is what we shall do," he replied.

"Okay." I glanced back at the crowd and rose on slightly trembling legs. I stepped down from the throne, mindful of Nektas's tail, and waited for Ash to join me.

Holding my gaze, he offered me his hand once more. Together, we crossed the dais.

"Sorry," I murmured to Rhain as we passed him. He watched in confusion as we stopped closer to the edge of the dais. The people below crowded forward. As I looked out over the gathering, I didn't take a breath, I didn't think. I just spoke.

"I'm sure many of you are wondering what we're doing right now," I said.

"I know I am," Bele muttered under her breath.

I pretended I didn't hear her as I continued. "I didn't feel comfortable sitting all the way back there and having to yell for any of you to hear me."

There was a wave of scattered chuckles, and I saw several quick grins and amused looks being exchanged. "Anyway,"—I cleared my throat—"we wanted to thank you all for coming together on such short notice," I said, ignoring the slight quiver in my voice. "I'm sure my Ascension has come as a surprise to many of you—or actually, all of you." My cheeks flushed, but I pushed on. "And many of you are uncertain of what is to come. We called you all here today to assuage those concerns."

I glanced at Ash, and he nodded for me to continue. "First, we wanted to say that we know the risks many of you took to travel to Lethe, and we are…inspired by that." My gaze flickered over the crowd, and my throat thickened with emotion that even caught *me* off guard. "And we are humbled. Truly. All of you are welcome here and are under our protection, as are all those who call Lethe their home. We are working on ensuring that each of you will have shelter and food."

"Land has already been set aside, and fields are being plowed to plant crops while additional housing is built," Ash continued, his voice far steadier than mine as he surveyed the crowd. "When winter comes, it may be a hard one."

"But there will be a winter thanks to our Queen!" a god shouted from somewhere in the gathering. Laughs and cheers of agreement traveled through the crowd. "And that is something to celebrate."

Ash nodded. "That, it is." He turned his head to me. "And we have Seraphena to thank for that."

Joyous shouts rose, sweeping over the coliseum and drawing a faint smile from Ash.

I lifted a hand, and they quieted so quickly I was a little taken aback. "It is not just I who is to thank for that. It is also Nyktos."

There were more exclamations, and they came in a great roar that brought a smile to my lips.

"I would not be here if not for him," I continued. "Our King."

It seemed like the entire crowd froze. If I had Ash's ability, I'd likely be drowning in shock.

"The realms will no longer be ruled by only the true Primal of Life," I announced. "That has ended. The realms shall thrive under the joint rule of a King and Queen."

"That will not be the only change. Iliseeum and the mortal realm will no longer suffer under tyrannical rule or cruel indifference," Ash said, his voice carrying. Ash wasn't threatening per se, but he *was* sending a message. "We *will* see Iliseeum as it once was under my father's rule. But better, where one can move among Courts without fear of punishment or leaving family and loved ones behind."

"We *will* have a future where mortals do not tremble in fear upon sight of us." I lifted my chin. "Or are treated as little more than sources of entertainment."

"These changes will not come easily. There will be resistance. Blood will be shed," Ash told them. "But we promise we will not give up until that future becomes the present."

Then Ash lifted our joined hands, the swirl of the golden imprint on the top of his left glittering in the sunlight.

A frenzy of cheers erupted across the coliseum floor, causing Nektas to lift his head. Their feet came down hard, thudding on the stone, matching the tempo of my heartbeat. My gaze flew to Ash's.

"I think they approve," he said as those in the crowd waved their arms in wild excitement. Voices clamored in unison, chanting…*mayeeh Liessa.*

Our Queen.

And shouting *mayeeh Liessar.*

Our King.

Blinking, I scanned faces filled with surprise. People were embracing one another, others *wept* as they pressed their hands to their cheeks or chests—women and men. My eyes widened in awe at the feverish outpouring of emotion from the crowd. My throat tightened but with good things instead of panic as I took in the joyful, beaming faces.

Ash tugged on my hand, drawing me to his side. I looked up, and his gaze swept over my face with intensity. "Thirty-six," he said, cupping my cheek with his other hand. "Just making sure they are all still there."

Then he kissed me.

And gods, there was no restraint or suppression of desire as I gripped the front of his tunic. Our tongues twined in a sensual dance as his sharp fangs grazed my lips. He kissed me as if it were just us, and for that fleeting moment, it truly was. But we weren't alone. Bawdy whistles and raucous shouts pierced the air.

I laughed against his lips, my face warming.

"I think they liked that even more," he said, folding his arms around me. As he held me, I swore the entire realm must have heard the cheers.

Closing my eyes, I rested my cheek against Ash's chest and soaked in the sound. I really hadn't known how today would go or what our reception would be. The possibilities had been endless. But I never expected this.

Though I probably should have. Most of those here knew that I had fought against the dakkais alongside Ash and had changed the landscape of the Shadowlands overnight. And I was, after all, the true Primal of Life, and Ash was beloved by his people. Of course, they would be ecstatic.

However, I'd never experienced anything like this in my entire life. I had not been known to my kingdom. I'd been nothing but a specter not fully formed yet drenched in blood. I wasn't that here. I was seen. Welcomed. Known.

When I pulled away, I peeked over my shoulder. Nektas was watching us. He huffed with a shake of his large head as Saion approached us.

"Your face is so red," Saion told me before addressing Ash. "The barrels of wine you had us bring are about to be rolled out."

"Perfect." Ash's hand slid down the center of my back.

"This went really well," I said as several soldiers began moving the large barrels out from the alcove of the colonnade.

Saion smiled. "Of course, it did."

Bele jogged down the dais steps, and something struck me as I looked over the mass of gods, godlings, and mortals. "No one is wearing masks like many did during the coronation."

"There is no need," Saion replied as the hum of string instruments reached my ears, the notes drifting through the air.

Faces blurred as I nodded. They hadn't felt the need to conceal their identities, not just because there were no other Primals in attendance but because they felt safe. Gods, that meant more to me than the cheers or being known.

And I would do everything to ensure they never lost that sense of security.

I let out a slow breath as the beat of drums joined the melodic dance. The rhythm grew louder, infusing the coliseum with infectious energy as I found Bele in the crowd. All I had to do was follow the wave of bows as the masses parted for the Primal goddess. She joined Aios, who stood with a petite woman dressed in a hooded, white gown with long sleeves who surveyed the revelers in front of her. It was Erlina.

The once-Chosen now had her own life, one where she wasn't subjected to the whims of another. I reminded myself that the others in Dalos and the other Courts would soon have that choice. Now, we just needed to meet with the Primals. Hopefully, that went as well as this had.

I wouldn't bet on it, but I also wouldn't dwell on it right now. There would be plenty of time for that tomorrow.

Nightmare.

Bars.

I was staring at bars made of gilded bones.

Soft material brushed against my legs as I staggered back a step, my feet sinking into soft fur. I looked down at the swath of ivory gauze and saw the darker pink tips of my breasts through the transparent garment.

"*No.*" My heart thudded heavily as my head jerked back around.

The golden chests.

The golden divan.

My head swung to the other side as pressure clamped down on my chest. I saw the large bed draped in gold blankets and white furs.

"I'm not here," I whispered hoarsely, my gaze slowly tracking to the bedposts and the floor at the foot of the bed.

Chains.

The air I breathed thinned as my eyes locked on the throne beyond the gilded cage set directly in front of the bed.

No. No. No.

This wasn't real.

"I'm not here," I repeated, closing my eyes. I wasn't here. I'd escaped. I was free. I wasn't here. I was safe.

Air stirred around me, raising the tiny hairs all over my body. Lilacs. I smelled *stale* lilacs.

"*I have been so damn lonely,* so'lis."

Every part of my body went rigid at the sound of that summery voice. *I'm not here.* I held myself completely still, keeping my eyes tightly closed. *I'm not here. I'm not—*

Arms tightened around me like a vise, digging into my sides. Against my back, *his* heart pounded faster than mine.

"*I just need to hold you,*" Kolis pleaded.

"No," I said—I know I said it. I felt the word rattle from my chest and claw at my throat. I felt my mouth move.

But I could no longer hear my voice.

I made no sound.

Nothing.

Suddenly, I wasn't standing anymore. He was sitting on the edge of the bed, and I was in his lap, my feet dangling above the floor. That single word shook my chest again and scratched my throat. My mouth moved once more, but I still had no voice.

Sweltering heat bore down on me as my fingers splayed.

"*That you would even speak his name,*" he hissed in my ear.

No. No. No—

Fangs tore into my skin, sending a jolt coursing through my entire being.

I screamed the word now, and it came from the depths of my being. It cut up my throat and split my mouth but I heard only the sounds of his muffled moans as he drew harder and deeper on the wound. His mouth moved. His body shifted under mine, and…oh, gods, I could feel him—

"*Liessa.*" A voice of shadows and velvet pierced the golden cage.

I would know that voice anywhere.

"*Ash*," I rasped, his name calming my heart and soothing my throat as my voice returned.

The bars before me disintegrated, and the chests and divan shattered into dust. The arms fell away from me, and the gown vanished…

"Wake up, Sera. *Please.*"

My eyes flew open with a jolt. I gulped in air. In the soft glow of the bedside table lamp, I saw silver streaked with eather, not gold-flecked eyes.

"It's okay." Ash was above me, a lock of chestnut hair hanging forward and brushing his jaw. "You had a nightmare."

Just a nightmare? It hadn't felt that way. I could still taste the fear and desperation in the back of my aching throat. Could he pick up on my emotions in dreams? Gods, that was an idiotic question. Of course, he could. I was probably projecting all over the bedchamber. And if I hadn't been, I could've said something. My throat felt like I'd screamed.

Screamed—

Panic exploded, dousing my body in suffocating, red-hot flames. I opened my mouth, but only a thin, wheezing sound parted my lips. I needed air. Space. Anything. I jerked up, nearly knocking my head into Ash's. A fist had my heart in its grip. My lungs clenched as my legs tangled in the blanket—

"Sera." Ash caught my shoulders, stopping me from toppling off the bed. "Look at me."

I strained against his hold, attempting to stand. "I can't…get air…in."

"I know, *liessa.* I'm going to help you. I just need you to look at me," he said. "Please."

My gaze flew to his.

His hands went to my cheeks, the feel of them cool against my too-hot skin. "Listen to me. You can breathe. You're just breathing too fast. Understand?"

I nodded as my hands spasmed.

Ash smiled. "Remember what I taught you before? Close your mouth and put your tongue against the back of your teeth. *Yes.* Just like that." His smile grew like a warm wind on a fall day. "Now, I need you to exhale nice and slow for the count of four. Can you do that?"

I nodded again, doing as he instructed.

"That's it." His eyes never left mine. "Now, you're going to inhale for four seconds. I'll count them. One. Two. Three. Four. Exhale now."

Ash kept counting, lifting his chin on an inhale and lowering it on an exhale. His patience didn't waver as the seconds turned to minutes. He stayed with me until my breathing slowed, and I was no longer gasping like a fish out of water.

Ash's thumbs swept across my chin. "How are you feeling?"

"Okay," I croaked, my face hot despite his cool touch. As my heart rate slowed, embarrassment rose. I closed my eyes. "I'm so—"

"Do not apologize for that." Shifting, he pulled me between his legs and held me to his chest. "Do not ever apologize for that. You have no reason to, nor any reason to feel embarrassment."

I pressed my cheek to his chest, not so sure about that. "I'm a Primal," I whispered hoarsely.

"A newly Ascended Primal."

"I'm still a grown-ass woman," I countered.

Ash's hand folded around the back of my head. "I don't think age has anything to do with it."

It should, because…seriously. How was I supposed to be the Queen of the Gods when a dumb nightmare could send me into a panic spiral? And why was I even having that nightmare? *Again*? It was…uncalled for.

I felt like a mess.

A hot, nauseous mess.

But I still relaxed into Ash's embrace, letting the coolness of his body beat back the flush in mine. I didn't know how much time passed before Ash tilted his head and pressed a kiss to my temple.

"You want to talk about it?" he asked.

Tension crept into my muscles. "Talk about what?"

He smoothed a hand down my back. "What you were dreaming about."

I closed my eyes even tighter, seeing bursts of white stars, but I still saw what I had in my dream. A gilded cage full of gold and…Kolis.

I just need to hold you.

Throat drying, I pulled back. My hands dropped to my lap as my gaze fell on the balcony doors. The curtains were drawn open, revealing the dark night sky beyond. "I don't remember what I was dreaming about."

"Not a single detail?"

"No." I forced a shrug. "Probably because it was nothing."

"Nothing," he whispered, watching me in a way that made it seem like he could see straight through me.

I nodded as I lay back down. "We should go back to sleep," I said, pulling the blanket up. "Morning will be here soon."

Ash didn't respond, and he didn't move as I rolled onto my side. After a few moments, I heard a click as he turned off the bedside lamp, plunging the chamber into darkness. The bed shifted as he reclined behind me, curling his arm around my waist. His lips brushed my shoulder, and then he settled. The tension didn't leave his body, though.

It didn't leave mine either as I stared into the darkness. Because I knew.

He didn't believe me.

I forced myself to finish the buttery scrambled eggs while Ash wrote in the Book of the Dead.

I had no appetite.

Which was weird because I was always hungry. But there was this strange, metallic, almost sour taste in my mouth.

I picked up the glass of juice as I peeked over at Ash's bowed head. He hadn't spoken much this morning, not even to ask me where I had disappeared to when I went out onto the Rise. I assumed his trip to Vathi consumed his thoughts. He'd be leaving soon, and when he got back, we planned to go to the Thyia Plains to speak with Keella. His quietness wasn't because of the night terror that had awakened us both in the middle of the night.

I hated that the nightmare had come after such a wonderful day. It felt as if it had tainted yesterday's success. And I hated myself even more for feeling as if the reception of our public address was somehow lessened because of it.

I shoved another forkful of eggs into my mouth and chewed as I scanned his office. Being back here was strange when I hadn't thought I would ever see the space again. It had changed. Though not a lot. There were two chairs in front of his desk, where only one had been before. An end table made of the same dark wood with hints of red as his desk had been placed to my right.

I glanced at Ash. Plans for additional insulas that Rhain had dropped off a little bit ago lay on the corner of the desktop.

Swallowing a sigh, I shifted my attention to the table before me. Beside my plate were two and a half glasses, strawberries, a cutting board, and a knife.

It was a very odd combination of things.

Ash had put the ledgers there, instructing me to move them around, open them, and turn pages without touching or tearing them. It was I who had brought in the other items. And the other half of one of the glasses was in pieces in the trash bin.

I had no idea why moving a glass without breaking it was so hard when I had harnessed the eather to free myself and Ash *before* I Ascended and could use it to restore life to an entire Court.

According to Ash, it was because I was thinking about it too much when it didn't come to, well, situations where I wasn't angry or excited about something. I was complicating it and not letting it come naturally.

"*Your thought is your will*," he'd said.

And that was about as helpful as my *no-shit* response.

"*Liessa*?"

"Hmm?"

"If you keep chewing on your fingers, you won't have any left."

I dropped my hand to my lap. "I'm not chewing on my fingers."

"Little liar," he murmured.

My eyes narrowed. He had his head bowed and tipped slightly to the side as he wrote in the Book of the Dead. "How would you even know? You're not even looking at me."

Ash lowered the quill and lifted his gaze. Wisps of eather spun in eyes that had become heated quicksilver. "I'm always looking at you, *liessa*."

A flush hit my skin as I returned my attention to my lessons. Summoning the eather as I stared at the knife, I willed it to lift—

The knife flew into the air, and I swallowed a shout.

Concentration broken, the knife plummeted back down. I leaned forward, catching it before the blade stabbed the innocent table.

I peeked over at Ash. His brow was furrowed, and I was sure I was being a distraction. My attention returned to the table. I'd really wanted the flavored water and had only managed to slice—or smash—two strawberries, so I quickly chopped one up and tossed it into the pitcher with my hands. Otherwise, I wouldn't have it until next year.

Placing the knife back down, I started to will it back into the air.

"*Liessa*?"

"Yes?"

"I'm curious," he said, the quill moving quickly over the page. "Why have you moved on from slaughtering innocent glasses to throwing sharp instruments?"

My lips pursed. "Maybe I thought I would be more comfortable working with a blade."

He smirked. "How's that idea working out for you?"

"Just perfect."

Ash chuckled as he closed the Book of the Dead. The quill vanished into thin air. "Perhaps you should stick to the ledgers and soft, non-pointy items."

"Perhaps you should mind your business."

"I would,"—he picked up one of the building plans—"except I am worried that this may end with you having to regrow an eye." He paused. "Or we'll end up without glasses to drink from."

I sighed. "Like I said before, maybe I'm faulty."

"You know, the more I think about it, the more I realize you might have a point."

My eyes narrowed as I pictured the knife flying through the parchment he held.

Ash's hand snapped up, catching the knife by the hilt right before it pierced the cream parchment. He slowly turned his head to me. "I assume you meant to do that."

I smiled broadly. "I did."

"Then what was different this time?" he asked.

"You annoyed me."

"Other than that."

I lifted a shoulder. "I wasn't…"

"Overthinking it?"

"Shut up," I muttered.

He grinned and placed the knife on the table. "I will, but that doesn't change the fact that you're overthinking."

He was right.

Whatever.

"Can I have my knife back?"

"I'm not sure you will behave yourself with it," he replied.

My lips parted.

Ash smiled as he turned his attention back to the plans.

I returned to moving the glasses around for a few more minutes, spilling some water and stopping one from flying off the table.

"Can I have the knife back now?" I asked.

"Nope."

I lifted my hand, and the blade flew off his desk, handle first. I easily caught it.

"Let me guess," he said. "You weren't—"

"If you say *overthinking it* one more time," I warned, pointing the blade at him.

Ash just grinned, and honestly, why wouldn't he? I was threatening him with a paltry paring knife.

I sighed. "I miss my dagger."

In the next several minutes, I finally stopped overthinking things. I managed to lift several strawberries and plop them into the glass of water before my attention shifted to the bare shelves as I wondered what could be placed on them. Ash wasn't the type to be into glass figurines as my stepfather had been. "You need knickknacks."

Ash half-laughed. "What?"

"Knickknacks," I repeated. "You know, small objects that are worthless to some but are something you enjoy."

"I know what knickknacks are, *liessa*." He looked up from the building plans. "What I don't know is why you're suggesting them."

"Your shelves are bare." I pointed at the walls. "My stepfather collected things made of spun glass. Or is it blown glass?" My nose scrunched. "Maybe they're the same thing."

"I don't believe so." Ash paused, looking to the side at the walls. "I never really thought about the shelves."

"I can tell," I replied dryly, taking a drink of the now-fruit-flavored water. "We'll have to get you some knickknacks."

"I'll add that to the list of things we must accomplish."

I looked at him with a frown. "We have a list?"

"We do." Rising, he set aside the building plans and returned the Book of the Dead to its drawer. "Speak with Attes. Summon the Primals. Plant more crops. Deal with Kolis. Spit on his close-to-dead-as-possible body." He ticked each item off as he walked around the desk, my brow rising with each item. "Rule the realms."

"That's an…impressive list," I slowly stated.

"I wasn't done."

"Oh."

"We also have to decide where we wish to live—here or in Dalos," he continued. I blinked, not having even considered a relocation. "Indulge in radek wine—"

"The kind that makes…"

"One incredibly aroused for extended periods of time?" A wolfish grin appeared. "Yes."

"Oh," I repeated. "I think I would like that."

Icy heat swirled in his eyes as he sat beside me on the light gray settee. "You will love it, *liessa*."

My gaze swept over his powerful body. I would be *obsessed* with that.

He glanced at the table that had been brought in for our breakfast. The heat faded from his stare. "Fates," he muttered, dragging a hand over his jaw.

"What?"

"What you're drinking," he said. "Or what you've made yourself. I completely forgot about this until now, but…"

"Your father used to do this," I finished for him.

His head cut to me. "How did you—?" He let out a soft laugh. "Foresight?"

It wasn't the *vadentia* but Kolis who had told me, but I smiled and nodded as I quickly looked away. I could feel his stare on me.

"It wasn't the *vadentia*, was it? It was Kolis." A moment passed. "Why wouldn't you just tell me that?"

I blew out a breath as I lifted a shoulder. "I just don't think it matters, and I don't want him to be associated with you remembering something about your father."

"It's kind of hard for him *not* to be associated with thoughts of my father, *liessa*." He reached over and tucked a curl back from my face. "But I do appreciate the consideration."

I relaxed. "It's pretty tasty. You should try it."

"I will." His attention shifted back to the table. "Are you finished eating?"

"Yep."

His brows furrowed. "You barely ate."

"Not true." I took another drink.

"You only ate half the eggs. Maybe a bite of the muffin." He picked up the napkin I'd tossed over a side dish, revealing the strips of fried meat. "And you didn't even touch the bacon."

I lifted a shoulder. "I guess I'm not that hungry."

"That's odd." Ash's frown deepened.

"What? Not being hungry?"

"Yeah." He leaned back and looked at me. "After an Ascension, one is typically hungrier than normal because the body is still going through changes. A lot of energy is expended."

"Oh," I said, cradling the glass to my chest. "Maybe I'm different because I was mortal."

"Maybe." His gaze tracked over my features. "When Kolis had you, was food restricted?"

I jerked, caught off guard by his question. "No. Food was provided. A lot of it." My hold on the glass tightened. "You think me not being hungry has to do with my time in Dalos?"

"Kolis has been known to use food as a form of reward and punishment," he said, and my stomach dropped. "I didn't know if that was the case with you."

"No. It wasn't." My gaze shifted to the plates. "I was…treated more like a guest than a prisoner."

Cold air blasted off Ash. "A guest kept in a cage?"

"A reluctant guest," I amended, feeling my chest knot. "But you don't have to worry about that. Kolis didn't do anything like that." A moment passed, then another. No longer thirsty, I placed the glass on the table. "Did he use food in that way with you?"

"He did."

I briefly closed my eyes as fury rose, stoking the embers. I had to take a deep breath. "I hate him," I said, folding my hand over his. "I really—wait." I looked down at our joined hands, realizing just then that his skin didn't feel as cold as it had the night before. Or this morning, when we woke, even. "Your skin is a little warmer."

He reached over and picked up the glass with his other hand. "Feels the same to me," he said, taking a sip. "It does taste good." He tipped the glass back, eyeing the contents. "Probably could get by with one or three less strawberries."

"I like it sweet," I murmured, sliding my hand up the corded muscle of his forearm. Maybe it was my imagination? It must have been because Ash hadn't fed since I'd awakened from stasis.

"While I don't mind that you're feeling up my arm," he drawled, "if you continue, I'm afraid I'll never make it to Vathi."

I pulled my hand away and cleared my throat. "I wish I could go with you."

"I wish you would talk to me."

My head cut to his. "About what?"

"That's another long list," he stated. "But we can start with what you were dreaming about last night."

A thin breath of air made it past my lips. "I already told you. I don't remember. So, you can go ahead and remove that from the list."

Tension bracketed his mouth as he looked away, and I knew that what I'd suspected last night was true.

He didn't believe me.

"Would you like me to remind you?" he said quietly.

I stared at him, my heart thumping as it began to race.

"You were screaming."

Shit.

A muscle flexed along his jaw. "You were screaming the word *no*."

Shit.

I swallowed. "I don't know why."

His gaze flicked to mine. "I think I have a pretty good idea."

Muscles all throughout my body began to tense as if I was preparing to leap from the settee and run. It was like the flight response kicking in, but I could feel the fight instinct gearing up to take over, and I didn't want that. Ash wasn't at fault here. He was only concerned. So, I took a moment to calm my ass down.

"I know you're worried about me," I started, and Ash's gaze returned to mine, "but I'm okay."

Several moments passed, the silence stretching between us. "It's all right, you know?" he said. "To not be okay. To not always be strong."

A jolt ran through my body as my hands curled around nothing but air. "Nektas said something like that."

"I'm sure he did. He's said it to me before."

I dropped my hands to my lap. "Why…why was he telling you that?"

"My father. Not knowing my mother. Kolis. Veses," he said, and my chest fisted with anger at merely the sound of her name. "I could keep going, but I think you get the point."

I did.

And I wished I didn't because it made my heart ache for everything he'd had to deal with.

That was why I wasn't going to tell him about the nightmare. He didn't need that living in the back of his head, haunting him, along with everything else.

"But you got through it because you had to, right?" I said. "And you were able to do that because you're strong. You're a survivor."

"So are you."

My brows snapped together. "I am, but that has nothing to do with survival."

"It has everything to do with surviving, *liessa*."

I shook my head, my palms beginning to sweat. How did we even end up having this conversation when we had far more important things to discuss? "I get what you're saying. I do. But I *am* okay. I'm not—" A sudden charge of energy bore down on me, pimpling my skin. I stiffened.

A frown pulled at his brow. "Sera?"

"I…I feel something. I don't know how to explain it. It's like I can feel the air changing. As if…"

Ash's chin dipped, and a low growl rumbled from him. "Is it fucking Kolis again?"

"No." Ash rose as I stood. "But it feels like something is coming." Eather throbbed in my chest. "Something powerful and…"

Old.

Something *Ancient.*

Sucking in a sharp breath, I spun toward the doors. No sooner had the thought finished than the air between the two shadowstone pillars warped.

Ash curled his arm around my waist and hauled me back as a sphere of eather materialized, rapidly swelling and elongating as it unfurled. But this was no random ball of eather. Instinct told me it was a tear in the very realm itself. An opening.

A portal.

The first thing I saw was skin. A whole lot of bare flesh and honed muscle in the shape of a tall, broad man with shoulder-length brown hair and skin a shade somewhere between the bronze of Ash's and the copper of Nektas's. The man *casually* walked out of the portal like he was merely taking a stroll in a park.

That was if one walked in the park only wearing loose-fitting, white linen pants and absolutely nothing else.

Well, he *was* wearing something else. Small gold rings in both of his brown nipples. I supposed that counted as some sort of attire.

I really needed to stop looking at his nipples.

I lifted my gaze. Scrolling vines similar to what adorned the throne room doors were tattooed up the sides of his throat, stopping at the curve of a jaw that could've been carved from granite. Except I didn't think that design was made of ink. It was a shade or two darker than his flesh and appeared to churn from *within* his skin, like the shadows often did in Ash's. I looked past sculpted lips, a chiseled nose, and arched cheekbones, momentarily distracted by the asymmetric features. And then I saw his eyes.

My lips parted. They were a kaleidoscope of colors: a warm shade of brown, the dewy green of the newly grown patches of grass outside, and the blue of the Stroud Sea. Bursts of silver were sprinkled throughout the colors like stars.

I'd seen those eyes before.

During my Ascension, when I'd seen how the realms were created.

"What the fuck?" Ash snarled, his flesh thinning. Shadows appeared along his throat.

The being's strange eyes flicked to Ash, his head moving in a way that sent a chill of unease down my spine. There was something utterly inhuman in that simple movement. Almost as if the entire realm shifted around him to accommodate the gesture. One side of his lips curled up, and instinct warned me that smile was not a good thing.

"It's okay." I stepped around Ash—or tried to. He sidestepped me. "He's an…" I trailed off as the being's gaze shifted to me. He waited to hear what I said. What I would reveal. My throat dried. "He's a Fate—an Arae."

The other side of the *Ancient's* lips rose then in a close-lipped smile. It reminded me of Kolis's smiles—the ones that were practiced and shallow as if he didn't understand the emotions behind smiling and was simply copying others' expressions.

How could Holland be an Ancient? He was nothing like this being standing in front of us.

"I don't give a fuck what he is," Ash fumed, the shadows deepening as they spread up his throat in nearly the same pattern as the one on the Ancient's skin. "I only know he had better have one good fucking reason for arriving unannounced and uninvited in our home."

Our home.

It was just two words, but they suddenly made me feel all warm inside—

The Ancient laughed.

Okay. Now was not the time to focus on how those words made me feel all ooey-gooey. Like, at all. Because the Ancient's laugh was even more creepy than his smile.

Dark tendrils of eather gathered on the floor, wrapping themselves around our legs. "I'm not sure what you find funny."

"Many things," the Ancient replied, his voice carrying a lilt I'd never heard before, one with a melodic quality.

The power growing around Ash caused the air to crackle and stirred the eather inside me. "You want to key us in on those things?" Ash said.

"You want to tell me why you speak for the true Primal of Life?" the Ancient countered.

I stiffened. "He doesn't speak for me."

The Ancient's head moved again, tilting to the side as he focused on me. "I suppose I should be relieved to hear that." He paused, his gaze moving over me in a way that said he was sizing up my worth and wasn't exactly impressed with the end result. My eyes narrowed. "But that is yet to be seen."

Between the tone that dripped disapproval and that look, it was like the Ancient had reached inside me and shattered any self-restraint I'd developed after my Ascension.

Eather rushed to the surface of my skin and seeped through. "I was wrong," I said as, out of the corner of my eye, I thought I saw wisps of silver-laced golden eather streaking through the dark shadows whirling on the floor. "He did just speak for me when he said you'd better have a good fucking reason for appearing in our home as if you belong here."

The churning colors stilled, and the bursts of eather brightened in the Ancient's eyes.

"Careful," he replied softly. "You may harness the eather of the realms, but you are only a…" The stars in his eyes pulsed, and while his lips didn't move when he spoke, I heard him clear as day anyway. Two words.

Baby Primal.

I sucked in a sharp breath and jerked. The shock collapsed my hold on the essence.

"You're the one who needs to be careful." Ash's chin dipped. "You may be a Fate, but that won't stop me from flaying the flesh from your body if I even perceive your words to be a threat to my wife."

Yet again, I felt myself melting inside, and really, *not* the appropriate response for several reasons. But most importantly?

Ash was a badass. But he could not defeat an Ancient.

Likely, none of us could.

That tight-lipped smile returned, almost as if the Ancient had heard my thoughts. "I do have a reason for being here," he announced as a shimmer of awareness swept through me.

"I suppose I'm relieved to hear that," Ash mimicked with a smile just as unfriendly. "But that is yet to be seen."

"Charming," the Ancient murmured, and a not-too-distant rumble echoed from outside. He glanced at the ceiling, and I could've sworn I saw a flicker of something skittering across his features. Not an emotion per se, but something like…wariness.

I thought about the dragon I'd seen taking out an Ancient during my Ascension. "Whatever your reason is, you'd best get to it." My lips curled into a smirk. "Because I think we're about to have company."

The eather dimmed in his eyes. "I've come to retrieve the Primal of Life."

My heart lurched. "What for?"

"You've been summoned," the Ancient answered. "By the true Primal of Death."

It was like the entire realm had ceased moving. I didn't even think Ash breathed as we stared at the Ancient. Kolis had awakened just the night before, and he already wanted to meet—already wanted to gain the upper hand. This was so like Kolis. I should've known he'd do something like this.

Then Ash spoke. "*What*?"

"The true Primal of Death has summoned the true Primal of Life," the Ancient repeated.

My heart began to pound. "I think we got that part. Why?"

"He wishes to speak."

"I don't give a fuck what he wishes," Ash growled.

The Ancient sighed. "If only it were that simple. If it were, I would not be here." He folded his arms across his chest. "As you already know."

My gaze darted to Ash's as instinct sparked, telling me what I didn't want to hear.

"He summoned an Arae to carry out the request," the Ancient added. "And to monitor the discussions, ensuring they remain peaceful."

Peaceful?

I laughed.

The Ancient's brow rose.

Shadows raced over Ash's cheeks. "What exactly does he want to discuss?"

"I do not know."

"Are you telling me that he summoned a Fate to broker a meeting but didn't tell you why?" Disbelief colored Ash's tone.

"He does not need to tell me why," the Ancient answered calmly. "Just as the Primal of Life would not need to tell me why."

"I'm sure we can hazard a few guesses as to why he wishes to meet," I said, turning to Ash. I lowered my voice when I spoke next. I wasn't sure what the point was. It wasn't like the Ancient wasn't standing *right* there. "He probably wants us to pledge our loyalty to him." He likely also wanted to know where Sotoria's soul was.

"Yeah, and we already know our answer," Ash seethed. "Starts with go and ends with fuck yourself." He shifted toward the Ancient. "You have our answer. Go tell him."

"It doesn't work that way," he said. "As you are fully aware." Those swirling eyes of color fixed on me. "It cannot be denied."

It…it couldn't.

Every part of my being knew that. I stepped to the side, thrusting my hand through my hair. "I know."

"Sera," Ash warned.

"You know it can't," I said.

"He does," the Ancient clarified.

"Thanks," I snapped, "but your input wasn't needed there."

That half-smile returned. "Equally charming."

My mind raced, trying to stay ahead of the riot of emotions, the shock of Kolis having recovered enough to do this. But how surprised could I be? I knew Kolis was strengthening. It was just faster than I'd expected. The anger and the fear that he would even dare summon me was stronger than the shock, though. Gods, the fear of feeling that desperation again hit me.

Shadows swirled faster around us as Ash's eyes locked with mine.

I took a breath that barely went anywhere. "This was bound to happen at some point, right? We knew we would have to come face-to-face with him eventually."

"On our terms," Ash spat. "Not his. Never his. And definitely not to fulfill whatever perverted entertainment value he will surely gain from this."

"I am not sure what perversion it is that you speak of," the Ancient stated. "But neither the Primal of Life nor the Primal of Death will be able to lash out at the other while in the presence of an Arae." The Ancient spoke as if he were speaking of squabbling children. "There will be no fighting or violence of any kind."

Ash didn't even look at the Ancient. "It is not physical violence I am worried about."

Air punched out of my chest. I knew what he meant. It was what Kolis could say. How he would make me feel.

"You do not need to concern yourself with any of it," the Ancient said. "The meeting is only between the Primal of Life and the Primal of Death."

The floor felt as if it shifted beneath me as Ash drew in a breath, but his chest didn't expand with an exhale.

I faced the Ancient. "Why?"

"He does not trust this Primal not to escalate the situation," the Ancient responded. "Nyktos cannot step one foot in Dalos during the meeting."

I almost laughed again.

"Are you fucking kidding me?" Ash bit out.

"And I can see why," the Ancient continued blithely. "He is nearly as temperamental as the creatures his father gave dual lives to."

"You're actually serious." Ash stepped toward the Ancient, causing my heart to stutter. "You're going to humor this son of a bitch, knowing what he has done?"

Reaching for Ash, I halted.

The Ancient's lips thinned. "I have no choice."

"You are a Fate!" Ash roared as twin arcs of shadowy eather exploded from his back. "You are not merely a messenger."

Something akin to emotion flashed in the Ancient's expression, startling me. "No, I am what ensures that balance remains."

Ash straightened, the skin of his throat turning the shade of shadowstone. "Forcing her to go before the monster who held her against her will is how you ensure balance? Are you fucking serious?"

"He's serious." My hands fisted until I felt my nails digging into my flesh. "But it's still a good question, especially because I'm willing to bet you know exactly what perversions he just spoke of."

The corners of the Ancient's mouth tightened, showing the faintest crack in his demeanor. "I will ensure that balance remains by any means necessary." Those variegated eyes shifted to mine. "That does not mean I enjoy doing so."

"Do you even know what it's like to enjoy anything?" I retorted.

"Does Holland?" the Ancient countered softly.

I snapped my mouth shut. How he said Holland's name sounded an awful lot like a threat.

"You know what is at stake," the Ancient reminded me.

I did.

Fuck.

The Ancient stiffened. "Speaking of *the* temperamental *creature*…"

The office doors flung open, and Nektas entered, his long hair flowing behind him. His stare didn't leave Ash or me as he prowled past the Ancient, not paying the being any mind.

On the other hand, the Ancient stepped back.

"What is going on?" Nektas asked.

The question was directed at me because Ash… I glanced at him. He was locked onto the Ancient like he was about to do something very unwise.

"Kolis summoned a Fate to broker a meeting between us," I said. "And only us."

Nektas's nostrils flared as he looked at Ash. "Son of a bitch," he muttered. The ridges across the bare flesh of his shoulders and chest were more pronounced than I'd ever seen them. "And you cannot change it?"

"No," the Ancient answered. "The summoner sets the terms. If they"—he indicated Ash and me—"had summoned an Arae first—"

"Don't," Nektas warned as he whirled on the Ancient. "Do not turn this back on them, Aydun."

The Ancient's nostrils flared at his name and sent a ripple of surprise through me.

"They would not seek to waste your time as Kolis would," Nektas said. "Which is exactly what will come of this."

Ash's low growl echoed through the chamber as the shadows solidified behind him. "Nothing will come of this."

"It doesn't have to be a waste of time," Aydun argued, his attention shifting to me. "Do you yearn for war? I do not believe you do."

I drew back. "Have you been listening in on us or something?"

"Do you?" he repeated.

"No."

"Why?"

"There has to be a reason?" I shook my head. "I don't want innocent people to die. Isn't that good enough?"

"Almost." The colors spun wildly around his pupils. "The future exists in several threads—"

"Do not start with that thread bullshit," Ash snarled.

The Ancient's head snapped toward Nektas. "I understand he cares for her. I know what that bond between them incites when the other is threatened, but you need to get him under control before I do."

I shot forward, stopped only by the arm Nektas flung out. Essence rushed through me, hot and violent. "You will do no such thing."

"For fuck's sake." Nektas edged me back. "Clearly, you don't know what that bond incites if you threaten either of them because you just did it."

"They are testing my patience," Aydun spat. "And I have been far too tolerant of both of them. So, get the one who is technically a Primal of no Court under control while I try to reason with the Primal who shouldn't even be a godsdamn Primal."

Ash lurched forward, but Nektas caught him. My head swung toward the draken as he shoved Ash back. "Stop," Nektas ordered.

Ash tried to sidestep him, knocking the table over. Glasses crashed. Pieces of eggs and bacon spilled across the floor. Nektas was on Ash, pushing him back again. The settee went flying as Nektas caged Ash in. The sound that came from the Primal would've sent anyone running as he bared his fangs at the draken.

Every part of me focused on Nektas. I knew he wouldn't hurt Ash. He would never do that. But the purely instinctive part of me didn't like it.

Energy was ramping up in Ash, causing the air to charge. Static crackled over my skin as the essence rose in response. One of the light bulbs exploded, sending fine shards of glass in every direction.

"Stop it," Nektas repeated, backing Ash up until he had him pinned to the wall by the credenza with his forearm across his chest. "You need to calm down."

A sound came from somewhere in the chamber. A hiss that was distinctively feline as I stepped toward Nektas and Ash, my hands opening and closing at my sides.

"For the sake of gods everywhere," muttered Aydun, "why did I have to be the one who answered the summons?"

"I need you to calm down before neither of us has a choice in you doing so." The muscles in Nektas's back flexed as he struggled to hold Ash back. "And preferably before the claws come out and Sera tears into me."

Claws come out…?

I jerked to a stop, only realizing then that I was just feet from Nektas, and my hands…felt weird. They tingled. I looked down, and my eyes went wide.

My nails had lengthened and sharpened. "What the…?"

"I know you're angry. I know you're scared," Nektas said, and that last part caught my attention. "But you go at that fucker over there and you know what will happen."

"Fucker?" muttered Aydun while I stared at Ash and Nektas. "That was uncalled for."

Whatever was happening with my hands fell to the wayside as a great sense of foreboding rose. Tiny bumps broke out across my skin. If Ash attacked Aydun, the Ancient would strike back. Nektas would defend Ash. So would I. But the Ancient…

Dread built as I looked at him. He would kill Nektas. My stomach pitched. He could kill Ash because, as Aydun had said, Ash was now the Primal of no Court. His death would impact Iliseeum and the mortal realm, but nothing as severe as what a death of any other Primal would cause.

Fear slammed into me, nearly taking my knees out from under me as the lights flickered wildly. "Ash," I whispered. "*Please.*"

Ash's pure silver gaze shot to me. Our eyes locked. A tense heartbeat passed, and then the shadows under his flesh thinned out. "I'm good."

"You sure about that?" Nektas still held him back. "Because I'm going to be really disappointed if I let go of you and you go at him."

"I won't." His eyes never strayed from mine. "I'm level. I just need to talk to Sera. Alone."

"The summons needs to be answered—"

"A couple of minutes isn't going to hurt anything," Nektas cut the Ancient off.

Aydun's jaw hardened as he looked away. "They have five minutes. That is all."

I bit my tongue, focusing on Ash. The dark tendrils of eather had mostly disappeared.

Nektas released Ash and slowly stepped back. He didn't take his eyes off the Primal as Ash pushed away from the wall. Neither did I as he stalked forward and clasped the nape of my neck. He pulled me to him, dropping his chin to the top of my head. My arms encircled his waist, and I held him tightly as tremors coursed through him.

"Outside," Nektas ordered.

There was a pause, and then the Ancient let out a deep sigh. "The only reason I'm following you is because it will only delay things further if I don't."

"Yeah," Nektas drawled. "That and the fact that you know I will rip your arms off and beat you over the head with them."

My eyes popped open.

Aydun chuckled, and it sounded different. Warm. Real enough that I lifted my head from Ash's chest. "You know, I've seen that happen before. Laugh every time I think about it."

"Why doesn't that surprise me?" Nektas muttered, the door swinging shut and muting whatever else he was saying.

"I don't even know what to say about that," I whispered, shaking my head. "I wonder how Nektas got to be on a first-name basis with him?"

"I don't know, and I don't care." Ash's fingers sank into my hair, and his chest rose sharply against mine. His features were stark—too stark. "I don't like this, Sera."

"Neither do I." I swallowed, but my throat felt dry. "But it is what it is." I tried to will my heart and mind to calm down so I could focus. "We know what Kolis will say. He'll demand our loyalty and, I imagine, command that I relinquish any claim to the throne. Is that even possible?"

Ash didn't answer as he stared at me, but the *vadentia* told me it was. Kind of. Instead of the true Primal of Life ruling, it would be the true Primal of Death. A first.

But a Queen of the Gods was also a first.

My fingers curled into the back of Ash's shirt as I exhaled slowly. "And I…I guess I'll tell Kolis to go fuck himself but in a more appropriate way. Then I'll—"

"I don't think I can allow this to happen," Ash said, speaking so quietly I wasn't even sure I'd heard him right.

But I had heard him.

I ignored it. "While I'm gone, you should go to Attes and tell him about Kolis. When I return, we will summon the Primals. Our plans haven't changed."

"I can't," he repeated. A faint glow of eather lit up the network of veins in his cheeks. "I can't let you go through with this." His eyes were full of so much essence the pupils were no longer visible as his gaze drifted to the doors behind me. The light in his veins ratcheted up. "I *won't*."

My heart stopped. "You have to."

His diamond-bright gaze swung back to me. "The only thing I have to do is keep you safe."

Letting go of his shirt, I grasped his cheeks. "If that's true, then you must let this happen."

Shadows seeped out from behind his shoulders. "That is the exact opposite of what I need to do."

"How will you keep me safe if you're dead?" I demanded, feeling my stomach pitch with each word. "Because that's what will happen if you try to stop this."

The line of his cheekbones sharpened. "You doubt the extent of what I'm willing to do for you."

"That's the thing, Ash. I don't doubt what you're willing to do." Panic seeded itself in the pit of my belly. "Listen to me. Please. We just got a second chance. One we had to fight for and will have to *keep* fighting for. And I am terrified of losing that—losing you."

His eyes went wide. "That is what you're terrified of?" More of his flesh disappeared. "You will never lose me, Sera. *Never.*"

"Then prove it," I whispered. "Please."

He inhaled sharply, his nostrils flaring. His eyes closed as another deep, quaking tremor ran through him. "Kolis… I know he scares you."

My breath caught as I dropped my hands to his chest. "He doesn't."

"Do not lie to me, Sera. Not now. Not about him." The tendrils of shadows arced. "I know what I felt from you when he had you. I choke on the taste of what you felt even now."

A part of me shriveled up right then because I didn't want to remember that he'd felt what I had. The fear. The panic. The desperation. And—

I stopped myself right before my lungs seized.

Ash's neck twisted like the Ancient's head had moved. Inhumanly. Otherworldly. The similarities between them and the Primals were uncanny. "*This*," Ash ground out, "is what I was talking about just minutes ago. You don't always have to be strong, Sera. And you *never* need to pretend with me."

"I'm not pretending."

"Do you think I don't know what you felt when you heard that Kolis had summoned you?" Ash demanded. "Do you really think I don't know what caused you to scream in the middle of the night? Do you?"

My body flashed cold and then hot as eather rose. I stepped back. "I am afraid of him. I'm fucking terrified of him and how he makes me feel like I have no control over anything. Okay? Does it make you happy to hear me say that?"

Ash flinched, the shadows stilling.

Shame scalded the back of my throat. I shouldn't have said that, but *fuck*. Now was not the time for this. "But I'm more terrified of losing you, and you know that is possible." I closed my eyes for a moment, then reopened them. "It hadn't occurred to me until Aydun spoke. Kolis's return as the true Primal of Death made you vulnerable. But I'm sure you were fully aware of that little fact."

Jaw working, he looked away.

"Yeah, you knew, and we're going to talk about that when I get back," I warned him. "Because I will be coming back, and I will probably be in a bad mood. So, be ready."

His head turned toward me. A moment passed, and then the smoky eather gathering around him collapsed into nothingness once more. "This isn't right."

"I know."

Ash held my stare, and then his mouth was on mine. His head tilted, and he parted my lips with a fierce stroke of his tongue. A desperate wildness claimed him. Us. We'd been here before. Too many times. So I recognized the madness in this kind of kiss. How it was a prayer and a curse. A promise and a release in a clash of teeth and tongues and searching lips. Desire flooded my senses. His. Mine. Pure, red-hot lust overwhelmed everything as his arm tightened around my waist. He lifted me onto the tips of my toes, and I could feel his hardness pressing against my belly. Desire pulsed through me, pooling between my thighs. I moaned into his kiss as I struggled to remember exactly what we were supposed to be doing at the moment. This wasn't it.

But damn, it felt so wrong to stop.

I wrenched my head away, panting. "We don't have time for this."

His pupils were visible now, but his eyes were no less bright. However, need fueled them now. "Fuck if we don't."

I gasped as Ash's hands went to the band of my leggings. He shoved them down, lacy undergarments and all. Somehow, he got one leg of the tight material over one boot.

"That was impressive," I murmured.

Rising, his lips curled into a shadowy, silky smile as he drew his hand up my leg, along my inner thigh. His mouth returned to mine, muffling my cry as his fingers delved between my thighs, parting the slick heat there. The contrast between my warmth and his coldness was startling.

Ash groaned into my mouth, and between his touch and that sound, I was undone. "Fuck it," I moaned. "We'll make time."

Gripping my hips, he lifted me. I wrapped my legs around his waist. His tongue danced with mine as he moved. My back hit the wall near the doors, as cold and hard as his body. I reached between us, grabbing the front of his breeches. Our hands fumbled until he grew frustrated and ripped the flap open. He shoved his pants down, and then he was filling me, inch by inch, his length and girth stretching me. The bite of pain was delicious, and we both shuddered.

There was nothing but an excess of pleasure and ecstasy, intensified by the deep, rumbling sounds he made as he thrust into me. Sinking my fingers into the soft strands of his hair, I reached up and clasped the shelf above me. Our mouths moved together, our tongues mirroring the pace of his hips. I thought I heard Nektas's deep voice, and then there was a sharp rap against the door.

"Five minutes are up," Aydun called out.

Holding me against the wall, Ash broke the kiss, his hips grinding against mine. "We're going to need—" His head fell back as I tightened on his cock. The tendons of his neck stood out starkly. "We need another minute."

"For fuck's sake, if they're—" His words cut off abruptly.

The inappropriateness of this. The ridiculousness. I bit down on my lip, but a short, high-pitched giggle snuck free.

Ash's head snapped forward, his veins pulsing with eather. "I love that sound." His hand curled around my chin as the fingers at my hip dug in. "I love your smiles. I love your throaty moans." His lips brushed mine. "I love how wet you are right now. And I especially love the way your pussy clamps down on my dick."

Another giggle parted my lips, and Ash captured the sound with his. Passion engulfed us, one not too different from what I'd felt when we were on the bank of my lake right before he took me into the water. I could feel my fangs throbbing. The desire for his blood rose, but that would require me to stop kissing him, and I couldn't even bear the thought.

This truly was madness.

And maybe how close we came to losing one another and what each of us was willing to do to keep the other safe was what drove us when Nektas and the Ancient waited only feet away. There was no way they didn't know what was happening, but in that minute, I didn't care. I was a fire in the flesh then, hungry for each thrust of his cock. Starving for him. He was greedy for each sweep of my tongue, each breath he tasted. He thrust hard and fast, and I met him just as fiercely.

And as the tension built and built until I didn't think I could exist for another second, and caught on that exquisite precipice, I knew that despite how treacherous our future would be, how uncertain everything was, one thing would remain constant. The tempest within us peaked, taking us both in the same heartbeat, and I knew there would always be us. Together. Always.

Ash's breathing was ragged as aftershocks of pleasure skittered through us. "*Liessa*," he rasped, pressing into me.

Several seconds passed—definitely more than a minute—but no sounds came from the hallway.

His forehead dropped against mine, and he swallowed hard. "He's going to ask about Sotoria."

"I know." I closed my eyes. "There's no way Kolis still believes I'm her. He would be dead if I was, and he knows that. He…" The look on his face as I drove the Ancient bone into him took shape.

"What?" Ash pressed quietly.

I shook my head. I couldn't say what I thought I'd seen in Kolis's expression. Resignation? Maybe even relief. It made me uncomfortable to even think about it. "He doesn't know where Sotoria's soul is."

"And we need to use that to our benefit. He needs to believe that it is still in you," he said, his body chilling against and inside mine. "Do and say whatever you need to convince him of such."

I kissed him, knowing how much it took for him to say that. I knew that taking what protection it offered me cut him up and would keep slicing at him. I hated this. All of it.

He gently separated our bodies and lowered me to the floor, ensuring I was steady before he pulled up his pants and then fixed mine. Neither of us spoke as he worked the legging up my leg and then straightened the dark gray blouse and vest I wore. When he was done, he smoothed the sides of my hair back, then tilted my chin until our eyes met.

Ash swept his thumb across my cheek. "Promise me," he said. "Promise me that whatever Kolis says or does, you won't let it leave a mark."

"I promise."

Splitting open the realm to travel from one location to another in a matter of seconds was what Ash had done in the past. It was a form of shadowstepping that only Primals and the oldest gods were capable of. And, of course, the Ancients. I just hadn't realized that was what Ash had been doing. I'd always closed my eyes, and even if I had kept them open, I probably wouldn't have been able to see past the whirling shadows.

I didn't close my eyes when the Ancient took my hand and the very fabric of the realm peeled back, revealing the shimmering, golden cluster of trees just beyond the City of the Gods and Cor Palace.

The very trees that Aios had created with her touch.

Glancing up at the graceful, sweeping branches and the glistening, fan-shaped leaves, I wondered if she would grow them in the Shadowlands now. I hoped so. They were beautiful, and I would never expect Aios to step foot in Dalos again.

Lowering my gaze, I peered through the sun-dappled trees. Nighttime had already come to pass between the time I'd been here and now. The air was still balmy, but it smelled even more of stale lilacs.

Of Death.

My lip curled as I shut down my emotions, locking them away. I didn't don the veil of nothingness, though. I would never do that again. I just became another part of who I was. A colder, calmer version of me.

"Let's get this over with." I started walking forward, my steps making no sound.

"Seraphena."

I stopped.

"We need to speak first."

I counted to five, though not because I was anxious. I wasn't walking out of these trees as I had the first time. I was irritated with the delay. "I don't want to linger." I faced the Ancient. "I need to return to the Shadowlands as soon as possible."

"Before your husband does something he'll regret?"

Well, yeah, that was the number-two reason. I doubted he'd left for Vathi, and the longer I was here, the more likely it was that he'd do something. But the number-one reason? "I didn't have such a great experience the last time I was in Dalos. I don't want to spend a moment longer here than necessary."

There it was again. A barely noticeable flinch in the skin around his eyes. "Nor do I."

"Then get on with it," I said before I could remind myself exactly what I was speaking to. "And I mean that in the most respectful way possible."

His lips curved slightly. "Holland warned me about you."

I stiffened, unsure how to respond. I had no idea if all the Ancients knew about his involvement or that thin, gray line Holland often walked.

"He warned me that you could have an…assertive personality," he continued. "I believe he said, 'aggressively assertive.'"

I winced. "I can't exactly deny that."

Aydun eyed me. "I'm not sure Holland knows you as well as he thinks he does, though. I expected more of a fight from you than Nyktos. He's always been calm. Practical. You, on the other hand…" Another emotionless, tight smile appeared. "But that is what emotion does."

"I disagree with that."

"Of course, you do. You were once mortal. That is not a part of you that you can carve out." He said it like he pitied me. "But you calmed quicker than Nyktos did. You understood. I didn't expect that."

I frowned. "Exactly what *did* Holland tell you?"

"Enough."

Shaking my head, I pushed my hair back. "I think the truth is that I didn't really know Holland."

"You know him better than most."

Then why isn't he the one here? I didn't ask that. It felt like it revealed too much. "His eyes looked nothing like yours."

"That's because your mind was incapable of seeing him for what he was," he explained as my brows inched up my forehead. "Only the true Primal of Life and the true Primal of Death possess the knowledge to see a Fate for what we are."

The fact that we could see them as they were because we knew what they were…kind of made sense. "I don't think you wanted to talk to me about Holland."

"No." He came forward, his feet gliding *over* the grass and mossy rock. "I have seen all the possible tomorrows. Some will surely come, and others are still unwritten. There are so many possibilities."

I dragged my gaze to his. The blue swirled into the green of his eyes. "Okay?"

"So many small choices can alter the outcome, as you are already well aware," he said, and my skin pimpled. "Something small and insignificant can change the course of the realms. That is why the future is never fully written."

I nodded slowly. "Pretty sure I've heard this before, so—"

"But there are possibilities that become events written in the essence of the realms," he said, his voice lowering as my breath snagged. "A series of steps and choices that will inevitably lead to only one outcome." The brown sliced through the blue as the stars grew in his eyes. "If war breaks out among the Primals, the balance will be unsettled in ways that will have dire consequences." The stars in his eyes brightened until they were almost painful to look at. "My brethren who went to ground will be disturbed."

A chill swept down my spine despite the humid wind. "They will awaken?"

"Consciousness will return to the oldest and strongest of them. That is no small step, but one of many that will lead to their Awakening." His head tilted. "Just as Kolis's betrayal of his brother was a step. What Eythos did altered it, but it was another step. The blood you took from Nyktos was one more."

I drew back, my skin warming. "I didn't realize Ancients were such…lurkers."

"There is a lot you don't realize."

Impatience snapped at me. "Why do I have a feeling you won't fill me in on all those things?"

"Balance," he purred. "But what I can tell you is that some things are inevitable. Eythos saw this, and he had a plan."

I crossed my arms. "And what a great plan that turned out to be."

"And you have a plan."

I laughed then, the sound biting. "I'm not sure what plan you think I have beyond figuring out a way to get rid of Kolis—"

"It's more than just him," he cut in. "Trust your instincts."

"You mean the *vadentia*?"

"I mean…" he said, pressing a finger to my chest, just below my collarbone.

I swatted his hand away. I couldn't have stopped myself from doing it even if I'd wanted to.

He was unfazed. "*Your* instincts."

"All right," I said, staring at him. I supposed he was talking about my gut instincts. "Thanks for…whatever this was."

The churning colors in his eyes slowed. "Preventing this war was a thread not seen, but neither were you originally. Do you understand what that means?"

I looked around at the trees Aios had created as if they held the answers. They didn't.

"You are what has been snipping those threads—ending some and weaving new ones. Trust your instincts," he said. "For if what comes from this meeting is war, it will not end, not until there is blood and bone."

Aydun's confusing warning haunted the back of my thoughts, but there wasn't time to really dwell on it. He took my hand once more and shadowstepped us smack-dab into the front courtyard of Cor Palace.

"A heads-up next time would be nice," I muttered, pressing a hand to my roiling stomach as the eather throbbed, alerting me to another Primal.

Aydun arched a brow. "I'll take that into consideration."

Not for one second did I believe him as I looked up. Four staggered crystal towers rose from the center of the palace. Cracks in the crystal fractured the sunlight. My gaze lowered to the diamond-encrusted stone fortress. Large and slimmer fissures ran the length of the columns and the walls behind them.

Someone must've done some housekeeping. There weren't bodies staked to the walls of the fortress or hanging from the trees this time. If there had been, there was a good chance I might've vomited all over the Ancient.

"You okay?" Aydun asked, glancing at my hand.

"Shadowstepping sometimes makes me nauseous." I dropped my arm. "This whole place nauseates me."

His left eye narrowed slightly, then the other side of his mouth curved up. "Interesting."

I shot him a look. The Ancient was…an odd one. I started for the colonnade steps.

"We must wait," Aydun stated. "To be allowed in."

Stopping, I blew out an aggravated breath. "And how long are we to wait?"

"As long as it takes for someone to receive us."

A low, rough laugh escaped me. "Oh, I know exactly what Kolis is doing."

"Hmm?"

"By making me wait outside, he's making it known that he doesn't consider me his equal," I bit out. "My mother used to do that when nobles she wasn't fond of from other kingdoms visited."

"Your mother sounds like a lovely person."

I snorted.

"Does this reception surprise you?"

"No." Temper rising, I crossed my arms before I used them to do something that would change Aydun's mind on who was the calmer one between Ash and me. There were no guards on the colonnade, but there hadn't been before. I looked over my shoulder, but the purplish-pink tops of the trees blocked my view of the Rise around Dalos. With everything that had happened, one would think the place would be teeming with guards.

It was kind of insulting that it wasn't.

"It shouldn't take long," Aydun said.

"Yeah, well, I'm not a patient person."

"It's something you will eventually learn to be," he replied.

I turned halfway to him. "Exactly how old are you?"

Aydun's head tilted sideways as his forehead creased. "How long has this realm existed?"

I frowned. "I have no idea."

"Neither do I." He shrugged. "But I'm that old."

My mouth dropped open. "Gods, you're even older than Nektas."

"All of us are," he stated.

I jerked, unable to even think of Holland as being that old. My brain simply couldn't process that as I turned back to the gold-trimmed doors. I shifted my weight back and forth from one foot to the other, wishing I had some sort of weapon on me.

Then I remembered. I did.

The eather.

I rolled my eyes at myself.

"Are you…dancing with yourself?" Aydun asked.

"I'm not dancing, you—" Eather throbbed intensely before fading out, warning me. I inhaled sharply. "Another Primal has arrived."

"They have."

I spun toward the Ancient. "I was unaware of other Primals being here."

Aydun plucked off a wilted leaf that had landed on his shoulder. "Only Nyktos was prohibited from attending."

"That's bullshit," I hissed, the wind picking up.

His eyes flashed to mine. "The summoner sets—"

"The rules. I heard you the first time." I turned back to the still-closed doors, not liking this one bit. Any number of Primals could've just arrived. My mind flashed to Kyn, then Veses, and the essence stirred wildly inside me. "What are the rules regarding the other Primals and fighting?"

"There can be no violence of any kind among the Primals." He came to stand beside me. "You have nothing to worry about."

"I'm not worried." I stared at those doors. "I'm disappointed."

His head swung toward me.

Fuck it.

I climbed the steps and crossed between two columns.

"What are you doing, Seraphena?"

"I'm not waiting." Focusing on the doors, I summoned the eather. The gold-plated doors swung open, slamming into the walls with a crash as they snapped off their top hinges. "Oops."

Aydun sighed.

Smiling a little, I strode into the palace. We hadn't entered this way when Ash and I came before. Attes had led us past some bungalows and brought us into the hall that led to the atrium, where I assumed Kolis would be. I glanced at the gold-cushioned settees lining the walls of the entryway. The foyer split into two wings.

I turned left. There really wasn't a reason for my choice, so I hoped it was the *vadentia* leading the way.

"We really should wait," Aydun suggested, following me.

"We've waited long enough." I entered a hall, passing several closed doors on one side and windows facing a courtyard on the other. Two doors were at the end of the hall. Of course, they were gold-plated, as were the ceiling and the wall sconces, the handles on the doors, and the windowsill trim. Gold veining even streaked through the marble floors.

Kolis was so fucking tacky.

"We waited a few minutes," Aydun pointed out.

"As I said, we waited…" I paused, sensing something…off. My steps slowed as my skin prickled. It was almost like what I'd felt right before the Ancient appeared, except this felt…*wrong*. Sacrilegious, even. Almost as if I had entered a Temple and cursed the god it served. My eyes narrowed on the doors ahead.

I didn't hear footsteps, but I knew something was near, and I was right.

The gold-plated doors swung open, and all I saw was gold—gold clothing, gold-painted wings, and golden hair.

My lip curled as a mixture of anger and unwanted empathy rose. "Well, now I know why I suddenly felt something profane."

Callum halted ahead of me, the painted wings on his face twitching a second before his expression smoothed into a smile as well-practiced as Kolis's. I didn't like the Revenant for a whole slew of reasons. The feelings were mutual, but what wasn't was the sorrow I couldn't help but feel for him. Sotoria's brother was a tragedy.

"Seraphena," he said, his tone level. Courteous, even. "I see you are as charming as ever." His eyes, which were such a pale shade of blue they were almost lifeless, drifted over me. "And as inappropriate."

"How so?"

"You're dressed worse than a common tavern wench and not fit to meet with the King," he replied. "And you were supposed to wait outside."

"Two things." I quickly glanced at the sheath and the golden hilt of the dagger on his left arm as I held up two fingers. "I got tired of waiting." I lowered my pointer finger, leaving the middle one still raised. "And I'm meeting no King today."

Callum's mouth tightened. "Charming."

I turned my hand around so my middle finger faced him.

"Very charming." He clasped his hands behind him. "But not as much as the last time I saw you. How are your arms feeling?"

Muscles throughout tensed. "Perfect." I smiled. "How is Kolis feeling? Last I saw, he had a few extra holes in him."

Callum tilted his head. "You will see for yourself soon enough." He stepped to the side and turned as he said, "Come."

I kept smiling, even though it hurt my face as I followed Callum through the doors, making sure I walked on his left side. We entered a wider hall lined with marble statues of… I saw a chiseled jaw and features similar to Ash's. "Kolis has statues of himself as decoration?"

"Of course he does." Callum stared ahead. "He is the King."

"Of tackiness?"

"And what are you the Queen of?" Callum responded, his chin tipping up a notch. "The Queen of Nothing? No, that doesn't sound right. How about the Queen of Lies?"

"To be honest, Queen of Lies has a nice ring to it." On my other side, Aydun frowned. "I kind of like it."

"You would." Callum's steps slowed as the hall curved. "I knew you were lying the whole time."

I said nothing as we passed more statues of Kolis.

"My sister…" His chest rose with a deep breath as stale air flowed in through an open window. "She had everything you will never have, starting with class."

"And yet, Kolis sought to dress her in a manner that exposed every part of her body?" I replied. "So classy."

Callum's jaw flexed. "Perhaps, deep down, he knew the truth."

"Ah, yes. That's exactly why." Anger pulsed. "He would never treat her that way. Never mind the fact that he sought to hold her captive *again* and force himself upon her."

Aydun's brows rose.

"You have no idea what you're talking about," Callum shot back, the veneer of civility cracking.

Just like before, disbelief rose. "I will never understand how you can justify Kolis's actions toward someone you clearly loved."

Callum went quiet.

"Then again, I will never understand how you can stand by while Kolis collects his favorites in an attempt to replace her, either."

"They were all sad attempts. Especially you. You were the saddest of them all." Callum's smile was sharper as he glanced at me. "Guess what I heard?" His voice lowered as if he were sharing a juicy secret. "Kolis is already building another cage."

My skin heated from the inside.

Callum chuckled as a rounded archway appeared, leading to a hall I recognized as the one we'd entered before. "Wonder who he plans to put in this one. You?"

My fingers twitched.

"Perhaps his nephew. Yes, it will likely be Nyktos." Callum nodded. "We know what will happen to you." He winked. "It's all Kyn can talk about."

The control I had on my temper snapped as we passed another fucking statue of Kolis. I pictured it doing exactly what I wanted to do to Callum and Kyn.

The statue shattered with a clap of thunder. Callum jumped as the Ancient jerked to a stop.

Slowly, both turned to look at me. "What?"

"You know what?" Callum spat. "That was disrespectful."

"Was it?" I angled my body toward Callum's.

"It was." A faint glow of eather appeared behind his pupils. "But not nearly as disrespectful as lying about Sotoria."

"Did I lie?"

"You're really going to try that route again?" Callum laughed. "It won't protect you."

I met his stare as my muscles loosened. "It wasn't your fault, you know. What happened to Sotoria was Kolis's fault and his alone. I wish you knew that. You likely would've led a normal life and passed on to the Vale. But everything done to her beyond that? You're just as complicit." I lowered my voice as he had. "And she feels the same as I do when it comes to you. She feels sorry for you, but she really fucking hates you."

Callum jerked his head back as if my words were a slap.

"That rule you spoke of," I said to the Ancient. "Does it apply to everyone?"

Aydun's lips actually curved up. "No, it does not."

"Good." I snapped forward, wrapping my hands around the grip of Callum's dagger.

His eyes widened as he twisted, grabbing for me, but I was faster than he was even *before* I Ascended.

And I was way faster now.

I yanked the dagger free and grabbed a fistful of his hair, jerking his head back so I could thrust the shadowstone blade through the underside of his jaw.

Callum was dead before I even tore the blade free.

"Gods," I said, watching him hit the floor like a sack of potatoes. "That felt good."

"What a strange thing for the true Primal of Life to say," Aydun stated dryly, glancing down at the crumpled form. An eyebrow rose. "And do."

"He had it coming." Kneeling, I quickly wiped the blade clean on his tunic. "And he'll come back."

"Unfortunately."

I looked at him as I rose. "Do the Ancients not approve of Kolis's creations?"

Aydun glanced down at the Revenant. "It's kept the balance."

I shoved the dagger into the back of my pants in case I needed it. "That's not an answer."

His gaze met mine. "What has kept the balance is a mockery of life. Reanimated flesh and bone and little else. This one is something more."

Yeah, he was.

I glanced through the door, past the shadowy alcoves to the golden curtains at the end of the hall. "What of the Ascended?"

"They are only a slight improvement," he answered. "They have souls."

My gaze flew back to his. I wasn't expecting him to say that.

"But neither were enough to keep the balance once you were born," he continued. "If you had died during your Ascension, taking the last true embers of life with you, what Nyktos saw in his vision would've come to fruition."

A chill broke out across my skin.

"He would've caused the Ancients in all the lands, both here and beyond the Primal Veil, to awaken," Aydun said. "Between him, his father, and his uncle, Nyktos is the one who came the closest to destroying the realms."

I stiffened. "But he didn't."

"He *could* have."

"He did what he did because he loves me," I insisted, anger rising once more.

"Selfishly," the Ancient tacked on. "He loves you *selfishly*, therefore risking the lives of nearly all who walk these realms." Stars burned in his eyes. "We got to where we are today because of another who loved so selfishly."

I stepped toward the Ancient without thinking. "Do not *ever* compare him to Kolis."

"I am not comparing them," he replied, utterly unbothered by my fury. "I'm pointing out what that kind of love is capable of."

"How…how can someone so old be so wrong?" I said, shaking my head. "What you're trying to compare? What Ash and I feel for one another and what Kolis felt for Sotoria? They are two very different things."

Aydun frowned, his head cocking. "How so?"

"What Kolis feels for Sotoria is an obsession."

"And there is a difference?" Curiosity filled his tone.

I stared at him, my mouth slightly agape. "How am I once again explaining what love is to a man who is fucking old enough to know better?"

Aydun looked even more confused.

"My gods," I muttered, searching for the kind of patience Ash had. "The difference is that I feel the same way for Nyktos as he does for me. Yeah, maybe he's obsessed with me, but I am also obsessed with him. It's consensual. Mutual. What *that* is?" I jabbed a finger in the direction of the golden curtains. "Is one-sided and twisted. Rot not much different than what affected my homeland. It's ugly. What Kolis feels *is* selfish, and I know firsthand just how *wrong* what he feels is." I stepped back, my throat thickening. "What Nyktos feels for me? It's beautiful. A miracle. It's…it's *hope*." I blinked tears from my eyes. "And I'm truly sorry that there are people, be them Ancients, gods, or mortals, who don't know there is a difference."

Aydun stared at me as I had done with him seconds ago, looking completely flummoxed.

And I didn't have the time or the desire to explain further.

Checking my emotions, I turned and entered the hall, glancing at one of the alcoves. No soft moans or deep groans came from them today, but a low hum of conversation drifted out from the chamber ahead, as did the sounds I expected to hear from the alcoves. My jaw clenched as my attention shifted there when the thud of awareness in my chest increased. The shadowstone dagger I'd helped myself to provided more comfort than the Primal essence did. Right or wrong, I was far more used to wielding a blade than eather. Maybe that would change someday, but for now, the feeling of the hilt digging into my back gave me strength as I pushed the curtains aside and stepped inside the wide, circular chamber. I came to a complete stop. It wasn't the Primal present that halted me, even though I should be focused on him.

It was the source of the raspy moans and groans.

My skin prickled as my gaze swept over the gold-painted ceiling, past the armored guards lining the walls, to the deep couches and settees sitting in front of the curtained windows of the atrium. They were mostly empty, except for a handful near the raised, columned dais framed by two closed archways. There weren't just gods on those couches with their faces buried in necks or between thighs.

My eyes locked with ones that had been warm brown but were now pitch-black with only a flicker of light deep within them. Gods, I recognized the fine features forever frozen in youth.

It was the Chosen I'd seen Kolis turn. Jove.

Aydun nearly walked into me as he entered the chamber, but I couldn't pull my eyes from Jove as my heart thumped.

What had Gemma said about the Chosen who disappeared? Some returned as something else—a cold creature never seen in the daylight.

The Ancient had said the Ascended had souls, but the eyes latched onto mine appeared vacant of such.

Jove's eyes closed as he drank deeply from a god's throat. The god's head fell back with a heavy, guttural moan echoed by another—a female goddess half-sprawled on the couch beside them, her golden gown hiked up to her waist. A pale head was nestled between her thighs.

I couldn't believe Jove was here. Not much time had passed since he'd been turned, and Kolis had made it sound like it could possibly take months for the Ascended to learn how to control their bloodlust and be trusted.

But maybe that wasn't the same for all of them, especially if they did have souls. That meant some small part of who they were before remained inside them. Perhaps how strong that part was determined how long it took them to control themselves.

"*Meyaah por-na*," rumbled a deep voice.

Violent energy pulsed within me as I pulled my gaze from the feeding and found the Primal of Peace and Vengeance. I understood what the bastard had said.

My whore.

Kyn was seated at a settee to the right of the dais and the gaudy, gilt and diamond throne, a woman draped in gold and ivory perched on his lap—one whose hair was a light shade of blond nearly as pale as mine. Static rippled down my arms, causing my fingers to twitch.

Kyn smiled at me, flashing long, sharp fangs. Two dimples appeared on his cheeks. "Show me the respect I'm due," he said, slipping his hand between the slit in the woman's gown. "And get on your knees."

A light, airy chuckle came from one of the other couches. Anger and disgust crashed together as I held Kyn's stare. I wanted nothing more than to lash out like I had with Callum, throwing the dagger at that smirk on his face.

I looked away from him and glanced at the large, prowling wolf carved into the floor, so similar to the one on the throne room doors in the House of Haides. It was their family crest, created by Eythos and Kolis's father.

"Did you not hear me, *por-na*?" Kyn's palm ran up the inside of the woman's leg. "On your knees."

I had no idea how Ash had maintained his composure among such a disgusting asshole like Kyn for years—decades—but he had.

And I would, too.

Sort of.

I smiled at Kyn. "Make me."

Aydun stiffened.

The hand delving under the skirt froze. Silence came from those on the couches.

Kyn's laugh was full of malice. "Oh, I plan to."

The Primal reminded me so much of the Lords of the Vodina Isles, and my smile grew. "I can't wait to see you try."

"You think Nyktos will be able to stop me?"

"He won't need to," I told him. "Because I will."

The air shifted, thickening as streaks of eather pierced Kyn's stare. The woman in his lap paled. She looked like she didn't dare breathe too deeply.

"Remember the rules." Aydun spoke up finally. "They do apply to other Primals. There will be no fighting."

"Lucky for you," I said to Kyn.

Aydun's head whipped toward me, a warning look in his glare. I ignored it, raising my brows at the Primal.

A muscle ticked in Kyn's jaw. Seconds passed with no further comment. Letting out a low laugh, I looked away, giving the guards a scan. Some of them were gods. A few had those pale, lifeless eyes.

Awareness throbbed through my body. A draken was near. More than one.

"Where is Kolis?" Aydun asked.

Kyn lifted a shoulder as his hand moved between the woman's legs. "He'll be here." His gaze shifted to me. "Why don't you come over and sit on my other leg?"

I wouldn't even dignify that with a response, but the Ancient examined the Primal with naked distaste.

"You created them," I muttered under my breath to the Ancient. "Well, you created his parents."

Aydun sneered. "I am not responsible for the bloodline that created that…creature."

I glanced back at Kyn. He stuck out his tongue, wiggling it in my direction. "Who did you create?"

"That is none of your business."

"Okay, then." I sighed.

"There's enough room for both of you," Kyn called out, and the woman giggled nervously. "And I've got two hands and a tongue."

"But no cock? Shocking," I retorted.

"You'll need to earn that, *por-na*." Kyn nipped at the woman's throat, and she gave another strained laugh.

I focused on the woman. I saw a faint glint of eather in her eyes before her lashes swept down. She was a godling. I had no idea how she'd ended up in Dalos, but I had a sinking suspicion that she wasn't from Vathi and also wasn't exactly thrilled to be where she was.

I thought of Evander and Jacinta. I'd read that situation wrong and killed an innocent god. This could very well be the same thing.

But…

But how much control did this woman even have? Like with the Chosen? Kolis gave them a choice, but what kind of choice was it at the end of the day? What kind of choice did this woman have with such an imbalance of power between her and Kyn?

Footsteps behind me drew my gaze. A bare-chested draken with long, wavy blond hair strode in. "I knew you'd arrived," Diaval said, "when I found him picking himself up off the floor."

Callum followed, his lips pressed together. He stopped beside me. Not close, though. He gave me a wide berth. "Give me back my dagger."

"No," I said, my attention moving to Diaval. The draken had dropped onto one of the couches, distracted by the Ascended feeding beside him. Or fucking. Man, that had escalated.

Callum crossed his arms like a petulant child as another draken walked in, one with light brown skin and dark, braided hair. Sax. I watched him walk to stand near Diaval, remembering what Ash had said. This had been one of his father's draken.

Did that mean…?

"You're a liar and a thief," Callum said.

"And the true Primal of Life," I replied. "Whose temper is currently worsening by the second. So how about you shut the fuck up?"

The Revenant turned his head to me. "Rude."

I moved to put Callum on the floor again, but a soft cry from the woman in Kyn's lap stopped me. Her eyes were squeezed shut, and her brow was tensed in pain. Kyn wasn't feeding. He was still staring at me with the fucking idiotic smirk on his face. My gaze dropped to where his hand was. He was hurting her.

I moved before I realized what I was doing.

"Seraphena," snapped Aydun.

I crossed the atrium. The woman's eyes had opened, and her lashes were wet as she ducked her chin.

Kyn's smile grew. "You changed your mind?"

I stopped in front of them, taking hold of the woman's chin. She gasped, her gaze flying to mine, and I knew. Perhaps it was because the *vadentia* was already growing stronger, or maybe it was just normal instinct. Either way, I *knew* the moment her eyes locked with mine.

I dropped her chin and then took her hand. It was limp in my grasp for only a heartbeat, then it firmed. I pulled her from Kyn's lap.

"Return to your home," I told her. "Now."

The godling didn't hesitate. She scurried across the chamber, and I hoped she listened to me and fled Dalos.

Kyn, the fucker, adjusted his crotch as he leaned back. "And here I thought I'd have to break you in." He patted a knee. "But don't be *too* willing. That takes the fun out of it."

It took everything in me to step back and not rip his dick off and shove it down his throat. It took everything and even more to turn away.

"Don't turn your back on me, *por-na*." The air stirred as Kyn shot to his feet.

I kept walking.

"You fucking bitch," Kyn snarled.

I couldn't see him, but I felt him grab for me. I spun back, but Kyn was faster. He caught my forearm, and his grip was cruel. The contact of his flesh against mine was worse than the pain, though. It turned my stomach with disgust.

Kyn said something repulsive about how he'd make Ash watch while he committed some hideous act of defilement, but I barely heard him. Eather-rich blood pounded in my ears as I lifted my gaze from his white-knuckled grip on my arm and met his.

Fuck the rules.

I smiled as the eather rose. Silvery light crept through the corners of my eyes as wisps of gold-laced eather seeped from my skin.

Kyn dropped my arm, jerking his hand back with a hiss of pain. Smoke wafted from his fingers, and the scent of charred flesh rose. His irises disappeared in a flash of silvery eather. "You fucking—"

"Enough!" Aydun threw out his hand.

Kyn's eyes widened, and then the space before me was empty.

What the…?

Kyn had simply been there one second and gone the next.

Confused, I looked around the chamber as the eather settled. I didn't see him anywhere. I turned back to the Ancient. "Um…"

"I put him in a time-out," Aydun bit out.

I blinked. "Would've been great if you'd done that earlier, like when…" I trailed off as the center of my chest throbbed intensely.

A sensation akin to thick oil coated my skin. The tiny hairs on the nape of my neck rose as eather stirred restlessly, pressing against my skin. I turned to the dais as Callum strode past me.

The true Primal of Death was here.

I was suddenly rooted to where I stood as the gold banners hanging between the two doors framing the back of the dais wall parted.

Guards in gold armor lined both sides of the wide hall I hadn't known was even there. They turned in unison, facing one another as they lifted gleaming swords to create an arch.

"Bow," Callum announced from the dais, his voice loud and chin held high. "Bow for the Great Protector, the Keeper of Common Men, and the Warden of the Gods. The true King of Men and Gods."

That was *not* his title. That belonged to Ash. These were just words strung together to inflate an already oversized ego, and it sounded ridiculous to me. Protector? Warden? It had to be a joke. A laugh bubbled up in my throat, but it didn't escape my lips as Kolis appeared in the hall and those throughout the atrium, even the Ascended, who had been feeding and otherwise engaged, stopped what they were doing and knelt. None of them had even stopped to fix their clothing.

Everyone except for the Ancient.

And me.

The swords swept down as Kolis passed beneath them, the top of his flaxen head nearly touching the ceiling—a head that bore no crown.

I didn't know what I felt as I watched him cross the dais, but he didn't look well.

Kolis was undeniably a beautiful man with his shaggy blond hair, cut jaw, and angular cheeks. He still was. But he appeared as a ghost of his former self. Thinner. Less…*shiny*. Dark shadows shaded the skin beneath his eyes and cheekbones. The Primal was still weakened.

That wasn't the only thing.

There was no hint of golden life in him now—no flecks of gold in his eyes or beneath his skin. Instead, there were slivers of deep, dark red in his silver eyes and churning slowly beneath his flesh. He even wore the true shade of death. Crimson.

The color of blood.

Kolis smiled down at me with one of those well-practiced, fake smiles that never ceased to make my skin crawl.

I didn't flinch, but I could *feel* his touch. I didn't wince, but I could *feel* the scrape of his fangs against my throat. I didn't move an inch, but I could *feel* his arms around me, his embrace too tight. At that very moment, I knew exactly what I felt. It wasn't nothing. It was a ruinous *everything*. I had to check myself again. I had to shut all of it down. No fear. No panic. No fury. And I did. I pushed it all down until I felt nothing but a simmering rage.

Until I could return his smile. "You look like shit," I said. "I'm guessing I woke you too early from stasis." My smile, just as skilled and fake as his, grew. "My apologies."

Behind me, the Ancient cursed under his breath, and the atrium went utterly silent.

Kolis's smile faltered. "And yet, you look extraordinarily well." His gaze moved to those kneeling. "Leave."

The Ascended and the various gods hurried from the space. The guards in the atrium and the hall, the draken, and Callum remained.

"You, too," Kolis said to the guards, then the draken. "Go."

Diaval grumbled as he rose. "And here I thought I would have some entertainment today."

As the heavy curtains along the back wall behind the dais swung shut, Sax followed the alabaster draken, his gaze briefly meeting mine before he quietly left. Then, it was just Callum, the Ancient, this fucker, and me.

Kolis turned his back on me, though. He slowly walked to the throne and lowered himself into the seat, his hands settling on the arms of the chair.

Silence stretched as the seconds ticked by, and for some damn reason, an image of him flashed in my mind when he lay sprawled on the floor with a look of…*relief* in his features.

Remembering that caused my stomach to clench and my non-existent patience to rear its head. "You wanted to talk," I said. "I'm here. So, talk."

Callum hissed. "Do not speak to the King—"

Kolis raised his hand, silencing the Revenant in an instant. And, gods, I wished I had that ability when it came to Callum.

"I did summon you here." Strands of blond hair fell against his jaw as he tilted his head. I didn't think the Primal had blinked once since he'd walked in. "You shouldn't have Ascended."

I said nothing.

"Which means you lied about Nyktos's *kardia*."

"I told the truth about his *kardia*," I said.

"And you continue to lie even now?" A half-grin appeared. It lacked the effort of making it look even somewhat real. "He risked dooming the realms to Ascend you. Only one in love would do such a thing, and one cannot be in love without a *kardia*, unless…" His chest rose with a sharp breath as his regard shifted to the Ancient. "Mates of the heart. Interesting."

Pettiness was the next to rear its head. I wanted to throw it in his face but speaking about something so beautiful and using it against someone like Kolis felt wrong. As if it would taint Ash and me. "I don't think that's what you wanted to discuss."

"No. It isn't." His fingers tightened around the arm of the throne as his focus returned to me. He fell silent again.

My hands fisted at my sides. "I assume you summoned me here so you can demand that I denounce any claim to the Throne of the Gods and pledge allegiance to you."

Kolis chuckled softly, the sound making my skin crawl. "I imagined you would demand something similar of me, except asking for me to return to my rightful place in the Shadowlands."

I said nothing because we did not even remotely plan to allow that.

"I have no intention of doing that," Kolis continued.

Catching the smile on Callum's face, I said, "Not a part of me is surprised to hear that."

"Then where does that leave us, Seraphena?" Kolis asked. "At war?"

My heart kicked against my chest as the Ancient stiffened beside me. "You don't want war."

Kolis was quiet yet again. Too quiet.

My heart started pounding faster. "Because you know what can happen if it comes to that." I jerked my chin at Aydun. "There will be no winners."

"Not necessarily true," he replied. "As long as the embers of life and death remain, there will be balance."

"But a war will disturb those who have gone to ground." I looked at Aydun for him to back me up, but the Ancient was frustratingly quiet.

"Perhaps." Kolis shifted on the throne. A moment passed, then another. The muscle by his temple ticked. "You do look like her."

I went rigid.

Wistfulness flashed across his features, causing my skin to crawl. "I can see parts of her in you, even now."

"But she is not her, Your Majesty," Callum interjected.

"I know." The skin over the knuckles of his left hand thinned, revealing a hint of crimson underneath. "But she was in there. Her soul, that is."

I showed nothing, even as unease festered.

"That's what my brother did, right? He placed her soul with the embers into your bloodline? But I imagine he intended for you to be reborn as Sotoria. That didn't happen. But her soul *was* in you."

"Her soul is where you cannot reach it," I said. "In me."

My lie was smooth enough that Callum stepped back, bumping into the dais.

Kolis's chin lowered as the shards of red grew in his eyes. "You took the Star diamond. I imagine my brother's soul was released, and that is where you have placed hers."

Fuck.

"We released Eythos's soul and then destroyed The Star." My thoughts raced. I had no idea if the diamond could be destroyed, but I remembered how it had been created. "Nektas did."

"Lies." Kolis laughed. "If you weren't clever enough to discover the importance of The Star, my nephew is. You have her soul in that diamond."

Fuck.

I could see I wouldn't be able to convince him otherwise. Which meant that any protection I may have gotten from Kolis believing that Sotoria was still inside me was gone.

Kolis's grip on the throne's gold arms eased. "I brought you here to make a deal, Seraphena."

Aydun stepped forward but remained silent. I imagined he wasn't supposed to speak. However, he was clearly interested in what Kolis had to say.

A small part of me was, too, but I doubted the deal would be anything but sadistic.

"You have nothing to say to that?" Kolis asked.

"Nope."

His nostrils flared, but only for a moment before his expression smoothed out. "I will not punish you or my nephew for what you have done."

"What we've done?" A wave of disbelief surged through my voice. "You held me against my will. You imprisoned Nyktos—"

"I imprisoned my nephew for attacking me and killing another Primal," he said. "And you claimed to want to be at my side. It is not my fault that I believed you."

I snapped my mouth shut.

"You manipulated me," he accused. "Likely believing that, with her soul inside you, you would be able to kill me."

Well, he was wrong about that. I knew I wouldn't be able to kill him when I attacked him. I just wanted to make him bleed.

"Thank the Fates you were wrong," he said, and my eyes nearly rolled out of the back of my head. "But as I was saying, I will not seek to punish you or my nephew. Those who conspired with you, however, *will* need to be punished. They cannot go without justice."

As if he knew anything about justice.

"But you may live out your *existence* as *a* Primal of Life*,"* he sneered, "with my nephew. Ensuring the balance remains."

I glanced at Callum. He showed no reaction to that as I'd expected. He had been all about Kolis taking the embers from me. Had he been telling the truth when he said his concern was for the balance?

"The realms will continue on as they have, except it will be under the rule of the Primal of Death as the King," Kolis said.

My mouth dropped open. "The Primal of Death has never ruled."

"Nor has a Queen," he replied.

Well, fuck me, he had me there.

His smile then was a little more real. "All you have to do is give me what I want."

Ice sloshed in my blood. He could not be serious, but he was. "Sotoria's soul?"

Kolis nodded. "Bring me The Star." He leaned forward. "That is all you have to do to prevent a war."

For a moment, all I could do was stand there while Aydun faced me as if imploring me to remember what he'd said under the trees. I hadn't forgotten. He'd told me that a war wouldn't be won until there was blood and bone. And while that made next to no sense to me, he had said that I needed to trust my instincts. He could've been talking about how far I believed Kolis would go. Or maybe he meant how I felt regarding using Sotoria's soul. How uncomfortable I was with the idea.

But what the Ancient had said or even how I felt about using her soul didn't matter. Giving Sotoria over to Kolis sickened me. He would have her reborn and would watch her grow—

Gods, I couldn't even finish that line of thought.

But was one soul—one life—worth hundreds? Thousands? My heart pounded erratically as I stood there.

My mouth dried. "And why should I believe you won't go back on this deal the moment you have what you want?"

"A deal is an oath. One that cannot be broken," Aydun advised me. "Doing so would force the realm to rectify."

That wasn't much of a reassurance considering Kolis had repeatedly done things that had to be rectified.

But I…gods, I could not do that to Sotoria. I couldn't do that to anyone.

"What is your offer?" Aydun prodded.

"What?" I breathed.

"He has offered a deal," the Ancient said. "You now must offer him one."

I inhaled sharply as I glanced between him and Kolis. Panic began to seed itself. Ash and I hadn't discussed this. We hadn't even considered it. Why hadn't Aydun mentioned this? Given me some time to come up with something. He had to have known this was possible.

It didn't matter. I had told Ash that I didn't want to make decisions without him. We were a team. I lifted my chin. "I need to discuss this with my King first."

"Your King?" Kolis laughed. "You are speaking to your King now."

My lip curled. "No, my King is Nyktos."

Kolis arched a brow. "I recognize no such thing. If you want to counter with a deal, you will do that now."

"Such deals are only made between the true Primal of Life and the true Primal of Death," Aydun stated. "You must offer one now."

Fuck. Fuck. *Fuck*.

"I'm waiting," Kolis announced.

Aydun sent a look toward the Primal of Death that I could barely decipher, but Kolis shut up. "Take your time."

It didn't matter how much time I had. I couldn't just come up with a deal of such magnitude on the spot. Gods, this was why I never should've been in this position. I wasn't good at negotiations and politics. I wasn't fit for this—

Stop.

My heart pounded as I forced myself to breathe in for the count of five. I glanced at Kolis, and this time, that fucking smirk was on his lips.

My chest squeezed. What had I said? That it was time to start having faith in myself? Panicking was not doing that. I held my breath. Whether or not I should've been in this position was irrelevant. I was here, and while I wasn't fit for this and clearly didn't have all that faith in myself, I was good at *pretending*. After all, I stood in front of Kolis and behaved as if no part of me feared him. So, I needed to hold it together. I needed to *think*. My heart slowed, along with my racing thoughts. *Think*. Some of the pressure left my chest.

And after what felt like an eternity, my first thought was that we would offer Kolis no such promise of safety.

I started to speak but then stopped. I knew that Kolis wanted to avoid war, and the lives of others had to be more important than our anger, right? A chance for peace had to be bigger than retribution, even if it went against the very core of who I was. That is what Eythos would've chosen, but it is not what I would choose for myself.

Fuck.

Okay. Go with my instincts? Wasn't that what Aydun had said? I briefly closed my eyes. I could not be as I was. I needed to be better. Less monstrous. There had to be a balance between those two things. One that protected the realms and was tolerable to all he victimized. There had to be.

And there was one that came close.

I opened my eyes. "I have a deal."

Kolis arched a brow. "And what is that?"

"You can keep Dalos, but you will not rule. You will remain as the Primal of Death, but you will have no authority over Iliseeum, the Shadowlands, or the mortal realm." I met his stare. "You will renounce the throne and not seek vengeance against any who have stood against you."

"Is that all?" Kolis asked, and I nodded. "What's in it for me?" he added.

"Balance will be kept, and you will get to live out your existence," I forced out, repeating what he'd offered.

"And Sotoria?" he asked.

The fucking creep… "My deal does not include Sotoria."

His fingers stretched outward and then slowly lowered onto the arm of the throne.

"You don't want war," I reminded him. "Neither do I."

"I'm not sure I believe that," Kolis countered. "Your nature is not all that different from mine."

I tensed. "I'm nothing like you."

"That's what you want to believe, but I've seen you as you truly are. I know the kind of violence you're capable of."

My tenuous grip on my anger started to slip. "You believe that because of what I did to you?"

"No." Kolis leaned forward, his lips curling upward. "I know it because of how eager you were to slay Evander."

My chest hollowed. *No.* Kolis was wrong. "I wasn't eager. Nor did I enjoy it. That is one of the many differences between us," I said, watching him shift back onto the throne. "Do you accept the deal or not?"

"You haven't accepted or rejected mine," Kolis pointed out.

"You do not need to right now," Aydun broke in. "Neither of you does. You both have time to think it over."

"That is true," the false King said. "But do you really need the time?"

"Do you?" I shot back.

Kolis's lips curled up in a poor replica of a smile, and then he towered over me, no more than a foot of space separating us. Gasping, I jerked back out of shock as my heart kicked violently against my ribs. Even with my newly heightened senses, I hadn't seen a flicker of movement from him. That was how quick he was.

Not even Ash could move that fast.

The bastard may look weak, but he was still incredibly powerful.

And I was…I was still very much afraid of him.

His smile widened, reaching silver eyes full of swirling crimson flecks. The tips of his fangs appeared. My stomach twisted sharply as my very insides flashed cold. An icy sensation crept down my spine, stroking the essence. It flared hotly as I forced myself to hold still and not back off, even though every instinct screamed for me to do just that.

"Kolis," Aydun warned, his voice low. "You know the rules."

"And I haven't violated a single one," Kolis replied, his gaze locked onto mine. "I'm only speaking to her."

"And that could not be done as you were before?" the Ancient countered.

"It could." Kolis's head tilted and lowered, sending a lock of hair falling against a sculpted cheek. He inhaled deeply, and his lip curled. "I can smell him on you."

Tiny bumps of dread broke out all over my skin. Revulsion rose, choking me.

That fucking smile grew even wider. "I could've punished you for the lives you took when you were here as a guest."

"A guest?" I sputtered.

"I could've punished Nyktos more severely for killing one of his brethren," he said, his voice clear but his lips barely moving. "And for attacking me, *his* King. I would even be within my rights to punish you for your blatant disavowal of my authority and for calling another 'King.' Wouldn't I be, Aydun?"

"You sit upon the Throne of the Gods," the Ancient replied stoically. "But she bears the Crown of Crowns."

The flesh beneath his eyes thinned until I could see a sheen of crimson bone. "I could've killed her many times over," Kolis answered, those swirling eyes still fixed on mine. "Easily. But I didn't. Does that not matter?"

Aydun may have answered, but I didn't hear him. I didn't even see anything beyond Kolis. It was almost like it was just him and me. *Breathe out.* And it didn't feel like we stood in Cor Palace's atrium. *Hold.* It felt like we were in the Sanctuary, in his private chambers, and I was—*no.* I was not caged. I was free.

"Instead, I was generous and kind," Kolis said, but I swore his lips didn't move. And—

Gold glinted *dully* from behind Kolis. My gaze darted over his shoulder. I didn't see the throne. Panic trickled through my veins as I saw bars, but that was impossible. *I'm not there.*

"I was gentle with you. Considerate." Kolis's voice *throbbed.* "Even *pleasing.*"

There had been nothing pleasing about what Kolis had done. I hadn't wanted to feel anything. He'd forced it. But I wasn't there. Kolis was standing in front of me—

Or was he? Panic surged like a trapped, wild animal because I could feel him behind me, beneath me, his arm too tight around my waist, and his hips rocking—

Every inch of my body was drenched in an icy downpour of raw, sharp fear as I felt that twisted tremor in his arms as he held me. Pressure settled on my chest, causing my breath to hitch as I felt the rapid pounding of his heart against my back, his hand sliding down my side, grazing my breast and clutching my hip. *Breathe in.* The essence swelled at the memory of the unwanted heat of his bite. *Hold.* My fingers twitched, tingling. *Breathe out.* I couldn't stop him. I couldn't do anything but sit there and take it, just as I had with Tavius, with all the training, with—

I was trapped.

"*Kolis.*" Aydun's voice suddenly thundered, snapping me into the present.

"That is enough."

Breathing heavily, I stepped back as I stared up at Kolis. We were in Cor Palace. The gold behind him was from the throne and all the other tacky décor. There were no bars. He was standing in front of me, and…

I glanced down. Was the floor trembling? My gaze flew around the atrium. The thick swaths of material covering the windows were swaying. A fine layer of dust drifted down from the ceiling as stone cracked like thunder somewhere in the chamber.

"Do I scare you, Seraphena?"

My head whipped back to Kolis as eather pulsed through me.

The skin under his eyes thickened, and the gleam of dull bone faded. "Clearly, I do."

"That is not her." Aydun faced me. "You need to calm yourself before Nyktos breaks with convention and shows himself."

It took a moment for the Ancient's advice to sink in. It wasn't me causing the palace to tremble.

It was Ash.

He was picking up on my emotions, even though I knew he was nowhere near us. I didn't feel his presence.

If Ash showed, he would bear some twisted consequence. My gaze swiveled back to Kolis. He smirked as he eyed me. That was exactly what he wanted.

Hands clenching, I focused on my breathing, taking slow and even breaths.

"And you." The Ancient turned to Kolis. "Using the essence against her in such a manner is unbecoming of one who calls himself King."

"I didn't harm her." Kolis tipped his flaxen head back as the swirling red shadows disappeared from his flesh. He began walking backward toward the dais. "Unbecoming or not, I violated no rules."

"Wait." I stiffened. "What are you—?"

"The true Primal of Death can root out one's trauma and what they fear, sending them back to that moment," Aydun answered before the *vadentia* could. What he spoke of was similar to what an *oneirou* could do—if an *oneirou* only manipulated negative emotions and created nightmares. "It's the *sybkik*—the unique ability associated with a Primal. And this one is reserved for those sentenced to the Abyss."

My lips parted on a quick inhale as I looked back at Kolis. He crossed the dais. He had…

He hadn't been able to do that before. The nape of my neck tingled as Kolis sat on his throne. When Kolis stole the embers, he'd upset the balance. And when the embers he'd stolen faded, even Kolis had weakened. But my Ascension had restored the embers of life and the balance.

And it would—or already was—restore the Primals' strength, including Kolis's, even though only a few embers of death remained in him after he made the transfer. The remaining embers were in Ash.

And all that meant was that Kolis would become even more powerful.

That should be the biggest concern. It was, but the fact that he had used that ability on me took center stage. Fury rose, erasing what filaments of fear and panic remained.

"What did you ask me?" I said. "Just a moment ago."

Kolis shifted, widening his sprawl on the throne. "I asked if I scared you."

Holding on to that rage, I smiled. "You fucking disgust me."

The flesh along his jaw and cheek thinned. Swirling cords of crimson reappeared, churning.

I wasn't done. "Just like you always disgusted Sotoria."

The waves of red shadows in his flesh stilled. Several seconds ticked by as the false King's gaze held mine, and the crimson faded from his flesh. "I would suggest that you use this time wisely, Seraphena."

Then, without another word, Kolis vanished from the throne.

The Ancient was quiet as we left the atrium and entered the empty hallway. I felt like I had just finished running up and down several flights of stairs—my knees were that weak as we reached the archway.

"Seraphena."

I should've kept walking as my name echoed down the hall.

I didn't.

"You should've accepted what Kolis offered," Callum said. "It was more than gracious of him."

A dry, cutting laugh parted my lips. Yes, Kolis was the epitome of *generosity*.

"If you are as wise as you think you are, you will accept it."

That wasn't going to happen, and Callum could likely tell that.

There was a moment of silence. "My sister does not belong to you."

"She doesn't belong to Kolis, either." My control fell to the wayside as the little monstrous part of me seized control. Reaching behind me, I grasped the grip of the dagger and spun. The blade left my hand with shocking speed. "You sick fuck."

The dagger pierced Callum in the center of the forehead, throwing him back. He hit the floor, dead for the second time today.

"Was that necessary?" the Ancient asked.

"Always."

Aydun took my hand instead of responding. Swirling mist suddenly surrounded us as he shadowstepped to the canopy of golden trees.

"Gods," I hissed, my head feeling like it was spinning. "Didn't I tell you that I would appreciate a heads-up next time?"

"I forgot," he replied. "Do you want to know how I think the meeting went?"

Exhaling roughly, I turned to him. A beam of sunlight sliced across his face. "Not particularly."

He looked unimpressed with my answer. "I believe it went as expected."

"What part went as expected? Him offering a deal? Me having to come up with one on the spot when I should've been warned of such before we got here?" I asked, my frustration nearly boiling over. "Or him exploiting what he did to—" I cut myself off and looked away, pressing my lips together.

"I was not certain that he would attempt to make a deal," Aydun stated. "But even if I was, advising you of the possibility would've been unfair."

I had to take an entire step back before I did something regretful. "You know what's unfair? Whatever the fuck your idea of balance and fairness is. Because to everyone but the Ancients, it really feels like none of that applies to Kolis."

"That is not the case."

"That's bullshit."

"Is it?" His unflinching stare held mine. "Does Kolis strike you as someone who is happy with their lot in life? Fulfilled?"

I opened my mouth but then closed it. The only time I could remotely say that I thought Kolis appeared even somewhat happy was when he believed I was Sotoria.

"Kolis was not always like he is now," Aydun continued after a moment, a far-off look settling across his features. "He was not without his flaws, but he was once fair and gentle. Kolis was feared, while his brother was welcomed. Dreaded, while Eythos was celebrated. Isolated and lonely, when his twin was surrounded by many. And while the other Primals could enter the mortal realm and spend time among them to retain some semblance of humanity, he could only do so for short periods and without interaction to avoid spreading death. He is the true Primal of Death, and mortals have never been able to come to terms with the knowledge that everything that begins must end. A millennium of that changed him. While many others are unable to see that, you have been able to."

My gaze cut back to him. Exactly how much were the Ancients able to see? Know?

"And that is no excuse for what he has done to others and you," he said, and I sucked in a reedy breath. "But he has not gone unpunished, Seraphena. Anything he has ever wanted or needed has been kept from him or eventually taken away."

"Maybe that is true," I started.

"It is," he cut in. "We cannot lie."

"Okay. So, that is true. He's been punished, but none of that has deterred him."

Aydun's gaze lowered. "I cannot argue against that."

It took me several moments to respond, and I only did so because I wanted to return to Ash. "How long do we have to answer whether or not we accept the deal?"

"I assume that means you already know your answer?"

"I do, and it is no."

Aydun nodded. "It is customary to give a full moon cycle."

"By mortal or Dalos standards?"

"Mortal."

So, a month. That was a long time to wait for an answer. My fangs scraped my pursed lips. But didn't I already know what the answer would be? I lifted my gaze to the Ancient. "You said that preventing war was a thread not seen. Has that changed?"

The Ancient laughed softly. "If it had, I could not tell you, and you know that."

I did, but that didn't mean I had to like it. Shaking my head, my gaze flickered over the golden leaves as I looked in the direction of Cor Palace. "Should I…?" I closed my eyes, not wanting to give the doubt a voice, but I couldn't stop myself. "Should I have just accepted his offer?"

"Did instinct tell you to do so?"

I shook my head.

"Then that is all that matters."

Aydun returned me—with warning this time—to the Shadowlands.

As the mist faded, I saw bare shelves.

Then, I was in Ash's arms, one wrapped around my waist while the fingers of his other sank into my hair. I held him just as tightly, feeling his heart pounding against my chest as I soaked in his citrusy fresh scent and the feel of his body.

"*Liessa*," he murmured, his mouth against the side of my head. Neither of us moved for several moments, and then he leaned back. Eather-drenched eyes searched mine. "What did he do?"

"He was…he was just being an asshole." My fingers splayed across his side. "Some of his abilities—like the *syhkik*—have returned to him. But I'm okay," I assured him before he answered. "I swear."

A faint shudder went through him, and then his lips found mine as he cupped my cheeks, tilting my head back. I rose onto the toes of my boots and placed my hands against his chest. The kiss deepened, and he tasted me, drank me in.

A throat cleared.

Ash slowly ended the kiss, but he didn't break away. His forehead rested against mine. He was breathing just as raggedly as I was.

I wet my lips. "I'm guessing you didn't leave for Vathi?"

"I think you know the answer to that," a gravelly voice drawled from behind Ash.

My fingers curled into Ash's tunic. "Did you have to sit on Ash to keep him here?"

"Pretty much," Nektas answered. "For a moment there, I didn't think I would be able to stop him."

"I'm sorry," I whispered to Ash. "I know it's not my fault, but I'm sure this couldn't have been easy for you."

His thumb swept over my cheek. "It wasn't." Lifting his head, he pressed a kiss to my forehead. "Do you need anything? Food? Something to drink?"

A wry smile tugged at my lips. "I wasn't gone that long."

"Any length of time is too long."

Feeling that in my soul, I smiled. "I'm good for now."

"If you change your mind, let me know." His lips touched my temple before he stepped aside.

Nektas sat in one of the chairs in front of the desk. Rhain was seated in the other. Both were watching us. The former had a small grin on his face. The god looked surprised. Again.

Feeling my cheeks warm, I cleared my throat. "Have you both—?" I stopped, looking behind me. The space was empty.

"If you're looking for the Fate," Rhain said, lifting a short glass to his lips and taking a sip, "he vanished the moment Nyktos reached you."

"Well, that's probably for the best." I glanced at Ash. His attention was fixed on me. "By the way, he now thinks I'm the calm one out of the two of us."

Rhain choked.

My narrowed gaze swung to the god. He was bent over in his chair, eyes watering. "Sorry," he gasped. "Went down the wrong pipe."

"Sure, it did," I replied dryly. "But that probably changed after the meeting."

Ash raised a brow. "How so?"

"I sort of might have killed Callum," I shared as Ash walked us toward the settee. "Twice."

Nektas snorted while Rhain wiped at his mouth with the back of his hand, and Ash sat, pulling me into his lap.

I felt a small jolt of unease, but I shut it down. I would not allow my fucked-up mind to do this to me. To us. I liked being this close to Ash, and it wasn't that long ago that he'd abhorred the touch of another. This openness between us was too important for me to ruin.

"What did he do?" Ash asked.

I forced myself to relax against his chest. "Breathe in my direction?"

"Besides that." Ash's hand slid from where it lay on my thigh to rest over my midsection.

"Honestly, he just annoyed me," I admitted. "I don't have a better reason than that."

The tips of Ash's fangs grazed his lower lip as he grinned. "Did anyone else annoy you?"

"Yes." The image of Kyn formed. "But none met the same fate." I tucked several thick curls behind my ear and decided to start with one of the more pressing issues. "Kolis looks like shit, by the way."

Ash's arm momentarily tightened, and Rhain's stare sharpened. "What do you mean?"

"His abilities are getting stronger, but I don't think he's fully recovered. He moved slowly. Looked thinner." I dropped my hand to the arm around my waist. "There were shadows under his eyes and below his cheekbones."

Rhain sat back with a shake of his head. "He should at least appear physically well by now." His eyes met mine. "Man, you must've really done a number on him."

"She did," Ash said, and the pride in his voice brought a smile to my lips even though I knew Kolis wouldn't remain that way. "What did he want?"

The smile faded. "He wanted to make a deal."

"A deal?" Rhain repeated.

"He offered what I assume he thought would be a truce."

"Did he now?" Ash's voice was level, but the temperature in the office dropped.

"He said he'd let us live out our lives in the Shadowlands and promised not to seek vengeance." I looked at Rhain and Nektas. "The others who have, as he put it, 'conspired against him,' would face punishment."

"And he would do what? Rule as the Primal of Death?" Rhain demanded.

I nodded.

The god leaned back, shaking his head as Ash asked, "And what did he want in return?"

My gaze met his. "Sotoria."

"Fucking Fates," he muttered, his jaw clenching.

"Wait a moment." Rhain lowered his glass to the knee of his dark gray breeches. "That's all he wanted?"

"All?" I sat straighter. "Yes, all he wants is the woman he got killed, brought back to life, assaulted, stalked—"

"Rhain meant no offense." Ash patted my belly.

"I didn't. Truly. I know Sotoria has suffered at his hands in ways I cannot imagine," the god was quick to say. "I didn't mean for it to be taken as if I thought that wasn't something significant. I just wasn't prepared for him to even offer a deal."

Realizing that I may have been a little too quick there, I nodded. "And he knows Sotoria's soul isn't in me."

Ash's head turned toward mine. "What?"

"He figured it out. The Star and your father's soul," I told him. Essence pulsed behind his pupils. Clearly, he wasn't happy to hear that. "I didn't accept the deal."

"I don't think any of us believed you would," Nektas stated.

Ash's head tilted as he eyed me. "Why do you sound like you're uncertain about that decision?"

"I'm not. I just..." I shook my head as I stared at Ash's forearm. "I mean, I didn't have a chance to accept or reject it, and I'll get to that in a moment, but before we entered Cor Palace, Aydun told me that preventing war among the Primals was not seen in any of the threads, but that I—I guess everything from my birth to my Ascension—kept snipping threads, ending some and changing others. It gave me the impression that I—or the choices I help make—could possibly prevent war."

The office was quiet.

"And he warned me that a war among the Primals would disturb the Ancients who'd gone to ground."

"Disturbing them is not the same as waking them," Ash pointed out.

"It's not, but I think it would make them more likely to awaken," I said. "He also said that the war wouldn't be won until there was blood and bone."

Ash frowned. "Won until life and death? What is that supposed to mean?"

"I don't know. And he wasn't into explaining things. Maybe he meant it in a figurative sense. Like the war wouldn't be won until there was life and death." My brow knitted. I knew he couldn't have been talking about a Primal of Blood and Bone because that wouldn't be helpful whatsoever. "But that doesn't really make sense."

"Unless he meant it in the sense that, for a war to end, the Primals of Life and Death must come together," Rhain suggested, his forehead creasing. "To no longer be at odds with each other."

"That's not going to happen," Ash said.

I couldn't stop the doubt from creeping in. "But by refusing to give him Sotoria, I'm choosing one person over potentially thousands, if not more."

Nektas leaned forward and rested his elbows on his knees. "If one life isn't important enough, then no lives are."

"It's not just that," Ash said. "There's no way he will honor the deal once he has what he wants."

"Aydun said that if Kolis went back on his deal, there would be consequences. That the realm would seek to rectify it," I said. "I guess it's like when an oath is made."

"Yeah, but none of that means he can't go back on it," Ash reminded me.

"I know. I thought the same." But would Kolis be willing to risk pissing off the Fates and have them do something to Sotoria? Possibly not.

Restless energy surged. "That's not all." I slipped from Ash's lap. He held on for a second before letting go. I walked past the end table and then turned back to them. "I had to counter. I wasn't happy about being unable to talk to you beforehand, but I…I made him a similar deal."

The office went quiet again.

My heart kicked against my ribs as I started to pace. "I figured that would be the response, and I know none of you believes that Kolis wants to avoid a war, but even if he plans to renege on the deal he offered, he is still showing restraint."

The air chilled even further.

"He is," I insisted, mostly to Ash. "He knows that Sotoria's soul is in The Star. He could simply tear apart the realm looking for it, which is an act that would erupt into war."

"She has a point there," Rhain said.

"Or he simply fears that if he were to do that, you would do something to The Star," Ash countered.

"True, but again, that shows he's being somewhat logical."

"What did you offer?" Nektas jumped in.

"My first thought was to offer him nothing, but that didn't seem like what a true Primal of Life would do. So, I offered that he could remain in Dalos but would not rule Iliseeum or the Shadowlands. He would renounce the throne and could not seek retribution against anyone," I told them. "In return, we would let him live out his life."

The three of them stared at me.

I started pacing again. "I know that's not desirable."

"That is the understatement of the century, Sera," Ash said.

"Yeah." I twisted my fingers around a strand of hair. "I know. But—"

"There's a but?" Ash questioned.

I stopped and met his stare. Or glare. The look was somewhere in between. "But I thought about Sotoria's soul and how I couldn't do that to her, even for a chance to ensure our safety. And I would do anything for that. Anything *but* that." My voice thickened. "And I realized that if one life is that important, then how can the lives of gods and mortals not be more important than our vengeance? Our anger? It can't be that way."

Silence greeted me, and what felt like my entire insides started to squirm. "Say something," I ordered Ash.

He leaned forward, propping his elbow on his knee. "You really, truly believe that Kolis doesn't want war?"

Obviously, I did. Well, I mostly did. Like, I was ninety-nine percent sure, but uncertainty rose. I wasn't sure how to answer. "I…I know you think my opinion is influenced by how he acted when he believed I was Sotoria, but even before that—the very first time I spoke to him in Dalos—he didn't speak of war."

"Instead, he spoke of killing all the Primals who stood against him," Ash countered. "How is that not war?"

"I see what you're saying, but I think…I think he was running his mouth. Wanting to scare me." My fingers tightened around my hair. "And I'm not saying his plan to kill those who stood against him changed, not even when he believed I was Sotoria. Later, he spoke of giving them the choice to stand with him instead of flat-out killing them. And yeah, that's not much of an option, but he also knew that most Primals would not go against him if he rose as the Primal of Blood and Bone."

Ash's expression was unreadable. "Kolis says a lot, Sera."

"I know. He is aware of his limitations, and I think he knows how tenuous his hold would become if another challenged his power. I mean, he absolutely hated when I used the eather around him, and I don't think it was because he was afraid of me or anything like that."

Nektas cocked his head. "What do you mean?"

"He doesn't like to be challenged."

Ash's jaw flexed. "That, I know."

"But it's about more than just his ego," I told him. "I think it was because he didn't want anyone else to see that I *could* challenge him."

Ash's head tilted. "And how does that have nothing to do with his ego?"

"I...I don't know. I'm not explaining it clearly enough." Frustrated, I shoved a curl away from my face, searching for how to convey what I felt when it came to dealing with Kolis. "Look, I don't think Kolis is reasonable when it comes to anything that doesn't line up with what he wants, but he knows what war would do to the realms. He doesn't want to rule over a pile of bones. He will seek to prevent that, which in his own shitty way, he's trying to do. If there's a sliver of a chance that he will abdicate the throne, then how can we not pursue that?"

Ash didn't respond for several long moments. "We spoke about entombing him. If we were to do that now, it would mean we've reneged."

My stomach churned. "I know." A muscle ticked in Ash's jaw, and my chest tightened. Did I make the right choices?

"There is no right or wrong choice," Nektas said, and I turned to him. Did I speak out loud? He was focused on Ash. "Peace should always be attempted first."

Ash sat back. "Even if that peace comes with a threat looming over our heads? Do we continue to live like that?"

"That's what your father would've chosen," Nektas said quietly.

"And look what that got him," Ash shot back.

"You think he didn't know the risks of refusing his brother? He did. But he had to think of everyone else. That is what a King does." Nektas held Ash's stare. "That has never been what Kolis has done, but that is what Sera is trying to do."

"I don't think Sera made the wrong choice," Ash insisted as he shifted toward me. "I don't."

Then what *did* he think? Because it sure didn't seem like he agreed with what I did.

"Okay." Rhain held up a hand. "What was his response?"

"He didn't accept or turn the deal down," I said. "Neither did I. I think Aydun likely sensed we were both going to say no, so he told us we had time to think it over. We have about a month."

"We should continue as we've planned then," Rhain said, setting his glass on the tray behind him. "Summon the Primals. Gain support. Nothing has changed."

Folding my arms over my waist, I nodded absently. Rhain was right. Nothing had changed.

But like before, I couldn't shake the feeling that everything had.

After Rhain and Nektas left, Ash and I sat in silence for a little while.

"Rhain is right. We should continue as planned," Ash said as he rose from the settee.

"Agreed." Nibbling on a fingernail, I watched him walk to the desk and pour himself a drink from the decanter.

It wasn't often that I wished I had his ability to sense emotion, but now was one of those times. I couldn't tell if he was angry or disappointed in me for offering the deal. If it was the former, I could deal with anger. Disappointment, though? My stomach churned. That would be harder to face.

But I knew he disagreed with what I'd decided. That much was clear.

He looked over at me. "Something to drink?"

"Water is fine."

"I will head to Vathi in the morning." Ash poured from the pitcher. "I think it would be wise to let Attes know about the deals."

I nodded. "He won't be happy to hear what Kolis asked for."

Lowering the decanter, Ash's head tilted, and his brow furrowed in perplexity.

"He knew her when Kolis brought her back and kept her captive. I don't know why Kolis allowed that, but Attes grew to care for her," I explained, folding my other arm over my waist. "I think it may have been more than that, honestly."

"If that is the case, then I feel bad for the bastard."

Well, I guessed feeling empathy for him was a step in the right direction. "I think it's also a good idea for Attes to keep The Star, at least for now, since Kolis believes we have it."

Ash nodded. "Would you like the water?" he asked as he approached. "Or would you like to continue chewing away at your finger?"

I narrowed my eyes at him and took the glass. "Thank you."

"Mm-hmm." He turned and took a drink. "Is that what you're anxious about?"

Holding the glass to my chest, I frowned. "What?"

"You're projecting anxiety. It tastes like syrup but carries the tartness of unease. It's not what I normally pick up from you when you're anxious."

Normally? I made a face.

Turning, he leaned against the edge of the desk. "Though I don't think it's Attes that has you this anxious."

It wasn't.

His eyes met mine over the rim of his glass. "Talk to me."

I took a drink, wishing I had opted for the whiskey. There were times when I was good at talking, especially when I was running my mouth, but these kinds of conversations? Well, I sucked at them.

But Ash was likely already aware of that.

Hand tightening around the glass, I looked up. "Are you…are you mad at me?"

A crease formed between his brows as he lowered his drink. "What?"

"Because of the deal I offered," I hurried on. "Or are you disappointed?"

"Sera," he said, setting his glass aside. "I'm not mad at you, nor am I disappointed in you."

I should've felt relief upon hearing that, but I didn't. "You're feeling something about it, though."

"Yeah." He laughed, thrusting a hand through his hair. "I'm feeling a lot of different things about it. Namely frustration."

"With me?"

"A little, but mostly with myself."

My head jerked back. "Why?"

"Because instead of spending time threatening the Arae and then fucking, I should've been thinking."

"I'm not sure I can agree with that second part," I said.

A wry grin appeared as he picked up his glass again. "If I had stopped for a moment to think about it, I would've realized there was a chance that Kolis would pull something like this. I could've prepared you for having to make an offer. We would've talked it through."

Could've. Would've. I hated those words. "I don't think any of us believed Kolis would demand a meeting or offer a deal," I reasoned.

"But I know him. I should have expected this." His gaze came back to mine. "From the moment we met in the Garden District, you have always been the stab-first-and-ask-questions-later type." He dropped his hand. "In both the figurative and literal senses."

My lips pursed.

"You'll strike first before anyone else can get the upper hand," he added. "You're not one to give many a chance."

"I can't exactly deny that," I said.

"That's changed.'"

"I…I don't think that's how a Queen would behave," I admitted.

He took a drink. "And how does a Queen behave, Sera?"

"I don't know." I shrugged. "But lashing out and potentially worsening the situation probably isn't it."

"Dealing with Kolis will always be a situation that worsens," he replied. "And what did I say before, when you said you didn't know how to be a Queen? I didn't say act how you think a Queen should. I told you to be yourself."

"I remember."

"Were you yourself when you offered him that deal?" he asked.

Yes? No? I wasn't sure. But what I did know, or at least what I thought I knew, was that I needed to be a less…stabby version of myself now that I was Queen.

"Are we going to accept his deal?" he asked in the silence.

My lip curled. "Absolutely, not."

"But what if Kolis accepts the deal, Sera?" he continued. "Are we really going to let him run around? Trust that he will keep to his word?"

I drew my tongue over the back of my teeth. "That's what I offered."

Ash's eyes flared with eather. "And?"

"And it won't be easy. Many will not be happy, but they will be… unhappily alive."

"Is that really what you want?" he asked.

"No." My free hand dropped to my side. "I want to make him bleed and dance in his blood. I want to fucking hurt him and, if I could, kill him. That is what I want."

A savage grin appeared. "That is the Sera I know."

"But does that make us better than him?" I asked. "I don't know if it does or doesn't, but if a war comes, I don't want it to be us who starts it," I said, and I wasn't sure if that was necessarily true. I wanted to attack, to go hard at Kolis, but I couldn't be that monstrous version of myself. "Even if the threat of disturbing the Ancients wasn't at stake, I don't want there to be a war at all."

"Neither do I."

"You don't, but you *have* been building an army and taking the necessary steps," I pointed out. "You were probably preparing for war before I was born. I haven't been. I haven't been preparing for any of this." I swept my arm out. "And I just did what I thought was right—"

"I don't think what you did was wrong."

"Yeah, you said that before, but I don't think that's the case."

"It is." His eyes met mine again. "And I'm sorry if I've given you the opposite impression. It's just…"

I watched him, waiting. "What?"

He looked away, a muscle ticking in his jaw. "It's almost like you trust him."

My mouth dropped open. "I do not trust him."

"Okay. That was the wrong word choice. It's more like you're giving him credit he does not deserve." Ash placed his drink down and pushed off the desk. He came to me and took my hand. Lifting it, he pressed a kiss to my palm—on the marriage imprint. "I know you believe he doesn't want war."

"But?" I whispered.

"As long as I've known Kolis, he's only wanted two things: Sotoria and to rule. His fear of harming you while taking the embers of life only held him back. Slowed him down. His plans never changed." Eather streaked across Ash's eyes. "His love for Sotoria, as twisted as it is, is powerful, but not as much as his thirst for power and search for retribution against those he believes wronged him."

I lowered my gaze. "I hope you're wrong."

"As do I." Mindful of the glass I held, he pulled me into his arms. "Because the Kolis I know would choose to see the realms burn before he relinquished control, and we should prepare for that."

"Did you or did you not," I began, holding the sword straight and steady, pointed directly at the fair-haired and muscular guard's throat—"offer to train me before?"

"I did." Kars' gaze darted left and right as he answered tentatively. "But that was before."

My lips pursed as I eyed him in the bright morning sunlight. "Why is now any different?"

"Well, you see…" He glanced desperately at the other guards filling the southwestern side of the courtyard. They offered no assistance. "It's because…"

"I'm now the Queen?" I supplied for him. "Because I'm the Primal of Life? Or is it because my husband is Nyktos?" I tipped the sword so it came within an inch of the underside of his jaw. "And you're more worried about what he will do to you if he learns you sparred with me than you are concerned with what *I* will do?"

"It's none of those reasons," Kars objected.

"He's lying."

Kars' narrowed-eye gaze swung to our left. "I am not lying."

"Yes, he is," the quiet voice came again. "I can smell it."

Frowning, I glanced over my shoulder at Reaver. He was seated on a large, gray boulder, his blond hair shielding most of his face as he eyed the burlap sack nestled in his lap.

Shortly after Ash had left for Vathi this morning, I'd crossed paths with Reaver and Jadis, and they had been by my side ever since. Well, he had been. Jadis…

My gaze flickered over the courtyard, looking for the girl. I found her in a few seconds.

Jadis was otherwise occupied.

The greenish-brown draken ran through the newly grown grass, trailing a strip of blue silk. I had no idea where she'd gotten that piece of cloth, which meant I probably should've kept a better eye on her than Pax, who trailed behind her.

It felt like forever since I'd seen the orphan Ash had brought into the Shadowlands nearly a decade ago. The fifteen-year-old now lived with a family in Lethe but spent a decent amount of time in the palace, doing odds-and-ends jobs. He eagerly tackled those tasks, and I thought it was because he liked being around Ash and wanted to prove himself useful. Maybe even show gratitude.

I refocused on Reaver. "You can smell it?"

"It's in his sweat." Reaver reached into the sack and rooted around. "The stench changes."

"What the fuck?" Kars muttered.

"Language," I warned him. "There are younglings present."

Kars' mouth dropped open. "Five minutes ago, you shouted that very same word."

"I did not."

"Really?" Kars replied dryly.

I had, in fact, yelled it. At the top of my lungs, too. But that was because I'd decided that my time was better spent training instead of pacing and waiting for Ash to return so we could go to the Thyia Plains and speak with Keella—who he'd sent word to this morning. When I first approached Bele and asked her to train with me, she had, without warning, thrown a godsdamn dagger at my head right before running back into the palace like some kind of psychotic woodland nymph—

Which reminded me of those Nektas and I had seen when we returned from the Vale. I wondered if they had changed after the balance was restored. Returning to…well, non-psychotic versions of themselves.

I needed to check on that later.

"You must be imagining things," I said.

Reaver giggled, and the sound was so unexpected that it drew Kars' and my attention.

The godling's lips curled into a smile. "By the way." Kars pointed his sword at Reaver. "I do not stink."

"You can't smell it, but I can." Reaver pulled a glistening red apple from the sack—his fourth or fifth of the morning. "Your scent becomes more… bitter."

I wondered if I should intervene with his snacking because that seemed like a whole lot of apples. But apples were healthy, weren't they?

"You are the Queen and the true Primal of Life. None of them will want to fight you," Reaver said, sounding far too wise for his age. He bit into the apple with a crunch. "And he's worried what Nyktos will do."

I faced Kars, raising an eyebrow.

"Someone needs to fight with her," Reaver added before Kars could respond. "If not, she's gonna start pacing again."

I would.

"It's because she worries a lot," he went on between mouthfuls of apple. "Even though she'll say she doesn't."

I opened my mouth.

Half the apple was already gone. "I can sense when you lie, too," he said, which I already knew. I was trying not to be anxious around him. "Your sweat changes, too." His upper lip curled. "It becomes tangy."

I stared at the draken, resisting the urge to sniff myself. "You know—"

A shrill screech interrupted us as one of the palace side doors opened, and Aios stepped out with Bele.

Well, I finally knew where Jadis had gotten that piece of silk. It matched the missing lower section of the blue gown Aios wore.

I shifted my attention back to Reaver. The little brat had been mostly correct with his earlier statement about my pacing. If I didn't do something, I would get stuck in my head, and I didn't want to be where I would stress over how things were going between Ash and Attes, if I had made the right choice by offering Kolis a deal, and how the upcoming meeting with the Primals would go. And if I wasn't thinking about any of that, I was half-afraid my mind would end up revisiting my time in Dalos.

And I didn't need that in my life.

I also didn't need Reaver pointing out every time I lied. "Perhaps you should assist with Jadis," I suggested.

Reaver's eyes widened. "I'd rather not." He clutched the burlap sack. "She'll want to eat all my apples."

"You mean there are actually some left?"

He nodded earnestly. "She always eats my apples."

"And would that be a problem? I think you've had enough," I said. "For a lifetime."

"Nek said you can't ever eat too many apples," he argued.

I started to explain that Nektas probably didn't mean he should eat a dozen of them but decided against it. I had a feeling I'd have an even harder time convincing Reaver of that than getting Kars to fight me.

Turning back to Kars, I spotted Saion. As he crossed the courtyard, he cut a striking figure in a sleeveless, dark gray tunic. I was surprised to see him since he had spoken of surveying some of the lands for crops after the meeting with Attes.

An easy smile appeared on his handsome face as he approached. "Heard you were looking to do some damage."

Curious as to exactly how he'd heard that, I shifted my grip on the sword. "I wouldn't say I was looking to do any damage."

The curve of his lips kicked up a notch as he nodded at Kars and then focused on me. "Walk with me?"

The look of relief on Kars' face didn't pass me by. "Sure."

Saion extended an arm toward the section of the Rise opposite where Jadis was. "You can leave the sword."

Sighing, I thrust the blade into the grass. The god ducked his chin, coughing faintly in a poor attempt to hide his laugh. I frowned as Kars pivoted, practically running toward the rest of the guards as they gradually dispersed.

"I'll be here," Reaver announced, pulling yet another apple from the bag. "Waiting."

Nodding, I joined Saion and fell into step beside him. "That has to be his sixth apple."

"Only six?"

My head snapped toward him.

"I've seen him eat fifteen in one sitting."

"Good gods," I murmured.

"Draken have crazy appetites," he reminded me, tilting his chin. The sunlight glanced off his warm brown cheek. "Especially when they're this young. They'll eat you out of house and home if you're unprepared."

"No doubt."

"By the way, a little bird told me what you were up to," he said, squinting as he turned his gaze to the pale blue sky.

"Uh-huh." My lips pursed. "And does this little bird also happen to be a guard?"

"I'll never tell." He winked, and my eyes rolled. "But the chirping this bird did wasn't out of malicious intent. Only concern."

"Can we stop pretending that you were speaking to a bird?" I asked. "And get to the point where I tell you I'm completely fine and capable of training, even though I just completed my Ascension?"

"Oh, I know you're more than capable of training and fighting." He stopped as we reached the shadow of the Rise. "The concern wasn't regarding your well-being."

"Kars?" When he nodded, my frown deepened. "Nyktos wouldn't have done anything to him." I saw the look of doubt cross his features. "Okay. I wouldn't allow him to do anything."

"No, you wouldn't allow that." He rested a hand on the hilt of the sword at his hip. "But I'm not talking about Nyktos."

"Then what…?" I stiffened. "You're talking about me? I wouldn't hurt Kars."

"You wouldn't *intend* to hurt him," he corrected gently. "But you could."

I opened my mouth.

"You brought life back to the Shadowlands overnight. That is how powerful you are now, and that kind of power will also affect you physically. You don't know your own strength, Sera. And that will take you a bit to learn. The same goes for a god once they complete their Ascension." His gaze met mine. "Even Nyktos didn't train with gods for a while after completing his Ascension. He had to make sure he fully understood his strength. What feels like a soft blow to him is like a sucker punch through the guts to one of us, and that's not an exaggeration," he said. "One hit from you, the *true* Primal of Life, and you would've likely broken Kars' arm."

If not worse went unsaid.

"I…" I didn't know what to say as my stomach sank. "I didn't know."

"Probably just hasn't been a topic that's come up yet."

I hadn't mentioned thinking about training to Ash before he left. He probably would have said something if I had, but… "It didn't even cross my mind." A bit of shame scalded my cheeks as I focused on the glossy surface of the Rise. I should've been more considerate. "And it should have, but I wasn't thinking beyond occupying my time." *And my mind*, I silently added. But it was more than that. "Nyktos doesn't rely on the essence when fighting. None of you do. I want to make sure I don't either."

"I get you." His chin lifted. "Fighting is a lot of muscle memory, but it's not something one retains any real skill for without practice."

"Yeah." I shifted my weight. "And I've been out of practice for…" I cleared my throat as I watched the clouds momentarily blot out the glimmer of the stars. Everyone knew how long. "It's been a while."

"Nyktos will work with you," he said. "After all, he enjoys getting his ass kicked by you."

Cracking a grin, I forced myself to meet his gaze. "Thank you for coming to say something. If you hadn't, I probably would've done some damage." I swallowed a sigh and scanned the sparring guards. "I think I owe Kars an apology."

"I don't know if that's necessary."

"It is." I inhaled deeply, squaring my shoulders. "He was trying to tell me why he couldn't train with me, but I wasn't listening. I should have."

Saion didn't respond. I glanced at him and found him watching me as if I'd sprouted a third hand from the center of my forehead. "What?" I asked.

"Nothing." He blinked and looked away. A moment passed. "You know what? It's not nothing. I was thinking that you've changed. You're not so irrational."

My brows shot up. "Wow."

A sheepish look crossed his features. "But then I realized you weren't always irrational. Just prone to moments of irrationality."

"If this is supposed to be a compliment, you're failing," I stated.

"You've always been thoughtful, though." His stare came back to mine. "Considerate of others. I don't think we always saw that. Except for Ector."

Feeling my heart squeeze, it was my turn to look away. "If I were truly considerate, you wouldn't have had to intervene."

"I don't agree with that." A moment passed. "Your Majesty."

I shot him an arch look.

"I don't think being considerate means always doing the right thing. If that were the case, none of us would be," Saion said, scratching his chin. "I think it sometimes means acknowledging when you should've been more considerate and then doing it. You—" A shout from across the courtyard drew our attention. "What the…?"

Jadis was hopping on her hind legs, clutching that strip of blue material in one hand as she spat short bursts of silver flames toward Bele. The Primal stood with her arms crossed, her features pinched in a way that said she was utterly done with whatever was happening while Pax grinned from where he sat, safely behind the draken.

"Jade, baby," Aios called out to the youngling. "Don't scare Bele."

Bele scowled, but Jadis stopped, screeching happily as she threw herself onto the several-inch-tall grass. Two thin legs stuck straight up as she waved the slip of blue material like a victory flag.

Pax grinned wider.

Behind Bele, Rhahar looked like he wanted to run face-first into the shadowstone wall.

"Man," I murmured, shaking my head. "Children—draken or not—are absolutely terrifying."

Saion chuckled. "That, they are." He glanced over at me. "By the way, I did have another reason for coming out here. Rhain is looking for you."

My stomach dipped. "What for?"

"Not sure," Saion said, "but he said it was important."

"*Seraphena*."

I opened my eyes. "What?"

"Have you been listening to me at all?" Rhain demanded.

"Of course." Tilting my head from where it rested on the arm of the chair, I slid a quick look at Reaver.

He grinned, returning his attention to the piece of parchment the god had given him that he'd been scribbling on. Reaver had followed me when I went to find Rhain while Jadis was still, well, I imagined terrorizing Aios and Bele.

I smiled.

"I find that hard to believe when you appear half-asleep," Rhain stated. "And rather uncomfortably."

"I'm not half-asleep, and it's perfectly comfortable," I grumbled, pushing up with an obnoxiously loud sigh. I then sat like an adult in the chair. "Happy?"

"Thrilled," he deadpanned.

My eyes narrowed on the god. We had vastly different ideas about what was important.

When Saion said that Rhain wanted to see me, my mind immediately went to the worst-case scenario: that he wanted to talk about how I had convinced Kolis to free him, even though that seemed unlikely. As it turned out, he'd wanted to go over the day-to-day functions of the palace.

Adjusting the bound parchment in his lap, Rhain leaned back. "Since you weren't half-asleep, you should be able to tell me what I've said."

"You were talking about…" What had he been talking about? "You were saying something about…cleaning."

One eyebrow rose.

"Is that wrong?"

"Technically? No."

I smirked.

"But you're only in the general vicinity of what I was talking about," he said, tapping the slender quill against the parchment. "I know you weren't listening. I called your name three times before you heard me."

I clamped my mouth shut, only grazing the inside of my lips with my fangs this time.

"I was speaking about how there really hasn't been any household management."

I nodded. I had heard him say something like that.

"No actual schedule for any of the staff, be it for cooking or *cleaning*," he continued. "In other Courts, it typically falls to the Chosen to organize such things." He stopped and frowned. "Or it used to. But it has been Aios and…was Ector," he said, and my heart twisted sharply, "who handled it in the past."

"I haven't seen any staff here besides Pax and Baines," I said, referencing the stable hand. "And I think I've only ever seen one of the cooks once. Valrie."

"Exactly," he replied. "That's my point. Nyktos has never really focused on those areas."

It wasn't for lack of caring. Instead, it was due to the exact opposite. Ash hadn't wanted staff in his house at all since Kolis could target them.

"I think it's time we establish household management."

My brows lifted. "And you thought I'd be the person to talk to about it?"

"I know a Queen doesn't oversee such—"

"It has nothing to do with being a Queen and everything to do with me having no household experience," I said. "I wasn't exactly raised to be a lady of the house."

Rhain pinched the bridge of his nose. "I wasn't suggesting that you personally oversee such things. And if you had been listening, you would know that."

"Oh," I murmured, starting to sink into my chair as Reaver's grin went up a notch.

"I said we'd hire someone to do it," he said. "And since you don't know the people here, and we will likely be busy in the coming weeks, I was also going to suggest we ask Aios to assist with that."

"You think she'll want to do that?"

"I wouldn't have suggested her if I didn't," he replied.

"Then it's fine with me."

Rhain wrote something down. "Whoever Aios determines is fit to run the household should live on-site, and the option to do so should be offered to any of the staff."

"Do you think it's wise for us to start bringing in staff now? All things considered?"

Rhain got what I was referencing without me having to say it. "I think it's time to start living free of Kolis's shadow."

I agreed with that sentiment, but we weren't free. We were far from it.

"I think we should bring in staff, as long as Nyktos is okay with it. But *things*," I said, nodding at Reaver's bowed head, "will need to be settled first before we allow anyone to live here."

"Agreed."

As Rhain reviewed how the staff would be paid, I watched Reaver scribbling away. We were making plans, which felt both amazing and terrifying. Even a bit risky. Like we might jinx ourselves.

"You're not listening again." Rhain sighed. "Look, I know you probably have a lot of stuff on your mind, and this feels like the last thing you need to be considering right now—"

"I wouldn't say it's the *last* thing." I tapped my fingers on the arms of the chair. "But yes, I do have a lot on my mind."

A moment passed, and then he asked, "Do you want to talk through those things?"

I huffed out a dry laugh.

"It's a genuine offer," Rhain insisted. "And not an entirely altruistic one."

"Really?" I drawled.

"Yes. Maybe you can focus if you get out whatever is on your mind." He paused. "Though I feel focusing isn't one of your strong suits."

I snorted.

With another heavy sigh, the tapping of his quill increased. Glancing over at him, our eyes met. We both quickly looked away. I rose from the chair. "That neat talent of yours? The telepathy? Do you always need to have an item belonging to the person to do it?"

His brows squished together. "What made you even think of that?"

"I don't know," I said, lifting a shoulder. "It just popped into my head."

He blinked slowly. "To answer your question, yes. I need a token or to be in contact with them."

I thought that over as my gaze swept along the bare shelves. "So, what token of Nyktos's do you have that allows you to communicate with him?"

"What makes you think I have something of his?"

I shot him a knowing look.

Two pink splotches appeared in the center of his cheeks. "I carry a medallion."

Interest sparked. "Can I see it?"

One more heavy, ground-shaking sigh left him as he reached into the breast pocket of his tunic. Opening his fingers, he held a small silver disc. A wolf's head had been carved into the metal. The detail was intricate, down to the tufts of fur.

"It's beautiful. Who made…?" I trailed off, lifting my gaze to his. The skin beneath my ear tingled. "You did."

Rhain's eyes widened.

I straightened. "You…you also made the box Ash keeps on his bedside table."

"How did you know that?" he demanded, then cursed.

"Foresight," Reaver said what Rhain had likely surmised.

"Yeah," Rhain said, clearing his throat. "I forgot."

Reaver nodded and then returned to his drawings.

"Do me a favor," Rhain stated. "Don't use that on me."

I arched a brow as I started walking. "Wasn't planning to."

"You just did."

"It was accidental. Sometimes, things just pop into my head," I told him, reaching the pillared doors again. "I'm still trying to get a handle on it, but I will do my best not to use it."

And I meant that. Even though I was really curious why he was so worried I would seek to know more about him. Then again, he could just simply value his privacy.

"Thank you," he said. "What else were you thinking about?"

"Oh, you know. Everything." Crossing my arms, I faced him.

Rhain eyed me for several moments, clearly waiting for me to elaborate. When I didn't, he glanced down at the bound parchment. "I'm sure you're nervous about meeting with the Primals."

"Obviously."

He grinned slightly, making me wonder how often Rhain actually smiled. "Being nervous is understandable, but just remember that you are the true Primal of Life and the Queen. I know that sounds easier said than done, but you have earned the title and the respect."

What he said struck me silent. *Had* I earned it? I guessed almost dying qualified as such, but I doubted many of the other Primals cared about that. To them, I was not only unproven, I also hadn't earned shit.

"There's just one more thing I didn't mention before regarding meeting with the Primals." Rhain closed the leather folio on the bound parchment. "Yesterday, you did amazing during the speech. I have every belief that you will do the same with the Primals as long as you keep your temper in check—"

"Yeah, I wasn't planning to threaten the Primals into siding with us, but thanks for the advice."

Rhain let out what was becoming one of his infamous sighs. "I'm being serious."

"So am I." I frowned. "Why would my temper be incited?"

"Does it need a reason?"

"Funny," I said. "But contrary to what you may think, I know when not to run my mouth."

The look on his face said he doubted that.

Irritation flared. "I know you've seen me lose my temper on more than one occasion, so I get why you're doubtful, but you also have to know that I wouldn't be standing here if I didn't know how to keep myself in check."

Reaver's quill stopped again as Rhain's head flinched back. "You're right. I do know that." His gaze lowered and then returned to mine. "I'm—"

"Don't apologize. It's not necessary," I cut him off, sounding like, well, Ash. "Thank you for helping me with all of this, but I think that is enough for now," I said, then winced at the bite in my tone. "And I do mean that. Thank you."

Rhain nodded awkwardly as he stood. He started for the door but stopped beside me. He appeared to want to say something more but changed his mind. Giving me a quick bow of his head, he left the office.

Pushing the last bit of conversation between Rhain and me aside, I began pacing the length of Ash's office.

My mind kept alternating between what Rhain had said and why Ash hadn't returned yet. I'd suspected that his trip to Vathi would be an in-and-out sort of thing. He'd been gone for almost two hours. But Ash was fine. He and Attes were likely just talking.

Honestly, I hoped he and Attes were genuinely speaking to each other and talking things through. They may not have been friends before, but there had been mutual respect between them.

I looked around the office. "I need to be doing something…queenly right now."

"I hope it's not more pacing," Reaver muttered.

I shot the little smart-ass a look, which earned me a boyish giggle. Grinning, I refocused. There had to be something I could be doing. I was Queen, right? I was to be this great Primal power—

"Wait," I whispered, my lips parting. "Great Primal power."

Reaver cocked his head to the side, his eyes alert.

"The prophecy," I told him, although I doubted he had any idea what I was talking about. I hadn't thought about it, not even when I was with

Aydun. "Kolis said there is a whole other part. Something about great powers stumbling and falling—" My eyes widened. "It was about the Primal of Life and Death."

"No such Primal exists," Reaver said.

"Right." I ran my fingers down my braid. "I totally forgot about that supposedly unknown part of the prophecy. The third part—the end—that wasn't seen by Penellaphe but dreamt by the Ancients."

Was it true, though? Kolis could've been lying, but I didn't think so. So, who did that part reference if he *was* speaking the truth? The one who would basically wipe out the other Primals. Because that was what Kolis had said he wanted to do—well, he'd claimed that initially.

And what had Aydun said? That a war among the Primals wouldn't be won until there was blood and bone. What the Ancient had said and the prophecy *felt* related. How, though? My intuition was unsurprisingly quiet, but I knew who'd probably know. Who could likely shine some light on what Eythos had been thinking when he devised his plan and would also know what could be done about Sotoria's soul and why Eythos had ended her second life.

"Holland," I announced, smiling. "And being the true Primal of Life, I can summon a Fate."

"Are you sure you want to do that?" Reaver asked, sounding nervous. "Summon a Fate?"

"It'll be okay," I promised. "Holland is…he's like family. The kind who spends your entire life lying to you, but still, family."

My words didn't seem to reassure Reaver, but I wasn't worried about Holland being a threat. He may be an Ancient, but he was still, well, Holland. And since he'd already talked openly about the prophecy with Ash and me, it had to be something the Fates didn't consider overstepping.

The question was, how did I summon him? Just…call out to him? The skin behind my left ear tingled. It wasn't just calling out to him. Doing so also involved using the essence. My will.

Stopping between the chair and the couch, I closed my eyes and focused on the faint thrum of eather. As an image of Holland formed in my mind, complete with the single crease between his brows, the essence pulsed intensely from my chest. "Holland," I spoke, my stomach twisting sharply as the resonance of my voice reverberated with the intertwined strands of power. "I would—" I shook my head curtly. "I need to speak with you." Pausing, I opened one eye. "Please."

Letting go of the eather, I felt it calm as I opened my other eye.

"Did it work?" Reaver asked as he scooted forward so his feet touched the floor.

"I'm not sure." I swept the tail of my braid over my chin. "I suppose we will need to wait and find out."

So, that's what we did.

We waited.

And waited some more.

Holland didn't magically appear before me.

"Maybe I did it wrong." I started to ask if I should try it again, but a sound came from the hall. A series of soft thuds.

My head swung to the closed doors, eyes narrowing. Wait, was my…?

A knock came.

"Aha!" I shouted, shoving a fist into the air. "My hearing is finally improving."

Reaver stared at me.

Grinning, I turned back to the doors. "Come in."

Reaver shifted forward as the doors opened, positioning himself so he stood half in front of me. It was a clear, protective move and made me want to hug him.

My two shadows, Rhahar and Kars, stood in the doorway. The latter shifted to the side. A guard with short, spiky dark hair and a complexion that reminded me of a smoky quartz appeared in the alcove of Ash's office. I was sure I hadn't met her before, but the name Iridessa came to mind. More information started to form, but I thought about Rhain's request not to use the foresight on him and stopped myself.

She bowed her head. "Your Majesty."

Rhahar raised a brow at me as I started to speak. "It's either that or *meyaah Liessa*," he informed me, and I snapped my mouth shut. "One or the other."

"Does it really have to be one or the other?" I countered, glancing between the two. "Because I'm not like Kolis. I don't need my ego repeatedly stroked."

"Kolis is greeted as such out of fear." Rhahar's hand fell to the hilt of his sword. "And because he demands it. We address you as such because it is owed. Deserved."

I started to argue that I hadn't done anything as their Queen to deserve such, but Reaver tugged on the sleeve of my tunic.

"Yes?"

"You are respected," he said in that quiet, far-too-wise voice for one as young as he was. "And Nek told me that acknowledging the thoughts and emotions of others is how you repay their respect with yours."

I stared at the youngling, my lips pursing. The fact that a ten-year-old was giving me sage advice was probably a good indication that I had a lot of maturing to do.

"Okay," I said, turning back to the two guards. "I won't continue to complain."

Rhahar ducked his chin, but not before I saw a look that said he didn't quite believe that.

Couldn't blame him.

I faced the other guard. "I don't believe we've met before."

"No, we haven't," she said, her bright amber gaze meeting mine. "I'm Iridessa."

"That's a pretty name," I said.

"Thank you." Pink blossomed on her cheeks, spreading across the small bridge of her nose. She was clearly as good at accepting compliments as I was. "Some visitors are quite insistent that they speak with you."

Rhahar's expression hardened at once. "Who is it?" he asked before I could.

"It is the goddess Penellaphe," answered Iridessa. "And a man named Ward."

My summons had worked.

Kind of.

The goddess Penellaphe had not only spoken large portions of the prophecy, but she was also intimately involved with Holland, and Vikter Ward was, well, I wasn't quite sure exactly what he was other than the first *viktor*—those who guarded someone the Fates believed would fulfill some purpose or bring about great change. Even mortals bound to commit terrible deeds could end up with a *viktor*, as messed up as that was, but the Arae used them to aid without upsetting their precious balance.

I still didn't see how sending in a *viktor* didn't upset the balance. Seemed like a loophole large enough that an entire kingdom could fall through it.

They weren't Holland, but as Reaver—in his draken form—and I were led to a chamber in a wing of the palace opposite Ash's office, I doubted their visit was coincidental.

Iridessa brought us to the space near the chamber that Jadis had almost burned down—one I doubted had been used in decades. I couldn't help but think about how Ector used to keep them clean despite their lack of use so Eythos could be remembered.

I supposed hiring someone to keep them clean was a way we could honor Ector.

As Iridessa opened the double doors and then stepped aside, bowing toward me before taking her leave, I swallowed the knot of sadness before it could expand.

Two figures sat on the ivory-cushioned settee. The male *viktor* placed something dark and square onto the thin table behind him as they rose. I wasn't sure what it was, but my gaze immediately went to the goddess. It was impossible for it not to.

Penellaphe stood out in stark contrast to the bare shadowstone walls and sterile white furniture. Everything about her was vibrant. The gown reminded me of the blades of grass now growing in the Shadowlands. She had long, honey-hued hair and bronzed skin, and her sea-blue eyes were nearly the same as the man's who had traveled with her.

Ward appeared as he had when he placed the charm on me, like a mortal who had seen several decades. Sending Reaver, who had flown in behind me, a wary look, he moved to stand beside the goddess.

They both began to lower themselves into deep bows. "You don't need…" The skin below my ear began to tingle as I stared at the sandy-haired male. It happened so fast, I couldn't even stop it. Thoughts began to form, coming together to answer what I hadn't known moments before.

"You were created," I blurted out.

Penellaphe's head lifted slightly. "Excuse me?"

"Ward." I gestured at him. "The Ancients created you. I mean, you were once mortal, but when you died and the Fates rewarded you, they created something entirely new out of you."

"Er…" Penellaphe murmured, glancing toward where Iridessa and Rhahar stood.

Ward's bowed head muffled his cleared throat. "Yes, that is correct."

That was also basically what they had told me, but there was more. The *viktors* were something otherworldly, like the riders, neither god nor mortal, alive nor dead. But he was…he was different.

I walked closer, focusing on him as Reaver landed on the low table between the settees. Eather hummed through me as I locked on Ward. Images formed in my mind. I saw…I saw glimpses of his many lives in the mortal realm. Him with his charges—those he was sent to watch over. But he was… "You were never reborn."

Ward's head jerked up then, his gaze finding mine and not moving away as if he'd been snared.

"The other *viktors* are reborn, but not you. Because you were *restored* by an Arae. Your lives in the mortal realm are fabrications. Convincing ones. You learned to live many lies, and you never lost your memories. And you're old. Older than some of the gods." Images and words flashed in my mind, coming so fast it was hard to make sense of them, but I saw him when he was mortal. "It was many centuries ago, and you were with a woman—a pregnant woman, not of noble birth. Her name was…" I frowned. "Phena?" That didn't sound right as I stopped in front of him. I lifted my hand, and before I even knew what in the world I was doing, I touched his cheek—

In my mind, I saw a woman with pale hair and a freckled, heart-shaped face. A woman who eventually gave birth to—

"Ronan," I whispered, jerking my hand as I took a step back. My heart thundered. Reaver unfurled his wings, lifting his head as he let out a low, deeper call. "Ronan Lesly." I sucked in a sharp breath, recognizing that surname. "There's no way…"

"I can explain," Ward said, straightening. "Or at least try to."

Unable to speak, I nodded for him to continue.

A heavy sigh left him. "Many, many years ago, when I was mortal, a Queen of a fledgling kingdom—"

"The Vodina Isles," I cut in.

He nodded. "The Queen knighted me, and I pledged to protect and serve her. I did so without hesitation," he said, his throat working on a swallow. "But her marriage was one of convenience. One to strengthen ties with other kingdoms. However, the King was already in love with another. A daughter of an aging bookkeeper. And the Queen was aware. She had her own..." Flushing at the throat, he glanced at Reaver. "She had her own suitors, but everything changed when a babe began to grow in the mistress's belly—one who was the illegitimate child of the King of Vodina. The Queen had yet to provide an heir, so she ordered the death of her husband's mistress and, therefore, their unborn child—unfortunately, something common in that time."

Knowing what had eventually become of the Vodina Isles, I imagined it was still common, but it didn't make much sense to me. "Why? It couldn't have been due to any fear that an illegitimate child would have some sort of claim to the throne."

"She feared she would be unable to produce an heir," Ward explained. "And yes, even if that were the case, an illegitimate child would still have no easy road to the throne. But it was more than that. It was an order born not of unrequited love but the desperation and fear of being tossed aside."

"Gods," I muttered, feeling just a tad bit sorry for the woman. If she hadn't been able to provide an heir, her fear would have likely come to fruition. Many kingdoms still operated that way to this day. It was a whole lot of patriarchal bullshit.

Bullshit that I could change, couldn't I?

I was pretty sure I could, but that was neither here nor there at the moment. "What happened?"

Ward's chin lifted. "As a knight, I'd delivered my fair share of death, but not to women and children. Others she could've gone to would have no such qualms. So the short of it is, I committed treason. I went to the bookkeeper's daughter, warned her of the threat, and protected her until the babe was born. But she was...unique for the time. She had no interest in simply being protected. She wanted to learn how to ensure her own safety. I taught her how to do just that."

"You succeeded."

Ward nodded.

"The Queen learned of your betrayal," I guessed.

"She did," he said. "The babe survived, and so did the mother. That was all that mattered."

"I don't think that is *all* that mattered," I said.

"But it was," Ward insisted. "For the bookkeeper's daughter eventually became Queen of Vodina."

My head cocked. "What happened to the first Queen?"

"Knowing the Queen would not stop until her child was dealt with, the bookkeeper's daughter slipped into the palace one night and…well, no one knows exactly what transpired. But come morning, the Queen was dead."

"Gee," I murmured. "I wonder what happened."

"I believe I may have been too successful in my training." Ward grimaced, causing the faint lines at the corners of his eyes to deepen. "Either way, the bookkeeper's daughter was the first non-noble to be placed on the throne. Her son, Ronan, eventually ruled Vodina, and the throne passed down through the family for centuries. It was the bloodline Ronan's birth began and then ended with—"

"With the last King Lesly, who only had a daughter. A princess married to…" I swallowed, unable to say it because it was too unbelievable. "After the marriage, King Lesly was overthrown by the Lords of the Vodina Isles, and a new King was installed."

"That is what I heard." His eyes searched mine. "You know who that princess was? Who she became?"

"I do," I said, my voice hoarse. "My mother."

"But you're wrong about the name of Ronan's mother. She *was* called Phena," Ward continued after a moment. "But that was a pet name the King called her. Her full name was Seraphena. Your namesake."

I knew this. I'd seen it. Heard it. But still, my eyes closed tight. It took me several moments to speak. "I…I didn't know that my mother had named me after her great…whatever."

"Then she did not tell you what Seraphena became known as?"

I gave a curt shake of my head and opened my eyes.

"The Silver Knight," he said. "The warrior Queen who fought alongside her husband and her people in battle. Her name, even now, is synonymous with honor and duty. A name that was never repeated throughout the annals of time until Calliphe, the once Princess of Vodina, named her only daughter such." A faint smile appeared. "And that is why I was rewarded all those years ago. By saving her and Ronan, I ensured that another bearing her name would eventually be born—one that would usher in great change."

Pressing my hands to my sides, I tried to speak but didn't know what to say.

I was shocked and wasn't sure which was more confounding. That Ward had become the first *viktor* because he'd saved my ancestor, ensuring that I was born generations later? Or that my mother had named me after someone who had clearly been a badass.

A murderous badass.

But the other Queen kind of had it coming.

"May I rise now?" Penellaphe asked.

"Oh, gods," I gasped. "Yes. I'm sorry."

"No need to apologize." Penellaphe straightened, smoothing her hands over the waist of her gown. "I see the Primal foresight is developing in you."

"When it wants to." I glanced at Ward. "I feel like I should thank you."

A faint smile appeared on his weathered face. "There is also no need for that. It's not like I knew what would come of the act. I just did what I felt was right."

"So few people do that," I murmured, thinking about…well, myself.

Penellaphe smiled. "You may wonder why we've come, but I must say something first. Before you tried to summon Holland, I felt…a ripple of power. Of *life*." She clasped a hand over her wrist. "I knew it had come from here, from you, so I expected something upon arriving. But I was still unprepared for what I saw here. I'm sure most people expect the Court ruled by death to be a dark and gloomy place, but that was never what the Shadowlands was. It's not what death is supposed to be. It has always been a place of beauty, even in its darkest corners. Part of me feared I would never see the Shadowlands as it was before." Her eyes glimmered, and her voice thickened. "But you restored it."

I didn't know what to say as I glanced between the two. Saying '*thank you*' felt weird. I shifted uncomfortably as Reaver watched me. "I just did what I felt I needed to," I finally said, clearing my throat. "And I didn't even know everything that would happen. I just wanted to restore the river." I cleared my throat. "Anyway, I assume Holland sent you?"

Penellaphe nodded. "He was unable to answer but hoped we may be of aid."

It was hard to extinguish the spark of annoyance and disappointment that Holland hadn't come himself, but Rhain would be proud to hear that I managed to find my manners. "Would either of you like something to drink?"

"That would be much appreciated," Penellaphe answered. "Shadow-stepping always makes me quite thirsty."

"And me nauseous," Ward remarked.

"I will make sure refreshments are sent," Rhahar announced and bowed curtly.

"Thank you."

The god turned, looping an arm around Kars. The godling was immobile, staring wide-eyed at Ward. Sending me a wink, Rhahar all but dragged Kars from the chamber as I wondered about Kars' reaction to Ward. It was a little odd.

As the doors clicked closed behind us, I faced the two. Both remained standing. I swallowed a sigh. "You can sit if you want."

"Thank you." Penellaphe returned to the settee, and Ward joined her. "I know there must be something you wish to know, but I need to ask how you are doing first."

"Other than being slightly unprepared for my new…place in things?" I said as I moved to the settee situated across from them. Sitting, I patted the cushion beside me. "I am well."

"That's a relief," she said, the corners of her mouth tightening. "I heard you met with Kolis."

"News travels fast," I drawled.

"Well, I overheard Embris speaking of it," she said, and as Reaver hopped over to the settee, I saw the shadows in her gaze. The same haunted look I saw in Aios's eyes when she spoke about Kolis. "I do not imagine that was easy to do."

"It isn't something I care to repeat," I said. "Did Embris tell you the details of my meeting with Kolis?"

"Only that he was confident Kolis could quell any notion of an uprising."

I arched a brow at that. "He offered me a deal," I told her, then shared what I'd offered in exchange. It felt right. Kolis had also held Penellaphe. She was another who likely wanted vengeance. "Negotiating with Kolis is the last thing I want to do, but if there's a small chance we can prevent a war…"

"Then it is a chance that needs to be taken," Penellaphe finished. "An attempt for peace must always be tried."

Relieved, I nodded. "By the way, did you know this was possible? My Ascension?"

"I'd hoped Nyktos would find a way to ensure you lived while also keeping Kolis from achieving what he wanted. But did I know? No. There has never been a Primal who was born mortal," she answered. "I still hoped, even after learning that Nyktos had his *kardia* removed, that you two were destined. Fated."

"Heartmates," I said as Reaver settled onto his belly.

"Yes. It is the only way any of this is possible." She smoothed a strand of hair back and tucked it behind her ear. "And if Holland knew, it's not something he shared with me. He wouldn't have been able to, even if he wanted to."

I wasn't so sure about that. "I know what the Fates are. They're Ancients," I said, scratching Reaver under the chin as I watched both Penellaphe and Ward closely. Neither showed even a flicker of surprise upon hearing that. "They made the rules."

"That doesn't mean they can break them, Your Majesty," Penellaphe countered quietly.

"And who would punish them for doing so? Who could stop them from changing the rules?" I countered. "And please, call me Sera."

Ward cracked a grin as he leaned back. "If you only knew how many times I have asked these same questions."

"Likely as many as I did when I first got to know Holland," Penellaphe said. "It took many years for me to understand what truly occurred when they created the Primals to establish the balance of power. In doing so, certain rules were established. Ones forged in the very essence that fills the realms.

Rules that became the air that is breathed, the water that is drunk, and the fruits of the soil that is harvested. When those rules are broken, the realms *know*. I had to see that for myself to understand."

I thought of what Aydun had said about the realms restoring balance, and a sense of knowing filled me. "When Kolis stole the embers…"

She nodded. "It wasn't the Arae who acted to restore balance. The very essence itself did."

The thought of the air around us consciously acting on its own sent a chill skating down my spine as I heard footsteps approaching the doors, ones carrying an uneven gait. A moment later, a soft knock followed.

"Come in," I called.

One side of the door inched open as Pax entered with a tray held tightly between his hands.

"Paxton." I rose, a smile spreading across my lips.

"Your Majesty," he said quietly, his voice carrying notes of the most northeastern kingdoms in the mortal realm. He halted to give me a quick bow. "I have refreshments."

I started to move toward him and take the tray, but Reaver nudged my hip. When I glanced down at him, he shook his scaled head.

Paxton approached. "Arik put some sugar and creamer in the little jars," he told us as he carefully placed the tray on the table, referencing one of the cooks who came to the palace during the day. "And added some soft biscuits he thought you all might like."

"Thank you." I sat.

He nodded. "Do you need anything else?"

"I think we're fine."

There was another quick jerk of his head, then Paxton straightened. He halted, lifting his chin just enough that I caught a glimpse of his brown eyes. "I didn't get a chance to speak to you this morning, but it's good to see…" Pink crept across his lower jaw, and his head dipped once more. "That you are well."

"It's good to see you again," I said, hoping he knew I meant it as I lowered my voice. "I can't wait to see if I can heat water with just a touch of my fingers now. I'll be sure to let you know."

Through the thick strands of hair, I saw his lips curve. "Okay."

Grinning, I watched him make his way out to where Iridessa and Rhahar waited. As the doors closed, I saw Iridessa tousle the boy's already messy hair.

"He's mortal," Ward noted.

"He is." I picked up the pitcher and poured the steaming liquid into three cups.

Curiosity filled Ward's features as he helped himself to some plain tea. No sugar. No cream. He seemed like the type. "How did he end up working in the home of a Primal of Death?"

"He was orphaned and living on the streets, pickpocketing to survive."

Lifting one of the lids, I used the small spoon to scoop up some sugar. "Which was how he met Nyktos."

Penellaphe's brows rose as she went for the creamer. "He attempted to pick Nyktos's pocket, an actual Primal of Death?"

"Yes." I grinned.

"That is not something you hear often," Ward remarked, shaking his head as he lifted the cup. It was…charming to see such dainty teaware held in large hands.

"I imagine not." Taking a sip of the hot tea, I knocked my fangs against the cup in the process. I peeked over at Penellaphe and Ward to see if they'd noticed. Neither appeared to have seen, but Reaver eyed me far too closely for him not to have witnessed it. I sighed. "He's very shy."

"I could tell." Penellaphe sat back. "But you're very good with him."

I shrugged. "Did Holland know why I tried to summon him?"

She shook her head. "He had an idea that it might have to do with the prophecy. It is why he asked me to come."

"Of course, he did," I replied dryly.

There was a slight tightening to the corners of her mouth. "May I be frank?"

"Sure." I offered my cup to Reaver, and he turned his entire head away. Apparently, he didn't like tea.

"You seem angry that Holland didn't answer," she stated.

Catching her sharp tone, I arched a brow. "I was under the impression that the true Primal of Life could summon the Fates and they would answer."

"They do when there is reason to," Ward said.

"You mean having a question is not a good enough reason?" I clarified.

"What Ward means is that there has to be a purpose, one with meaning beyond a personal need," Penellaphe explained. "You summoned Holland when you could have summoned any Fate. If Holland had answered, it could've been seen as him showing you favor."

My eyes narrowed. So, if I had summoned any old Arae, could he have answered? "That is…"

"Ridiculous?" Penellaphe finished for me, taking a sip of tea. "Yes. I agree. But he wanted to. Truly."

She tipped her body toward me, holding the teacup level to her chest. "He would be here if he'd been sure that answering your summons would not have caused any issues."

"Then why didn't he broker the meeting between Kolis and me?" I asked. "It was Kolis who summoned the Arae."

"You know he's walked a fine line with you. The others know this, too." A look of sympathy crossed her features. "He's very fond of you, Sera, and he was overjoyed when he learned of your Ascension. It brought him to tears."

My gaze fell to the muddy tea as I rubbed my thumb along the smooth porcelain. I pressed my lips together. The sharp sting of my fangs against the insides of my lips was nothing compared to the burn in my throat. I already knew why Aydun had been the one to handle Kolis and me. I was being a brat, but anger was a much easier emotion to deal with than disappointment and sadness. Still, Holland…well, despite the secrets he'd kept, deserved better from me.

"I know that he cares for me. It's just that…" The drink of tea I took did little to soothe the burn. "He feels like he's part of the family I had from my life before. And I…I miss them. I miss him." Shaking my head, I glanced up. The sympathy in both their stares made me want to throw myself behind the settee. "Okay. Enough of that." I blew out a long breath. "I learned something about the prophecy while I was in Dalos."

Penellaphe blinked a few times. "From Kolis? I'm not sure what he could've said. He had no knowledge of my vision before—"

"He lied," I stated bluntly, causing Penellaphe to jerk. "Kolis knew about the prophecy before you saw it. He just didn't want you to know that."

"I…I don't understand." Penellaphe lowered her cup to the saucer she held. "How is that possible?"

"It would only be possible if another had seen it before you," Ward surmised, squinting. "Someone who, conveniently, was unable to speak of it."

"But why would he act as if he had no understanding of my vision?" she asked, twisting toward Ward. "Why would he question me incessantly about what I saw—?" The cup she held rattled against the plate. "Every little detail?"

"He wanted to make sure you didn't know the complete vision," I told her. "And it was good that you didn't. Ward is right. I got the impression that others knew of it and might be no more, including the last oracle born. And Eythos."

Eather pulsed behind her pupils. "Wait. Are you saying there was more to what the Ancients dreamt?"

"According to Kolis, there is." I took a drink of the tea and then leaned forward, placing the cup on the table. "He claimed there were three parts—a beginning, a middle, and an end. The first part was what you know. The desperation of golden crowns and all that. I don't remember it word for word."

"I do. I'll never forget it," Penellaphe whispered, clearing her throat. "From the desperation of golden crowns and born of mortal flesh, a great primal power rises as the heir to the lands and seas, to the skies and all the realms. A shadow in the ember, a light in the flame, to become a fire in the flesh." She exhaled raggedly as she stared, her eyes unfocused.

"When the stars fall from the night, the great mountains crumble into the seas, and old bones raise their swords beside the gods, the false one will be stripped from glory until two born of the same misdeeds, born of the same great and Primal power in the mortal realm. A first daughter, with blood full of fire, fated for the once-promised King." She cleared her throat.

"And the second daughter, with blood full of ash and ice, the other half of the future King. Together, they will remake the realms as they usher in the end. And so it will begin with the last Chosen blood spilled, the great conspirator birthed from the flesh and fire of the Primals will awaken as the Harbinger and the Bringer of Death and Destruction to the lands gifted by the gods. Beware, for the end will come from the west to destroy the east and lay waste to all which lies between."

Another chill curled its way down my spine, raising the small hairs on my nape. "There is another part," I said. "A part Kolis claims is the end of the vision. It's about the one born of blood and ash, and the bearer of two crowns. I wish I remembered it exactly, but the title I was given was included in that part. The part about being *bathed in the flames*—"

"Of the brightest moon." Penellaphe stood suddenly. "Keella."

Reaver lifted his head, watching the goddess as I frowned. "What?"

"It was something she said during your coronation." Penellaphe bent, placing her cup and saucer on the table. "She reacted strongly to the title Nyktos gave you, especially the brightest-moon part."

I stiffened, remembering they had been sitting together during the coronation. "She inquired about that when she approached us, asking why he had chosen that."

"Clearly, that part references you. The bearer of two crowns," Penellaphe stated. "The rightful heir to Lasania, and you as the Consort."

"That's what Kolis believes."

"Is there more?" Ward asked, his forehead creased.

"Yes, and it's pretty…creepy." My fingers pressed into my knees. Closing my eyes, I concentrated hard on what Kolis had said. "Great…great powers will stumble and fall. Those left standing will tremble as they kneel, will weaken as they become forgotten. For finally, the Primal rises, the giver of blood and the bringer of bone, the Primal of Blood and Ash." I opened my eyes. "That's not the whole thing exactly, but it's the general gist of it."

Penellaphe stared at me, her lips parted. For a moment, I wasn't sure if she breathed.

"He thinks it's talking about him," I continued. "That he will make the great powers stumble and fall as he rises as the Primal of Blood and Bone."

Penellaphe continued to stare.

"Are you all right?" Ward asked, touching her arm. A moment passed before she nodded. "Then can you sit?"

Her gown billowed around her as she did as he asked.

"And maybe speak?" I added. "You're starting to make me nervous."

Penellaphe blinked rapidly. "He…he says that's the end of the prophecy?"

"Yes."

Her hands curled into tight fists as strands of eather lashed through her eyes. "He's wrong."

"I know what I saw. Wars yet to take place. Cities yet to fall and rise once more. I saw *them* hundreds of years from now. Longer. A near millennium. I saw *her*. The Queen of Flesh and Fire in the mortal realm, where blood trees grow."

"I remember you speaking of her and a King." I racked my memory. "You said they…felt right."

"They felt like hope," she whispered, squeezing her eyes tight. "This part he speaks of? The giver of blood and the bringer of bone? I think I know what that means. Blood symbolizes life."

"Bone represents death," I murmured, my mind flashing to when I stood with Aydun beneath Aios's trees.

"Yes. Life and death. Blood and bone," Penellaphe said, her knuckles turning white as she fisted the skirt of her gown. "That part speaks of a Primal of Life and Death."

"That's what we figured, too. And the giver of blood and the bringer of bone?" I frowned. "You think that's referencing something or someone else?"

Her gaze lowered as she shook her head. "Possibly. It makes sense. But what I do know is that what I saw happens in the future. The part that involves the two daughters?" Her lashes swept up. Eather pulsed brightly in her eyes. "It is they who will remake the realms. They will usher in the end. Not Kolis."

"That whole usher-in-the-end part still sounds as bad as it did the first time I heard it," I said, even more confused. "How can you be sure that's the end of the vision?"

"Because all that occurs after our awakening, and we haven't gone to sleep yet," she said. "That is when the realms are remade. Not before."

I shifted closer to Reaver. "You saw yourself sleeping? Going into stasis?"

"I saw most of the gods going into stasis. A long one," she told me. "I didn't elaborate on that part when Holland and I first spoke to you and Nyktos. I didn't think it was an important detail."

My stomach twisted. "And when does this happen? *Why* would it happen?"

"It won't happen for quite some time. When? I can't say for sure, but I know of things that have yet to occur. Things that will." Her right hand fluttered to her stomach. "And why? That, I also can't say. But it didn't feel bad. It felt natural. Like it was time."

Now, it was I who stared at her.

She laughed lightly. "I know that going into stasis for hundreds of years can sound frightening."

"*Hundreds* of years?" I mumbled.

"But I've heard it passes as quickly as a handful of nights."

"Uh-huh," was all I could say.

Ward turned his head but not quickly enough that I missed his grin.

"But what's important is that Kolis is wrong. What he thinks is the end—that it's him rising? He's wrong," she repeated, her voice steadying and becoming more confident. "He is."

Maybe… "Or you're both right."

Her brows pinched. "What do you mean?"

"You believed that the great conspirator was Kolis, right? I always thought it sounded like he would reawaken." Unnerved, I resisted the urge to rise and begin pacing. "And you said the gods go into stasis. Who's to say that Kolis doesn't, too? And the end you saw is when he awakens."

As soon as I said that, I thought about Ash's and my original plan to entomb Kolis, and the unsettled feeling grew. "The Ancient who brokered the meeting between Kolis and me—Aydun? Do you know him?"

"I've only seen him a few times in passing," she said. "I do not enter Mount Lotho, where they live. Not even with Holland."

"Well, he said something before I spoke with Kolis. That war between the Primals could only be won once there was blood and bone. And I can't shake the feeling that it ties into the prophecy."

A slight frown appeared. "Why did he say that?"

"I honestly don't know, other than it seemed like he was urging me to find a way to prevent war." I brushed a crumb from Reaver's foreleg. "He said that, in all the threads he'd seen, war wasn't prevented. But that me Ascending as the true Primal of Life was changing some threads." My head tilted. "Which is strange. Why would I be that unexpected considering you," I said to Ward, "were made a *viktor* because you helped create my bloodline?"

"But that was just the thread that started yours," Penellaphe said.

"And yeah, it seemed like I wouldn't Ascend, but…" I shook my head. "The whole fate and thread stuff makes my head hurt."

"Same," Ward murmured, looking at Penellaphe as she fell silent.

Her honey-hued hair swayed as she shook her head. "That part about the bearer of two crowns? He believes that is referencing you. What about the great Primal power rising? He believes that is him? But it can't be. The phrasing—*giver* of blood and the *bringer* of bone doesn't make sense. It would mean that he brings about—or brings into creation—the Primal of Blood and Bone. Not that he becomes that."

"I could be repeating it wrong." Frustration rose. "That's completely possible."

But if I hadn't?

"That could be the case." Ward leaned forward, resting his elbows on his knees. "But it sounds like someone may know exactly what that part of the prophecy states. Someone other than Kolis."

My gaze darted to Penellaphe, and I knew the moment she realized the same thing I did.

She smiled. "Keella." Excitement glimmered in Penellaphe's ocean-blue eyes. "She's old enough that she could've learned about the Ancients' dream and was clever enough to keep Kolis from realizing it."

I nodded in agreement, more than hopeful. It had been clear to me that Keella had known something when she approached Ash and me at the coronation and spoke about my title. Could it be the vision? And could that possibly mean that she not only knows what it means but also its correct order?

"Nyktos is currently asking Attes to assist with summoning the Primals," I shared with them. "We already plan to visit the Thyia Plains afterward to speak with Keella about the Ancients." I forced a heavy exhale. Patience had never been a virtue of mine. I wanted to go to the Thyia Plains right now, but I needed to be smart instead of impatient. Which was also not normally a part of my nature. "I will ask her then."

"Now, this summoning-the-Primals business?" The goddess picked up her cup. "Are you asking them to come to the Shadowlands?"

"We are." From the corner of my eye, I saw Reaver take note of the biscuits. "We know it will be risky, but we decided it was important for us to know who will stand with us and who will rise against us."

"*We*." Penellaphe gave a delicate shudder. "You have no idea how long it has been since any of us has heard the Primal of Life use the word *we* when speaking of decisions being made. It's positively orgasmic."

Ward arched a brow and gave her a sideways look.

Grinning wryly, I leaned forward and picked up one of the flaky biscuits. "There was something else I wanted to talk to Holland about." Sitting back, I tore a small piece of the pastry off and said, "I wanted to ask him about Eythos's plan and Sotoria's soul."

"Oh, I'm not sure what I can tell you about that." Surprise flickered across her lovely features as she looked between Ward and me. "But I can try."

"I don't understand what Eythos was thinking when he developed this plan of his," I began, trying to make sense of my thoughts as I offered a piece of the biscuit to Reaver. He took it quickly and without taking my fingers in the process. "He placed the embers of life and Sotoria's soul together to create a weapon that could kill Kolis."

A frown tugged at Penellaphe's brow. "Yes. That is how I understand it."

"But he had to know that Kolis cannot be killed unless another can be Ascended to take his place. Kolis made sure that wasn't possible. Which is something Eythos knew," I said as Reaver reached over and snatched the remainder of the pastry. I hoped he wasn't listening too closely to us. "I assume he believed that I, as Sotoria, would succeed in killing Kolis, and then his son would Ascend as the true Primal of Life—which is a huge risk to take on just an assumption. He would have had to believe that I would not only want to kill Kolis but would also be capable of doing so. And perhaps that is also why he went to Holland in the first place. Hoping the Fates would get involved somehow and prepare me."

Penellaphe's frown deepened.

"But that doesn't address the fact that with Kolis's death, his essence would return to the realms. It would cause untold destruction and upset the balance. And I know what happens when the balance is so greatly uneven."

"That is true," Penellaphe began, returning her cup to the saucer, "but only if the last of the true embers of Death aren't removed from Kolis and transferred to another strong enough to withstand the power of them and Ascend. That is not the same as a natural Ascension, but it should work since the Arae are the ones who obtained the Star diamond for a situation such as this."

I rocked back. "I hadn't even considered that," I admitted. Had Ash? "If no gods can rise to take the embers, transferring them is sort of a loophole," I murmured. That made sense, but… "But it's still a huge risk. One that leaves no room for error. Eythos would've been working off the assumption that not only could I manage to kill Kolis without getting taken out in the process, but also that it would be done after we learned about something like the Star diamond, located it, and then used it to transfer the embers. All at the same time his son took the ones from me. Eythos couldn't have been *that* reckless."

"But you did learn of The Star. Things happen for a reason," she stressed, her stare meeting mine. "Some things work out, whether it is the Arae or the essence itself."

"And that is what Eythos was banking on?"

"I think Eythos may have believed that Nyktos would take the embers from you before they were impossible to remove," she reminded me, sending a glance at Reaver, who was happily chowing down on his second biscuit. "Removing the embers wouldn't have removed Sotoria's soul. You would have still been able to weaken Kolis enough for the embers to be transferred."

"In other words, Eythos never expected his son to fall in love with the weapon he created. Or my recklessness," I said, thinking about how the tiny bit of blood I'd taken from Ash the first night we were together had changed everything.

"But your recklessness also saved you, did it not?" Penellaphe asked. "You may not have survived the Culling either way, and you wouldn't have Ascended to become the true Primal of Life."

Holland had once suggested something similar.

"But his plan didn't work in more ways than one. I'm not Sotoria. Her soul only resided in me. Even if everything else had gone as planned, I may have been able to weaken him but not kill him." I fell quiet upon realizing that Penellaphe was gaping at me. "Did Holland not tell you? He had to know that I wasn't her. Attes knew. So did Callum."

"There is only so much Holland can tell me unless I happen upon the information myself," she said. "And even then, he must walk a fine line regarding what he confirms."

I blew out a heavy breath. "That would drive me insane."

Penellaphe laughed softly. "It has been…trying, but I love him."

My breath caught. The way she said that—so simply. As if it were the only reason needed.

And it was.

It really was.

"Attes said the Fates could've intervened and made it so Sotoria and I were not one and the same as a way to restore the balance," I said. "But I got the impression that Holland believed I *was* Sotoria."

"As did I," Penellaphe admitted, creases forming in her brow again. "But if he knew or even suspected that what Eythos did hadn't worked, and depending on what that kind of knowledge may have impacted, he would not have been able to say anything."

My jaw tightened. "I don't like it, but I get it. Especially in this situation where both Eythos and Kolis did a number on fate and balance." I was rather proud of my response. What came out of my mouth next ruined it, though. "It's still fucking annoying."

Penellaphe's lips twitched.

"Her soul?" Ward cut in, drawing my attention. Tension bracketed his mouth. "Does it still remain in you?"

"I didn't want her soul in me when it came time for Nyktos to take the embers," I shared. "I thought I was going to die, and her soul…"

"It would've been lost," Penellaphe finished, her voice troubled. "*She* would've been lost." Her eyes widened. "You found The Star. Is that…?" The goddess blanched as if she couldn't bring herself to say it.

"Yes. Her soul is in there. For now." Rubbing the heels of my palms over my knees, I thought everything over. I had more questions than I'd had before. Frustration rose, but I knew it wasn't Penellaphe's fault. "Which means using The Star to transfer the embers anytime soon is out of the question."

"Back to the part about Eythos's plan," Ward began after a moment, stretching out a long leg. "I know I don't know much."

"That's not true." Penellaphe's smile turned fond. "You often figure things out before I do."

"We'll have to disagree on that," he replied, and I had to think, for someone who lived as long as he had and would, there *was* likely a lot he knew. "But what if we're wrong about what Eythos actually planned? Sometimes, we start off thinking one thing and stick with it despite new information or evidence that points to the contrary of what we believe."

Reaver eyed him and then lifted his head, listening intently.

"And in this case?" Ward dragged the back of his hand over his chin, the creases at the corners of his eyes deepening. "We believe that Eythos planned for you to become this weapon, armed with the embers and Sotoria's soul. But what if we were wrong about what he intended?"

Penellaphe twisted toward him. "What do you mean?"

"I have to admit, I, too, have a hard time wrapping my head around all the risks Eythos took. Though I never met the man." His gaze flicked to the goddess before returning to me. "I heard he could be impulsive," he continued, and I thought about the *lyrue* he'd created. "But he was also very smart. This plan we believe to be his? It's full of so many holes I could fall through it." Ward dropped his hand to his thigh. "What if this—or a part of this— is what he intended all along? That either you or Sotoria Ascended as the true Primal of Life, therefore truly making you the weapon he intended? One that could go toe to toe with Kolis and make sure another could take on the embers."

Like Ash? Could Eythos have intended that for his son instead of him becoming the true Primal of Life?

"This," Ward repeated, his sea-blue eyes meeting mine, "could've been his plan all along."

And if it was, then…

Kolis knew how The Star worked, and he knew we had it. He'd even said that Ash would be clever enough to figure out its importance. Kolis would expect us to use The Star against him, and for Ash to take the true Primal of Death embers.

My heart felt like it stopped as my gaze fell on the marriage imprint. Although Ash and I hadn't discussed the fact that he was a Primal of no Court, I hadn't forgotten that realization.

I wasn't a threat to Kolis.

Ash was.

And that put a target on him.

Shooting to my feet, I startled the goddess and the *viktor*. "I need to go."

Reaver rocked back on his hind legs, lifting his wings. He rose into the air and followed me.

"It's all right," I told him, not wanting him to worry.

"Is it?" Penellaphe asked.

"Yes," I said, about to make damn sure everything was fine. "I'm sorry to end this meeting abruptly."

"It's okay." Penellaphe scooted forward. "Is there anything we can help you with?"

I shook my head as I opened the door. There was a good chance I was overreacting. As long as Ash remained in Essaly, Kyn wouldn't sense his presence. But…

My skin prickled, and I thought back to right after Rhain and I had parted ways. I'd been pacing, and yeah, I was almost always moving or fidgeting, but there had been an undercurrent of edginess there. One I thought had been fueled by not doing something proactive.

What if I had been wrong?

I looked down at the shimmering swirl on my right hand as I opened the door. The sight of it quelled some of my fears.

But not all of them.

Reaver flew out behind me as Rhahar pushed off the wall, and Kars stiffened. The godling took one look at me and went on alert. "What's going on?"

"I don't know." I stopped, sparing a quick glance down the hall as Reaver circled above. "It's probably nothing, but I have this…feeling. I need to see Nyktos."

A frown pinched Rhahar's brow. "He's still in Vathi."

Reaver landed beside me. *Is it the* vadentia*?* I heard the question in my head.

"I'm not sure," I said aloud, my fingers twitching. "But I need to go to Vathi."

Kars and Rhahar exchanged a look. "Lailah is with him, and so is Nektas," the god reminded me.

"I know." I pivoted halfway and started down the hall toward the foyer. "But I still need to go."

"I'm not sure that's wise." Kars hurried behind me. "We can get Bele or Rhain to check on—"

My gut clenched. If something was happening or about to, there was no way I would risk endangering any of them. "No."

I want to go with you. Reaver's voice reached me.

Immediately, the image of his limp body after Veses had so viciously hurt him flashed in my mind. "Absolutely not."

Reaver dipped down, extending his wings. He landed in front of me, squawking as his cobalt eyes narrowed until only a hint of the slit-shaped pupils were visible. He straightened to his tallest height possible. *But I can help you.*

"I know you can." I knelt and cupped Reaver's scaled cheek. "But you cannot go with me."

I need to be where mayeeh Liessa *is*, he insisted. *I may be small, but I am brave.*

"I know you're brave." My heart squeezed as if he'd wrapped himself around it, and in a way, he had. "Isn't Jadis here?"

Reaver gave me a reluctant nod.

"While I'm gone, I would feel better knowing you are here to keep her safe. Just in case anything happens," I said.

His wings arced high and then swept down, tucking close to his body. He turned his head away.

My hand lowered to my knee. "What is it?"

He shook his head.

"When you and Nyktos were…gone last time," Rhahar said quietly from behind us, "Reaver thought he could've prevented what happened."

Oh, gods.

"This isn't like that. I promise." I gently curved my fingers around his chin, guiding his gaze back to mine. "And there was nothing you or anyone else could've done. Do you understand?"

Bright, glimmering blue eyes met mine, and that brought tears to my own eyes. *I do.*

I didn't think he did, and that was something Ash and I would have to make sure he understood. "You'll keep Jadis safe while I'm gone?"

Always.

"That's my Reaver-butt." I pressed a quick kiss to the top of his head, right beneath the nubs of his newly sprouted horns.

"Sera—" Kars began.

I rose. "I'm going to Vathi." I faced them, pulling the Queen card. "No one else is going, and that is an order."

Rhahar's jaw hardened. "Got it."

"Perfect." I turned.

"Just one question," he continued. "Exactly how are you getting there?"

I stiffened. Good gods, that hadn't even crossed my mind.

"You haven't shadowstepped that far, right? And even if you have, you don't know where you're going to move that fast. So, you're on horseback. That will take hours. And that's the shortest route, which puts you smack-dab in the middle of the territory controlled by Kyn," Rhahar continued. "To go to where Attes is, you've got to cross over Mount Rhee. You're looking at a day's ride at least."

My stomach gave another twist at the mere thought of doing that alone, especially since it wasn't the kind of shadowstepping that was as simple as moving really fast. It was shadowstepping through the eather, basically tearing open the realms, and I had no idea how to do that. But I knew how to find out. "How do you shadowstep between realms?"

"I don't know how to explain it," Rhahar caged his response.

But I wasn't asking him.

I'd asked myself.

The skin behind my left ear tingled, and the knowledge came to me, much like remembering something I hadn't thought of in a while.

Shadowstepping between Courts or even realms was like using the Primal essence for anything else. It was a result of *my will.* I just needed to think of where I wanted to go and then will it.

Except I didn't know exactly where Ash was in Vathi. He could be at the palace or somewhere else, but could I shadowstep to where Ash was?

The answer came to me in an instant.

Running my palm over the top of Reaver's head, I turned to Kars and Rhahar as I pictured Ash in my mind. "Keep an eye on things."

"Damn it," Kars exploded.

Smiling, I grabbed onto the image of Ash as I harnessed the Primal essence.

"Seraphena!" Rhahar lurched forward.

Power surged through me like a fiery torrent as I willed myself to Ash's side.

Strands of gold and silver spilled out from me, forcing Rhahar back as the tendrils of eather whipped against the air, ripping open a blinding tear.

I walked through it without a second thought.

Eather spun maddeningly as a fierce rush of pine-and-sea-scented wind enveloped me, tossing the wisps of hair that had escaped my braid across my face. Awareness throbbed in the center of my chest, and I felt *him*.

Then I heard Lailah gasp and say, "Fates." Through the essence, I briefly saw her staggering to the side. I may have nearly shadowstepped *into* her.

Whoops.

The tendrils of gold-and-silver-streaked eather slowed and faded, revealing slivers of stone, ivory walls covered in bright-green ivy that glistened in the sunlight, and comfortable-looking brown leather settees. Several people were there, but at first, I only saw him.

Ash stood only a few feet from me, a shadowstone dagger strapped across his broad chest. He crossed that space in half a heartbeat.

"Sera." He clasped my cheeks, and a charge of energy shifted between us. "What are you doing—?"

"Is everything all right?" I cut in as Nektas appeared to Ash's left. We were on some sort of veranda.

"Of course."

"That's debatable," muttered Attes in his familiar, deep voice just as I heard the distant sound of barking dogs.

"What do you mean it's debatable?" I started to turn my head toward Attes.

Ash wasn't having it. He kept my attention on him. "Forget about him."

"That's rude," the Primal remarked as Lailah crossed between Ash and Nektas, holding a bronze cup.

"You shadowstepped *here*?" Ash stated. "By yourself?"

The way he said it, like I was a child not old enough to ride a horse by myself, stroked my already frayed nerves. And not in a good way. "Three things."

Behind Ash, Nektas pressed his lips together and sat on one of the wicker settees.

"Number one," I said, holding up my hand, "I obviously shadowstepped here. Number two, I'm also *clearly* capable of doing so by myself."

Ash straightened. "Number three?"

"I'm not a child," I snapped and saw Lailah's eyes double in size as she lifted the cup to her lips.

"Trust me, *liessa*," Ash drawled, his voice dropping to a shadowy, silky tone that stroked all the *right* nerves. "I know you are no child."

I ignored the simmering heat curling low in my stomach. Now was not the time for that nonsense. "Good to know we're on the same page, but I wasn't done. I came here because I was worried about you."

"*Liessa*..." The line of his jaw softened. "That was four things."

"Don't even try being cute," I warned him. "I should've just ignored the feeling I had."

"Sometimes, I think, '*Hey, I'm feeling lonely. Maybe I should look for something more long-term*,'" Attes said to no one in particular. "But then I'm always quickly reminded of why I'm more into the short-term."

Lailah huffed out a dry laugh. "As if that is a choice," she said under her breath.

A throat cleared behind me. This time, Ash didn't stop me from turning. Before I could even meet his gaze or speak, Attes lowered himself to one knee and placed his empty hand over his chest.

"*Meyaah Liessa*," he said, his head bowed so deeply that his hair tumbled forward in waves.

"That's not necessary," I said for what felt like the hundredth time.

"It's completely necessary," Ash drawled.

I shot him an arch look. He simply winked at me.

"I agree with Nyktos," Attes replied. "I'm honored to do so. It has been far too long since I have felt pleasure upon paying such respect."

The air chilled behind me.

"I would gladly spend a hundred years on my knee before you," Attes continued, his tone turning to silk. "Both of them if you so requested that of me."

"Well, *that's* really not necessary at all." I fought a grin as the temperature in the antechamber cooled more. "You can rise, you know."

"Your wish is my command." Attes rose, lifting his head. A flicker of surprise washed over his face as he blinked—correction...as he blinked *one* eye.

My mouth dropped open. It wasn't the shallow scar running from his hairline, across the bridge of his nose, and down his left cheek that had caught my attention. His right eye was swollen shut, and the skin around it and the lid were a gruesome shade of reddish-purple. "What happened to your eye?"

"Oh, this? It's courtesy of that one." He jerked his chin toward Ash. "Your dear husband."

My mouth fell open for the second time. I slowly turned my head to Ash.

"My fist slipped."

"It must've slipped really hard to leave that bruise." I crossed my arms.

"It did," he replied, his gaze sweeping over me.

"And did you hit him before or after he agreed to attend this meeting?"

"Does it look like he hit me only once?" Attes countered.

"You hit him twice?" I screeched.

"No," Ash said, dragging his lower lip between his teeth. "Three times."

I stared at him in disbelief. There were far more important things to focus on, but I couldn't believe he'd hit Attes three—

"It was more like four," Lailah corrected.

I turned to her. "I thought you were here to make sure they behaved."

"She tried, but she was unsuccessful," Attes said. "And that's kind of your fault. Since you declared him King—which I agree with, by the way—he demanded that she not interfere."

Ash smiled tightly. "I did do that."

Nektas snorted.

My head swung back to the draken. "And you couldn't stop him?"

"I could have." Nektas took a drink from his cup. "But Attes had it coming."

"Oh, my gods," I muttered, turning back to Attes. "And you were somehow unable to defend yourself?"

"What was I to do?" Attes tilted his head, sending a lock of sandy hair against a cheek also mottled, though a less violent shade of red. "Striking a King would be considered treasonous."

"That is true," Ash said.

I took a deep, calming breath. "That looks painful."

"It feels about ten times more painful than it looks," he said.

Ash huffed. "Don't waste your time feeling sorry for him. He could heal it. He's just not doing it."

"Why are you—?"

"Because he's attention-starved," Lailah interrupted.

I turned back to the Primal. The bruises did look terrible, but the Primal of Accord and War was a strikingly handsome man, even with the bruised and swollen eye. Not even the scar detracted from the chiseled features. But when I looked at the scar, I couldn't stop myself from thinking about how he'd gotten it. He'd been trying to stop Kolis from killing his children.

Gods, how fucking terrible was that? Kolis had harmed so many people, and all because he'd lost what was never his in the first place.

Sotoria.

Now that the shock of seeing Attes's black eye had faded, all sorts of messy emotions rose in me. I was happy to see him. Attes had helped me when I was held in Dalos, but he had seen a lot, and that brought forth so much anxiety it was no wonder I'd felt like I might vomit earlier. His presence also stirred up shame. And no matter how much I knew I shouldn't feel that, I couldn't stop my skin from feeling like it was crawling.

I looked away and drew in a shallow breath. "I feel the need to apologize for my husband's *ill-advised* actions."

"There is no need," Attes said.

"*That*, we can agree on," Ash remarked.

Attes stepped closer. "Your eyes. I've never seen anything like them."

My ears prickled at the low rumble of warning coming from Ash.

A gleam sparkled in Attes's one good eye, and it had nothing to do with the eather. "They are absolutely beautiful," he went on as if completely oblivious to the dark energy ramping up on the veranda. "Stunning."

"Thanks," I said. "I guess they happened because there's never been a true Primal of Life who was born mortal, so…" I gave a one-shouldered shrug.

"No," Attes said, practically purring the word. "There has not."

"You're showing a little *too* much respect," Ash advised coolly. "Keep it up and you'll find yourself neutered."

I nearly choked. "Really?"

"Really."

"That's a painful process I hope not to experience." Attes chuckled, and a deep dimple appeared on his right cheek amid the bruises. The glint of devilry faded from his smile. It was then that I noticed the shadows under his eyes. A pang lit up my chest. He didn't look like he'd gotten a lot of sleep, and I figured that had to do with his brother.

His enemy.

He took my hand, and two things happened. A faint charge of energy passed between us. And the Primal behind me growled.

"Ash," I snapped, exasperated.

"It's all right. He's only being protective of you. As he should," Attes said. I wasn't sure I agreed with that, especially considering Ash knew better. "I am glad to see that you are well. When I saw you last…"

I swallowed thickly, nodding at what went unsaid. When we were at the Primal Keella's residence in the Thyia Plains, I'd clearly been dying. I hadn't thought I would see him again, either.

"But here you stand, alive and the true Primal of Life. I could not be happier." He glanced at Ash. "And that is all because of you."

Ash said nothing as he stepped up and slipped an arm around my waist.

"And because of you." I squeezed Attes's hand. "I don't remember if I thanked you for your aid while I was in Dalos. But even if I did…thank you."

"There's no need."

"There is," I insisted. Ash's cool chest brushed my back. "If you hadn't taken the risk and told me I wasn't Sotoria, I would've seriously tried to kill Kolis. And it wouldn't have worked. He would've known the truth, and I would either be dead or…"

Or worse.

That also went unsaid.

Ash's lips brushed my cheek. "She speaks the truth."

Attes's smile was small and heartfelt, but there, as he released my hand. "He already thanked me once. No need to do it again."

Raising a brow, I looked over my shoulder at Ash. "You actually thanked him?"

"Yes." He kissed my temple. "I told you. We worked things out."

"With your fists," I muttered.

"He actually thanked me before he hit me," Attes said. "Or was it between the first and second punch?"

"It was between them," Ash said.

I shook my head. "I do not understand either of you."

"We understand each other," Attes interjected.

I supposed that was all that mattered.

I started to turn back to Ash when a shiver of unease coursed through me, each hair on my body standing on end. Instinct kicked in—the kind that had nothing to do with the *vadentia* and everything to do with the primitive part of my consciousness that sensed…

That death was in the air.

My eyes flew to Ash's.

He stilled, eather flaring brightly in his silver eyes as he picked up on my emotions.

Nektas rose, his chin lifting as he inhaled deeply.

Eather flooded my veins as I spun, scanning the thick, sweeping pines crowding the foothills of the snowcapped mountains. My heart began to pound.

"If you're feeling something, I'm not," Attes said as I walked forward.

"Neither am I," Nektas said. "But I do *smell* something."

Attes's booted feet hitting the stone as he walked echoed across the veranda as I eyed the dark shadows between the tightly packed trees.

I squinted, straining to see as far as I could into the vast forest. There was something about the darker splotches farther back. They didn't seem right. They were too thick and suddenly seemed closer. The barking from Essaly—in the opposite direction of the forest—picked up in a nervous, almost frantic chorus.

"What do you smell?" Ash asked.

I stopped at the edge of the veranda. What I saw weren't shadows. They were solid and prowled between the trees. I tensed as I suddenly saw a pair of amber orbs reflecting back at me. Dozens of them. But they weren't orbs.

They were *eyes.*

"I smell wet dog," Nektas answered as the luminous, predatory glow blinked out of existence.

"Son of a bitch," Attes growled as branches low to the ground rattled.

The barking ceased.

My lips parted as a…dog trotted out from the forest, its fur shining a deep reddish brown in the sunlight—if dogs could grow to be a size somewhere between a kiyou wolf and a dakkai, that was. And if they looked like they had been bred with a barrat.

The creature was ugly, and not in a it's-so-cute-it's-ugly kind of way. Fur rose in spikes all along its back—not because it was matted into that form but because it just naturally grew that way—or so it appeared. There was no fur on the pointy, twitching ears or on most of its tail, except for a frizzy ball at the end. And its face? Well, that was where the barrat part came in. It had the face of an overgrown rodent, whiskers and all.

"*Kynakos,*" I murmured, eyes widening. "Dogs of War."

The creature started prowling toward us, sniffing the air.

Attes was suddenly standing between us and the creature. "*Stasi dato,*" he ordered.

The dog's upper lip curled as it growled, baring teeth that would make a dakkai nervous.

Ash was beside me at once. "I don't think it's standing down."

"*Stasi dato nori,*" Attes shouted.

The creature's yellow eyes flickered over Attes to where Ash and I stood. Its powerful muscles rolled along its sides and back a heartbeat before it leapt into the sky. I jerked forward.

Ash caught my arm, and Attes cursed, moving blindingly fast. He caught the dog around the neck.

My eyes slammed shut, and I winced at the yelp and the sharp, sudden crack of bone I heard. "Poor puppy," I murmured.

"That's not a puppy, *liessa,*" Ash said, his hand sliding from my arm to my waist. "They're venomous beasts."

But it still looked and sounded like a dog. Kind of.

I cracked open one eye just in time to see Attes laying the hound down. He did so almost reverently.

"I assume that's not one of yours," Nektas said.

"No." Attes rose, his back still to us. "I stopped breeding them ages ago. They have the temperament of a starving dakkai, and you almost always have to put them down to avoid unnecessary bloodshed."

My hands closed at my sides. "Kyn."

Attes nodded. "He never stopped breeding them. But they've always listened to me. They're bred only to obey a Primal of Vathi."

The eather hummed violently as I lifted my gaze to the forest. It had gone eerily quiet. Had I overreacted by coming here? "Did my presence draw it here?"

"No," Attes answered. "The *kynakos* are fast, but it would take an hour or so for any of them to make their way here from Vangar, where Kyn resides. Unless…"

"Unless what?" Ash's arm tightened around me.

"The forests here are thick enough that damn near anything could be inside them and it wouldn't be seen from the sky," he said, looking down at the *kynakos*. "He hasn't tried it before."

"But things are different now," I said. "He knows who you've allied with, and he was in Dalos yesterday. He could've sent one of them to keep an eye on you."

"And with you spending your free time shit-faced," Lailah said, her chest rising with a sharp inhale as Attes's head jerked up, "you wouldn't be paying close enough attention to know if one of them was near your home."

I half-expected him to give her some playful or witty retort, but he didn't. A muscle flexed in his jaw.

"Let's hope it was just one of them." Lailah had drawn closer as she rubbed the heel of her palm against her chest. "No one wants to face a pack of war dogs on the hunt."

On the hunt…

If they hadn't been lurking nearby, and it would take them an hour or so to get there…?

My hand went to Ash's arm. Energy throbbed as I lifted my gaze to the pines once more. It was still so quiet. The prickly sensation remained, telling me I hadn't overreacted. Attes started to turn, the breeze ruffling his hair, and I remembered. I had been urged to come here for a reason. That…

The pine branches began to rattle again.

"There's not only one." My fingers dug into Ash's arm.

Attes swore, whipping his attention back to the pines. "Get inside the palace. Now."

It happened so fast that it left no time for escape. The Dogs of War exploded out of the forest—dozens of them. They raced across the field, jaws snapping and tails thumping.

"Motherfucker," Lailah muttered, withdrawing her sword.

As Ash pulled his shadowstone blade from its baldric, my right hand flew to my thigh but came up empty. "Shit," I muttered.

"Stay back," Ash said, flipping the dagger. "You have no weapon, and their bite is nasty as fuck, even to a Primal."

"You have two daggers," I pointed out. "And I have the eather."

"You just used a whole lot of it to restore the Shadowlands," he reminded me. "And you're still a—"

"Baby Primal," Attes threw out as he whirled.

"Exactly," Ash said as my eyes narrowed. His gaze met mine. "We've got this."

My hands curled into fists. "Have I mentioned how much I miss my dagger?"

Attes dipped, catching one of the beasts around the shoulders as another rushed him.

"Attes!" Lailah shouted, darting forward. "Behind you!"

He cranked his head around as a *kynakos* leapt over the Primal as if he were just an obstacle in its way.

Clumps of grass kicked up as the Dog of War landed near the steps, its yellow eyes fixed on—

Bone cracked as Ash stepped forward and launched a shadowstone dagger at the *kynakos,* striking it square between the eyes. It fell back, dead before it hit the ground. "Do I have two daggers?" he responded.

"Asshole," I muttered as another shot past Attes, saliva dripping from its gaping mouth.

Nektas stalked toward the veranda just as Lailah spun, her long, dark braids fanning out as she brought her sword down on the back of the *kynakos's* neck. Dark red blood spurted and mixed with smoke as Nektas's chin lowered—

"Holy shit." I jerked back as a powerful stream of silver flames erupted from the draken's very mortal mouth.

The funnel of fire slammed into the beast, engulfing the creature within a heartbeat.

I stared at Nektas while Attes tackled another war dog. "You just spit fire from your mouth."

"I did," Nektas replied, wisps of smoke wafting out from the corners of his lips.

"Yeah," I whispered, blinking rapidly. Never in my life had I seen anything like that.

"I wish you could see your face right now." Ash pulled his dagger free from the *kynakos* and tossed a grin over his shoulder. "It's quite adorable." He whirled, releasing the other dagger. The blade struck the *kynakos* Attes had pinned to the ground.

Lailah cursed as one of the beasts dodged her. "What?" She straightened, her grip firming on the hilt of her sword. "Do I not look tasty?"

"You always look tasty." Attes grunted as he snatched another *kynakos.* "Exceptionally so."

"I didn't ask for your opinion," Lailah retorted, stalking past Attes.

Attes replied to her as he twisted the beast's neck, but I didn't hear what he said. That prickly, unnerving feeling remained as silver flames swallowed another Dog of War. The scent of burning fur and charred flesh filled the air as my gaze flitted from one *kynakos* to the next. My fingers twitched as one after another avoided injury, their focus singular. The *kynakos* were on the hunt. Another skidded to the side as flames pummeled the ground.

On the hunt…

A *kynakos* barreled past Nektas, its jaws snapping at the air as Ash turned, the length of his blade soaked in blood. Like before, the beast ignored closer targets.

"The Primal of no Court," I murmured, my stomach dipping as Attes grabbed the *kynakos* around its waist. Fear punched through my chest.

Ash shoved the dagger under the massive beast's jaw and turned his head toward me.

"I didn't overreact." Red-hot fury replaced the fear and had me stalking toward the veranda steps. "They're hunting you."

Nektas's gaze shot to mine. Understanding flared. "Fuck."

The corners of my vision turned white as power swelled inside me. Summoning eather to fight wasn't something I'd done often. When I used the eather against Kolis before my Ascension, it had been instinctual, born of panic and rage. The essence had just responded to my emotions—

No, it wasn't only that.

It had also responded to my will, just as it had when I summoned the water to fill the rivers. Even before my Ascension, the essence responded to what I wanted. Yes, it could be stoked by my emotions, and I had lost control before, but I wielded it. The eather didn't have power over me, and I was no longer just a vessel.

I controlled it.

Me.

No one else.

I lifted my hand, and the essence responded immediately to my summons. I understood the downside of using the essence, but these furry bastards were hunting *my* heartmate. And if I had to choose between him and anything—anyone—else, I would *always* choose him.

Bands of gold-tipped silvery light sparked, swirling down my arm. My will formed in my mind, and within a second, it transformed into raw energy. Eather erupted from my fingertips, forming several torrents of hissing, twisting gold-and-silver energy bolts. The tendrils of eather snaked through the air, casting flickering light and shadows across the grass.

Ash whipped around as a *kynakos* launched itself at him. The first current of eather slammed into the beast, and because I willed it a quick, *soundless* death, the Dog of War was snuffed out. Obliterated.

"Fuck," rasped Ash, tracking the essence as my gaze flicked to the right. Eather caught a *kynakos* mid-jump as a branch of energy spun between him and Nektas, arcing and then diving—

Attes swore, springing toward Lailah. He grabbed her around the waist.

"What the—?" she exclaimed as he lifted and spun her away from the tendrils of eather. "Was that even necessary?"

Attes held her several feet off the ground. "I don't want you to get hurt."

Coils of crackling essence formed a web and streaked above the grass, fanning out in every direction. The moment the energy brushed up against a *kynakos,* it was extinguished in a flash of bright light, leaving nothing behind but a shower of glittering dust. That, too, disappeared.

The field was empty, but I didn't call the eather back to me. The twists of pulsing power reared back, poised to strike.

"*Liessa*," Ash said, coming up the veranda steps. "I think you got them all."

Nodding, I scanned the forest once more, seeing nothing. The sharp, uncomfortable feeling of apprehension had eased. It wasn't completely gone, but it was nothing like before.

My heart still pounded, but I released the eather. The strands of essence flickered out. I met Ash's stare as he approached. "They were after you."

Ash's jaw hardened as he hooked an arm around my shoulders and drew me to his chest. He pressed a kiss to my forehead.

"Fucking Kolis," Lailah growled.

"I don't think that was him," Attes said, and I frowned. "And trust me, I'm not giving him a pass, but he's never demanded that we use the *kynakos* to do his bidding."

"There's always a first," Nektas muttered.

"Yeah, there is." Attes's voice was closer. "But it's more likely that my brother was trying to earn Kolis's praise."

Fury rose in my chest as I pulled away from Ash and faced the other Primal. "I *really* do not like your brother."

He thrust his fingers through his hair. "Don't blame you."

"I assume you realize that summoning Kyn for the meeting is off the table now," Ash stated, and I breathed a sigh of relief. "I don't give a fuck about proving shit to him."

Attes nodded and dropped his hand. "I understand," he said, his voice heavy. "And I agree."

A pang of sorrow sliced through my chest. I wished it wasn't this way for Attes.

Lailah cleared her throat. "You said you had a feeling that drove you here?" she asked, glancing in Attes's direction. The Primal was staring off toward the forest. "Was it like the *vadentia*?"

"The answer to that will have to wait," Ash said before I could reply. "I need to speak with my wife."

My belly did a series of little wiggles and flops as I dragged my gaze from the bushes. I didn't know if I should be worried.

Or excited.

Ash's voice dropped, sounding full of smoldering flames as he added, "In private."

Excited.

I was definitely feeling *excited* as my eyes locked on his molten silver gaze. But there were important things to discuss. Lots of things. Ignoring his rich scent, I forced myself to act responsibly. "We need to talk about what just happened—"

"That can also wait." Ash took my hand as he stepped into me. I felt him then, thick and hard against my belly. Our gazes collided, and he didn't look away as he said, "Lailah?"

"I'm good."

"As am I," Nektas shared, and my heart started to pound for a wholly different reason than it had before as a shadowy mist unfurled around us.

"Perfect."

I didn't even see the essence rise as Ash's mouth descended on mine, his tongue parting my lips with one fierce, wicked promise of what was to come.

"I really hope Kars and Rhahar didn't head to Vathi," I said as I slipped from Ash's embrace, a little breathless from the kiss. He had shadowstepped us back to his office in the Shadowlands.

"So, they knew where you were going?" he asked. The lock engaged with a metallic click. My gaze shot to Ash's. The intensity in his stare bore into me, causing my already erratic pulse to speed up.

"Yes." I backed up some more.

"Did they try to stop you?"

"They tried." I drew in a deep breath, catching the thicker, heavier scent of arousal.

Oh, gods.

"And failed." He prowled forward, each step fluid and precise.

"Would you expect anything less?"

One side of his mouth curled up. "Absolutely fucking not."

I inched back a step and bumped into his desk. "We need to talk."

"We do," Ash agreed. "That's why we're here."

I blinked hard, surprised. "Talking is clearly not what you're communicating."

"I suppose I need to work on that."

"Yeah—" I gasped.

Without warning, he closed the distance between us. He was right in front of me, one cool hand cupping my cheek and tilting my head.

His mouth returned to mine with unerring accuracy, interrupting my steady stream of questions—though he'd ask more questions than I did. There was nothing gentle or tentative about the kiss or my body's immediate response. The flick of his tongue along the seam of my mouth was like a lightning bolt to my senses, electric and intense. His touch was cool, but it evoked a rush of sultry heat.

Ash's lips lifted from mine, but not far. "You taste like sugar." A deep and dark growl rumbled from him. "I like."

"It's from the tea I had earlier." Or at least I thought it was. I couldn't be sure now. His kiss had scattered my thoughts, and he wasn't done doing so.

He kissed me again, and this time, his tongue parted my lips and swept inside, dancing with mine. "My brave, beautiful wife." His lips coasted over mine. "Still so frightened by a snake."

"That will never change."

"Good. I find it adorable." His other hand landed on my hip. "I know you were upset when you saw Attes's face, but I didn't hurt him too badly."

I gripped the front of his shirt. "You shouldn't have hurt him at all."

His lips brushed mine as he moved his large hand over the curve of my backside. "I enjoy the way you look in these pants." His fingers followed the thin seam over the center of my ass. "But I love the way your body feels in them."

Heart thumping, I lifted my gaze to his. "I can tell."

"Can you?" A wolfish grin appeared. A wicked gleam in his stare joined the devilish expression. "How about…?" His questing fingers dipped lower, dragging a ragged gasp from me. "Now?"

Raw, sharp sensation curled tightly in my core as my fingers splayed across the soft linen of his shirt.

His chuckle was like silk against my skin, and his kiss was more languid and intoxicating this time. I started to lean into him, wanting to give in to the captivating pulse of pleasure his kiss and touch elicited.

But we *did* need to talk.

Mustering up what little self-restraint I had, I lightly pushed against his chest. "Yes, I can definitely tell you're fond of these pants, but we need to behave responsibly at the moment. So you need to forget about them," I said, ignoring the breathy note in my voice. "What did Attes think about us wanting to meet with the Primals?"

"He thought it was a good idea." The grip on my ass tightened as he dropped a quick kiss to the corner of my mouth and then my cheek. "If he heads out to the other Courts when he said he would, we'll hear from him within a day."

My stomach dipped once more. "That's quick."

"It is." He slid the hand from my cheek and down the side of my throat. His palm glided over the thick braid of hair, and his fingers skimmed the curve of my breast where it was lifted from the tight vest. I inhaled sharply. "I'm betting Lailah will go with him."

"Re—" I gasped as his thumb drifted over the tip of my breast. The layers of clothing provided little barrier to the coolness of his touch. "Really?"

"Mm-hmm," he murmured, bringing both hands to my hips. "Before you arrived, she offered to back him up in case of any problems." His lips found the hollow beneath my jaw, sending a tight—almost too tight—shiver down my spine. "Which he eagerly accepted."

"Oh, no." I drew my lip between my teeth as I stared at the ceiling. My heart felt like it was a trapped hummingbird. "Theon won't be pleased to hear that."

"I wasn't exactly pleased myself." Ash nipped at my chin. "But my Queen informed me that I was only to ensure that Attes behaved if Lailah wanted that, and it seemed to me that she had no interest in my intervention."

"I have so many questions about those two."

"They had a thing some time ago," he said. I'd already figured that much out myself. "It did not end well."

Concern took root. I grasped his cheek and guided his gaze to mine. "Is she safe with him?"

"A part of me wants to say no, just to see what you would do to Attes. I'm sure it would be bloody and violent." A quick, savage grin appeared as his fingers dipped under the band of my leggings. "But you said we needed to be responsible. Lailah is safer with him than she is with anyone else."

I was relieved to hear that. "You don't seem to be behaving all that responsibly right now."

"I'm being completely responsible." He nipped at my lower lip. "I was gone longer than I wanted to be. I missed you, *liessa*."

A swelling motion filled my chest as I admitted, "I missed you, too."

His nose brushed mine. "Of course, you did."

My eyes narrowed as I stepped an inch or two away from the desk. "Let's back up a second—or five. You really shouldn't have hit Attes three times."

"It was four."

"You probably shouldn't have corrected that statement."

One side of his lips curved up as he drew my right hand from his chest. Kissing the center of my palm, he turned his head. His gaze slid to mine as his tongue flicked over the golden imprint. "It wasn't entirely intentional. My arm may have moved on its own at some point." He caught the tip of my finger with his teeth. The sharp prick and tight draw of his mouth conjured a heady mix of reactions that had my heart pounding in anticipation and—

Letting go of my finger, he lifted his head. "Attes deserved it." The essence stilled in his eyes as they met mine. "He knows that."

What Lailah had said about Attes choosing not to heal himself filled my mind. "But he can't keep deserving it every time you see him."

"Debatable."

"Ash." I sighed.

"The way your voice lowers when you're annoyed makes my dick hard," he countered. "I'm not sure that's the desired effect."

"It's not."

"You sure?" His body pressed into mine, inching me back against the desk, and I felt against my belly just how *much* he was telling the truth. "I can practically taste your arousal."

My blood heated as every single one of my nerve endings hummed.

"Sunshine," he murmured, threading his fingers through mine. "Attes and I talked things through and came to an understanding."

"But not forgiveness?"

"Forgiveness is nothing more than a benefit to the forgiver," he reminded me. "Because it is easy, it does so very little. Understanding is much harder. It allows for a chance to move forward, which is what we will do."

The next breath I took came a little easier. "I'm glad to hear that."

"I knew you would be. That is why I made an effort to understand."

"After punching him? A few times?"

"No." Ash smirked. "That happened *after* we came to an understanding."

"Oh, my gods."

"I know I should probably apologize."

"But you wouldn't mean it," I said, and he gave me another half-grin. "I think it's better if we stop talking about Attes."

"Agreed," he murmured, nipping at another finger. "You said you had a feeling that drove you to Vathi? Was it the *vadentia*?"

"I don't know. I mean, it had to be that, but it felt different. I'm not sure how to explain it. It started when I was talking to Penellaphe and Ward and realized—"

"Wait a second." Eather swirled in his irises. "You were talking to Penellaphe and that *viktor*?"

"Yes. I tried to summon Holland."

Ash pressed a kiss to the golden imprint. "Was it because you missed him? Or was there another reason?"

My head tilted slightly. "Both."

"You're surprised." His lashes swept down. "It's cool against my throat."

I blinked. "I…I just didn't expect you to think of that. Of me missing him," I admitted.

His chest rose with a heavy breath. "Sometimes, I forget how lucky I am to have had a kind and involved father." His gaze lifted to mine. "I hate that basic consideration comes as a surprise to you. I wish I could change that."

"You are," I whispered.

"And I will continue to do so." Dipping his head, he kissed me. "I'm sorry he did not answer."

"Me, too," I whispered, my throat stinging like it had when I spoke with Penellaphe but for a different reason this time.

His stare pierced mine. "I am beginning to dislike Holland as much as your mother."

"It's not his fault. My reasons were personal," I said, defending him as Penellaphe had. "And since I summoned him directly, it could have been seen as favoritism if he'd come."

"That makes little sense," Ash said. "Therefore, it is likely true."

I cracked a grin.

His features warmed as he looked down at me. "What was your reason? Other than wanting to see him."

I lowered my hands to my sides. "I remembered something while you were gone." I paused as he lifted a hand from my hip. His fingers walked their way up the line of clasps on my vest. "It's about what Kolis said regarding the vision Penellaphe had."

A muscle flexed in his jaw—the only sign that he hadn't missed a word I'd said. "What was that?"

"Kolis said her vision wasn't complete. That there was another part, which he believed was the end of it, but—what are you doing?" I asked as he unhooked one of the clasps.

"Nothing." Another clasp came undone. Then another. "Please, continue."

It didn't seem like he was doing *nothing*, but I continued. This playfulness was still so rare, and the ease with which he now interacted with me, without any reservations or stiffness, showed how comfortable he was. He trusted me. And that made me feel…well, it made me feel like I was *seen*. Accepted. And about a hundred other things. So, I told him what I could remember of that part of the prophecy and how Penellaphe believed Kolis wasn't correct. By the time I finished, he had the top six clasps undone, and the vest had slipped a half inch or so. "There is a chance Keella knows about the prophecy."

"She's old enough to have knowledge of it." He moved on to the string at the collar of my blouse, loosening it. "And based on what she asked at the coronation," he added, following the same line of thought I had taken when I spoke about her earlier, "it seems like she's heard that phrasing before."

"That's what I…I was thinking." I gripped the edge of the desk as he drew the sleeves of my blouse down, inch by inch. "You are definitely up to something."

"I have no idea what you're speaking of." The sleeves gathered at my elbows as the blouse slipped. Cool air followed, teasing my skin. A husky sound rumbled from his chest. "Beautiful."

I looked down, my breath catching. Ash had bared my breasts, and with the vest positioned just below them, they were shoved up, boldly offering the beaded nipples to his perusal.

"My beautiful wife." One cool finger swept over a rosy peak. "My beautiful Queen." His lips parted, revealing a hint of fang. "We will need to speak to Keella about this."

Brows knitting, I lifted my gaze to Ash's. "What?"

"You're not paying attention."

"Yes, I am."

A brief smile appeared. "I said we will need to speak to Keella about the vision and her knowledge of it."

"Oh. Yes." My skin tingled. "That's not the only thing we discussed."

"Tell me." His hands returned to my hips.

I jumped as his fingers slid beneath the waistband. The sound he made told me he enjoyed how the movement caused my breasts to jiggle. "I'm trying to, but you're being very distracting."

Thick lashes lifted, and eather-streaked eyes met mine. "Your failure to maintain focus is not a reflection upon my actions."

I sucked in a short laugh at the obvious callback to when we'd been in this very office, and I'd been doing my level best—and succeeding—to distract him. "I see what sort of poor comparison you're attempting to make, but when you couldn't concentrate, I wasn't in the process of undressing you."

"This time you speak of…you had your lovely breasts shoved in my face," he countered. "How is that any different than now?"

My lips pursed.

"I've gotten better at multitasking since then." He kissed me. "I do love you in these pants." His lips brushed the curve of my cheek as he tilted his head, his mouth lining up with my ear. His voice was a silk-draped whisper as he said, "But do you know what I love more?"

Muscles coiled tight and low in my stomach. "No."

"You out of them."

A laugh burst from me. "I can't believe you said that."

"Believe it." Without warning, he whipped the leggings down to where they snagged on my boots, right below my knees. "Now, please continue with what else you discussed."

I gaped at him.

"Please." His fingers skated up my now-bare thighs. "Continue."

"It was about your father," I said, gasping as a cool finger slipped over my thin undergarment. "And what he planned for the embers and Sotoria's soul."

"What about it?" His fingers danced over the lace.

"Just that it was too risky and…" A taut, hot shiver curled deep inside me.

His lashes shielded his gaze again, but I felt the intensity of his stare upon my breasts and his hand between my thighs. "And?"

Throat dry, I struggled to remember exactly what had been said. "That none of it worked out as he planned. They agreed."

"Who wouldn't?" Ash questioned. "My father's plan wasn't well-thought-out. Clearly."

"But what if it was, and we were wrong about what he planned?"

Ash's exploring fingers stilled, and his lashes lifted.

"What if this—or at least some of this—is what he planned? For me to become the true Primal of Life."

Ash didn't speak for a long moment. "If he believed you would be Sotoria reborn, it would make sense. You would be a true weapon and able to fully stand against Kolis."

"Ward thought there was a chance Eythos wanted you to become the true Primal of Death. That it would be possible by using The Star," I told him, watching a crease form between his brows. "But that's the part that didn't go as planned. I'm not Sotoria, and The Star…"

"Is already in use," he finished.

My gaze searched his features as seedlings of concern rooted themselves. "How does that make you feel? The possibility that he might not have intended for you to be the true Primal of Life."

The skin between his brows smoothed. "I feel nothing."

Doubt crept into my tone. "Nothing?"

"Nothing," Ash confirmed, and the furrow returned. He studied me. "Did you think I would be disappointed to learn that?"

"I don't know. Maybe? It should—"

"You're no longer allowed to say that." Essence streaked through his eyes.

I snapped my mouth shut, mostly out of surprise.

"And I mean that as respectfully as possible," he tacked on. "It never mattered to me if it was my birthright. What did was stopping Kolis. That was all that mattered to me."

"Mattered? As in past tense?"

"Yes, *liessa*, as in past tense. Because you are the true Primal of Life, and stopping Kolis is no longer all that matters to me," he said. "You do."

My lips parted on a soft inhale as I stared up at him.

"And I do mean that, Sera. Everything else is now a byproduct of that. Not a single part of me gives a fuck if that's wrong. Besides, it sounds to me like we need to transfer his embers to me. With the exception of those embers being death instead of life, that's what I planned. Yeah, it's complicated since The Star is in use, but it was complicated before."

True.

"We need to entomb Kolis until Sotoria is reborn. Then we'll take the embers."

My heart sped up. "So, that's the plan?" It was the most sensible one. But releasing Sotoria's soul to be reborn meant she wouldn't have control over her future. Just like before. Just like me. I exhaled slowly. "Then you will be the true Primal of Death. And I, the true Primal of Life."

Ash nodded. "Yes."

We were in agreement, but I didn't want that for Sotoria.

"Glad it's decided," he said, his voice lowering as he ran a long, cool finger along the edge of my undergarment. "What I don't understand is how this led you to Vathi."

It took me a moment to think past how that featherlight touch sent pleasure dancing up and down my spine. When I did, the passion cooled in the rise of unease. "You're a Primal of no Court."

His exploration ceased, and his gaze lifted to mine. "*Liessa*..."

A knot lodged in my chest. "You know what that means. You've *always* known what that would mean."

"Sera," he began.

I gripped his shirt again. "Kolis knows we have The Star, Ash. And he also knows what can be done with it."

"That doesn't matter."

"Yes, it does. Kolis is clever enough to expect us to use The Star in the same way he did. And he has to know that you could take the true embers of death. That makes you a target." My heart felt like it had stopped—just like when I realized it before. "You can be killed without any huge impact on the mortal realm, and I know you realized that. Why didn't you tell me?"

"Why would I make you worry?" His eyes searched mine. "Over nothing."

"Nothing?" I nearly screeched the word. "Confidence is sexy, Ash, but not when it becomes idiotic. You're a target. That's when I got the feeling that something bad was about to happen. And I was right. What just happened with the Dogs of War is evidence of that. If not Kolis, then another Primal will come for you."

A lock of hair fell against his cheek. "I've always been a target."

"But this is different—"

"You're right. It is different now," he cut in. "Because of *you*. Because of *us*." He cupped my cheek. "Do you really think I would allow anyone to take me out when I have you to fight and survive for? That I would allow anything or anyone to steal our future? That's never going to happen, Sera. Never." Strands of eather spun as he held my stare. "I am a Primal of Death. You are the fucking true Primal of Life. No two beings in any realm are safer than we are. Because I also know that you won't allow that to happen. Or am I wrong?"

"No," I whispered, anxiety swirling.

His eyes flashed pure silver for an instant. "Say it like you mean it, Sera."

"I do..." I stopped and took a deep breath. Ash was right. He wouldn't allow it. Neither would I. None of that meant I would suddenly cease worrying about something possibly happening to Ash—that wasn't in my personality. But determination was. Resolve poured in, crowding out the fear as eather hummed through me, turning the corners of my vision white. "*No*."

"That's my wife." He kissed me and then drew back, his gaze lowering. "This is such a pretty slip of lace. Did Erlina make you many of these?"

I blinked, caught off guard by the subject change. "I think so."

"Good." With a quick jerk of his hands, he tore the undergarment in half.

"Ash," I gasped.

"I'll make sure to pay her double if you find yourself in need of more." Grasping my hips, he lifted me with shocking ease and placed me so my ass was on the edge of his desk. He cupped my nape and guided me so my hips were angled upward. "*Liessa*?" His lips made their way to my ear. "I want to fuck you."

Oh, gods.

"I have wanted to fuck you from the moment you shadowstepped into Vathi." His cool breath against the skin beneath my ear sent a taut, enticing shiver coursing through me. "And I definitely wanted to fuck you when you took out the *kynakos.* You were so powerful. So beautiful. Fucking glorious," he said. "But I need to taste you first."

A full-body shudder took me. I watched him draw back, and my chest tightened, but for the most delicious reasons.

"And speaking of things I've wanted to do…" He dropped to his knees before me. Seeing him like that always left me breathless. "When you sought to distract me as I wrote names in the Book of the Dead?" he said, tugging off my boots and then my leggings. "I wanted to toss that gown up and get between your thighs."

I was going to melt. Right here. "I wouldn't have stopped you."

"You should have." Spreading my thighs, he looked up at me. A lock of chestnut hair fell forward, softening the brutal hardness of his jaw. "I wasn't as deserving of you then."

Before I could protest, he was on me. His mouth. His tongue. His fangs. He licked and sucked, drawing my hips off the desk, and when his tongue dipped, the most needful sound rumbled from deep within him.

Ash was…*insatiable.*

He tasted me—no, he *feasted*—and all I could do was hold on to the edge of the desk and try to keep my precarious balance. Tension coiled tight with each plunge of his tongue, drawing me closer and closer to the edge of release. I shook with need, caught on an almost painful precipice as he lifted his head.

"Sunshine," he murmured, his lips glossy as he kissed my inner thigh.

He rose with the quick grace of a wolf hunting its prey, and as he shoved his pants down, I wanted nothing more than to be devoured.

"Ash?"

His hand halted, and his eyes flashed to mine. "*Liessa*?"

"Are you going to fuck me now?"

Shadows appeared beneath his flesh, swirling as madly as the eather in his eyes. "Nothing will stop me."

Pure want made me a little dizzy. "Prove it."

An inhuman growl came from him—a sound no mortal could make. Probably not even most gods. It should scare me. But it only excited me as he freed his thick, rigid length. A small bead of liquid glistened at the tip.

Then his hips were between my thighs, spreading them. Deep, sharp pleasure twisted inside me as I felt the cool pressure of his cock. Sliding an arm around my back, he clasped my hip with his other hand. A stuttered heartbeat later, the way he held me kept me from sliding backward under the force of the deep, hard thrust. I cried out, shaking as my body opened for him.

There was no space between our bodies. Seated fully inside me, he didn't move as I curled my legs around his hips. Even as his arm trembled, he held himself still for a moment. And then another.

"Ash?" I whispered against his lips, my pulse thumping erratically.

He lifted his head. Our eyes locked. There was a sudden wildness in his silvery gaze. My breath stalled a little.

I touched his chest, concerned. "Are you okay?"

"Yeah." The eather brightened, whirling through his irises. His hand left my hip, and he caressed my cheek. "I just sometimes remember how close I came to losing you."

My heart ached. "But you didn't."

"And I won't." He drew his thumb across my lower lip. "Not ever. That is the promise we're making to each other."

Ash began to move then, thrusting deeper into me, filling me up. His pace increased until it became a frenetic tempo I thought might tear me apart, given the pleasure.

Then he suddenly lifted me off the desk, his large hand cradling the back of my head. I gasped, stunned by his sheer strength as his hips plunged upward. I grasped his shoulders, my senses overwhelmed.

Potent desire spread through me. I arched in his embrace, my body aching and tense.

"Please," I heard myself whisper—beg.

Ash answered without hesitation, knowing what I wanted. Needed. He moved faster, grinding against me as he took me right to that slick edge and then over it. I let out a scream as hot, tight spasms shook me.

Ash's head kicked back as he drew me down on his cock. A roar of release escaped his throat while he held me tight to his chest. It was a sound that must have shaken the walls of the palace.

One last shudder ran through my body as I clung to him, trembling with aftershocks of pleasure. Moments passed, and I became aware of the fact that he'd lowered me to the edge of the desk again, but was still deep inside me, cool and throbbing.

He kissed me. The one before had been that of unyielding need. This was a gentle and languid benediction.

His fingers trailed down my cheek as he eased himself from me and stepped back. Wavy strands of hair fell against a slightly flushed cheek as he pulled his pants up, his chin pointed downward.

Was he blushing?

I thought so, and there was such a sweetness to it that I felt my heart do several little skips.

Leaving his pants unbuttoned, he looked over at me. Only the thinnest streaks of eather were visible as one side of his lips curled up. "I wish to paint you," he said, crossing the distance between us. "With you like this."

I glanced down at myself. "You wish to paint me topless—*wait.*" Surprise jolted me. "You can paint?"

One shoulder lifted. "I used to when I was younger. Can't say I was any good at it."

I gaped at him. "What have you painted?"

"Landscapes—mostly Mount Rhee," he said while pulling my blouse sleeves back up, referencing where the draken resided. "And how the meadows would look if filled with poppies. Sometimes, I did portraits."

My mouth was still hanging open. "I can't believe you're just now telling me you can paint."

"It's not something I honestly thought of before." He tugged some hair free from under my shirt collar. "Truthfully, it's not something I even thought of until now. I haven't painted in years."

Years likely meant decades. All I could do was stare at him in stunned silence. Honestly, I shouldn't have been surprised. Those long fingers of his *were* talented, and I'd always thought they were far too graceful for someone who had only ever handled a sword or dagger. I knew—

"Portraits?" I asked. "You said you've painted portraits?"

Ash nodded.

A sudden sense of knowing filled me. "You painted the portraits of your parents."

He didn't answer immediately. "I did."

I was once more staring open-mouthed at him.

"When Kolis killed my mother, he also ensured that all traces of her were destroyed," he said after a moment. "My father was too preoccupied with a babe he never planned on rearing alone and grieving to stop it."

A bitter knot of grief settled like a stone in my chest.

"So, there were no portraits of her. When my father was killed, there was nothing left behind of him either. I already had no real image of my mother in my mind, and I knew that as the years passed, I would forget what my father looked like, too. I didn't want that." His forehead creased. "I painted him first—when the memories were still fresh. Then, with Nektas's help, I painted my mother. It was the last time I painted."

Sadness mingled with awe as I murmured, "My gods."

Grabbing hold of the sides of my vest, Ash's gaze met mine. "What?"

"It's just…beautiful and tragic," I said, breathing through the sting in the back of my throat. "I wish I had better, more eloquent words."

He paused to kiss me. "Your words are always good enough."

Actually, *his* were. Mine were poor imitations. "You can paint, Ash."

He gave me another half-shrug.

"Seriously," I insisted. "Your mother looks real."

Pausing, he frowned. "That's because she was real, *liessa*."

"I know. That's not what I meant. I never would've guessed that someone who hadn't seen her—who only had the memories of another to go from—was the one who had painted her. That takes real skill. You're not just good," I told him. "You're really, *really* good."

Ash was quiet.

"And I'm not just saying that because I can't draw a straight line."

His lips twitched. "I'm sure you can draw a straight line."

"No, I can't. If you don't believe me, ask Ezra the next time we see her." As soon as I said her name, I yearned to see her. It was hard to move past it. "She's witnessed my poor attempts at doodling. I'm bad, like really, *really* bad."

A grin finally appeared. "I wish to see just how bad you are at drawing."

"No, you don't." I eyed him, suddenly thinking about all the bare walls in the many chambers. "Do you still have those other paintings?"

He nodded.

"Where are they?"

"In one of the chambers you apparently haven't entered yet," he answered.

"Take me to them. Right now," I demanded. "I want to see them."

"I would be glad to. But not right now."

My eyes narrowed. "Why not?"

He chuckled as he came back to me. "Besides the fact that you remain without pants," he murmured, nipping at my lower lip, "you need to feed."

Thoughts of seeing his paintings vanished as those four words elicited a sudden throbbing in my upper jaw. Until that moment, I hadn't felt like I needed to feed.

My gaze dropped to his throat, and the ache moved to my chest and then my stomach, reminding me of hunger pains. Muscles tensed, and I could've sworn I saw his pulse beating beneath his flesh. My throat dried with the sudden need to feed. I started to lean forward, but my thoughts decided to go in an unwanted direction.

An image of Veses flashed in my mind—her at Ash's throat, taking from him as she straddled him. *Used* him.

I drew back, my heart thumping unsteadily. I didn't want to do that to him. "I feel fine," I said.

"I know you do." He cupped my cheek. "But we don't know how much essence you used against the *kynakos*. And even if you hadn't been in that fight, you would still need to feed every couple of days for a bit as your body continues to adapt to the Ascension," he reminded me as he smoothed his thumb across my cheekbone. "If you don't, you'll feel as exhausted as you did while in your Culling." His eyes met mine as he fixed my shirt. "I don't want to risk that."

"You're right. I remember. It's the whole baby-Primal thing."

His eyes searched mine. "Then why do you hesitate?"

"I…I guess I'm not used to it. I don't find it repulsive or anything," I quickly added. "It's just…"

"Different." He moved on to the vest, his fingers as nimble and quick as they had been when he unhooked the clasps. "That's understandable. It's not yet natural to you."

"But it will be," I murmured, running my tongue along the back of my teeth. The pulsing sensation returned, more intense than before.

Ash watched me, his eyes halfway closed. "I enjoyed it when you fed from me before. Thoroughly."

I stopped messing with my fangs.

"And when you were at my vein, it was only you I thought of."

I went completely still.

"I knew it was your fangs piercing my skin. Your mouth that moved against my throat," he continued. "I knew it was you I willingly gave my blood to. Not her."

A tremor ran through me. Gods, how had he known? I didn't think sensing what I felt could've filled in the gaps like that. A mix of emotions swirled through me. I was relieved that he hadn't thought about her when I fed from him and was clearly far better at dealing with certain things than I was. But that relief carried the bitter edge of guilt.

Eather pulsed brightly in his eyes. "Sera."

I squeezed my eyes shut. "I didn't want to, you know, make you feel like I'm using you."

"I would never think that, Sera."

"I hate that I even caused you to think of her," I whispered. "That's not what I wanted."

"I know." His lips brushed my forehead. "But I'm glad you did."

My eyes flew open. "You sure about that?"

"Yes." He drew back. "Because now I can make sure you know that when you feed from me, I'm not thinking of her." His fingers slid into the hair above my loosened braid. "When I'm with you, she doesn't even exist. That's what you do for me. And that is an exquisite gift. Let me do this for you."

I knew he spoke the truth, so when he guided my mouth to his exposed throat, I didn't resist.

I'd just come out of stasis the last time I fed from him. I'd been acting on pure instinct fueled by hunger. But nature did take over as soon as my lips brushed the steady beat of his pulse. My body knew what it was doing even though my mind wasn't exactly sure.

My head tipped, and my lips peeled back. My eyes fell closed once more, and instinct took over. I struck. His body jerked as I pierced his vein, and then mine did the same as the first drop of his blood rolled over my tongue.

Gods, the taste of him… The flavor of his blood filled my mouth and coursed down my throat. I swallowed, and it was like every cell in my body woke up and stretched in response. I took more of him into me.

"*Liessa*," he said roughly. "Release your fangs."

I obeyed, pulling them from his skin.

"That's my Queen." Ash's hand fisted my hair. "Keep drinking."

I did.

My mouth sealed hungrily over the wound I'd created. Maybe I really *had* needed to feed. I drank deeply, my fingers pressing into the taut flesh of his waist. Gods, there was nothing like his smoky flavor and how the awe-inspiring power of his blood felt like a jolt to every sense, strengthening me. Empowering me.

But his blood was doing even more than that.

Each draw on his vein created a languid, thick heat. I pressed against him, skin tingling all over as I moaned. My fingers dug into his shirt. My blood hummed as it pounded through me. Heightened desire pooled between my thighs, and my body reacted. I strained to get closer to him, needing him.

"I know," Ash groaned, the arm around my waist tightening as he lifted me. "Don't stop feeding."

I drank, vaguely aware of him moving us to the settee. As he sat, I pushed on his shoulders, forcing him onto his back. A thick, husky chuckle stirred the hair at my temple and then ended in a moan as his rigid length parted my flesh.

I had no idea how we'd gotten turned around on the settee or when he'd ended up flat on his back. All I could concentrate on was the feel of his cock filling me as the power of his blood did the same. The combination drove me wild. I ground against him, keeping him deeply seated in me.

"That's it." His voice was a sensual snarl as one hand cradled the back of my head and the other fell to my hip. His fingers pressed into the flesh there. "Ride me."

His demand fanned the flames. I fucked him, drinking and drinking. And, gods, I wanted to keep drinking. I wanted to drown in his taste. I felt my release barreling down on me, but I knew where that could lead—even for a Primal. Especially a newly risen Primal.

Bloodlust.

Though it wasn't easy, I forced myself to lift my head. When I did, Ash wrenched my mouth to his. Our lips and fangs crashed together as I came, and he followed with a thrust of his hips.

"Do you need more?" he asked after a few moments, his voice richer.

"No." A fine sheen of sweat dampened my brow as I drew back and opened my eyes. Two small, angry red marks marred his flesh. Instinct took over once more. I nicked my tongue with a fang and then licked the wounds. Ash shuddered as I sealed the punctures.

My grip on his shoulders relaxed as I wiggled down, resting my cheek on his chest. "Thank you."

"I feel like I need to be the one thanking you," he replied.

A tired smile pulled at my lips as a faint quiver danced from muscle to muscle.

"I want you to make me a promise," he said after a moment. "That you won't run off and start searching every inch of the palace for my paintings the first moment you get."

"I wasn't planning to do that." I lied because that was likely exactly what I would do.

"*Liessa,*" he murmured, his voice heavy with knowing amusement.

"Whatever," I muttered. "I won't go searching for them."

"Thank you." He tucked a strand of hair behind my ear. "I want to be with you when you see them."

The quiet way he said that and the fact that he wanted to be there when I saw them eased my impatience a whole lot. I smiled up at him. "I love you," I told him. "Even though I'm thoroughly jealous of this hidden talent of yours."

He laughed softly. "I'm sure I can help you improve."

"I wouldn't be so certain of that."

"Trust me," he murmured, smoothing his fingers over my hair. "I will have you drawing straight lines in no time."

Smiling, I turned my head and dropped a kiss onto his chest—his cold chest.

Concern sliced through the pleasant fog in my brain. I sat up. His eyes were open, and the glow of eather was bright behind his pupils. He looked the same. The hollows of his cheeks weren't stark. His features weren't drawn, but…

"Do *you* need to feed?" The moment the question left my lips, a messy mix of emotions swept through me once again. There was blade-sharp anticipation, partly due to the sensuality of the act itself but also because I wanted to give him what he'd given me. Power. Life. But there was something else beneath the longing. Something oppressive and choking.

Fear.

And it was so godsdamn ridiculous. I had no reason to feel it. Ash had taken my blood at my lake. He hadn't hurt me. He never had. And I hadn't thought about my time in Dalos then or what had been done to me. There was no reason to assume I would now.

Ash smoothed his hand up my back. "No, *liessa.*"

I swallowed, barely tasting him anymore. "I took a lot of blood from you when I awakened. And this wasn't a little bit either."

"My body will quickly make up for it," he told me.

I stared at him, uncertain. I knew that as long as he wasn't injured, consumed food, and rested, he would replenish what was lost. But I also knew that his body was still playing catch-up—and I knew that because I'd seen it before when Veses fed on him. I just hadn't known the cause then.

"Are you sure?" I asked.

"Yes, *liessa.*"

I didn't move as a different kind of need filled me and urged me to prove that I was being silly. That I wasn't afraid. That my time in Dalos wouldn't have any lasting effects on me.

That I was right.

Nothing had really happened to me.

My mouth felt dry. "Ash?"

"Mmm?" His eyes were closed.

My heart thundered as I touched his chin. "I want to do for you what you did for me."

"I know, *liessa*." He tilted his head and kissed the tip of the finger that had been on his chin. "But if I drink from you, I'm going to fuck you again."

Desire fisted deep inside me. "Sounds like a good plan to me."

A deep rumble radiated from him as he hooked his arm around me and pulled me back down to his chest. "If that happens, we'll end up breaking this couch, and I'd hate to have to explain how that happened."

Well, that *would* be awkward.

"We could always move to our bedchamber, where there is a very nice large bed," I suggested, unwilling to give in quite yet. "And maybe you could, you know, control yourself."

"Like you just did?"

"Touché," I murmured. "Sorry about that."

He chuckled. "Don't apologize, *liessa.* I love that greedy pussy of yours."

I choked on a laugh.

One side of his lips curled. "Plus, if I feed, we'll never make it to the Thyia Plains."

I nodded. "You're right.

"Always."

I laughed, but I didn't feel it as my stomach churned with the guilt that flared to life the moment I felt relief at Ash's refusal to feed.

We planned to leave for the Thyia Plains after sharing a quick meal.

But that didn't happen.

Attes arrived in the Shadowlands instead.

Concern grew as we neared the main hall, and it didn't help the churning in my stomach since I'd finished eating. There was no way Attes had finished with the Primals already. As Ash and I saw Rhain and Saion, he squeezed my hand. Just that small gesture calmed some of the worry.

"He's in the throne room," Rhain announced.

Ash sighed as we turned left. "What is he doing in there?"

"I have no idea," Saion said. "But he's not alone. Thierran is with him."

Ash stopped abruptly, his head cutting toward the gods. "What the fuck?"

Saion laughed. "That was pretty much my response."

"Who is Thierran?" I asked.

A faint grin appeared on Ash's lips. "A walking nightmare, in both the literal and physical senses. He's an *oneirou*."

I wasn't expecting that to be the answer. At all.

"Thierran has a lot of sway over the remaining *oneirou,* even though they tend to stay out of Court politics," Ash quickly explained. "Which is normally a good thing. But it also begs the question of *why* he is here with Attes."

"Maybe Attes came upon him when he went to Lotho," I suggested. "I assume he can be trusted?"

"Trusted in the general sense? Absolutely fucking not," Ash said as we began walking again. "But when it comes to Kolis? Thierran's never been a loyalist."

I wasn't exactly reassured by that, but I didn't think Attes would bring the god here if he believed he was dangerous.

We walked through the open double doors between two pillars and entered the throne room.

Thousands of candles jutted from the smooth, black walls of the vast, circular chamber, and hundreds more hovered above the main floor, scattered throughout despite the sunlight pouring in from the open ceiling.

My gaze immediately landed on the *oneirou.* Hair as dark as the shadowstone around us lay against his chin, shielding his face. He stood to the left of the center aisle, between the rows of benches, and was almost as tall as Ash. What held my attention was the sword strapped to his back, the daggers sheathed to his upper arms, and the hilt of another blade I saw tucked into the shaft of his boot.

Good gods, this god carried a small arsenal on him—one Bele would be impressed by.

He looked up then, turning his head slightly toward us, and my back straightened. The man appeared to be in his twenties—there wasn't a single crease or line in his skin, which was a color somewhere between sun-kissed and olive. His features looked like they'd been carved from some fine stone by a master sculptor. Every feature was perfectly symmetrical—the angular cheekbones and jaw, the blade-straight nose, and the dark, arched brows matching his sculpted lips and framing the most beautiful eyes I'd ever seen. They tapered upward at the outer corners and tipped down toward the bridge of his nose at the inner. The irises were a shade of bluish-purple so deep and dark it bordered on amethyst, and he looked like he'd come very close to losing both eyes.

Two eerily straight lines had been gouged into his skin, starting at the center of his forehead and slicing through his eyebrows just before the arch, then running down his cheeks to end at the corners of his lips.

I could feel it happening—what I'd done when I looked into Vikter's eyes. I was trying—albeit failing—not to do it whenever I pleased. My senses stretched out. In the back of my mind, I knew I shouldn't be doing what I was—it was a huge invasion of privacy. But my curiosity got the better of me. Focusing on him, I tried to *read* him as I had with the *viktor* and…

Saw and felt nothing.

Absolutely nothing.

But I had the distinct impression that if I *pushed*, I could discover what I wanted to know.

One side of those almost-too-perfect lips curved up, creating a dimple that partly disappeared into a scar. I suddenly had the distinct impression that this stranger would like to see me try.

There was a challenge in his blue-purple eyes and he wore a grin bordering on a smirk.

He bowed gracefully at the waist and folded a black-gloved hand over his heart. "*Meyaah Liessa.*" He spoke in a velvety voice I was sure had led many down a path of very bad, yet fun, decisions.

I acknowledged his greeting with a nod as Attes looked over his shoulder.

"I'm trying to think of the last time I stood in this space and saw sunlight reflected off the thrones." Attes stood in the center aisle, his back to us. "It was so long ago I can't remember."

My gaze followed Attes's to the hauntingly beautiful thrones carved from blocks of shadowstone, their backs stretching into wings that touched at the tips.

"It's been a little over two decades since the sun rose here," Ash replied as Saion and Rhain closed the doors to the space.

"Yeah," Attes replied. "But it has to be at least two centuries since I entered the throne room."

Ash's attention shifted to the god. "Thierran."

The *oneirou* bowed again. "Asher."

My attention sharpened at his response, but Ash merely gave a dry laugh. I relaxed—a little.

Attes turned to us then. Shadowstone armor covered his chest. That wasn't the only thing different about him. His eye was no longer swollen, proving what Lailah had claimed about him purposely not healing it. "I'm sure you're wondering why I'm back so soon and why I brought…a friend with me."

"Yes," I said. "But where's Lailah?"

"I believe she returned to your training fields to take out her anger on some poor, unknowing soldier," Attes replied. "Apparently, spending even a short amount of time with me incites such a need."

"That it does," Ash replied dryly, still focused on the *oneirou.* "I'm surprised to see you here."

"As am I to be here." Thierran shrugged. "But when I heard—"

"Heard?" Attes interrupted, his eyes narrowing.

Thierran flashed him a downright devilish grin. "When I *figured out* what Attes and Lailah were up to, I invited myself along."

"And why would you do that?" Ash asked.

"Besides wanting to see the Queen in person?" His bright, bejeweled gaze drifted to me. "I have to admit," he said, and I arched a brow at the purr in his tone, "one look, and I can safely say that serving you will be far more…*pleasing*."

"Careful," Ash warned softly.

Thierran chuckled, but the sound lacked humor. "I'm always careful."

"And if I remember correctly, you've always been an opportunist, too," Ash replied. "One who wields a sword when it benefits him."

"That hasn't changed," Thierran acknowledged, standing unsettlingly still. With his black attire and hair, he looked like he was seeping into the shadowstone all around him. "Removing Kolis from the throne *does* benefit me."

"True," Ash said after a moment. "I imagine you will be lingering in Lethe, then?"

"Unless I want to face an untimely death, I will. Some of us aren't so privileged as to have a Fate at our beck and call," he said, clearly referencing Penellaphe—and, by extension, Holland.

"Fine," Ash said after a moment. "You're more than welcome."

"Thank you." Thierran inclined his head.

"But," Ash continued, and I tensed, recognizing that too-low, too-level tone, "if you try any of your shit, I will do worse to you than Kolis could even imagine."

Well, I was pretty sure I knew who had given Thierran those scars.

And I really wanted to know what his *shit* was.

"I don't have a death wish," Thierran replied, his gaze briefly flickering to me. "I'm the least of your concerns."

Air lodged in my throat. Something about how he'd said that…

I shook my head. "Would either of you like something to drink?"

"I'm good," Attes answered.

I looked at Thierran. "You?"

"I'll never turn down an offered drink," he said. "It's bad manners to do so."

Attes snorted.

"I'll grab something from the dining hall," Rhain said, jogging from the room.

I returned my attention to the *oneirou*. "Exactly how did you figure out what they were up to?"

"Many of the Courts are abuzz with news of your Ascension—lots of talk about what it means, what will happen, and so on," he said, each word rolling smoothly off his tongue. "Then Attes showed up in Lotho with a goddess linked to the Asher, and since I can't remember a time he visited Lotho, it wasn't hard to put two and two together." He paused, and the grin returned. "That is if one is clever and pays attention."

"Or snoops in others' dreams," Ash stated.

The other side of Thierran's lips curled up just as Rhain returned with a bottle of wine and a glass. "That, too."

My lips parted slightly. I had a feeling the latter had much more to do with Thierran putting two and two together than simply him paying attention.

"Though I can't imagine why Attes would bother with Embris," Thierran continued. "He's so far up the King's ass, it would take the Fates to remove him."

I didn't like the sound of that for several reasons. "You mean he's so far up the *false* King's ass since the true King is standing beside me."

"Oh, really?" Eather pulsed through Thierran's eyes.

"Yes. There is no just-a-Queen or just-a-King bullshit," I said. "There is us."

"I like you," the *oneirou* said softly. "A lot."

Ash's narrowed-eye glare shot to the dream god.

"And I mean that in the most respectful manner possible," Thierran corrected, bowing his head. "*Meyaah Liessar.*"

My King.

My lips curved into a smile as I looked up at Ash. "I really do like the sound of that."

He returned my smile. "It does have a nice ring to it."

"That it does," Attes agreed, drawing our attention to him. "Bringing Thierran here isn't the only reason I returned," Attes began as the *oneirou* took the glass and bottle from Rhain. "Lailah and I got a later start heading to the Courts than anticipated."

"Interesting," I remarked, my eyes narrowing. "Does that have anything to do with why Lailah is taking her anger out on some innocent soldier?"

Attes started to grin but apparently thought better of it. "You'd have to ask her," he replied smoothly. "I had just shadowstepped into Lotho when I ran into this fucker." He jerked his chin at the god. "Then Lailah mentioned something you failed to tell me about."

"And what is that?" Ash let go of my hand and crossed his arms.

"You forgot to tell me that a deal was offered."

"I didn't forget," Ash replied. "I told you Kolis summoned her. I just never got to the point where details were shared."

I glanced between them. "How much time did you spend punching him?"

Thierran glanced up curiously from the glass of wine he was pouring.

"Not enough," Ash muttered, and I rolled my eyes. "Kolis offered her a bullshit deal, and she had to offer him one in return."

Attes's gaze flicked to me. "And what was that deal exactly?"

"That he had to abdicate the throne and agree not to seek vengeance," I said. "Then he could live out the rest of his existence."

Attes stared at me.

Unease slithered down my spine as I gripped the tail of my braid. I glanced at Ash. The eather had stilled in his eyes as he gave me a small nod. I took a deep breath. "We want to do everything we can to prevent as much bloodshed as possible. And I don't believe Kolis wants an all-out war. A part of him understands that there are…bigger issues at hand than what he believes he's entitled to." I met Attes's gaze. "Like the Ancients."

A muscle ticked in Attes's jaw. "When we spoke while you were still in Dalos, I told you I wanted to prevent the kind of war Kolis would wage."

I felt Ash's attention turn to me as I nodded. "I remember."

"That is partly why. So, I agree with doing whatever we can to lessen the bloodshed. But then what?" Attes pressed. "What if Kolis refuses your offer? Because what Nyktos was able to tell me didn't go past meeting with the other Primals," he finished.

"The plan is to force him to accept a version of the deal I offered. One in which we keep him alive until we can take the embers from him and place them in Nyktos."

Understanding dawned. "The Star." His jaw hardened. "But that's currently in use."

"I know," I said, once more uncomfortable with the idea of Sotoria being trapped in The Star. It bothered me as much as forcing her to be reborn did. "That leaves us with only one option. Just like the Ancients, Kolis needs to be subdued."

"And you think he will willingly allow that?" Attes asked, glancing at Ash.

"No," Ash answered, and the other Primal's gaze returned to me.

"I don't either. I know there will be a fight, but I want that to be a decision the Primals who support us are involved in," I said. "And I want them all to agree that we cannot allow this to extend into the mortal realm. Whatever war we fight, we do among us."

"I see what you're attempting." Attes pursed his lips. "You want some level of accord while knowing there will also be some level of war. That's not impossible, but it is extremely difficult to achieve." His stare rose. "And there's still much to be decided."

There was.

"I'm also about to give you another thing to consider," Attes said. "As highly unlikely as it is, what if Kolis accepts the deal you offered? That is much like an oath, Seraphena. Breaking it would have consequences."

"I know." I took another deeper breath, knowing I had to own up to what I'd done. "It wouldn't be what any of us wants, but I had to offer something. And if he does accept it? I will…" Bile gathered in the back of my throat. "I will honor it because my hatred of him and my need for vengeance cannot be greater than the lives of countless others. None of our anger can be greater than peace."

A wistfulness filled Attes's gaze. "You sounded so much like Eythos just then." He shook his head. "When the Ancients created the Primals, they did so to protect the collective—all living beings—from themselves. That was our role. We were to be protectors. Guardians of men, gods, and all that is in between. And we were, for a time." Attes's gaze returned to the blue skies above. "I do not believe it was all emotions that changed it—changed *us*. I believe it was hatred, jealousy, and apathy." His gaze lifted to mine. "Vengeance and retribution."

"And that started with Kolis," Ash stated.

Attes nodded. "And it's a damn shame. Like my brother, he wasn't always like this. I know it's hard to believe, but neither he nor Kolis were like this before."

"I believe you," I said, feeling Ash's stare. "I saw glimpses of who he was."

Attes nodded slowly. "Your father believed Kolis could be saved."

"And look what that got him." Ash's fingers stilled.

"I know," Attes replied. "You're not your father. Neither are you," he said to me. "If Kolis accepts the deal and then breaks it, neither of you will give him another chance—or keep giving him chances. You will not falter like Eythos did." He sighed. "Either way, I do not believe that any of the Primals who will potentially ally with us would fault you for attempting to make peace. Sacrifices should always be made for that. Our emotions and lives should never be greater than the collective."

Some of the tension eased from my muscles. "That is a relief."

Attes gave me a faint smile that didn't reveal a dimple. "As I said, I doubt Kolis will accept the deal, but it does change things."

I tensed. "Like what?"

"He didn't accept or reject the deal, right? Neither did you?"

"Correct." Ash frowned. "We have a little less than a month to make a decision."

"That's what I was afraid of." Attes thrust a hand through his sandy hair. "We've now entered an *eirini*."

"Fuck," Ash spat, turning sideways.

Rhain leaned forward. "We haven't entered into a truce, so how can there be an *eirini*?"

"But you did when neither deal was rejected or accepted," Attes explained, tension bracketing the corners of his mouth. "I assume the Fate who oversaw the meeting didn't remind you of the *eirini*?"

"No, he did not." My fingers moved fast around the tail of my braid.

"Fucking Fates," Thierran muttered, pouring what had to be at least his second glass of wine. Maybe his third. "There are rules during an *eirini*."

The hair on the back of my neck rose as Ash cursed again. "For example, neither party is allowed to attempt to sway the other Primals and their Courts to raise arms against the other, which means Kolis didn't order Kyn to use his Dogs of War."

Attes's upper lip curled. "Knowing my brother, he likely believed he could either capture or wound Nyktos, thus gaining Kolis's approval."

"I should've thought about that possibility." Ash dragged a hand down his face.

"But an *eirini* has rarely been needed," Attes said. "It's understandable that it would be forgotten. It didn't even cross my mind until Lailah mentioned the deal."

"Yeah, but it's more than just not being able to sway the other Primals." A muscle ticked in Ash's jaw. "The *eirini* mostly applies to the one who was first offered a deal."

Attes nodded, and Saion shook his head. "Meaning you can't do shit, while the same doesn't apply to Kolis."

My mouth dropped open. "That…that's bullshit!" Eather hummed through me.

"Yeah, well, if you ask the Fates, I'm sure they'll say it's to keep the balance by ensuring that any deal is made in good faith," Thierran said, sitting down.

I started to pace. "And I'm betting Kolis was fully aware of this."

"I'm sure he was," Attes said. "There's even a chance he hoped that neither of you knew about the *eirini*. If you were to proceed with your plan to meet with the Primals, there would be consequences. And knowing the Fates, it would be something really fucked up."

I walked toward the dais, needing space. How could Aydun forget to mention this? Better yet, why hadn't the *vadentia* warned me? It had to be because it didn't work when it came to my actions. "So, what are we supposed to do? Sit around and do nothing?"

Attes turned. "You can do anything that does not involve calling Primals to arms." He paused. "And you cannot attack during the *eirini*."

"Of course," I spat, stopping at the dais. "Haven't we already broken the *eirini*? By involving you?"

"No, because I pledged allegiance to you before the *eirini*," Attes answered. "The rule doesn't apply to me."

"What about him?" I nodded at Thierran.

"You asked nothing of me." Thierran propped his boots on the bench in front of him. "I invited myself along." He took a drink. "And I've never been what one would consider loyal to Kolis. And he knows that."

"How have you managed to stay alive with Kolis knowing that?" I questioned.

"Because he knows if he tries to come at me, I'll do worse to him," Thierran stated, eather burning behind his eyes.

I raised my brows. "Worse than death?"

He smiled. "I'll take his dreams."

Air whooshed out of my lungs as I held Thierran's stare. I suspected that *was* worse than death because Kolis likely only dreamed of one person.

Sotoria.

"Real convenient of Aydun to fail to mention any of this," Ash gritted out. "Considering how *understandable* it is that an *eirini* would be forgotten."

"Yeah." I leaned against the dais and let my head fall back. Why did it almost always feel like the Fates were actively screwing us over? It didn't make sense. Aydun wanted me to avoid war, but why didn't he ensure I knew the rules? "Shit."

"It's not a big deal," Attes began.

I laughed.

"It's really not," he insisted as Ash approached the dais. "You just cannot involve the other Primals or attack. That's it."

"He's right." Ash stopped in front of me, taking my hands. "We can still proceed with figuring out how to entomb Kolis."

"There's really only one option for that," Attes said, sitting on one of the benches opposite Rhain. "You will definitely need the bones of an Ancient."

"We know," I said.

"And we also know we need more than just that," Ash said, turning as he slid between me and the dais. He looped his arms around my waist. "But regarding the bones, Kolis has most—but not all—of the stash."

"He does," Rhain said, squinting.

"Most of it was in the Carcers," Attes said. "I doubt it still is."

"Damn it." I closed my eyes. "When I destroyed the prison Ash was being held in, I likely destroyed all the Ancient bones there, too."

"We wouldn't need a lot, right?" Saion set his glass on one of the stone benches. "Enough to make chains and probably some spikes."

"As you said, Kolis has most of it. But not all. The Primals who've stayed in his favor have bone weapons. I have a spear. So does Kyn. And I know he has at least one chain. I'm betting Veses has some, too. Maybe even Embris."

"Are you suggesting we just go to their Courts and take it?"

Attes met my stare from where he sat. "If it comes to that, yes."

My stomach dipped as I started to respond, but the sudden throb of an arriving Primal snapped my attention to the doors. The feeling was intense, meaning the Primal was close. Too close—

"Son of a bitch," Ash growled, and Attes shot to his feet.

"No," rasped Attes. "He can't be this fucking idiotic."

The doors to the throne room swung open, and the Primal God of Peace and Vengeance entered.

Wisps of shadow whirled around Ash's legs as he stepped forward. "If he's harmed a single guard outside," he said to Attes in a low voice, "he will not be leaving here conscious."

If Kyn had harmed any of our people, he wouldn't be leaving here in one piece.

Shoulders tense, Attes nodded. "Understood."

Kyn strolled down the center aisle. "Don't worry. I didn't touch a single hair on any guard's head."

Attes grabbed Rhain by the arm and shoved him behind him as he demanded, "What are you doing here?"

Rapidly fading sunlight glinted off the bronze-and-shadowstone armor covering Kyn's chest. "I could ask you the same question, brother."

"He's welcome here. You are not." The air in the throne room dropped several degrees. "So, you have less than a minute to explain why you'd make such an unwise decision as entering the Shadowlands uninvited."

Kyn stopped halfway down the aisle. "I came to demand payment for what was done to my hounds."

Anger and disbelief combined, forming a searing knot in the center of my chest. "The hounds you sent after Nyktos?"

Kyn's eather-soaked gaze flicked to me. "I wasn't speaking to you."

"You should be," I said. "Since I'm the one who killed most of them."

"Interesting." Kyn's steps slowed. "I'll make sure to let the King know you've admitted to slaughtering my hounds."

"You go ahead and do that," I retorted.

That fucking grin of his faded a notch as he looked away from me. And then it completely disappeared when he noticed Thierran, who remained seated, his feet still on the bench in front of him, ankles crossed. "What the fuck are you doing here?"

Thierran cocked his head and raised a brow. "Acknowledging your presence already isn't worth my very precious time," he said, sipping from his glass. "Let alone answering your questions."

Kyn halted, his flesh thinning until I saw hints of gray beneath. My skin prickled as energy ramped up. He lifted his left arm, eather sparking.

Essence flooded my body in a hot rush as I stepped forward. I didn't rein the power back in. Gold-tinged silver filled the corners of my vision. A glow pulsed around me, and several strands of hair began lifting off my shoulders. "Don't even think it, Kyn."

He slowly turned his gaze to me. Our eyes locked as brilliant strands of gold-and-silver eather streaked from my legs. One side of his lips curled up. "Weren't you in a cage the last time I—"

"Finish that sentence, and I will rip out your tongue and then feed it to you," Ash growled, his shadows snaking out and streaming between the rows of benches.

Holding Kyn's gaze, I smiled. "Finish it."

Kyn's nostrils flared.

"Don't finish that sentence," Attes intervened, holding up a hand as he glanced over his shoulder at Ash and me. "Let me handle this."

The hazy outline of wings appeared behind Ash's back, stretching out. "If by *handle this*, you mean removing him from my sight, then you'd better do it quick."

"I want payment for my hounds," Kyn demanded, glancing to where Rhain stood. "He'll do. We have some unfinished business to attend to, anyway."

"Try it." Rhain's nostrils flared as Saion moved closer to him, his hand going to his sword.

"Stop it." Attes blocked his brother. "Fucking Fates, what are you thinking? You shouldn't be here."

"Neither should you," Kyn retorted. "And you definitely should not have freed her."

"He didn't," I said, fingers twitching. "I freed myself."

"Congratulations." Kyn blew me a kiss.

"I'm going to fucking disembowel you," Ash promised.

"Can't wait." Kyn turned back to his brother. "You should be before our King, begging for his forgiveness after the shit you pulled."

"That's not going to happen." Attes moved toward his brother.

"Preferably on your knees." Kyn ignored Attes. "Something I'm sure some of you are well versed in."

Anger pumped through me. "Your insults are only slightly less amusing than Veses'."

Kyn huffed out a laugh. "What's going to be amusing is seeing you try to repeat that with a dick in your—" He grunted, sliding back several feet before catching himself. Eather lit up the veins in his cheeks, and his head jerked back toward me.

I stood several feet from where I'd been standing before. My reaction had been immediate, the eather rising to meet my will seamlessly. "Watch your mouth."

Kyn straightened. "That was a cute parlor trick."

"Did you see what I did to Kolis?" I asked, lowering my hand as I felt the throbbing awareness of a draken. "Was that a cute parlor trick?"

"No, that was what we like to call an act of treason." He focused on his brother. "And that is exactly what you're doing by being here."

"Actually, it's not, considering I no longer recognize Kolis as my King," Attes replied. "And I didn't long before she Ascended."

"You…you fucking idiot." Kyn's jaw throbbed, and he inhaled sharply. "You're endangering your Court, Nyktos."

"Is that so?" Ash replied in a voice that was too quiet.

"Kolis won't stay my hand now." A glint of eagerness sharpened his features. "He will order your Court to be returned to dust." His gaze shot to the dais as the door leading to what I called the war room opened. "Along with your draken." He let out a cutting laugh. "Even you."

"Sure, he will." Nektas crossed the dais and jumped down. He exchanged a look with Ash and then planted himself before me.

My narrowed-eye gaze landed on Ash. We would have to talk about that later—like after the trash had been dealt with.

"Kyn," warned Attes, creeping closer to his brother, "you need to leave. Now."

He wasn't listening. Instead, he said, "And I will gladly see it carried out."

"No, you will not." Attes planted a hand on Kyn's shoulder, shoving him back. "You aren't going to do shit."

Kyn laughed. "I always thought you were a little soft. But this? I never believed you capable of being this much of a fool."

"It is not I who is the fool." Attes followed as Kyn stepped to the side. "You need to leave."

"But I just got here." Kyn edged to the side more. "And I haven't received my payment. Nor any thanks."

"And what do you think we need to thank you for?" Ash asked.

I couldn't wait to hear this.

"For staying out of the goodness of my heart and attempting to talk some sense into you."

"Do any of us look like we need that?" Thierran asked.

"You always look like you need that." Kyn shadowstepped, passing his brother.

Shadows spun across the floor, rising within inches of Kyn, forcing him back a foot.

Ash's wings thickened behind him. "I thought you were going to handle him."

"Yeah, well, it's taking me a minute," Attes muttered.

"If you stand against Kolis,"—Kyn lifted a hand, sending his brother skidding backward—"you will spend the next several centuries regretting it."

"Do you think we haven't already spent centuries doing just that?" Attes spat, a pale shade of gray appearing just under his flesh.

Kyn's lips peeled back. "Kolis has only done what was necessary."

"Are you serious?" I demanded. "If you're going to support him, then at least be truthful about who you are supporting."

"And what would that truth be?"

"That he's a monster," I hissed, eather crackling from my skin as I sidestepped Nektas. "And the worst parts of you have benefited from that."

"It doesn't have to continue to be that way," Attes said, clasping Kyn's shoulder from behind. He spun him around. "You weren't always this—"

"This what?" Kyn shrugged off his brother's grasp.

"Violent," Attes answered without hesitation. "Aggressive. Bitter. Demeaning—"

"He's always been annoying as fuck," Ash cut in, shadows swirling rapidly around his legs. "Just wanted to throw that out there."

Kyn's head whipped toward Ash. "Fuck you."

"You weren't always hungry for vengeance," Attes rushed on. "You used to live for peace. Both of us did. What you've become is Kolis's fault. His actions have corrupted you."

"You have no idea what you're talking about," Kyn snarled. "If his actions corrupted me, then it would've done the same to you."

"You think I haven't felt his influence? I have," Attes shouted. "All of us have. You know I speak the truth, and the Fates know I should've spoken it earlier than this." Attes's voice roughened. "I should've stepped in centuries ago. But it's not too late to stop this."

"It might be too late for you, brother." Kyn extended his arms. "For all of you."

"It's about to be too late for your ass if you don't get the fuck out of my Court," Ash warned.

Kyn spun, baring his fangs. Eather swelled inside me, pressing against my skin.

"Look, I get it." Kyn drew back, his body moving in a disturbingly serpentine manner. "Kolis took your mother. Your father." He smiled. "Then your Consort."

The shadows stilled around Ash.

"Of course, you're angry. You've always been angry. But you, brother? You may feel a little regret here and there, but you live. You still prospered. All because of Kolis. All because he kept the balance."

"Balance he had to maintain because of *his* actions," Attes argued, his eyes wide. "Are you fucking serious right now?"

Kyn smirked. "Not to sound cliché, but I'm deadly serious."

"And you're also worried," I said. "I remember what you said to Kolis. You were concerned that his idea of creating life wouldn't continue to maintain the balance."

Kyn stiffened. "I have no idea what you're talking about."

I laughed. "Yeah, you do. You tried to hide just how concerned you were in front of Kolis because you're afraid of him."

"And you're not?"

"Who wouldn't be?" Shadows throbbed around us.

Kyn stared at me for a moment. "Brother, did you swear an oath to *her*?"

My muscles locked up as Nektas edged closer to me, his hair shielding his face as he dipped his chin.

"I did." Attes grabbed his brother. "Before she Ascended and rose as the true Primal of Life. Before the *eirini*."

"And what exactly do you think she can do for you? For Iliseeum?" Kyn's laugh sounded like blades being dragged against each other. "She is a mortal."

My brows lifted as Saion sighed. "She is not quite mortal any longer."

"It's kind of embarrassing that you even have to state that," Ash drawled.

Kyn shoved Attes back once more to fully face Ash. "You want to know what's embarrassing, Nyktos?"

Attes held up a hand. "Don't say another word."

"No." Ash's voice was soft, his lips curving into a smile as cool wind blew through the throne room. The faint sound of crackling came from the walls as the candles were snuffed out. "Please, continue."

"*You*." Kyn tilted his head. "I'm embarrassed for you."

Attes paled. "Shut the fuck up, Kyn."

"Because you stand here," Kyn continued, his words slithering over my skin, "beside *her*. When only a few weeks ago, your Consort was Kolis's whore."

My heart stopped. Everything in and around me did.

"And I cannot wait for Kolis to fulfill his promise to me, and she becomes my—"

Ash was a blur of shadows and icy rage, slamming into Kyn in a heartbeat. He had shifted, his skin the color of midnight streaked with pure silver bolts of eather. Twin, sweeping arcs similar to the wings of a draken rose as Ash lifted Kyn into the air. Attes was shouting, but all I heard was the wet splatter of shimmery, bluish-red blood and tissue against the stone floor.

Ash had driven his hand through Kyn's stomach.

The Primal of Peace and Vengeance roared, his body jerking. Blood splattered the table.

"Stop this!" Attes yelled as Thierran reached for his bottle of wine, yanking it clear of the carnage.

Kyn's flesh turned a deep shade of stone gray. Leathery wings sprouted from his back, and he gripped Ash by the arms.

"Don't worry," Kyn spat, shaking Ash off. He flew back, the jagged tear in his stomach healing. "I'll give her back to you," he said, and I flinched.

"Stupid fuck," Nektas bit out, thin traces of smoke following his words. "Such a stupid *fuck*."

"That is," Kyn hissed, "if anything is left of her."

Ash laughed.

He *laughed*.

Then he was on Kyn, their bodies crashing together in a clap of thunder. Kyn's fangs flashed as his head snapped down, aiming for Ash's throat.

Kyn was ages older than Ash, but Ash was enraged, and that fury set the candles aflame again, the fire racing upward. He was possibly even furious enough to kill his second Primal as he jerked his head to the side, avoiding Kyn's bite.

Gripping Kyn's jaw, Ash forced his mouth open. "What did I promise you?"

"Fuck—"

"That's not it." Ash's hand moved as quick as lightning.

Blood poured from Kyn's mouth as Ash held something pink and limp.

It was Kyn's tongue.

His actual tongue.

Just as Ash had promised, he shoved it back into Kyn's gaping mouth.

"Stop this." Attes whirled toward me. "You have to stop this, Seraphena."

I knew I should. No god had been Ascended to take Kyn's place. Not only would killing Kyn kickstart a bloodbath, but it would also damage the mortal realm.

But I did nothing.

Rhain turned to me. "If Kyn falls here and not in battle, it will send the exact opposite message you want to extend to the other Primals and gods."

I knew that.

Kyn hadn't done anything but run his mouth—not exactly a good reason to kill someone.

But still, I did nothing.

Ash's arm jerked back and then thrust forward again. The other Primal's eyes went wide, and his body became rigid as he let out a guttural scream, throwing his head back.

Ash flew up to the ceiling and yanked his arm back. Kyn's wings collapsed.

"Holy shit," Thierran murmured, taking a drink of his wine.

Ash now held Kyn's beating heart in his hand. The shadows moving through Ash's flesh stilled, leaving silver streaks across Ash's cheeks as his all-silver eyes locked with mine.

Ash bit into the heart, tearing through the muscle. Blood spurted, running from the corners of his mouth. He lifted his head and then spat the blood into Kyn's face as his hand closed around the heart, crushing it.

Then he let go of Kyn.

I watched the Primal plummet to the floor. He hit a stone bench, cracking his back.

Thierran winced. "Ouch."

A giggle crawled up my throat, but I squelched it as Attes closed his eyes, letting out a long breath. I wasn't sure it was one of relief, even though his brother still lived since he still had a head. It was probably more a mixture of that and dread.

Ash lowered himself, landing between Attes and me. Nektas stepped out of his way and moved back as Ash's wings evaporated.

"I don't care what you do with him as long as you get him the fuck out of here," Ash bit out, turning to the others. "This meeting is over."

The blood and gore weren't visible on his shadowstone-hued flesh as Ash faced me. His eyes met mine, and he stalked toward me, silently taking my hand and shadowstepping us from the throne room.

Cool fingers brushed my cheek, catching several curls and tucking them behind my ear. "What are you thinking, *liessa*?"

I sat on the side of the tub Ash occupied, my chin resting on my forearm. The water had turned red with blood, but it had since been emptied and fresh had been brought in.

"Many things," I murmured.

"What's the most pressing?"

They all felt equally pressing as my gaze lifted to Ash's. The striking lines of his face were relaxed and showed no sign of him having ripped the heart from another Primal's chest.

And then bit into it.

"I was thinking about the *eirini* and how close we came to breaking it," I said, trailing my fingers through the water. My gaze briefly lifted to his. "I was thinking about Attes. Everything with Kyn must be so hard for him."

"It would've been less so if he'd gotten the fucker out of there."

"It's his brother." I watched the suds swirling over Ash's thigh. "He was trying to do it without hurting him."

"And that's a problem." The tips of Ash's fingers smoothed over a strand of my hair. "Because, at some point, he will need to hurt his brother."

"I know." I pulled my fingers from the water and straightened. "And he knows that."

He huffed. "You sure about that?"

"He knows what happened when Eythos gave Kolis too many chances."

His gaze tracked the strand of hair he threaded through his fingers. "Yeah, and I think he was more so reminding himself."

"Possibly," I murmured. A huge part of me childishly hoped that Kyn and Attes wouldn't have to come up against each other, but the very real possibility weighed heavily on my mind and heart. I had to shift my thoughts to something else. "So, Thierran? There's something…"

"Not quite right about him?" Ash suggested.

"Yes." I grinned. "I tried to read him but saw and felt nothing."

Ash's fingers stilled in my hair. "I would strongly advise against attempting that again."

My frown returned. "Well, after that dire piece of advice, I want to try it again."

Ash sent me a look of warning. "The *oneirou* can do more than just invade someone's dreams."

"They can steal them."

"It is more than that. They are known by another name: *Sōl Eder.*"

The translation caused my stomach to dip. "Soul Eater?"

"Yes. They can manipulate the emotions of their targets—including gods and Primals—both when they sleep and while they're awake."

My lips parted. "I think I know what kind of shit you were talking about now when you warned him."

"They are the only gods that can mess with us if they catch us off guard," he said, as serious as when he ripped out Kyn's heart. "Most are smart enough not to try it. But if they catch you in their heads, it's in their nature to do the same in return. And what they can do is far more than learning details about a person. They can create an emotion out of nothing, including manifesting and amplifying fear. They can drive someone mad in their sleep and send a god fleeing before a sword is even raised."

What did it say about me that I thought that ability was kind of interesting? Creepy, but definitely interesting.

"You don't fuck with them, Sera. Not unless you plan to end them immediately after doing so."

I swallowed. "Message received."

"Good." He exhaled heavily.

"You were sort of fucking with him out there. In case you didn't realize," I pointed out.

"That's because Thierran has just enough common sense to know I will do exactly as I warned without hesitation."

"Oh." My lips pursed. "I'm guessing they're really good at blocking their minds from others?"

"Yes. Not even I can easily read their emotions without making it known that I am doing so. And I know what I'm doing." His gaze met mine.

"You're still figuring out your abilities."

"I said I wouldn't."

He didn't look away. "And I also know you're incredibly curious and impulsive."

"I'm not—you know, I can't even deny that," I said, and Ash chuckled. "Do you think we can still go to the Thyia Plains?"

"I think so. We just need to be careful with what we say."

I was relieved to hear that, and then I got a little distracted by all the sleek flesh on display. After he dried off, we talked a little about the *eirini* and what it meant. He stressed again that it wasn't that big of a deal, but it made me feel like we were spinning our wheels. Then he briefly checked in with Rhain—something I felt was actually expected of *me*. I kept forgetting. When he returned, I had just finished readying myself for bed. I stepped out of the bathing chamber in a thin, silky nightgown that reminded me of the color of Aios's hair.

Ash's eyes flared to a heated silver as he crossed the chamber. "Beautiful," he murmured, stopping near me.

He kissed the skin beside the gown's thin strap. The tips of my breasts tightened, and I shivered at the touch. "I'll be right back."

I nodded as he entered the bathing chamber. Dragging my hair over my shoulder, I climbed into bed and pulled the blanket up.

Ash returned, drawing to a halt as he saw me. An eyebrow rose. "Are you okay?"

"Yeah." I frowned. "Why?"

"You're holding the blanket to your chin."

"Oh." I looked down to see that I was, in fact, clutching the soft fur to my chin. I eased up on my grip as Ash undressed.

I expected him to join me, but he didn't until he pulled on a pair of loose-fitting linen pants, keeping his back to me. That was odd. Or was it? He didn't always sleep nude. Prodding at a fang, I watched as he settled in beside me.

He didn't roll onto his side to face me, which also felt strange. I glanced over at him, my mouth opening and then closing. A knot lodged in my throat.

"I think we need to talk about Kyn." Ash shattered the silence.

I tried to swallow as I quickly averted my gaze, but it was difficult. "About what happened earlier? I probably should've stopped you."

Ash snorted. "You really think that?"

"Both Attes and Rhain asked me to."

"Why didn't you?"

I lifted a shoulder and peeked over at him. "I didn't want to."

"I'm glad you didn't. I thoroughly enjoyed shutting the fucker up." One side of his lips curled up, but it didn't soften the tension around his mouth. "But I thought for a moment that I might kill him. He's not Hanan, but I was angry enough to do it—at least, it felt that way."

I pressed my lips together.

"What he was saying?" Ash's voice was level, but my essence throbbed in response to the angry rise in his tone. "About Kolis offering you to him? That wasn't the first time I heard that."

I squeezed my eyes shut, knowing where he'd heard it, even though I did my best to forget it. Kolis used to talk to Ash when he visited him in the Carcers. So did Kyn.

"It was said in front of you, wasn't it?" he asked.

"Yes." I opened my eyes and willed my heart to slow. "It was before Ione gave Kolis the confirmation that I was Sotoria."

Ash went quiet for a moment. "I'm sorry."

A tremor shot through me. "You don't need to apologize. It was just a threat—an empty one at that."

"It wasn't empty," he said, his voice roughening. "It was before Ione? That means you had no idea she would lie for you. His threat was a real possibility. And that…" He cleared his throat. "It had to be terrifying and enraging."

It had been.

"And you must have felt trapped."

I had.

I'd felt cornered and helpless.

"I know I did when he ordered me to feed—and to keep feeding—until there was no life left in those he turned me on after I pissed him off for something so irrelevant I can't even recall what instigated his fury now."

My breath caught as I looked at him.

"Sometimes, it was gods who hadn't even entered their Culling. I used to wonder what they'd done to earn such a fate until I realized they had likely done nothing—or something insignificant." He stared at the ceiling, his hands resting just below his chest. "If I refused—which I had before, though only once—I learned quickly."

"What…what did he do when you refused?"

"He killed three gods."

"Gods," I rasped.

Ash's chest rose with a heavy breath. "So, that was my choice. Were three lives worth me refusing to take one? I decided it couldn't be. And for a long time, I didn't know if I had made the right decision."

"That's an impossible choice to make," I told him, my heart aching. "I would've chosen the same."

"Yeah, and you would also wonder if you had made the right decision," he said, and I didn't need to confirm that. He was right.

"How many times did he make you do that?"

"Hundreds."

Shock doused the rising anger, but I could still feel it building in the air around me. It took me a moment to get it under control. "I want to kill him."

"As do I."

"Those deaths are not on your hands, though." My fingers dug into the blanket.

"I know that." A muscle ticked in his jaw. "But every so often, I dream of being in Dalos, feeding and feeling the heart stutter and stop. Feeling the anger and desperation as I searched for a way out of what I was being made to do. I don't think about it as much as before, but yeah, that shit can haunt."

"I'm so sorry." Tears stung my throat. "But I was lucky, Ash," I whispered. "I wasn't forced to do anything like that."

He was quiet for a moment. "Evander?"

A jolt of surprise ran through me. "How do you know about him?"

"Keella told me when we were in the Thyia Plains before you woke up."

Gods.

I couldn't be mad at Keella, but I wished she hadn't said anything. "It wasn't like that."

"What *was* it like?"

"It was…it was when Kolis brought me to court. There were Chosen there who had shed their veils and acted as servants. Some were rather friendly with the gods, but it was hard to tell, you know? The gods would just grab the Chosen."

Ash said nothing as an image of Evander filled my mind, his eyes widening with shock. "I got angry at the way the Chosen were being treated, and when Evander grabbed one—Jacinta—and bit her… It was right after—" I cut myself off with a shake of my head. "Kolis led me to believe that Evander was forcing himself on Jacinta and told me I could stop him. So, I did." The sight of the life fading from those shocked eyes filled my mind, and I flinched. "Then Jacinta started screaming. That's when I realized he'd played me. Easily. *Too* easily. I should've known better."

"How could you have?" Ash asked.

"Everyone speaks about how manipulative Kolis is. I saw it myself."

"That doesn't mean anything, Sera. Every situation is different, and I've seen him manipulate gods three times older than me."

I didn't want that to make me feel better because I had taken a life. Likely a purely innocent one.

"So, just like you're sorry I experienced that,"—his head turned toward mine, and our eyes locked—"I'm sorry you experienced what you did. Okay?"

The tears stung my eyes now. "Okay."

He held my gaze for a moment and then looked away. The lights flickered off, plunging the chamber into darkness. A moment passed, and then the bed shifted as he rolled onto his side. His arm came around me. I felt his lips brush my cheek and closed my eyes against the rush of rising emotion, refusing to allow it to be freed. It wouldn't help anything, and it would only worry Ash more.

I wouldn't cry.

I *wouldn't.*

Guards adorned in violet-hued armor bowed as a godling led us through the wide, windowed hall. The male kept stealing glances behind him as we followed, his gaze often dipping to where Ash's hand was wrapped tightly around mine. I tried smiling at him, but when bright pink infused his cheeks, I wasn't sure it had helped.

The godling stopped before a rounded archway. "Her Highness is waiting for you inside."

"Thank you," Ash said.

He bowed his fair head as we walked through the archway and into a chamber open to the outside.

The Primal Goddess of Rebirth stood in the center of the room, her curly, russet-colored hair unbound and flowing over her shoulders and back.

"Your Majesty," she said, the length of the bluish-gray robes she wore pooling on the terracotta floors as she began to lower herself.

"Please, don't," I stopped her, lifting a hand. "That isn't necessary."

"But it is, Seraphena," she replied.

I snapped my mouth shut as Ash gently squeezed my hand.

Keella placed one hand over her chest and flattened her other palm on the floor. Curls spilled forward as she bowed her head deeply. "It is an honor to bow before the *Queen* of the Gods."

My cheeks warmed as I shifted from one foot to the other, immediately thinking about the god, Evander—previously of the Thyia Plains, Keella's Court. I pushed those thoughts aside. "It…it honors me that you feel that way," I said, hoping that sounded like an appropriate response—because I meant it. "You may rise."

Keella did so with regal grace. The Primal goddess was nothing but pure, stunning elegance.

"And you do not need to do that again," I quickly added.

The corners of her full lips twitched. "Is that an order?"

"It is."

She gave me a small nod of acknowledgment. "I must say that your first order to me as my Queen is quite…refreshing."

"I'm sure it is," I said, thinking only the gods knew all the horrible things Kolis had ordered her to do in the past.

"We apologize that we were unable to make it yesterday," Ash said. "But thank you so much for making time to see us today."

"Of course." Clasping her hands, her quicksilver gaze moved to where Ash's hand still held mine, and a warm smile appeared. "I am so incredibly relieved to see you again—both of you," she said. "But especially you, Seraphena." She laughed softly. "No offense, Nyktos."

He chuckled. "None taken."

"You look very healthy and strong," Keella said, her smile broadening. "And so…" Thick, dusky lashes lowered. "So full of life."

Something about how she said that felt a little odd, but I couldn't quite put my finger on why.

"Come and sit," Keella offered, stepping aside to reveal a table between two settees displaying an array of refreshments. "I must admit I was surprised to hear that you two had sought to speak with me and not the remaining Primals."

"We're in a period of *eirini*," Ash said as we sat on one of the thickly cushioned settees. "Until it ends, we will not be summoning them."

A flicker of surprise skittered across the smoky, reddish-brown skin of her face. "So, some sort of deal of resolution has been offered between Kolis and you?"

"Between Kolis and *us*," I corrected. "I do not rule alone. If I am the Queen, then Nyktos is the King."

A pleased look filled her expression. "I am curious to learn how the deal came about."

My gaze swept over the chamber as Ash gave her a short rundown of the meeting Kolis had initiated. The warm white walls were bare. Past another sitting area and beyond the parted gauzy curtains, I saw tall, violet-hued trees swaying in the sweet, heady breeze that filled the tranquil space.

"Interesting," Keella remarked once Ash had finished. "I wish I could say more, but I dare not tempt the Fates."

I raised a brow. "Neither do we. So, please excuse our vagueness about some of what we wish to ask you."

"Understood." She leaned forward and picked up a porcelain pitcher. "But I imagine I can guess what your answer will be at the end of the *eirini*."

Ash smirked. "I'm sure you're right."

"Tea?" she offered.

"Thank you," I said as she poured three cups. "There are two separate things we were hoping you could assist us with."

"We don't want to take up a lot of your time or have the Fates get the impression we're doing something we shouldn't, so I think it's best if we get right to it."

"Agreed."

"We had a question about the Ancients," Ash said, deciding to start with what felt like the most important thing. "Other than Kolis, you would likely be the only one old enough to remember them and the war."

Curiosity filled her eyes. "Sometimes, I wish I didn't. That was a time of violence and bloodshed. A time best forgotten but necessary to remember." She took a sip. "What questions could you have about them?"

"I know that not all passed on to Arcadia," I said, swallowing. The tea was sweet, just the way I liked it. "And some that could not be forced to go were entombed."

There was a slight widening of her eyes.

"I learned that during my Ascension," I explained, and she nodded in understanding. I chose my words wisely so as not to violate the *eirini*. "Ancients are incredibly powerful, more so than any Primal, so I am curious as to how they were entombed."

"Especially when it would be difficult to keep a Primal in the ground for thousands of years," Ash added. "We thought you might know how that was done and would be willing to share."

"For curiosity's sake," I added, just in case a Fate was lurking unseen somewhere or the essence itself was listening in.

Keella's gaze drifted between us, and a slight grin briefly appeared before vanishing. "Yes, for the sake of curiosity," she said, clearing her throat. "I do remember. It was something that took quite some time to figure out, lengthening the war each time one of them broke free of the bonds of their brethren."

So, the bones of an Ancient were definitely involved.

"You see, the bones weakened them, but as you well know, the ground seeks to protect us—and them," she continued. "Neither shadowstone nor bone can block the strength of the eather that fills the very air we breathe and the soil we rest in. But there is something that acts as a…" Her nose wrinkled. "A shield of sorts." She inhaled deeply and slowly. "Other than Kolis, no other Primal alive today knows of it."

"What is it?" Ash asked.

"Celastite," she said.

Ash frowned as he glanced at me. I had no idea what that was. My *vadentia* was silent as a tomb, which could only mean… Excitement sparked. My intuition wasn't working, so it had to be something.

"It's a naturally occurring mineral that can be found where the Ancients first slept and matured," Keella explained, and I knew she was speaking of where the Ancients had first fallen as stars. "There are many places, but they are all in the mortal realm."

"Really?"

She nodded. "There are at least a dozen entombed in the mortal realm that I can remember."

That such a powerful being could've been beneath Wayfair or some other place I'd been was unsettling.

Then the other thing she said struck me. At least a dozen? Good gods. I reached out and picked up a piece of sliced cheese.

Ash leaned forward. "So, these places where the Ancients are entombed must contain some kind of impact area."

She nodded. "Over the years, they became underground caverns. Recognizing one as such wouldn't be hard. You see, the celastite is oddly colored. It carries a burnt-red sheen."

Nibbling on the cheese, I nearly choked. "A burnt-red sheen?"

"Yes. The mineral often looks damp, as if it is weeping."

Ash eyed me. "Have you seen something like that?"

"I haven't seen it, but I do know of at least one place," I said. "In Oak Ambler." I twisted toward Ash. "It's near Massene—a port city." I stiffened. "I have heard of there being caves along the bluffs, and that Castle Red Rock was built from the stone mined from that area."

"Well, I guess we know where the castle got its name." Ash met my stare, and I knew what he was thinking. That we may have found a location. "What if an Ancient has already been entombed there?"

"You would feel it if they are there," Keella said. "It would bring upon a great sense of unease that even mortals would pick up on."

"That's good to know," Ash murmured.

"If you do get curious about these locations," Keella said, tilting her head, "I suggest you don't spend too long exploring them. They can weaken you. Just being inside one and near the celastite can affect you."

"We'll keep that in mind," Ash said. "Thank you."

Keella's smile was knowing. "Was there something else you wanted to ask?"

"Yes." I switched gears. "We wanted to ask you about a prophecy."

Keella's whole demeanor swiftly changed as she stiffened. It caused my skin to prickle.

"It is a prophecy spoken by Penellaphe," I said. "And the last oracle."

"We've come to learn that my father knew about it," Ash said, leaning back and resting an ankle on his opposite knee. "And we suspect you are also aware of it."

Keella remained quiet.

"Penellaphe shared it with us, but when I was…" I took a quick sip of tea. "When I was in Dalos, Kolis told me there was a third part of the prophecy that Penellaphe didn't know about until I shared it with her recently." I then told Keella what I'd shared with Penellaphe. "She thinks Kolis has the prophecy in the wrong order."

"Apparently, he believes it is about him becoming a Primal of Blood and Bone," Ash said.

Keella snorted. "Of course, he would. After all, he thinks everything is about him."

A short, dry laugh left me. "So, the prophecy isn't about him?"

"Oh, it is. At least, some of it." Several moments passed, and a slight tremor ran up her arm as she took a sip of her tea. Her gaze rose to meet Ash's. "Your father shared it with me. It was one of the reasons I helped him when it came to Sotoria." She lowered her cup to her lap. "I'm sure you can imagine the other reasons."

I took a drink. Despite the sweetness of the tea, it still soured in my stomach. Unfortunately, I *could* imagine the reasons.

"What does Sotoria have to do with this prophecy?" Ash asked.

"Everything," Keella said in a voice barely above a whisper. "She is, after all, the Harbinger and the Bringer."

"Of Death and Destruction?" My insides flashed cold. I wasn't expecting that. Nor did it feel right.

"She is not death and destruction," Keella said, putting her cup on the table. "At least given what Eythos and I understood of the vision."

Ash's eyes narrowed. "Then her being a harbinger and a bringer means she is…what? A warning?"

Keella's chest rose with a shallow breath. "Where she goes, death and destruction follow."

Tension crept into my muscles. "Kolis."

"He is the true Primal of Death, who often has a habit of creating destruction," Keella said. "Does he not?"

"Then neither Penellaphe nor Kolis was right about the order of the prophecy. Because Sotoria's time…" No, Sotoria's time hadn't truly passed. Her soul was still alive. She could be reborn. "Did you know there was more to the prophecy than what Penellaphe saw?"

She nodded. "Only because Eythos did."

"And how did my father come to learn the information?"

"He, like his brother, heard the dreams of the Ancients," she said, clasping her hands once more. "Eythos said it was all they dreamed until they stopped."

"Stopped dreaming?" I asked.

She nodded.

I placed my cup on the table but didn't sit back. "I'm not sure why that creeps me out, but it does."

"Do you know the order?" Ash asked as he began rubbing the center of my back.

"I do not speak it. Call me superstitious, but I fear doing so breathes life into it." She stood. "One moment."

We watched her go to a narrow cabinet along the wall and open a drawer. As she stood still, her hand moving quickly across a piece of parchment she had pulled out, Ash ran his hand up under my hair to clasp the back of my neck. I looked over at him.

"You okay?" he asked.

I nodded, thinking about what he had shared with me last night. I didn't want him to worry, so I smiled, even though my chest ached just thinking about what Ash had told me. What Kolis had put him through was unimaginable. And, gods, a part of me hoped he refused the deal because stripping him of power wasn't enough. It wasn't the kind of justice I wanted to dish out.

And that was a good indication that my whole our-vengeance-can't-be-more-important-than-the-lives-of-others speech was a whole lot of, well… bullshit.

Also, it was an on-the-nose example of why I wasn't cut out for the true Primal of Life stuff.

Because I also wanted to kill Kyn. Really badly.

Why did that bastard have to tell Ash what Kolis had offered when I was at Dalos? Better yet, how could anyone find pleasure in doing so?

Ash dipped his head and kissed my temple.

Keella returned to us, holding the parchment. Dropping his hand, Ash took it and held it so we could both read it.

"Your penmanship is beautiful," I murmured.

"Thank you." Keella returned to her seat.

Taking a shallow breath, I began reading the prophecy.

From the desperation of golden crowns and born of mortal flesh, a great primal power rises as the heir to the lands and seas, to the skies and all the realms. A shadow in the ember, a light in the flame, to become a fire in the flesh. For the one born of the blood and the ash, the bearer of two crowns, and the bringer of life to mortal, god, and draken. A silver beast with blood seeping from its jaws of fire, bathed in the flames of the brightest moon to ever be birthed, will become one.

When the stars fall from the night, the great mountains crumble into the seas, and old bones raise their swords beside the gods, the false one will be stripped from glory as the great powers will stumble and fall, some all at once, and they will fall through the fires into a void of nothing. Those left standing will tremble as they kneel, will weaken as they become small, as they become forgotten. For finally, the Primal rises, the giver of blood and the bringer of bone, the Primal of Blood and Ash.

Two born of the same misdeeds, born of the same great and Primal power in the mortal realm. A first daughter, with blood full of fire, fated for the once-promised King. And the second daughter, with blood full of ash and ice, the other half of the future King. Together, they will remake the realms as they usher in the end. And so it will begin with the last Chosen blood spilled, the great conspirator birthed from the flesh and fire of the Primals will awaken as the Harbinger and the Bringer of Death and Destruction to the lands gifted by the gods. Beware, for the end will come from the west to destroy the east and lay waste to all which lies between.

I sat back, glancing at Ash as my heart pounded. "Kolis was wrong." I looked over at Keella. "And he didn't know the part about the two daughters."

The Primal goddess said nothing.

I rubbed my palms over my knees, suddenly feeling anxious. I should feel relief that Kolis had been wrong about the order of the prophecy, but that meant Penellaphe had been correct, and my suspicions regarding how it sounded might also be on point. "Kolis said that the part about the bearer of two crowns and the born-of-blood-and-ash part was about me."

The Primal goddess was quiet for several more moments. "I wasn't sure if it was referencing you," she said, holding her hands together so tightly I saw her knuckles bleaching of color. "Not until your coronation."

"The brightest moon," Ash murmured, still staring at the paper he held. "It was just something that popped into my head. And it made sense." He looked up then, his eyes meeting mine. "Your hair always reminded me of moonlight." He let out a rough laugh, his gaze moving to Keella. "That is why you said it made you feel hopeful."

Delfai, the God of Divination, had said the same thing. "Kolis also thought I was the silver beast, but…"

"'*A silver beast with blood seeping from its jaws of fire, bathed in the flames of the brightest moon to ever be birthed, will become one,*'" Ash read aloud. His throat worked on a swallow. "I'm the silver beast."

"And you have become one," Keella said.

Ash blinked, shaking his head. "It's crazy. I had…" He trailed off, clearing his throat. "Then this means the false one—Kolis—will be stripped. Will be defeated."

"That's not the only thing it says." I rose, unable to stay seated. "I've always thought the prophecy sounded like Kolis would be defeated but then return." I walked behind the settee. "That he was the false one and also the great conspirator. And we—" I stopped myself before I spoke about our plans.

Ash got where I was going with it, though. He nodded. "But this also sounds like the Primal of Blood and Bone will rise. If that's not Kolis, then who is it?"

I stopped walking as I reached the opening to the outside. A knot lodged in my chest. I turned back to where Keella and Ash sat. "What is that part again? After it says, '*as they become forgotten*?'"

Ash turned his attention back to the parchment. "'*For, finally, the Primal rises, the giver of blood and the bringer of bone, the Primal of Blood and Bone.*'"

"Will become one," I murmured. My breath caught, and my head snapped up. "Could that part about the giver of life actually be about me?" My heart lurched. "I mean, I had the embers of life inside me even before I Ascended. I was the giver of life. But I'm not the bringer of death."

"You're not?" Keella questioned. "You are the bringer of *a* death."

"Not Kolis," I whispered. "But..."

"Me," Ash finished.

I glanced down at the golden swirl on the top of my hand, and my chest hollowed. "Then could the prophecy mean that Nyktos and I are the giver and bringer of the Primal of Blood and Bone?"

"I believe so," Keella said. "I believe the prophecy was always speaking about you, Nyktos, and Sotoria. Eythos thought the same."

"But that doesn't make sense," Ash argued. "We are not truly one. And that doesn't explain who these two daughters are." He frowned, dropping the parchment onto the table. "I can't shake the feeling that the answer is right in front of us."

"Isn't it usually?" Keella leaned forward and picked up a slice of cantaloupe. "But with prophecies, sometimes you must read between the lines."

The thing was, though, Ward had been correct. This was what Eythos had planned. And that had to mean he knew exactly what the prophecy meant.

"You said that some of the prophecy is about Kolis?" Ash asked.

"Yes, but he is too arrogant to realize what role he'll play in the end."

My stomach hollowed. "In the end?"

"*That* is what the prophecy warns of," she said, her voice dropping. "It is the end of all that is known. The rise of a Primal of Blood and Bone and the Awakening of the Ancients."

Walking toward Ash's office the following morning, I tugged on the lacing of my vest. For some reason, the top felt tighter. Either that or my breasts were way more sensitive than usual.

I stopped messing with it as I came upon the shadowstone pillars and heard Ash speaking with Attes. He'd sent word to the Primal last night to come when he could so we could share with him what we'd learned from Keella.

Attes rose from where he sat before Ash's desk and faced me. "I didn't get a chance to do this, but I need to apologize for my brother's behavior—"

"Let me stop you right there," I interrupted. "You're the last person who needs to apologize for him. You're not responsible for what he has done, and his behavior does not reflect upon you."

Attes exhaled heavily, nodding. "Thank you." He cleared his throat and returned to his seat. "Nyktos was just telling me you guys might have found an answer to one of our most pressing problems."

"Yeah." I sat on the edge of the desk, not liking the idea of talking to Attes's back if I had chosen the settee. We really needed more chairs. "Is this the first you've heard of celastite?"

"It is." Attes leaned back, resting one leather-encased ankle atop the other knee. "Kind of ironic that the location of where the Ancients first arrived can nullify their essence."

"I'm sure it has something to do with balance and makes no sense," I remarked.

"Saion is heading out to Oak Ambler today to see if he can locate the caverns," Ash shared. "Crolee is going with him. If he can find them, he'll see how deep they are."

"We don't want Kolis any place near the surface," I added. "The last thing we want is for someone to stumble upon him."

"Sounds like a plan," Attes said. "I can send some of my gods to help if we need to go deeper."

"That would be good. Thank you," Ash said, and I was happy to hear those two words come out of his mouth.

Saion and Rhain showed up then, and Attes rose to leave and wrangle a few of his most trusted gods.

As Ash spoke with Rhain and Saion, I followed Attes out into the hall. I'd thought of something during our quick meeting—something I believed he could answer for me.

There was also something I wanted to say to him.

Attes raised an eyebrow as I fell into step beside him. "You do realize that your husband will likely make good on his earlier threat when he realizes you are out here with me."

I smiled. "He wouldn't."

Attes sent me a knowing look.

"I won't let him," I amended. "There's something I wanted to ask you. In private."

As we walked, Attes ran his fingers over his chest. A faint ripple of silvery light washed over his sleeveless gray tunic, revealing a bronze-and-shadowstone chestplate when it receded.

"Neat ability," I remarked.

"Isn't it?" Attes stopped behind one of the chairs from the right side of the table. "It ensures that I am always prepared for battle. Figured it would be wise to don the armor just in case you're not faster than Nyktos." He smiled, but it was a little empty.

I looked up at him. There were deep shadows under his eyes, and I didn't need the *vadentia* to tell me the cause. "I'm sorry."

His head jerked toward me. "For what?"

"For your brother."

Attes quickly looked away. "Fuck, Seraphena, don't apologize for him."

"I know Eythos still loved his brother. That was how Kolis was able to kill him." I stared ahead. "And I know you still love yours, even though he's a fucking asshole."

He remained silent.

A lump formed in the back of my throat, and tears stung my eyes because there wasn't a single part of me that doubted Attes's oath to Ash and me, nor the very real likelihood that he would find himself facing off against his brother.

I cleared my throat. "There is something else I need to tell you about him."

He inhaled sharply, his eyes flashing pure silver for a heartbeat. "Did he do something to you? Before Kolis believed you were Sotoria?"

I recoiled, taking a step back. "No. Gods, no. Why would—? Never mind. I know why you would ask that." My voice was low as my stomach churned. "You know exactly who your brother is."

"I know exactly who he has become," Attes corrected softly.

I wanted to apologize again, but I didn't think it would make anything easier. "I didn't get a chance to say something before, but I swore an oath that Kyn would face justice for what he did to the people here."

Attes stopped near the main hall, his eyes closing.

"Is that why you didn't stop Nyktos?" he asked quietly.

I considered lying. "No. I simply wanted to see Kyn hurt."

His chin lowered. "I get that."

"I won't try to carry through on that oath during the *eirini*."

He glanced over at me. "But you will eventually."

"I will." I crossed my arms. "I felt like I needed to tell you that."

Attes's chest rose with a heavy breath. "I can understand such an oath being made, Seraphena."

"That's why I'm sorry," I said. "And you can call me Sera."

His jaw worked as he nodded. Swallowing, he opened his eyes. Only a faint glow of eather pulsed behind his pupils. "Is telling me this why you're currently risking getting my balls cut off?"

I arched a brow. "Yes, but there are other reasons. I wanted to ask you about Sotoria."

It seemed impossible, but Attes stiffened further. "What about her?"

"I assume you have The Star somewhere safe?"

"I do." He was silent for a moment. "And I assume *you* want to be in possession of it."

I nodded. "But I think it's better if you keep her. I'm sure Kolis believes I have The Star, so she's safer with you. I know you will protect her."

Something flickered across his face, too fast for me to read. "I will."

I glanced back toward the chambers. "When I was in Dalos, the Star diamond was above me. It looked different then," I said, even though Attes knew. "But I often saw this light moving around inside it. I thought my mind was playing tricks on me, but it was Eythos's soul. He was…active. Aware. I was wondering if it's the same with Sotoria."

"Does the *vadentia* not tell you?"

I shook my head. "I think it's because her soul was in me."

Two lines formed between his brows. "I cannot say for sure, but there is a light—her soul—inside the diamond. It doesn't move around, though."

"I hope that means she's like…asleep," I said. "That's how she was most of the time she was inside me."

"I hope that, too." He cleared his throat. "At least, that is what I tell myself."

Neither of us liked the idea of her being trapped in The Star, but that was better than her being reborn and Kolis getting his hands on her.

"There is also something else Kolis said," I continued. "And I think he spoke the truth, but I don't understand why."

Attes folded his arms across his chest. "What was it?"

I glanced down the hall. It was empty, but I still lowered my voice. "Kolis said it was Eythos who caused Sotoria's second death."

Attes's gaze flew to mine. A moment passed. "Your suspicions regarding that are true."

I knew they were. But hearing Attes confirm it still felt like a gut punch. "Why?

"Because it was what she wanted," Attes stated flatly. "Sotoria asked him to do it."

A fortnight had passed since Ash and I spoke with Keella. In that time, Saion had found the caverns. Even now, he was there with Crolee and the gods Attes had sent, excavating to get as deep as the celastite would allow. As we'd said when we talked to Attes, we didn't want Kolis entombed anywhere near the surface.

I still couldn't shake what Ash had said when we spoke about the prophecy. That the key to fully understanding it was right in front of us. Every so often, it felt like it was on the tip of my tongue, but the knowledge slipped away when I tried to voice it.

Thankfully, things had been calm in the last two weeks. Almost normal. Crops were growing faster than expected, the framework for the insulas had been built, and evenings were spent sharing dinners with the others. Ash and I trained together, working on controlling the eather and swordplay. There was lots of laughter and even some quiet moments where it was just us. It was a beautiful taste of what we could expect from life once we dealt with Kolis.

But I kept finding myself back in Dalos when I slept. Not every night, but enough that I wanted to pray that my screams wouldn't wake Ash. But they did.

A giggle drew me from my thoughts. Jadis walked—or perhaps bounced—a floppy doll across the floor toward Reaver.

He looked at her and the doll as if he was half-afraid. And, honestly, I couldn't blame him. The doll looked like half its leg had been chewed off, and what remained of its yellow yarn hair stuck out in every direction, charred at the ends.

The doll *was* disturbing.

But the little girl was adorable.

I rarely saw her in her mortal form while awake, but she'd arrived this morning as Ash and I finished breakfast, wearing a simple deep blue cotton gown, her hand held tightly in Reaver's, and that doll dangling from her other hand.

I glanced at the door, wondering how long Ash would be gone. Shortly after he had finished writing the names of the recently deceased in the Book of the Dead, he'd been summoned to the Pillars of Asphodel. We'd planned to do more training today, and I looked forward to it. I needed the exhaustion—the brain drain—that came from doing something physical.

"I don't want to comb its hair," Reaver said. When I looked, a beautiful comb with green and black jewels down its spine lay on the floor between them.

It was a bit too fancy for a child, and I had a feeling it had probably belonged to her mother.

"Brush!" she demanded excitedly, thumping the doll's head off the floor.

Reaver curled his lip. "I'm not touching that thing. It'll fall apart, and you'll blame me."

"Nuh-uh." She bopped the doll's head off Reaver's leg.

Reaver moved his leg away. "You were supposed to comb *your* hair. Not your doll's."

I arched a brow as I eyed Jadis. Clearly, she had not.

Her hair reminded me of mine. It looked like it had been caught in a cyclone. The long, waist-length brown locks were tangled and most definitely knotted.

She stopped banging the doll off Reaver's knee. "No."

"Nek told you to brush your hair." Reaver picked up the comb and handed it to her. Leaning back against the base of the settee, he folded his thin arms. "If you don't, you're gonna get in trouble."

Her chin dipped, and her eyes narrowed until only a thin slit of those vertical pupils was visible.

Oh, no.

I recognized that look, even if she was in her mortal form.

The hand that held the comb cocked back, and like a girl after my own heart, she threw it without an ounce of hesitation.

Snapping forward, I caught the comb before it smacked into Reaver's face. "Let's not do that."

Jadis's head swung in my direction, and I saw big, fat tears welling up in her diamond-bright eyes.

"How about I get the knots out?" I suggested, patting the spot on the floor before me. "I promise I won't pull on your hair."

The little draken glanced between me and her doll and then crawled over, sitting cross-legged in front of me. I guessed that was the go-ahead since Jadis was far less talkative in this form and much clearer when using the *te'lepe*—which I supposed made sense since it was more about communicating her thoughts instead of finding the right words to go with them.

Hoping I was half as good as Ash at doing this, I separated her hair into three sections and carefully began combing the tangles free. There were a lot of things I could be doing right now. I needed to practice shadowstepping and work on using the essence for more precise, delicate tasks since I still struggled with moving a glass without shattering it. I could have handed the young draken over to Aios and went to train with Bele since she was around, but gods, it wasn't that long ago that I had feared I would never see the younglings again. Spending time with them was just as important as anything else.

As I worked on Jadis's hair, she let out these little peals of giggles that tugged at my lips. It took me far longer than it should have to get the knots out, but as Reaver distracted her with the creepy doll, wagging it back and forth, my thoughts wandered. I wasn't sure how I ended up thinking about the father I'd never known. It sort of snuck up on me and then struck me that I could visit him.

My soul felt like it left my body at the mere thought.

I didn't need the *vadentia* to warn me that going into the Vale to find him—an act far too easy for me to do so as the true Primal of Life—was something the Fates would frown upon.

The dead were dead.

The living were alive.

Any interaction would upset the balance. But could I at least see him? Not speak to him, but just discover if the portrait of him was accurate? Maybe even hear his voice? I imagined it would be the same as it had been while he was alive. I didn't see any harm in that.

I pressed my lips together as I ran the comb through Jadis's hair. Either way, it wasn't something I could do now. It would have to keep for later.

"Thank you," Jadis said in her singsong, little-girl voice.

"You're welcome, sweetheart."

Her face broke out in a wide, beautiful smile, and then she planted the wettest, sweetest kiss on me. Gods, I melted right there, and even more when she scrambled toward Reaver and curled up in his lap. He didn't shove her away. Instead, he moved the doll in tune with the melody she hummed under her breath. It was just as rare to see the two of them like this as it was to see her in her mortal form.

I placed the comb on the desk, my gaze falling on the Book of the Dead. Ash had forgotten to put it away when he was summoned. Three glasses of juice, all of them somehow belonging to Jadis, were next to it, and I picked them up in case the moment of tranquility ended. I turned and scanned the chamber. Other than an end table, which wasn't exactly a large surface, there were only the shelves.

It was once more clear how rarely Ash had used his office—or any of the spaces in the palace, for that matter—for any length of time that required refreshments.

But that was changing.

So, there needed to be more furniture in here.

And knickknacks.

I placed the glasses on a nearby shelf and then turned, my gaze returning to the Book of the Dead. I returned to the desk.

Curiosity swelled, and I reached for the book, even though I was unsure if I should pry. Just as my fingers brushed it, I stopped. The back of my neck tingled as I heard my voice in my mind as clearly as if I had spoken out loud. *The Book of the Dead is for the dead. Not the living.* I pulled my hand back, my fingers curling inward. I had an innate feeling that I would cross an invisible line if I opened the book that Ash wrote the names of the dead in—in his blood.

True Primal of Life or not, I still found that unbelievably creepy, but their souls couldn't cross through the Pillars until Ash wrote their names. Or, technically, Kolis could now be the one to write their names, but that obviously wasn't happening. The only reason Ash could continue doing so was because of the true embers of Death inside him.

All of this made me wonder what had happened when he was held prisoner. Did no souls cross over? Intuition told me they did, but I didn't understand how.

I did know who often took Ash's place at the Pillars. It was the same god standing outside the office right now. I spun toward the office doors and shouted, "Rhahar!"

The god opened the door a moment later, his starlit dark brown gaze darting between the young draken and me. "Yes, *mey—*" He caught himself, his hand firming on the hilt of his sword. "Yes, Seraphena?"

"Sera is just fine," I told him. "I have a random question for you."

"I hope it doesn't end in you shadowstepping somewhere," he remarked. "Or asking me to train with you."

Reaver let out a little laugh and then ducked his head, whispering something to Jadis.

"No," I sighed. "And I'm sorry about that."

"You already apologized three times," he replied. "You don't need to keep doing so. Just take one of us with you next time. So, what's your question?"

I grinned. "Did any souls pass through the Pillars while Nyktos was held in Dalos?"

An eyebrow rose. "That really is a random question, but yes, souls crossed over."

"How?" Picking up the tail of my braid, I leaned against the desk. "From what I understand, souls can't cross between the Pillars unless Nyktos writes their names in the book."

"That was the case. Souls would get stuck waiting outside the Pillars if Nyktos was…unavailable." He shifted, widening his stance. "Sometimes, for a few days. The longest was a couple of weeks."

If Ash couldn't write the names for days or weeks, it was because of Kolis. My gaze landed on the couch. Or possibly even Veses. The anger that always occupied my thoughts of her was stronger now that I'd seen her in Dalos. Knew what she went through.

Reaver's head lifted, his alert gaze swinging toward me. The *notam*. It wasn't just my anxiety he could feel. Instinct told me it was any extreme emotion. I checked on Jadis, but she was still humming, thankfully oblivious to what I felt.

I breathed deeply through my nose and then exhaled slowly, tamping down the anger the best I could. "Did he come up with some sort of bypass?"

"He did a few years ago so the souls wouldn't have to dwell in a state of purgatory." Rhahar leaned against the doorframe. "When Nyktos is…unable to write the names, I do it for him."

Surprise flickered through me as I curled my arm back, cupping the back of Reaver's neck. "How is that…?" I trailed off as the answer to my question rapidly formed. "Because he took your soul when Phanos wanted to punish you and your cousin, and then…he *did* release it back to you."

Rhahar's eyes widened. "How did you know that?"

"Foresight." I tapped my finger off my temple. "Or something like that. Supposedly, Eythos had something similar."

"I'd heard that he had keen foresight. Something close to precognition." Rhahar swallowed. "If you could figure it out, why did you ask?"

"This intuition thing is really hit or miss," I said. "And by that, I mean it's mostly a miss."

His lips pinched, and then he blinked several times. "Yes, he did release Saion's and my soul back to us."

"Knew it," I murmured. "Because your soul was held by him, it allows you to know the names of the deceased."

"Yes, but that's not the only reason. I had to take his blood, and it only works when I'm holding the Book of the Dead. Rhain can also do it." He idly scratched his chin. "Just in case something should happen while we're both out of pocket."

"That was very smart of him," I said.

Rhahar's chin lifted. "Nyktos is one of the smartest beings I know."

I smiled, affected by Rhahar's loyalty and moved by his willingness to share this information with me. It hadn't always been this way. "Thank you."

"No need to thank me," he said, inclining his head. "Is there anything else you need?"

"No, but this was…nice." Warmth crept into my cheeks. "I mean, talking with you. About Ash and stuff," I stammered as Reaver slowly turned his head toward me once more. My neck continued to heat. "I know we really haven't had the time in the past, and, well…things are different now."

"It has been nice." A moment passed. "And things *are* different now."

"Because I'm the true Primal of Life and the Queen," I surmised.

"The foresight thing truly is more of a miss than a hit." A faint smile appeared on his handsome face. "It has little to do with that."

"Really?" I drawled.

He nodded. "You risked your life for Nyktos and the Shadowlands." Stepping farther into the office, he lowered his voice. "And for Rhain."

My stomach hollowed, and the heat drained from my skin.

"I…I don't know how you convinced Kolis to release him alive, and Rhain has never gone into a lot of detail…" he said, pressing his right palm to his chest as he glanced at the younglings. "But I know it must have come at some cost to you. You had no reason to do it—not for him. Not even for the Shadowlands when Kyn attacked."

"That's not true," I whispered.

"But it is." Eather pulsed in his eyes. "We never gave you a reason to, yet you continued giving us ones." His shoulders squared. "That is why things are different now."

I opened my mouth but didn't know what to say. I always sort of wanted to crawl into myself when confronted with these types of situations, where someone said something nice and there were no expectations. No strings attached. But even more so with this. And it had little to do with Nektas being correct when he said I was terrible at accepting praise of any kind.

Luckily, the sound of approaching footsteps put an end to my awkwardness.

For a brief second.

The very auburn-haired god Rhahar had just spoken about appeared in the doorway. I tamped down the wariness that came with his presence. It wasn't his fault. It was mine. All mine.

"If you're looking for Nyktos, he's at the Pillars," I told him as Rhahar faced the other god.

"I know." Rhain cleared his throat. "I'm here to see if Rhahar wanted something for lunch."

"You saved some for me this time?" Rhahar laughed. "I'm shocked."

"Next time, I'll make sure I forget," Rhain replied before glancing into the office. "What about you all?"

"I'm good," I said, turning to the younglings. "I'm sure they're hungry, though."

Both Jadis and Reaver nodded eagerly. The former waved at Rhain, and he smiled down at her, his dark amber eyes warming.

"All right. I'll go grab something for you all." He started to turn away, then stopped. "I almost forgot. Just a heads-up, Thierran is staying in one of the rooms on the second floor until one of the insulas becomes available."

I nodded.

"I doubt you'll see much of him," Rhain quickly assured me.

Realizing my thoughts showed on my face, I shook my head. "It's not that. Did we not have space available for him in Lethe?"

"We have space, but we've been saving it for those we don't want to put in a…" He glanced at the younglings. "Complicated situation."

He meant a *dangerous* situation in case a war broke out, which made me laugh.

Rhain's brows rose.

"I'm sorry," I said. "It's just funny that we're okay with putting Thierran in a potentially *complicated* situation."

Rhahar snorted. "You met him, right?"

I nodded. "He seems nice."

Both gods stared at me.

"What?"

Rhahar curtly shook his head. "I've just never heard anyone describe Thierran as *nice*."

"Or any *oneirou*," Rhain muttered and then said louder, "but especially that one. You saw him when that thing went down in the throne room. He was more worried about getting—" His lips pursed as he realized Reaver was listening intently. "He was more worried about getting stuff in his wine."

My lips curved up. "Yeah, he was."

"And that amuses you." Rhain coughed. "All right, then. I think I'll leave now." He turned, frowning at the glasses on the shelf.

"Oh! I have a tiny job for you." I clasped my hands together as Rhain faced me. "Is there a small table or something we can bring in here to place refreshments and stuff on? And have it not be removed like the other tables? I would do it myself, but I'm not sure I should randomly take a table from another room."

Rhain tilted his head. "I can find one for you."

"Great."

"Is that all?" he asked.

I nodded and then thought differently. "Maybe an additional chair? Or two?"

Rhain stopped at the doors. "Two chairs?" he repeated, and I nodded. "Nyktos tends to be a minimalist regarding the spaces he spends time in."

Didn't I know it. "The space is big enough, isn't it, Reaver?"

He nodded. "It is."

"We could maybe place them across from the settee," I suggested. "I'm sure Nyktos won't even notice."

"He'll notice," Rhain stated flatly.

"It'll be okay," I assured him.

Rhahar grinned. "We'll get some chairs."

"A table and two chairs," Rhain said. "Is that all?"

"Yes."

He hesitated. "You sure?"

I nodded. "Thank you." Then I gave him a wave, which Jadis mimicked, nearly smacking Reaver in the face.

My redecoration plans took center stage as I watched Jadis and Reaver, who quickly devoured the sandwiches Rhain had returned with. It was nice to think about something so mundane. Figuring that at least Jadis would soon be taking a nap, I found her blanket in the credenza and tossed it onto the couch. Her eyes were getting heavy-lidded—

My chest suddenly hummed, causing me to stiffen. I knew what that feeling meant.

A Primal was here.

And I knew in my bones it wasn't Ash.

30

The humming intensified as instinct warned me this wasn't Attes either. I spun toward the younglings. "Stay here."

"A Primal is here." Reaver halted in the process of lifting Jadis. She giggled as her feet dangled above the floor. "And you're worried."

Damn that *notam*.

I crossed the distance between us and knelt. "I am, and that's why I need you to stay here with Jadis."

His stubborn gaze met mine as he set Jadis aside. "But you are *meyaah Liessa*—"

Jadis had stopped laughing, having picked up on the swift changes in the chamber. She dropped her doll and pressed herself against Reaver, wrapping her arms around him. "Scary," she whispered, her eyes bigger and rounder than I'd ever seen them.

"It's okay," I assured her, placing a hand on each of their cheeks. "You don't need to be scared, sweetheart. Not when Reaver is with you. He will keep you safe." My gaze shifted to Reaver. "Right? Remember what I asked of you before?"

He glanced between us and nodded. "Always," he said. "I promised you."

"That's right." I kissed his forehead and then Jadis's.

Reaver folded an arm over Jadis's shoulders as I rose and turned. Forcing myself not to bolt from the chamber and scare Jadis further, I walked out of Ash's office.

Damn it. I shouldn't have been thinking about how calm things were. I'd jinxed myself.

I closed the doors behind me. "A Primal has arrived," I told Rhahar, who now stood with Kars. "And it's not Ash or Attes."

Then I ran.

"Sera!" Rhahar exclaimed.

I didn't slow down as I raced down the corridor, picking up speed as I reached the closest exit. Kars' curse got lost in the pounding of my heart. I willed the door open, catching it before it crashed against the shadowstone wall.

I spotted Aios in the courtyard, speaking with Bele. Her buttercream-colored gown fluttered around her slippered feet as she turned toward me, just as Bele's eyes flashed an intense silver.

"Fuck," Bele spat, her hand going to the sheath on her forearm. "I feel them."

It occurred to me then that I'd picked up on the Primal's arrival before any of them had, just as I had felt Kyn's presence before even his brother did, but there was no time to boast. "Aios," I said, slowing. "Make sure Reaver and Jadis remain inside. They are in the office."

Aios nodded, grabbed fistfuls of her skirt, and without hesitation, took off in the direction I'd come from just as a horn blew at the entrance of the Rise, snapping my head around. My hands fisted. The Primal was at the gates. I started for them but stopped as Kars and Rhahar poured out the door.

"Do you know who it is?" Bele asked.

I shook my head. "I want to see them before they see me." I pivoted back to the side of the Rise that faced the Dying Woods. "Go to the gates and ensure that no one gets past them," I ordered.

A savage smile appeared as eather lit up the veins under her eyes. "You got it."

Bele was a blur of black and gray as I turned to Rhahar and Kars. "The same—"

"Nyktos is at the Pillars," Rhahar cut in. "He's bound to them until he finishes. That means we back you up whether you like it or not," Rhahar cut in. "That is our duty."

"Fine," I bit out. "Stay below and *behind* the Rise, at least."

I didn't wait for their answer, knowing they would obey. Quickly climbing the steep staircase, I reached the top and started running again, heading for the gates. The hair Ash had braided this morning thumped off my back as I rounded the corner of the Rise, Rhahar and Kars keeping pace with me on the ground below. I spotted archers already in their nests, shadowstone-tipped arrowheads pointed down.

Fuck.

Whoever had arrived was definitely not someone like Keella.

Gods, if it was Kyn returning for his payment again…

It would be bad.

Because while Ash had been able to stop himself yesterday, I wasn't sure I could.

The front of the courtyard came into view as the area between my shoulder blades twinged. Several guards stood at the ready at the closed gates, their swords glinting in the sunlight. Bele was with them. My gaze flicked up as an auburn-haired god ascended the steep stairs.

Rhain didn't look in my direction as he walked toward the lower wall above the gate, but he lifted a hand as if to warn me off. I slowed, hidden behind the narrow wall of the battlement. But if I felt this Primal?

They felt me.

Several guards bowed as I passed. I wanted to tell them to stop, but I kept my mouth shut for once.

Rhain moved to the battlement, where it curved out, and exposed himself from the waist up. He placed his hands on the ledge before him as the not-too-distant rumble of warning came from the sky. "*Veses.*"

I jerked to a stop so fast I nearly lost my balance, my body flashing cold and then hot—*red-hot.* Something was wrong with my ears because there was no way I had heard that name. There was no way she would come here.

I would've preferred fucking Kyn over her.

"I want to see Nyktos."

At the sound of the sultry, raspy voice, whatever restraint I had snapped.

The world around me blurred in a haze of gold and silver as I headed down the Rise, moving so fast I ended up shadowstepping to the battlement.

Rhain staggered to the side in surprise. "Fates," he muttered.

The Primal Goddess of Rites and Prosperity came into view as I stalked to the ledge.

Veses stood below, her head tipped back, and her long, blond ringlets cascading down. The golden sunlight only heightened the beauty of her delicate features.

"You're not Nyktos," Veses stated.

"No shit." I pressed my palms to the ledge, letting the warmth of the stone seep into me as I saw a deep shadow coasting through the scattered clouds above the road. It struck me then that Veses couldn't sense that Ash wasn't at the palace. My mind raced over the different times Ash had sensed another Primal's arrival. He knew the moment they entered the Shadowlands. Either that meant Ash was more powerful than Veses, even though she was significantly older, or my presence somehow blocked that. There was no time to allow for my intuition to kick in as I stared down at the Primal goddess. "You must be out of your mind to come here, Veses."

Her full lips, painted to match her crimson gown, thinned.

"What?" I challenged. "No bitchy retort?"

"Sera," Rhain warned under his breath. Then he spoke louder to Veses. "What do you want?"

"I already told you." Her chin lifted a notch, and my muscles tensed. "I am here for Nyktos."

Hearing her say that twice? When all I saw was her in Ash's lap, feeding from him? Using him? Fury seized control. I shifted my weight forward and drew my legs up. Rhain cursed, and I felt his fingers graze my arm, but I was so very fast now.

I launched myself off the battlement of the Rise. Cool air reached me, catching the sleeves of my blouse in a rush. There were only a few heartbeats of weightlessness as the hard ground raced up to greet me.

Instinct took over. My body relaxed, even as my knees bent. I landed with my feet shoulder-width apart, sinking into a crouch as the jarring impact traveled up my spine. Air punched out of my lungs. Dull pain flared in my hips but quickly faded. My gaze locked with Veses' as I straightened.

Her eyes widened for a fraction of a second, then her expression smoothed out into bland indifference. "Impressive," she purred.

I smirked. "I know."

A large shadow broke free of the rapidly gathering clouds, its widespread wings casting a foreboding silhouette over the road leading to the Rise.

Several guards scattered as the onyx-hued draken landed beside me, Ehthawn's sword-sharp talons digging into the newly grown grass beside the road. His long, sinuous tail coiled, whipping across dirt and stone as he stretched his thick neck past me. His horned head was only a few feet from Veses as he let out a body-shaking roar, exposing large, bone-crunching teeth. Sparks of silver fire danced in the space between him and the Primal goddess.

Her chest rose sharply, straining the thin material of her gown as the glow of eather pulsed behind her pupils.

"You're not welcome here," I told her.

Her gaze lowered, tracking over the vest and pants I wore. One side of her lip curled in distaste. "Nyktos has welcomed me here many, many times in the past."

I took a step forward, smiling as she retreated. "The keywords there are *in the past.*"

She huffed. "That could change, especially when Nyktos grows tired—"

"That won't happen," I cut her off. "I know that seems foreign to you since you have no idea what it feels like to have someone love you."

Her lips thinned, and the eather pulsed brightly, proving I'd struck a nerve with my admittedly nasty barb.

But fuck her.

For real.

"You know what I know?" Veses' expression smoothed out.

"Can't wait to hear it."

She smiled. "I know how fickle the heart is."

"That should tell you something, shouldn't it? That a fickle heart is what you know?" I sighed. "Gods, I do feel sorry for you, Veses."

She flinched as if I'd slapped her. "You're a fool if you do. There is no reason—"

"There are several reasons to feel empathy for you, Veses." I eyed the Primal goddess, remembering our conversation after I'd intervened on her behalf in Dalos. "And you know each one of them."

Some of the color drained from her face.

"But let me make one thing clear. Even though I feel sorry for you, I still want to kill you, and you know exactly why."

The skin above her eyebrow twitched as her eyes rose to mine.

"And you also know I'm fully capable of doing so," I tacked on as the gates opened behind me. "I'm *the* Queen, Veses. No one would stop me, yet you came here to speak to my *husband*. So, who is the fool?"

She stiffened. "You are no Queen."

"I'm the true Primal of Life." The essence rippled through me as Ehthawn reared his head back. Silver embers fell to the stone. "Look around you. How can you deny that?"

Her gaze darted left and right, passing over the land now ripe with life. "You redecorated. How lovely. It means nothing."

"It means everything," I said. "Your failure to accept that, just like your failure to realize that Kolis is a piece of shit who, just like Nyktos, doesn't want you, doesn't change the reality."

Her pretty face twisted into a sneer. "Then why don't you kill me, Seraphena?"

"I'm trying to be a better person." My hands curled into fists.

"Better than who?" Her finely arched brows rose. "Nyktos? I saw what he did to Kyn."

"How—? You know, I don't even care."

"He needed blood," she answered anyway. "After what was done to him."

"You fed him after what he did to you?"

She shot forward as quick as a pit viper. "I told you before, I like—" Her hair blew away from her face as she skidded back several feet. "*Bitch.*"

"I remember what you said. You liked it." I lowered my hand and stared at her. I would never understand her. Ever. "And to answer your question? No, I'm not better than Nyktos. He held back."

Her hair fell back over her shoulders in perfect ringlets. Another reason to hate her. "You think you're better than me," she spat.

"I don't have to try to be better than you."

"Cute." Her nostrils flared. "Especially when you have no idea."

"About what? You? I know everything I need to know."

"You don't know shit, *Consort.*"

Rhain shot forward. "She is no Consort." His voice vibrated with anger. "She is *the* Queen."

Veses laughed, the sound like wind chimes. "I recognize no such title or crown."

Rhain stiffened. "That would be considered—"

"It's okay." Lifting a hand, I stopped Rhain. "At the end of the day, her acknowledgment means nothing to me." I lowered my arm, refocusing on Veses.

"Is that so?" Her head moved in a serpentine manner. "When you call yourself Queen and refuse to acknowledge the King?"

My eyes narrowed. Clearly, someone had been talking to Kolis or Callum. "Because I *am* Queen, and Kolis is no King." Violent energy ramped up. Clouds gathered above us, thickening and dimming the sunlight. "Are you here on his behalf, acting as his little lapdog? Eager to please him despite his abuse?"

Her cheeks flushed pink as the sound of footsteps closed in behind me. "No, I'm not here on his behalf. But speaking of *the* King," she said, "I'm sure he would reward me greatly if I brought you back to him as a gift."

The air charged around me. "I would love to see you try."

Her gaze flicked behind me, and then her voice lowered. I could feel her…essence and the anger feeding it. "After Kolis is done with you," she said, "Kyn has big plans for you."

In an instant, all I could see was silver-laced gold.

"Fucking Fates," Bele hissed from behind me. "Do you *want* to die?"

"I'm not talking to you," Veses snapped.

"Exactly," replied Bele.

Veses rolled her eyes before refocusing on me. "I was right, you know. About you. I knew you weren't her." Her lips spread into a cruel smile. "Let's not forget what Kolis promised if you turned out not to be Sotoria."

My fingers straightened as Ehthawn growled.

"By the way, does Nyktos know how that one was freed?" she asked, nodding at where Rhain had come to stand a few feet behind me. "Have you told him how far you were willing to go to convince Kolis that you were Sotoria?"

My heart stopped, barely aware of the curse echoing from Rhain.

"I heard all about that." She tsked under her breath as she stepped forward. "So don't pretend you're better than me. You're nothing more than a caged whore."

A storm built inside me as the wind picked up around us, playing with her ringlets. It wasn't even the whore part that caused my skin to feel as if it were suddenly too tight. It was the caged part. Because, in my mind, I saw bars made of the gilded bones of the Ancients, and my heart lurched, then sped up. My fingers curled, pressing into my palms. Eather hummed in my ears, and my throat shrank—

The clean whisper of shadowstone swords being drawn pulled me from my thoughts. Time slowed. Or maybe my thoughts raced too fast as the scene taking place around me became clear. Swords were being drawn in the courtyard below and before the Rise. Bowstrings were pulled taut, and the crushing feeling of suffocation shifted deep inside me, coming from the same area in my chest that had cracked open the night I'd attempted to flee the Shadowlands. What seeped out was hot, endless fury.

I caught the slight twitch of the muscle above her right eye as dark, ominous clouds gathered overhead. I saw the unconscious flinch as the air around me charged, filling with the luminous, silver-tinged gold light. And I…

Gods, I wanted to lash out. To make her eat her words. To level her.

"Now," she continued smugly, her chin rising once more, "I've come to speak to Nyktos and hopefully talk some sense into him. Because despite *your* failure to realize how this will end for you, it doesn't change reality."

Eather throbbed beneath my skin as Ehthawn's spiked tail thumped off the road.

"And in case you don't know how this will end, let me break it down for you," she said, her voice dripping with false sweetness. "It ends with you on your knees and every hole being used to serve every god, draken, and dakkai." Veses winked, and I heard a swift inhale behind me. "Maybe you'll like it."

I laughed, and the sound reminded me of a summer storm. "You silly bitch."

Her brows shot up. "Excuse me?"

I shot forward. Veses threw out her hand as silvery streaks of eather poured into her veins, but I was the true Primal of Life, and I knew how to fight *dirty*.

Catching her arm, I grabbed a fistful of those blond ringlets and yanked her head down as I raised my leg. My knee connected with her face, and the sound of bone crunching sent a surge of satisfaction through me. She yelped, the shock of pain causing her to lose her hold on the essence.

I jerked her head back. Shimmery bluish-red blood gushed from her now-crooked nose. "I think you forgot something." I jerked her head back until we were at eye level. "I'm no longer caged."

Her eyes flashed pure silver a heartbeat before I twisted, lifting her by the hair. I spun and threw her. She screamed, hitting the stone of the road and rolling in a tangle of red and long limbs.

Blond strands dangled from my fingers, burning away as eather crackled over my hand.

"Ouch." Bele laughed.

I stalked toward Veses as she rose onto her hands and knees, tendrils of eather dripping from my fingertips. I drove my booted foot into her side, knocking her down. I grabbed her hair again, flipping her onto her back as I moved to stand over her. She grunted as I knelt, digging my knee into her chest.

"I could forgive you for your poor choices in men, your pathetic insults, and even for loving someone as hideous as Kolis." Currents of raw, powerful energy built inside me, fueled by rage. It was the kind of power designed to create life, but that was not what I intended to use it for. I inhaled her rose scent as I lowered my head to her blood-streaked face. "But I can never forgive you for how you hurt Reaver, and I will never forgive you for what you did to Nyktos."

Her all-silver eyes widened as I *felt* her essence. This time, it wasn't anger that threaded through the eather in her. It was fear.

"Tell me." My voice was a scorching whisper. "Tell me what you see in my eyes, Veses. It's not life, is it? It's death." The essence swelled inside me as I swung my right hand down—

"Sera." Rhain caught my arm, and my head jerked toward him. The glow of gold-and-silver eather danced over his angular cheeks. "Don't kill her."

Veses swung her arm, eather spitting from her fingertips. The heat of the energy stung my cheek as I caught her wrist an inch from my face. I twisted until I heard bone break.

"Bitch," she gasped.

"And exactly why should I not kill her?" I asked Rhain.

Rhain still held on to my arm. "You know why."

Fury dug its claws into me as I met his stare. "And *you* know why she deserves nothing less than death," I hissed, my voice low.

"You're right," he said. "She deserves nothing but death."

"Then don't stop—"

You won't do it.

My gaze flew back to Veses'. That voice… She hadn't spoken out loud. It had been *inside* my head.

Not because you're better than me or Kolis. Veses' lips curved into a bloody smile. *It's because you're weak. So godsdamn weak. That's why you're not any better. Claiming to be so is nothing more than an act.*

I sucked in an unsteady breath as I was thrust back to when I was caged, and Veses had been on the outside. When she said we weren't that different.

And she had been right.

We both reacted violently when it came to the ones we loved. It was the monstrous part of us both. And she was right about me not being a better person.

But she was wrong about why.

"I know what she's doing. She's in your head. Don't listen to her." Rhain's grip on my arm firmed as he knelt beside me. "You don't want war, Sera, but if you kill her, that's exactly what you will start."

It would absolutely start a war. What had I said to Ash? I didn't want us to be the ones who started the war. But as the anger pumped hotly through me, I couldn't give two shits about what I'd said. The hairs all over my body rose as a strange, shivery heat ran down my spine and arms, shocking my fingers.

Veses winced.

And I smiled, wanting to strip the flesh from her bones and then break every one. Slowly. I wanted to kill her over and over. My hold on her shattered wrist tightened as my fingers—my *nails*—cut into her skin, drawing blood.

Is vengeance worth the price?

I stiffened, feeling another draken's echo or imprint. It was...earthy. Wild. In the back of my mind, I knew the sensation was unique to only one draken, but it was Rhain's voice that intruded, mingling with my thoughts. I stared down at Veses, the rose-scented breeze tossing wisps of my hair across my face.

Was vengeance worth the price?

Yes.

Yes, it was.

"It's more than vengeance," I said. "It's justice."

"The difference between the two is a fine line." Another voice, a deeper, gravelly one, reached me.

My gaze shot up as Nektas crossed onto the road, the ridges on his shoulders fading as loose pants manifested.

Wind whipped his hair as he knelt behind the Primal goddess's head. "And no one walks it without stepping over that line."

No one? Nektas was wrong. Ash would walk that fine line. He'd done so with Kyn. He always had. It was me who couldn't.

The true Primal of Life.

The Queen.

"Ash sent me," Nektas said, his voice gentling as Rhain released my arm. "He was worried."

It took a moment for what he said to break through. Ash must've picked up on my emotions while at the Pillars. A shudder went through me.

"How sweet," rasped Veses.

My lips peeled back, and a sound I didn't recognize came from deep within me. Before I knew what I was doing, my head snapped down, fangs bared. I tore into Veses' throat, and there was nothing clean or quick about the bite. I wanted to cause pain.

And I did.

Veses screamed, her back arching as thick blood poured into my mouth and down my throat. Her blood was sweet—too sweet—and tasted of roses.

Tearing through the delicate flesh of her throat, I reared back and then spat a mouthful of blood in Veses' face.

Bele laughed.

Veses fell back against the stone, panting.

I forced myself to lift my fingers from her wrist, catching a glimpse of the deep, crescent-shaped slices in her skin that my nails had left behind. Then I made myself stand and back away from her as the strange tingling sensation faded from my skin.

I dragged the back of my hand across my mouth, wiping away the blood as Rhain and Nektas rose. "Get up and get the fuck out of here," I bit out. "And do not ever come back looking for Nyktos. If you do, I will prove you right."

Breathing heavily, she sat up. Bloodstained curls fell across her chest as she looked at me.

"That this *is* an act," I said and felt Nektas's questioning stare on me.

The Primal stood with far more grace than I would've thought capable, especially with her throat torn open and her right hand hanging askew from her broken wrist. Her damn nose had already healed, though.

Veses turned and then stopped.

"Whatever you're thinking about saying or doing," Nektas drawled as Ehthawn rose behind him, "I would strongly advise against doing so."

Veses' back stiffened, but she faced me, her blood-smeared lips pressed into a thin line. "Kolis offered you a deal," she said, her voice hoarse. "That's why I came here. To get Nyktos to convince you to take the deal offered to you."

"And you thought you could accomplish that?" I stated, not having the mental capacity to wonder if what she said was true.

A subtle flicker of emotion skittered across her face, and a slight tremor hit her hands before she straightened the fingers on her uninjured side. "If you don't accept the deal, you will regret not doing so."

Rhain cursed.

A rush of heat traveled up my spine as my eyes locked with hers. "Is that a threat?"

"No," Veses answered as mist rose, swirling around her legs. "It's only the truth."

"Can I talk to you?" Rhain asked as I stalked toward one of the side doors.

Taking a deep breath, I stopped and nodded. It was probably a blessing that Rhain was delaying my return to the younglings. With or without the *notam*, I didn't need to be anywhere near them in my current mood…or with Veses' blood smeared across my chin.

Yuck.

"Can you give us a moment?" Rhain asked Rhahar, who had been trailing behind us.

I stiffened, knowing what was coming as Rhahar gave a way-too-elaborate bow before backing off. "I know I didn't control my temper out there. You don't have to tell me."

"That's not what I was going to bring up," he said, much to my surprise. "I…I just wanted to let you know that nothing has changed." His gaze briefly met mine. "I haven't told anyone what you did for me, and I won't."

I took a step back without realizing it. Denials rose to the tip of my tongue and spilled over. "There's nothing you could really tell them. You were unconscious—"

"I know you made a deal with Kolis," Rhain interrupted, his voice low. "I don't need to know the specifics of what that deal entailed to *understand*."

My skin flashed hot with prickly, stinging heat. Pressure clamped down on my chest.

Rhain stepped in closer. "Have you told Nyktos?"

The tightness moved to my throat.

Rhain took my silence as an answer. "That's what I thought." He looked across the courtyard, and then his gaze returned to mine. "I know you're not asking for my advice, and I also know it isn't my place to say shit, but those details won't stay between you and Kolis." His voice dropped even lower. "Kyn was still there, wasn't he? He knows, and he clearly told Veses."

The ground felt like it shifted beneath me. "It doesn't matter. I know you don't believe me, but nothing happened."

"Sera—"

"It's the truth."

"Diaval knows." Eather pulsed through his dark golden-brown eyes. "The damn draken overheard everything. I know what Kolis asked for in exchange for my freedom."

Tonight, we'll share the same bed.

I couldn't feel my feet. "Nothing happened," I insisted. "Kolis only wanted to sleep in the same bed. He didn't try anything." The essence sparked within me, and I had to count to five to quell it. "It was nothing, and that is the truth."

"I…" Rhain swallowed and looked away. "It doesn't matter if that is the truth when it's not what others believe. Maybe that is wrong of me to say, but it's reality. And maybe what I'm about to say is also wrong." His eyes met mine. "Talk to Nyktos. Tell him before someone takes what should be your words to share and weaponizes them."

31

Standing on the balcony outside the chamber connected to our bedchambers, I felt Ash's return from the Pillars as I watched a draken with violet-tinged scales and two curled horns fly over the courtyard. Based on Reaver's description, I assumed it was Hymeria, one of the five female draken. She landed on the Rise beside Ehthawn, and the larger draken brushed his head over hers like I'd seen Reaver once do with Jadis. I pushed the damp hair from my face and then turned, grateful that Ash hadn't come back when I'd been vomiting up Veses' too-sweet, flowery blood.

I walked into the antechamber as the main doors opened, stopping at the side of the oval table. An aura of power flooded the space, and the room seemed to shudder in the heartbeats before Ash entered.

Thin wisps of shadowy eather swirled around his leather-encased legs as he stalked forward, his chin down. Strands of thick hair brushed the hard line of his jaw.

"I'm okay," I was quick to assure him.

Ash said nothing, just stepped onto the dais. He crossed the distance between us, clasping my cheeks and tilting my head back. "That is not true."

"It is—"

His flesh began to thin. "There are red marks on your left cheek that weren't there before."

I jolted, not having noticed that when I washed my face earlier. It had to be from when Veses' eather had skimmed my face. "They don't hurt."

"I'm relieved to hear that."

Tiny bumps broke out all over my skin in response to the chill. "You sure about that?"

"Yes." Eather lit up the veins in his jaw.

I folded my hands over his forearms. "I'm completely fine."

"There is blood in your hair, Sera."

"Shit," I muttered. "I thought I got it all out." Shadows appeared beneath his skin, and I hastily added, "It's not my blood. It's Veses'."

Ash's eyes flashed pure silver as the shadows deepened and moved faster. "So, *that* was the cause of what you felt?"

"What exactly did you feel?"

"Anger," he growled as the room's temperature dropped even more. "I tasted hot, acidic anger."

My stomach churned. "That doesn't sound pleasant."

"What was she doing here?"

"She wanted to see you." Little misty puffs punctuated my words. I slid my hands to his chest, hoping to ease his anger. "Obviously, I didn't take too kindly to that, but…" I glanced at the wall beside us and did a double-take. A fine layer of glittering ice spread across the sleek shadowstone. "Is that *frost*?" My gaze shifted back to Ash. Little of his bronze flesh was visible now. I grabbed his dark gray tunic. "I'm completely okay. I promise. Veses, on the other hand… Not so much."

His eather-drenched eyes searched mine. "Honestly?"

"Yes." I rose on tiptoe and kissed his icy lips. "There is no need to worry."

A shudder went through him. "I feared it was…"

My heart cracked. "You had to know it wasn't Kolis."

"It wasn't him I was thinking of."

I started to ask who, but then I knew. Kyn. Veses' taunt slithered through my thoughts. "You don't need to worry about him either. I don't want you to worry at all."

Ash's arms went around me, and he lifted me clear off my feet, holding me tightly to him. "I will never not worry about you, *liessa*."

Looping my arms around his shoulders, I buried my face in his neck. His hand cradled the back of my head as he turned, leaning against the iced-over wall. He slid down until his ass was on the floor, and I was facing him, my knees pressed against the wall.

"Tell me what happened."

"Do you promise not to freeze us if I do?"

His fingers curled into my hair, loosening the braid. "I'll do my best."

I kissed the space above his pulse. "I was with Jadis and Reaver when I felt a Primal arrive. I knew it wasn't you or Attes, and I wanted to see who it was."

"You knew it wasn't Attes?" Surprise filled his tone.

"Mm-hmm," I murmured against his throat.

"Your Primal senses are really kicking in. Soon, you'll be able to tell which Primal it is before they arrive."

My brows knitted. "Really? How?"

"I'll explain, but you need to tell me what happened first."

I was half-tempted to give my intuition time to answer for me, but the room was only beginning to warm. It would have to wait. "I went out onto the Rise, and Rhain was there. Veses didn't seem to know you weren't here—like she couldn't sense your presence."

"You were likely blocking her. She would have to be closer to tell if I was here or not," he answered, confirming my theory. "It can happen when the true Primal of Death is near, too. You and Kolis would be the only ones unaffected by it." His palm smoothed up my back. "What led to the blood in your hair?"

I cringed a little against his neck. "When I heard her say she wanted to see you, I sort of…you know, had one of those knee-jerk reactions."

A rough chuckle shook both of us. "I am not surprised to hear that."

"You probably also won't be surprised to hear that Veses was being a bitch," I said and then told him what'd happened.

Well, I told him everything except her taunts about how Rhain had been freed, despite Rhain's advice. It wasn't like I didn't understand what he had been trying to tell me, but what would Ash do with that knowledge? Other than be enraged. "She was running her mouth, and I kind of lost it. I broke her nose."

Another short laugh rumbled from Ash. "I assume with your fist?"

"More like my knee." I rubbed my nose along the still-cold skin of his neck.

"Nice technique."

"And I threw her down onto the road," I continued. "By her hair."

Ash fell silent.

"Then I kicked her, and I think I grabbed her by the hair again."

He was still quiet, but I detected faint tremors along his shoulders and chest. He was…laughing.

I plopped my forehead on his shoulder. "And then—"

"There's more?" he cut in.

"There is," I muttered. "I broke her wrist."

"Okay."

I closed my eyes. "And I also bit her."

The hand on my back stilled.

My hands fell to my thighs. I didn't think he was angry since my knees were damp from where the frost had melted away. Or at least he wasn't as angry as before. "That's probably how I got her blood in my hair. I wasn't exactly…precise when I did it. I kind of tore her throat open. Her blood tastes gross, by the way."

Silence.

I squeezed my already closed eyes shut tighter. "Anyway, I then spit the blood in her face."

Another beat of silence passed.

"Is that all?"

"Yeah?" Unease swirled.

Ash's hand swept back down my back. "You aren't confident in that answer." As his hand moved back up, it curled around my braid. He gently tugged my face out of his shoulder, and his eyes met mine. Only faint streaks of eather were visible. "What are you not telling me?"

I slumped a little. "I wanted to kill her."

His brows shot up. "That's what you were holding back?"

"I mean, I would've killed her if Nektas hadn't shown up—even after Rhain tried to talk sense into me, reminding me that I didn't want war." I shook my head. "And I really would have, Ash. I was that"—I held up my thumb and pointer finger, spacing them less than an inch apart—"close."

"But you didn't."

"Only because Nektas was there. So, I'm not sure that counts."

"It does." His other hand ran along my jaw. "I wouldn't have blamed you if you had."

My mouth dropped open.

"I held back with Kyn, but it seems you've forgotten that I killed a Primal in anger. And I don't regret doing it," he continued. "I can tell you right now that Nektas wouldn't have been able to stay my hand. Not when Hanan was standing between you and me." He ran his thumb across my lower lip. "But he was able to reach you. So don't feel too bad about it."

I let what he said sink in. Ash hadn't walked that line between vengeance and justice as well as I believed. And that made me feel a little better about what had almost happened, as messed up as that was.

So, I let go of the guilt and shifted my focus to what had preyed upon my mind as I stood out on the balcony. "As much as I hate to admit this, I think Veses was telling the truth about coming here to get you to talk me into taking Kolis's deal."

He tucked a shorter strand of my hair back behind an ear. "What makes you think that?"

I fixed the collar of his tunic. "Like I said before, she…cares about you—in her own twisted, messed-up way." I quickly moved past that point before I slipped into a rage spiral. "She said I would regret not taking the deal."

His jaw flexed. "Did she say this before or after you handed her ass to her?"

My lips twitched as I glanced down at my hands. "After I…" I frowned, staring at my nails. I had thought I'd gotten all the blood out from under them, but a tiny speck of dark red remained. It wasn't that which caused my spine to straighten, though. "My nails grew."

He looked down at my hands. "They look normal to me."

"I know, but they lengthened and sharpened." My eyes widened as I remembered what had happened when Aydun first showed. What had Nektas said then? Something about the…claws coming out. "Today wasn't the first time that happened. I wonder if that means I'll be able to shift sooner than you could."

Lifting my left hand, he kissed the center of my palm. "Wouldn't that make you special?"

"More special than you. Yes."

He chuckled. "That's okay. My fangs are still substantially more impressive than yours."

I grinned, thoroughly enjoying his teasing because, gods, I really hadn't realized how badly I'd missed the side of him I'd seen in the mortal realm. When he was just Ash, able to shed the weight of responsibility and forget the cause of the blood drops inked into his flesh for a little while. But that *was* who he was. He was once more that Ash.

A wide, likely half-crazed-looking smile spread across my lips, and I didn't care about how I looked because this was us. Who we had been when we were strangers, then friends, enemies, and now…lovers. This was simply who we were when we were together. And if he was reading my emotions now, he would taste nothing but the sweetest, chocolate-dipped strawberries.

Nothing but love.

Veses' warning followed me as the day progressed. It was hard not to think about it, even as Ash and I spent the better part of the day in the courtyard training alongside the guards.

The tension in my muscles that accompanied each swing of the sword and even the impact of the blades meeting felt so damn good. I broke a sweat but didn't tire as I had before I Ascended. Not even after switching off with Bele, who managed to knock me on my ass. It had taken hours for me to tap out. Never in my life had I trained for that long.

Holland, wherever he was, would be proud.

We'd spent the evening with the Shadowlands gods, discussing battle strategy in case things went south and a full-scale war broke out. Where we would attack first, if we would. The best way to lay siege to Dalos. It wasn't an easy conversation to have without knowing who our allies or enemies were.

I hated the fucking *eirini*.

With each passing day, it was getting harder not to think like Bele. To call for a meeting and reject Kolis's offer.

But that wouldn't be wise. It'd be reckless and a slew of other bad things. As much as I loathed the *eirini*, it gave us time to prepare the tomb beneath Oak Ambler.

It gave *us* time.

Gods, I should be asleep instead of staring at the ceiling.

At least I wasn't staring at Ash like a creeper.

My mind wouldn't shut down, alternating between, well…everything. Would Kolis wait out the *eirini*? How would he respond once I summoned the Primals? What about the prophecy? Then there was the confusing storm of conflicting emotions that had reared its head once more this evening when I fed from Ash, and he'd declined my offer. I'd felt relief and disappointment at the same time. Then shame. That still scalded each breath I took.

And if I wasn't thinking about all of that, it was what Attes had confirmed about Sotoria when I saw him last and how desperate she must have been to ask such a thing of Eythos.

And how hard it had to be for Eythos to carry out her request.

It also made me think about how close I had come to the very same thing but for vastly different reasons—and by my own hand. Had Sotoria's soul been aware of what I had done when I took too much of the sleeping aid? I didn't think so, and I was grateful for that.

I didn't want to dwell on Sotoria. It made me so godsdamn sad. And thinking about Sotoria—what was expected of her—made me angry. Obviously, we needed her to be reborn if we hoped to kill Kolis. None of the Primals were powerful enough to do it—at least not now. Maybe one day. But even if we succeeded in entombing Kolis, there would always be a risk to Sotoria.

I eventually shifted my thoughts to the reason behind spending the day training with mortal weapons. Not only was it important to keep those reflexes honed, but fighting with the essence against another Primal could spell disaster for the mortal realm. Still, there would be times when using the Primal essence was inevitable—when violence fueled the will behind it.

But there had been an impact when I'd used the eather against Kolis, and I worried about how that had played out in the mortal realm. What would the repercussions of anything that happened from here on out be?

I worried about my family.

And something else also occupied the back of my mind as I watched the silvery glow of starlight ripple across the ceiling. It was a feeling that I was supposed to remember something.

Something really important.

I searched my thoughts. They raced and came together like run-on sentences. I ended up back on the prophecy. Frustrated, I blew out an aggravated breath.

"*Liessa*," Ash murmured, his sleep-roughened voice startling me. "Why are you not asleep?"

My lips pursed. "I am sleeping."

His chuckle was low and throaty. "Want to try answering that again?"

I crossed my arms over the soft, knit blanket. "I'm just thinking."

"About?"

"Everything."

"I'm not sure it's possible to think about everything."

"My brain would like to disagree with that assumption." I tilted my head to the side. In the darkness, I could see that his eyes were closed. "And how did you know I was awake?"

"I just did."

My brows rose. "Care to elaborate?"

"I can't explain it better than that." He brushed several strands of hair back from his face. "I just knew you were awake, so I woke up."

"That's…different."

"Is it?" The bed shifted as Ash rolled onto his side to face me. "Want to tell me what one of those things you were thinking about was?"

I started to tell him but stopped. "It's not important enough to keep you awake."

"Now I'm the one who gets to disagree." Ash's arm came around my waist. "If it's important enough to keep you awake, it's important enough for me to know."

Gods.

That statement wasn't just sweet. It was perfect.

"*Liessa*?"

Drawing in a shallow breath, I plucked out what felt most important at the moment. It likely wasn't, but it mattered to me. "If we cannot prevent a full-scale war, what kind of damage could we be looking at?"

"A lot of energy is created when Primals fight, which builds up in the area," he answered instead of asking why I had been thinking of that in the middle of the night. "It disperses, spreading throughout the realms. Just using the eather in the mortal realm can have an impact, depending on how much is expended." His cold hand moved over the blanket and across my hand in smooth, slow circles. "Iliseeum is heavily warded and has been since the time of the Ancients. Those wards are tied to the Primal of each Court. As long as the Primal remains standing, the Courts are mostly protected, but the area where the Primals fight will sustain damage."

"Like in Dalos," I said, remembering how both fights had cracked walls and leveled trees. "And the mortal realm?" I knew the answer. I knew the answers to all of these questions. "It can manifest in several ways."

"The release of energy, if big enough, can create tsunamis, earthquakes, and violent storms," he said. "The severity depends on how intense the fight is. If a Primal falls without another being able to rise? You're looking at all of those things but amplified."

"Gods." The muscles in my neck tightened. "Where would the impact hit? Across all the kingdoms?"

His hand stilled briefly. "Your foresight didn't tell you what would happen?"

"No," I whispered. There was nothing but silence then. My throat dried.

"I don't know why. It has nothing to do with me or the Fates unless…"

Ash was silent for a moment. "Unless it does."

I closed my eyes. "Meaning it will happen."

"We don't know that." Ash's hand began to move again. "Remember what Holland said about threads. There is more than one way things can play out."

I knew that, but the fact that it was even a possibility horrified me. As did the knowledge that every decision, action, reaction, and inaction, no matter how small, could drastically change things.

"Nothing is set in stone, *liessa*." His lips brushed my temple. "We are proof of that. Don't forget."

"I won't, but there is still a chance. And I want to warn Ezra. Because even if we prevent a war…" I didn't need to finish. Ash knew there would be a fight, no matter what. "Lasania is a coastal kingdom."

"You're the true Primal of Life." Ash's leg curled under the blankets. The short, rough hairs of his leg tickled mine. "If you wish to warn the mortal realm, you can."

"I know, but I want your advice," I told him. "Being in a position to make these kinds of decisions is new to me. And even if it wasn't, I wouldn't—I don't—want to be the only one deciding. Especially since my desire comes from a purely emotional place. Plus, even though warning them feels right, what if it causes unnecessary panic?"

"I think that is a risk, but you have to weigh that against what you already know. There will be disruption to the mortals' lives," he said. "I think it's fine to warn them."

Relieved that he thought so, some of the tightness eased from my muscles. "When do you want to do it?"

"When do *you* want to do it?" he countered.

"Tomorrow?"

Laughing under his breath, he pressed a kiss to my cheek. "Then do it."

Excitement filled me, and it kind of felt wrong to feel that, considering what message I had to share. But I would get to see Ezra and maybe even my mother.

"But," Ash added, and my anticipation wilted, "we both cannot go. With everything that is happening, one of us needs to remain here. And that should be me."

I pressed my lips together. "That makes sense, especially considering what happened the last time we returned from the mortal realm."

Ash stiffened against me. "That's not going to happen again."

I wanted to believe that, but the mere fact that we both couldn't leave said differently.

"I don't want you to go anywhere without me. And yeah, I know how that sounds, and I don't care." Ash relaxed a little against me. "I'm going to be…"

I knew how it would be for him while I was gone. He'd be sick with worry, as would I.

And the fact that he didn't want me to go without him didn't bother me. It didn't come across as overbearing or overprotective because I knew he had a real reason to be concerned, but I also knew he wouldn't prevent me from going.

"I know you can take care of yourself, but I want Nektas to go with you." He paused. "And I will ask Attes to be here while you're in the mortal realm, just in case."

Just in case things went sideways, which was always possible. "Okay."

"That shouldn't be a problem unless it becomes a problem. Meaning Nektas will do anything and everything to protect you, including taking on his true form."

My brows lifted as I imagined everyone's reaction to seeing a draken. Or tried to. It would be pure chaos. A tiny, evil part of me wanted to see that.

I shook my head at myself. "I understand. I won't be gone long. I promise."

"I know." His lips touched the corner of mine, and they felt colder than they had earlier. "Anything else on your mind?"

"No," I lied.

"Then you're going to sleep?"

I nodded.

His lips found mine for a quick kiss. "Good night, *liessa*."

"Good night," I murmured.

Ash settled beside me, the slow, comforting circles of his hand slowing and then stopping altogether after a few moments. I concentrated on where our skin met. His leg felt colder, didn't it? So did where his chest met my shoulder.

My heart kicked around in my chest. He'd given me so much blood since I'd awakened. My throat dried as anxiety rose, but I pushed past it. He needed to feed, and I needed to provide for him. "Ash."

"If you're saying my name, you can't be sleeping."

"I haven't fallen asleep yet."

"No shit," he replied dryly.

I rolled my eyes. "I'm not a guy. I can't close my eyes and fall asleep in five seconds."

"Have you thought about trying?"

"You'll be shocked to learn I have, but that's not what I'm thinking about."

"So shocked," he drawled.

I took a deep breath and exhaled loudly.

Ash ignored it.

I stared at the ceiling once more. Several minutes passed. "Ash?"

"Close your eyes."

My lips turned down at the corners.

"And go to sleep."

My eyes narrowed. "It's important."

"No, it's not."

I turned my head toward his. "You just said that whatever was important enough to keep me awake was important enough to keep you awake."

"What you're thinking about now is not important."

My frown deepened. "And how do you know what I'm thinking?"

"I'm all-knowing." Ash snuggled in closer, working a *cold* thigh between mine. "It's a new ability."

"Uh-huh," I muttered, then my eyes widened. "Wait. You'd better be joking."

"I'm all-knowing when it comes to you," he amended with a chuckle.

"You're not funny," I grumbled.

"And you're not sleeping." His arm tightened around me. "You need your rest, *liessa*, and I'm prepared to ensure you get your sleep."

I huffed out a short laugh. "And exactly how are you going to do that?"

"Quite easily."

"Whatever." I sighed obnoxiously. A few moments ticked by. "You know, I'm thinking about you—" I squeaked as Ash rolled atop me. My wide eyes locked with his. Bright streaks of starlight swirled wildly in them. "What are you doing?"

"What I said I'd do," he answered. "I'm going to ensure you get your much-needed rest."

"How?" I tried to move my arms, but his chest trapped them against me. "By squishing me to sleep?"

"No." His lips coasted over mine. "I'm going to fuck you so hard that the only thing you can do afterward is sleep."

My mouth dropped open, but he captured whatever I was about to say with a stroke of his tongue, and then he did as he warned.

Ash fucked me hard, face-to-face, and then flipped me onto my belly, driving into me until I was limp and sated. And he was successful.

Within five seconds of closing my eyes, I fell right to sleep.

32

Stomach roiling, I stopped at the bottom of the staircase as I heard footsteps coming down the main hall. I focused on my breathing until the churning settled.

The last thing I needed to do was vomit all over Ash's desk after clutching the rim of the sink as I dry-heaved for what seemed like a small eternity. He would never agree to me leaving for Lasania today if I did that.

It had to be the bacon.

Why? I had no idea. I loved the stuff and was in a long-term relationship with it, but the moment I'd smelled the fried meat, I'd thought I might vomit all over the table.

It was probably also the fact that Ash had woken me from another nightmare this morning. When he asked me about it, I'd pretended to have no idea what he was talking about.

He had let it go.

But he'd known.

"Sera?"

I looked up, seeing Bele and Aios coming down the main hall.

No two people could look more different than they did.

Bele was dressed in black from head to toe, her dark hair swept back from her face. Aios wore a bright yellow tunic and white pants, and her cherry-red hair flowed to the middle of her back.

"Why are you just…staring at the floor?" Bele asked, striding into the library.

"I wasn't—" I stopped myself. I *had* been staring at the floor. "Never mind."

"Exactly." Bele smiled brightly. "By the way, you don't look so good."

I frowned. "Thanks."

"You're welcome."

I stepped away from the stairs and placed my hand against my cheek. I looked over at Aios. "Do I look bad?"

The goddess shook her head.

"She's lying," Bele said. "Only because she's nice."

"Wow." I raised an eyebrow.

"You don't look ill," Aios assured. "You just look a little pale."

"A little?" Bele mumbled under her breath.

"Bele," Aios snapped.

"What?" Bele threw up her hands. "You just said she looked pale."

"I was trying to be supportive," Aios hissed.

"So was I." Bele crossed her arms.

"Wait," I interrupted. "I really look ill?"

"No," Aios quickly answered.

"Yes," Bele said a second later.

"Fates," Aios exclaimed. "I love you. You know I do."

My heart gave a happy little squeeze at the proclamation.

A radiant smile appeared on Bele's face. "I know."

"But you," Aios continued, pointing at her, "seriously need to work on your people skills."

Bele's smile faded.

I smirked even though I felt a wee bit of sympathy for the *baby* Primal. I, too, needed to work on those skills.

Still, my shoulders slumped thinking about what we'd been talking about. I had looked a little pale, and there had been faint shadows under my eyes when I left the bathing chamber, but I didn't think it was that bad.

The hem of Aios's sunny tunic fluttered at her knees as she spun toward me. "You don't look ill." Behind her, Bele's eyes widened, and her lips squeezed together as she stared at the floor. I knew Aios was just being nice. "You just look like you…didn't sleep well."

"I think I ate something that didn't agree with me," I said, and Aios's brows knitted. "I was feeling a little nauseous—"

"No sh—" Bele caught herself as Aios's head nearly spun on her shoulders. "—*ush*. No, *shush* it." Bele clasped her hands together, giving me a big, closed-lipped smile. "You look so, so energetic."

"That's what you were going to say?" I crossed my arms. "Really?"

"Yes." Bele nodded, the curve of her lips growing. Her voice then reached a pitch I'd never heard from her. "*Yes.* You look well-rested and lively."

"Please stop smiling at me like that."

Bele's smile slowly faded.

"What do you mean you ate something that didn't agree with you?" Aios asked.

I shrugged. "I just felt nauseous after breakfast."

"I've never known a Primal to get sick from food." Her forehead creased. "But then again, you just Ascended." She glanced at Bele. "You felt sick to your stomach a few times afterward, right?"

Bele nodded. "But I never looked like I was half-dead."

"Sweet Fates." Aios's head fell back.

Resisting the urge to will the chandelier to come down on Bele's head, I focused on Aios. "You truly are the most gracious goddess there is."

Her chin lowered, and a small, confused grin appeared. "Well, thank you."

Bele's eyes narrowed on me. "Are you flirting with Aios? Right in front of me?"

"Yes. That's exactly what I'm doing while married to a Primal of Death." I pinned her with a dry look, catching the glimmer of amusement in her silver eyes. "I'm just pointing out how gracious she is for putting up with you."

Aios laughed softly.

Bele pressed a hand to her chest. "You wound me, *mey*—"

"Shut up," I cut her off.

"Yes." Bele paused dramatically. "Your Majesty."

I sighed.

Aios pulled Bele's hand from her chest. Their fingers immediately twined. "She's not always so antagonizing."

Bele snorted. "You don't have to lie for me, *so'vit*," she said, causing me to jerk toward her. She dipped her head and dropped a kiss on Aios's temple. "I excel at being antagonizing. It's like a special ability."

A chill crawled its way down my spine. What Bele had called Aios was so close to *so'lis*, which meant *my soul*. But it wasn't the same. It was actually sweet. So, I ignored the feeling of spiders crawling over my skin. "My life," I murmured, clearing my throat. "You're adorable, Bele."

She extended the middle finger of her free hand, the nail painted black. "Is this adorable?"

"It makes me want to flirt with *you* now," I replied.

Bele laughed as I glanced at Aios. She was watching me, her lips mashed together as if she were physically restraining herself from saying something.

I quickly looked away and ran my fingers down my braid. "I need to get going."

"Heading to talk to Attes?" The humor vanished from Bele's striking features. "I was in the office when Ash told him about Veses showing up. He was pissed. I hope he fucking destroys her. Does that make me a bad person?"

"Yes," Aios and I said at the same time, even though I was kind of hoping the same thing.

The Primal pouted. "I expected that response from her." She nodded at Aios. "But you used to be more fun."

I arched a brow. "How would you know if I was more fun? You don't really know me, Bele."

"Oh, I know you." She wrapped her arms around Aios's waist and moved to stand behind her. "My absurdity recognizes your absurdity."

Fingers halting on my braid, I stared at her.

"Or it used to." Bele rested her chin on Aios's shoulder. She squinted her eyes at me. "Wait a second. Your absurdity is still in there. It's just leashed."

"I don't know if I should feel complimented or insulted," I drawled.

"Well," Bele began.

"Or just really confused," I added.

Aios lightly smacked the arm around her waist. "What Bele is trying to say is that she senses your…temperament."

"It comes with the Court lineage. The whole Hunt and Divine Justice thing," Bele explained. "Sensing one's temperament—"

"Allows you to be a better hunter," I finished for her, either my foresight or my knowledge kicking in.

"And to deliver divine justice," Bele said as Aios smoothed a hand across her arm. "Sensing someone's natural temperament helps to know if someone's act was a one-off or something in their nature."

"Makes sense." Twisting the end of my braid, I shifted my weight from one foot to the other. "So, my *absurdity*? What exactly does that mean? And what does it tell you?"

"It means you're someone who would shadowstep to a whole-ass different Court without ever shadowstepping anywhere by yourself before."

"I knew I would be fine," I denied.

Both of Bele's brows rose. "Sure," she said, and I rolled my eyes. "Anyway, you're impulsive."

Knee-jerk reactions. Ash would agree with her.

"You're easily distracted." Bele's words snapped my attention back to her. She smirked. "Hot-tempered. Violent if provoked. And, sometimes, even when you're *not* all that provoked."

"I feel attacked," I muttered.

Streaks of eather flared in Bele's eyes. "You're wild and reckless in a way that borders on having a death wish," she continued, her voice carrying a hum of power. "You have a vengeful nature."

My nose scrunched. "You can stop now."

"Good luck with that," Aios murmured, leaning into Bele. "She's in the zone."

She was definitely somewhere…creepy. Her stare was unblinking, and a faint luminous glow filled the veins of her cheeks as she fixated on me—or looked *into* me. "You don't think enough, yet you're an overthinker. You can switch from joy to rage in a snap. The only thing predictable about you is that you're unpredictable."

Our gazes met. The silky threads of power in her voice and the swirling wisps of eather were eerily mesmerizing.

"But you're also loyal and dedicated. Caring. You have a strong sense of what is wrong and what is right, even if you operate in the middle." Bele blinked, and the eather dimmed. When she spoke again, the tendrils of power were gone. "Your nature is in juxtaposition with itself. A certain brand of absurdity just like mine—poor people skills included." She winked before nipping at Aios's neck, causing the goddess to squeak. "But as I said before, you've got a lot of that leashed right now."

I honestly had no idea what to say to any of that. What she said felt really spot-on, but for some reason, I was uncomfortable with what she'd sensed. She'd missed an adjective in her long list. Monstrous. But maybe that was the part I had leashed. And if so, shouldn't that make me happy? I should be less impulsive, or in Bele's words, less my own personal brand of absurd—

I stopped myself. "Why am I even standing here talking about this with you?"

"I was wondering the same thing," Bele said.

"Gods, you're annoying." I smiled at Aios. "You are not."

The goddess grinned.

"You're welcome, by the way," Bele shouted. "You don't look half-dead anymore."

I flipped her off and walked past the empty pedestal—I *really* needed to put something on that thing.

Ignoring the new Primal's laughter, I made my way down the hall. My stomach *had* stopped turning over. Maybe Bele's caustic attitude had an oddly calming effect on me.

The doors to Ash's office were open, and my gaze, like always, immediately connected with his. He sat with his booted feet resting on the edge of the desk and one hand on the dark surface. Long fingers tapped slowly as his eyes narrowed slightly. I hoped I didn't still look pale or, according to Bele, like death warmed over.

Pulling my gaze from Ash's, I took stock of the office. The items I'd requested the day before now occupied some of the space. Two dove-gray chairs had been placed across from the settee, and Saion sat on one. But that wasn't all. Another end table, this one round, had been positioned between the chairs. And they weren't the only new additions. A table had been brought in and put behind the settee, where Rhain sat. Two pitchers and several glasses were on the narrow stand.

I mouthed *thank you* to Rhain as I walked through the pillared alcove. He gave me a quick nod in return as Ash motioned me to him with a curled finger.

I walked around the desk, spying a slender black box almost the length of my forearm on the credenza.

"Attes said he had some news to share." Ash dropped his other foot to the floor and took my hand. He tugged me down until I sat in his lap. "We were waiting for you to join us."

My stomach flipped unsteadily, and the response had nothing to do with my earlier nausea. Still, I breathed in deeply. Fresh citrus and clean air surrounded me—not choking, stale lilacs.

Ash leaned in, speaking low as Rhain rose and retrieved the pitcher from the stand, pouring two glasses of water. "Are you feeling well?"

So I still looked like death warmed over. Great.

Sighing, I nodded.

He kissed my temple before leaning back and turning his focus to Attes. "What is your news?" Ash asked, his hand curving over my hip.

"I still have eyes in Dalos," Attes began. "And I know that Kolis hasn't been seen at court as much as usual."

Attes still had a spy in Dalos? It wasn't Elias, who had become one of Kolis's trusted guards. He was now in Attes's Court. So, who was it?

The skin beneath my left ear tingled, and an image of a goddess with long, dark hair and rich, brown skin formed in my mind. "Dametria."

Attes stiffened. "How did you—?" His shoulders relaxed. "*Vadentia.*"

I nodded. "I met her briefly and thought she acted different than the other gods who visited Kolis. She didn't…" I trailed off as memories of how Kolis had put me on display threatened to surface. I didn't want to think about any of that. I didn't *need* to.

"She didn't what?" Ash asked quietly.

"She didn't act like an asshole," I told him, which was true. "She's safe there?"

"For now," Attes said. That wasn't exactly reassuring. "Word is his favorite golden fuck has been running interference for him, along with Varus."

I knew the golden fuck was Callum, but the second one was unfamiliar.

"Varus of Kithreia?" Ash stiffened behind me as Attes nodded. "My father entombed him."

"I know. I aided him in doing so, along with…my brother." Attes picked up his glass and drank deeply. "I believe he must've escaped when Veses had her draken attack the Red Woods."

Rhahar cursed. "We checked and double-checked to make sure we got all those who were entombed."

"We must've assumed he was one of the ones killed without much left behind," Rhain said, shaking his head. "I'm sorry. We should—"

"It's okay." Ash lifted a hand. "It would be impossible to know for sure that all who escaped were recaptured. The blame for this does not lay at the feet of anyone in this room."

It was Veses' fault.

Anger sparked, causing eather to throb hotly through me. A charge of energy stroked the air, drawing the Primals' gazes to me.

Attes raised a brow. "You okay?"

"Yeah, sorry about that."

A quick grin appeared on Attes's face. "While Callum and Varus have been speaking for Kolis, one particular visitor has spent a lot of time with him, in what I can only assume is an attempt to ensure he has their support." Attes shifted back in his chair. "Phanos."

"First off," I began, "it pisses me off that he is having meetings. And secondly, there is no way Phanos will give him support."

"I wouldn't be too sure of that," Saion stated.

"Seriously?" Shock filled my voice. "Kolis made Phanos sacrifice so many of the ceeren—something he obviously wasn't thrilled with. I saw the sorrow in his eyes."

A muscle ticked in Saion's jaw. "Phanos doesn't like to make waves."

"Nice pun," Attes noted.

"Thank you." Saion then continued. "Look, Phanos doesn't particularly like Kolis. I don't think any of the Primals do."

"Except his brother," Rhain pointed out with a nod at Attes.

"Clearly, I was the twin born with intelligence and good looks," Attes said, but his usual humor was missing from his voice.

Saion smirked at that. "But Phanos can be very…self-involved."

"Name one Primal who *isn't* self-involved," I said, and when Attes opened his mouth, I added, "Besides Nyktos."

Attes pressed a palm to his chest as if he were wounded. I rolled my eyes.

"Oh, I'm self-involved," Ash said, his arm briefly tightening around me. "And I am just as selfish." His eyes met mine when I looked over my shoulder. "And you know that."

Denial rose to the tip of my tongue, but I wouldn't be sitting here if he wasn't selfish. Then again, was saving my life really *that* selfish? Yes? No? Probably a little of both.

"Do not forget that, at the end of the day, this is the same Primal who drowned a city," Saion reminded me. "Simply because those living there ceased to honor him by endangering their lives."

"I haven't forgotten that." Blowing out an aggravated breath, I drew the braid over my shoulder. "He was upset about the loss of those ceeren. Why would he not want justice for that? Or, at the very least, want to avoid being put in that situation again?"

Rhahar rubbed his chin and shook his head. "Because seeking that justice could negatively affect him."

"And not seeking it will still negatively affect him," I pointed out. "It's not like we're going anywhere. No matter what side he chooses, if Kolis doesn't take the offered deal, there are still two sides."

"Exactly," Ash said, moving his thumb down the curve of my hip. "Phanos may see himself as damned if he does, and damned if he doesn't. Most in that situation would side with who they believe poses the least risk."

"Then what?" I started twisting the end of my braid between my fingers.

"That's basically saying he believes Kolis will remain as he was."

"He has no reason not to think that. Phanos doesn't know you. He doesn't know what you are and aren't capable of," Ash stated. "But he knows Kolis. And he knows how vindictive he can be."

Pressing my lips together, I turned my attention to the empty shelves. Phanos had to feel what happened here in the Shadowlands when I brought the river back. So he knew I was capable of *something*. But I'd suspected that, hadn't I? That many of the Primals wouldn't immediately jump on board and be okay with the idea of me being Queen. Ash and I had even discussed it.

"Phanos knows you, though," Rhain spoke to Ash. "He has to be worried about standing against you if it comes down to it."

Ash's tone was pure ice and shadows when he said, "He'd better be."

"What we need to keep in mind is that Phanos may side with Kolis now, but you will have a chance to convince him otherwise," Attes reminded. "Both of you will once the *eirini* ends."

I nodded slowly. "You're right." I met Ash's gaze. "We will."

Because we had to.

Phanos had the second-largest army, and if it came down to war, we needed him on our side.

I stared at the small, oval dining table that had been brought into Ash's office as I waited for Nektas to arrive. Attes had heard Lailah's voice and roamed off.

There were several ledgers on the table and a pitcher of water.

Nervous energy buzzed through me, making it hard to pay attention to any one thing.

I would see Ezra and Marisol in a few short hours. Maybe even my mother.

Excitement and anxiety crashed together. How would they respond to seeing me when, thanks to my eyes and fangs, it wasn't like I could hide that I had changed? And should I share with them what I'd become? I knew I could if I wanted to, but I didn't want them to see me differently—well, more so than they likely already would.

Ash looked up from where he sat behind his desk. "What's on your mind?"

"Nothing."

Head tilting, his gaze shifted back to the parchment. "You sure about that?"

I nodded.

"I feel like we're about to have a repeat of last night," he remarked.

"Which part of last night?"

Ash's gaze flicked up, once more meeting mine. "Both."

Heat hit my blood as my mind bypassed the talking portion of last night and went straight to the fucking-me-until-I-fell-asleep part.

Ash started to lower the parchment as his citrusy scent reached me.

Reminding myself that Nektas would be showing soon, I forced my mind to more appropriate things. Once my blood had cooled, I refocused on my eather *lessons*.

"Shit." Ash's head jerked back. "I forgot."

"Forgot what?" Curiosity surged as Ash didn't answer but instead rose and turned to the credenza. When he faced me, he held the slim, black box I'd seen earlier.

He sat beside me. "I can't believe I forgot this." He offered me the box. "It's for you."

I took it. The weight immediately felt familiar. The whole thing did, except it had been Ector who had delivered it the first time. My eyes flew to Ash's as my heart skipped a beat.

"Open it," he urged.

I unfolded my legs and ran my thumb along the seam of the smooth wood. Slowly, I cracked it open.

A slight tremor ran down my arm as I stared at the stunning dagger cradled in the same cream cloth. It was somehow more beautiful than the last one he'd gifted me. The hilt was crafted from the same kind of lightweight, white material, but that was where the similarities ended. The pommel had been carved into a full moon, and etched into the grip were silver flames. Carved into the cross guard was the same swirling vine pattern as seen on the throne doors.

Wordless, I gripped the hilt and began pulling it free of its black sheath.

"Careful with the blade," Ash warned.

The moment I saw it, I understood. My lips parted. This was no shadowstone dagger. The blade was slender and a dull white, sharpened into a fine, deadly point.

"This is made from the bone of an Ancient, isn't it?" I whispered, my voice hoarse.

"It is."

I swallowed, but a knot formed in my throat anyway. "How…?"

"Attes cleaved it from his bone spear," he said. "And yes, he agreed to do it without me having to punch him."

A shaky laugh escaped me as I stared down at the dagger. The blade wasn't bare. Carefully chiseled into the bone with meticulous attention to detail in each stroke of fur and curve of ear was a wolf, its jaws open, baring teeth and breathing fire.

"He…he made this?" I asked, the piece of art blurring.

"He did," Ash said. "Carvings and all. I asked him if he could the last time he was here."

Wonder filled me as I shook my head. "Wow."

He caught a stray curl and tucked it behind my ear. "I thought this one would be more personalized and symbolic." His fingers lingered for a moment and then glided down my arm. "You're the hand that wields the blade."

My breath snagged. "'A silver beast with blood seeping from its jaws of fire…'"

"'Bathed in the flames of the brightest moon,'" he finished, his head tilting slightly. "Are you all right?"

Sucking in a shallow breath, I blinked several times. "Yes. It's so beautiful, and I'm just…" I struggled to contain the riot of emotions building in me. "I don't remember if I told you this or not, but I was never given gifts. Not during the Rites or for my birthday. It didn't bother me before—or at least that was what I told myself."

Ash had fallen silent as I spoke. I cleared my throat. "It seemed silly to feel bad about not getting gifts when so many people went to bed with empty bellies and no roofs over their heads, but I did care. Not because I wanted things. I just wanted to…"

"You wanted to be thought of," he said.

I nodded, feeling my chest squeeze. "The shadowstone dagger you gave me before was my first gift. It will always be special to me." Our eyes met. "Just as this one will be. Thank you."

"You're welcome." He dipped his head and kissed me. When his mouth lifted, he rested his head on mine. "Have I told you today how much I loathe your mother?"

"Not today."

Ash was quiet for a moment. "Do you think you will see her later?"

"I…I don't know. It all depends on if she is with Ezra."

"And if she isn't?" he asked. "Will you look for her?"

"I'm not sure." Things were complicated between my mother and me. I hoped we could maybe repair our relationship someday, but Ash's anger on my behalf went a long way to healing some of those long-festering wounds. Maybe that was a little messed up, but it was true. And it also made me want to be better—better at being Queen, the Primal of Life…at everything. But most importantly, his wife. His partner. I knew where to start. Well, I knew several *ways* to start.

"I promise I won't throw this one at you," I swore.

Ash let out a loud and deep laugh. "I don't know if I should be pleased or disappointed to hear that."

Careful not to touch the bone, I slid the dagger back into its sheath and put it and the wooden box on the table before turning to him. My heart was pounding even faster. "Do you need to feed?"

Thick lashes lowered. "No, *liessa*."

The same messy mix of relief and disappointment hit me, leaving me feeling as if my skin was too tight. "Are you sure?"

"I am."

I clasped his cheeks. His skin was cool but didn't feel as cold as before. "Is it my imagination again, or does your skin not feel as cold?"

"It's not your imagination." Turning his head, he kissed my palm. "It's just my blood regenerating."

My brows knitted. "That's faster than normal."

"I believe it's because of you rising as the true Primal of Life," he explained. "The essence is already strengthening in me."

Which meant it was already strengthening in the other Primals. Including Kolis.

There wasn't much time to dwell on the realization that the Primals were all strengthening. Rhain and Nektas joined us soon after.

The god didn't look all that thrilled by the news of where I was headed. I knew he was thinking about what had happened the last time we'd left for the mortal realm.

"I won't be gone long," I assured Rhain like I had last night with Ash.

He nodded from where he stood by the doors, his arms crossed.

"And I promise I won't get into any fights," I added, seeking to ease his obvious concern. "Or even tell anyone who I am now."

"*Liessa*," Ash drawled. "Any mortal who crosses paths with you will know."

"Because they will sense it?" I figured.

"That,"—his lips twitched—"and your eyes."

I frowned. "Oh, yeah."

"Did you forget about that?"

"No." I laughed.

Ash arched a brow.

"I didn't. Anyway…" I drew out the word. "Are we traveling to the gateway?"

"You're a Primal now." Ash tucked the same curl behind my ear. "You don't need to use the gateways. You can shadowstep."

"Oh." I smoothed my hands over my hips, suddenly nervous. My right hand moved lower, brushing over the hilt of the bone dagger. Ash had found a thigh sheath for me. Touching the grip calmed me a little. "Like when I shadowstepped into Vathi?"

"Wait." Nektas stepped forward, his brow furrowed. "This will only be your second time shadowstepping?"

I folded my arms. "Maybe."

"It's easy," Ash said.

"More like it's going to be interesting," Nektas remarked.

"Well, that's really helpful." I saw Rhain's lips split into a grin, and my eyes narrowed on the god.

"You know what to do," Ash began. "All you have to do is focus."

"Good luck with that," Rhain said.

"You know,"—I started turning toward him—"your presence here isn't really necessary—"

"You will focus," Ash repeated, curling his fingers around my chin and guiding my gaze back to his. "And think of where you want to go. Then will yourself there."

"I know."

Ash's chin dipped. "Just don't overthink it."

"I'm not."

"*Liessa*," he murmured.

"Whatever." I exhaled loudly, trying to shake off the nerves. "I know what to do. Will it and get it."

Ash nodded. "Coming back is no different." His gaze swept over my features. "It should only take you seconds."

I nodded, trying to shake off the nerves. I knew what to do. I understood how moving between the realms worked, but shadowstepping into the mortal realm felt vastly different than stepping into Vathi. And yeah, I hadn't thought about doing it when I went to Vathi. I just did it. Now, I had to think about it, and the damn draken wasn't helping.

"Why did Nektas say this should be interesting if it's so easy and we're basically just moving super-fast?"

Ash shot a glare over my head. "Because he was being an ass."

"True," the draken replied.

"Ignore him." Ash sent Nektas one last look of warning before cupping my cheeks. "Think of someplace within the grounds of the palace. That way, you won't have to worry about getting past any guards." His eyes searched mine. "Okay?"

"Okay."

"You've got this." Ash held my gaze for a moment longer, then his lips met mine. The kiss was soft and infinitely tender. It was a kiss of sweet devotion.

He pressed his forehead to mine. "I'll be waiting."

"I know," I whispered, stepping back as he let go.

I turned to Nektas and took a deep breath, holding it for five seconds. "You ready?"

The draken raised a brow. "Are you?"

"Yes."

Nektas lifted his hands for me to take. Feeling his slightly rough, warm palms against mine, I thought of the one place I knew I could conjure up a realistic image of.

The garden.

I pictured the silvery green bushes with their purplish-blue spikes and the stone bench before them. Nepeta blue, my mother had called them.

The flowers my father had favored.

Holding on to that image, I summoned the eather. It rose in a hot rush and spread throughout my entire body. I took another shallow breath and then willed us to Wayfair Palace's gardens.

Streaks of silver-and-gold essence swirled through the thick mist, whirling around Nektas and me as the floor seemed to drop out from under us for a heartbeat.

My stomach pitched as I tried to peer through the spinning eather. I caught glimpses of pitch-blackness for several seconds—

A flash of whitish-silver light broke up the nothingness as the space between the realms split open. I caught the brief scent of fresh lilacs, and then the sea's briny breath enveloped us, but Nektas's wild, earthy scent remained strong. The crackling light faded until only a thin line was visible, and that too quickly faded, revealing the silver-tipped green bushes and faded purplish-blue spikes of the nepeta blue in the throes of a late-season bloom. Inhaling the hint of the bush's earthy, slightly sweet aroma, I looked up at the clouds that had taken on dusk's rosy, ethereal glow.

A breeze tossed some curls across my cheeks, and my heart skipped a beat. "The breeze," I whispered, looking up at Nektas. "It's *cool*."

His head tilted slightly. "It is."

"It never felt this cool." Letting go of his hands, I stepped back and turned toward the bench I'd seen my mother sit upon. "At least, not that I remember. The Rot affected the weather."

"But not anymore."

"No." I swallowed. "I knew the Rot was gone, but feeling it?" I exhaled roughly. There were no words as my gaze shifted back to the gently swaying spikes of flowers, just soaking in the feeling of the air without the suffocating humidity.

Nektas waited quietly beside me for many seconds—maybe even minutes—before he spoke. "We should find your sister."

Drawing my gaze from the nepeta blue, I scanned the yellow snapdragons and scarlet asters at the foot of a marble statue of Maia, and the sweet alyssum that carpeted the ground on either side of the stone pathway like snow. I got my bearings. "We can enter the palace through the garden doors."

"Lead the way, *meyaah Liessa.*"

I started to move but stopped, looking up at the draken. "Earthy."

His brows rose.

"Your scent," I explained. "It's earthy. I never really noticed it before, but I…sense it before you are even near me. When I do, it's not really a smell or a taste. More like a sensation."

His head tilted. "Is there a question in there for me?"

"I'm not sure." I cracked a grin. "I can tell when it's you, and I think I'm starting to know the other draken before even seeing them, too. Ash said it's like I'm picking up on an echo."

"What he and the other Primals feel is an echo, but what you're sensing is our imprint," he said. "There's a difference. Only the true Primal of Life and the true Primal of Death can pick up on our imprints and use them to communicate with us."

My brows shot up. "You mean like I can talk in your head."

"Part of me wants to tell you no."

"That's rude."

"But yes, if we open ourselves to it," he said. When I started to speak, he cut me off. "Let's talk about this more when we're not standing in the mortal realm."

Blinking, I jolted. Good gods, for a moment there, I'd actually forgotten what I was doing and where I was. Nektas's grin showed he knew.

"Come on." I sighed, tabling my new discovery for later. I edged around the bench and followed the darkening path. "I'm thinking we'll be able to find Ezra in the dining hall." At least, I hoped so.

Passing another statue of Maia, we walked out onto the main pathway. The golden light of the veranda peeked through the sweeping branches heavy with pink blossoms.

"There appear to be guards ahead," Nektas commented.

I could see their shadowy forms standing at the open doors. "I'm not sure if any of them would recognize me."

"I find that hard to believe," he said. "With your hair and freckles, you have quite recognizable features."

I lightly dragged my fangs over my lower lip as my steps slowed. "I…I wasn't seen a lot. I usually used the servant's stairs and halls, and honestly, half the guards here probably thought I was a servant, so it's quite possible none of them would recognize me. And I doubt they would just let me enter the dining hall." I thought about the last time Ash and I had visited. "Most of the guards don't even know my name."

"That's…" Nektas trailed off. When I looked over my shoulder, I saw that his jaw was set in a hard line.

"Just the way it was," I said, facing forward.

"More like unacceptable."

"Yeah," I sighed. "That, too. But because of the deal, I guess it was easier to keep my identity hidden so no one had to explain why I wasn't available to marry or wonder what happened when I eventually disappeared."

"As if that was the only option," Nektas noted, his gravelly voice flat.

It wasn't.

But it had been the easiest for my mother. My shoulders tightened as I focused ahead. We had far more important things to think about at the moment. "When we were here last, Ash basically scared the guards into leaving us alone."

Nektas laughed. "Sounds about right."

I smiled as I stopped near the last of the autumn-blooming cherry trees. "I don't think I'll have the same effect," I said, speaking low. "So, I guess I could use compulsion." My lip curled at the thought of that.

"I think you underestimate your presence if you think you won't have the same impact."

I looked back at Nektas and arched a brow.

His head lowered. "You're the true Primal of Life, Sera. What would the guards do if you showed them that?"

"Freak out?" I glanced back at the veranda.

"That and allow you to go wherever you want."

I thought that over. "Ash didn't really reveal who he was when he was here."

"You do not seem to like the idea of compelling someone." Nektas picked up on that. "If you like, I can scare them as Ash did."

I snorted. "I don't know if we should do that." I squinted. "I guess I could just compel them not to see us. I mean, that's not like making them do anything, right?"

Nektas hesitated. "I suppose."

"You don't sound entirely convinced of my thought process," I pointed out.

"You have a unique thought process."

"That's a nice way of putting it."

"But I think it would be wise for our presence to go largely unnoticed so we do not cause a scene," he added, his voice carrying a hint of amusement. "So, yes. Do not compel these guards by compelling them."

I rolled my eyes.

"There is a third option," he said. "Allow them to see you. As Ash said, they will know you are at least a god and would likely allow you to dance on their backs if that is what you wished."

"Good point," I muttered. "I keep forgetting that."

"Understandable."

I got myself moving. The gardens were quiet as I glanced back at

Nektas, realizing only then that he was dressed as he normally was—meaning he only wore loose black pants. No boots. And no shirt.

I hoped no parties were being held.

Lifting the tree's lower branches out of the way for him, I walked out from the coverage, and the two guards came into full view.

Once again, I was happy to see that neither wore the obnoxious puffed waistcoats or pantaloons. Their tunics and breeches were still plum-colored, but their new uniforms were leagues above the former.

"I'll tell you what," one guard said as he turned to look over the garden. "That one is an odd snob—*shit.*" The guard reached for the sword at his waist as he limped forward with a wince. Tension bracketed his mouth, turning the corners white. "Stop right there."

"The fact that I made it to the steps without either of you noticing is kind of concerning," I remarked, glancing at the second guard. I recognized the fair-haired man in his third decade of life. Jamison was his name. "Don't you think?"

"Listen here, miss, I don't know where you come from, but..." Jamison's eyes went wide the moment Nektas appeared behind me. His head tipped back as Nektas came up the steps. "Dear gods, you're...enormous."

"Thank you," Nektas replied.

"Enormous or not," the other gaunt-faced guard cut in as I opened my senses to him. His name came to me. Wil Tovar. That was all I allowed myself to know about the slender, dark-haired mortal. "Where is the rest of your clothing, my man?"

"Mortals." Nektas laughed softly. "Always so preoccupied by the flesh that they don't see what is right in front of them."

"Mortals?" Jamison repeated with a chuckle, sharing a long look with the other guard. "I think my man has been in his cups tonight."

Tovar's laugh faded as I reached the top of the steps and stepped into the light of the lamps lining the wall. Our eyes met, and the man staggered back. "Good gods," he gasped.

I smiled. I probably shouldn't have seeing how Tovar paled, but it wasn't often that I incited that kind of response.

I'd have to think long and hard later about why that amused me.

"What is your problem?" Jamison frowned. "Maybe you're deep in your cu—"

"Shut up, you prick," Tovar hissed, bowing his head.

"Don't call me a prick, you fuck." Jamison moved toward Tovar, his cheeks flushing.

"Look at her." Tovar lowered himself, his face contorting as he pressed a hand to his side. "Look at her eyes, you fool."

Jamison turned to me as I arched a brow. He squinted and then went rigid. "Oh..." His mouth fell open. "Shit."

"The security here is impressive," Nektas drawled from behind me.

I almost laughed, except these two shouldn't be entrusted with guarding a bale of hay. "The bowing…" My lips pursed as they both dropped to their knees, Jamison moving much faster than Tovar—he seemed pained by his movements. "Is not necessary."

"We are s-sorry." Tovar's voice quaked. "We didn't know."

"Yes." Jamison's head bobbed frantically. "Please forgive us. We did not mean to disrespect you."

Whatever humor I felt vanished as I stared at the two clearly frightened men. Their response wasn't exactly shocking. Most mortals behaved this way when confronted by a god. I could only imagine what they'd do if they knew I was a Primal.

Nektas frowned as he stared down at the two men. "It has been a long time since I have been around those in this realm," he said, drawing a quick peek from Jamison. "I do not remember them behaving this way."

"How did they behave before?" I asked.

"With joy upon seeing a god," he answered. "Not nearly sick with fear."

I imagined that wasn't the case toward the end of the time when the Ancients ruled. He was likely speaking about when Eythos reigned as the true Primal of Life.

"Crossing paths with gods usually doesn't end well," I said, thinking about what the gods had done in the Garden District the night I'd been with Ash. Even if gods were in the mortal realm for different reasons, they tended to do as they pleased. "It shouldn't be this way."

"No, it shouldn't," Nektas agreed.

This wasn't the first time I'd thought that, but I'd never been in a position to do a damn thing about it before.

Now, I could.

"It's all right. You have not shown disrespect," I assured them.

"Debatable," Nektas murmured.

I shot him a look as neither man moved.

Nektas crossed his arms.

"Ignore him," I said, turning to them again. Tovar was trembling. "It's all right. I promise." I ventured forward, doing something I rarely did in the mortal realm. I reached out and touched the man's warm cheek.

Tovar's head jerked up, his eyes widening even more.

"You may rise," I insisted. "Both of you."

The guard's chest rose sharply as he inhaled. For a moment, neither of us moved. Tovar didn't even exhale as he stared. My senses snapped open, and before I could stop myself, I…connected with the man.

I wasn't sure what was happening. I didn't see into his mind or his soul, and I wasn't reading him, but I did sense…something. Pain. A sickness that had been spreading, eating him up from the inside…long before he felt the first twinges in his gut. An ache that eventually stole his appetite.

Only seconds had passed, but I knew the man was dying slowly and painfully. And my touch…

The tips of my fingers glowed faintly with eather.

Oh, shit.

Before I could pull my hand away, the essence seeped into the man's skin.

"What the…?" Jamison rasped, having risen.

Golden light lit up Tovar's veins, all along his throat and down his chest, arms, and stomach. Tovar stiffened as if strings had been attached to his tendons and pulled. His gaze was unfocused for a heartbeat, and then it cleared. The tension that had drawn the color from the corners of his mouth loosened. The aching hollowness of his face eased as my touch…

Healed him.

I'd never healed anyone from a sickness before.

But I was the *true* Primal of Life now. Emphasis on *life*. I pulled my hand away.

Tovar's eyes glistened as he shook, but this time, it wasn't from fear or pain. It was from relief. "Thank you," he uttered hoarsely, tears filling those dark eyes and spilling over to course down his cheeks. "I prayed each night in the Temple, but there was no relief. I stopped praying. Thinking, you know, maybe I…I wasn't worthy. That I'd done something to deserve it—"

"You haven't," I said, even though I hadn't allowed myself to see anything about him. But I didn't think many deserved the kind of sickness that was a different type of rot.

His eyes shuttered closed. "Thank you."

"Don't mention it." I stepped back and glanced at Nektas.

The draken stared at me blandly.

"Whoops."

"Whoops, indeed," he replied dryly.

"I have no idea what is happening." Jamison scratched his head, his gaze bouncing back and forth between Tovar and us. And Tovar, he was…

Well, he was just rocking back and forth, thanking me over and over.

There was a good chance I probably shouldn't have done that. Actually, I had no idea if I should've done that or not, but I doubted healing him would cause any cosmic imbalance.

Or at least I hoped it wouldn't.

Either way, I couldn't regret it after seeing the relief on the man's face.

Nektas touched my arm, reminding me that we had a reason for being here, and this wasn't it.

I pulled my gaze from Tovar. "I need to speak with the Queen."

"Her Majesty is in the dining hall," Jamison answered.

"Thank you." I gave Tovar one last look and felt compelled to say something. "Make your life a worthy one."

"Of course. Yes. I will." Tovar folded his hands together beneath his chin. "I swear to you."

Nodding, I entered the hall adorned with mauve banners bearing the insignia of the Mierel family, a crown with a sword slicing through it.

"I didn't mean to do that," I said after a moment.

There was no answer, but I knew Nektas had followed me. I stopped and turned.

He stood in front of one of the banners, his brow pinched.

"What are you doing?" I asked.

"The crest. It's an odd symbol."

"It is." I glanced down the empty hall. "It's supposed to represent strength and leadership. Except it looks like someone getting stabbed through the head."

"Strength and leadership? That's not what it means. Not originally," he said with a slight shake of his head. "The leaves? Those are not laurel. They're elm."

My brows lifted. "I'll have to take your word for that."

"Do you know the significance of elm trees to the Ancients?"

The nape of my neck tingled. "Life."

"Yes. And the sword? It symbolizes many things—power, strength, courage." Nektas paused. "Truth."

A fine shiver broke out over my skin. If the crown represented life and the sword could be truth, then… "True Life? True Primal of Life?" I laughed. "No. That has to be a coincidence and a stretch."

"I do not believe in coincidences, nor do I believe that is all this insignia represents. Look at the positioning of the sword." Nektas pointed. "It's slanted. Not entirely straight." He looked at me. "That should be familiar to you."

I stared at the crest, frowning. All I could see was someone being stabbed in the head and dying…

Dying.

My lips parted as I staggered back, just as the guards had moments ago. I'd seen a similar symbol in the Shadow Temple. "Death. That is the symbol for death."

"No. *That*," Nektas said, pointing again, "is a symbol representing both life *and* death, on the crest of the same bloodline that eventually birthed a mortal who became the true Primal of Life. Who also happens to be the mate of a Primal of Death."

"Well, when you put it that way, it doesn't seem like a coincidence, but…"

But that damn prophecy.

While the Fates couldn't see the entirety of the future, they could see the many possibilities that lay in wait.

"The Mierel Crest is only a few hundred years old. It started with…" My eyes narrowed. "Motherfucker."

"That's who it started with?"

"It started with Roderick Mierel." My head whipped toward him. "He only became the recognized King of Lasania after the deal."

Nektas turned his attention back to the crest.

"None of this means Eythos gave Roderick the design, but…" A strangled laugh left me. "He must have."

Nektas exhaled slowly. "This is not the symbol that represents the inevitability of life and death and the importance of both."

"The crescent moon," I murmured, my skin pimpling. "'A Maiden as the Fates promised.'"

Nektas's head cut toward me.

"'And you shall leave this realm touched by life and death.'" My voice was hoarse when I spoke. "That was something my old nursemaid Odetta said to me." I reached back and touched the back of my left shoulder. "I have a birthmark that's kind of shaped like a crescent moon."

"Fate marked you at birth," he said, mirroring Odetta's claim. "With the symbol of the equal power of life and death."

Unsettled, I slid my hand away.

"But if Eythos left some sort of hint behind, it would be the symbol of life. This insignia could represent something other than you and Ash. It could be—"

"Life and Death not joined," I cut in. "But one and the same."

A silver beast with blood seeping from its jaws of fire, bathed in the flames of the brightest moon to ever be birthed, will become one.

A chill went through me as I stared at the crest. If this symbol, representing life and death as one, never existed before, how could Eythos have had anything to do with it? And why? The *vadentia* was eerily quiet. Which meant…

It either involved the Fates or something close to me—to my present or future.

For finally, the Primal rises, the giver of blood and the bringer of bone, the Primal of Blood and Ash.

Another chill went through me. "None of this makes sense or even matters right now," I said. Nektas nodded, but there was a strange edginess to him. I turned and started walking toward the dining hall. "And you know why it doesn't matter?"

"Why?" Nektas followed me this time.

"Because trying to figure all of that out," I said, gesturing at the banners as I took the hall to my right, "makes my head feel like it's going to explode. Like, go splat all over those banners."

"We don't want that to happen."

I stalked forward, passing the curved archways of numerous unnecessary chambers.

"The idea of all this being connected angers you," Nektas commented.

"It annoys me." I entered a narrow hall where the walls had been painted white and were lit by gas lamps. "Because it makes it feel like things are predestined. I guess that's sometimes not bad, right? If you like the outcome. But other times, it is bad. Either way, it makes you wonder what the point is if what's to come will happen one way or another."

"Nothing is written in stone."

"Yeah, everyone keeps saying that." The corridor curved, and at the end of the absurdly long hall, the doors bearing the crest came into view. "But it sure as fuck doesn't feel…"

A prickly sensation erupted all over me. The cause wasn't because nobody was guarding the door. That wasn't all that surprising. Ezra wouldn't demand guards stand outside each and every chamber she occupied, and I got that. I was of like mind. But she was mortal, and Lasania was not without enemies, especially the Vodina Isles Lords—thanks to me following through on my mother's orders. But it wasn't that.

"Ash put wards up when he first brought me into the Shadowlands," I said. "Ones meant to keep my family safe." Foresight told me I knew the answer, but I needed to hear it. "They would still be working, right?"

"They may have weakened a little while Ash was in stasis, but they will remain as long as he lives."

I nodded but picked up my pace because those wards protected my family against gods who sought to harm them.

Not anything that wasn't a god.

Not Primals.

Essence throbbed hotly in my chest as I breathed deeply. There was a smell in the air—one that shouldn't be here. Not anymore.

Stale lilacs.

I broke into a run, my hair streaming out behind me. I didn't slow down as the stench of death increased. I willed the doors open. They swung apart, slamming into the stone walls on either side, causing those in the long, rectangular chamber situated in the center of the sunken space to gasp.

A chair fell over as my gaze swept past the familiar faces—

All I saw was *gold.*

Gold hair.

Gold tunic.

Gold-painted *wings.*

Eyes a shade of blue so pale they would've bordered on lifeless if not for the spark of eather behind the pupils as they locked with mine.

Callum sat at the dinner table with my family and *smiled.*

"Seraphena," he drawled, plucking the napkin from his lap and dropping the mauve cloth onto the table. "What a lovely surprise to see you here."

Eather swelled with my rage, rushing to the surface of my skin. As silvery-gold light filled the corners of my vision, I saw Ezra skirt the table's edge and stand behind my stunned mother. Marisol started to move toward the male I recognized as her father, her dark gaze darting nervously between

Callum and…not me. She was looking behind me.

A low growl rumbled from Nektas.

"Wait. You two know each other?" Ezra asked, her voice calm like usual. It was as if she wasn't even surprised to see me barge into the dining hall. "I thought you only saw one another in passing."

"Oh, we are well acquainted," Callum drawled, winking.

The bastard actually winked.

Heat poured into my veins. The part of my brain that still operated as a mortal shut off. I shadowstepped from the top of the rounded steps to the side of the table. Lady Faber let out a little shriek of surprise and bounced against the table. Wine glasses toppled, splashing red liquid over the white cloth.

Callum started to rise, but I was faster.

Gripping the back of his chair, I ripped it out from under him and threw it across the chamber. It smashed into the wall, shattering into pieces as he hit the floor on his ass.

"Seraphena!" My mother found her voice then, clutching the ruby at her throat. "What are—?" She jerked back in her chair as my head cut toward her. The blood drained from her face. "My gods."

Callum chuckled from the floor. "Well, not quite."

"Shut up," I hissed, grabbing him by the back collar of his tunic.

Hauling him to his feet, I flung the fucker in the same direction as the chair. He hit the wall with a satisfying thud and fell forward.

"My word," Ezra murmured.

Callum caught himself before he face-planted on the floor. "Ouch." He started to push up.

I was on him before he could take a step.

Slamming my hand into his chest, I shoved him into the wall, cracking the stone. Plumes of dust rose and shuddered to the floor as his head bounced off the stone.

"Sera," Ezra spoke again. "Can you please tell me what is going on? Preferably starting with why you just *tossed* a god across the chamber."

"He is not a god," I snarled, smashing Callum's head against the wall again just because I felt like it.

"Okay. Then can you tell me what is happening and, at some point, explain why your skin is…" She paused. When she spoke again, her voice sounded closer. "Actually, I don't even know what your skin is doing, but you…you look like a god. Were you Ascended?"

"I'll explain everything in a second, but I need you to get back." I spared a brief glance at Nektas. "Protect them."

"You are my priority."

"*Nektas.*"

The draken sighed. "As you wish, *meyaah Liessa.*"

"*Meyaah…Liessa*?" mumbled Marisol, and then Lady Faber's squeak told me that Nektas had moved closer to them.

I focused on Callum. "What are you doing here?" Streaks of essence swirled down my arm, and sparks crackled from my fingertips. "Do not make me ask you twice."

Blood trickled from behind his ear. "You asked me to be quiet—well, you demanded that I do so." He smiled, red smearing his teeth. "And kind of rudely, too."

I pulled him away from the wall and then thrust him back, cracking more stone. "Don't try to be clever, Callum, because you're not."

"Maybe not." His head rolled on his shoulders in a way that made me think I'd done some damage to a few important muscles back there. "But I'm smarter than you."

"The fact that you're here tells me you're not." I pushed him back as he tried to gain his footing.

"I was just chatting with some old friends," he said, his gaze darting down for half a heartbeat. "Catching up."

"They are not your friends."

"That's not true," Callum coughed out. "The former Queen and I go way back."

"Yeah, you do." I breathed in, attempting to quell my temper. "What were you chatting about?"

"You," he whispered, the dull glow of eather flickering behind his pupils. "And what a lying whore her daughter is."

"I'm really curious to see what kind of effect fire has on you," Nektas growled. "So you'd better watch your mouth, you little fuck."

Callum's nostrils flared.

I smiled.

His arm snapped out, going for the dagger at my thigh.

I caught his arm. "Once again." I twisted, breaking the bone. My smile grew as his eyes squeezed shut. "You're clearly not clever."

Spitting a mouthful of blood onto the floor, he lifted his head. "You were much easier to deal with when you were caged."

Fury gathered in the back of my throat, tasting of ash. I gripped his chin as the air around me charged.

"Sera," Nektas called. "He wouldn't have been able to shadowstep into this realm. He was brought here."

I inhaled sharply. Nektas was right. I'd been too angry to consider that. "Who brought you here?"

Callum didn't answer, his gaze focused on the eather singeing his flesh.

"Did he come with another?" Nektas demanded of those at the table.

"Not that we are aware of," Ezra answered. "He's been here for a couple of days, though."

My brows raised. "You've been here that long? What the fuck, Callum?"

"There was a lot to tell them," he rasped. "You know, like how you looked behind gilded bars."

That was it.

Callum knew it, too. His eyes flared wide. "Shit."

Eather erupted from my fingers, burning the skin of his chin. I willed the essence inside the Revenant like I'd seen Ash do. I *pushed* it in, flooding him.

Callum jerked wildly, his arms flying out from his sides. A scream of pain tore from his throat as the eather pounded through his veins. His body stiffened as the silvery-gold stream of eather pouring from his mouth cut off his scream. His eyes *sizzled*, then popped. Thick globs of watery red liquid spilled down his cheeks and over my fingers.

"I think…" Marisol gagged. "I think I'm going to be sick."

Callum went limp.

I released him, watching him fall to the floor in a crumpled heap, smoke drifting from his ears and the charred holes where his eyes had been.

A body hit the floor behind me, and Lord Faber shouted as Marisol yelled, "Mother!"

Nektas's heavy sigh echoed through the chamber as I knelt, wiping my fingers clean on the front of Callum's tunic. I rose then and turned.

"Is he dead?" Ezra asked as she clutched Marisol's back. Lord Faber held his wife's prone form in his lap as Marisol knelt beside them, dabbing a damp napkin at her mother's temples.

I focused on Ezra. Her white knuckles were the only indication that she wasn't as calm as she appeared. "Unfortunately, no."

"Unfortunately?" my mother repeated, her eyes wide and the skin at her mouth white as she stared at my hand.

"He'll be back to his obnoxious self sooner rather than later." I glanced down, thinking I had missed some gore but hadn't. She was staring because gold swirled along the flesh of my hand and arm. Probably my face, too. I willed the eather to calm. "Well." I sighed. "This wasn't how I expected to break the news. I'm sure you are all a bit confused."

"Confused?" Mother laughed in a way I'd never heard her before. She sounded nervous and…horrified. "What are you?"

I stiffened, bracing myself against the old, familiar sting. I'd known it was coming, but fuck, it still burned.

Nektas stepped forward. "This is your mother?"

I cleared my throat, blinking rapidly. "Yes."

"I see the resemblance." A curtain of red-streaked hair fell over one bare shoulder. "And yet you clearly don't know who your daughter is." His head straightened. "But you're about to find out."

I started to frown, but then I felt it. The throb of awareness I didn't just feel in the center of my chest but also in my bones and soul.

Uh-oh.

The chamber started to shake, stirring Lady Faber from her faint. "What is…what is happening now?"

Marisol grasped her hand. "I'm not entirely sure."

The dishes began to rattle, and thin fissures appeared in the marble tile. A blast of thunder shook the chamber, exploding the glasses on the table.

"Oh, no." Ezra threw up her hands, causing her short, ivory waistcoat to rise above her slender hips. "We just repaired the Great Hall from the last time."

I shot her an incredulous look as a laugh built in my throat.

"It was horridly loud—the stone and hammers," she said. "And I swear they only banged those damn hammers when I got a few minutes to read."

"Really, Ezra?" Marisol said under her breath. "Is now a good time to mention that? When another god is about to appear?"

"God?" Ezra laughed lightly. "That is no god coming. It is a Primal."

Lord Faber's mouth dropped open.

Cracks ran up the walls and over the ceiling, sending dust falling. I winced, thinking there would be far more banging hammers in Ezra's future.

A gust of cold wind whipped through the dining hall as shadowy mist began seeping from the small cracks in the floor.

"What have we done to anger the gods?" Lady Faber whispered, staring up at me as her husband and daughter helped her to her feet.

"It wasn't you." Nektas looked pointedly in my mother's direction.

She didn't move.

"Does he really need to do all of this?" I asked.

Nektas smiled. "He does like to make an entrance."

The air warped a few feet to my right and a ball of crackling eather appeared. The orb expanded, thinning and stretching to roughly accommodate the height of a damn giant. Icy power drenched the dining hall as the tear in the realms split wide open. Thick mist rolled out, pooling on the floor as Ash arrived, dressed as he had been when I'd left him in the Shadowlands: black breeches and a loose, linen shirt. He looked every inch a Primal of Death.

Ash's eather-streaked gaze immediately found mine. "What happened?"

Pursing my lips, I crossed my arms. "Was that really necessary?"

"I felt your anger but decided to let it go. I knew you were okay." He frowned, glancing at the others. All of them had lowered themselves to their knees, including my mother. At least, I believed she had. I couldn't see her anymore, so she was either on her knees or hiding beneath the table. "But then I felt your pain."

"I'm not hurt," I told him.

Ash was in front of me in a heartbeat, his hand on my cheek. "It was not physical pain."

My breath snagged. "This one-way-sensing-emotion thing is so damn annoying."

"What…?" Ash's eyes narrowed as he finally became aware of Callum's body. "What the fuck is he doing here?"

"That's what I was trying to figure out before you decided to show off," I told him. "Well, before I did that to him anyway."

Ash's gaze swung back to mine, and his voice was barely above a whisper when he spoke. "I know it cannot be him who caused that reaction."

"It wasn't," Nektas interjected. "And you arrived at the perfect time. I was about to explain to her so-called mother who her daughter is."

Eather swirled madly through Ash's eyes, and his jaw hardened.

His gaze remained fastened to mine as he said, "Rise."

I tensed because I knew that tone of voice.

Gowns whispered over marble, and feet shuffled as I touched his arm. "Ash."

His thumb smoothed over my lower lip. "I love you."

I opened my mouth, but he silenced me with a kiss. And, gods, he kissed me like a man coming out of a drought, sipping and savoring until I felt a bit weak in the knees. There was no reason for him to kiss me like that in front of everyone, including my *mother*. Not that I was complaining, but my face felt like it was on fire.

Ash lowered his hand and stepped back. He faced those now standing at the table. Poor Lady Faber looked like she might pass out again as she smoothed a trembling hand over her gray-streaked midnight hair.

Lady Faber need not worry, though. Ash was focused on my mother like a predator when they spotted their prey.

"Your daughter is brave. More courageous than most. She is loyal, even to those who do not deserve such," Ash said, and his tone said he was talking about the present company as he stepped toward the table. Shadows peeled away from the corner of the lamplit chamber and gathered at Ash's booted feet. "And she cares deeply for others, even for those who, yet again, are not deserving."

Mother flinched.

"Your daughter cares deeply." Ash's low voice echoed throughout the chamber, bringing frost with it. "Even when doing so hurts her."

My chest lurched. "It's okay."

"No, it is not." Ash lifted a hand, and the table flipped high into the air, sending bowls and platters of food flying. It came back down, right on Callum. "Because none of those things has anything to do with who she has become."

"Ash," I said, stepping forward.

"Did any of them bow when you entered?" Ash asked.

"No," Nektas answered with a smug smile before I could point out that I hadn't given them time to or that there were far more important things to discuss.

"Perfect." Shadows rose up Ash's legs. "Bow."

Everyone at the table began to lower themselves before him.

"Not to me," Ash stopped them, swiping his arm toward me. "Bow to *her*, the One who is born of Blood and Ash, *the* Light and the Fire, and *the* Brightest Moon, the *true* Primal of Life and the *Queen* of the Gods and Common Man."

"Oh, my gods," whispered Marisol as she lowered herself to one knee, her mouth hanging open. Her parents did the same.

Everyone looked shocked. My mother couldn't even move. But Ezra…

She smiled and shook her head as she lowered to her knee. "It makes sense," she whispered, glancing at Marisol. Her eyes glistened as her gaze swung back to me.

"You do not bow?" Ash's voice was like the crack of thunder that had torn through the room earlier. "Do I need to repeat myself for you to understand?"

"You do not." My mother trembled, her throat working on a swallow. "I understood what you said. All of it."

I stiffened, my back becoming as unbendable as an iron rod while my mother lowered herself to her knees. She bowed her head, blue jewels glittering in the mass of icy pinned curls.

I jerked as Ash shadowstepped to my mother's side. "*Ash.*" I hurried forward. "Do not hurt her."

He knelt at my mother's side as smoky tendrils whipped inches from her cheek. "It is only by the grace of my wife that you live. I have told you that already," he said as small bits of ice clung to the hem of her gown. "But I am willing to face her anger to ensure that your sharp tongue leaves no more cuts." His head tilted. "Do you understand me?"

Trembling, my mother nodded.

"Ash," I repeated. "That's enough."

The curve of his lips was achingly cold. "For now, it is."

I opened my mouth, but Ash was suddenly in front of me. "Be angry with me later," he requested, kissing me again. "I need to return."

I wasn't sure if I was all that angry. Still, I nodded. "Callum—"

"I'll take him," he said. "And I will ensure he's given our best accommodations."

Knowing he was talking about the dungeon, I snorted.

Ash left my side and raised a hand. The table flipped over, revealing a sprawled but no-longer-leaking Callum.

The Revenant was already healing.

Ash gripped him by the back of the neck as his silvery gaze briefly met mine. He then looked past me to where my mother remained kneeling. "Remember what I said."

My mother's head rose. She didn't look at Ash. Her gaze was fastened on me. "I will."

"Sorry about the table," I said. Ash had returned to the Shadowlands with Callum, and we'd moved to one of the nearby sitting chambers. "I hope you all at least finished supper."

Ezra arched a brow and lowered herself onto a forest-green settee. Marisol had accompanied her parents to a separate chamber in an attempt to calm them.

"And for the new cracks in the walls," I added.

Nektas snorted from where he stood by the doors. I didn't have to look at him to know he was eyeing my mother.

"We had just finished supper, and I suppose the dining hall was in need of a remodel." Ezra smoothed the front of her waistcoat. There was nothing wrong with it. What she was doing was a nervous habit—the only sign she was disquieted by, well…everything. "So, you're the Primal of Life? How is that even possible?"

The simple bluntness of her question made me grin. I didn't think anyone would be able to handle this kind of news as well as she was, but then again, she'd known I had the power to restore life. As she had said in the dining hall, it made sense to her.

"It's kind of a long story, and I don't have much time," I said.

"Can you not make some?" Ezra countered.

I laughed dryly. "There isn't enough time in the realms for me to tell you everything. But I…" I sat on the edge of the chair across from her. "But I'll tell you as much as I can."

And I did, skipping over a lot, like how I'd been held captive, as well as Sotoria and her soul. I glossed over how close I'd come to dying. I also had to silence Ezra's understandable questions regarding the part about who Kolis really was.

By the time I got to my Ascension and awakening as the true Primal of Life, Marisol had returned and sat next to her wife. She stared at me like she had never seen me before.

I couldn't quite blame her for that as I smoothed my hands down my thighs. "So, yeah. That's it."

Ezra blinked and cleared her throat. "I am positive that is *not* it."

I smiled. "It is for now—"

"I believed you had died," Mother said.

My breath snagged as my gaze flew to where she sat. She hadn't spoken—not once until now—but I kept hearing what she'd said to Ash.

Nektas unfolded his arms, but my mother continued.

"The Rot disappeared in a flash. It was just gone." Her hands were still in her lap, but her knuckles were as white as Ezra's had been. "Only one thing could've done that. I figured you'd somehow fulfilled what we believed to be your duty—"

"If I had succeeded in killing who we believed to be the true Primal of Death, it would have been a catastrophe," I interrupted.

"I understand," my mother replied. "But we didn't know there was another way for the Rot to end. We'd only ever been told that the Rot would not lift until you killed the Primal of Death."

"I thought the same," Ezra said, drawing my attention back to her. "That you had succeeded by killing…" Her brows furrowed. "The correct one." She gave a small shake of her head. "And we knew…"

"I wouldn't have survived that," I murmured. "I get it."

"And Kolis?" Marisol asked, tucking a short strand of dark hair behind her ear. "He's the true Primal of Death?"

"Yes. And he's still alive. That's why I came here today. But I need to know what Callum was doing here." I cleared my throat. "And what he said."

"He arrived two days ago, I believe. We'd just returned from Massene, where we celebrated the Rite with Princess Kayleigh and her family," she said, and I tried not to think about the fate of the Chosen. Marisol's fingers dropped to her cream-colored blouse. "I didn't speak very much with him." She glanced at Ezra.

"Neither did I," Ezra told me. "He joined us for supper each night and mostly kept to himself outside of that."

Which meant…

I twisted in my seat. "He is the one who told you how a Primal can be killed."

My mother nodded curtly. "He arrived a few years after you were born and claimed he wanted to help us," she said, staring at the gold and mauve wallpaper. "He knew about the deal, so I…I believed him."

"He was right. That *is* how a Primal can be killed," I said. "Did you speak to him?"

"A few times." She swallowed. "He told me the Rot had lifted because you'd succeeded."

"What?" I exclaimed at the same time Ezra did.

"You never told me that." Ezra pitched forward to look around her wife.

"You already assumed she was dead," my mother replied, the corners of her mouth tightening. "But I knew you harbored some hope that she still lived. I didn't want to take that from you." She looked at me then. "He spoke the truth about that."

Confused, I rose from the chair. "He did. And that makes utterly no sense."

"Did he tell you she killed Nyktos?" Nektas asked.

My mother shook her head. "No. I asked." She glanced between the two of us. "But he said he could not tell me how. I thought—well, you know what I thought."

What in the world was Callum up to? Part of me wanted to leave right then and beat him until he returned to life and answered my questions.

I began to pace. "What else did he say?"

"He talked about nothing of importance. He mostly seemed content with company, even if it was quiet," she said. "But when he wasn't here, he spent his time at the Cliffs of Sorrow."

Of course, he would spend time there, where his sister had died. "Gods," I murmured, hating the pang in my chest. I didn't want to feel empathy for him. Especially now. Not when I knew that fucker had a reason to be here. Still, I couldn't stop myself.

"You said he wasn't a god." Ezra spoke. "Then what is he?"

"An atrocity," I said, pulling my gaze from my mother's elegant profile. "The dead reanimated."

Marisol sat back. "You're saying Callum is *that*?"

Callum was different, but I didn't see the point in getting into that when it would likely only confuse them further. "They are neither god nor mortal, created to serve only Kolis. And as you saw, they are very hard to kill."

"What if he comes back here?" Ezra asked.

"Summon—shit." My pace picked up as Ezra and Marisol tracked my movements. "I haven't felt any summonses yet, and Kolis is likely still sending gods loyal to him to the Temples." Frustration rose. "There has to be another way…" I stopped, closing my eyes as I concentrated. There *was* another way.

"Sera?" Nektas called.

"I'm okay. I'm just thinking." I knew the answer was in all the information I'd received during my Ascension. I knew it was—I spun back toward my mother, startling her. "Call my name."

"Excuse me?" Her eyes lifted to mine.

"If you need me, all you have to do is call my name, and I will hear you." Eather hummed throughout my body. "No matter what."

"That's all?" Doubt colored Ezra's tone. "She just shouts your name, and you'll come?"

"I don't think you need to shout it, but yes." Glancing at my mother, I exhaled slowly. "It's because we share blood."

"That makes sense," Nektas remarked.

"It does?" Ezra questioned wryly, and then her gaze sharpened on the draken. I had a feeling I knew what she would ask next.

I jumped in. "Promise me you will call for me if Callum shows again."

My mother nodded after a moment. "I promise."

A little relieved, I nodded.

"May we back up a moment? To Callum? I don't understand. I mean, I *do* on a basic level that I will likely be thoroughly confused about later when I think about it more…" Ezra said, and a small grin appeared on Marisol's face. "But if Callum serves Kolis, why would he tell anyone how to kill a Primal?"

"Trust me, I have the same question. And I plan to get the answer from him." That and the reason he was here just hanging out.

"That's not the only thing I'm confused about," Marisol said. "You said that gods loyal to Kolis were still answering the Temple summonses, but you're the true Primal of Life—" She laughed nervously. "And even as bizarre as that sounds, I don't feel all that surprised by it." She shook her head as Ezra and I shared a quick glance. "Anyway, I'm guessing Kolis won't remain the false King?"

"He won't. And that is why I'm here." I moved to a chair and sat. "I haven't gone into much detail about the horrors Kolis has committed, but when I say he has little respect for mortal life, I am not exaggerating. He cannot be allowed to rule." I was very careful about what I said next. "Nyktos and I are doing all we can to prevent a major conflict in Iliseeum."

Ezra went still. "By conflict, do you mean a war?"

"Yes." I leaned forward. "But no matter what, there will be a fight, and it will be felt in the mortal realm. You have likely already felt it."

Marisol frowned. "There was a very bad storm a bit ago. I'd never seen anything like it. We lost a few ships."

I winced, guessing that had been a result of Hanan's death.

"There was also what appeared to be a bad lightning storm," Ezra added, her brows drawn. "One that seemed to linger only over the Dark Elms."

That was likely when I Ascended.

"You could see more of that," I continued. "Maybe even earthquakes and landslides."

Ezra swallowed and then did what she always did. She pulled herself together and nodded. "That will be unfortunate."

"Very much so." I curved my hands over my knees. "I want you all to be prepared over the next couple of weeks—maybe even months." I shifted my focus to Marisol. "I know this isn't easy to plan."

"It's not." Marisol took Ezra's hand in hers. "However, we won't be blindsided. We can prepare by upping our food storage and moving faster on our plans to improve the tenements." Her gaze met Ezra's. "They would be most at risk in the event of an earthquake."

"And we can begin creating temporary shelters," Ezra said slowly. "Winter is only a few weeks away, and while it will not be freezing like in the north or east, the people here aren't used to anything but hot and humid weather. They're enjoying things now," she was quick to add. "But winter…"

Winter, even a mild one, would be difficult for those unused to it.

Marisol's gaze swung back to mine. "What about the other kingdoms? Can we warn them?"

"We can send the missives all at once," Ezra said, lifting Marisol's hand to press a kiss atop it.

I had to fight my smile as I stared at them. They weren't just thinking of themselves but others—people they had never met and likely never would.

"Are we allowed to do so?" Ezra asked.

I glanced at Nektas.

"You're the Queen," he replied. "You can do as you wish."

"You sound like Nyktos," I muttered, shifting my attention to the two before me. "I don't see why not, but I would advise against going into a lot of detail or bringing up Kolis. He can be very vindictive, and I do not want anyone catching his attention unintentionally."

"We won't," Ezra assured, slipping her hand free of Marisol's. "But what of you? Will you be okay?"

"Yes," I said. Not just because I didn't want to worry her but because I would be, damn it.

Ezra exhaled heavily. "Thank you for warning us."

"I wish I could do more."

"I know. And I also know that you must leave soon. But I do have one more question." Ezra clasped her hands together. "Though it's not for you."

I glanced between her and Marisol. "Okay."

Ezra's head turned to the rounded archway of the door. "You are not a god, are you?"

My eyes widened slightly.

"I am not," Nektas said.

"How did you know he wasn't a god?" I asked.

"His skin," she explained. "When we were in the dining hall, I saw…ridges appear in his flesh in the shape of scales."

"You're too observant for your own good," Nektas remarked.

"I do not believe one can ever be *too* observant," she countered, and I saw the corners of Nektas's lips rise. "Are you a draken?"

Marisol gave a full-body jerk, and for a second, I feared she might end up on the floor like her mother.

"I am the *first* draken," Nektas stated.

Ezra's mouth formed a perfect circle.

"Okay. Well, that's enough for today." I rose, knowing there were likely a hundred questions forming in Ezra's mind right now.

And I was right. "But—"

"I will return," I interrupted. "As soon as everything is settled. You can ask all your questions then."

Ezra huffed out an irritated breath. "You swear?"

"Did I not promise that I would return the last time?"

"You did." Ezra rose. "Do not break the promise this time because I will have a written list of questions ready for you."

I laughed. "You likely will."

"Your laugh." Ezra stepped toward me and then stopped. "I have never heard you laugh like that before."

"Really?" I felt my cheeks warming.

Her eyes glimmered. "You and Nyktos? He called you his wife."

"He did." Now my cheeks were *really* burning. "We are married."

"And you love him?"

"I do."

Ezra smiled. "That is lovely to hear when he's clearly besotted with you."

Then Ezra shocked me.

She reached between us and took my hand in hers. I experienced a rolling tremor as I felt her warm skin against my palm.

"I am happy for you, sister."

Sister.

"Thank you," I said hoarsely.

She released my hand, and I turned away, still feeling her skin against mine. I said goodbye to Marisol, or at least I thought I did. I was in a state of shock.

Ezra had touched me and had done it so casually. I could count on one hand how many times she had done that in the past.

If she had only done so because of who I was now, I didn't care. It didn't matter.

"Seraphena." My mother rose in a quiet rustle of silk. "May we speak? In private?"

Age-old tension crept in, erasing the shock. My feelings when it came to my mother were still as complicated as ever, even though I had a little better understanding of why she was who she was. Still, I was about to say no because I didn't need to continue allowing her to hurt me.

And that was both for my sake and hers.

But I remembered what I had seen snippets of, and what Ward had shared.

My namesake.

"We can," I said, and Nektas didn't look even remotely thrilled about that. "It's okay," I told him. "Can you give us a couple of minutes?"

"Do I have to?" Nektas didn't take his eyes off my mother.

"Yes." I walked past him, touching his arm. His bright gaze met mine. "Do not scare them."

He huffed.

Without even looking back at Ezra, I *knew* she was brimming with excitement about the prospect of having a few moments alone with the very first draken.

Actually, as I closed the doors behind me, I was more worried about him than I was about her.

My mother waited across the hall, standing at one of the windows overlooking the moonlit gardens. She faced me, expression without emotion in the soft, buttery light of the gas lamps.

Maybe I should be worried about myself.

"Thank you for speaking with me," she said.

I stopped a few feet from her.

She clasped her hands together and cleared her throat. "I don't know where to start, and we surely do not have enough time for that."

"No, we don't."

A faint smile appeared. "Is it true? You love him?"

Her question surprised me, and it took me a moment to answer. "I love him with everything I have in me."

She nodded, her gaze skittering over my face, and I wondered if she saw any of herself in me. Or if she only saw my father.

"I didn't mean to…upset you earlier when I asked what you were. Seeing you was a surprise. Seeing what you can do was a shock. I know that is no excuse," she went on quickly. "And I also know that how I treated you was not right."

"If you're attempting to apologize, it's not necessary," I said. "Or needed."

"But it is."

"For you?"

"No." She held my stare. "For you."

Shaking my head, I started to turn away.

"I wasn't a terrible mother to you," she said. "I wasn't a mother at all."

Halting, I slowly turned back to her.

"You grew up without a mother, even though I was under the same roof." Her lower lip trembled and then ceased. "I wish it had been different. That I had been better. Paid attention. Spent time with you. I just—" She cut herself off, her shoulders tensing. "It doesn't matter why."

But it did, didn't it? Yes, and no.

Her gaze flicked to the lit gardens. "When I believed you had died, all I felt was anger. Not at you, but at me." Her chin lifted a notch. "I just want you to know that."

I eyed her, unsure if she spoke the truth. If I wanted to, I could look into her soul like I had done with Eamon, the guard, but I resisted doing so. It wouldn't tell me if she was being truthful or attempting to get into my good graces now that I was the true Primal of Life, but…

"Why did you name me after the Queen of the Vodina Isles?"

Her gaze cut back to mine. "How…?"

"It doesn't matter how," I said. "Only why."

She stared at me for several moments, then blinked. "Your father. He told me about the deal before we married. He wanted to give me a chance to back out, but I was already so very much in love with him." Her voice cracked, and she inhaled sharply. "Most would not have shared what he did, but he was a good man. Caring. Thoughtful. Loyal. You have all his good traits." She blinked several more times, and I felt the air leave my lungs. "I knew what I was agreeing to if we had a daughter. Like a child, I hoped that we would not, but that was not what fate had in store for us." She swallowed again.

"When I held you, you didn't cry. You just looked up at me with your father's eyes, and I knew what you would face. I knew—or at least I believed—how it would end for you. You would need to be strong, tenacious, and even vicious to succeed. Just like the warrior Queen—the Silver Knight—who fought beside her King and slayed her enemies." Her fingers fluttered to the jewel at her neck. "I thought it would be a fitting name."

It was.

In more ways than one.

I tipped my head back, seeing the gold veining in the ceiling. Gods, I didn't know what to say or how to even feel. I wanted to let it go like I had with Ezra, but my mother was different.

However, I was also different now.

"I get it," I said, closing my eyes. "On some level, I get why you were the way you were. The deal. My father." Lowering my chin, I opened my eyes and met her stare. "But I don't know if I can ever forget all of that."

"I know," she whispered.

The back of my throat stung, and what I admitted to her next shocked me. "But I…I don't think I would have survived all I have—and, gods, it has been a lot,"—my voice broke as my thoughts flashed to Kolis and then Tavius—"if I only had my father's traits. They didn't get me through any of it. My stubbornness and will? Even my temper?" I laughed hoarsely. "Those weren't only the traits of the Queen you named me after. They are also yours."

My mother had gone completely still and silent.

"I'm not sure what that says or even means at the end of the day, but I…I would like to be able to forget. To let it all go," I said. And, gods, the truth I spoke did something miraculous. A little bit of the weight that was always on my chest lifted. I took a deeper breath. "I don't know much about my father and would like to learn more. Perhaps you can tell me about him when I return."

The former Queen of Lasania—the last Princess of the Vodina Isles, my mother—didn't hesitate. "I would like that," she said. "I would like that very much."

35

"You're very quiet," Nektas noted as we entered the gardens.

"I'm just thinking."

"Are they good thoughts?"

Passing the statue of Maia, I nodded. "They are."

"Relieved to hear that," he said. "Your mother is…"

"Something else?"

The sound that came from him was part laugh and part growl. "That is one way of putting it."

A surprisingly wry grin tugged at my lips. I was still processing everything that had happened with my mother. We hadn't talked long, but it felt like a major step in a good direction. I wasn't sure what the outcome would be. There was a lot of messy stuff to sift through, but I meant what I said. I wanted to move on. Let go. And I wanted to have real conversations with her. Maybe I would tell her what had happened before my father died, what he'd attempted to do. Though I didn't think that would bring her any peace.

"Your sister is very inquisitive," he said as we stopped near the nepeta blue.

My grin turned a lot larger then. "How many questions did she manage to ask?"

The cool breeze lifted the long strands of his hair, tossing them across his face and chest. "Far more than a mortal should've been capable of doing in such a short period of time."

I laughed. "Sorry about that."

A dark brow rose. "No need to apologize. The Queen is…amusing. And her wife is extraordinarily polite." He offered his hands. "They both handled the news of who you are fairly well."

"Ezra's known about my ability to restore life for a while, and she's always been very…pragmatic," I explained, taking his warm hands in mine. "And her wife? She was the first person I brought back to life. That was before I knew that restoring a mortal's life meant another paid the price. She doesn't know. And I don't want her ever finding out."

"Understandable." His fingers curled around mine.

"But I think she…kind of senses something. I don't know what, but maybe she knows on some kind of unconscious level," I said, glancing back at the castle's lit windows.

For the first time since…well, forever, I didn't feel an overwhelming sense of anger, inadequacy, or hurt. All of that was still there. One decent conversation with my mother wouldn't erase all of it, but it was muted by something new. Hope.

I pulled my gaze from Wayfair. "Ready?"

Nektas nodded.

I had originally hoped to visit Cauldra Manor—the ancestral Balfour home in Massene—to see if Delfai was still there. Him knowing how the Ancients had been entombed was a long shot, but it was the best we had. However, that was before I'd found Callum having *supper* with my family. Discovering what the fuck he was up to was the priority now.

Clearing my mind, I pictured the damn empty pedestal in the foyer as eather swelled. Tendrils of gold-streaked silver essence rose from the ground beneath us. The mist thickened and swirled, spinning up our legs. The vanilla scent of the purplish-blue flowers faded as we shadowstepped into the House of Haides.

The throbbing sensation of another Primal echoed in my chest before the mist evaporated. The feeling felt…familiar as I let go of Nektas's hands and turned, glancing at the closed main doors past the pointed archways.

"A Primal is here," I announced as I started down the hall, heading for the underground level.

"There is." Nektas brushed red-and-black strands back over his shoulder. "It's Attes."

Well, that kind of explained why the awareness felt familiar. I had totally forgotten that Ash had said he would ask Attes to be here.

As we entered the left hall, I spotted Rhahar and Kars at the end, guarding the door near the back stairwell. Rhain stood with them.

The auburn-haired god turned as we passed Ash's office. He waited until we were almost upon them to ask, "How did things go?"

"Other than finding an unexpected visitor with them? Good. My step—my sister is going to alert the other kingdoms of possible impact." I stopped before them. "Do you know if the Revenant has come to?"

"I'm not sure, but we're about to find out," Rhain answered as Rhahar opened the door. "After we're finished down here, there's something I need to show you and Nyktos."

I nodded as I entered the narrow, torchlit stairwell. The musty scent of the underground lair surrounded me as I thought about the underground pool and wished that was the source of my visit to the dank space as goldish-red flames danced off the damp walls.

That prickly sensation of unnaturalness returned as I followed the curve in the stairwell, our boots thudding softly off the stone. Remembering the steepness of the last step, I managed not to trip and fall flat on my face as my gaze flickered over the rows of bleached, twisted…*bone.*

The bones weren't gold nor carved from those of an Ancient, but my stomach still roiled upon seeing them. I dragged in a breath, forcing my gaze forward.

Ash drew his booted foot off one of the bars and rose from the wooden chair he'd been seated in as Attes turned.

Ash was before me in an instant, his arms around me and his mouth cool and firm against mine. He kissed me as he had before. Fierce. Hungry.

A throat cleared, but Ash was in no rush. I gripped the front of his shirt as he slowly ended the kiss, drawing my bottom lip between his. "How did things go?" he asked, resting his forehead against mine.

I closed my eyes, soaking in the feel of him. "Okay."

"Don't mind any of us," Attes drawled. "Take your time. We'll just stand here and wait."

"Shut your damn mouth," Ash said, and I grinned. His hands slid over my cheeks and into my hair. "I'm going to need more details when we have time." He tilted his head and kissed me once more. "I hope you're not too angry with me over my interference with your mother."

I may have been a little irritated by his unexpected presence, but the moment he'd said why he had come? How could I be upset with him? He'd felt that deep, cutting pain and defended me. I couldn't love him *more* for that. "I'm not angry with you."

His fingers curled into my hair. "I missed you, *liessa*."

Gods.

Every beat of my heart was his. "Show me how much you missed me later."

The deep, sexy rumble that came from him sent a heated thrill through my blood. "I can't wait."

Neither could I.

Pressing one last kiss to my forehead, Ash stepped back and turned. Down the hall, Rhain was studying the floor as if it held the answers to life.

I cleared my throat. "Has he woken up?"

"He did right after I got him here," Ash said as we walked ahead.

"Huh," I murmured, scanning a cell that looked like a tree bear had burst through it, leaving several rows of bars shattered. A rusty dark color stained the floor of what had to be Veses' cell. I looked over the etchings in the broken bones. Primal wards. They were powerful, just as the bones were, and would even hold a weakened Primal, but they were not unbreakable.

Veses was proof of that. "He's a little too quiet to still be conscious."

Attes snorted. "That's because he started running his mouth, and Ash quickly grew annoyed."

I glanced up at Ash as the faint stench of stale lilacs reached me. "What did you do?"

One side of his lips curved up as we stopped in front of a cell. "Quieted him."

I faced the narrow cell. There were no cots or chairs. Just bone chains connected to the back wall—

I squinted. Something dark and wet was splattered on the back wall. My gaze lowered to where Callum lay sprawled on his back in the middle of the torchlit floor. The entire front of his gold tunic was drenched in blood, and there was a large puddle beneath him.

"Exactly *how* did you quiet him?" I asked, spotting a rather straight, pinkish-red line across Callum's throat.

"Removed his head," Ash answered.

I slowly turned to him. "You did *what*?"

"Decapitated him," Ash said as if he were listing an uninteresting step in a recipe. "With a sword."

"His head reattached itself," Attes shared, folding his arms over his armor-covered chest. "It was quite disturbing to watch the tendons and muscles do their thing. They sort of crept and slithered across the floor until they reached his head." He sent me a grin as the picture he painted formed in my mind. "You should've seen it."

"I'm glad I didn't." Nausea rose so sharply I thought for a moment I might vomit all over Ash, but as my stomach calmed, I remembered something. "You threatened Callum once," I said to Attes. I couldn't believe I'd forgotten this. "You said you knew how to kill a Revenant."

A dimple appeared on Attes's cheek as he grinned. "I do, but it's not pretty. Kolis calls it the Fire of the Gods."

Ash frowned. "Draken fire?"

"I've seen that work on a fresh Revenant," he said, and I immediately wondered exactly how that had come about. "But ones that have been around for a while? They have to be burned beyond just a crisp, and they take longer to die that way. They need to be turned to ash. But what Kolis was talking about—the Fire of the Gods—it's draken blood. *Ingested* draken blood. Burns them up from the inside."

Nektas's brow rose. "Makes sense. Just coming into contact with our blood kills or severely wounds most. Ingesting our blood would kill almost anything."

But not a Primal or Ancient. Instinct told me that draken blood did something else entirely in that case. Something not good.

"I'm not sure I'm entirely comfortable asking the draken to open their veins for us," I said.

Nektas shrugged. "As long as it doesn't require much, it wouldn't be a problem. Our bodies heal quickly." The draken peered into the cell and smiled. "We can test it out with that one."

"You can open your vein and force-feed Callum, but that won't work with every Revenant out there," Attes pointed out. "We would need to have it bottled, and as you well know, storing draken blood isn't easy since it also burns through most fireproof stone. The only thing it doesn't is—"

"Basalt," Nektas cut in. "Another type of shadowstone."

My stomach churned. "You mean more slag?"

"The slaggiest of slag," Ash corrected, causing my lip to curl. "It's where dragon fire impacts a surface and the temperature is at its highest, creating a medium to dark gray stone. The problem is, it's been a really long time since dragon fire has touched anything. Whatever is out there would've been long since buried."

Frustration started to rise, but then I stiffened. "I saw the creation of the Star diamond when I was in stasis—dragon fire killed an Ancient, leaving behind that diamond, but also—"

"Basalt," Ash finished, a slow grin appearing. "The Undying Hills."

I nodded. "I've never seen them before—well, in real life. But Delfai said the Fates erupted the mountain to get to the diamond, leaving the area and surrounding hills barren."

"Barren and gray." Attes squinted as he turned back to the cell. "I saw the Undying Hills a long time ago."

"I've been there," Ash said. "There was a lot of rock—rock that definitely could be basalt since the Arae erupted the mountain, likely unearthing it."

"I'll get on it as soon as we're done here," Attes offered. "Which we have to be, sooner rather than later."

I narrowed my eyes and glanced back at Callum. "Why is that?"

"The *eirini*," Ash spat. "Attes was kind enough to explain that keeping Callum could be seen as a violation since he serves Kolis."

My nostrils flared with a surge of anger. "Well, there goes killing him."

"Unfortunately," Ash said. "But he needs to be free before the moon rises."

"Which is less than an hour from now," Rhain said.

I shook my head. "I know I've said this before, but I'm going to say it again. The *eirini* is bullshit."

"That it is," Rhain remarked.

"Too bad we don't have more time. If we did, we could let Thierran at him." Attes glanced over. "He's still here, right?"

"Yeah, but he's been keeping a low profile," Ash said.

So low, I had entirely forgotten the *oneirou* was here.

Rhain shifted, angling his body away from the cell. "Was your family able to say why Callum was there?"

"Not really." I sighed. "Apparently, he was there for a few days and mostly kept to himself."

The skin between Attes's brows creased. "That's odd."

"He's odd." I stepped forward as the fingers on Callum's left hand twitched. My gaze flicked up to his throat. The line there was barely visible. "He's waking up."

An intense silver glow filled the symbols etched into the bone bars with a wave of Ash's hand. As the light faded, a section of the bars swung open.

Ash followed as I walked into the cell, mindful of the blood and chains that secured Callum's slim wrists and ankles. The bonds were taut, preventing him from doing much more than wiggling around. I knelt at Callum's side. His features were still slack under the golden paint. I looked back to those in the hall. "Can someone grab me some water and a rag, please?"

"On it." Rhain took off in a blur.

Kneeling at Callum's head, Ash asked, "Please, tell me you're going to smother him with the rag and then drown him?"

I snorted. "That wasn't exactly what I planned."

"That's disappointing."

A low laugh escaped me as I looked Callum over, noting the width of his shoulders and the stark, tapered waist. He was thinner than I remembered.

I kept a close eye on him until Rhain returned with a bucket and a cloth. Ash rose to retrieve the items. The metal bucket clanged off the floor as he set it by me. I quietly took the rag from his hand and dipped the cloth into the icy water.

Faint tremors ran along the Revenant's body, but he didn't stir. Not even when I scrubbed a little harder to remove the thick paint from his face, revealing a smattering of freckles along the bridge of his nose and across the tops of his cheeks. He didn't have nearly as many as I did, but the sight of them was unsettling. I wiped at his brow, removing the paint there, and then I leaned back, taking in his heart-shaped face, angular cheeks, and full mouth—

I jerked my hand back as I stared at him. "Please, tell me you don't see what I do and that I'm imagining things."

Ash was silent for a few moments. "He looks…he looks like you."

My heart started pounding as I dropped the cloth onto the floor. Not only that. He looked *young*. He couldn't have been more than twenty—if that—when his life had ended and he'd been restored, forever frozen on the cusp of adulthood.

Attes moved closer to the bars. "But he looks more like Sotoria. Except for the hair, he's damn near the spitting image of her." A moment passed. "You two look like you could be cousins."

"I always thought it was weird that I resembled Sotoria. Like having her soul placed in my bloodline somehow influenced my features," I said. "I have my mother's face for the most part. Except for the freckles. That's all my father. His hair…" I thought of the painting and felt my stomach twist. My head cut to Attes. "I've only seen a painting of my father, but his hair was a deep reddish-brown color. Not the same as Nyktos's. More like red wine."

Attes jaw clenched. "Sotoria's hair was that color."

"Her soul was in your bloodline for hundreds of years on the Mierel side," Ash said softly. "It's possible that influenced more than just your appearance."

"Could be," Nektas considered. "Or you are of the same bloodline as Sotoria."

My eyes flew to Ash's. He shook his head. "If the *vadentia* doesn't tell you," he said. "Then only the Fates can."

I nodded slowly. Either way, it was disturbing because I didn't like the golden fuck.

With that thought in mind, I picked up the bucket of water and dumped it over Callum's head.

The Revenant's eyes opened wide, his back bowing as he drew in a ragged breath. "*Fuck.*" Gasping, he sputtered, spitting water as his arms curled. The chains clanged off the stone floor.

"You were taking too long to wake," I said.

His head cut toward me.

Smiling, I wiggled my fingers at him. "Hello."

Water dripped off his nose, and he inhaled sharply. "Bitch."

Ash struck as fast as lightning. He grasped a handful of hair and jerked Callum's head back as far as possible without snapping his neck.

"Fuck," Callum repeated.

"Watch your mouth," Ash warned. "Or we will get to see how your arms and legs reattach themselves."

"I would like to avoid that," I said. "So, as long as you behave yourself, we will."

Callum's lips peeled back over his teeth. His canines were longer than a mortal's but shorter than mine. However, they looked sharp. "You're violating the *eirini.*"

"Are we?" I raised my brows. "If that's the case, we may as well just kill you. You know, might as well fully commit or some shit."

Ash forced the Revenant's attention back to him. "And guess what, fucker?" His smile was pure smoke and ice. "We know how to kill you."

Nektas neared the bars. "I'm more than willing to open a vein."

"He's helpful like that," I said as Ash released the Revenant's hair and stood.

Unease skittered across Callum's features, tightening the skin at the corners of his eyes and mouth.

"Or we can return you to Dalos before we've actually violated anything," I said. "But to do that, you're going to need to answer some questions."

Callum said nothing as his glare locked on me.

"Why were you at Wayfair?" I asked.

"Why are you still alive?" he replied.

Ash slammed his booted foot down on Callum's hand. The crack of several bones made me wince as the Revenant shouted. "For each question you refuse, another bone gets broken." A lock of hair fell against his cheek. "Understand?"

Callum clamped his mouth shut.

Ash tsked softly under his breath. "Let me ask you again." He ground his boot down. Blood drained from Callum's face. "Do you understand?"

"Yes," Callum rasped.

"Thank you." Ash lifted his boot, and his eyes met mine. "Go ahead."

"Why do I find you so…hot right now?" I asked.

"Fucking Fates," Rhain muttered from the hall.

Ash winked, and that didn't really help me behave appropriately.

I shook my head as he began circling Callum's body. "Why were you there?"

"I wanted to visit your mother," he said. "I find her quite interesting."

My head tilted to the side. "Come on, now."

The sharp crack of bone drew a shout from Callum. Ash had stomped his foot. "I…I answered her question."

"You're spewing bullshit." Slowly, Ash lifted his boot. "That's not going to fly either. Keep it up, and the femur bone will be next. That's the most painful one to break." Edges of his hair slid across his jaw. "It's my favorite."

Callum's lifeless blue eyes darted between Ash and me. "You two…are perfect for each other."

My smile was more genuine. "Aren't we, though?"

Sweat beaded Callum's upper lip as he shuddered. "I visit Carsodonia whenever I…I can." His stare fixed on the ceiling. "It's where I'm from."

"I know where you're from, jackass." I sat beside him. "That doesn't explain why you were at Wayfair."

Callum's gaze darted to where Ash had stopped. He stood by his hip and thigh. "Kolis didn't…ask me to go."

"Okay…" I waited for more of an answer.

"You'd better keep talking," Attes advised. "Nyktos is eyeing that bone of yours."

"You're a traitor." Callum lifted his head. "A fucking—"

I snapped my fingers in Callum's face. "Focus."

"I already told you the truth," he spat. "The former Queen makes for an enjoyable companion."

Ash lifted his boot.

"She does! She requires no idle chit-chat when with her," he said in a rush. "I can just walk the gardens or sit with her in fucking silence."

I held up a hand, stopping Ash. "You could do that by yourself."

"And where would I stay? It's not like there are many places there with spare rooms, and your inns are shit." The faint glow of eather pulsed behind his pupils. "They were shit when I lived there." His upper lip curled. "Besides, I wanted to see her once more."

I lowered my hand as the sensation of cold fingers tiptoed down my spine. "Once more? What does that mean?"

His stare held mine for a moment and then flicked away. "I figured I wouldn't be making many trips to the mortal realm for the foreseeable future." He closed his eyes, his features tensing. "And your mother? She respects me."

"Because she thought you were a god."

"So?" Tension bracketed the corners of his mouth. "I didn't think you would show up. I figured you'd be busy making…bad choices."

Someone who sounded like Attes chuckled under his breath.

I eyed the Revenant. My foresight was silent, so I looked at Nektas, remembering how sensitive the draken's senses were. "What do you think?"

"All I smell is the stench of pain and death," he said. "It's masking everything else."

Callum wheezed out a laugh. "You make it…sound like I smell bad."

I pressed my lips together. Part of me thought Callum was telling the truth, and that was kind of sad. "Why weren't you by Kolis's side?"

"He's been…in a mood." Callum tracked Ash as the Primal resumed his prowling. "I bet you can guess why."

Attes had said that Kolis hadn't shown up at Court, most likely holing up in the Sanctuary alone. But…

"It seems rather strange that you'd take a vacation while Kolis is about to lose his authority," I pointed out.

"Seems rather strange to me that…" Callum drew in a ragged breath. "That you think Kolis will lose anything."

Ash stepped on Callum's broken hand.

The Revenant howled, kicking his head back. "Fuck."

"He is going to lose everything," I said.

Breathing heavily, Callum turned his head toward me. "I want…my sister's soul."

"Why?" Out of the corner of my eye, I saw Attes move toward the cell. "So she can be reborn and terrorized by Kolis? Held captive?" My anger rose. "Stripped of all choice and free will? Assaulted? That's what you want? Fuck you."

His nostrils flared as he looked away.

I had to rein in my anger. We were running out of time, and there was something I needed to know. "Why did you tell my mother how a Primal can be killed?"

"That is a very interesting question," Attes noted.

"I don't know what you're talking about," Callum answered.

"Bullshit," I spat. "You told my mother that a Primal can be killed by someone they love. Something no mortal knew until you opened your mouth."

Callum's eyes closed. "I didn't say shit."

Spinning, Ash drove his foot down on Callum's left thigh. The sickening crack of bone, and the Revenant's hoarse shout, echoed through the underground lair.

"Clearly, you're worried about Kolis finding out what you did. He's not your problem right now, though. We are. So, do you want to rethink that answer?" I suggested.

The Revenant's flesh was pasty and damp with sweat. "There's… nothing to rethink."

Callum's other thigh snapped, followed by his right hand and left arm. By the time Rhain warned us about the time, every bone in his limbs had been shattered.

And still, the bastard kept up with the lie.

The realization that I wasn't going to get an answer from him drove me to my feet. Rhain had started to pace nervously in the hall.

"Sera," Ash warned softly.

"I know." Anger rippled through me as I once more knelt by Callum's head. "You still conscious?"

"How can I not be?" Each breath was ragged. "When…someone keeps breaking my bones."

I gripped his chin, forcing his head toward me. Two watery blue eyes locked on mine. "I want you to listen to me, Callum. If you go near my family again, for any reason, I *will* kill you. *Eirini* be damned. Do you understand me?"

"Yes," he gritted out between clenched teeth.

"Thank you." I released his jaw and unsheathed the Ancient-bone dagger.

And drove it through the center of his forehead.

He didn't say a word or even have a chance to blink. He died for the…who knew what time today, his eyes open wide.

Wrenching the dagger free, I cleaned the blade on an unstained section of his tunic. "I hope he wakes up with a headache. Otherwise, this was a giant waste of time."

"You think he was telling the truth about his reason for being in Lasania?" Ash asked as he released Callum's limp body from the chains.

"Who knows?" I muttered, sheathing the dagger.

"I wouldn't be surprised if he was telling the truth," Attes said, entering the cell. "He's not openly disrespected in Dalos, but none of the gods who frequent the Court like him. They don't like anyone they view as being favored by Kolis."

"Poor him." I turned to Attes. "Can you take him?"

Attes nodded. "I'll drop him off somewhere." He flashed a grin. "Somewhere really inconvenient."

"As long as it doesn't interfere with the *eirini*," Ash said, "you can drop him off in the Lassa Sea."

"Actually..." Attes's smile grew as he picked up the Revenant's lifeless body and tossed it over his shoulder. "That sounds like a good idea."

I woke with a jolt, essence thrumming through my body, along with an overpowering sense of something off in the air.

Something wrong.

Something *unnatural.*

I opened my eyes. The cool weight of Ash's arm remained around my waist, and his chest rose against my back as my vision adjusted to the darkness of the chamber. I lay there in silence, waiting for the sensation to subside. It didn't.

Did I have a nightmare? I had no recollection of such, but it wouldn't be entirely surprising if I had.

Scanning our surroundings, I didn't see anything wrong about the space. I looked at the balcony doors, holding myself completely still. I heard and saw nothing, but the sensation of some sort of...shift in the realm continued to rise. Hair slipped over my shoulders, falling into my face and across my chest as I rose halfway onto my elbow.

The arm around my waist curled. "*Liessa*?" Ash's voice was gruff with sleep. "Is it a nightmare?"

I was so fixed on the sensation, I didn't have much of a reaction to his assumption. "No." I peered at the heavy curtains blocking the balcony door. "Do you feel it?"

In an instant, Ash was sitting upright. When he spoke again, all traces of sleep were gone. "Feel what?"

"I'm not sure, but it feels like there's something in the air that shouldn't be—something that shouldn't be *here*." Confused, I shoved tangled strands back from my face. "You don't feel anything?"

"I don't feel anything." Ash's chest brushed my arm.

Confused, I searched the silence and stillness of the chamber. What was I feeling?

Ash leaned in, dropping a kiss on my shoulder. "Do you still—?" He stiffened against me, going so quiet that unease blossomed.

I twisted toward him, my stomach dipping when I saw streaks of eather lighting up his eyes in the darkness.

"Shit," he growled, tossing the blanket aside. He swung his legs off the bed and was on his feet in a heartbeat.

"What is it?"

"I feel it now." Moving to the wardrobe, he pulled on a pair of breeches. Two of the wall sconces flickered to life, casting a soft glow into the chamber. His skin had thinned.

My hands fisted in the blanket. "Is it Kolis?"

"No," he snarled, shadows swirling across the hard line of his jaw. "It's the Abyss."

36

Relief and concern whirled together as I scooted to the edge of the bed. "That was not at all what I expected you to say."

"And I didn't expect you to feel that before me." Pulling the pants up to his hips, he looked up and over at me. "Your senses are continuing to progress impressively."

"I'm going to hold off on bragging about that until you tell me exactly what I felt that involves the Abyss."

"I'm not sure." He tugged a tunic over his head. "I can only feel the unrest radiating from there, though that is not entirely uncommon. Sometimes, it's an escaped soul."

I supposed that would explain why it felt like something was here that didn't belong. "And when it's not that?"

His gaze met mine. "Other times, when a soul makes it out, it stirs up the rest and becomes an uprising of sorts."

I didn't need any foresight to know that an uprising in the Abyss, where souls paid for every evil deed they committed while alive, wasn't good.

I rose. "I just need to find something to wear."

Ash grabbed the leather straps of his baldric. "That won't be necessary."

I turned my head toward him. Did he really expect me to stand back when he wasn't? Oh, he *knew* better than that. "What do you mean it won't be necessary? And don't say it's because I can't enter the Abyss. I know I can," I said, having had no knowledge of that before it came out of my mouth.

"Yes, you can." Draping one of the straps over his shoulder, his fingers moved expertly over the baldric. "But that doesn't mean you should."

Crossing my arms, irritation flared to life. "Is it because the Abyss is your thing, and you're, like, asserting boundaries or something?"

He paused, brows snapping together. "Seriously?"

I lifted a shoulder. "It's a valid question. I mean, that is your arena."

He stared at me for a moment, then curtly shook his head. "It has nothing to do with that. Especially since you're the true Primal of Life, Sera. *All* the realm is your thing."

My chest squeezed, and not because that was still overwhelming to hear. And it was. But it was how he looked at me. As if he couldn't believe I would suggest such a thing. I hadn't meant to offend him with my question, but perhaps I had. I shifted, uncomfortable. "Then why?"

"Would you like one reason or many?"

My eyes narrowed as my guilt over possibly upsetting him vanished. "Would you like me to give you one reason or many to explain the anger I'm sure I'm projecting all over you?"

I swore I saw him grin as he turned his head to the side. "You're the Queen."

"And you're the King."

"Yes, but you're *the* Queen." He buckled the harness, looking up. "The *true* Primal of Life."

"Whose senses are progressing impressively, according to you," I snapped. "And it's not like I just Ascended yesterday, so it isn't like I need to be resting and eating and feeding every five seconds."

"That has nothing... *Fuck*." Eather pulsed behind his pupils as his gaze swept over me. His lips parted, revealing a hint of fang as his citrus scent increased. "I'm not sure how I'm supposed to reason with you," he said, his voice smoothening and deepening. "Not when you're standing before me gloriously naked."

Sultry heat hit my veins as my body happily responded to his arousal, but every other part of me was so not on board. "Well, you'd better figure it out." I watched him cross the space between us. "I can help, Ash, and I refuse to sit back and do nothing while you put yourself in danger just because I'm the...whatever. That is not how this is going to play out."

"I would never expect you to do that. I wouldn't even want that." He caught a strand of hair that had fallen against my cheek. "It thrills me that you have my back. You have to know that. But you are the Primal of Life."

I stared up at him, my frustration rising. "I know. That's been repeatedly established, Ash."

"But you haven't really thought about it." He clasped the nape of my neck. "You would be entering the Abyss, Sera. Not just the outskirts, where the riders had you, but deep within the Abyss. Every soul there will sense you—will be drawn to you."

I immediately thought about the Shades gathering at the edges of the Dying Woods.

"That alone will cause things to escalate," he continued. "But it's more than that. You're already worried about not being able to stop yourself from bringing someone back. And remember what I said about my father struggling against his instinct to intervene when near the Pillars and how much it saddened him? Being there could be overwhelming for you."

I clamped my jaw shut, causing my fangs to scrape the insides of my mouth. "Ouch," I muttered, touching my lip. "These godsdamn fangs."

"Careful with them. I like the way they feel." Ash cupped my cheek, tilting my head back. "I need to go."

The rational side of me knew he was right. My presence would make things worse, and my already tenuous restraint on my ability to restore life would be tested. Then again, I wasn't sure I'd be all that inclined to bring those in the Abyss back to life.

And that part of me also knew I was wasting time. I exhaled roughly. "I hate the idea of you going out there and facing who knows what when I can't be there with you."

"I know." He dipped his head and captured my lips with his. The kiss was fierce and hard, igniting a throbbing ache I probably should've been a little ashamed of but wasn't. "Just as I hated it when you entered the mortal realm without me."

"But I had Nektas with me."

"And I will have Crolee and many guards."

Closing my eyes, I grasped the front of his tunic. "Be careful."

"Always." His mouth found mine once more.

I forced myself to let go of his tunic. Sitting on the edge of the bed, I watched him step back. Wisps of shadows seeped from him, swirling around his legs.

Then he was gone, shadowstepping from the chamber.

I threw myself back until I was flat on my back. Prone, I stared at the glossy ceiling.

"Ash will be okay," I reminded myself. Problems at the Pillars of Asphodel were common, and he said it was the same at the Abyss. There was no reason for me to be so anxious.

Knowing there was no way I would be able to go back to sleep, I rose again. Worry gnawed at me, coating my skin like thick oil. This wasn't as bad as being stuck in the cage and unable to do anything, but the waiting and not knowing what was happening was just as stifling.

I plucked up the pale, silky nightgown from the floor and slipped it on. My gaze went to the balcony doors, and then I made my way over to the wardrobe. Two robes hung there, one the dark gray robe made of crushed velvet I'd already worn. The other was a shade of deep violet. A pattern of ivy had been stitched in black along the lower portion of the robe and the chest, framing the delicate pearl-capped buttons on both. The amount of time it must have taken for Erlina to create something like this on a piece of clothing one usually only wore in their bedchamber had to be staggering.

I reached for the pretty garment and then froze. Tiny bumps rose all over my body. Slowly, I turned to the balcony doors once more and held still. The palace was completely silent. Whatever was occurring in the Abyss had no effect here.

But…

I grabbed the dark gray robe and shoved my arms into the sleeves. As I buttoned it, I crossed the chamber. Pushing the drapes aside, I opened the doors and stepped out. My fingers tingled strangely as I looked up. The night sky was as black as shadowstone, but it was blanketed by brilliant stars that cast silvery light over the courtyard and the Rise. Breathing in the rich scent of soil and a faint trace of woodsmoke, I walked to the railing. I could make out the forms of a dozen or so guards patrolling the wall.

The feeling of *unnaturalness* thickened, causing more tiny bumps to spread across my skin. Eather stirred, almost like a warning. Adrenaline flooded my body as I scanned the courtyard and then the Rise, finding a handful of guards along the northwestern portion of the wall, an area that bordered the Red Woods and the road to the Pillars of Asphodel. There were also several farther south.

But something was wrong.

Something was wrong *here*.

My skin continued to prickle as I looked at the sky once more. Stars winked in and out, momentarily obscured by…

Leaning forward, I squinted. More stars flickered. The sensation of wrongness coated my skin now, igniting the most primitive instincts. My lips parted as I stared, making out shapes in the sky. Fast-moving shapes with *wings*—

A shocking sound shattered the silence, a shriek so chilling I thought it would freeze the very air. I jerked back from the railing. Shrill, piercing screams followed in a macabre chorus as the guards along the Rise spun toward the road leading to the Pillars.

A jolt of surprise rippled through me. I'd heard those shrieks before. When I came out of the cavernous tunnel along the outskirts of the Abyss. There had been flames, and these creatures were flying above them.

I stiffened as one of the shapes flew closer, moving as fast as a draken. I caught a glimpse of a wingspan larger than Reaver's. "What in the—?"

In the blink of an eye, *something* came at the guard closest to the road. There was a blur of talons, dark-feathered legs, long, straggly hair, and…a vaguely mortal-like body. The creature dug its talons into the man's back. The guard let out a pained, *wet* sound as he was lifted into the air and flown out over the courtyard, thrashing and screaming the whole time.

The thing dropped the guard.

Out of reflex, I shot toward the railing and tracked the guard's rapid descent. The heavy smack of a body hitting the ground turned my stomach. My heartbeat stuttered. The guard must have been a godling because heat flared against my palms when the all-too-familiar urge to intervene, to steal the guard's life away from death, slammed into me.

My hands curled into fists as the thing flew up, letting out a grating, crackling noise. But I was locked to where I stood, staring at the guard on the ground as I reminded myself that I couldn't intervene. *I couldn't.* I started to force myself to look away, but something was happening.

A flicker of light seeped out from the guard, forming a small orb of softly glowing golden light. What was I seeing? The skin of my neck tickled as the small ball of light floated up several feet before fading. Instinct told me the light hadn't really disappeared.

It had only moved to the Pillars, where it would take the shape of the man once more.

I'd never seen anything like that before, but I'd heard what it was called here and in every realm—even the ones beyond the Primal Veil. It was the *spirit* of an individual. Their inner *consciousness*. The *psyche*. The *self*. *Sóls*. The *soul*.

I'd finally seen what I'd always sensed upon death. The separation of the soul from the body.

"Get to low ground!" a guard shouted from farther down the Rise. "Everyone."

My head snapped up. Now was not the time to be distracted by what I'd seen. I knew what this creature was. I'd seen them after I'd been with the riders. It was a *sekya*, and they were not allowed to leave the…

To leave the Abyss.

Shit.

This was what I'd felt upon waking. They were the source of the unrest Ash had eventually sensed. No souls were trying to escape the consequences of their crimes. Instead, it was those delving out the punishment.

The *sekya* flew toward the palace as others drew closer, their shrieks rising with my fury.

Guards flooded the courtyard, one of them shouting in a voice I recognized as Kars'. "Get off the Rise! Now! Go! Go!"

My heart lurched as the guards on the Rise ran for the nearest steps, scattering in each direction, but I knew—gods, I knew they wouldn't make it. The *sekya* were too fast, and it didn't matter what they were called, because there were rules…

Rules that had nothing to do with the *eirini* and were a part of all that information fed to me during the Ascension. There were so many godsdamn rules, but only one was important to me at the moment.

The *sekya* were not supposed to attack the living—be they Primals, gods, mortals, or anything in between.

But like with the dakkais, they could only be controlled to a certain point.

Several reached the Rise, chasing down the guards there. Half of them dropped from the sky as the first tucked its wings back, diving straight for the guards in the courtyard.

A Rise guard's scream was cut short. The awareness of death pressed down on me as pieces fell to the ground. *Pieces* of what remained of the guard.

Kars threw a shadowstone dagger, striking the *sekya* in the chest. It let out a howl of pain and folded its wings as it got knocked back. It spiraled down to the hard earth. I didn't feel its death, nor did I see its soul.

But the others echoed its cry. The whole damn mess of them veered, following the ones aiming for the palace.

A flash of intense silver cut through the darkness of the courtyard—an arrow of pure Primal essence. My head jerked to the left.

Rushing across the courtyard, Bele leapt onto a boulder, her shoulder-length braid slapping against her rounded cheek. She crouched, one arm outstretched as she held a bow made of crackling essence.

"What ugly…" She pulled the string of eather taut and released another arrow. "Motherfuckers."

I would've laughed, except I could see we were outnumbered—even with Bele's arrival. I sensed another death. With every blow landed against a *sekya*, another came from the sky, more pissed off than before.

I had to do something. If not, the courtyard would be littered with *pieces*. Possibly even Primal ones. I turned to the bedchamber doors just as the eather thudded heavily in my chest. A wail of pain stopped me, and my anger took hold.

There wasn't time.

Eather pounded through my veins. The corners of my vision turned silvery-gold as I spun back to the railing. I grabbed it, and energy ramped up inside me as I sprang forward.

Cool night air rushed up, catching the sides of the robe while the *sekya* shrieked overhead, and the guards shouted from below.

Like before, my body knew what to do. My knees bent to lessen the shock of the impact as the rest of my body relaxed.

My landing still knocked the wind out of me.

Kars staggered back a step with a gasp, "Good gods."

The flash of pain was even duller and faded quicker than before.

Wishing Ash had been here to see what I was confident had to be one badass landing, I rose.

Kars stared, his mouth hanging open.

"I'm not going to use the stairs ever again," I told him.

He lowered his sword. "Uh-huh."

"Show-off," Bele yelled from where she was perched on the boulder. "Nice to see you joining us. Hopefully, you're going to do something other than stand there looking proud of yourself."

I grinned. "Honestly? I hadn't thought past jumping."

"That's reassuring," Kars replied.

"What did I say?" Bele released another eather arrow. "About your absurdity?"

A shrill yelp of pain silenced whatever I was about to say to her. I *had* come down here to do more than look proud of myself.

Drawing in a deep breath, I focused on the *sekya* as one flew under Bele's arrow, aiming straight for where I stood before the guards. I had no more moments to waste. No time to overthink.

Summoning the eather, it responded in a heady rush. Power surged through me as I lifted my hand. My skin warmed. Silver light seeped out from under the sleeves of my robe—silver light laced with gold.

Energy erupted from my palm. Like a bolt of lightning, it sliced through the air, striking one of the creatures in the chest. Its wings collapsed as it fell, spinning in midair. The *sekya* crashed into the ground, kicking up dirt and dust as it rolled, coming to a stop a few feet from where we stood. Realizing that, like with the dakkais, I didn't feel its death, I looked down. Smoke wafted from the charred skin of its chest—a rather *voluptuous*, bare chest. My gaze shifted. Its scraggly hair was blown back from a pasty gray face. Its eyes were vacant, empty of life, and the color of heated gold, matching the streaks zigzagging through the undersides of her onyx wings. The creature's mouth hung open in a silent scream, revealing a row of teeth shaped like daggers.

The *sekya* looked like the Ancients had drunk too much whiskey when they constructed the creatures, seeming to want to create a new breed of bird, then changing their mind halfway through and giving them a vaguely mortal appearance.

But the *sekya* wasn't hideous. Her features were still somehow delicate. Beautiful, even. And that made the thing all the more disturbing.

An arrow of eather blazed through the sky, snapping my attention from the bizarre creature. Two *sekya* dodged the eather as at least half a dozen more flew over the courtyard, speeding toward us.

Flipping my palms outward, every part of my being fixed on them. Gold-tinged silver light once more sparked from beneath the sleeves of my robe. Wisps of eather swirled around my wrists and then my palms, moving faster as a silvery web of eather formed in my mind, stretching toward them like bony fingers.

The air vibrated as thin arcs of silver laced with gold seeped from my fingers, dripping to the ground as I walked forward. Tendrils took shape, rapidly spreading across the ground and lifting. The eather erupted into the web I'd conjured, each branch ripping through the sky almost faster than the eye could track. Veins of eather struck the *sekya*, one after another, catching them in mid-flight and sending them falling to the ground. I pulled the eather back—

A hot, dry hand clasped my ankle, jerking me back. I gasped, twisting at the waist.

The *sekya* Bele had first taken out smiled up at me. I froze in confusion, just for a second, but that was all it took. The creature pulled, throwing me off balance. I went down hard, landing on my back with a grunt.

The thing hissed like a feline and then leapt.

"Shit," I grunted, throwing my hands up. I caught the *sekya* by the upper arms a heartbeat before it landed on me, holding it back. "How are you not dead?"

It screeched, its face and gnashing teeth inches from mine.

"Seriously?" I glanced down at the thing's chest to make sure Bele had struck it with the essence, and…yep, there was a charred hole between the creature's flat breasts. "I'm so confused right now."

The *sekya* drew up a feathered leg. My eyes widened as I got an up-close-and-personal look at its taloned feet. Cursing, I drove my knee into its thigh, blocking it just as its talons snagged the robe.

"If you tear my robe—"

The tip of a sword suddenly burst through its chest, creating another hole as hot, musky-smelling liquid sprayed me.

Ugh.

Kars jerked the sword and *sekya* back. Turning, he kicked it free of his blade. The creature fell face-first onto the ground.

"Thank you." I sat up, wiping at my face.

"You're welcome." He offered me his hand.

Taking it, I stood. Behind Kars, I saw Bele straightening, her eyes widening. I turned.

All around us, the fallen *sekya* rose, shaking dirt from their feathered bodies and wings.

Bele looked over at me, her brows raised.

"What?" I threw up my hands. "I don't know how they're not dead!"

But I should, shouldn't I? I knew what they were called and who had created them, but I didn't know how they could be killed.

"Because I assumed I knew how. Obviously, I was wrong," I mumbled to myself. The skin behind my ear tingled as my thoughts raced, and a *sekya* lunged toward a guard, avoiding the sweep of his sword, and another took to the air.

"I…I can't kill them," I whispered, my hands falling to my sides.

Kars cursed, darting to the side as I scowled. He glanced at me. "For real?"

"That can't be right. I'm the fucking true Primal of Life." Annoyed, I spun toward a *sekya* and summoned the essence. It responded in a hot rush, joining my will. "How can I not kill one of these things?"

A flash of eather funneled from my palm, slamming into the *sekya's* chest, knocking it to the ground. I didn't retract the eather as I stalked toward it. I kept the stream of power bearing down on it until I reached where it had fallen.

I closed my hand, able to see the charred edges of its now-split rib cage and the ground through the massive hole in its chest. "Let's see you get up from that."

"They shouldn't be getting up at all." Bele fired another blast of eather and then jumped from the boulder, narrowly avoiding a swooping *sekya*. "Hey, *meyaah Liessa*." She crouched. "To your right."

"Don't call me—damn it!" I jumped to the side as a *sekya* dove at me. The thing swept back up, *cackling* as I glanced down to make sure the one on the ground wasn't moving. The unblinking stare looked dead to me. "I think I got—"

The eyes *changed*.

It was barely noticeable, just a faint glow returning to its golden eyes. The *sekya* gave me a bloody smile.

"Son of a bitch!" I shouted as the *sekya* rose, its wings spreading as it lifted into the air. "I can see Kars through your godsdamn chest! How is this possible?"

Kars turned, his head jerking as he blinked. "Well, that is not something you hear or see often."

"Their head!" Rhain shouted as he rounded the side of the palace. "You have to destroy their heads!"

"Now, you tell us?" Bele snapped, the crackling bow dissipating as she reached to her hip and drew a shadowstone sword.

"I just got here." Rhain skidded to a stop, his jaw unlocking as he saw me. "What are you doing out here?"

"Being unhelpful," Bele retorted.

Lifting an arm, I extended my middle finger toward her. "The head, you said?" I grinned tightly. "All right, then." My chin dipped as I summoned the eather. Thrusting out my hand, spitting and hissing eather streaked out.

The eather split the *sekya's* head right down to its neck. My lip curled as it once more landed in a messy heap—an even messier heap. "I think I might vomit."

Rhain rushed to my side. "What are you doing out here?" he repeated.

"Killing *sekya*." I frowned. "Or trying to."

"Yeah, I see that." He stepped in, lowering his voice. "You shouldn't be out here."

I ignored him, not taking my eyes off the thing on the ground for more than a second. "I know. There's no way this thing is going to—"

Rhain grabbed my arm, shoving me behind him as he rammed his sword through the underside of a *sekya's* chin, catching it in midair. He grunted, taking its weight. Withdrawing his sword, he had already faced me as the thing hit the ground and *shattered* into ash. Rhain was speaking, but I wasn't listening as I slowly turned back to the other *sekya*. That one hadn't broken apart. I looked down, and my mouth dropped open.

Filaments of tissue stretched out from the two halves of the split head. The fibers connected and twisted around one another, drawing the two sides together.

"You've got to be kidding me!" I shouted.

Rhain paled as the head stitched itself back together. "That is…" He swallowed hard, stepping forward and bringing his sword down on its head.

The *sekya* broke apart in a musty shower of ash.

Eather pulsed in my chest, warning me that death was afoot. "I really can't kill them!"

His brows knitted. "Then you should get inside," he instructed. "We've got this handled."

A sword fell between us, bouncing off the ground. A body followed, smacking with a wet, fleshy sound.

I raised my brows.

"We'll get it under control," he amended with a wince. "Nyktos should be here shortly. Go inside."

"That is not happening." I dipped, not looking at the guard's stomach or what was hanging out of it as I picked up the fallen shadowstone sword. "I can still use this, right?"

"I...I guess so." Rhain frowned. "But I also don't know why you can't kill them with eather. That's what Nyktos does."

"Of course, he can kill them," I muttered, turning around as my grasp on the sword firmed. The answer to why I couldn't was somewhere in my head, but I really didn't have time to figure it out.

A *sekya* had taken notice of me from where it hovered. Raising my free hand, I wiggled my fingers. It cocked its head to the side. The *sekya* smiled, baring its dagger-like teeth.

I returned the smile.

Letting out a powerful shriek, it flew toward me. I waited until it was inches from me, and then I moved. Twisting to the side, I popped up behind it as its talons dug into the ground. Stepping forward, I drove the sword through the back of its head. The feeling of the shadowstone meeting little resistance brought forth a twisted surge of satisfaction. It felt like forever since I'd held and used a sword outside of training. The last time... I wasn't going to think about the last time. I watched with relief as the *sekya* shattered.

Ignoring Rhain's glare, the robe's hem snapped at my ankles as I spun toward the cluster of guards hacking away at the *sekya*. One of the creatures with a shadowstone arrow protruding from its chest swooped down, aiming for Kars. I rushed forward and grabbed the first thing I could get my hands on. Fingers sank into the surprisingly soft wings, and I jerked the creature back.

The *sekya's* screech ended abruptly as I jabbed the sharp edge of the blade through the back of its skull. It spasmed and then disintegrated into a fine, dusty mist.

"Fates," Bele snarled, cleaving a head from a *sekya's* shoulders. She stared northwest. "What is going on?"

The rich, metallic scent filling the courtyard settled in the pit of my stomach as I followed her gaze. My heart sank. Another dozen or so *sekya* neared the Rise. Nearly the same number of guards stood, but many were injured, and the creatures were fast with their talons and teeth. This was about to get really bad.

I turned to the guard I quickly recognized as Eamon. "Help get the injured inside." He gave me a quick nod and I spun back to the others. "I'll take them down. While they're out, go for their heads," I instructed, the eather throbbing in my chest. "Be quick."

"Done," Kars shouted.

I was already walking forward, raising my right hand. The air around me hummed with power as fine threads of silvery-gold eather drifted from my fingers, covering the ground. The web of eather formed, its branches clawing at the sky like ascending stars. I willed the essence toward the *sekya*—

Suddenly, the realm became silent.

Still.

Everything north of the wall turned black as the night sky seemed to deepen and come alive with dark, violent power. The pulse of awareness in my chest intensified as the air charged, raising the fine hairs all over my body.

Several of the *sekya* in the sky shrieked, their wings pounding rapidly at the air as thick shadows rippled over crackling arcs of energy, snuffing out the light—*my light.*

My mouth dropped open as I slowly lowered my hand. All across the courtyard, the *sekya* on the ground spun toward the smoky mass.

Whirling shadows poured down the side of the Rise and the *sekya* scrambled in different directions. They were fast.

But *he* was faster.

Dark tendrils snaked out from the void of churning nothingness, streaking across the sky and the ground. Strands of thick shadows wrapped themselves around the bodies of the airborne *sekya.* Funnels of whirling, coal-black mist raced across the ground, and the shrieks rose to an ear-piercing volume. Threads of silvery eather spun through the swirling darkness, slamming into the *sekya.* Their shrieks were cut short, one after the other, as my gaze fixed on the center of the shadowy mass above the Rise.

Ash lowered to the courtyard with immense widespread wings made of sparking eather and unrelenting shadows. His skin reminded me of the darkest hour of night pierced by streaks of starlight. The tunic he'd donned earlier was gone. Silver energy leapt from his white-as-snow eyes and outstretched palms.

The breath I took went nowhere. I couldn't look away as the *sekya* continued to fall around us, their bodies shattering. His feet touched the ground, sending shadows billowing all around him. This was *Nyktos,* a Primal of Death, in his true form.

And I was in awe.

Delicate tremors coursed up and down my body as he stalked toward me. Shadowy wisps bled into the air around him at his approach. The kaleidoscope of shadows and silvery eather swirling through his flesh slowed.

Behind him, the last of the *sekya* splintered, their feathered wings fragmenting, and half-mortal bodies becoming nothing more than faintly glowing embers. Ash's wings dissipated. Tension surged in the air as a brutal harshness etched itself into his striking features.

I remained where I stood, having flashbacks of the night some of the entombed gods had been freed. My breath quickened as those unnerving silvery pools locked onto my eyes. He looked as he had then.

Terrifying.

Beautiful.

And furious.

A saner person would've probably tucked their tail and run. I was not a saner person. I stood there, vaguely aware of Rhain and Bele backing off.

Tendrils of shadows swirled around Ash's legs as he stalked toward me. "Are you all right?"

"Yes." My gaze swept over him, and I watched the shadows in his flesh start to recede. "I'm fine."

"There is blood on you."

"It's not mine." I watched a muscle in his jaw flex. "Are you okay?"

He gave me a curt nod, his attention shifting to the gore scattered about the courtyard. Static crackled, and I wasn't so sure he was all right, even though I saw no signs of injury on him.

To our right, Bele rose from where she had crouched by a fallen guard. I looked away quickly. I had to. I wasn't sure I could walk away without intervening if I saw their face.

"What in the world just happened with the *sekya*?" Bele asked. "They've always served you."

"They have," Ash answered as my intuition sparked, whispering what he spoke. "But I am not the true Primal of Death. Kolis is."

And while these creatures had been content to continue as is all these years, something had changed. My eyes flew to Ash.

"Kolis summoned them." He lifted his gaze from the fallen guard and met mine. Only a hint of his irises appeared. "He's strengthening his defenses."

"The *sekya*..." Rhain said, shattering the tense silence. "Did all of them leave the Abyss?"

"They did." Ash looked up as two draken flew overhead, their shadows deepening the night as they landed on the Rise.

My heart lurched. "How many were there?"

His attention returned to the guard's remains. "About a thousand, give or take a couple hundred."

Good gods. "Do I want to know how many made it out of the Shadowlands?"

"I would say about seventy-five percent," he answered.

"I almost regret asking," I murmured. "I couldn't kill them with eather."

"No, you could not. Only a Primal of Death can kill them with eather," Ash explained. "And I have just enough of those embers to get the job done."

I glanced at the draken. It was Ehthawn and Crolee. "Not even the draken?"

"Not even them," he confirmed. "The *sekya* would've swarmed any draken who came to our aid, and they're capable of severely injuring even one as old as Nektas."

"Gods," I muttered.

Ash's eather-drenched gaze locked on mine. "And they can do a lot of damage to a Primal, especially a newly Ascended one," he said, his gaze sweeping over me. "Without a weapon."

I tensed as my thoughts went immediately to the dagger he'd gifted me.

"She held her own and then some," Bele spoke up. "With or without a weapon."

Ash's gaze slid to the Primal while I shifted from one foot to the other. I appreciated Bele coming to my defense, but the thing was, I had come out to fight without a weapon, and that was idiotic.

The essence in me swirled, responding to Ash's. Outwardly, he appeared to be calming—the shadows weren't as thick. But the inside was a different story, and his barely leashed anger had much more to do with what had happened here than it did with me.

These were our people strewn across the courtyard, and even if Kolis had only summoned the *sekya* to him without giving them orders to attack, he knew that many of them would. Because intuition told me the creatures' bloodline was old. They had been created by the Ancients themselves. Just as the dakkais were. And their nature reflected that of their creators.

Hunger and cruelty.

This was Kolis's fault, and I was sure that knowledge fueled Ash's rage. It fed mine as I turned. Kolis was strengthening his defenses, likely in preparation for giving his answer to the offer I made. There was still time left in the *eirini*—at least a week—but he was already preparing for us.

For war.

I stood there for several moments in the moonlight, staring at the splashes of blood tainting the newly grown grass. The wildly churning essence calmed as a sudden prickling sensation erupted along the nape of my neck. Before I knew it, I was crossing the courtyard. I entered the palace, the stone cold beneath my feet. It was as if I were being urged forward. I didn't think it was my heightened intuition. It felt more like the eather inside me. The Primal essence continued to intensify, throbbing in the pit of my chest. I walked beneath the crystal chandelier, making out the low murmur of several voices and another sound—one too muffled for me to make out.

Crossing under the wide, sharply pointed archway, I smelled the iron-rich scent of blood. I passed the empty, white marble pedestal and the closed doors on either side of the area. Reaching where the hall split in two, I went right without much thought. It was like I already knew where to go.

And I was right.

The sound of voices picked up as I entered the palace's right wing, where the doors to the various, mostly unused chambers were closed. I kept going, reaching another branch in the hall, one where one path led outside and the other to a narrower hall with fewer but larger spaces. They had been completely empty when I'd explored the palace with Jadis and Reaver.

I went down the hall, my fingers digging into the soft velvet of my robe. Halfway down, I saw that two doors were open. I picked up my pace, the eather buzzing hotly through my veins. I jerked to a halt when I stepped into the dull light spilling out of the chamber.

I took in the horror of the space. Gods were extraordinarily hard to kill, given only a handful of things *could* kill them—shadowstone to the heart or the head, a blast of eather from a stronger god or Primal, draken fire.

And massive bodily damage inflicted by any creature created by the Ancients.

The dakkais and *sekya* were only two of them. The knowledge I'd gained during my Ascension warned me there were more—truly nightmarish things. But gods weren't infallible.

And this room was proof of that.

The large chamber had quickly been converted into an infirmary. Those wounded from the attack were laid out on thin cots—about a dozen of them. Most of the injured were unconscious. Moans came from those who weren't as Aios hurried between the cots, her arms full of bandages. She wasn't alone. A tall man with a large brown satchel was crouched beside one of the unconscious guards. I needed no introduction to recognize the light-yellowish-brown-skinned man as Kye, the Healer.

Aios had likely already been here with Bele. I had no idea how the Healer had gotten here so quickly, but I was grateful to see him.

I fully entered the chamber, my attention shifting to a guard lying just beyond the doors. She wasn't awake, but her features were still contorted in pain.

I recognized her.

It was the guard with the pretty name.

Iridessa.

Beside her shredded tunic, a pile of blood-soaked linens lay on the floor, and bright, shimmering blue-tinged red already stained the bandage across her chest.

Iridessa was alive—but barely. And I doubted whatever vial Kye had pulled from his satchel while he assisted another could reverse the damage of the *sekya's* claws.

A faint series of tingles erupted behind my left ear as I knelt at Iridessa's side, careful to avoid the mess on the floor. Like with the guard on the Rise, knowledge of her filled my thoughts.

She was a *fighter*. A goddess who'd originally served Hanan, having defected from his Court a few years back after guards sworn to protect the people of Sirta slaughtered her family. She was young compared to the others. Younger than even Ash. She'd seen a hard century of life.

Lifting my hand, I placed my palm on her uncovered shoulder. Her skin was damp beneath mine as I closed my eyes. Summoning the essence, I felt it rush to the surface. It came to me easier when used for this than it did when using it as a weapon or to move objects. I didn't really have to think much about it as I channeled the energy into the goddess. *Sekya* talons had punctured her lungs, her left arm was broken, and several vertebrae were cracked. The essence repaired those injuries.

The reason this was easier didn't really occur to me until Iridessa's brow smoothed out and her breathing deepened. The eather was designed to protect life. To heal. And that had shaped Eythos and even Ash before the embers were removed from him. It wasn't as strong as in his father, but the essence of life had played a role in who they each were at the very core of their being. Because it belonged to them. And that was why Eythos could forgive his brother. Why Ash felt each and every death so deeply.

Aware that my presence had gained attention, I rose and moved to the cot of another unconscious guard. Something else occurred to me. It was also why I hadn't slain the monster while with the riders.

Using the eather to heal or restore life was natural to me only because it was natural to the energy itself. But it hadn't shaped my nature.

Only I could.

If I could.

As I healed the guard beside Iridessa, I thought about what Odetta had said to me. That I had been touched by both life and death. Really, it was Sotoria's soul that had been touched by death.

Time blurred as I healed the injuries of several more guards. While doing that, I felt Ash's presence. He watched me as intently as one of Attes's silver hawks. He didn't try to stop me, simply gave me space as I moved from one cot to the next. Neither did Kye or Aios, the former flushing pinker each time I drew closer to him. When Rhahar arrived, I heard him informing Ash that the *sekya* hadn't headed toward Lethe. That brought me some relief.

The arm beneath my hand trembled as I healed wounds not as deep as some of the others. This guard had awakened upon my approach. His name was Liam. He was only a little older than Iridessa, and his past was nearly the same as hers, except he'd escaped Kyn to join the Shadowlands. I didn't speak as the pallor of death eased, revealing his olive-toned complexion. Neither did he. Not until I made to leave.

Liam clasped my hand. "Thank you," he rasped.

I nodded, not wanting his gratitude, as I moved to the last of the unconscious guards. My skin chilled as I reached the godling's side. Blood stained his hair to the point where I couldn't tell if the strands were normally coppery. There had been a reason I'd been avoiding him.

He was no longer with us.

His soul had left him before I entered the chamber—possibly only seconds beforehand—because Kye and Aios still seemed unaware of his passing.

I lowered myself to my knees and swept my gaze over him. His injuries were significant. If he had been mortal, his body would've been in even worse condition. Still, even as a godling, it was bad. If I had to guess, I'd say he'd been one of the guards dropped from the Rise.

Eather swelled as I stared at him. My body tensed, and then I reached for him.

A cool hand caught mine, startling my heart into skipping. My gaze flew to a pair of beautiful silver eyes. Holding my stare, Ash drew his thumb over the imprint on my palm. In the silence that followed, I realized something.

"It must be hard for you," I whispered hoarsely, thinking of his abilities. "To be around so much pain and be able to feel it."

"It's manageable," he assured me, but I couldn't see how. He had to be drowning in it.

Drawing in a shallow breath, I looked back at the man. I knew his name. The Court he originally served. How old he had been. I didn't want to know those things. I wanted him to remain a faceless, nameless stranger. It was easier that way.

Ash's other hand wrapped around mine, causing me to look down. A ripple of surprise went through me as he threaded his fingers through mine. I hadn't even realized I'd lifted my left hand.

"He's gone, *liessa*," Ash stated quietly. "His soul is no longer with him."

"I know."

"Do you?" he asked quietly.

A knot lodged in my throat. I nodded.

Ash pressed a kiss to my left hand, then my right. "You've done more than enough." He straightened, holding on to one of my hands as he helped me to my feet.

As I rose, I caught Aios's gaze fastening on the fallen guard as she gathered some soiled linens. Her eyes glimmered with unshed tears. The knot in my throat increased as Ash and I turned to the doors.

The Healer stood before us. "Your Majesty." Placing a palm over his chest, Kye bowed. "Thank you for your aid."

I thought I said something appropriate and didn't just stand there, staring at him with a slack jaw. At least, I hoped I did. Kye glanced at Ash and then nodded, stepping aside.

Ash led me toward the hall, and as I looked over my shoulder when we reached the doors, I saw Kye draping a sheet over the guard.

Once in the narrow hall, Ash folded an arm around my shoulders. Wisps of shadowy eather spun out, coiling around our legs. He said nothing as we shadowstepped back to our bedchamber.

I looked up at him and remembered the anger I'd seen in his features in the courtyard. I didn't think all of it was directed at Kolis. A good ten percent was likely due to me getting involved in the *sekya* attack while relatively weaponless.

And, honestly, I deserved to be taken to task for that. It had been foolish of me to rush out without a weapon.

"I know what you're about to say," I began.

"I doubt you do," he said, his voice rumbling as tendrils of night coiled around his legs.

My spine stiffened. "I'm pretty sure I—" I squeaked.

Ash moved faster than I could track. His cool hand clasped my cheek, and he tilted my head back. The scent of leather mingled with citrus and iron.

Within a heartbeat, his mouth was on mine, our lips melding.

The kiss was so untamed and relentless in its passion it left my senses spinning. It wasn't just hungry. It was *starved.* And every part of my being immediately responded. The realm around us and all its problems vanished in an instant. His kiss had that kind of power.

Our teeth gnashed. His fangs grazed my lip, drawing an illicit shiver from somewhere deep inside me. Lifting me onto the tips of my toes and pulling me against his chest, his lips parted mine. I grasped the nape of his neck, kissing him back just as fiercely.

Ash's palm slid down, trailing over the side of my throat and then my shoulder. He backed me up and drew my tongue into his mouth, sending waves of pleasure cascading through me.

Surprise rippled as my lower back abruptly came into contact with the hard edge of a table. Ash's chest left mine, and I felt his fingers there, quickly undoing the robe's buttons. A heartbeat later, the sides gapped, and he grabbed hold of my hands, lowering them.

"Ash," I gasped.

He shoved the sleeves of the robe down, letting the garment fall to the floor. "Hmm?"

Cool air danced over the bare skin of my arms. "What are you doing?"

His mouth moved over mine once more as his hands went to my waist and then my hips. "What does it look like?"

"It looks like you're undressing me." I tipped my head back. The sight of him sent my already racing heart to fluttering.

Ash appeared mortal, but he also didn't.

Shadows churned under his skin like storm clouds. Tendrils of eather still seeped from his body. His irises were now visible, but streaks of eather pierced the silver.

He looked stunningly otherworldly as he stared at me. "That's exactly what I'm doing." Thick lashes swept down. "Unless you'd prefer I not." His head cocked as he inhaled deeply, his nostrils flaring. The tips of his fangs became visible, causing muscles low in my stomach to curl. "Though I sense you have absolutely no issue with me doing so."

The deep rumble coming from his chest heated my blood. "I don't."

"I know." His hand coasted up my side.

"I'm just surprised," I said, sucking in a shallow breath as his hand drifted higher. The thin, silk nightgown was no barrier against the coolness of his touch. A wave of shivers followed in the wake of his movements. "I didn't think undressing was what you had in mind."

"Undressing you is always what I have in mind." Cupping my breast, he grinned, and my breath caught.

My lips felt swollen as they parted. "I figured you were going to lecture me about being outside."

He drew his thumb over the peak of my breast, the hollows of his cheeks becoming sharper as my nipple beaded. "I told you that you had no idea what I was going to say."

"I sensed—" I gave a little jerk as his other hand folded around my right breast. "You were angry when you first returned."

"Was I?" he asked, watching himself draw the same response as he had seconds earlier.

A heaviness settled in my chest. It wasn't the all-too-familiar warning of anxiety but a thick, languid sensation that also bloomed between my thighs. "Yes."

"Perhaps..." he murmured, lowering himself to his knees.

My heart thudded as my hands fell to the table on either side of my hips. The sight of Ash on his knees before me never failed to stun me into silence.

He stretched a little, his head now level with my chest. "I was wrong earlier."

"About—?" I swallowed, and my entire body bowed as his mouth closed over my breast. The combination of the silk and his cool mouth was downright sinful. "About what?"

His head lifted, and he pressed a kiss to the swell of flesh above the lace. "About your senses developing faster than I expected."

It took a moment for the meaning of what he said to pierce the fog of desire. "What?"

"There is no way you sensed anger from me."

Before I could respond, his mouth moved to my right breast. He sucked deeply as his thumb and forefinger closed around the still-tingling nipple, drawing a sharp burst of dual pleasure from me. My hips twitched when he did something rather wicked with his fingers.

The shadows beneath his flesh thickened and spread. "Anger was the very last thing I was feeling."

Gripping the table, my chin fell forward as I struggled to focus on what we were talking about. "I never said I sensed anger from you."

He chuckled, nipping at my skin through the silk. "Yes, you did."

"I misspoke, then." I was breathing fast as Ash rose with fluid grace, his stare fixing on mine. The heat in his eyes scorched my skin. "You *looked* angry."

Tsking under his breath, he shook his head and stepped into me. His chest brushed my already sensitized breasts. "That is not how I appeared when I looked at you."

I had to crane my neck back to hold his stare. He towered over me. Anyone else crowding my space like this would've drawn out my temper, but he caused an entirely different reaction. My body throbbed with arousal as my gaze soaked in the brutal lines of his features. It was almost the same expression I'd seen in the courtyard. "You sure about that? You look the same now."

"I was angry when I saw what had happened to our people. You are correct in that sense, but that's not what I felt when I looked at *you*. Nor is it what I feel when I look at you now." His fingers curled under the thin straps of my nightgown. His head dipped as he tugged the lacy straps down, baring my breasts to the featherlight touch of his chest. When he spoke, his lips brushed mine. "Want to wager a guess at what I'm feeling?"

I didn't even attempt to do so as his fingers left the straps at my wrists and grazed the sides of my breasts. Nor did I try to put a stop to what he was doing. There were important things to be discussed: the *sekya.* Kolis. Those wounded and lost. But it was almost as if his touch, the sound of his voice, and his words had woven a sensual spell.

"When I saw you, I wasn't thinking about you being out in the courtyard, fighting alongside our people," he said against my mouth. "I asked you not to come to the Abyss, and while I would have preferred that you stayed out of trouble—"

I opened my mouth.

Ash took that exact moment to kiss me, silencing my protests regarding *staying out of trouble.* "I do not expect you to stand by and do nothing while those you care about are under attack." His lips brushed mine. "The moment I learned that the *sekya* had attacked the palace, I knew my Queen would be out there, holding her own. That is what I expect from you."

Good gods. That was possibly the hottest thing anyone had ever said to me.

"*Always*," he added, dragging strands of my hair over my breasts. "What I *didn't* expect was what I would see when I saw you."

The way he said that caught my scattered attention. "What...what do you mean?"

"You were shining. Gold. Silver. You were ethereal." His palms coasted across my waist. "It was as if the moon and the sun had finally come together. I saw you, only you, and you were the most beautiful being I'd ever seen."

My eyes drifted shut. I leaned into the table as he urged the nightgown farther down.

"And all I could think about was how badly I wanted to be inside you," he said, and I felt his lips curve upward at the breathy sound that left me. "How I *needed* to be inside you."

I shuddered as desire twisted sharply deep inside my core.

His hands settled on my hips. "That was what I was thinking about in the courtyard. And as fucked up as this is, it was also what I was thinking about when I found you with the injured. You were luminous then, too. It's also what I'm thinking about now."

Without warning, he spun me around and slid one hand to my stomach. My eyes flew open as he pressed his hips against my rear. I could feel him, thick and hard. The sudden change of position had a startling effect, stirring that hidden part of me that loved it when Ash took control. It brought forth a rush of wet heat and a little seed of trepidation. The unwanted anxiety was like a noxious weed, threatening to take root, but the feel of *him*—of Ash and no one else—against my back kept me grounded. His hold on me was firm yet comforting as his thumb moved over my skin, just below my navel. The caress was soothing, and after a few moments, the fires that burned with a dark, welcoming heat beat back the apprehension.

When Ash dominated, I didn't know why it aroused me to a fever pitch. Or maybe I did know why I liked it like this and wasn't yet willing to face it. But I knew why I allowed him to take my hands and place them on the table. I knew why I didn't put up a fight when he bent me forward, forcing me onto the tips of my toes. I understood how I didn't panic when his large hand smoothed down the center of my back, pushing me onto the cool, glossy surface of the table.

I could give up control and let go.

Ash could take me.

And I could allow it.

Because he understood. I trusted him, and I knew I was always safe with him.

"Just do me a favor next time and take the dagger with you," he said, working his forearm between the table and my cheek.

"I…I can do that."

"Good." Ash leaned into me. His lips were cool against my jaw. "*Liessa*?"

"Yes?" I breathed, staring at the open doors of the balcony beyond the pitcher and empty glasses on the table.

He lifted my gown, running his rough, calloused palm up my thigh as he used his knee to spread my legs. "I'm going to fuck my Queen."

Oh, gods.

His hand delved between my thighs, and I bit my lip hard enough to draw blood at the contrast of his cool fingers and my damp heat. At the rumble of approval that radiated from him and vibrated against my back. I shivered as his fingers brushed the taut bundle of nerves. My hips jerked, and I felt the thick head of his cock against me.

"And I'm going to do it"—his voice was a silky whisper in my ear—"just as you like it."

And he did.

I cried out as he began thrusting into me. Every inch of him sent a wave of pleasure so powerful through me that it bordered on pain. My breath quickened as he continued to fill me until not an inch of space remained between us. Gods, he…he felt bigger. I looked down at the arm beneath me, the one protecting my cheek, and saw that his shadows had nearly solidified. I could feel myself tightening all around him, and then he began to move, and the glasses started to clink softly against one another.

There was nothing slow or tentative about the way Ash took me. Each plunge of his hips was indescribable—each pull and push stimulating every nerve ending I had. I wanted to meet his thrusts, but his weight held me in place as his lips brushed across my cheek and jawline.

"I can taste your desire." His lips neared the shell of my ear as his strong body caged me in. "I'm drowning in its sweetness."

Fingers curling against the wood, I moaned as ribbons of shadows swirled along the surface of the table and around my hands. My eyes closed as I whispered, "Harder."

"Fuck," he grunted, picking up his pace and going deeper, *harder*. "Like this?"

"Yes," I panted, pinned firmly between him and the table, completely at his mercy. "*Yes*."

He drove into me with such intensity it was both a punishment and a reward. And, gods, I *loved* it.

Muscles tightened low in my stomach, and I felt myself rushing toward release when Ash suddenly shifted behind me.

He straightened, folding one arm between my breasts and the other across my waist, sealing me to his chest. My feet no longer touched the floor as Ash drove into me, seamlessly stopping and thrusting, grinding against me between pushes. His fingers curled around my chin, and I clasped his arms.

The rising friction created an incredible wave of pleasure that quickly swelled. Able to move my hips just a bit, I rocked against him. It was a raw need, caressing me like soft flames, arousing a blazing fire as intense as any before it.

A tight knot of tension formed, curling and unfurling. Ash drew me down on his length, hard, holding me tightly against him.

"*Liessa*," he rasped against the flesh beneath my jaw.

His head dipped, and I felt the sharp graze of his fangs at the space between my shoulder and neck as he started to shudder. It was all too much. Ash's release sent me over the edge, and I fell with a throaty shout. I came apart, fragmenting into ecstasy-soaked waves that rose and crested for what felt like a small eternity. Ash held me the entire time. He didn't let go until his breathing slowed, and he then kissed my shoulder.

"Sera," he murmured, his lips coasting up my throat and over my still wildly beating pulse.

A dual burst of lust and anxiety sliced through me. My eyes flew open as pressure clamped down on my chest, punching the air out of my lungs.

I saw gold.

Gold bars.

And I felt heat against my back. Oppressive heat instead of the comforting chill of Ash's flesh. Just for a second—no more than a heartbeat—my breath lodged in my throat—

Stop this.

I squeezed my eyes shut. *Stop this now. I'm not there.* I held my breath for five seconds. *I am here.* I exhaled slowly. *I'm with Ash.* I inhaled. *I'm not there.* As the panic loosened its grip, I slowly became aware of Ash's hand rubbing the center of my back through my nightgown. That didn't make sense. I hadn't pulled it up. Had he?

My throat tight, I opened my eyes and realized I was gripping his arm and once more staring at the open balcony doors, but it was from a much lower position, and I could feel Ash's heart pounding against my arm. It took a moment to realize that not only had Ash turned me in his arms without me realizing it and fixed the nightgown so I was covered, he'd also sat us on the couch.

Good gods. How long had I been freaking out? My heart turned over heavily. It had felt like only seconds, but clearly, it had been longer than that because I…I was in his lap, my feet dangling a few inches above the floor, and his hand was in my hair. Then I smelled—

"Lilacs," I rasped, my body shaking. "I smell stale lilacs."

Terror seized me in one breath, and shame scalded me in the other. My muscles locked up and then moved all at once. I had no control over them—over myself. I sprang from Ash's lap so fast I nearly lost my balance as I bumped into the table, knocking over a glass.

"Sera?" Ash said my name quietly, but there was no mistaking the heavy threads of concern in his voice.

Calm down. I needed to calm down. *I'm not there. I'm being foolish. I'm not there.*

Managing to take a deep enough breath, I closed my eyes and focused on breathing. "I'm okay." I was. "I'm fine."

Ash didn't respond, and the silence drove my eyes open.

He was on the edge of the couch, frozen as if he had been in the process of standing. His right hand was on the arm, his knuckles bleached white.

My chest rose and fell with a ragged breath, and I could've sworn his chest did the same.

"You're okay?" he said, the skin of his chest thinning.

I nodded, pressing my shaking hands to my hips.

His throat worked on a swallow. "What just happened?"

"Nothing." I took another step back and turned halfway to the table, staring at the overturned glass. "You didn't hurt me or anything—"

"I know I didn't hurt you." Ash had gone completely still. "I also know that wasn't nothing."

I stared harder at the glass.

"You smelled lilacs. Stale lilacs," he continued, his voice low. "That is what death—true death—smells like."

The temperature around me plummeted, and I swung my head back to him.

"That is what Kolis smells like."

A shudder went through me, and I forced myself to move. I started toward the table. "Yeah, he does."

His body trembled, too. "Sera…"

My skin stretched tight as I reached for the fallen glass. "What?"

"Talk to me," he said. "Please."

I swallowed, my heart squeezing. My hand was still shaking as I righted the glass. "About what?"

"About what you're feeling right now."

"I'm feeling kind of tired right now," I answered, forcing a yawn. "Shouldn't we be sleeping?"

"Sera."

Feeling backed into a corner, I reacted like any caged animal. "*What*?" I snapped. "What do you want me to say? I freaked out for a minute. It's no big deal."

"I didn't say it was."

"You're acting as if it is!" The wall sconces flickered as essence rose, but I wasn't sure if he or I did it.

"I don't mean to," he said, his voice softer. Calmer. "I'm sorry if I did."

Gods, my heart hurt as if his apology had been a dagger plunged straight into it. "You have nothing to apologize for." I moved away from the table and bent to pick up my robe. Once it was in my hands, I had no idea what to do with it, so I simply held it. "I'm just tired, Ash. That is all."

There was a stretch of silence and then he said, "Do you remember the cavern I took you to so you could clean up?"

His question caught me off guard enough that I turned to him. He'd let go of the arm of the couch. "Yes."

His skin had stopped thinning. "I told you then that I know it's still you."

I froze.

"You didn't need to remind me that it was still you," he said, his body still on the edge of the couch. "I know it's still you, no matter what has happened."

Pressure descended onto my chest, and all I could hear for a moment was the pounding of my heart. "Nothing happened, though."

His eyes slammed shut as he twisted his head to the side.

"I told you that before." My grip tightened on the robe. "Kolis didn't—"

"And I told *you* before that I know better." His head whipped to the front, and his flesh thinned once more. Shadows began blossoming on his chest, spinning at a rapid, dizzying speed. "I felt your anger. Every time I was conscious, I felt your pain. I felt your—" He inhaled sharply. "I felt your desperation."

The floor felt like it was moving beneath my feet. I hadn't forgotten any of that. I'd just refused to allow myself to think about how he had clawed at his flesh to get to me. That he knew, even though I pretended he didn't.

"He took from you," Ash seethed, and those four words fell like frozen rain against my skin. A sheen of white frost appeared at the corners of the walls. "He took your blood."

"I told you I stopped him."

"You stopped him *that time*." His head twisted again, the tendons in his neck standing out. "Please do not lie to me, Sera. You don't need to."

I shook.

"Don't you understand that?" His gaze swung back to mine. Eather crackled from his irises. "I know."

I jerked. "Know what?"

Frost spread over the wall, crackling. "I know how he is. I know exactly what he is capable of. And I know what he did to others he put in those cages."

I stiffened as my mind flashed from the things in the chest to how Kolis's throne was set so he had a perfect view of the bed. I thought about the chains. The chair by the bathing tub. How he'd *displayed* me. How he'd offered me to Kyn. How he'd found *release* as he held me to him, feeding from me. The stitches of the robe loosened beneath my fingers as I took another step back. Gods, I could feel the…the dampness even now.

Ash's body seemed to vibrate as he took a deep breath. The frost retreated a few inches. "I know you tried to convince him you were Sotoria. I know…" His lids lowered, and the skin around his eyes creased. "I know you did everything you could to get him to free me."

When he opened his eyes, they glimmered. "I *know*."

But he couldn't know everything. There was no way unless Kolis had said something…

My skin burned. I knew Kyn had told him what Kolis had offered, but Ash wasn't talking about that. "What did he say?"

"It doesn't matter."

"What did he say*!?*" I shouted, the robe slipping from my fingers. Panic blossomed in the pit of my stomach. "Yes, I pretended to be Sotoria. I told him I would consider things with him if he released you. He agreed but found every reason not to." A jagged laugh crawled its way out of me, and then the words came out in a rush. "It didn't matter how much I pretended I didn't want to rip his throat out whenever I had to listen to him. He always found a reason not to let you go. You were too angry. I was too mouthy—too stubborn." My hands opened and closed. "So, yes, I pretended to enjoy his presence and often failed at doing so because he—" I stopped. Kolis's anger at me asking about Ash's release after Ione confirmed that I was Sotoria resurfaced and struck like a pit viper. Just as his fangs had. I lifted my hands and then lowered them. "I told him you didn't love me."

Ash had gone quiet. His eyes never left me, but I didn't really see him. I didn't see anything. "He knew I cared for you. I…I think he knew it was more than that, even though I played it off." The breath I took felt insuf-ficient. "I told him you had your *kardia* removed. If I hadn't told him that, he..."

"I know what he would've done," Ash said, his voice sounding as pained as I felt on the inside. "He would've put me into stasis, and I may still be in it. But you protected me. You saved me."

I had.

I *had.*

I'd saved him.

"You saved yourself," he said.

I had.

I *had.*

"I saved myself before it was..." I trailed off, my mind flashing to Gemma, Aios, and all the other nameless, faceless *favorites.*

"Before what?" Ash questioned. "Before it was too late?"

"Yes," I whispered hoarsely, backing up and then walking forward. "It doesn't feel like it, though." I turned, then stopped. "Why does it feel that way? Nothing happened."

"Stop saying that nothing happened, Sera!"

"It's the truth, godsdamnit!" I screamed.

And it was the truth.

Nothing had really happened to me. I was *lucky.*

Ash was on his feet in the blink of an eye, the faint outline of wings appearing behind him. "And I know that isn't true!" he yelled back, causing every item in the room to tremble. Everything except me. "I saw the bruises, and I don't give a shit how he controlled his anger the next time." Shadows spun beneath the flesh of his cheeks. "He *hurt* you, Sera. He *threatened* you. He *showed* you off. And I know what Kolis said he'd do to you if you turned out *not* to be Sotoria."

I wanted to look away, but I couldn't.

"I know Kolis fed from you." His lips peeled back in a low snarl. "And I know—" He stopped himself, his eyes closing again. "I know he is why fear seizes you when you feel my fangs—when you never allowed fear to stop you before."

The breath I exhaled formed a misty cloud.

"He took that from you," he seethed. "Whatever you experienced with him, Sera? It wasn't nothing. Because I know a part of you is still there." His voice trembled. "Still in that cage."

The breath I took evaporated, and like flint struck against oil, panic exploded, stoking the Primal essence. It rose in response, flooding my blood.

A faint tremor rocked the chamber as my fingers began to tingle. And... gods, I could feel all these *parts* inside of me thinning, becoming fragile and brittle. A tremor ran through me.

Ash stiffened, and then everything about him changed. The hazy outline of his wings collapsed. The frost retreated. The temperature increased. But that...

That last part wasn't him.

It was me.

"It's okay." Ash spoke, but he sounded a hundred miles away. "Everything is okay, *liessa*." He stepped toward me, lifting his left arm. There was something on his skin—something bluish-red.

Blood.

Dried blood that had seeped from small, half-moon cuts in his arm. My mouth dried. My nails…

I'd done that.

I'd done that to him. I just hadn't seen it until now.

Violent energy surged through me, seeping into the air. The glow of the wall sconces flared through the chamber, brightening until the entire space was filled with light. Bulbs exploded, one after another.

Wind whipped through the open doors, lifting the curtains and knocking the glasses off the table, causing them to roll against each other. Causing them to rattle like the chains had as they'd been lifted, stretching my arms until I felt as if they would be torn from their sockets. My chest heaved, but nothing but the thinnest breath seemed to get through.

"Sera," Ash said softly as the chandelier swayed above me, casting strange, dancing shapes against the walls. "I need you to slow your breathing. Take a deep breath and hold it."

I heard him. I understood. But all I could think about as I stared at him was that he *knew*. His features were stark, and…

And I felt like I was going to break.

I couldn't.

I couldn't break.

I *wouldn't*.

My lungs seized. There was no air as the chasm that had cracked open in the Dying Woods split wide, sending a rush of every emotion through me. But it wasn't the long-buried pain and loneliness that rose, rearing its head and taking shape like a wraith that haunted every thought. It was anger, sorrow, and shame that coated my skin like thick, choking oil. The fury of being made helpless. The sorrow of all those who had come before me and the control, freedom, and everything else Kolis had taken from me—from us. The godsdamn shame I knew—I fucking *knew*—shouldn't be mine but still was because that fucking voice in the back of my head whispered that I *should've been* smarter when I dealt with Kolis. I *should've* prepared myself better. I *should've been* stronger. If I had, I could've handled Kolis better. I would've realized that The Star was above me the whole time. I would've freed Ash sooner. If I had been stronger, he never would have felt my desperation and torn at his flesh to get to me. If I was stronger, there wouldn't still be a piece of me locked in that cage.

I would've been able to deal with this. Would have gotten over it.

All of it was too much.

My throat sealed. Panicked, I started to back away. I couldn't breathe.

I needed to get away from here—from it. I had to. I had to. I had—

The panic was snuffed out instantly, crushed by something feral and powerful. Instinct took over, and it was primal. Ancient. Wild.

And it wanted out. Needed to take back control.

Ash's eyes were wide and bright—too bright. "I've got you," he swore. "Always."

I could feel that wild, primal, ancient thing inside me stretching, and I knew it understood Ash's words.

A hum suddenly filled my ears. My blood. Heat swamped every part of my body. I noticed Ash's mouth moving and his features sharpening until I saw the pores of his skin and the faint shadows beneath it. I saw the blood pumping in the veins of his neck as a distant rumble jerked his head toward the balcony doors. My skin vibrated. Every part of me buzzed, and in the back of my mind, I knew something was happening.

Something was changing inside me.

A fire hit my flesh, filling my mouth with the taste of blood and ash. My chest rumbled as the vibration intensified. Gold-tinged silver light dots appeared on my hands and arms, and then they were everywhere.

Pain flared along the sides of my face as my jaw stretched and expanded, peeling my lips back. Canines grew. My nose flattened. My body spasmed, doubling me over. My lips peeled back more as my jaw popped out of its socket. My knees cracked and changed shape. My fingers shrank and thickened. Strands of silver-tipped gold fur sprang from my flesh, rapidly covering my hand as my nails grew and sharpened. The straps of my nightgown snapped. Silk slipped from my body as I contorted, bones cracking at the joints and then fusing back together. My back bowed as I changed. Shifted. I fell forward, my…paws landing on the stone floor with a soft thud.

My breathing slowed.

My heart calmed.

Taking a step back, I shook myself. The feeling was *amazing*. I did it again, letting out a pleased purr.

The air shifted around me, and I reacted. Sinking back, my tail swooshed over the smooth stone, and a sound came from within me that turned deeper and raspier. I bared my fangs, my muscles tensing as I prepared to leap—

The threat backed off, giving me space. Muscles twitched as I held myself still, staring at leather-clad legs. Neither of us moved for several moments.

A cool breeze sifted through my fur, drawing my attention to the swaying drapes. To the outside. Muscles twitched more. Anticipation pounded through me, becoming a need.

My claws rapped off the stone as I moved slowly toward the doors, and then I took off.

Crossing the balcony, I leapt onto the railing, balancing myself as I quickly scanned my surroundings. I jumped, landing on the ground below.

I didn't even feel the impact.

This time?

I shook my head. It didn't matter. I was free. I picked up my pace, breaking out into a run.

"Open the gates!" a voice shouted from behind me. "Now."

A deep voice brimming with authority. One accustomed to giving commands and being obeyed.

A familiar one.

An important one.

The cork shoved deep into the neck of the vessel loosened. I started to slow down.

Ahead, the gates swung open, and bodies scattered. The urge to give chase, to hunt them down, hit me, but the desire to run was greater.

So, I did.

I ran.

I passed the gates and the different scents. I sprinted down the road, my ears twitching as I processed the sounds around me. Leaves rustled, shaken by the breeze. Farther up, near the starlight, wings beat the air. But closer, I heard the rush of water over rocks. I followed that sound, veering off the road. A channel of water came into view, and on the other side, a forest. There. I wanted to be there.

Steering clear of the crimson-and-silver flowers, taller grass grazed the sides of my stomach. I neared the river and eyed the churning water, searching for a way across. I found it in a series of rocks jutting from the surface. I dashed down the riverbank, my paws sinking into the softer, damp ground. Reaching the edge, I jumped, landing on a slick rock and sliding an inch or two. Cold water lapped at my legs and dampened my tail. Inching to the edge, I sank down and batted at the flying droplets until I focused on my clawed paw.

In the starlight, I could see that the fur appeared silver, but when the breeze ruffled the strands, I saw the gold underneath.

Sound caught my attention, and I flattened my ears. It was barely audible over the babbling of the water, but I heard something on all fours. Something running. Something larger than me.

I leapt to the next boulder and then the third before making the longer jump.

Water splashed, soaking my lower body as I landed in the shallow water near the riverbank. Making my way onto dry land, I shook the water from my fur and then took off once more.

I ran through the trees, leaping over rocks and fallen limbs. I ran straight into the thick darkness of the deeper forest, dashing between the trunks. I picked up different scents as I ran. Earthy tones. Floral notes of blossoming flowers. The hint of rain and sea salt. I ran right and then left.

I ran and ran, my taut muscles stretching and burning. Seconds turned to minutes. Minutes became hours. And still, I ran, my lungs taking in deep, filling breaths as the sky through the trees lightened to a deep violet-blue. I kept running, stopping every so often to inspect a small mound of rocks or investigate a strange scent.

A cluster of small, white-petaled flowers caught my eye. I sank down on my belly before them. They were some sort of daisy. My tail swished over the mossy forest floor as my ears picked up the sound of buzzing. Insects. I tracked a small, black bug hopping from petal to petal—

A different sound reached me. Heavier, repetitive thuds.

I rose, darting around the flowers. I ran, enjoying the feel of the wind in my fur, the air in my lungs, and the dirt beneath my paws. Eventually, the trees thinned, and the scent of the sea grew stronger. I slowed, crossing a meadow of thin reeds taller than me. The land dipped and then rose again as the sky above continued to lighten. I rushed up the hill, spotting a faint mist at the top—

Dirt crumbled under my feet. Hissing, I scrambled back from the edge of a cliff—a bluff. Staying on much more stable ground, I sank low to the ground and squinted. Through the mist, I saw blue.

A new scent reached me. I swung around, tracking the movement of the reeds several yards away. I prowled to the left. The stalks shuddered, foot by foot.

Throwing myself to the side, I dug into the ground and ran again, racing along the bluff. I picked up speed. It didn't feel like I even touched the ground. I ran until the mist seeped over the cliff, forcing me back a few feet and into the reeds. Then I kept running, bursting from the reeds and onto a road.

A wall of thick, swirling mist rose in front of me. I skidded, kicking up loose dirt. The thick hairs all over my body stood on end as I eyed the mist. I knew this place.

I crept along the barrier, picking up the sound of something else in the reeds, moving closer. My muscles tensed. I'd been here before. This was a gateway to the mortal realm, to my…

To my lake.

Home?

Yes.

And no.

Pieces of me started fusing back together. Pieces I wanted. Others I didn't as I stopped in front of the thickest part of the Primal mist. Behind me, the reeds continued brushing against one another, swishing in time with my heartbeat.

I could will the Primal mist to part. I could open the gateway. I could because I could do anything I wanted—

A scent reached me. Fresh and citrusy and stronger than before. I spun, a low growl rumbling from my throat as the reeds shook and parted.

A wolf stalked out onto the road, its fur a glossy silver in the dimming starlight and lavender-streaked skies. The beast was huge, a good head taller than me, broader at the shoulders. And a predator to his core.

But he was a beautiful creature, and I wanted to run again because I knew he would give chase. He'd been doing so for hours, tracking me across the river and into the woods. It was in his nature to do so.

But he hadn't been hunting me. I knew this, even in my…*nota* form. He'd been watching over me, as he had done for most of my life.

The silver beast drew closer, its intelligent gaze locking with mine. Silver eyes.

I froze.

The wolf stopped a foot from me and then changed. It was like the stars themselves danced over the wolf's fur in a wave of shimmering, silvery light that lasted for only a second or two. The silver fur retracted. Hard, golden-bronze flesh appeared. Muscles lengthened, becoming leaner. Paws shrank and thinned, becoming fingers. Legs with a dusting of dark hair formed, and then arms.

His scent…

A man now crouched before me in the same place the wolf had been—a russet-haired man I knew was tall even though he wasn't standing.

My gaze flickered over his features. The high, broad cheekbones were familiar. So was the full mouth. I…I knew those lips. Had felt them on my skin. Heard them whisper sweet words. But this was no mere man. He was powerful.

Primal.

A Primal of Death.

And he was…

The mist drifted over the road, drawing my attention back to the wall. To the gateway.

"*Liessa*," he spoke, and I shuddered at the shadowy sound of his voice. "You can't go through there. Not like this."

My head snapped back to his, and our eyes locked.

"Plus, you must be tired," he said, keeping his voice low. Gentle. "You've been running for hours." He glanced up at the pink-and-purple-streaked sky. "Dawn is approaching." His chest rose in a shallow breath, and then he extended a hand. "Let's go home."

Home.

I leaned forward and sniffed his hand. Fresh air. Citrus. His scent.

My other half.

My heartmate.

My King.

Husband.

My everything.

He was *mine*, and I was *his*.

The cork in the neck of the vessel loosened even more. I became more of myself and less the wild, free animal. My gaze shot to his arm. The four half-moon cuts were gone. So was the blood, but I could still see it in my mind. My head lowered.

He dropped his arm. "I'm fine, *liessa*," he assured me, somehow sensing where my mind had gone. "But I'll be perfect once you come back to me."

I wanted that, but I…

I wanted to be free. There was no looming war or crown I didn't even want. I was stronger in this form. I was myself. Nothing could gain the upper hand. If they tried, they wouldn't have a hand—or a head. In this form, I could be the monster.

He lifted his arm again, once more extending a hand to me.

Hissing, I swiped out a paw in warning.

He didn't even flinch.

His hand didn't waver.

"Come back to me." He tilted his head, and a lock of hair kissed his cheek. "Will you do that? Please?"

A shudder went through me. I was never able to deny him when he said please. No matter what. No matter what form I took—unless it was for something I wasn't ready to share.

I stepped toward him and then stopped. I wasn't even sure how I'd turned into this or why it had happened, so I didn't know how to come back to him.

"All you have to do is will it." A charge of energy passed between us as his fingers sifted through the fur on my cheek. "Like you do when using the eather. Just want it, *liessa*."

Something beautiful.

Something powerful.

Closing my eyes, I nuzzled his palm and then concentrated. I wanted it, so I willed it.

The change came at me faster than before. Silvery light appeared all over my limbs and then washed over my body just as it had done with Ash. The process was far more fluid. Tendons loosened as my bones contracted, snapping back into place. My fingers thinned and lengthened, and my jaw shrank. I felt my hair slide over my shoulders, but I never felt the roughness of the road beneath my bare knees.

Ash didn't allow that.

He swept me up in his arms and rose. He didn't speak as he held me tightly against him, his cool body a relief against my overly hot skin. For several moments, I just focused on his thumb smoothing back and forth along my side, but inevitably, the reality of the situation rose.

"I…" Wincing, I cleared my throat. "I don't know what happened."

"It was your *nota*." One hand ran up my back, slipping under my hair.

"The *nota* is still you, but it's the most instinctual part of your Primal being. Just like with the eather, it can respond to your emotions or a potential threat."

"Great," I murmured. "So, what you're saying is that the next time I'm anxious, I'm just going to shift into a cave cat and eventually end up naked somewhere?"

"Not necessarily, *liessa*." His tone had lightened, but only for a too-quick moment. "It has to be pretty severe for that to happen. At least, now. After the first time you shift, you have more control over it."

That would be a relief, except for the fact that I clearly had no control over my anxiety, my breathing…or my own head.

Turning, I looked down at his arm once more. I couldn't believe I'd hurt him. I couldn't believe I'd done any of that.

Shame scalded my cheeks. "I'm…I'm sorry."

His arms tightened around my waist. "*Liessa*, you have nothing to apologize for."

Gods, that wasn't true. "I scratched you."

"Barely."

"You bled."

"You've stabbed me before," he reminded me.

"But that was intentional. Kind of."

A rough chuckle teased the wisps of hair at my temple. The sound of his laugh caused the corners of my lips to tip up, but the humor was all too brief.

I really couldn't believe what had happened. That I had freaked out like that and lost control. That he knew I was afraid of him feeding. That I *was* even afraid of that. That I could somehow forget that it was Ash I was with.

That he knew a piece of me remained in that cage.

"I'm tired," I said hoarsely, and it was true. A bone-deep exhaustion had settled over me.

Without saying a word, Ash shadowstepped us back to the bedchamber and then took me to bed. I was sure I had dirt on me, and the gods only knew what else, but I rolled onto my side and folded my arms over my chest.

Lying down behind me, Ash pulled the blanket up over us. A moment passed, and then I felt the weight of his arm on my waist. Immediately, my mind wanted to go back to when I was in Dalos, to when—

No. I pressed my lips together, welcoming the sting of pain as my fangs scraped my lip. It stopped me from putting space between us. Even if it felt like I did at that moment, I didn't want that. We slept like this all the time because the feeling of him touching me was comforting. Grounding. It was my thoughts that weren't.

His chest rose against my back once more. "Sera…"

I heard it all in his voice. "I don't want to talk about it," I whispered, feeling my nostrils burn.

"Okay. We won't," Ash said without hesitation, but I felt the fine tremor that went through him. "There is something I need to say, though. Something you need to hear. You don't have to respond. You don't have to say anything."

I squeezed my eyes shut.

"I would give anything to be able to go back and take your place. Fucking anything," he swore. "But I can't."

And I was glad he couldn't because I knew he would.

"All I can do is tell you that nothing—absolutely nothing—has changed between us," he said. "No matter what happened, it hasn't changed how I see you. You're still the same brave, strong Seraphena I saw that night in the Shadow Temple. It hasn't changed how I feel about you. Nothing can. Nothing ever will."

Sourness lingered in the back of my mouth as I stood in the dimly lit library.

There had been no *almost* vomiting this time. The late lunch/half-supper I'd eaten hadn't stayed in me for long.

The only blessing was that Ash hadn't been present for it, and it had happened so quickly there hadn't been time for me to feel any sort of anxiety over it. He'd been with Rhain…or maybe Saion and Rhahar. Either way, Ash was now just beyond Lethe, where the army trained. At least, that was what Rhahar had said Ash was doing when I left the bedchamber.

He'd been gone when I woke.

Waking up without him by my side reminded me of how it had been when I'd first slept in his bedchamber. He was never there in the mornings.

My throat thickened as I stared up at the portraits of Ash's parents. I'd slept late. Well into the afternoon—no dreams, no nightmares.

I was positive the vomiting had everything to do with last night. Okay. Mostly everything. I was also nervous about the prospect of randomly shifting again. At this point, anything was possible.

I transferred my weight from one foot to the other, wincing at the dull ache in my thighs and stomach. My muscles were definitely sore from either the change or all the running.

Hurling noodles and rice everywhere probably also had something to do with the twinge in my side.

My gaze drifted over Eythos's familiar features. Gods, I still couldn't believe Ash had been the one to paint these.

I wasn't even sure why I'd come here. The library was a dark, cavernous place where sadness seemed to cling like dust to the tomes lining the shelves, the portraits, and the furniture. My attention shifted to Mycella.

She was beautiful, and there was little doubt the kindness in her eyes and the curve of her lips had been exactly as Nektas described.

And she had, at one time, harbored feelings for Kolis.

Disgust rolled through me, and I had to remind myself that was before Kolis became who he was today. Even I had seen brief—*very* brief—moments of who he used to be.

I didn't even know why I was thinking about this.

Actually, that wasn't true. It was because I was doing everything in my power not to think about the fact that Ash knew way more than I realized or wanted to acknowledge. And I didn't know how to deal with that. I didn't even know how to deal with myself, other than wanting to take a wire brush to my skin. And maybe my brain.

It hasn't changed how I feel about you.

I believed him. I know he loves me. How could I not? He had been willing to set the realms on fire to save me.

But how couldn't it change the way he saw me? Because it had changed the way I saw myself.

I'd thought I had been prepared to handle Kolis. That I could separate who I was from who I needed to be. After all, I had been groomed to do just that since I was old enough to be sent to the Mistresses of the Jade. To lie. Manipulate. Seduce. I should have been able to handle everything that happened and then some.

It wasn't like I'd actually *enjoyed* learning the art of seduction before I was even of appropriate age to be married, for crying out loud. It had been awkward and embarrassing to go from not even speaking about sex to discussing it in great, graphic detail with strangers, and then learning how to do it. It had been confusing and even scary at times.

My gaze lowered to the flickering flames above the candles set out under the portraits. Even now, my cheeks burned thinking about it. One didn't learn how to seduce with simple words. You were shown. You *practiced*, acting out what you were taught. And, well, the body didn't always agree with the mind. What I had felt when the courtesan showed me how to pleasure another while pleasing myself, and then later, when I *pretended*, had been a confusing-as-fuck mix of emotions. It had felt good, and it had also felt wrong. I had been curious, and I had also dreaded the sessions and the look on Holland's face when he knew I'd begun that portion of my training. All in all, it wasn't a great experience. I had gotten over it.

But I really hadn't gotten over that either, had I?

Pressing my lips together, I reached down and brushed my fingers over the hilt of the bone dagger. The feeling of it on my thigh was calming and helped me refocus my thoughts. My training didn't matter. What did was that, despite all of it, it seemed I couldn't deal.

It didn't make sense. Sure, Kolis had bitten me twice—almost three times. The first time had been mind-numbingly painful. The second time… He hadn't made it hurt. He had ejaculated, but whatever pleasure the bite had forced upon me had been brief. He'd slept beside me. He'd held me. He'd looked at me, seeing far more than I ever wanted, and he'd touched me. But it wasn't like I'd been raped. Nor was I like Veses, who had to pretend that she enjoyed being degraded. Kolis had known I didn't like what he was doing. I hadn't experienced what Ash had, repeatedly having to allow Veses to feed off him, either. And given what little I knew of Veses, she'd likely made it hurt as many times as she'd made it feel good. Then, there was everything Ash had experienced due to Kolis. I hadn't spent decades under the threat of the gods only knew what.

But I *had* spent years with the threat of Tavius lingering in the shadows of every corridor and his cruelty that bordered on sadism. I'd had to deal with the leering, too-long looks that started when I was far too young to be on the receiving end of *any* sort of attention like that. It hadn't been until the end that he'd gotten bold—and idiotic—enough to attempt to touch me. My last day in Lasania—the last day of his life—he would've tried more if he hadn't spent the night celebrating his father's untimely passing.

At the end of the day, though, none of that should affect me like it was because it was…

I closed my eyes, still able to hear Ash shout, "*Stop saying that nothing happened!*" He had been wrong, though. In comparison, what I had experienced *was* nothing.

But as I stood there, I wondered what I would say to someone else if they'd experienced what I had. Would I tell them it was nothing? Would I even think that?

But I should be different.

I had to be.

Because I couldn't let this be my ruination, and that was exactly what it felt like.

Awareness throbbed through me, drawing me from my thoughts. I tilted my head and listened. I didn't hear any footsteps, but even though Ash was shockingly quiet for someone his size, I knew it wasn't him.

Tiny hairs rose on the back of my neck as I turned. A shock of surprise ran through me as I saw the God of Dreams, dressed in black, standing in the doorway.

Dark hair shielded his face as he bowed. "I did not mean to startle you, *meyaah Liessa*."

"It's all right." I watched the *oneirou* straighten. Despite him staying at the palace, this was the first time I'd seen him since Kyn was here, and I kept forgetting that he *was* here.

"A library," he remarked curiously. Those startling eyes that bordered on amethyst swept over the chamber before returning to me. "May I?"

I nodded, reminding myself of what Ash had warned me before I even got the urge to read the god.

"Thank you." Thierran entered, once more eyeing the tomes lining the shelves.

After an awkward moment of silence, I found my manners. "I hope your stay at the palace has been pleasant."

"It has been, for the most part."

Hearing his response, I was a little taken aback. "For the most part?"

"I have not slept well here."

"I'm sorry to hear that," I said.

"Apology accepted."

I managed to stop the laugh before it escaped. I didn't know if I should be insulted or amused.

"The doors to this space have always been closed," Thierran spoke. "So, I wondered if it was another sitting chamber or something more exciting."

"I imagine discovering that it is only a library is disappointing."

His laugh was soft—airy, even—as he walked along the rows of books. "Quite the opposite, *meyaah Liessa.* I've always found libraries enjoyable."

"Then you must prefer the peace of one," I guessed, noting the sheathed daggers on each of his forearms.

"Typically." He stopped halfway, dark brows furrowing. "Though I'm not sure I would find this one all that peaceful. There's a…sadness to it."

Once again, a wave of surprise rippled through me. "There is."

"My awareness of such has caught you off guard."

"It has." I quickly racked my brain for what knowledge it contained on the *oneirou* as he began walking again.

"All *oneirou*—what is left of us, that is—are sensitive to…impressions left behind. Emotions leave an imprint," he shared, his attention shifting to the candlelit portraits. "Especially extreme ones."

My gaze followed his to the painting of Mycella. Ash's mother and Aios were cousins, so either her aunt or uncle was from Kithreia. I knew Mycella wasn't from there, though.

"Mycella was from Lotho," I said.

Thierran nodded.

"Many who live near Mount Lotho are gifted with unique talents. Walking in dreams. Prophesizing." He glanced over his shoulder. "Sensing emotion."

"And manipulating it?"

"That, too." He turned back to the paintings. "Mycella's father was an *oneirou*, one of the oldest. From what I knew of her, she could not enter other's dreams, but she could read emotions and control them if she so wished." He paused. "She passed down half of those abilities to her son."

"She did."

"The *oneirou* blood is strong, though. Known to skip a generation, only to reappear again," he said. "If you and Nyktos were to have a child, it's quite possible they would have the same abilities as Nyktos, or even those of his mother's father."

My heart skipped a beat as his words tugged at a memory. Something I should have remembered—

"But that's neither here nor there." Thierran faced me. "When we first met, you tried to read me."

Tension crept into my neck. "I did."

One side of his lips turned up, pulling the scar on his left cheek taut. "You failed."

"Correct." My shoulders squared. "I didn't try it on purpose. It sort of just happened. However, I didn't exactly attempt to stop myself from doing it either."

He stared at me for what felt like an entire minute. "Your honesty is refreshing. Besides your husband, who is still very young…" It was odd hearing him say that, considering he looked the same age as Ash. "Most Primals tend to be untruthful, even when it is not necessary. Which is amusing since the Ancients could not lie." His head cocked. "Did Nyktos tell you how I was scarred?"

"He did not." The swift change of subject left me a little unsettled. His unflinching stare was far more unnerving, though. "But I figured Kolis was responsible."

"He was."

I waited for him to continue. He didn't. "Are you going to share why?"

"No."

"All right, then." I was too tired and stressed to play polite Queen and hostess. "You're more than welcome to linger here for as long as you'd like, but please close the doors when you leave." I started to turn.

"I was actually looking for you."

I stopped. "For what? To complain about your lack of sleep?"

His chuckle was low and velvety. "I was."

My already non-existent patience thinned. "I'm not sure what you expect me to do about that."

"Deal with whatever troubles you."

I drew back. "Excuse me?"

"Whatever plagues you upon waking follows you into your sleep and calls to me," he stated, and I felt the blood drain from my face. "I can usually ignore it, but I was unprepared for the…intensity of such emotion. I need to stay awake to resist." A strand of midnight hair slid against his cut jaw. "You see, when someone dreams vividly, it's a siren's call to an *oneirou.* It prods at our most basic instincts to feed. Not on blood, but on emotion."

My stomach turned over, and my body flashed cold and then hot as eather stirred.

"The first night here, I was pulled into your dream."

I inhaled sharply. "You did what?"

"Like you, it wasn't intentional. It's not easy for us to resist the call when we are asleep," he continued. "I did not feed, nor did I linger."

I didn't even care about the feeding part because, dear gods, what had he seen? The golden bars flashed in my mind. "Am I supposed to thank you for that?"

"No. I'm just letting you know before you blast me into Arcadia." He smiled. "Which you appear to be about to do."

It was then that I realized I'd taken a step toward him, and my skin was likely starting to do that glowing thing it did. "I'm not going to blast you into Arcadia," I said, forcing my hands to unclench. "Through the wall, though? That's still up in the air."

His smile spread then, revealing a hint of fang, but it quickly disappeared, taking with it the ever-present glint of devilment in his eyes. "I did not tell you this to upset or offend you. That is the very last thing I want to do." Dark, thick lashes swept down. "What troubles you while awake will not give you peace in sleep, *meyaah Liessa*."

It wasn't like I didn't already know that. "And I'm guessing your reasoning for telling me this is because you would like some restful sleep?"

"That's not the sole reason, but yes, some restful sleep would be welcomed. I'm not a purely altruistic being." His lashes lifted, and there it was again, that twinkle in his eyes. But once more, it disappeared. "When someone, especially a Primal, cannot find peace while awake or asleep, it shows itself in their actions, decisions, and temperament, as the realms already know."

Eather throbbed as my eyes locked onto him. I didn't try to read him, but I *knew*. "That is how you got those scars."

Thierran said nothing.

"You were in Kolis's dreams, and he found out," I said. "I can only imagine what you saw."

"You likely know what he dreams about."

"Sotoria?"

Thierran nodded. "He dreams about finding her and then losing her. Over and over."

A savage sense of satisfaction filled me. "Good."

"I agree. The only downside was that he believed I was responsible for such."

"Were you?"

Thierran's chin dipped, and that glimmer returned to his eyes. "Not then."

An idea occurred to me. "Exactly how much damage can you do with another's emotions?"

"For example? I could take all the hate one feels for another and turn it back on them. Let it consume them," he said. "But if I can get my hands on someone, I can do much more."

"Like what?"

"I can put someone into a waking nightmare."

"Even a Primal—an old and powerful one?" I asked. Ash had said as much, but I wanted to hear Thierran say it.

"Even one of them." He glanced at me. "What are you thinking?"

"Would you like to get into Kolis's head?"

Thierran smiled. "I would love nothing more."

"Good," I murmured, filing that piece of information away as awareness suddenly coursed through me. My gaze flew toward the doors as I felt Ash draw near. It wasn't the same as being alerted by another Primal's presence. I was once again amazed by how some innate part of me recognized that he was closer.

A mixture of anticipation and nervousness swelled inside me, and I wanted to run toward the doors at the same time I wanted to hide. What I did was stand there, hands clasped. I saw the moment Thierran felt him. The *oneirou* stepped back, and his gaze went to the doors.

The stagnant air of the library shifted ahead of Ash, coming alive in the seconds before he appeared in the doorway.

My breath caught at the sight of him. I was immediately reminded of the night of my coronation. The curve of his hard jaw was the same. The lines of his features just as striking. His hair was free, brushing his dark gray tunic. Silver scrollwork lined the collar and cut diagonally across his broad chest. Leather pants the same hue as the tunic molded to his body. The cuff on his upper arm glinted despite the dim lightning.

Ash nodded in Thierran's direction. "I would like to speak with my wife," he said, and my heart did a hundred different silly things, including plummeting to my toes when he added, "Alone."

Thierran skedaddled right out of the library without another word. He clearly sensed the tension, which meant there was *definitely* tension.

My legs felt numb as the doors swung shut behind Thierran, closing quietly.

"I'm surprised to find you in here," he said, his attention fastened on the portraits. "With Thierran."

"You and me both." I smoothed my hands over my hips. "He was walking by and saw me in here. Apparently, he was curious about what this chamber was."

Ash stopped beside me, his hands clasped behind his back. "I can only imagine what kind of conversation took place."

I really hoped he couldn't, at least when it came to what Thierran said before Ash arrived. "We actually talked about your mother. I didn't know she was *oneirou*."

"Half *oneirou*," he corrected.

"It surprised me initially, but it makes sense—your abilities and all." I looked up at her painting. "He said your mother wasn't someone to mess with."

"She could affect other's emotions," he confirmed. "Though my father said it was rare that she did so. She felt the same way about it as you do with compulsion." He was quiet for a moment. "What drew you to the library? This space is usually empty."

Everyone seemed to avoid this room, likely due to the sadness Thierran had spoken of. Except for today. "It's quiet."

"That it is."

I stared up at his unreadable profile. There wasn't any coldness to his voice, but his tone was nearly the same as it had been after I found Veses feeding on him and demanded to be set free once Kolis was taken care of. He sounded…closed off. Like a wall had been erected.

My stomach hollowed, and I quickly looked away from him. Or was it my imagination? My fears that, despite what he'd said to me in the early morning hours, he wouldn't look at me the same. My gaze inched back to him. But that didn't make sense. Ash had known. He'd always known. And I'd just been over here pretending he didn't.

But I hadn't seen him all afternoon or evening, and that wasn't like him. Not anymore. And I…

I wanted to ask if he was upset, but the words wouldn't come to my tongue. I just wanted him to look at me.

"How are you feeling?" he asked.

"A little sore. I mean, my muscles," I quickly amended, the back of my throat burning. "From all the running." I took a shallow breath as my gaze dropped to my hands. "I don't think I've ever run that much in my life. And I hate running."

"Your *nota* appears to love doing so," he remarked.

I nodded, staring at the golden swirl on the top of my hand. "Will it always be like that? Running for hours?"

"Likely not. The first time is always intense and driven by animal instinct."

"I didn't realize running aimlessly was a part of a cave cat's instinct." I ran a finger over the swirl. "Would've thought hunting would be the first item on the list."

"I suppose we should be glad it wasn't."

My lips quirked at that. "Yeah. That could've been a problem."

There was a beat of silence. "I didn't think you'd be able to shift so soon," he said. "Either way, I wish your first time in your *nota* form was different. I wanted it to be a good experience for you."

"It was." I looked up. Silvery eyes locked with mine, and my heart started pounding. "I mean, it wasn't bad. It was kind of freeing. Even the running. I wasn't thinking…"

Wisps of eather appeared in his eyes. "About?"

"Anything. My mind was quiet," I admitted. "It's never quiet." I cleared my throat. "Anyway, I saw Bele and Aios a little bit ago. I'm surprised they didn't know I shifted last night. I would've thought the guards would have said something."

"The guards saw nothing out of the ordinary last night."

"Uh…"

"That is if they wish to keep their eyes and tongues," he added.

My mouth dropped open. "You threatened them to keep silent."

"I would never," he murmured.

"Ash," I said, my brows lifting. "There really wasn't any reason to do that. What bad things could they have said about seeing me in my *nota* form?"

"Nothing," he said. "But if they talked, and those they told talked, you would hear about it. I know we haven't had much time with each other, but I know how your mind works." He paused. "Mostly. But in this case, you would've worried that others were speaking about what they saw last night. You would begin thinking they somehow knew what caused it."

"That's not…" My lips pursed. "Okay. You're completely right."

Ash smirked, looking back at the paintings.

"Thank you."

"Not necessary." He tipped up his chin.

But it was.

It was sweet and thoughtful of him to ensure that no one spoke about my wild run through the courtyard and beyond. I probably shouldn't think him threatening others was sweet, but he *was* protecting me, even if just from words and speculation.

And gods, that made me feel like I wasn't worthy of him—not in a self-deprecating way, but in how it made me want to be *better* in every way.

And I knew how to start.

I'd always known.

Taking a deep breath, I looked up at him. I needed to talk to him. Ash watched me, the glow of eather vivid behind his pupils.

His mouth opened, but awareness throbbed through me, and a few seconds later, I saw that he felt it. "A Primal has arrived." He glanced at the door. "Do you know who it is?"

Clearing my mind took a few moments, but as I focused on the fading throb of awareness, the hazy image of the Primal of Accord and War formed in my mind. "Attes."

"Correct."

"Huh," I murmured. "So, that's how you know who it is before seeing them. That's shockingly easy."

"It is if you give yourself time to pay attention," he remarked.

I snorted. Meaning it would require a conscious effort from me.

"I'll see to him," Ash said, then hesitated. His gaze flickered over my face. "I'll find you afterward."

A hundred different things rose to the tip of my tongue. It was all of that being-better stuff, but Ash dipped his head and pressed a kiss to my cheek.

Then, he was gone.

Ash went to meet with Attes, who likely wanted to update him on what he'd found in the Undying Hills, but I didn't leave the library. However, I wasn't alone for long. This time, I heard the footsteps nearing the chamber.

"Sera?" Bele's voice floated in from the hall.

I turned, seeing both her and Aios in the doorway. "Hey."

"What are you doing in here?" Bele asked, drifting into the library.

I shrugged. "I was looking for something to read."

The Primal's eyes narrowed on me. "You…are so boring now."

"Bele." Aios sighed, smoothing a hand over her peach tunic. She brushed past Bele, her eyes filling with concern. "Are you feeling unwell?"

"I'm so glad you asked that." Bele crossed her arms. "I was wondering the same, but figured I'd get yelled at for saying you look like you haven't slept in a week."

My stomach twisted sharply. Had they heard about my wild, late-night run? Other than Rhahar, I hadn't seen anyone else. They must have. Guards had seen me, and who wouldn't talk about a large silver cave cat sprinting across the courtyard? "I shifted into my *nota* late last night and ended up running around for…" I trailed off, noticing both goddesses were gaping at me. "So, you *didn't* hear about that?"

"No." Bele drew out the word.

"I thought maybe you hadn't gotten much sleep because of the attack," Aios stated.

Gods, I wanted to smack myself. Somehow, that had completely slipped my mind. Still, I was surprised they hadn't heard.

"What is your *nota*?" Bele demanded.

"A cave cat." My head cocked. "Yours?"

"An owl. Just like Hanan." Her eyes rolled. "What the fuck am I supposed to do with that?"

Aios placed a hand on Bele's side. "Be a beautiful, wise huntress."

"Owls are creepy," I said.

"No, they're not," Aios insisted, shooting me what could only be described as a look of desperation. "They are wonderful creatures."

"I don't know about that," I went on. "How they turn their heads is weird."

Bele looked like she wanted to do more than give me the middle finger.

"Thanks," Aios grumbled.

I fought a smile. "What are you two up to?"

"I'm taking Aios to Sirta. That's where we were headed when I saw you standing in here, being all weird." Bele took Aios's hand and started backing up. "I would ask you to join us, but I'm mad at you, so I'm not."

Worry rose as I glanced between the two. "Is it safe for her to be there?"

Bele stopped, her dark brows rising. "I wouldn't take her there if it wasn't."

I winced, realizing how that had likely come across. Guilt prodded at me. "I'm sorry. I know that. I'm just…a worrier."

"It's okay," Aios was quick to say. "We appreciate the fact that you worry." She looked up at Bele. "Don't we?"

"Yeah."

That didn't sound convincing at all. "Wait. Why are you walking past the library if you're taking her to Sirta? Wouldn't you just shadowstep to your Court?"

"I don't like shadowstepping between Courts when I'm inside a building," Bele answered. "It's weird."

My brow furrowed. "Why is that weird?"

"I feel like I'm going to accidentally step through or into a wall." Bele shuddered. "And get stuck in it."

I stared at her. "That is…actually the weirdest thing."

"I say this with the deepest respect possible," Bele replied. "Fuck you, *meyaah Liessa*."

"All right." Aios tugged on Bele's hand. "Let's go before you end up getting thrown through a wall."

Bele blew me a kiss, and I smiled as Aios dragged her toward the doors. I started to turn back to the portraits when I heard Aios say, "Can you give us a moment?"

Thinking she was talking to me, I turned, only to realize she was speaking to Bele.

"A moment where I can't be involved?" Bele asked.

"Yep."

"Why—?" Aios cut Bele off with a kiss.

"Please?"

"How can I say no after you kiss me?" Bele grumbled. "That's an unfair tactic." She stepped back, looking over Aios's head toward me for a moment.

"I'll be outside."

"Thank you, love."

I looked away and saw an all-too-familiar heated look fill Bele's stare. Several moments passed before I heard the library doors close.

"What's up?" I said, looking over my shoulder.

Aios's face flushed prettily. She came forward, and her chest rose with a deep breath. "Was Nyktos surprised you shifted already?"

Not expecting that question, I faced her. "Yeah, I guess so. Why?"

"It's just that I've never heard of any Primal shifting as soon as you did. Bele just did it recently, only once, and even her shifting so soon was a surprise."

"The embers were already mature when placed inside me," I said with a halfhearted shrug.

Aios nodded, clasping her hands. "With Bele, she shifted because she was upset. We were talking about everything that happened when Kyn attacked." Her gaze moved from me to the portraits. "It was the first time Bele actually brought it up and talked about how she felt when she heard that I had…that I died." She sent me a quick smile. "She's not big on opening up—like someone else I know."

A faint smile reached my lips. "I guess Bele and I have more in common than we thought."

"Yes." She was quiet for a moment. "You know, when you were taken, I knew Nyktos would find a way to save you."

I raised my brows. "You did?"

"I wasn't awake yet when Nyktos left the Shadowlands to bring you back, but I heard how he couldn't be talked out of it. Not even Nektas could convince him to wait until the Shadowland's forces could join him," she said, causing my chest to squeeze. "None of that surprised me, though. His reaction—his need to get to you as soon as he could—that is. I've seen the way he's looked at you—from the moment he brought you here. Even when he was angry. I saw how he looked at you the night of your coronation, and I knew what that look of want that goes bone-deep meant."

"You did?" I whispered.

"He looked at you in the same manner I used to catch Bele watching me during one of our off periods. It was how I knew I looked at her." Her smile was sweet. "His love for you was so clear, etched into every inch of his flesh."

My breath caught.

"And I saw it on your face. I saw it long before then," she continued, sending a dose of surprise through me. "I heard it in your voice the night of your coronation when you asked if I'd ever been in love—what it felt like."

I remembered exactly what she had told me. "You said it feels like being home, even in an unfamiliar place."

"Was I not correct?"

"You were." My eyes searched hers. "You spoke then in the past tense—"

"Remember when I said yes and no as my answer to whether my relationship with Bele was new?" she said. "We've only recently rekindled."

I started to speak but stopped myself.

"What?" Aios prodded.

"I was going to be nosy."

"Please, do so."

I didn't need to be given permission twice. "What happened that you spent the last two decades apart when it sounds to me like you were both still in love with each other?"

"It's hard to say." Aios sighed. "Bele can be…"

"Difficult?" I suggested.

She laughed. "I was going to say she can be so strong that it's hard not to feel weak in comparison."

"Oh." My lips pursed. "Sorry." I leaned toward her. "You're not weak, Aios."

"I know that." She paused. "Now. But to answer your question, it wasn't just that." Her shoulders lifted in a shrug. "I don't think either of our heads was in the right place."

"I'm happy to see it appears you're both in the right space now."

"We are." Her smile grew, and she tilted her head. A moment passed. "And you probably think it was Bele who wasn't in the right headspace. It wasn't. It was me."

I quieted, watching her.

Her gaze was fixed forward, but I didn't think she saw anything before her. "It took a long time for me to move past what happened when Kolis held me. And even longer for me to realize that I hadn't yet when I believed I *had.* Like I was able to move on in certain areas but not others. And…" She shook her head. "Like you—like probably *everyone* who has ever gone through something like that—I didn't like talking about it. Especially with someone I loved. I didn't want her to…"

"See you differently?" I whispered.

Aios nodded. "I knew she wouldn't." Her gaze briefly met mine. "And you know Nyktos won't. But I also know it's hard to stop those kinds of thoughts."

"It's not that," I said, my voice hoarse. "I mean, it was. And maybe there is still a part of me that fears that. But it's me. I'm the problem." I gave a short laugh. "I don't want to look at myself differently. That's the problem because…" I dragged my hand over my face. "I can't even deal with what happened."

"With what happened while you were in Dalos?" Aios asked quietly.

I shook my head, throat thickening. My gaze dropped to my hands. Several moments passed as I ran my fingers over the marriage imprint. Maybe even minutes. And I didn't even know why I said what I did next. "He hadn't been with anyone since Sotoria."

Aios hesitated. Only for a heartbeat. "That doesn't surprise me. As I told you before, he never touched any of us."

"But he liked to…he liked to watch." My fingers curled inward. "Remember, I found the chest of *toys*."

"He did." Aios's inhalation—like her exhalation—was long and slow. "Did he make use of them this time?"

"No. Probably because I used one as a weapon." The smile that memory brought was quick. "And I think because he believed I was Sotoria. He wouldn't…disrespect me. At least, that's what he probably thought in that fucking messed-up head of his."

I ran my tongue over the back of my teeth. "He…he did touch me, though. The first time was at the beginning when I tried to escape." My cheeks warmed, and I hated that. The feeling. The thoughts behind it. "He used compulsion to make me behave."

"Was that the only time?"

I shook my head and then quickly looked at her. "He didn't go too far."

Her chin lowered, along with her voice. "He went too far the first moment he laid a finger on you."

"I know." I looked away, my nose and throat stinging. "He didn't rape me. That is not a lie."

"I believe you, and I am relieved to hear that," she said and then fell quiet. She let the silence stretch between us again. Giving me time.

Space.

At some point in that time and space, I told her everything. It was almost like I wasn't there. My lips and tongue moved without conscious effort. I stood without realizing it, and everything just came out of me. And when I was done…

"I thought I would feel better after saying something." A ragged laugh left me as I sat, my spine stiff. "I don't feel better. Fuck, I feel *worse* because saying all of that out loud makes me feel like I'm back there. I can even *smell* him. And it also makes me feel like I'm overreacting. That I didn't have it as bad as far too many others did."

"Fates, Sera, you are so wrong about that," Aios said, sitting beside me, though not too close, like she knew I needed a good foot of space around me. Because, of course, she knew. "Yes, some of us experienced worse when he tired of us and tossed us aside, but that does not mean that what you went through is less than. He held you against your will. Put you on display and threatened you. Repeatedly. He manipulated you and abused you. He forced you to do things you didn't want to do. He assaulted you. And if you hadn't freed yourself when you did, he would've taken what he wanted. I know he would have. *That* is not nothing."

Flinching, I closed my eyes. "I know. I know it's not nothing. I do." I folded an arm over my waist. "I think the hardest thing for me is the lack of complete…control. I had none. And…" I pressed my lips together. "Yeah, that's the part I keep getting hung up on."

"That's understandable, Sera. I felt the same way. We couldn't even choose what we wore or when we ate. But we both have control now."

We did.

"Last night, I had…I don't know. It was like I was suddenly back there. I lost control, and the *nota* took over." I pressed my lips together. "Nyktos hasn't fed from me since I returned. I've offered, but he says he doesn't need to, and I know that's not why. I freeze up every time, but…" I trailed off, remembering how his lips and flesh had felt earlier. Once again, his skin hadn't been as cold as it normally was when he didn't feed, and I didn't think it was his body replenishing itself. So, how…?

The nape of my neck tingled, and an image of Rhain formed in my mind.

Oh, my gods.

I jumped up, startling Aios. "I'm sorry. I need to go."

Aios rose, concern filling her expression. "Is everything okay?"

"Yeah. I just need to talk to Rhain." My heart thumped as I turned to the door but then forced myself to stop. "Thank you for talking to me. I…I know it didn't make me feel better now, but I think it will."

"It will," she said. A moment passed. "I promise."

Rhain looked up from the parchments he held as I all but burst into the chamber a few doors down and across the hall from Ash's.

"Seraphena." The skin between his brows puckered. "Has something happened?"

"No." I quietly closed the door behind me and crossed the lamplit chamber. My eyes were glued to him, searching for evidence that I hadn't hallucinated what my instinct told me. "I need to ask you something."

"Okay."

I sat on the cream settee across from the one he was seated on. "And I need you to be honest."

His expression immediately smoothed out. "All right." He placed the parchments down on the cushion beside him. "What is this question?"

I eyed him, spotting the sudden tension bracketing the corners of his mouth. "I think you know what I'm about to ask."

Rhain folded a knee over the other. "It would be impossible for me to know what you are thinking or about to ask."

"Not this time." I leaned forward, keeping my voice low because I knew Ash was just down the hall. "And I'm asking you to be honest, not because I am your Queen, but because I am *Nyktos's* wife."

The lines around his mouth deepened.

"I haven't fed him since I returned from Dalos, but there have been times when it's felt like he's fed. His skin isn't as cold. He told me it was because his body was replenishing itself, but I don't think that's always the case." I watched how Rhain kept his expression blank the moment I started speaking. "Have you been feeding him?"

The truth was instantaneous. It was in the slight twitch of his right eye.

My heart cracked. "You have been."

Rhain paled. "You don't—"

"No, I do know. I do," I stressed, and Rhain fell quiet. "I'm not reading you. But, gods, I…I still know."

His jaw flexed, and his gaze moved to the door. "It hasn't been often."

Another cut sliced across my chest. "Once is too many."

Rhain's head swung back to mine.

"And I'm sorry you had to do that," I said, my heart twisting until my chest hurt.

His mouth dropped open. "You cannot be angry with him."

"Oh, my gods." I stiffened. "I'm not angry with him. Or you. I'm…I'm angry with myself."

Rhain snapped his mouth shut.

"This is…" I rose, thrusting a hand through my hair. "I've offered to feed him, but he…" I dropped my hand to my stomach. "I locked up. And he…he knows why. That is my fault. I am his wife. It should—" My voice cracked. "It should be me feeding him. Taking care of him and providing for him as he does for me."

"No." Rhain scooted forward. "This is not your fault. It's Kolis's."

"Maybe in the beginning." I swallowed, looking at the door. I shook my head. "But…"

"Listen to me." Rhain rose and stepped in front of me. "Whatever hang-ups you have with that? Not your fault."

"I—"

"Shut up and listen to me."

I snapped my mouth closed, my eyes widening.

"And I mean that with all due respect," he tacked on, cheeks flushing pink. "Do you know how Kolis made Nyktos feed until he killed?"

Just hearing that sent a wild whip of anger through me. "Yes."

"And do you know that, afterward, Nyktos would refuse to feed? For months. He almost made it half a year before he got so sick, so weak, that he was maybe one breath away from stasis. It got so bad, especially after Veses started paying him visits that we feared he would slip into stasis, and we wouldn't be able to wake him. Or that he would be driven mad by bloodlust."

The air left my body. I knew it had gotten bad, but not *that* bad.

Rhain's eyes were an intense gold. "And I'm sure you remember how close he came to the latter the night the gods attacked you in the throne room."

I nodded.

"He only started feeding normally again after you came into his life, and he had a hard time even then, which I'm sure you also know."

I did.

"But if he has to feed from anyone else? Like while you were in stasis? He struggles to make himself do it. His hang-up when it came to feeding was due to what Kolis did to him—forced him to do," he said. "Do you think that is his fault?"

"No," I exclaimed. "Gods, no."

His brows rose. "Then why the fuck do you think this is *your* fault?"

"I…" I closed my mouth. "Gods."

"What?"

"You're right." I sighed and plopped back down on the settee.

He frowned. "You don't need to sound so disappointed."

I laughed hoarsely. "I'm not. It's just…when it's my fault, I can fix it, you know? I have control over it. At least, that is what I tell myself."

Rhain studied me for a few seconds and then returned to the settee across from me. "I've never seen Nyktos behave like he does around you." A faint smile appeared. "He still doesn't like to be touched by others. Nektas once said he was like that even as a child, but he is different with you. He always was. And it is more than that. Seeing him openly affectionate with anyone? I didn't think I'd ever see that, and I know I wasn't the only one."

I thought about all the times Rhain had looked stunned by Ash's displays of affection. His reactions always stood out to me.

"He loved you before he realized he could. And him coming to me to feed him—something he struggles with even now—is something he does because of his love for you."

"I know," I whispered, feeling tears crowd my eyes. I tried to push them down because I didn't want Ash to sense my emotions and worry.

"That is how he is changing what was done to him. It wasn't his fault, but he's fixing it," Rhain stated. "And even though this isn't your fault, you can still fix it. Fates, Sera, you even know how."

Gods, did I ever know how.

And it was well past time I did it.

Because we were supposed to be a team. Partners. We stood by each other's side. We would change the realms.

But not if I continued this way. Not if I didn't start trusting myself. And that was it, wasn't it? The key. It wasn't that I didn't trust Ash. I trusted him with everything—my joy and sorrow, my pleasure and pain. Like I'd said to Aios, it was never about him seeing me differently. It was always about me thinking of myself differently. That was the problem I needed to face. With Ash. And it couldn't wait. Thank the gods I no longer sensed Attes so I could.

Some of the rawness eased. "Thank you." I cleared my throat. "Thank you for providing for my husband and telling me to shut up."

"You're welcome. I think." His head cocked when I rose. "What are you going to do now?"

"Find my husband and talk—" I jerked as a horrifying scream pierced the air, cutting through the atmosphere like a blade. Concern surged through me, and my gaze flew to Rhain's.

He was still looking at me, brows raised, waiting for me to continue. It was like he hadn't…

"Didn't you hear that?" I asked, my voice barely above a whisper.

"Hear what?" he asked.

"A…a scream." Throat suddenly dry, I tried to swallow.

A look of worry settled onto his face. "What?"

I stared at him in confusion. There was no way he hadn't heard what I did. My skin was still pimpled from the sound. "I heard a scream—a kind I've never heard before."

Rhain rose, the look of worry increasing in his expression. "Sera, I didn't hear anything."

That was impossible unless my hearing had improved that much. But it sounded close, almost as if the person were standing right beside me.

"Sera?" Rhain inquired. He reached out to place a hand on my shoulder, but I stepped back. "What's going on?"

"I…I don't know." Turning, I quickly crossed the chamber and wrenched open the door. "Something—"

Another scream echoed through the palace halls, causing me to stagger back. It wasn't just a scream. There were many. A terrifying chorus of them. Hundreds. *Thousands* of screams brimming with pure terror and desperation.

My heart hammered in my chest, threatening to break free of its cage. My wild gaze met Rhain's. "You can't hear them?"

"No. I don't hear anything." He said more, but the cacophony of guttural wails and agonized shrieks drowned him out. It was as if every tortured soul in existence had converged in…

Oh, my gods. It was in *my* head. And the screams were so loud, blending together to form a symphony of brutal terror. My hands flew to my ears in a futile attempt to dampen the sound. The screams felt as if they were tearing through my mind, sending sharp, pulsing pain between my temples and shooting down my spine. I doubled over, my fingernails digging into my scalp.

Rhain reached for me, grasping my arms. My knees went out. I didn't even feel myself hit the shadowstone floor. I rocked forward as Rhain released me, rushing toward the door. His shout was muffled by the screams, each wave more gut-wrenching than the last. It was like the very realms themselves were crying out. There were shrill cries that sounded like nails on a chalkboard and low moans that evoked images of bodies writhing in pain. I slammed my hands against the sides of my head, but they still came. The intensity of the screams seemed to amplify, the sheer volume of suffering they conveyed becoming nearly unbearable as hundreds of them—thousands—wailed, pleading between gasps punctuated by sobs as they *fell.* And I *felt* them. I *saw* them. A mother's cry when her child was torn from her arms. A guard's anguished shout as an unseen enemy struck him down. A lover's desperate sob as they clung to the lifeless body of their beloved. The sheer breadth of the pain was staggering until the screams were abruptly silenced. They all fell, one after another…

Eather throbbed in my chest, so intense that it stole my breath. The essence kept pulsing—as if I sensed death.

A warm hand cupped the back of my neck, startling me. I looked up to see Nektas crouched before me, fainter screams still causing me to flinch.

"*Meyaah Liessa.*" His rough, gravelly voice caused me to wince.

"Where is Nyktos?" Rhain demanded.

"He was summoned to the Pillars of Asphodel," Rhahar said, his fisted hand at his chest.

His cousin stood beside him. "The souls can wait—"

"You don't understand," Rhahar interrupted. Nektas helped me stand. "He was *pulled* to the Pillars."

Breathing raggedly, I felt my stomach hollow. I'd never seen the draken look so pale—so disturbed.

Rhain stumbled back and understanding dawned on his face. "*No.*"

Saion's worried gaze darted between his cousin and Rhain. "What the fuck is happening?"

"As a Primal of Death, it is a summons he has no choice but to obey." The corners of Nektas's mouth were pinched white. "There are…" He looked away, his jaw clenching. He closed his eyes.

"Too many souls have arrived at the Pillars to be judged by them," Rhain answered.

Saion stiffened. "What?"

"Souls," I whispered, my hands trembling as I suddenly understood what had taken my legs out from under me. "Hundreds." A shudder went through me. "*Thousands* of souls. So many I could hear them. I can *still* hear them. Can feel their deaths."

"Fates," Saion breathed. "What could've caused that?"

"A…a disaster in the environment?" Rhain suggested numbly. "Like a massive quake?"

"No," I whispered, the nape of my neck tingling. "It wasn't that. There was nothing natural about this. It was…" I inhaled sharply. "I have to go."

Nektas's stare snapped in my direction. "No, you do not."

Shaking my head, I backed up, the essence thrumming. "I *have* to."

Rhain's eyes went wide. "Don't—"

The part of me that still operated as if I were mortal simply clicked off. There was no hesitation, no overthinking anything.

Following the cries of the dying, I shadowstepped into the mortal realm—into a waking nightmare that had once been my home.

Lasania.

Death was everywhere.

It was all I could smell when I shadowstepped to different parts of the kingdom. All I could see. All I could hear amid the wailing of those who remained. No matter where I looked. No matter where I shadowstepped. Death had come in the moonlight, during the quietest, softest hours, and reigned with supremacy over Lasania's capital. Neither wealth, power, nor age protected them.

And even though I couldn't believe what I was seeing, I knew. Gods, I knew whose screams I had heard first.

But I couldn't believe it as I kept moving throughout Carsodonia and saw every one of their faces, each with waxy, stunned expressions. A bone-deep fury sparked.

Bodies hung from blown-out windows. They lay in their gardens in pairs, faces forever frozen in horror, and crowded the narrow streets of Croft's Cross, having fallen one atop the other. They choked the Nye River and washed in with the tide, some getting snagged on the rocks while others got pulled back out to be forever lost in the Stroud Sea. Bodies dotted the beach's white sand, their arms and legs twisted. They bunched in scattered heaps along the battlements, forms broken from the fall.

And all the while, shadows moved silently through the city like wraiths, seeking to hide. But I saw them. I saw all of them. And I felt others I hadn't yet seen. I was not alone here.

My gaze lifted to the towers and turrets of the castle, and I *knew*. Gods, I already knew what I would find when I shadowstepped beyond walls that had done nothing—absolutely fucking nothing—to prevent the horror that had come this night. Still, what I saw in the courtyard brought me to my knees.

I saw them between the flashes of lightning—silver-and-gold strikes that tore through the night sky. Impaled to the walls of Wayfair just as the gods had been on the Rise outside the House of Haides, staked through the hands and chest with shadowstone. Their heads were tilted back, forced into unnatural poses that exposed their faces as if they wanted to be seen. Needed to be.

I didn't want to look. A tremor started deep within me, and I made myself see them—see the faces of the servants and guards, maids and stewards I recognized. I saw the dark-haired, pale-skinned serving girl who'd baited me into a trap the day I returned from assisting Ezra at the Healers. I saw the cook Orlando, the mountain of a man reduced to nothing but lifeless flesh and bone.

I saw Lady Kala.

My mother's most trusted Lady in Wait, who'd made that long walk with me through the corridors of the Shadow Temple upon my seventeenth birthday. Who was always with—

Long, blond strands danced in the wind, tangling with Lady Kala's brown hair. My chest compressed. A citrine hairpin glittered in the sunlight. A pretty, once buttery-yellow gown now glistened with streaks of red, but I heard her voice as if her lips moved.

I would like that…

I would like that very much.

A spasm jerked me forward onto my hands. There would be no future meetings. No desperately needed conversations. No attempts to try to understand each other. To forgive. No moving forward. Allowing time to tell new stories. No—

I rocked forward, lowering my head and squeezing my eyes shut. It did nothing to stop the rush of raw emotion. My cheeks dampened. I sucked in a metallic-coated breath, opening my eyes. A teardrop fell from my cheek and splattered off my hand.

Red.

It was red.

Another fell. Then another. The blood tears were no longer coming from me but from above.

I lurched to my feet, mouth and throat dry. I stumbled over a prone guard's legs—a Royal Guard. And there were more. They'd died quickly, their necks broken, as had those I'd seen in the city.

Eather throbbed and pressed against my flesh. I searched faces through the crimson-tinted rain, feeling pieces of me break away with each sight of mouths stretched wide in silent screams. Beige and brown faces. Pale and pink ones. Olive-toned and—

My throat constricted. My steps faltered, and I fell to my knees once more. My vision went black and then came back as I stared up at a jaw that was no longer stubborn. An awareness pressed upon me, but more pieces of me broke away when I saw none of the compassion and cleverness in her beautiful, once-warm brown eyes. I shook when I saw the pinstriped waistcoat, now black-and-red instead of black-and-white.

Beside my sister was her wife, her head turned slightly to Ezra as if Marisol had turned to see her love in the very last moments of her life.

They'd died side by side. Together. And I hadn't been here this time for Marisol. I hadn't been here for any of them.

Everyone at Wayfair was dead.

All of them.

And more than half the city now rotted in the rapidly forming red puddles. I couldn't comprehend the senselessness. Never in my darkest nightmares could I have imagined this kind of horror. This kind of—

Movement from the castle caught my attention. Too-dark and thick shadows filled doorways and moved in the breezeways. They were no longer seeking to hide.

They were how so many had been killed so quickly. Because what I saw weren't shadows. They were Cimmerian—senturion warriors that could pull from the darkest hours of night to cloak their actions. And they would've done just that, sweeping through the city like a plague of nightmares, leaving indiscriminate ruin and despair in their wake. Most had served Hanan but defected once Bele Ascended.

I knew exactly where they had gone.

The air around me charged, reacting to the energy sparking from my pores. A bolt of lightning struck the coast of Carsodonia. The night deepened, and my attention shifted to my kind, smart *sister.* At the Queen and Consort Lasania had needed. And then I thought about what Callum had said. How he'd wanted to visit with my mother one last time.

He'd known.

I'd told them all they had to do was call my name. Why didn't Ezra do that?

Electricity rolled down my splayed fingers as I stared at the loss of hope. Of a future. Eather seeped from my fingertips. I couldn't breathe, but that was okay. Grief gave way to fury.

The distant howls of the living faded, and awareness thudded in a hollow echo through me. The storm inside me spilled into the realm. Wisps of eather crackled around my arms.

"Kolis has come to a decision regarding the deal you offered. You now have his answer."

Muscles locked all along my spine. My heart stopped. My mind clicked off. Wind heavy with salt and blood whipped through the courtyard, stirring the stained silk gowns and mauve banners. Thick, dark clouds rolled in, blotting out the moonlight. I forced my stare from the faces of the dead and looked over my shoulder at Kyn.

Our eyes locked across the field of dented armor, bent shields, and still-sheathed swords. He'd finally gotten what he'd wanted, even though this wasn't the Shadowlands.

Vengeance had been unleashed.

And it would continue.

"He apologizes for not waiting until the *eirini* ended but he has grown rather impatient." Kyn's bronze helmet dulled underneath the clouds the starlight couldn't penetrate. A long spear was embedded in the ground beside him, its blade a milky white. "What did you think would happen? That he would accept your deal? That you would somehow rule? Win? You cannot win against Death. He is inevitable." Through the drenching blood rain, Kyn's lips formed a cruel smirk as he chuckled. "Life is not."

That laugh ended me.

I was no longer who I once was or was now. I was made of the anger and sorrow of my sister's tortured expression and my mother's forever-silenced voice. I was nothing but the fury and wasted hope of those small bodies left in gutters like trash and the souls lost at sea. I was nothing but a vessel of rage and the anguish of the great, unforgivable loss of all those who'd perished.

I rose, not as the true Primal of Life but as a Primal of devastating ruin and wrath.

That combustible mix poured into every fiber of my being. I turned to see Kyn and the Primal God of Wisdom, Loyalty, and Duty flanking him. An aura of silver and gold pulsed as a shockwave of ruinous wrath erupted from me. The ground began to tremble. Fissures appeared in the battlements. Dust clouds rose from streets and homes, and roofs peeled back, shattering in the wind, and walls collapsed. Flashes of vibrant orange, yellow, and brilliant, flickering red flames funneled into the sky above the capital. The earth beneath my feet cracked as I took a step forward.

"And you will soon learn that for yourself," Kyn promised, wrenching the bone spear from the ground.

The land stopped trembling. The wind ceased. Blood rain no longer fell. The very air itself contracted. I saw the flash of unease loosening the corners of Kyn's mouth, erasing his fucking smirk, and Embris's eyes widened. All the violent, devastating energy came roaring back to its creator. Me.

My head jerked back as the pressure built and built, joining my will.

"Shit," Kyn growled, launching the spear.

Eather streaked from my hands, slamming into the ground and then lifting. The energy rammed into the spear, shattering the bone.

"Fuck," Embris rasped, moving fast. His hands were a blur.

Hot, stinging pain erupted in my shoulders, causing me to stagger back. I looked down to see two hilts vibrating from where the daggers were now embedded.

Reaching up, I pulled the first dagger free, wincing as pain radiated down both arms. I tore the second one out. The midnight blades were slick with shimmery, blueish-red blood. I lifted my head, breathed in the pain, and let it become part of me.

I laughed.

And the wall around Wayfair turned to dust.

Stepping forward, I threw the shadowstone daggers. Kyn cursed and spun. Embris lurched to the side. One grazed Kyn's arm. The other struck Embris in the chest.

Too bad.

I'd been aiming for the head.

"Fates," seethed Embris, yanking the dagger free.

"Well, now I think you just pissed her off," Kyn spat, his head jerking to the right as he shouted a command.

Cimmerian peeled away from the walls and raced from the now tomb-like halls of Wayfair. More ran past where the wall had once stood. Hundreds of them. They rushed toward their end as the two Primals stood back.

Cowards.

They were fucking cowards.

Blood dripped from my arms when I thrust them forward. Bands of eather rippled out and split as I pictured the essence forming tendrils. They snaked across the ground, glancing over bodies before rising like vipers, striking their targets to my left and right.

Screams once more tore through the air when the streams of eather funneled through the Cimmerian's chests and heads. The cloak of night fell away from each of them, and I raised my arms, lifting them into the sky. The warriors squirmed, shouting as strips of their flesh burned off.

Kyn's glare met mine.

I smiled and closed my fists.

The screaming ceased when I crushed their throats. The sound of cracking bones radiated over the capital like thunder.

I stalked forward, bursts of eather appearing over the courtyard like dazzling, silvery fireworks. Blood dripped from my fingers, splashing off the soil. My chest throbbed with echoes of death. I didn't falter as what remained of the Cimmerian fell to the ground in clumps and pieces.

Ancient instinct fueled me, and a great howling wind picked up. I pulled the essence from the very air itself, as well as the deepest parts of the ocean. All across the land, dots of silvery essence appeared. The realm contracted.

Kyn started backing up, lifting his hand to blow me a kiss. "Later."

Shooting forward, I willed the eather toward him. Primal mist poured out of Kyn. The realm split open, and streaks of eather whipped out, slicing through the thick mist.

The essence slammed into nothing as Kyn shadowstepped back to Iliseeum.

I turned to Embris.

A thin, silvery line tore open behind the Primal, and he shadowstepped. He was fast, but my rage was unending—madness pouring from a bottomless well deep inside me.

I rushed forward, grabbing Embris's arm just as Lasania fell away. Violent power tore through the empty air with a scream, collapsing the mist swirling around Embris's legs.

I fell from the sky into a field of corn, landing on my knees. I didn't feel the pain as I rose, though. Looking around, I saw the green, rolling hills of the kingdom of Terra.

Ahead, stalks of corn shuddered, and Embris staggered to his feet. He whipped around to face me. I prowled forward, and the energy ramped up, building as stalks of corn bent sideways.

Embris shouted, and the air opened behind him once more, this time revealing the stunning violet clouds surrounding the lush green hills of Lotho. Staggering, high-pitched draken calls could be heard.

The ground cracked under my feet, golden wisps of essence rising from the fissures. Eather as brilliant as the summer sun streaked out, searing the ground. The eather stretched between us, closing the distance between Embris and me. Essence rose, wrapping itself around his legs.

The tear in the realm flickered and then sealed, silencing the draken calls.

Embris's head jerked around, his eyes widening. "You can't do this!" he roared, flesh thinning. Tendrils of eather snapped around his wrists, stretching his arms out until his back bowed. "You can't—"

I lifted my hand, silencing him with a twist of my wrist, shattering his jaw. "You will die in this realm."

My words set fire to the corn, and the hills lit with an orange glow. The sky above me cracked open just as my heart had done when I saw Ezra's face. Eather rushed down my arm, crackling and spitting.

All around me, the realm screamed, and I thought I heard my name in the loudest of them.

The valley shuddered when I rose from the ground, gripping Embris's boyish curls. I twisted his head back and then struck, sinking my fangs into his throat.

The Primal shouted, and his energy lashed out at me, stinging me through my shirt and breeches. But I didn't care. I drank deeply, taking in his blood—the very essence of the realms. I didn't care that I had never really spoken to this Primal. I drank until I felt him weakening, felt his breaths becoming labored, and his heart falter. Only then did I tear my fangs free.

Silvery eather lit Embris's veins, but it quickly turned golden. Blood leaked from the Primal's ears, nostrils, and mouth, then seeped from his pores.

"You will not pass into Arcadia." My lips brushed his cheek, peeling layers of his skin back. I dragged him into the air and away from the trembling walls surrounding Masadonia, the capital of Terra. I took him as far from the city as possible—from the bells I now heard ringing within the city's walls. "There will be no long rest for you. No peace. You deserve *nothing*. You will cease to exist."

The flesh of Embris's throat had begun to flake off, golden eather flooding the rest of his body. I forced him to his knees.

"I am the One who is born of Blood and Ash, *the* Light and the Fire, and *the* Brightest Moon, the *true* Primal of Life and the *Queen* of the Gods and Common Man. I will give you what you deserve," I whispered, but all in the realm, from the west to the east, heard my words. My skin tightened as I lifted my right arm. "I condemn you to the final death."

Lightning erupted from the sky, striking my right palm. A jagged bolt formed, as hot as the Pits of Endless Flames of the Abyss. Guided by instinct, I jerked his head back and slammed the lightning bolt through the underside of his jaw.

The end of the Primal of Wisdom, Loyalty, and Duty wasn't instantaneous.

Embris's flesh tore away, and what was left of his blood fell to the ground, boiling until it eventually evaporated and his muscles and tendons dried out. He experienced the disintegration of every fucking inch of his body, starting with his lower half. I left his head—his eyes—for last, making sure his very last second of existence was just as terrifying as Ezra's and Marisol's had likely been—as my mother's, the servants', the guards', and all those who were now gone were.

I let go, and his head shattered into a cloud of shimmery dust that spread across the cornfield.

Embris was gone.

And it did nothing to assuage my rage or sorrow. It only grew.

I stepped back as particles of eather began pulsing and expanding where Embris once knelt, coming together to form a ball of softly glowing energy.

Something was happening.

Tiny hairs rose all over my body, and energy pressed down, forcing me to move back even farther.

The ball of energy drifted into the sky and climbed until it was among the stars, throbbing all the while.

Everything stopped.

My breath.

My heart.

The realms.

Eather seeped from the top and bottom of the orb, then from its left and right. What remained of Embris's essence shuddered—

Then erupted in a blinding light, streaking to the north and south, then the west and east of the realms.

In the distance, half the Masadonia Rise came down. I could hear windows shattering as a scorching wind blew through Terra. For a brief second, I saw pink trees similar to those lining the Golden Bridge, as well as the moonlight-kissed thatched roofs of farmsteads and villages. I saw people running in the hazy glow across the fields. Women. Men. Children. They all ran in a desperate attempt to escape, but then it all went up like they were nothing but dried-out tinder. The trees. The farms. Villages. The people. The orange-lit hills—the lower mountains of the Undying Hills—that stretched all the way to the city of Masadonia crumbled into the sea, sending out a thunderous shockwave. A great wave rose, one as high as any mountain and as wide as the entire coast of the mortal realm. It blocked out the stars and moon—

A flash of intense silver cut through the night sky, and the arrival of another Primal thudded in my chest. In the shadow of the still-rising, deadly tsunami, I saw Phanos's silhouette. He thrust his essence-lit trident into the wave with a shout, calling forth a roar of powerful wind from all directions. Eather erupted from the trident, exploding into a silvery web that pushed the wave down.

The ground trembled where I stood once more, making me drag my gaze from Phanos. Where the villagers had fallen, shells of packed, hard ash now encased them. Hundreds of them were forever frozen, some sprawled on the ground in clusters. Families. Others were alone on their knees, their arms shielding their heads or raised as if they'd spent their last seconds praying to gods who would not answer.

Because we had brought this ruin upon them.

Fine fissures appeared where Embris had knelt and spread all the way into Masadonia. Small saplings wiggled free of the cracks all around me, growing, expanding, and rapidly becoming thick trunks with glossy, bleeding bark. Hundreds of trees. Thousands. Limbs sprouted like bony fingers, misshapen and bent. Buds sprouted from branches and unfurled.

From where the lower mountains of the Undying Hills once stood to the half-shattered Rise of Masadonia, a forest of dark crimson leaves and glistening bark rose forebodingly in the stark moonlight.

The once bountiful fields of Terra were no more. In their place was a forest birthed from soil drenched in Primal essence and mortal blood. A tomb.

The temperature dropped until I could see my breath, but it did nothing to cool my fury. Dark, choking rage rose like a seething storm, swallowing me. It was like a tempest of darkness roaring through my veins, consuming everything in its path, urging me to crush. Obliterate. It was in every heartbeat, like an echo of wrath with a name as I opened a tear in the realm.

Kolis.

I walked along the sun-streaked golden road, the scent of blood and death clinging to me.

Ahead, the polished marble and diamond Rise stood tall.

Through the mist shrouding what lay beyond, guards in golden armor rushed along the top of the wall. Several lifted gold-plated bows, aiming shadowstone-tipped arrows in my direction. Others exchanged wary looks. They inched back, their attention shifting to the dark clouds above them. It was almost as if they had been expecting me.

"Halt!" a guard shouted from above the gate.

That would not happen.

Eather swelled inside, and I lifted my hands. Gold-laced essence streaked out from my fingertips and raced across the ground. The clouds above continued to thicken, blotting out the sun. Some guards ran. Others fired arrows.

But it was too late for them all.

Wisps of eather rose, shattering the arrows as the thicker strands of energy poured into the diamond-encrusted Rise. Gold-tinged silver light spread, forming a network of veins that traveled the length of the wall surrounding Dalos.

I snapped my hands into fists.

The crack was like a blast of thunder, freezing the guards where they stood. All across the Rise, gold-winged faces contorted in shock and disappeared. The Rise exploded into fragments of stone and ash.

Lightning struck the ground as I walked forward, the diamonds beneath my feet shattering. Wind tore the purplish-pink trees from their roots and twisted their limbs until they broke. The smaller wall around Cor Palace came into view. It, too, turned to dust. I toppled the trees that bodies had once hung from.

The palace went next as I called for Death to show himself. I shattered the glass doors and peeled back roofs. I brought the walls down, and all that answered was a chorus of short-lived screams.

Chest throbbing, I closed my eyes and shadowstepped farther into Dalos, appearing just outside the sprawling fortress and before a line of ready guards.

Several arrowheads hit their marks, but I didn't care. I welcomed the pain and gave myself over to it because it was nothing compared to what I felt inside. I stalked forward, sending a crackling web of energy ahead of me. The lines of guards fell. I lifted my hand, ripping the heavy, gold-plated doors from their hinges.

"Kolis!" I shouted, entering the Sanctuary and ripping arrows from where they were stuck. This part of Kolis's domain had remained unscathed after I escaped.

It would not stay that way.

He'd taken my control. My sense of self. My *family*. I would take all he had taken from me—threefold.

A bolt of eather came at me when I passed the gold-adorned archways. I spun to the left, spotting several armed gods.

I sent one through the glass and another through a wall as I shot forward, dipping under a raised shadowstone sword. Catching the god's arm, I rose behind her. "Where is Kolis?"

"Fuck you," she spat.

"No, thank you." I tore into her throat, drinking deeply. Hot, thick blood poured into my mouth, and footsteps pounded.

Still latched onto her neck, I spun around just as a shadowstone dagger tore through the air. The blade struck the goddess between the eyes. Catching her sword as it fell, I released her body.

And locked eyes with another god. The stupid fucker charged me. Deflecting the blow, I landed a vicious kick to his knee, shattering it. He shouted, going down. I drove the sword through his skull and threw out my left hand. Streams of eather hissed through the air, hitting another guard as a pale-eyed Revenant took his place.

I yanked the shadowstone sword free as the Revenant came at me.

I didn't have time for their shit.

Twisting, I swung the sword in a high arc, cleaving the Rev's head from its shoulders. Remembering what I'd been told about Callum's head reattaching itself, I kicked this one down the hall.

"Kolis!" I screamed. The door to my right opened.

A blast of eather knocked the sword from my grasp, spinning me back a few feet. I caught myself before I went down. My skin smoked, my flesh charred, and I couldn't feel my blood-soaked hand. I lifted my head.

A god stood before me, breathing heavily. I thought he looked familiar as he lifted both hands and took a tentative step back, a lock of brown hair falling across his forehead.

"I'm not going to fight you," he began.

"Shut up," I said, snapping forward. I gripped his throat with my ruined hand. It hurt, but I drowned myself in the pain and sent a rush of eather through him.

The god's head kicked back, and he screamed, eather pouring out of his open mouth.

I dropped him, throwing out my hands. Eather spread across the interior wall. "Kolis!" I yelled. "You wanted this! Face me!"

He didn't appear, even as I moved deeper into the building, leaving a path of ruin in my wake. Panting, my steps slowed when I entered a windowless hall. I'd been here before.

I stopped and listened. The fingers of my good hand twitched, and my head tilted. There were sounds. There had been noises the entire time. Quiet ones. Moans. Whimpers. Some louder. But I didn't hear the rumble of a draken as my stare fixed on the wall.

Kolis wasn't here.

The son of a bitch likely suspected I would come for him and took his draken and most of his Revenants.

But I knew what he *didn't* take.

My chin lowered, and I pulled the essence to the surface. It pulsed and then crawled over the wall. I tore the innermost wall of the Sanctuary down, block by fucking block, exposing what Kolis kept inside to the sun.

There were many of them. Hundreds of Ascended. Most started to run, their skin smoking. Some came at me. Others headed for parts of the Sanctuary that still stood. None made it, their flesh catching fire. My gaze collided with the fine features of one not much older than me.

Jove.

I couldn't look away as his face contorted in pain—the same features I'd seen fear in not that long ago.

He'd been a Chosen.

But he hadn't chosen this. He hadn't chosen any of this.

The throbbing in my chest intensified. I staggered sideways and turned. Jove fell in a fiery heap. My gaze landed on the path of destruction I had left as the smell of burnt flesh filled the air.

Through the smoke and crumbled stone, I saw a section of the Sanctuary still standing with strips of white rippling in the wind. I walked through the smoke, jerking to a stop.

A group of Chosen stood huddled together, pressed against one of the walls. Most were veiled, but others were not, their faces masks of fear and horror as they…

As they stared at me.

"It's okay," I assured them, lifting a hand.

They shrank back, some even screaming. My gaze fell to my hand, where eather still swirled around my bloody, charred fingers, wisps licking the air. Through the gore, I saw the still-shimmering golden swirl of my marriage imprint on the top of my right hand.

Every muscle in my body locked up as patches of shiny new pink flesh appeared. What…What was I doing?

My gaze flew back to the Chosen—to those I would give a real choice to once I'd dealt with Kolis. They could serve as intended without fear of exploitation or return to the mortal realm. I would set them free. Not harm them. But it was clear they were terrified of me. And this time I…

I had given them a reason to be.

I reeled back, inhaling sharply, and shook my head in disbelief. Of course, Kolis wouldn't have taken them. He'd known I would come. All the guards were proof of that. Yet he *still* left them here. He didn't care about life.

Did I?

The strips of white billowed as the clouds overhead began to break apart. The sight of them cowering in fear was startling, but the realization of all that'd led me here was *monstrous.*

I'd taken lives. Countless lives.

Oh, gods.

I stumbled, my heart thumping. "I'm sorry," I whispered, my chest seizing. In my mind, I saw the villagers, their arms raised to a sky I'd brought down on them in an act of justice.

An act of vengeance.

I kept walking backward, hands and arms trembling. My thoughts raced. I had to fix this. I had to. I could. I *would.*

I returned to Terra. The bells of Masadonia had ceased ringing as I walked into the blood-drenched forest. Slivers of moonlight filtered through the heavy canopy of crimson leaves, reflecting off the ash-hardened shells of the fallen villagers.

I knelt by one and saw there were two. A man or a woman with another beneath them—a desperate attempt to shield a child.

"I'm sorry," I whispered, lightly placing my bloody hand on the shell. "I'll fix this."

I put my other hand on the ground. I didn't know what I was doing—it was instinctual. I summoned the eather, and it responded in a hot rush. My skin tingled with warmth, and gold-laced eather seeped from my pores and dripped onto the ground beside drops of blood that had fallen from me. I lifted my head and stared at the forest floor through strands of pale, bloodied hair. Tendrils of eather rolled out, casting a glow as the essence swirled under and over the shells of the dead, leaving glittering daylight in its wake. My fingers dug into the soil. Wisps of Primal mist seeped beneath them, curling and spreading across the ground.

Beside me, the shells shuddered, and the ash flaked off. Patches of pink flesh and ragged clothing appeared. Singed blond hair. My eyes locked with wide, blue ones full of fear and awe, reflecting the golden glow of eather. I pulled my hand back, and ash mixed with blood, smearing my fingertips.

"Momma?" a small voice trembled. "I had a bad nightmare."

The woman's attention immediately shifted to the small one in her arms. A sob shook her body as she held the little boy close.

I rose slowly, my body aching. Villagers stood throughout the forest, their faces pale or marked with confusion as they shook ash from their hair and clothing. They moved slowly, helping others stand, and some stood transfixed as the gold-laced silver tendrils disappeared into the mist, still gathering along the forest floor—

"Thank you," a man whispered, dropping to his knees, the weathered skin of his jaw slack. "Thank you, my—"

"No." I flinched as the man looked up at me how that guard Wil Tovar had. Others followed suit. Like I was a blessing. A miracle bestowed upon them. A benevolent Primal Goddess of Life. But I wasn't. I was the opposite. The nightmare the boy had spoken of. I had not earned their praise or worship. I deserved their fear.

"Rise and leave," I said, pushing with my voice—with my eather—until all were standing and backing away from me. "Leave this place." The corners of my vision were filled with silvery, golden light. "Leave this place and never return. There is nothing but death here—in the Blood Forest."

As they fled, I left and returned to Wayfair. To my family.

It was not quiet here. Deep, hollow bells rang from the Shadow Temple in a solemn rhythm of death as I limped forward. My gaze lifted to where Ezra remained impaled to the now-cracked wall.

My heart shattered again.

But I would fix it. I was the true Primal of Life.

I could bring them back.

All of them.

My clever, fair sister and her kind, loyal wife. My mother, who had named me after the brave and revered Queen of the Vodina Isles. The small ones in the gutters. Those in the sea, lying in the streets, and beyond Lasania. I would return them to what they were, just as I had with the villagers in Terra.

I moved fast, summoning the eather to draw the spikes from the bodies of those impaled and gently lowered them to the ground. I kept Ezra and Marisol side by side, not changing the direction in which Marisol looked. It didn't feel right as I knelt beside my sister.

Purpose filled me, and the humming eather rose once more. I reached for Ezra's hand—

"Sera?"

I spun, eather crackling from my fingertips.

Awash in a fiery glow, Holland stood before me, the heated wind tugging at the white linen pants and tunic he wore. Somehow, the pristine material remained unblemished as he stood among the dead—those he'd shared suppers and stories with. His ageless face mirrored those scattered around him. His expression showed horror. He wasn't looking at me. He was looking at everything around us.

Seeing him stunned me and conjured a wealth of emotions and memories—from when I was just a young girl holding a blade for the first time up to the last time I'd seen him in the throne room. In an instant, I was some other version of me. A mixture of that young girl and the woman he'd raised like a daughter.

The eather fizzled out. Pain flared all along the length of my body, and I took a stumbling step toward him.

His head turned back to me, and I saw that his once hickory-hued irises were now like Aydun's—bursts of silver sprinkled through the colors, appearing like the stars they had come from. "What have you done?"

I jerked to a halt with a wince. I didn't understand what he was asking. "What have I done?"

"You killed a Primal, Sera."

I drew back in disbelief. That is what he had to say to me? *That*? After everything? It took several moments for me to snap out of my stupor. "Do you not see what Kolis did? To everyone here? To my mother? To Marisol and Ezra?" My voice cracked, and, gods, it hurt. It hurt even worse to see Holland's gaze flicker behind me and witness his flinch. "I gave him a chance. I made him an offer. This was his answer. He nearly killed everyone in the city. He acted, and I am reacting."

Holland's chest rose with a deep breath, and he returned his gaze to mine. "And you killed nearly as many."

My head jerked back as if I had been slapped, even though I knew I had unleashed ruin upon those here and beyond. I inhaled through my stinging nose. "I'm fixing that." I started walking backward. "I'm going to undo—"

Holland took a step forward. "You cannot do that. You have already brought Marisol back once," he said. "You cannot do it again. Her soul is now beyond your reach and can only be released by Death—the true Primal of Death. Why do you think Eythos hid Sotoria's soul?"

Shaking my head, I looked back at Marisol, unable to see past how she had turned her head toward Ezra in her final moments.

"It is how the balance is kept," Holland continued. "You already gave Marisol a second chance. The realms prevent that from happening again." His voice roughened. "She is gone."

I didn't want to believe Holland, but instinct told me he wasn't lying. My shoulders curved inward, and a heavy ache settled in my chest. Only Kolis could release Marisol's soul now. I briefly closed my eyes as sorrow threatened to overwhelm me. I couldn't allow that. My hands fisted, and eather pressed against my skin. I opened my eyes and turned my attention to Ezra. I could almost believe she was sleeping if I didn't look at her face. "He doesn't hold the souls of the others."

"You cannot bring them back, Sera."

I whipped around. "I can't? I'm the true Primal of Life."

"I know what you are, but just because you *can* do something doesn't mean you *should*."

I inhaled sharply. "Do not start with that philosophical bullshit, Holland. My family is dead." Anger pulsed through me. "My city is nearly gone."

"I know. I know this hurts." He lifted his hands, and when he spoke next, his voice had gentled. "And I'm sorry. I truly am. This shouldn't have happened. It's not fair."

"You're right. This shouldn't have happened, and it's *not* fair. That's why I'm going to make it right."

"But you won't, Sera. You will just end up repeating everything that led to this very moment. You've already started to with those you brought back."

"This is different," I insisted.

"Listen to me. Please," he said, the stars in his eyes brightening. "You know what happens if you bring them back. Other lives will be forfeited to take their place."

Oh, gods.

I hadn't even thought of that. How many villagers had I brought back? A hundred? No, more… Two hundred? Three? That meant…

I briefly closed my eyes. "I don't care." I turned back to Ezra.

"You must care," Holland insisted. "It is the only way balance can be kept."

"Fuck balance!" I screamed, and lightning streaked overhead. "Where were you to remind Kolis of balance when he ordered this? Where were any of you? Where—*wait*." My entire body jerked. "Did you see this, Holland?"

Holland's eyes closed.

"Did you know this would happen?" I shouted. "And do nothing? You knew these people! You knew Ezra—" My voice gave out, and my hands fisted.

"Sera," he rasped, pain etching his features. "There are many threads, many possible outcomes. Ones we cannot interfere in—"

"Are you fucking kidding me right now?" I had to force myself to move back and look away from Holland before I lost control.

"I'm sorry," he repeated.

I looked down at Ezra and then swung my gaze to where my mother now lay on the ground. A shudder went through me. The gnawing pain seemed endless as another lightning bolt raced across the smoke-filled sky. "I told them to call my name. Said I would come. Ezra didn't do it. But I heard her shrieks—" I cut myself off. Anger and anguish flooded my senses. "Why didn't she call for me?" I looked back at Ezra. "Why didn't you do what I told you? Godsdamnit!" I screamed. "Why?"

"You know why," Holland said softly, sadly. "She would never willingly endanger you."

That made it worse.

Because this—all of this—wasn't just Kolis's fault.

"Ezra will be with Marisol and her father once more," Holland said. "You need to let her go."

I shook. "My mother…"

"You need to let them all go, Sera." His voice was closer. "This is not where you are needed, and you're in no condition to continue as you are."

Tremors ran up and down my arms as I closed my eyes again. "And where *am* I needed?"

"A god who serves in Lotho must be Ascended soon," he said. "The energy Embris's death released is making its way across all the realms. It must return to a vessel before it circles back—"

"I know what will happen," I cut him off. "That doesn't change what I must do. I have to bring Ezra back. I have to bring them all back."

Holland's sigh was heavy. "I don't want to hurt you, Sera."

Crushing agony formed a tight ball in my chest. I opened my eyes, slowly faced him, and all I saw at that moment was an Ancient standing before me. One who had known all along that those he'd laughed and fought beside would die like this.

Streaks of swirling eather brimmed beneath his flesh. "Eythos once found himself in a similar position. A plague struck down a village he favored. He brought them back—all of them—even though that was not what the realms needed. And he continued to do so, each restored life leading to others believing there would always be a second chance. And each life cost another theirs until he had ended the lives of as many as he restored. By the time he realized his folly, it was already too late. It was expected from him. You need to be better than that, Sera."

"I don't care what Eythos did," I spat. "Nor do I care about being better than him or anyone. That is what led to this!"

"How?" Holland shook his head. "How can you think that?"

"Because trying to be better is what stopped me from going after Kolis. Trying to be better is what prevented me from refusing his deal and entering the *eirini*." My wounded hand ached as I lifted my fists. "Trying to be what I'm not is what allowed this."

"And what are you, Sera?"

"What you trained me to be," I snarled. "A fighter. A killer. Not some fucking benevolent ball of goodness." I shook. "If I had just listened to my gut from the beginning—"

"Things would've been different?" he finished. "Maybe. Perhaps if you had rejected Kolis's offer, this never would've happened. Or maybe you would've lost those here and more in the battles that followed. Maybe if Kolis hadn't kept all his pain to himself, he would've turned out differently. Maybe if you hadn't held in all your pain, you wouldn't have given in to it now. Many things could've been different, but this is what happened," he said. "Now, you must do what is right for the realms."

"I don't give a fuck about the realms."

The bands of churning eather stilled in his flesh. "You don't mean that."

"Believe what you want."

The skin of his cheeks began to thin. "I will not allow you to make the same mistakes those who came before you made."

That was the wrong thing to say. Grief gave way to ruinous fury. Eather spilled from my fingertips, pooling on the blood-soaked ground. "Try," I whispered—or yelled. I wasn't sure. But my voice was both everywhere and nowhere. "Try to stop me."

Mist drifted from him, spilling onto the ground. It sparked with a thousand dazzling stars as Holland *changed*, became taller and broader. His features sharpened. His flesh became starlight as the mist formed wings and then thickened, solidifying until I thought I saw glossy, black *feathers* in the glow of the nearby fires.

"What in the actual fuck?" I whispered.

Holland shot forward, and instinct kicked in. I spun to the right, summoning the eather. I didn't want to hurt him, either, but I wouldn't allow him to stop me. I threw my arm out, and eather erupted from my fingertips. The raw energy slammed into Holland, rippling over his body before seeping *into* him.

His now hairless head tilted. When next he spoke, his mouth was full of starlight, and his voice boomed like thunder, rattling my bones. "You know better than that."

My lips parted as he rose into the air, his massive wings stretched high. Wisps of pure white eather swirled around his arms.

I took a breath.

That was all.

And then I was no longer in the courtyard but standing on the white limestone and granite steps of the Temple of Keella. I was in the heart of Croft's Cross.

Or what was left of it.

Holland grasped my shoulder. "Look."

The tall, narrow tenements had been reduced to piles of rubble. The already uneven cobblestones were shattered. Bodies lay everywhere. Survivors scrambled up heaps of jagged stone. There were screams for help, pleas for the gods to bring aid, and among the chaos, a dark-haired woman robed in white stood in the cluttered roadway, cradling a limp babe against her chest. She hummed and smoothed her hand over a pale cheek.

I recognized her.

She was the Priestess I'd seen when I came to retrieve Norbert's children, Nate and Ellie. The one who had said the age of the Golden King was over and that no Mierel sat on the throne.

And never would again.

The Priestess's sorrow-filled gaze lifted, meeting mine.

My body jerked, and then we were suddenly in the Garden District, bells chiming. The air was thick with smoke, and the destruction was vast. Homes were leveled. Fires raged. Survivors rushed toward crushed hills of stone as pale, gaunt, black-robed Priests moved through the debris, ringing the death knell.

"Look," Holland ordered. "Look at what has already happened to the people you were willing to die to protect." His fingers dug into my shoulder. "Are you willing to exchange their lives for your Ezra? Are you willing to take their lives?" He turned me to the left.

A man and woman huddled on the ground, their arms around two small children. They were all wounded, smudged with dirt and blood, but they were alive, a family still intact.

"Them?" demanded Holland. "That is who will pay the price. Everyone who walks will."

My chest cracked, somehow deeper and more unforgiving than before.

"And do you think those you bring back will not know the price that was paid?" His massive wings stirred the thick billow of smoke. "They have been dead long enough to know, just as many of the villagers were. They will return to see their family and friends dead in their place. Do you think they'd want that? Do you think those you've sentenced to that fate wanted that?"

My lungs burned when I dragged in a stuttered breath. My heart pounded as I stared at the family, the death knell continuing to ring.

I couldn't do that to them.

And that made the pain unbearable.

I wrenched myself free of Holland's grasp, trying to swallow, but it got stuck. I saw that he no longer looked like such an otherworldly being. His wings were gone, and his skin was no longer full of starlight. I recognized every inch of his features and saw sorrow in the kaleidoscope of colors in those eyes. I couldn't bear to look at him.

I turned to the once beautiful garden. Men and women, children, and the elderly were strewn about, their necks broken and twisted at unnatural angles.

This was Kolis's fault, but…

I couldn't let myself finish that thought. I *couldn't*. But I had to. Because Holland was right. Not only Kolis's choices had led to this moment. Mine had, too.

Pressing my hands to my temples, my chest tightened.

So many lives had been lost.

So many.

What have you done?

What I'd done was right in front of me.

Oh, gods.

A shudder went through me, and I stumbled forward. My legs went out from under me. I didn't hit the cracked streets. Instead, my knees pressed into damp soil as the weight of it all fell upon me. Each act of vengeance and retribution fell like the stones I had torn down and the mountains I had crumbled. I pitched forward, placing my hands on the grass.

Oh, gods.

Nightmarish images rose as I stared at the Blood Forest I had shadow-stepped into. Toppled homes and burning forests. Deep crevices in streets and beneath homes and people's feet. In my mind, I saw the Priestess cradling the small child—one whose life I might have inadvertently taken in anger. The hills alight with fire. The screams I'd heard after ending Embris.

They were the screams of the dying. Lives *I* had taken. Maybe not thousands, but hundreds. And that…oh, gods, that was just as bad. It was just as monstrous as what Kolis did.

What had I done?

My fingers dug into the clumps of grass, and I trembled. Kolis had acted.

And I had *re*acted.

I summoned the eather, and the power responded to my will, stretching out and wrapping itself around each blood tree. I destroyed them one by one, unable to bear the sight of what I'd done. I destroyed all but a small cluster that stood at the foot of what remained of the Undying Hills.

I focused on them, but the eather rolled off them. Nothing I did removed the twenty or so trees that remained. I tried until I was exhausted. My gaze swept over the now-barren fields before returning to the remaining blood trees. For some reason, I could still see them covering the landscape as if all those haunting trees would one day return.

I pressed my forehead against the tainted ground, dragging in air. It tasted of the ruin I had caused.

The line between acting in rightful justice and lashing out in wrathful vengeance was a fine one. Incredibly thin and so easy to cross. I needed no *vadentia* to know that. I'd always known that. But I hadn't just crossed that line.

I'd destroyed it.

And had become a true monster in the process.

What rose then was just as choking as the rage. It, too, was an all-consuming tempest, and every heartbeat was an echo of ravenous sorrow.

I broke.

I rocked back, bloody hands fisting in my hair as I screamed. Tears coursed down my cheeks and fell from the sky. I screamed until I thought I might rip apart, until my voice gave out, and there was nothing.

I didn't know how long I remained on my knees, arms limp at my sides. I heard and saw nothing until I registered someone calling my name over and over.

Hands grasped my arms, shaking me. "Sera!"

Numbly, I opened my eyes, expecting to see Holland, but it wasn't him.

Attes was crouched in front of me, red soaking his hair and streaming down his face. "Sera? Can you hear me?" He squeezed my arms. "Do you understand me?"

"I…" I rasped hoarsely. "Look…at what I did."

The Primal shook his head and swallowed thickly. "That doesn't matter right now."

How could he say that? My gaze drifted behind him to the crimson leaves.

"Look at me." He caught my chin, forcing my gaze back to his. "I need you to focus on me and listen. If you don't, there will be more death and destruction. Lotho needs a Primal, and only you can Ascend one. If you don't do it and do it now, the essence will circle back, and there will be even more damage. You must stop this."

The screams…

Those lost when Embris's essence was released. I flinched, and Attes cursed. Their blood was on my hands.

"Sera," Attes pleaded.

"I know," I croaked.

Relief poured into his features, and he helped me stand. As the blood leaves swayed in the wind, we shadowstepped to Mount Lotho.

43

At any other time, I would've marveled at the beauty of the Athanien Palace. The sweeping structure had been built into the side of Mount Lotho and consisted of far too many floors to even count, connected by spiraling outdoor staircases that looked like death traps to me.

The palace wasn't the only building that climbed to the heights of the mountain. Tall towers lined Mount Lotho and disappeared into the clouds. I knew that was where the Fates resided.

But there was nothing beautiful about the Court now. It was storming violently. Lightning continuously pierced the dark violet and charcoal clouds, revealing glimpses of the pitched roofs and rain-soaked marble streets of the cities sprawling along the hills and the steep inclines of Mount Lotho.

Draken swarmed the palace, their staggering calls those of restlessness, confusion, and anger. There was also concern.

So much rain had fallen that the gods clustered outside the doors feared mudslides would soon follow. Several were out there now, using essence to hold back the unstable ground. I closed my eyes. It reminded me of Phanos fighting the tidal wave my actions had caused.

"Sera," Attes called softly.

I turned from the window to see him entering the atrium with Penellaphe.

The goddess's light brown skin had taken on an ashen hue. "Sera," she whispered, crossing the distance between us. "Fates, are you all—?"

"There isn't time for that," I cut her off. What I said wasn't a lie, but I also didn't want her concern. "Are you willing to accept the position of Primal of this Court?"

She stopped short, her fingers curling into the lace on the collar of her blouse. "I am, but there are other gods older than me—more deserving."

"I don't know them. I know you."

Penellaphe took a deep breath. "Then I accept."

Attes led us to a nearby chair. I'd been relieved when I realized the crimson now dried in streaks over his face and matting his hair was from the blood rain and not something else. It hadn't just fallen throughout the mortal realm. It also drenched the Courts of Iliseeum. "Do you know how to do this?"

I nodded. "Your wrist?"

Penellaphe extended her arm, and Attes's worried gaze lingered on me. I took the goddess's hand. The sight of my blood-and-dirt-smeared fingers against her clean, unblemished skin caused me to flinch. Whose blood was that? Mine? Embris's? The unknown gods I'd killed?

"Sera?" Attes said quietly.

I shook myself free of those thoughts. The wind and rain lashed the walls. Lifting her wrist, I didn't waste any time. I bit into her vein. Her sharp inhale reminded me to release my fangs. I hadn't done that when I'd torn into Embris's throat. The taste of Penellaphe's blood reminded me of cherries as I drank deeply and as quickly as I could, hoping I wasn't causing her pain. I'd already brought about enough of that to last a lifetime. At some point, Penellaphe sat, or Attes guided her to do so. I wasn't sure which. Soon, I became aware of the pulse beneath my fingertips and its echo in her blood. When it slowed, I closed the wound and then bit into my wrist. Red-hot pain radiated up and down my left arm, and Attes winced. I hadn't been as clean with myself as with Penellaphe. It wasn't on purpose. At least, I didn't think so.

Blood welled and ran down my arm. I lifted my wrist. "Drink."

Her hands shook when she grasped my arm. Rain-slicked hair fell forward. She sealed her mouth to the wound and drank as I stood there. I didn't really feel it or know how long it took, but Penellaphe suddenly released my arm and jerked her head back. Warmth had returned to her skin.

"Rise," I said, guided by the instincts of a Primal of Life. "Rise as the Primal Goddess of Wisdom, Loyalty, and Duty."

Ruby-red stained her lips, and her eyes widened. She pressed a hand to her chest, the veins along the top lit with a golden glow. "Oh…"

Lowering my arm, I stepped back. A sudden wave of dizziness swept through me. I forced out a long, slow breath. A level of detached curiosity filled me as I watched the essence travel through her veins, disappearing under the sleeves at her wrists to reappear along her throat.

"Sera." Attes touched my arm, his voice low. "Close your wound."

I started to lift my arm but halted when eather filled the veins of Penellaphe's cheeks. Her eyes got even wider, filling with eather until her pupils were no longer visible. Her chest rose sharply, and then she shot to her feet, knocking the chair over.

The air shifted around us, thickening and charging with all the combustible energy. Particles of eather lit up all around Penellaphe, moving throughout the atrium and beyond the palace. The Court of Lotho burned with silver light. Arcs of eather erupted from the particles, slamming into

Penellaphe and returning to a source, a home.

Penellaphe's head jerked back, and she threw out her arms. Blinding light streaked from her, sparking and hissing. She rose into the air, reaching the ceiling. The glow was so intense my eyes watered as eather enveloped her entire body. The howling wind and rain ceased. Through the windows, I saw the thick clouds breaking apart to reveal the clear night sky.

There was silence and then the staggering high-pitched call of a draken. Then another. And another.

The eather around and inside Penellaphe throbbed and then flickered out. She dropped from the air, but Holland was there before Attes or I could do anything. He caught Penellaphe, cradling her limp body in his arms. I was…so out of it that I hadn't even felt his arrival.

Nice of him to show up.

"I got you," he murmured, brushing his lips over her brow before lifting his gaze to mine.

"Sera," Holland called. His painfully familiar features were tense, but his gaze was soft. "Thank you."

My eyes slammed shut, violent emotions swirling dangerously inside me. I stepped back and turned away, swaying slightly.

"Sera," Attes started.

"I'm fine."

"No, you're not." He caught my arm, irritation and concern filling his tone. "You're dizzy, aren't you? Don't even bother lying. You're walking like you've drunk a fifth of whiskey."

"Then why did you ask?"

"Because I have no idea what you plan to do next, and I doubt you realize the vulnerable state you're in right now." The angles of his face were tense and smeared with dried blood, making his scar stand out more. "You're a fledgling Primal and have used way too much eather."

"I'm fine. I drank from Embris," I said, wincing.

"And you just Ascended Penellaphe. Whatever you gained will deplete quickly." Attes folded an arm around me, swearing under his breath. "Come on, I'm taking you home."

I didn't protest, not even when he tugged me against his side. I was…I was done. And I was tired—

Awareness of another Primal throbbed in my chest as the mist began to lift from the floor. My head shot up. I recognized that sensation—the imprint. A hazy image of—

"Motherfucker," Attes roared, sensing his brother.

My heart lurched, pumping adrenaline through me. I wrenched myself free of Attes, spinning to where Holland held Penellaphe. My eyes locked with Holland's. His were wide, and the bright silver pupils had dilated until no color was visible.

"I didn't see this," he rasped. "This was not a thread."

The breath I took froze in my chest. Gods. Holland…a Fate, an *Ancient*, sounded *afraid.*

Why would he be afraid of Kyn?

Holland rose swiftly, holding Penellaphe tighter to him. "Do not fight," he said through gritted teeth. "You will not win, Seraphena."

He vanished with the new Primal.

The glass walls of the palace exploded, sending shards through the atrium. Attes flung out a hand and grabbed my arm. A wall of silvery eather went up, shattering more glass.

"Fuck," he snarled, pulling me back to him. Mist whipped around us.

A burst of energy reverberated through the large chamber, piercing the mist. Without warning, we were moving in opposite directions. I slid across the floor, boots slipping. I fell to my knees just as the horned tail of a draken whipped through the atrium, right above my head, before slamming into Attes. The Primal flew across the chamber, hitting a marble pillar with a fleshy smack. I jumped to my feet, and he fell to his knees, catching himself.

"Fuck you, Thrax," Attes grunted. "That was unnecessary."

I started for him—

Bad life choice.

Who I assumed was Thrax swept his tail back, and *I* was in its path. I hit the floor, holding my breath as the tail skimmed over me. One of the spikes grazed my shoulder, ripping my shirt, and only by the grace of the Fates, missed catching any skin in the process.

The ceiling tore back, claws ripping through glass and stone. A draken with fiery red-and-black scales descended into the ruined chamber, its wings beating at the dust in the air as its claws slammed down behind me.

Oh, shit.

I rolled to the right with only seconds to spare.

Massive forelegs landed where I'd been with a force that would've crushed me. Mouth dry, I popped to my feet. The draken snarled, its lips vibrating as they pulled back over sharp teeth. Thrax wasn't nearly as big as Nektas, but he was fast with that fucking tail. He caught me in the back, sending me flying. I hit the floor with a groan. It knocked the air out of me, but I rolled, coming to a stop on my belly. Air—too much air—surrounded me. I turned my head, gasping and seeing nothing but the darkness of a steep drop-off on the side of Mount Lotho.

Why did Embris have to build his palace on a fucking cliff?

I shoved to my feet. Wind roared through the trembling palace, blowing my hair back. My chest suddenly warmed with the echo of death. The flare came again and again as Thrax snapped at Attes. I didn't see Kyn, but I knew he was close. He was in the palace somewhere—likely the source of the death I felt.

I summoned the eather, feeling it pulse wildly—too wildly. A bolt erupted from my palm, nowhere near as strong as earlier. The silvery-gold stream arced across the chamber, striking the draken in the side.

Thrax yelped and lurched toward me. His jaws opened as he roared, the force sending me back about half a foot, the stench of sulfur and blood choking me.

I pulled the essence to the surface when I saw Attes's armor appear. The Primal rose into the air, eather crackling and spitting from his splayed hands. Thrax huffed, drew his neck back, and started to turn back to Attes.

"Hey, you fucker," I shouted. "Your breath smells like your mouth has been up Kyn's ass!"

Thrax halted and then turned his attention back to me, eyes narrowing.

A stream of bright eather slammed into Thrax. The draken reared back, spraying shimmery blood. I darted out of its path, but Attes was close, continuing to slam the draken with eather. The armor protected his chest, but the sleeves of his tunic burned off, and his flesh smoked.

Thrax went for Attes, releasing a stream of silvery fire. Attes lurched to the side, throwing a bolt of eather that hit the draken in the face. Thrax shot back—

Icy fingers trailed down my spine. I sucked in a shrill breath, catching the scent of stale lilacs—death. The hairs along the back of my neck rose. Everything inside me stopped except for my heart. It beat steadily. Calmly, even. I turned around and saw Attes and the draken spill over the edge where the glass walls had stood, falling over the cliff. There was a shout of pain, but all I saw was the figure in the center of a whirling mass of crimson-streaked shadows in the sky.

"*Kolis*," I hissed, feeling a violent rush of energy surge through me. Fury sank its claws into me, climbing my spine and filling my limbs. It filled my heart and wrapped itself around my fingers. So, I seized it. I stalked forward, the marble tile cracking under my steps. Throwing out my hand, golden-silver light rippled down my arm.

Seeing my family's faces and the horror forever etched into their features, feral rage fueled me, and eather exploded from my palm, racing through the sky. A savage smile lit up my face when the essence struck Kolis, scattering the shadows around him. His head kicked back, and the eather raced across his bare chest, singeing his crimson pants. I lifted my left arm, wanting to cause him pain, wanting to *destroy* him—

A dark, cold laugh slithered through the air and over my flesh. Kolis's chin lowered. Crimson-streaked tendrils rose once more in the ink-black sky, writhing and swirling, his eyes gleaming like ruby jewels. All along the cliffs, great elms and pines bent back as if to escape the weight of his power and presence.

A reddish-silver pulse of light rippled across the realm, revealing the draken that had taken flight from the palace. I saw them when the sky growled, a deep rumble building in intensity until it reached a deafening crescendo. Bright bolts of crimson-laced eather erupted from Kolis and danced across the horizon, splitting into multiple veins that streaked through the clouds like writhing serpents.

From the valley below, a draken's panicked call sent dread cascading through me. The draken in the sky veered sharply and dove to the ground—to safety.

"No," I whispered. I had no idea if the draken were now loyal to Penellaphe or not, but I didn't want to see what I knew was coming.

A scream lodged in my throat. The eather struck draken after draken. Horror swamped me as they twisted and writhed in the sky, their wings crumbling and then disappearing. Essence flared in me, one, two, three…eight times as the draken shifted into their mortal forms, their bodies limp as they fell…

I couldn't believe what I'd just seen. Shock paralyzed me when the draken on the ground let out anguished wails. Kolis had nearly wiped out all the draken of the Court in less than a minute. I didn't think I would be capable of something like that even if I wasn't a fledgling Primal. The kind of power it took to kill a draken…

His laughter ceased. Then, he began to *sing*, his voice traveling through the air like a sinister requiem that became a somber song. My entire being recoiled instinctually as the very realm shuddered, and the haunting hymn rose…

Something fell from above too fast for me to tell what it was, but it was too small to be another draken. I jerked, something else plummeting from above. Warmth flared in my chest. I looked up, the heat quickly returning as another object fell, then another, and another…

I saw *things* climbing out of windows and over balcony rails on the upper floors of the sweeping ivory palace, opening their arms wide and embracing the call of death.

Oh, my gods.

Horror rose. Gods and godlings, mortals and servants, embraced death. The fall from Mount Lotho would kill a god. It would likely even do serious damage to a Primal.

"You sick bastard!" I screamed, willing the eather to the surface to try to catch the ones I could, but the essence merely sparked and flickered. The delay was costly, and the fall was too quick. "Stop!"

The chilling song ceased.

My furious glare fixed on Kolis as another echo of death haunted me. "Why? Why would you do that?" I shouted. I didn't know if I was asking about those he'd called to their deaths or if I was demanding to know why he'd taken my family. I wasn't sure why I was asking either. I knew the answer. He was a walking nightmare. Still, I screamed, "Why?"

"You should know," Kolis said, his voice no longer carrying the winds of summer. Now, it brought with it the nothingness of death.

"Other than you being absolutely demented," I seethed, "do you even know why you are this way?"

A heartbeat passed, and then Kolis was directly in front of me. I didn't even see the blow coming. His fist slammed into my jaw, the force cranking my head back.

Pain erupted, and blood filled my mouth, but I somehow managed to keep my footing.

"Did you really think that would hurt me? A Primal a millennium old?" Kolis's laugh sounded like dry bones rubbing together. "You silly cunt."

Head ringing, I straightened and faced him, spitting a mouthful of blood directly in his face.

Kolis smiled, and there was nothing fake about it. He licked the blood from his lips. "Tasty." Crimson shadows blossomed under the flesh of his chest. "I should thank you for Ascending a Primal to take Embris's place. I would've chosen someone different, but she…" His smile spread, and red swirled in his eyes. "She will be so lovely when she kneels before me and pledges her allegiance. Not as fulfilling as when you do, but still enjoyable."

It was almost like his words were a different sort of siren's call to me. Common sense jumped right off the cliff, along with Holland's advice. Rage was an unending fire in my blood, even as instinct warned me that I needed to be careful. I had to put space between us. Kolis was old. He was stronger and faster. I had been weakened substantially, and the pain from my numerous injuries was no longer so dull. Tiny stings and sharp pricks joined the throbbing in my jaw, but all the drowning anger and sorrow was far greater, as was the knowledge that I was no longer afraid of him.

The palace trembled under my wrath, and I launched myself at Kolis, summoning the eather.

All he did was lift his arm, and it was like I fucking jumped throat-first into his palm. "As much as it pains me even to admit this, Seraphena,"—his grip on my throat tightened—"I admire your tenacity. If things were different, you would've sat at my right hand as my most vicious ally."

"Thanks," I bit out, grasping his wrist. "My life is complete hearing that—"

He squeezed, silencing me and cutting off my next breath. "Your mouth, however, is a different story."

I managed a smirk and lifted my left hand, extending my middle finger.

Kolis sighed. "I shouldn't be surprised that you'd throw yourself at me. That's what whores do."

Then he threw me down with enough force to knock the trapped air out of my lungs again. The impact hurt, but I could still breathe. Wheezing and coughing, I rolled onto my side.

"And that is all you are. A whore with stolen power." He stood over me, planting one foot on either side of me. He grabbed my hair, wrapping the strands around his fist. Jerking my head back, he forced me to meet his stare "A mortal pretending to be a Primal, who doesn't know her place."

"Or doesn't know when to shut up?"

"Acknowledging the problem is half the battle, isn't it?" He smirked. "You thought yourself so much better than me, didn't you? Just like Eythos. But look at what you've done."

I flinched.

"You killed tonight, Sera. You murdered coldly and without thought or care," he said. "You're no better than me."

I couldn't think about that right now: the truth in his words. I grabbed his arm, my nails breaking off as they dug into his flesh. I summoned the eather, but…it only pulsed weakly. My heart stuttered, and my gaze flew to his. Fuck.

"What? Come on, Seraphena. Lash out at me," he goaded, an achingly frigid smile playing on his lips. Out of the corner of my eye, I saw guards beyond the interior archway leveling their bows. "Fight me like the Primal you think you are," he pouted. "Or can't you get it up?"

"That sounds more like your problem." I gave him a bloody smile.

His nostrils flared. "You fucking—"

Holding on to his arm, I kicked out hard, slamming the heel of my boot into his stomach. He bent over just as a high-pitched whistle hit the air—several of them.

Kolis looked at them.

That was all he did.

The arrows shattered into dust, and the guards' heads snapped abruptly.

I briefly closed my eyes against the pulse of death.

"How quickly loyalties change," Kolis remarked with a shrug. "Embris would be rolling in his grave, as they say." He twisted the hair in his grip, sending a fiery wave of pain across my skull. "Still nothing?"

My pulse pounded, and I could feel the eather struggling to ignite inside me.

Kolis chuckled darkly. "That's what I thought. Pitiful." He yanked my head back until sharp, stabbing pain shot down my spine. "I want you to know one thing, Seraphena." The dull gleam of red bone appeared along his jaw. "It was neither Kyn nor Embris who entered Wayfair. Who listened to the pleas for mercy. Nor was it they who killed the Queen of Lasania. It was me."

Everything inside me stopped once more as a tempest of fury surged through my veins, and pulsating rage roared in my ears.

"I was the last face they saw. The last voice they heard." His head lowered to mine, and I shuddered, feeling his lips against my cheek. "And it felt so good to place my hands on them and hear their necks snap." His tongue snaked along my cheek to my ear. "You brought this on yourself."

My mind clicked off. There was nothing Primal or mortal about what I did next. It was pure, animalistic, unbridled rage. I snapped my head forward, not even feeling the strands of hair I tore out in the process, and went for the closest part of him, sinking my fangs into the side of his throat.

Kolis roared and jerked his head back. His flesh ripped, spilling even more blood. It coursed down his neck and my chin. I didn't even have a chance to swallow it.

Suddenly, I was flying.

The floor was up, and the sky was down for a few brief seconds. I crashed into a pillar and fell forward, stunned as agony radiated down the length of my body.

Get up.

I needed to get up and breathe. I flattened my palms, and lightning streaked the sky, momentarily turning night to day. *Breathe in.* I needed to get up because this was the true Primal of Death. I may have thought I'd faced him before, but I hadn't. I'd squared off with a weaker version of him.

Kolis stopped, looking up as heavy thunder rolled. He laughed. "You are so incredibly easy to provoke," he said, voice thickening. "So incredibly easy to play."

Hold. I took the time to rest and take stock of the situation while he blabbed on. Using eather wasn't an option, but I wasn't weaponless. I pushed onto my knees. *Breathe out.* Another bolt of lightning cut through the sky. *Hold.* The air cooled, the temperature dropping until I could see my breath.

"Perfect," he said. "Nyktos can feel you right now, even though he's at the Pillars. Blood isn't that powerful. The blessing of a heart bond, though? He can feel everything and do nothing." He paused. "I do hope he sends his draken. I would love nothing more than to send Nektas's body back to him."

The lightning. The temperature. It was Ash.

"Believe it or not, I enjoyed escorting souls through the Pillars. Seeing their lives. Their pain. How they loved. Hated. Their mistakes and successes. I lived vicariously through them for eons," he said. "But I do not miss being tied to them."

I shuddered and breathed out. Tiny snowflakes had begun to fall, swirling gently to the ruined floor. Silvery flashes of light began pulsing in the valley below.

"You're nothing but a fledgling Primal without my nephew by your side," he continued. "Or a so-called Fate to make sure your mouth doesn't get you into trouble."

I lifted my head, meeting his stare as realization sank in. All of this… Kolis had set a trap, and I had rushed right into it.

"Ah, I see you're finally figuring it out." He raised his brows, and crimson shadows swirled across his cheeks. "Admittedly, you killing Embris did catch me a little off guard. I didn't think you'd be able to harness that kind of power yet. That angered me." Chunks of stone lifted and slid away as he strode toward me. "But having you unleash your rage and take quite a few people's lives in the process was also surprisingly arousing."

"Fucking creep," I rasped.

"What did you say?"

I rose to my feet, holding my breath for five seconds. "I said, you are—"

Kolis shot forward and grabbed my throat. He lifted me, slamming me into the wall. "I'm sorry. What did you say? I couldn't hear you."

"Fucking creep!" I screamed.

His eyes flashed pure crimson as he pressed into me. Fucking gods, he hadn't been lying a few seconds ago. My stomach roiled. "I gave you a chance, Seraphena. All you had to do was give me what I wanted. I would've left you and my nephew alone. I wouldn't have gone after your family. I would've had my everything." His mouth brushed my chin when he spoke, his voice as soft and gentle as the most peaceful death. But his body shook with anger. "I would've been happy!" he shouted. "I would've been whole for the first time in my fucking life!"

I tried to turn my head away, but he tightened his grip. Over his shoulder, I saw a draken drawing nearer. I didn't know if it was one of his or one that now belonged to Penellaphe, and I had no idea where Attes was.

"I would have what you and my nephew have." Kolis inhaled deeply. "But you had to be this way. You had to ruin everything. You had to test me."

Without even looking, he threw out his left hand. A bolt of crimson-and-black eather streamed out, thick like oil, striking the draken. Its scream stole my breath, its wings crumbling before it fell.

"You just had to make it difficult." He rested his forehead against mine and sighed. "So, now I'm going to make it difficult."

I swung my arm, grabbing a fistful of his hair. Strands snapped when I jerked his head back. "Do you ever not blame yourself for anything? Oh, wait. You have. You blame yourself for your brother's death."

His lips peeled back in a snarl. "You have no idea what you're talking about."

"You and I both know that's bullshit, Kolis," I hissed. "You loved him. He loved you. And you murdered him."

"Shut up."

"By accident," I spat.

Hollow bone appeared along his jaw. His lips thinned until there was no flesh as he leaned back.

"Tell me, Kolis." I laughed, spitting blood. "Do you really want to live? Because I know what I saw when I drove the bone through your chest. *Relief.*"

"Shut the fuck up!"

I swung my knee up. Kolis moved at the last second, and the blow connected with his chest. He grunted and released me. I reached for the bone dagger at my thigh, unsheathing it. I thrust out, aiming for the fucker's head—

Kolis caught my wrist, looked down at what I held, and tilted his head. "Drop it," he ordered, his voice guttural.

"Fuck you," I spat, swinging out with my other arm.

"Maybe later." He caught my left arm. Flesh returned, and the crimson bone retreated. "I think I'm owed that, aren't I?"

I struggled to push past his hold. "I thought you were waiting for Sotoria."

"I was." He twisted my right wrist, snapping the bone. I couldn't suppress the scream as my fingers sprang open, and the dagger slipped free. "It's not like I'd be betraying Sotoria. I don't desire you or your body. I desire your pain and submission. Your humiliation. And since I know her soul is in The Star, I also know she's not out there waiting for me."

"Waiting for you?" I gasped, my arm throbbing. "You mean hiding from you, willing to end her life to escape you?"

Kolis turned sharply, throwing me like a sack of potatoes. I hit the floor, crashing into stone. I groaned when thudding agony rolled through my right arm. I couldn't move as I felt the essence slipping from my chest and pooling in my stomach.

I really should've listened to Holland.

"You and I are really going to need to work on watching that mouth of yours." Kolis was kneeling over me before I could even move. He grabbed my nape and flipped me onto my back. "Because you and I?" He caught my wrists, grinding the broken bones together as he pinned my arms above my head. He straddled my legs, trapping them. "We're going to be spending a lot of time together."

"Get off me, you piece of shit!" I screamed, eather flickering frantically. He switched the hold on my wrists to one hand. "Get off me—"

He slapped his free hand down on my mouth, his fingers more bone than flesh and cutting into my skin. "I have a feeling I'm going to have to cut out your tongue, and that would be a shame. I'm sure once Kyn finishes with his brother, he'll want a taste of that sharp tongue." A spasm shuddered through him as he rolled his neck. "I need you to listen to me when I tell you how this will go."

I glared at him, wishing my stare could burn him alive.

"First and foremost, you will give me The Star," he said. "But that will no longer satisfy me. You will give me more than that."

I strained against his hold, rage choking me.

"You will give me retribution," he whispered, blood dripping from his throat onto my face, even though the wound had healed. "I will keep you alive until Sotoria matures, and then I will drain every drop of blood and essence from you and rise as the Primal of Ash and Blood." He lowered his head, and my body went rigid. I felt his fangs against my throat. "That will take years, Seraphena. *Years.* And in those years, you will feel what I have. What it's like to have the one thing you only ever wanted repeatedly taken from you. Do you know how that feels? You should have gotten a taste of it since I've already begun." He lifted my upper body when I didn't answer and slammed me back down. My head cracked off the floor. He removed his hand from my mouth. "Do you?"

"Fuck off!" I shouted as panic, icy and slick, coated my skin, and my vision blinked in and out. I couldn't pass out. I couldn't.

Kolis gripped my chin. Snow fell in larger flakes, coming down faster.

"Every day without her kills a piece of me," he said, real emotion creeping into his voice, thickening it. "And I want *that* for you. I want you to drown in it. Choke on it. I want each and every day you live to be coated in sorrow and regret, while knowing you could've prevented it by giving her to me." He slammed my head back once more, and my vision faded again. "I want Nyktos's death."

My heart stopped, and my struggles ceased. "No," I seethed, feeling the essence trying to rise. "I will not allow it."

"You are no longer in a position to decide what you will allow." He tipped my head back until my neck protested. "But I don't want a quick death for him. He will live as long as you so that he, too, can feel that loss every day. So that he can feel everything done to you, just as he feels this right now. And as I said before, Seraphena, I have so much planned for you."

My insides flashed cold, and our eyes locked. I thought I heard footsteps, but I had to be imagining it because he didn't react.

"And because I am a kind and gracious King, I will allow you two to leave this existence together," he said, eyes burning like coals. A shadow moved out of the corner of my eye. He was zeroed in on me and only me. "But by then, I imagine both of you will be begging for death."

He shifted his lower body, and my entire being flinched. "Should we start now?"

I refused to look away from him. I refused to cower—to beg or disappear.

"I'm going to ask you once more," he said, slipping his hand from my chin and running it down my chest. I clamped my jaw as he squeezed, swallowing the cry of pain. "Do I scare you?" His hand twisted, and I kicked my head back. A wave of agony washed over me. "Do I?"

I panted through the pain. My head was spinning. Another flash of lightning radiated through the sky, reflecting off a blade of dull white. I didn't understand what I was seeing in the falling snow until my eyes locked with ones the color of the Stroud Sea. "No," I rasped. "You don't scare me anymore. I feel absolutely nothing when it comes to you."

Kolis lifted his head, eyes narrowing. "We'll have to change that, won't we?"

I smiled. "I think…I'll pass on that offer."

Crimson eather flared in his eyes, and I knew he was about to do something terrible.

He didn't get the chance.

The bone dagger I'd dropped sliced clear through Kolis's throat as his head was jerked back. Hot, shimmery blood sprayed my face, and the Primal reared, his shout ending in an abrupt crunch of bone as Ward, the first *viktor*, cut the fucker's head clean off his shoulders.

The release of energy came in a flash of intense whitish-silver light.

It wasn't a destructive discharge of power, but it still threw Ward back and knocked the air out of me.

I'd been wrong.

Ward hadn't sliced Kolis's head completely off. And I wished I hadn't been wrong for several reasons. The least important one—but the only reason I could focus on at the moment—was the fact that Kolis's head had *flopped* to the side, lying against his shoulder, exposing torn sinew and bone. His head was only hanging on by threads of flesh.

He blinked at me, his mouth stretched wide in a silent, bloody snarl.

I would never *unsee* this. And there was a good chance I might vomit, but I needed to snap out of it. He staggered to his feet, and mist poured from him, opening a tear in the realm. I groaned, rolling onto my side and trying to stand. Kolis was severely weakened, and that kind of injury wouldn't heal right away. The tomb in Oak Ambler wasn't ready, and we didn't have enough Ancient bone to hold him. But if we could keep him—

The entire realm seemed to flicker into nothingness—either that or I passed out because the next thing I knew, Ward was hovering over me, his sandy-blond hair damp with fallen snow. Concern was clearly etched into the sun-weathered lines of his face.

"Say something," he said, his cold hand on my cheek.

I swallowed, wincing as pain flared in my throat. "Hi?"

His brows shot up. "Say something a little more complex than that."

"You almost cut Kolis's head off."

"Feels strange to be relieved to hear you say that," he said. "But yes, I did."

"He's gone, isn't he?"

Ward nodded.

I swore, squeezing my eyes shut. Kolis would likely be down for the count, but…

"Thank you," I said.

"No need to thank me."

But there was. If he hadn't shown up…

Ward worked an arm under my shoulders and apologized. I winced. "You need to get out—" He cursed, ducking his head when a large, green-and-brown-scaled draken landed on the edge of the ruined chamber. "Godsdamnit," he muttered, glaring at the draken, who stared back at us with vivid sapphire eyes.

"What is it with…you and draken?" I asked as he helped me stand. The…the *imprint* of that draken was familiar. Aurelia? Attes's draken?

"They breathe fiery eather," he quipped. "Enough said."

I figured he had a point. "Aurelia?"

The draken nodded.

"She won't hurt you," I said, taking a deep breath that hurt my ribs, spine…everything.

"Sure." Ward sounded doubtful.

The valley below was illuminated with streaks of eather once more, drawing my attention. I stiffened. Aurelia's neck swiveled gracefully. She peered down into the valley, letting out a low whimper. I pulled away from the *viktor* and limped toward the edge of the atrium. Snow continued to fall in heavy sheets, coating the rooftops and the once rain-slicked streets. It wasn't the only thing that littered the tops of buildings and roads. Bodies did, too. Lotho residents moved in the streets, seeing to the fallen.

I turned away from the sight. The reminder of the true extent of Kolis's power was painful. "Is it Attes and Kyn?"

Yes, came Aurelia's response. It wasn't as loud or clear as when I heard Nektas or even Reaver, but the worry in her soft voice was evident.

My hands closed into fists. "I need to get down there and help Attes." I tried to summon the eather, but the pulse of power was weak. "I don't think I can shadowstep."

"Going down there would be unwise," Ward stated.

"Agreed," another voice intruded, snapping my head toward the still-standing interior wall.

Thierran strode forward, the hood of his cloak shielding his head from the precipitation. The footprints the *oneirou* left in the snow were red. Blood. He carried a short sword at his side, the tip also dripping blood.

"How did you get here?" I demanded, tensing as I reached out, taking the bone dagger from Ward's hand. Ash said Thierran could be trusted. Somewhat. But I wasn't taking any chances.

"Trust no one. Smart girl," he murmured, eyeing the dagger. His gaze lifted to mine. "I could sense…something going on down here, other than the obvious," he said. "Since I am from Lotho, I can enter without it causing a stir. No one else from the Shadowlands could do that, so Rhain sent me."

It made sense, but I kept the dagger in my hand. "You had trouble coming in?"

His head tilted. "More like I figured it was time to settle some old scores on my way up."

Ward grunted something under his breath and crossed his arms. I eyed the *oneirou.* What had Ash said? He'd called Thierran an opportunist. A low laugh left me.

The *oneirou*'s violet eyes glittered with amusement. "You're wounded." He paused. "And you smell of Death."

"Thanks," I murmured. "Kolis was here."

"That's who did this?" He looked over the side of the mountain and his jaw tensed. "He finally almost succeeded."

"In what?" I noticed the snow had slowed.

"Eradicating the *oneirou.*" He sheathed his sword. "I am the last."

Gods. The weight of that was almost too much to bear as it stacked on top of all the other losses. "I'm sorry."

Thierran's gaze met mine. There was nothing to be gained from his expression. "Thank you," he said finally, bowing his head.

Kyn tucked tail and ran, Aurelia said through the *notam*, each word laced with disgust. *Even left his wounded draken here.*

The draken.

I sucked in a shrill breath when images of the falling draken filled my mind. "Lotho had how many draken?"

"Ten, I believe," Thierran answered.

There were only two now. I shuddered.

Aurelia lowered her head when Attes appeared. He looked as bad as I felt. The armor across his chest was dented, fresh blood coursed down his arms, and his leather pants were charred in several places.

"Where the fuck is Kolis?" he growled.

"Likely gone to ground." I sheathed the bone dagger. "Ward here snuck up on him and nearly decapitated him."

"Wouldn't have been able to do it if he hadn't been so focused on you," Ward replied.

Attes's gaze shot to mine, and I looked away. He reached out and ran his palm over Aurelia's scaled jaw. "Come on." He came to my side, and Aurelia took off, rising into the sky. "Let's get you home before any other asshole decides to show up."

I nodded but then turned to the *oneirou.* "Are you coming back?"

"Eventually. No need to rush now that Embris is no more." A grin appeared, curving the straight lines of his scars. "Can't say I am even remotely upset about that."

"We can agree on that," Ward said gruffly, and my chest hollowed. He bowed his head toward me. "If you will excuse me, I would like to check on

Penellaphe."

"Thank you again," I said, weariness settling in. And now that the adrenaline was gone, I could feel the cracks in my restraint starting to form.

Ward waved my gratitude off, walking away. Attes folded an arm around my waist and told Thierran, "Stay out of trouble."

The *oneirou* smiled in a way that told me he planned to use this time to settle more scores. I wanted to laugh again.

Attes shadowstepped us back to the House of Haides, and as the mist around us faded, I saw familiar faces in the palace's foyer. Solemn expressions. Worried eyes.

It was Rhain who stepped forward. "Sera?"

"Where is Nyktos?" Attes demanded.

"He's still at the Pillars," Rhain said, his gaze fixed on me. "Rhahar joined him to help. There's been…"

There had been even more souls passing through the Pillars.

Because of me.

Because of Kolis.

A tremor coursed through me.

"I'll have fresh water sent to your chambers," Aios said, drawing away from a shockingly quiet Bele. "We'll get you cleaned up."

I said nothing, just started to go with Attes and Rhain as they led me toward the stairs. Some distant part of my brain clicked back on, and I remembered what the events of tonight actually meant. I needed to keep it together. For just a little bit longer.

"Are the Shadowlands secured?" I asked, barely recognizing my voice.

"Yes," Lailah answered. "Soldiers are on the Rise surrounding Lethe and the palace since this…this began."

"Has Theon been notified to watch for any movement?"

"Yes," she said.

"Good." I pressed my hand to my lower stomach, my mind racing. "We…should send someone to Mount Lotho," I said, truly having no idea how much Holland would intervene if there was another attack. "There are only two draken remaining. Penellaphe's Court will be vulnerable until she awakens."

Lailah's inhale was swift. "Only two?"

"Kolis," I said, and that was all I could say about that.

"I'm already on it," Attes assured me. "Aurelia will send Elias and several of my most trusted guards."

"Sera." Saion moved into my line of sight. "What are the orders if we see ships entering the Lassa Sea?"

I met his stare, but all I saw were the people of Lotho leaping to their deaths. "If they do not swear allegiance to the true Queen and King, destroy them."

"Are you sure?" Attes asked.

"I think she was pretty clear," Bele growled, eather pooling in her eyes.

Rhain turned to me. "There will be no turning back if that is what we do."

"We are already past that point, and that was before Kolis had my family slaughtered," I hissed, and Bele gasped. The shock radiating through each of their faces told me they hadn't learned about that yet. Energy ramped up inside me. "We were already past that point. I just didn't see it until now."

"Fates," Rhain rasped.

Attes hung his head in shame that didn't belong to him.

"I will no longer risk the lives of those I care for," I told them. "If any forces are perceived as a threat, destroy them."

Saion nodded, anger mixing with the disbelief in his expression. "Understood and agreed."

Lailah joined him, thumping her fist off her chest. "We will gladly follow those orders."

I inhaled through the burning in my throat and eyes.

"Bele," Attes said. "You need to protect your Court's boundaries."

Bele's nostrils flared. "I need to protect my Queen—"

"You will be doing just that by making sure your Court doesn't fall into Kolis's hands," I said.

Bele's jaw flexed, but she nodded. "I promise that will not happen."

"I know." I forced a swallow. "Kolis is wounded. He will be out, but I don't know for how long. And I assume Kyn isn't in much better shape."

"He's not," Attes confirmed.

"But we should plan for either of them to make a move at any point," I continued, glancing at Rhain. "We need to send forces to Sirta to back up Bele."

There were several nods.

"I will also send a division." Attes tugged on my waist. "Come."

Kars moved away from the pedestal and stopped in front of us. He lowered himself to one knee and bowed his head. "I am sorry for your loss," he said, his voice thick. "May your family be welcomed into the arms of those waiting for them in the Vale."

Tears clogged my throat and stung my eyes. I felt myself begin to shake and crack further. "Thank you."

I had no idea how I ended up in my bedchambers, whether I had walked or Attes had shadowstepped us—for all I knew, he could've carried me. But we were there.

I looked around the space. Everything looked different now.

Attes stood in front of me and took my left hand in his. "Sera—"

Closing my eyes, I immediately regretted doing so. All I saw was the fear on the Chosen's faces. The bodies of my family, strangers, and gods—bodies *I* had left in my wake.

I sucked in a short breath, stumbling back a step as I freed my hand from his grasp. "Dametria," I gasped.

Attes frowned. "What?"

Part of me didn't want to ask because if I'd done something to her... "Was she in Dalos? At Cor Palace or the Sanctuary?"

Understanding flickered across his features. "No, she was not. She has not been harmed."

Thank the gods.

Attes inched closer. "You still haven't closed this wound. It will not heal until you do."

"Really haven't had time." In truth, I had completely forgotten about it.

"You need to close your wound."

I stared at the ragged puncture wounds, feeling Nektas draw closer. There was so much blood on my arm, I had no idea who it actually belonged to.

"I swear to the Fates, Sera, if I have to force your mouth open to do so, I will," Attes growled. "I'm giving you one more chance to do it yourself because Nyktos doesn't need to return to see your wrist torn half-open."

Nyktos.

Ash.

Hearing his name pierced my chest far more painfully than any arrow or dagger tonight. Gods, what would he think of me now? Would he still say that I was kind and loyal? That I thought of others before myself? That I wasn't a monster? And the panic he must've felt while I fought Kolis... A shudder ran through me as I lifted my wrist and sealed the wounds.

"Thank you." Attes thrust his hand through his hair and then dropped it. "Sera, I..." He briefly closed his eyes and then shook his head. "Nyktos will punch me three times more than last time for being in your bedchambers with you," he joked, but the teasing didn't reach his eyes or his tone. He exhaled heavily and then clasped the back of my neck. "I'm sorry, Sera. I'm so fucking sorry about everything."

Everything.

I didn't want to hear that because how could I apologize to all those who'd lost people they cared for today? I stepped away from him, my throat tightening.

"Kolis said none of this would've happened if I had given him Sotoria."

Attes's features tensed. "Sera—"

"You need to make sure she's safe," I said, my breath thinning. "If he gets to her, then all the deaths will have been for nothing."

Eather streaked across his eyes. "He will not have her."

Nektas pushed open the balcony doors. He crossed the distance, his long hair streaming behind him.

"*Meyaah Liessa.*"

I flinched at the sound of his gravelly voice. Gods, I didn't want to see him right now. I didn't want to see anyone because I knew I needed to keep it together. Kolis could attack at any moment. I had to be ready while Ash dealt with all those souls—some of which I had sent his way. The next breath I took got stuck.

The draken's gaze swept over me. The blue in his eyes turned luminous. "You've been injured."

A strangled sort of laugh escaped me. He was worried about me? Me?

Nektas stopped in front of me and grabbed my right hand. The flesh there was still pink and raw. He leaned in, sniffing, and growled low in his throat. "You're bleeding."

"What?" Attes demanded. A moment later, I felt his hands running up my back, searching for a wound.

"I'm fine." I pulled myself away from them.

Nektas's eyes narrowed. "No, you're not. You haven't healed completely."

"That doesn't make sense." Worry filled Attes's tone and stare. "Were you wounded by Ancient bone?"

"No. I don't think so." The room felt too small with them here. "It doesn't matter."

"Disagree," Nektas stated.

My hands were trembling as I ran them down my face. "I am the last person either of you needs to worry about right now. Kolis—"

"Fuck Kolis," snarled Nektas, his pupils contracted further into slits. "Attes, summon the Healer."

"No!" I shouted, feeling the tenuous hold I had beginning to slip. "I don't need the Healer. I don't need either of you with me. I just need to be alone right now."

"Attes." Nektas ignored me. "Go—"

"Do you all know what I did? Why Ash is stuck at the Pillars? It wasn't just Kolis. It was also me! I killed!" I screamed, my control completely snapping. I turned, finding Attes standing behind me. "I killed so many innocent people tonight!"

"Kyn killed more," Attes said. "So did Embris. They did it on Kolis's orders—"

"That doesn't change what I did. I tried to fix it. I tried—" I stiffened, horrific images filling my head. Anger and sorrow pumped through me so intensely that, for a moment, I couldn't breathe. In the distance, I heard another draken let out a series of staggered, anxious calls.

Images of the fire-lit hills and villages flashed before me, replacing those of my family. I saw the guards on Dalos's Rise. The one who'd said he wouldn't fight me. I saw Jove. I saw the Chosen huddled together in fear. The Priestess and all the destruction.

You murdered coldly and without thought or care. You're no better than me.

"What did I do?" I whispered, my body shaking. "What have I become?"

Attes reached for me. "Sera—"

I pushed him away. The Primal stumbled back, and I doubled over, clutching my head. There were screams again, but this time, they were mine. My chest tightened. Nektas was speaking, but I couldn't hear him. There were other voices now. I felt Nektas's arms around my waist. I heard more draken as lightning flashed outside the balcony doors. I couldn't breathe when I saw Jove. My entire body shook as I saw the limp babe in the Priestess's arms. Ezra and Marisol. My mother. The ruined homes, broken streets, and leveled villages. The nameless, faceless lives I'd exchanged for those I'd brought back.

I was losing control again.

Breaking.

Pressure descended on my chest, and wind battered the walls, blowing open the balcony doors. I suddenly remembered what Veses had said when she came here. She'd warned me. She'd fucking *warned* me. Lights all along the wall flickered, and the bulbs burst. The bed rattled. I couldn't calm myself. Couldn't hold myself together like I knew I should. I couldn't be stronger. Better. I didn't even try.

I screamed.

I screamed until a hum filled every part of my being. My skin began to vibrate. Fire erupted along my flesh. Clothing tore. The sheath on my thigh snapped. My bones cracked and then fused back together as I shifted.

The *nota* took over.

The draken held me in his arms as I struggled, snapping and clawing at him. He didn't let go, not even when I brought him to his knees. He held on, my claws scraping against the shadowstone, chipping the floor. I needed to be free. To run. To *not* think or feel.

"I'm not letting you go," the draken grunted. I tried to throw my weight against him. "I'm sorry, Sera. I know you think that's what you need right now, but it's not safe."

I growled, hissing and straining against him. I hurt. Outside. Inside. It was too much.

"Should I summon Kye?" a softer voice asked. "He could give her a sedative."

"Is she still bleeding?" a deeper voice asked, carrying Primal power. My head snapped in his direction. I bared my fangs at the scarred Primal. His brows shot up.

"Either she is, or I am," the draken said. "Actually, both of us are."

"Then we don't want to sedate her until we find out why she hasn't healed completely." The Primal watched me warily. "Plus, I'm half-afraid she'll try to eat the Healer."

"I think you need to be more worried about her eating *you*," another voice came. I twisted my head to the far right, snarling at the auburn-haired god. "Please, do not let her go."

"Trying not to." The draken managed to work an arm under my chin, clamping my head against his chest. "I think it's best if you leave."

The clicking in the back of my throat grew into a roar.

"You sure about that?" the Primal asked.

"I have her under control," the draken shouted, and I could smell the others' doubt as I hissed at the Primal, feeling my fur rise. "Or she'll tire herself out first. Either way, get the fuck out of here."

The Primal nodded, taking the dark-skinned goddess's arm. "We won't be far."

The draken cursed again. "And do not let Aios in here."

I started to dig my back paws into the floor as the draken rolled his weight, pushing me down onto my belly. I didn't like that. Neither…neither part of me did.

"Sera, listen to me," the draken said, his head pressed against the back of my neck. "You need to get control of your *nota*. I'm not going to hurt you. You know that."

I whined, trying to shake him off, but he didn't budge an inch.

"Stop." His arms tightened. "Stop and listen to me. I know you're hurting. I know you're in pain, and I know that's not just the physical."

I panted, trying to get my legs under me. I managed to lift myself about an inch.

"Fucking Fates, Sera," the draken groaned. "At any other time, I'd find your strength impressive."

The draken moved then, nearly lying completely on me. I grunted, going flat once more.

"Let's try this again," he said, shifting his head. A curtain of black and red hair fell over my face, tickling my whiskers. I opened my mouth. "You know—"

"Do not grab my hair, Sera. That would be rude," he snapped.

I grabbed a mouthful of his hair and jerked. The draken swore, and for a moment, I thought I had him and twisted my head, preparing to shake him.

"You need to control your *nota*, Sera," he growled. "If not for me, then for Ash."

My muscles tensed as my jaw tightened around the thick strands of hair.

"He can feel all of this," the draken said, his voice filling with gravel. "He's been feeling everything you have, and he can't come to you."

Ash.

The name echoed in my head, followed by images of silvery eyes that warmed whenever he was with me. *Ash.* He was mine. My world. My King. My heart.

"You know what it's doing to him." The draken's voice had lowered but thickened. "It's eating him up. Cutting into him. I don't want that happening to him."

A loud whimper left me.

"I don't want this happening to you." His ragged breath stirred the fur of my neck. "Please, Sera. I'm here for you. Just like I promised. Remember? When we came back from the Pools? We don't have to talk. You don't even have to shift back if that's not what you want, but I'm here for you. Remember?"

I…I remembered.

I wasn't sure what got through to me. The reminder that Ash was feeling everything I was? Or the reminder of the promise Nektas had made on the road back to the palace from the Pools of Divanash. Whatever it was, I stopped fighting. I went limp, breathing heavily, the last of the fight-or-flight adrenaline leaving me.

"Can you do me a favor?" Nektas said after a moment. "And let go of my hair?"

Feeling guilt gather in the back of my throat, I spat out the mouthful of hair.

"Thank you." He lifted his head, and after a moment, shifted his weight off me, but he didn't let go. Several moments passed. "Sera?"

I made a chuffing sound as I stared forward. Through the open balcony doors, I saw that deep blue had begun to penetrate the night sky.

"There you are."

I didn't respond to that, just lay there, exhausted, my heart pounding. We remained that way until dawn broke. Eventually, Nektas sat up. With his back against the foot of the bed, he pulled my head into his lap. I didn't look at him as I stared outside.

He ran his hand between my ears and continued stroking my fur, the ridges on his palm soothing. By the time he spoke, the sun had risen.

"You should eat something," he said softly.

I wasn't hungry.

Nektas seemed to sense the meaning behind my lack of response. "Okay. We'll try again later."

He stayed with me, continuing to run his fingers through my fur. My eyes closed when the sunlight began creeping over the shadowstone. I didn't sleep. Instead, I played every decision I'd made since rising as a Primal over in my mind. Every choice that'd led me to this moment. Where had things gone so terribly wrong? Because I had played a role in what'd happened. I hadn't listened to my instincts when it came to Kolis. I'd been too determined to be different. To be more like…like how I thought a Queen should be. How I thought Eythos would handle himself, even though I knew that, in the end, that had sealed his fate. Since I'd awakened, I'd tried to have…less knee-jerk reactions. I'd tried to be less impulsive. Less reckless. Less absurd. Less like who I was.

Less like a monster.

Less like…less like Kolis.

But as the day wore on, I…I accepted what I had always known. What even Nektas had known when he said the monstrous side of me could one day save me.

The truth was, I *was* like Kolis.

Maybe it was the embers I'd been born with. How I'd been raised. Maybe it was the training and the grooming. Maybe it was all the choices I'd made in my life that allowed me to act with cold violence on one hand and heal with the next. Or maybe it was because I'd been touched by life and death at birth. Perhaps that ensured I wouldn't end up like Eythos. Too forgiving. Too hopeful. Too loyal. Because those things were just as bad as being too harsh and too unforgiving. Both blinded you in different ways.

The why didn't matter.

Because, all along, I'd fought my instincts instead of learning when to listen to them and when to heed the counsel of others. I hadn't truly had faith in myself.

And Ezra had paid that price. So did Marisol. My mother. Those Kyn and Embris had killed on Kolis's orders.

And those I slaughtered when I tipped over that line between justice and vengeance—when I let myself be consumed by rage and sorrow that had built inside me for days, weeks, months, and years.

What happened wasn't just the end result of Kolis's actions. Or me trying to be better. What had Holland said? *Maybe if you hadn't held in all your pain, you wouldn't have given in to it now.* He'd never trained me to be a cold killer. He'd trained me to always be compassionate, even in death. I owed a part of what I'd done to all that anger—the fury, panic, and desperation I'd bottled up inside me.

This…this was as much Kolis's fault as it was mine.

How would I live with that? I didn't know.

At some point, I heard a quiet knock on the door. It was Rhain. He told us things were still quiet, before sharing that the Primal goddess Maia had entered the mortal realm to check on the *state of things*. That surprised me. It also bothered me. I should be there. The…how did Rhain put it? The *event* had subsided. He'd asked if I would eat. If he should try to bring the Healer in now. My body hurt, but I'd stopped bleeding, and there was no reason to send for the Healer, especially since I was still in my *nota* state. Aios came by. She sat with Nektas, petting my side. Like him, she didn't talk. She didn't leave until night fell and Rhain returned. I smelled food.

"Any word from the Pillars?" Nektas asked, keeping his voice low, even though I doubted he believed I was asleep.

"No," Rhain answered. "I've never known it to take this long, but he shouldn't be much longer."

Nektas didn't respond. We both knew why it had never taken this long. A Primal had never been killed in the mortal realm before. The death toll was…high.

It was Attes who delivered both relief and heartbreak.

He knelt beside Nektas and me, gently touching my jaw. "I went to Wayfair," he said, fingers sinking into my fur. "I didn't know which ones were your family, but I made sure all who were on the grounds were given burial rites."

I nosed his hand, unable to even huff my gratitude. The pain and relief were too great. I slipped further into my *nota*, returning to the last time I'd seen them. How they'd looked. Ezra's questions. Marisol's smiles. My last conversation with my mother. The fragile hope that we could maybe repair our relationship. I stayed there with the future that should've been.

Nektas tried to get me to eat several times. I wasn't hungry. He let it go, and silence reigned until the doors opened again. This time, it was small footsteps that neared us but then stopped.

"It's okay," Nektas said. "You can come closer. It will do some good."

There was one set of footsteps, then another, much lighter pair.

"Sera?" Reaver called in a small voice. I lifted a paw. He took it and sat beside me. "Is…is she okay?"

Tiny hands landed near Nektas's palm, fisting my fur. The smell of peaches and sugar reached me. "Sad," Jadis whispered.

"Yes, she is sad," Nektas answered.

I felt Jadis move closer and then her lips against the bridge of my nose. "There. Better."

"I don't think that works," Reaver said solemnly.

"Uh-huh," Jadis cried.

"She'll be better," Nektas assured them, somehow quieting them both with three words. "She will."

Reaver lay beside me, still holding my paw. Jadis managed to get herself between him and me, curling into a little ball against my stomach. Their warmth calmed the unending rush of thoughts, allowing me to slip into quiet numbness.

Nektas stayed where he was. I didn't know how he did it. He didn't leave once. Not even to take care of personal needs. He stayed, simply stroking my head. No one else entered the chamber. No one tried to talk to me. I didn't know how much time passed before my body and mind simply gave out. I fell asleep. I didn't dream. There was just…nothing.

Until cool fingers threaded through my fur and the scent of citrus and fresh air reached me. "*Liessa*," Ash called softly. "Come back to me."

Ash knelt before me, his fingers sifting through the fur beneath my chin as he lifted my head. Exhaustion was etched into the lines of his face and the shadows under his stunning eyes. "Please," he said, the sound of his voice raw, several strands of shoulder-length hair slipping forward to kiss his jaw. "Please come back to me."

His words were like magic. And as his gaze held mine, I willed myself to shift back into my mortal form with a shudder.

"Ash," I rasped, my throat scratchy.

He made a sound that seemed to come from the depths of his soul. Gathering me in his arms, he sat back, pulling me between his legs and against his chest. Pain roared in the moment I returned to myself, and how tightly Ash held me didn't help. But I ignored it, needing to be close to him. Neither of us spoke as he held me. As I clung to him. I had no idea where Nektas and the younglings had gone, but I knew we were alone.

I buried my face in the crook of his neck. I couldn't seem to get close enough. I needed to feel his heart beating against my chest. When his arm loosened around my waist, I whimpered.

"Shhh," he murmured. "I'm not going anywhere. I'm just getting you a blanket. You're cold."

A moment later, soft fur draped over my shoulders, and his arm returned to my waist. He clasped the back of my head, his fingers curling into the tangled strands of my hair.

"Sera," he whispered, his large body trembling. He tightened his arms around me. "I'm so sorry. I'm so fucking sorry."

My fingers clenched the soft linen of his shirt. The breath I took burned my throat and nose. The blanket slipped down my back as I started to pull away.

Ash's inhale was rough and stunted as he stared at me. I didn't know what had caused that reaction until I looked down. Under the dried blood, there were bruises up and down my arms, some of them still an ugly shade of purplish-red. Others were an array of blues. Strangely, my lower stomach was the only area I could see that didn't appear marked. Though I wondered what my throat looked like based on how he was staring at it. But then his gaze lowered to my chest. The bruise there was one of those ugly shades, darker than the areola.

Ash became rigid, his flesh thinning. "He touched you." The tendons in his neck stood out starkly. "He hurt you."

I didn't deny it. I didn't say anything. I closed the distance between us and rested my cheek on his shoulder.

Ash didn't move for what felt like an hour, but then he tugged the blanket back up and folded his arms around me again. He didn't hold me as tightly, though. "I want a Healer to look you over. The bruises should be gone by now."

"No."

"Sera—"

"I don't want a Healer. I'm fine. I just used a lot of eather." My voice still sounded hoarse. "I would like a bath."

Ash wasn't happy about my choice, but he relented. "I can do that." He kissed the top of my head. "Hold on."

He rose, carrying me into the bathing chamber. I could've walked, but I didn't protest. He set me on the ledge and then placed his hand in the now-cold water, heating it. I shrugged off the blanket and stepped in. A breathy sigh left me as I sank down and reached for the soap.

"Let me." Ash had rolled up his sleeves. He took the soap, setting it aside before cupping his hands in the water.

Warm liquid cascaded over my skin, and I watched crimson ribbons swirl away from my body, staining the water. Ash's hands were gentle, traveling across the planes of my back, washing away the blood.

He had to be exhausted. He likely wanted nothing more than to wash the last two days from *his* body, but he took his time, running his soapy hands down both of my arms. He took care with my hands and fingers, erasing any traces of blood that lingered. He didn't speak, but so much was said in how he methodically rinsed my hair, his fingers combing through the tangled curls with a tenderness I didn't feel I deserved. Each time the water turned pink with evidence of the night's violence, he drained the tub, only to refill it with clear, clean warmth from the unused buckets that had been brought in. He washed every part of me twice, almost as if he sought to cleanse away more than just the physical evidence of all that had happened. It was like he was also trying to remove the stains upon my soul, offering absolution I was too shattered to ask for.

He lifted me from the tub, and I caught only a glimpse of my reflection as he dried me off. My face was a mess. Bruises marred the skin around my mouth, and my throat showed deep fingerprints.

Ash took me back into the bedchamber and placed me on the bed. He replaced the towel he had wrapped around me with a blanket made of soft-spun yarn.

"I'll be right back," he promised, brushing his lips over my forehead. "Rest."

I nodded, tucking my legs up under the blanket. He grabbed pants from the wardrobe, and I sat there, eyes glued to the bathing chamber. He left the door open, and I saw him strip down. His movements were quick. When he stepped out of my line of sight, I heard water splash. I knew he wouldn't take nearly as long with himself.

I was right.

Within a handful of minutes, he was once more in the bedchamber, the loose cotton pants clinging to the skin he hadn't dried thoroughly. Water still dripped from his hair when he came toward me, roughly rubbing the towel over his head.

"Ash?" I whispered.

He tossed the towel back into the bathing chamber, then started toward me but stopped as my anxiety spiked. "It'll be okay, Sera."

A tremor went through me. "How?"

"Because we will make it okay."

It wasn't that simple.

I forced myself to meet his gaze. It was hard. So many emotions and too many thoughts crowded every part of my being. "You know what I did?"

He didn't look away as he sat on the floor a few feet from the bed. "I do."

"How do we make that okay?" I asked, my heart rate picking up. "I—I can't…"

"You can't what?" he asked quietly.

I shook my head, pressure starting to build in my chest. "I…I can't believe what I did." The words tore at my chest, rattling me. "I can't believe what I caused."

Ash…flinched. "*Liessa*—"

"Part of the reason you were trapped at the Pillars for almost two days was because of what I did."

"Sera, that's—"

"It's true." Tears crowded my eyes, and I stood on numb legs, wrapping the blanket around me. "I lost control. I killed people—innocent people, Ash."

Eather streaked across his eyes, and his body tensed. "You did."

You did.

He wasn't denying what I'd done. I didn't want him to, but a small, childish part of me wanted him to be oblivious to it. How fucked up was that? I started to turn from him.

"Don't," he said. "Don't shut down. We need to talk about this. No bullshit, Sera. No lies. No half-truths. No hiding."

My lips trembled, and I pressed them together to stop them.

"Okay?" His eyes searched mine. "Sera?"

"Okay." I closed my eyes. A storm of emotions brewing inside me, stirring the eather. "I…I should've listened to you. You said Kolis would do something terrible if he felt threatened. You were right. I knew you were right, and I should've listened, but I didn't think he would do *that*."

But that wasn't entirely true, was it? I knew Kolis could be horrifically cruel.

"I didn't want to believe it," I admitted.

"Who would?" He looked up at me. "Who would want to believe he would do that?"

"Who would want to believe what I did?" My legs shook.

The air around us dropped several degrees when Ash's anger rose to the surface. "What you did is not the same as what Kolis did."

"I knew what would happen if I killed a Primal without there being another to take their place, and I still did it." I opened my eyes, and eather gathered like a knot in my chest. "And if I had caught Kyn, I would've done the same to him." My breath came in short, shallow pants. "Do you know I went to Dalos? I destroyed the Rise."

Something close to pride filled his gaze.

I shook my head. "Don't look at me like that. I killed every guard on the wall."

"Guards loyal to Kolis, Sera."

They had been, and the guilt I felt wasn't for them. "I leveled Cor Palace. There were gods in there. Then I tore down the Sanctuary. I slaughtered gods who said they wouldn't fight me. I destroyed his Ascended."

"I know. There were Ascended at the Pillars."

I flinched at the reminder that they still had souls—that many, if not all of them, would have never chosen their fates. My chest rose and fell rapidly. I searched for anger and disappointment in his features, but all I saw was sorrow. Compassion. Love.

I looked away from it. "Was there…?" I swallowed and pushed past my cowardice. "Were there Chosen at the Pillars? Kolis left them there. I…I didn't know. I didn't stop to even think about them."

"I don't know, and that is the truth," he said. "There were many souls there. When that happened, the Pillars couldn't perform their duty. I wrote many names, but I did not personally handle any Chosen. Rhahar could have."

A shudder rocked me, and I lowered myself to the floor, needing to be closer to him. "I… When Embris died, it destroyed most of Terra. There were…entire villages were wiped out. Whole families. They were…" Images of their ash-encased bodies filled my mind, and I shook my head. "I brought them back without even thinking of the price. I saved them and, in the same breath, sentenced others to death. Even before that, when I first saw what they had done to—" My voice broke, and Ash tipped his head down, resting his forehead against mine. "I couldn't control my rage. It became this tangible storm that continued to wreak havoc on those in Lasania—in Carsodonia. I don't even know how many I killed tonight."

"Does it matter?" His eyes met mine. "One is enough. You've said as much yourself. Whether it was ten, a hundred, or a thousand, it will not change how you feel right now."

The weight continued pressing down on me. "Then tell me I was wrong. Tell me I fucked up! Tell me that—"

"I understand," he cut me off. "That's not what you want to hear, but it is what you need to hear."

I stared at him in disbelief. "How can you understand what I did, Ash?" The pressure amplified. "How can you even stand to look at me?"

His eyes widened, and his skin thinned. The temperature dropped even more. "Are you…?" Eather swirled in his eyes, and shadows blossomed under his flesh. "Are you fucking serious right now? You're honestly asking that question?"

"I am the true Primal of Life—"

"You are Seraphena Mierel!" His eyes flashed pure silver for a heartbeat, and the walls trembled, causing the chandelier to sway. "You are my wife. My fucking everything. I've told you this before, and it remains the same. There is *nothing* you could do that would *ever* change what I see or how I feel when I look at you."

I sucked in a staggered breath. I knew that. Of course, I did.

"And I *do* understand what you did because, right or wrong, I would've done the same."

"No, you wouldn't have. You are better—"

"I am not better than that!" he shouted, pitching forward to plant his hands on the floor in front of him. For a moment, I thought he might take his wolf form. That was how he looked. "I am not better than you, Sera. You keep forgetting what I would've done if I'd lost you. I would've destroyed both realms. I would've become the end of everything, and the Fates know I wouldn't have thought twice," he snarled, his fangs bared. "Do you really think I didn't try to kill Kolis after he murdered my father? I did. Even though I wasn't powerful enough to do so, I fully intended to while knowing the consequences. I tried to kill him when he had you in Dalos, or did you forget that, too?"

I shivered. "I haven't forgotten, Ash, but this isn't the same, and you know it's not."

"What I know is that realms would be on fire if I had lost you," he swore. "And even though you know that to be true, it does not change how you feel about me. Just because I have you doesn't change what my intent would've been." He took a deep breath, visibly attempting to calm himself. "I know what you want. What you think you need. You think you deserve to be punished. That something should be taken from you."

"Would I be wrong?" I cried.

"Your guilt? Your remorse? It is choking me, so I know it must be suffocating you." His voice cracked, and a glistening sheen of tears reflected in his eyes. "And I know it's not going to be something that will magically disappear tomorrow. And there *will be* a tomorrow, Sera. There will be a thousand and more tomorrows. And I know your remorse will still be there with you no matter how many tomorrows there are. *That* is punishment enough."

Was it, though?

He closed his eyes, and when they reopened, his lashes were damp. "What you did is not the same as Kolis."

"What I did started as an act of justice, but it turned into nothing more than vengeance," I said, disgust and shame lacing each word I spoke. "And once that happens, no one is on the right side. I went too far, and people paid with their lives."

"Listen to me, Sera. Two things can be true at the same time. You went too far, but you are not Kolis. That doesn't absolve you of responsibility, but it is not the same."

I shook my head, a wail of grief welling up in me.

Shadows crawled up his neck and spread across his jaw. "Did you intend to kill? I'm not talking about Embris or the guards. Not even the Ascended. Did you intend to kill mortals?"

I drew back. "Gods, no."

"Did Kolis intend to do so?"

"Yes."

"*That* is the difference, and I can tell you right now, Kolis doesn't feel an ounce of regret for what he ordered," he said. "That is another difference."

A tremor started building deep inside me. "But how…how do I live with this?"

"You don't just live with it," he said, his hands trembling when he tipped my head back. "You accept what you did. You learn from it."

Accept it? A thousand years could pass, and I would still be horrified by what I'd caused. But I…

"I'm already learning," I said. "I didn't listen to my instincts. I should've listened to you and the others. I never should've believed that Kolis would put the realms before himself and his wants. I should've refused to offer him a deal instead of wanting to be better—less like who I was. Less like Kolis and more like your father. But that's the thing, Ash. I *am* like Kolis."

His nostrils flared. "I swear to the fucking Fates—"

"I am, Ash. That's what you don't want to accept." I shook even harder. "I am not him or Veses, but I am *not* a benevolent person. I'm not cruel, but I don't regret killing Embris for his role in taking my family from me. I never even really spoke to him, and he was more than happy to carry out Kolis's orders and help kill innocent people. Or maybe he wasn't happy to do so. Maybe he was threatened or scared. I don't care. I'm glad I saw the life go out of his eyes." I couldn't sit still any longer, so I rose again.

As Ash stared up at me in silence, I took a deep breath and willed my heart to settle. "I am not a forgiving person. I try to be, but I can be monstrous. More so than you, and I am capable of horrific violence."

"So am I." He leaned back, bending one knee.

"You are when it comes to me or Kolis, but you would not have done what I did if I wasn't threatened." I held the blanket tighter around me. "You said no lies. No bullshit or half-truths. You would've stopped yourself. You know that."

Ash looked away, a muscle ticking in his jaw.

"I never should've tried to handle this like I thought Eythos would have. I should have—" I stopped myself. Should have. Could have. Would have. I *fucking* hated them.

"What are you saying?" Ash asked.

"I'm saying I…I need to be me."

His gaze met mine. "That's all I've ever wanted. That is all the realms need."

I stared at him, the clarity of his words driving me down. I sat on the edge of the bed. Gods. Ash…he'd always known what I was. What I was capable of. The good. The bad. The beautiful and the ugly. He had always accepted me. I'd just never accepted that. I hadn't wanted to face it. Just like I…

I hadn't faced so much in my life. It hadn't made me stronger. It had only made me weaker.

He rose and knelt in front of me. "*You* are who I fell in love with, Sera. *Every* part of you. Not just the easy stuff but the complicated, messy aspects, too. I love each part of you equally. You will always be what I cherish most, *liessa*." Clasping my cheeks, he kissed the top of my head. "Nothing will ever change that."

Wrapped in a deep violet robe with pretty embroidery and pearls, I sat on the balcony's daybed, staring up at the star-strewn night sky, despite it being cold enough to need to tuck my legs beneath the heavy folds of the robe. The chill in the air made me think that snow may soon fall.

An entire day had passed since Ash coaxed me out of my *nota*, and we'd spent most of that time sleeping—actually, he was *still* sleeping. Both of us were exhausted to a bone-deep level and were lucky things were quiet, giving us time to rest. I couldn't sense the true Primal of Death. It was like before he'd awakened from stasis the last time. I felt nothing, no intuition concerning his current state. I had to assume he was still in stasis.

That allowed me to relax. A little. I should be resting, too, but when my eyes had opened, memories of what I'd done came to the forefront, and I hadn't been able to fall back to sleep.

So, here I sat, watching the guards patrol the Rise, thinking about everything Ash had said. He'd been right. A thousand tomorrows would come, and I would still carry the guilt with me. Sure, it would lessen as time passed, and I accepted it.

But it would always be there, haunting the back of my mind like the spirits lingering in the Dark Elms, refusing to cross over.

And that wasn't the only thing haunting me.

When we were awake earlier, it had only been long enough to eat and for Ash to check in with the others. He hadn't been gone for more than ten minutes—I honestly didn't think he'd even left the fourth floor. But when he returned, his flesh was noticeably warmer. Ash had given me his blood then, which was why I was sitting outside, possibly turning into a Primal ice cube.

I remembered what I'd learned before…everything happened.

Ash had been feeding from Rhain.

A shaky breath left me, and I closed my eyes. That wasn't the only thing

I'd been thinking about, though. What I'd done occupied my thoughts, as did what Ash had said to me. He had been right. I had to face it, accept it—even though it would be painful—and live with it. Accepting it also meant facing a harsh truth about myself.

And what I'd been through.

Not just with Kolis but also with Tavius and my *training*. I forced myself to sit with it just like I had that day in the library. To acknowledge things I hadn't shared with Aios. Moments I'd convinced myself weren't happening when they were, and still pretended to this very moment hadn't occurred. But no amount of refusing to acknowledge what had really taken place when Kolis fed from me stopped the truth from haunting the farthest recesses of my mind or finding me in sleep.

When Kolis bit me the second time, he hadn't just held me as he found pleasure. I counted my breaths.

One.

Two.

Three.

Four.

Five.

He had touched me as he fed from me. He'd held me in his lap, my feet unable to touch the floor, and the hand that skimmed over the fucking poor excuse for a dress had slipped under.

My hands were clenched as tightly now as they had been then. No matter how far I had retreated in my mind as part of him invaded me, my subconscious still remembered. My body could still feel the rough, scalding jab of his fingers. Mentally, I hadn't been there when it happened, but a part of my soul had been there every single fucking day since. And telling myself it could've been worse no longer helped. Saying that it wasn't assault just because he'd used his fangs and fingers instead of his dick didn't change that it was. It didn't change who I was. Didn't change that I had been a victim.

My nails dug into my palms as I counted. One, two, three, four, five. Being a victim wasn't a weakness, a stain, or something to be ashamed of. All those ugly things were bestowed upon the victimizer. That wasn't on me.

"Sera."

My eyes flew open at the sound of Ash's voice. I'd been so lost in my thoughts I hadn't heard him walk out onto the balcony or felt how close he was, standing only a few feet from me.

His hair lay free, brushing his bare shoulders and that hard-as-granite jawline. He moved as if to come closer but halted, his eyes burning brightly under the starlight. "What are you doing out here, *liessa*?"

I swallowed. "Thinking."

He stared at me intently, like he did every so often, and I suspected he was checking to see if all the bruises had faded. Most of them had. Just a few pale blue ones remained, and I knew it bothered him. The bruises should be completely gone by now, and I was willing to bet I would be having a one-on-one with the Healer tomorrow if they weren't.

"And freezing while doing so?" he said finally.

A wan smile tugged at my lips. "It's not that cold." My gaze moved, taking in the hard-packed muscles of his chest and abdomen. Even his feet were bare. "I have far more clothing on than you do."

"Good point," he acknowledged with a tilt of his head. "But I don't feel the cold like you do."

It was strange that Kolis now felt as cold as Ash, but Kolis's frigidness hurt to come into contact with. Ash's never did. My gaze swept over his face. There were still faint shadows of weariness under his eyes.

His chest rose with a deep breath. "How long have you been awake?"

"I don't know." I glanced at the sky, seeing no hints of dawn. "A couple of hours."

Concern flickered across his features. "You've been out here this whole time?"

"I couldn't sleep and didn't want to wake you."

"I'd rather you *had* awakened me." He came forward then, sitting beside me.

"You're tired, Ash, and you need your sleep. The fact that you didn't wake up when I left is evidence of that."

"You need your rest, too." His gaze dropped to my hands in my lap. "More so than I do."

Ash reached over and picked up my hands. He carefully straightened my fingers, stiffening when he saw the three little crescent-shaped marks on each of my palms left behind by my fingernails.

"*Liessa*," he murmured, and my heart ached as he lifted my hands and brushed his lips over the fading marks.

As he smoothed calloused thumbs over my palms, I had a feeling I was projecting a whole mess of emotions onto him. And it was a mess because I felt *everything* right now. Sorrow. Anger. Nervousness. I knew I needed to talk to Ash. Really talk. But there was nothing easy about that for me. I was never the talking type. I hadn't been raised that way. It wasn't an excuse. It was just the truth. When it came to something important, I could rehearse everything I wanted to say a hundred times, but the moment I opened my mouth, something entirely different came out. Even more so when it came to this.

But I had to.

Because what I'd gone through was slowly chipping away pieces of me. Eventually, I would be left with nothing.

"It's not true, you know." I stared at our hands. "I don't need more rest than you."

"What makes you think that?"

"I fed from you a handful of hours ago," I said.

He said nothing, opting to kiss my palms again. Then he placed my hands back in my lap and rose. He went to the railing and leaned against the shadowstone. The muscles along his shoulders bulged as he eyed a guard in the distance. "Is that what you've been thinking about while sitting out here?"

"Yes, and no. I've been thinking about a lot of stuff."

He faced me. "You going to tell me what you've been thinking about?"

Talk to me.

That's what he always said. When I didn't, he didn't push, except for the night of the *sekya* attack. I doubted he would push now. I wanted to talk. Needed to. I just didn't know where to start because this—all of this inside me—hadn't been birthed into creation when Kolis captured me. It had started long before then.

Ash drew in a heavy breath and pushed away from the railing. "Will you at least come back to bed with me?"

My gaze flew to his, and my chest seized. Words bubbled up, shaken free. Ones I had only ever shared with Nektas. "I tried to end my life once."

Ash's entire body jerked back, and he bumped into the railing. "What?"

Part of me couldn't believe that was where I'd started—that I had just hurled that at him with no warning. He hadn't been prepared to hear it. The shock in his expression was proof. "I'm sorry. I probably should've given you some sort of heads-up on that."

Ash stared at me. His hands had returned to the railing, and he held on to it as if he needed the support.

I looked away from his hands, focusing on mine. "I drank a vial of sleeping draft—far more than necessary. And convinced myself for so long that it was accidental. That it wasn't on purpose. But…" My nose and eyes stung. "It was. I didn't want to wake up."

"Why?" he asked hoarsely.

"I don't know," I said with a shaky sigh and peeked up at him. His eyes were closed tightly. "That's not entirely true. There wasn't one reason. I don't think there was even one reason—specifically what he believed my fate to be—for why my father took his life. It's never that simple."

A spasm ran through him, and his lashes lifted. When he spoke, his voice sounded as choked as mine felt. "When did you try that?"

"I know what you're thinking. That it's because you rejected me."

His jaw clenched. "That wasn't a reason?"

"It doesn't matter, Ash. You're not responsible for that. Just like I know I'm not responsible for my father, even though I spent most of my life feeling like I was. I just…I felt like I was failing everyone and myself. I didn't like who I was because I was no one. I was this blank canvas, taught to act and behave like someone. To not really have feelings. Like I couldn't be mad or even happy. I was just to be whatever I *needed* to be." I knew I was rambling, but I couldn't stop myself. "But I wasn't good at that, so I had to pretend how my mother acted didn't affect me. I made myself okay with the fact that no one, except Odetta and Holland, really touched me. I just had to deal with

Tavius and him thinking he could do whatever he wanted to me."

My fingers curled inward again. "I couldn't refuse training, whether it came to mastering a sword or seduction, and I had no one, not even Holland, that I could really talk to."

"This training? To seduce?" Ash sounded like each word cut his throat to speak. "How old were you when it began?"

"Not old enough to be able to deal with it," I admitted quietly. "I was scared at first. I remember begging Holland to not let me go, but…" I closed my eyes and shook my head. "That part of my life was so…weird."

"I can think of a better word than weird," he bit out.

"I mean, I felt embarrassed to be doing the things I was being taught and didn't know how to feel about it. Sometimes, it felt good, but it…it also felt wrong."

"Because it *was* wrong," he said.

"I know." I sighed. "I think maybe I knew it then, too. But I couldn't say no. I couldn't say I didn't want to do it. I didn't have a choice in anything. And I…I didn't want to do it anymore. So, the draft."

Ash looked stricken, as if someone had plunged a dagger into his chest.

"I regretted it as soon as I woke up. I was embarrassed. And I hated that I felt that way." My lips peeled back with a low growl. "I still hate that my head just doesn't work like it should. You know? Like there were—and still are—others with worse childhoods and experiences, and they never once thought about trying or doing something like that." I laughed, but there was no humor in it. "But I did."

"I'm so damn sorry, Sera," he whispered. "All those times I said you had no regard for your life. I didn't know. If I had, I would never have said that."

"You don't need to apologize because it's true. Or was," I said, holding the edge of the blanket to my chin. "I didn't value my life. Not until I decided I wanted to live—when it felt like it was too late. You're part of the reason. I mean, it's not just you. It was also gaining control. A sense of self. I was no longer an empty vessel. I was becoming someone, and you helped me do that. And I…"

I lifted my head to find Ash watching me from where he stood by the railing, his eyes glittering.

I wet my dry lips. "You…you've been feeding from Rhain."

Ash went completely still.

"That's why you don't feel as cold sometimes," I said, my chest aching anew. "You had to go to him because I couldn't provide for you."

"Sera." Ash jerked away from the railing. "You provide for me. You give me everything I could ever want."

"Except the one thing you need to survive. It's okay—" I winced. "No, it's not okay. What I'm saying is that I'm not mad at you or anything. It makes me love you even more because I know how hard it is for you to feed from others. I'm angry with myself."

His hands fisted at his sides. "Do not be angry with yourself. Kolis—"

"He took that from me. From us. I know. You were right when you said that."

"I don't care about being right." He came forward and lowered himself to his knees before me. "I will do anything for you not to feel fear, Sera."

"I know." The pressure was crushing then, my chest squeezing as if a giant hand was trying to pinch off my breath. "You never caused me fear. I know you won't hurt me. I just... My mind goes back there to Kolis. To being in that fucking cage, and him..."

Ash reached for me but placed his hands on either side of me instead. "And him...?"

I opened my mouth when more words slithered their way up my throat. "Him having complete control. In what I wore. What I ate. Where I went. He put me on display as if I was some kind of token. Or a pet. Even when he held court. And you know what the fucked-up thing was? He liked it when I tried to escape, or he scared me. He enjoyed it. And not because he's a fucking piece of shit, but because it reminded him of Sotoria. Gods..." I tugged at the stitching on my robe. "He didn't like it when I mouthed off. Because there were times, Ash, when I couldn't pretend. I just couldn't. And when that happened, it didn't matter that he believed I was Sotoria."

"What?" His voice was steady but thin. "What did he do?"

"He almost always controlled himself, and gods, that was somehow scarier. Seeing him get to that edge and then pull back? It left me feeling like I was constantly on the cliff's edge. I know that doesn't make sense, but that...that was worse than the chains."

Ash's inhale was audible. "The chains?"

"I..." I stared at his shoulder. "It was because of Veses."

"I will kill that bitch."

"It wasn't her fault," I said with a humorless laugh. "He punished her. Gave her to Kyn in front of everyone." I almost gagged, disgust rolling through me. "And, gods, I hate her. I hate her as much as I hate him. But that wasn't right. I don't care what Veses says. It was disgusting. I told him as much, and I'd already mouthed off at him more than once that day. I just couldn't..." I shook my head. "He hung me by my arms."

The temperature plummeted. I could see my breath. A thin layer of ice spread from Ash's knees and crept across the balcony floor. My gaze flew to his.

There were no pupils visible in his eyes.

"Ash," I whispered.

"I'm fine."

"No, you're not."

His neck twisted to the side. "I still look like me, don't I?"

I nodded.

"Then I'm okay." The eather retreated a bit from his eyes. "Please.

Please, keep talking."

"I don't think that's a good idea."

"It is. I need you to." His shoulders rolled. "You need to."

"I don't want this stuff in your head, Ash. You already have enough."

"It's been in my head, Sera," he said hoarsely, his features stark. "It's in my head every night you scream. It's there when I feel you lock up against me. When I can tell you're fighting not to pull away from me. It's already there."

Pain lanced my chest. "I don't want that."

"I know." He took a breath, and the ice began to melt. "Tell me how Rhain ended up freed."

My heart stuttered. "You don't know?"

"I don't know what I know. Or what I don't."

I glanced down at his hands. The knuckles were bleached white. "Kolis was going to have Rhain killed, and I…I couldn't allow that. I told him that it would only worsen tensions if he killed Rhain. That is true."

"But that wasn't the only thing."

"No." I focused on the golden imprint on my hand. "I told him I would do anything. That I was willing to make a deal." I looked up at Ash. "What I'm about to tell you is the truth. I'm not omitting anything. I'm being completely honest, and I need you to believe that."

His eyes searched mine. "I'll believe you."

I took a breath and counted to five. "He agreed to free Rhain if I allowed him to sleep with me—"

Ash's eyes flashed pure silver.

"All he meant was sleeping next to me," I quickly added. "That was all. He wanted to…" My lip curled. "Hold me while he slept."

"Did you think that was what he meant?" he asked after several tense moments.

"No," I whispered, feeling daggers in my gut. "All I could think about was saving Rhain. I panicked, and I agreed. I'm sorry—"

"Fates, do not apologize." He sank back on his haunches. "You have nothing to apologize for."

"But—"

"No," he snarled, shadows appearing and then disappearing beneath his skin. "Even if he wanted more and you agreed to it, you would have done so under duress. That's not true consent. Ask me how I know."

"I don't need to ask," I said. "I know how you know."

"Then do not waste a fucking second on guilt."

My chest rose deeply. "I…I won't. You're right."

He twisted his neck again. "Is that the only time he wanted to sleep beside you?"

I shook my head.

Ash took a breath. I wasn't sure if he took another after that.

"He has remained celibate since Sotoria." I watched his chest, looking for movement. "How incredibly creepy is that?"

The chest rose then. "I don't even know what to say."

I nodded.

"There's more," he said quietly.

I nodded again, my mind returning to when I first woke up in Dalos. "You…you know he fed from me the first time. That time it hurt. It was so painful, and I was relieved." I closed my eyes. "When he did it again, it was…it was after Ione told him I was Sotoria. He didn't make it hurt for long."

"But he did at first?"

"He was mad. I asked about freeing you, and he was so angry that I brought up your name while he…held me," I said, anger rising. "That's when he bit me again. But then he was…gentle because he thought I was Sotoria." Revulsion churned through me. Telling Aios this part hadn't been easy, but every word took so much damn effort now. "And that was worse. It didn't feel bad, and I hated that. I fucking hated it."

"It's not your fault, Sera. Even if you felt pleasure, it's not something you can control," he said quietly. "I couldn't control it when Veses fed from me."

"I know," I whispered for what felt like the hundredth time. I could feel his hands shaking on the daybed beside me. "I do know. But sometimes, I can…I can feel him behind me. *Moving*," I spat, my stomach churning. "I can feel him against me, and I'm suddenly back there, unable to stop him. Unable to do anything but let it happen. Wait it out as he finds pleasure and…"

"And what?" Ash asked—or begged.

My throat burned. "He…he touched me. It wasn't the first time. He used compulsion against me in the beginning, right after I stabbed him. He'd had enough of my mouth and antics, and when he returned me to Dalos, he touched me like he was unfamiliar with a woman's body or something." Words rushed out of me then like a flood overflowing the banks of a river. "But he didn't go too far, not like he did when he fed from me. Then, he put his hands on me, inside me—" I smacked my hands over my face, choking on what spilled out of me. And it wasn't just what Kolis had done that tore itself from me now. It was how Tavius had tried to put his hands on me. How he'd pinned me to my bed that fateful morning Ash finally came for me. I spat out the knowledge that if I had remained in Wayfair Castle a day longer, Tavius would've likely followed through on his threats.

And it just kept flooding out of me, pumping from that chasm in my chest. I didn't even know what I was saying. I jumped from Kolis to Tavius to the training to fucking Kyn and his crudeness until I was panting for breath. Until what I thought while Kolis assaulted me became words I whispered. "I hate him. I hate Kolis, and I hate Eythos for creating that situation. I hate the Fates for preventing him from telling you the truth, and I fucking loathe how much everything reminds me of Tavius."

Ash's cool fingers folded around my wrists. "Sera, love—"

"I hate them!" I screamed, my throat convulsing. I screamed as the knot of sorrow lodged in my chest, too big to pass. Ash moved swiftly, lifting me into his arms and folding his hand against the back of my head. I screamed into his chest when he carried me inside, and the doors closed behind us as he brought me to the floor beside the bed. "I hate them!"

I couldn't stop as Ash held me tightly to his chest. I shrieked my hatred against him as the floors trembled and the call of worried draken drew closer to the palace. I raged until my anger gave way to grief, and the tears no longer choked me but ran down my face. I broke, my screams turning into sobs that shook my entire body. At some point, those cries took on a different source.

Ash held me, his cheek pressed to the top of my head. He rocked us, assuring me it would be okay. That he was there and would always be there. Reminding me that he loved me. Telling me to let it out as tears fell for Ezra and Marisol. For all the lives Kolis had taken and the ones who'd perished because of my actions. I grieved for who I was before Kolis. Who we had been. Clutching Ash's arms, I howled the agony of losing my mother and the small spark of hope that had been extinguished. And I *mourned.*

I mourned the knowledge that the realms would never be the same because of me.

Ash smoothed his hand over my head and ran his fingers through my hair. He'd been doing that for…I didn't know how long.

We were still on the floor, me in his arms, my tear-stained cheek plastered to his chest. My head ached a little, but I had stopped crying. Finally. I had shed so many tears I didn't think it was possible for me to ever cry again.

Like with Aios, I didn't feel better after telling Ash everything, but I knew I would eventually.

We were quiet for so long that I flinched when I broke the silence with my hoarse voice. "Ash?"

He kissed the top of my head. "*Liessa*?"

The breath I exhaled was shaky. I was a little afraid to ask what I did next. "My mother…where is she now?"

Ash brushed his lips over my forehead this time. "She's in the Vale," he said. "I don't think that's what she deserves, but I thought that was what you would want."

I squeezed my eyes closed. I was wrong. There *were* more tears. "Thank you," I whispered, knowing how hard it must have been for him to send her to the Vale.

His arm tightened around me, and we fell into another stretch of silence. The weight of his hand and the feel of his fingers sifting through my hair were soothing, allowing my mind to clear. There was something else I needed to tell Ash, something I'd realized while in my *nota* form and had come to accept.

I would never be able to slay the monstrous side of me. I would only ever be able to wound it. It would always be a part of me.

Drawing in a breath, I sat back. Ash's eyes opened and immediately found mine. "There's something I need to say."

His hand left my hair and swept down my back. "I'm listening."

"I don't want to lose control like I did again, but I know me," I said. "I need you to promise me something, Ash."

His hand halted on my lower back. "What do you want me to promise, Sera?"

A wry smile tugged at my lips. "You didn't automatically say, '*anything*.'"

"I know better than to say that right now." Tension bracketed his mouth. "What do you want me to promise?"

"I want you to promise you'll stop me," I said, and his features took on a blade-sharp edge. "I know me. I…I *will* lose control again, especially when it comes to Kolis." I drew in a shallow breath. "When he came to Lotho, he…he killed almost all the draken there. He didn't even seem to care if they remained loyal to Embris—to him—or not. Then he laughed, and—" I swallowed the lingering taste of horror. "He *sang*, and gods and godlings leapt to their deaths, Ash. Dozens of them. Maybe more. Thierran is the last *oneirou* now." The hardest words came next, the reason it would erase every good intention I had. I rose, needing space to say what I had to. "He…he killed Ezra and Marisol. He snapped my mother's neck with his hands."

Ash tipped his head back, his jaw tensing.

"There's more," I said, my voice trembling as I spoke, even further proof of why I couldn't be trusted to quell my rage. "He doesn't just want Sotoria's soul. He wants us to suffer like he has, and in the most messed-up way that I truly do not need to go into details with."

Ash didn't blink. He didn't breathe. But his eyes turned into pure silver orbs.

"I cannot promise I will not lose control again because of that. I wish I were different, but I'm not," I told him. "I need you to intervene if I get to that point."

His entire body jerked back with a swift inhale. "Sera—"

"I know that what I'm asking is horrible. I *know*. And I hate that I'm asking you this. That I'm putting you in this situation." Tears blurred his features. I turned and sat on the edge of the bed. "But you cannot allow me to seek vengeance because I will not be able to live with doing something like that again."

He twisted toward me. "I will help you ensure it doesn't get to that point."

"I hope you do. But if you can't?"

"I *will*," he growled, pushing to his feet. He stepped back and thrust a hand through his hair.

I squeezed my eyes shut. "But if you can't, Ash, I need you to stop me by…by any means necessary."

He swore, and an icy wind whipped through the bedchamber, tossing my hair across my face. "Do you realize what you're asking of me?"

"I do."

"I would have to put you in the ground, Sera. Into stasis. I would have to—" Eyes closing, his fisted hand went to his heart. "I would have to hurt you."

I could see that this was hurting *him*. "I'm sorry. I know what it would do to you, and I hate that. I hate that I'm even asking this. But whatever pain you would cause would be momentary. The pain I would cause if I lost control again would end me, Ash. It would. I wouldn't be able to come back from it. Please," I whispered. "Please, promise me."

He was kneeling before me in a heartbeat, the tips of his fingers chasing away the tears. Hands trembling, he rested his forehead against mine and shuddered.

Neither of us spoke for several long moments. When he did, pain coated each word, but so did love. Not the blind, foolish sort, but *real* love. The hard kind. "I promise," he rasped, his voice thickening with barely checked agony. "I swear I will stop you—" His voice cracked, and I felt the dampness of his tears mixing with mine. "I will stop you from seeking vengeance."

The air shifted and charged, responding to the oath made by a Primal. I felt it in my bones—the promise becoming an unbreakable vow that would remain until we entered Arcadia.

47

"Did you eat enough?" Ash asked, striding into the antechamber and pulling a white linen shirt over his head.

"Yes." This morning, he'd asked if I'd slept enough. The answer was the same, even though I could count on one hand how many hours of sleep I'd actually gotten. But I'd slept deeply, apparently having cried myself into exhaustion.

Ash eyed the array of dishes he'd arranged for me like he had when I said I'd gotten enough sleep. I'd eaten something from every plate and bowl. He looked worried when he stepped onto the raised platform. "You sure?"

"I ate two helpings of the sausage." I patted my belly. "I'm stuffed."

One side of his lips curled up, and he stopped at my side. He bent, kissed my cheek, and then stepped back. His gaze roamed over my face before fixing on my throat. Eather pierced his eyes as he opened his mouth.

"I know what you're going to say," I jumped in. "It's the same thing you said this morning."

He sat in the chair to my right. "That hasn't changed, *liessa.* Those bruises should've healed by now. I want Kye to look you over."

"I don't know why the bruises haven't completely faded, but I feel fine, Ash." I took a drink of the citrus juice. "I promise."

Ash didn't say anything, just picked up the last strip of bacon he hadn't eaten before he'd left to change.

"And we have too much to do today to waste time summoning a Healer," I added.

He glanced over at me. "Making sure you're healthy will never be a waste of time, Sera."

"It is when I'm okay." I sat back in the chair, resting my hands on the arms. "We need to decide what we're doing. I'm pretty sure Kolis is still in stasis, but I doubt he will be for much longer. We need to…"

Wiping his fingers, he then tossed the napkin onto his plate. "Strike before he awakens?"

I nodded. "That's what I should've agreed to when we first had this conversation."

His eyes found mine. "What you decided the first time wasn't wrong, Sera."

My fingers pressed onto the wooden arms. "Can I ask you something? And will you give me your honest answer?"

"Always."

I swallowed. "When you agreed to try to go the somewhat peaceful route first, was that what you really wanted? Or did you agree because it was what I suggested?"

"That's a question with a complicated answer." He rested his elbow on the arm of his chair. "I, too, wanted to avoid a full-scale war. Too many people would've died, both here and in the mortal realm. That's why I agreed."

"But?"

He was quiet for a moment. "But you know what I thought. That once Kolis felt truly threatened, he would strike out." He drew his thumb over his chin. "I just prayed it would not be in the manner in which he did."

Swallowing again, I nodded once more.

"So, yes, I did agree because it was the right route to go," he continued. "I had my reservations, especially about the deals, but that is in the past. There's no point in dwelling there. We don't have time for that."

I exhaled slowly. "Agreed."

He took a drink of his coffee. "You said last night that you were now going to be yourself. You. Not who you thought you should be. I think I know the answer, but I want to hear it from you. How do *you* think we should proceed?"

I didn't even have to think about it. "I think we should go straight to Dalos and take out anyone who stands in our way."

"That's what I thought." He set his cup down. "But that will not work. As of right now, we still do not know who our allies are, and Kolis's armies outnumber ours, even with you Ascending Penellaphe."

I tensed. "You've gotten an update from Lotho?"

"Thierran gave me a brief update when he returned last night," he said. "Nearly half the army has defected and fled to Dalos."

I closed my eyes. Our numbers were closer to Kolis's, but he still had more unless a Primal like Phanos joined us. "I wonder if Thierran settled all the scores he needed to," I murmured.

Ash's brows rose. "Do I even want to know?"

"Probably not." The royal blue tunic I'd donned settled around my thighs as I rose from the chair and walked toward the open balcony doors. My gaze fell on the sunlight reflecting off the Rise walls. "We still need to summon the Primals."

"Agreed."

"We need to do that today." I crossed my arms over my chest. "And we need to summon all the Primals, including Kyn and Veses. I want to make a statement."

I didn't even have to finish what I was saying. Ash knew, and a savage glint filled his eyes. He nodded and then asked, "Will you be able to handle that? There are rules when all the Primals are summoned into one's home. They cannot be harmed unless it is in self-defense."

"It won't be easy. I…I may need your help with staying calm," I admitted, feeling my cheeks burn.

He raised a brow. "You do realize I'm not the best person to rely on when it comes to that son of a bitch and keeping calm."

"You will stop yourself. You've done it before," I reminded him.

His eyes flashed with luminous eather. "That was before."

Before he knew everything.

"We won't mess this up. We will make sure we control ourselves," he said after a moment. "Are we still planning to establish a council of sorts after Kolis is dealt with?"

"Yes. I still believe in that." I tucked a curl back. "More now than ever."

He was quiet as he rolled up his sleeves. "Are we giving the Primals an ultimatum? Swear allegiance to us or die?"

I turned halfway to him. "I don't like it," I admitted, twisting the ends of my hair. "It sounds like something Kolis would do. With Phanos, I would like to give him the chance to stand down, but…"

"You want to do that because of what the ceeren did for you."

I nodded. "I saw his pain at their loss, Ash. It was real."

"I'm sure it was." He exhaled heavily. "But isn't Kolis capable of experiencing emotional pain?"

My fingers stilled.

"Veses? Kyn?" he continued. "That doesn't change who they are at their cores, Sera. You know that."

"I do." I let go of my hair. "Thinking anything different would mean making another mistake. The same mistakes. We have to end this, and we need to do it in a manner that lessens the impact on the mortal realm."

He inclined his head, catching what I wasn't saying. That I could no longer hold back in an attempt to lessen the lives lost in Iliseeum. "That will solve our problem of acquiring enough Ancient bones. Either the Primals will give us what they have, or we will take it."

That was what Attes had suggested. Take the bones from the Courts.

"You do know that we cannot just kill the Primals who refuse to join us," he said quietly.

"I know." I tipped my head back against the cool wall. "I could Ascend a member of their Court just in case. We already have Aios if Maia remains loyal to Kolis. I could Ascend either Theon or Lailah to replace Kyn. We also have Saion and Rhahar."

"Rhahar will not want to rule the Triton Isles," he said.

My gaze flicked to him. "Then we will ask Saion."

He nodded. "That leaves us with Veses' Court."

"Rhain won't take her Court." I pushed away from the wall. "And there truly isn't a single god there we can trust?"

"I do not believe so."

I made my way back to him, my chest heavy. "Does that mean we have to…?" I stopped searching for a less harsh word. I couldn't pretty up the eradication of an entire Court. My chin lifted. "Does that mean we have to kill every god there?"

"The ones old enough to become an issue." His jaw ticked. "Yes."

Shaking my head, I glanced up at the ceiling. There had to be another way. Not trusting any of the gods to rule as a Primal didn't mean they were incapable of changing. "There will be an impact on the mortal realm if we do that. With no Primal of Rites and Prosperity, we'd plunge all the kingdoms into ruin."

"We would."

I stopped in front of Ash, wanting to be close to him. There was no reason for me *not* to be. Ash knew nearly *everything* now, and he'd held me close as I slept. And as I got ready this morning, he hadn't tried to hide his hungry stare when I undressed. Nothing had changed—well, that wasn't entirely true. Everything had changed, but not in a bad way. It was almost like there was a new type of understanding between us. That didn't mean I ever wanted to talk about what Kolis had done to me again, but I knew I *could* if I needed to. I nudged Ash's leg with my knee.

He looked up at me and turned his body to the side. "You sure?"

I didn't even have to say anything, and he knew. That was one of the many reasons I loved him so much. I offered him my hand.

He took it at once, folding his much larger hand around mine, and tugged me down so I sat in his lap. There was a moment when my mind wanted to go someplace else, but I nestled against Ash's chest instead when he wrapped an arm around me.

"This helps you think better?" he asked.

"Mm-hmm," I murmured, wiggling until I could rest my head under his chin. "It's another of your hidden talents."

He chuckled, burying a hand in my hair. "One even hidden to me."

I smiled. "Do you remember during the last meeting when we talked about how the true Primal of Life could take on a Court?"

He kissed the top of my head. "Yes."

"What if I take the Callasta Isles?" I said. "I know it's never been done before, but that has to be better than what feels like genocide that leaves no one but orphans behind—children who will then grow up, likely hating us for slaughtering their parents without really giving them a chance to be able to change."

"Giving them a chance can leave us vulnerable to rebellion and attacks," he said, finding a curl.

I thought about that. "I'd rather deal with that than proceed as if it's a foregone conclusion."

"I would prefer that also," he said, wrapping the strand around his finger. "As long as we know we cannot continue to tolerate attacks."

"Yeah, I know." Sunlight crept over the interior walls. "But maybe there will be a god we can trust to rise at some point."

"One can hope," he said warily.

I trailed my fingers down his forearm, tracing the tendons and bone. "We need to remove as many of Kolis's allies as we can before going after him. Once that's done, we'll have to…what did Attes say? Be the ones to act and not the ones to react?"

"Yes." He straightened the curl out. "What are you thinking?"

"I'm thinking there is no way there won't be a clash of armies, no matter what we do. I can only hope that Ez—" I sucked in a reedy breath as Ash's arm tightened around me. I pushed through the burn of grief. "I can only hope Ezra was able to warn the other kingdoms to prepare or that they will after what happened in Lasania and Terra."

Ash's arm tightened even more, and that also made it hard to push through the burn. I cleared my throat. "It's not like Kolis won't know what we're up to."

Ash let the curl bounce into its normal shape. "He will strike back quickly."

"We still need the upper hand. Something that will catch him off guard. And we already have it."

Ash didn't even need to guess. "Sotoria."

I nodded.

"He is also unaware of what we've been doing in Oak Ambler," he said. "That will be finished any day now."

"Yes." I sat up, not leaving his embrace but meeting his gaze. "But we need to draw him out and away from everyone else. He won't expect us to hand The Star over, and even if he suspects it to be some sort of trick, he'll still come. He'll do anything to get her back."

"As disgusting and disturbing as that is, it's the truth."

But there was another truth.

The one thing I hadn't opened up to Ash about yet. The only thing left unsaid between us but something that had occupied my thoughts from the moment I knew Sotoria's soul was inside me and what it meant.

I took a deep breath. "But I cannot allow him to have her."

A slight frown pulled at Ash's brows. "I didn't expect you would."

I placed my hand on his chest. "I also can't allow Sotoria to be forced into another life where she has no control. One where she runs the risk of Kolis somehow escaping his entombment and getting his hands on her before she can end him." What Kolis wanted both of us to suffer replayed in my mind. "I…I never want him to see her again."

His eyes widened. "I want that, too. Fates, do I ever. But she is the only one who can end him."

"But it's not fair to Sotoria," I said. "For her to be reborn yet again, only to have to deal with Kolis once more."

"Not if we do it right." Ash disentangled his fingers from my hair. "For Sotoria to be successful, Kolis just has to be conscious, not free."

"And you think it will be that easy? That it will be as simple as waking him long enough for Sotoria to plunge a bone dagger through his heart?" I challenged. "We don't know that. What we do know is that the moment Kolis sees Sotoria as he remembers her, he will tear himself limb from limb to get to her. I don't want to risk that."

A moment passed. "Then what do you suggest?"

"What we already planned to do until Sotoria was ready. Entomb Kolis," I told him. "Look, the Ancients have been entombed for thousands of years and are more powerful than he is. There is no reason we can't do that and then release Sotoria's soul so she can find peace. He won't be dead. Balance will remain. You will still be a Primal of Death and the King."

"I don't care about being King or a true Primal. That's not my concern." Dragging his fangs over his lower lip, he turned his head. "You're right. There's no reason we can't do that."

I didn't let hope spark. "But?"

"But the prophecy, Sera. By choosing not to end him, we are fulfilling that part of the prophecy."

"I know, but we're going into it knowing there's a chance he could reawaken," I argued, even as I felt a tiny kernel of doubt. "We simply have to prevent that from happening, which isn't impossible. Not when the Ancients have been entombed for so long."

His gaze came back to me. "The only thing is, we would have to be okay with him still being alive."

The thought of Kolis still being alive, even if entombed, made me want to scream, but… "But if I have to choose between Sotoria and him, I can deal with him being alive. I can deal with the possibility that he could somehow awaken in a thousand years. Because you know what? We will be ready for him when he does. We won't let him usher in the end."

"I get what you're saying. But, Sera—Fates, the only thing I want is for there to be a future where you never have to think about that bastard again," he said, cupping my cheek. "Where he is no longer a threat, not even a distant one."

"And I want that for Sotoria. I want her to have a choice—to find peace or live a life without the threat of Kolis."

Ash inhaled deeply, the muscle in his temple ticking.

"I know she is only one girl. In the grand scheme of things, she's just one life. But she has suffered over countless lives because of him. She has suffered to the point where the last time Kolis had her, she asked your father to end her life," I said, and Ash's eyes widened. "Kolis told me that. I didn't want to believe it, but Attes confirmed it. And, Ash, I know what it feels like to get to that point. Yet I still don't know how bad it got for her. I've never been okay with using Sotoria. Never," I told him. "She doesn't deserve this."

His head fell back, and he exhaled heavily. "No, she doesn't deserve this."

I let the spark of hope grow a little. "Will you be able to live with this?"

"I can live with whatever brings you happiness."

"Ash, I'm being serious."

"So am I." His chin lowered. "You're the most important thing to me. Your happiness is everything, and if that means keeping that fucker alive but entombed and us doing everything to keep him that way for you not to carry the guilt of forcing Sotoria to be reborn, then I can easily deal."

My breath snagged. "Truly?"

He smoothed his thumb over my bottom lip. "Truly."

"I think I'm going to cry."

"Please, don't." He pressed his forehead to mine. "I want to burn things when you cry."

"But they're happy tears."

"Tears are tears."

I laughed shakily. "Okay. I won't cry." I cradled his cheeks. "I love you."

He kissed me softly, so tenderly my chest swelled. "I suggest we not leave this open for debate," he said, leaning back. "Most of the Primals don't even know about her. We should keep it that way."

I nodded. "I want to tell Attes, though. He will support this."

"I don't doubt it." He slipped his hand from my cheek and moved it to the nape of my neck. "We need to run this past the others."

My stomach dropped a little. "Okay," I said, and his eyes narrowed immediately. I sighed. "You're reading me."

He didn't even deny it. "What about meeting with the others made you anxious when summoning the Primals didn't?"

"I…" I pressed my lips together to give myself a moment. "What if they think of me differently because of what I did? What if they're scared of me?" I tensed. "That…that would hurt because they…they are the only family I have now."

"Oh, *liessa*, they've always known who you are at your core." His gaze met mine. "While it may have been rough in the beginning…"

I snorted.

A grin appeared. "They accepted you. Just like I did. They will not think of you differently because they know you."

The breath I exhaled, while not free of guilt or shame, was lighter. "Thank you for reminding me."

"I will always remind you of that." He kissed me again, and I felt like I could float right up to the ceiling. "Before I get everyone in here, I need to know one thing. Are you going to be okay with all of this when it's over? Even the harsh parts?"

I knew what he was talking about. The deaths that would be at both of our hands. "This is different than me losing control, but it will bother me. It'll haunt you. Both of us. But I have to be okay with it, and…and I will be."

"So, we're in agreement, then?" Ash asked, his fingers tapping softly against the wood. "We summon the Primals today and then proceed accordingly."

Holding the fork with a slice of melon for the little draken in my lap, I smiled faintly as Jadis took the fruit without staring the fork down for five minutes.

Progress.

She held on to my hand without digging her claws in when I speared another piece of fruit. Reaver was at our side in his draken form, and I didn't think he'd taken his eyes off either of us since everyone arrived.

I glanced up as Jadis guided my hand, and therefore the fork, toward her mouth. There were nods of agreement.

Everyone was here.

Despite Ash's assurances, seeing all of them had been hard at first. I wasn't just worried that they would think of me differently or be scared of me. I'd also feared they'd feel pity because there was no way that those within the palace had not heard me rage screaming last night.

But while their eyes and words had been compassionate, none of them had acted strangely. Well, except for Bele. She'd patted the top of my head when she passed.

My gaze swept past Nektas to Attes. Drinks had been brought in, but he hadn't touched the coffee or gone for one of the decanters of whiskey or sherry. Sure, it was early, but I doubted that would've stopped him in the past. He also hadn't said much.

I cleared my throat. "I know our plan is…brutal and not at all what I originally wanted, but this is the only way we believe we can lessen the impact on the mortal realm."

"Doesn't sound brutal to me," Bele said, tucking a strand of dark hair behind her ear. "Sounds like a good time."

Lailah and Aios frowned at Bele. "It's not brutal. It's actually smart,"

Lailah said. And it was. It was what we should've done at the beginning. "If we can pull this off, we will have the upper hand when it comes to Kolis."

"Agreed," Rhain said, rising. "If you will excuse me, I should go ahead and begin preparing for the Primal summonses."

"Thank you," I said. Jadis pushed my hand away, letting me know she was done.

Meeting my gaze, Rhain gave me a small smile and nodded. Jadis peered over my shoulder, watching him leave. I patted her scaled back.

Ash shifted his attention to the *oneirou*. "You think you'll be able to do your thing?" Ash asked. I'd told him about what I had thought of when I spoke with Thierran in the library.

"You get Kolis alone?" A lock of black hair tumbled over his forehead. "I will do my thing and then some."

Ash's smile was tight as he looked at the twins. "Theon, I want you in the Bonelands while we have this meeting, just in case." Jadis turned in my lap, stretching her arms toward him and letting out a little chirp. He reached over and placed her on his lap.

"I feel so unloved," Nektas remarked as his daughter pressed her head against Ash's chest.

Ash snorted. "Lailah, I want you at the Black Bay."

The siblings nodded, and Nektas handed a blanket and what appeared to be a nightgown to Ash. As they rose to leave, Lailah sent Attes a worried glance.

He didn't even seem to be aware that they'd left.

"Saion, Rhahar, you will remain here," Ash continued, attempting to pull the nightgown over Jadis's head, but she kept lifting her wings. Nektas grinned.

"Sounds good to me." Saion looked at his cousin.

Rhahar nodded. "You really think any of them will come at either of you?"

"They'd have to be very foolish," I commented, scratching Reaver under the chin. Ash finally got the nightgown on Jadis and covered her with the blanket. "They may not have known what I was capable of before, but they do now," I said without the hint of smugness that would normally fill my tone. But that was before. Now, I knew this was nothing to boast about.

Bele was silent for a moment, surprisingly not responding with one of her customary quips. "They're not going to be here, right?" She jerked her chin toward Reaver.

The draken narrowed his eyes.

"I will take the younglings to Mount Rhee before the meeting," Nektas said, propping a bare foot up on the edge of the desk.

I didn't think I'd ever seen Nektas in shoes.

"I doubt anything will happen," Ash said, adjusting the little draken in his arms. Jadis was already asleep. "But I don't want you near the throne room, Aios."

Aios frowned. "I am not happy with that."

"I am." Bele smiled at her, and the look she gave the Primal immediately erased the smile. "We done here for now?"

Ash nodded. "Stay close."

"Will do." She rose and took Aios's hand. "Let's go so you can yell at me in private."

Attes actually chuckled at that as he started to stand.

"Attes," I said. "Can you stay for a few moments?"

"Of course." He settled back.

"Come, Reaver." Nektas stood, taking his sleeping daughter from Ash's arms. "We need to go."

The draken hesitated, his cerulean gaze darting between Nektas and me. *I don't want to leave you.*

Even his voice in my mind was filled with dread. "It'll be okay." Bending at the waist, I cupped Reaver's jaw and kissed the top of his warm head between the horns that would soon grow. "Go with Nektas."

His heavy sigh echoed in my thoughts, bringing a grin to my lips. He rocked back, extending his wings and taking to the air.

Once it was just the three of us, I got up. As I passed Ash, I briefly stopped to kiss his cheek. His gaze tracked me when I sat in the chair Nektas had occupied.

Attes's wary gaze slid to mine. "Don't look at me like that."

I arched a brow. "Like what?"

"Like you're worried about me," he replied. "It makes me uncomfortable."

"It shouldn't, considering you saw me having a complete breakdown."

"Are you going to say that doesn't make you uncomfortable?"

"It does," I admitted and felt Ash's hand on my lower back. "But I am worried about you."

A ghost of a smile appeared. "There is no need, Sera. I know why you wanted to speak with me in private, and while I appreciate the thoughtfulness, I've known this day was coming, even when I didn't want to know." He inhaled deeply. "Kyn will not survive this."

I wanted to look away, but it felt wrong. Weak in a way I couldn't be.

"No," Ash said from behind me. "He will not."

Attes nodded, his lashes lowering. "He…he truly wasn't always like this," he said roughly before clearing his throat. "He once lived for times of peace. He had a heart. He laughed and loved. He lusted for life and not cruelty." His gaze turned distant as if he were seeing far into the past. "His care for the younglings remained through the centuries, the only thing that reminded me of who he used to be. The only hope I had that he could still be saved. Kolis took that when he had you kill Thad," he said, and my eyes closed. "When I could finally tell him that his youngling draken still lived, it was too late. My brother was gone."

"I'm sorry," I said. When I felt his hand on mine, I opened my eyes.

He lowered his head so we were at eye level. "As am I." He squeezed my hand and then straightened. "But it is what it is."

Ash's hand moved in slow circles on my back. "We will need to Ascend someone to take his place."

"Lailah," Attes said without hesitation. "She has the temperament, and she's ready."

I glanced over my shoulder at Ash. He eyed Attes closely. "And you're suggesting Lailah because you truly believe this," he asked. "Or because you want her?"

I raised my brows at Ash's bluntness.

Attes huffed out a low laugh. "Her being a goddess hasn't stopped me from wanting her, has it?"

Oh, my.

Ash made a sound that might've been a laugh. Or maybe a growl. I couldn't be sure.

"Besides," Attes went on, "I aim to rest after this."

Heart dropping, I stiffened.

"I don't plan to enter Arcadia," he said, seeing my reaction. "Not yet, at least. Nor will I go to ground immediately afterward. You will need my aid in the transition. But I will need to rest." His gaze flickered away. "I need that time."

"I understand," Ash said, and so did I, even though it made my heart ache.

"I will assign Theon to oversee things in my place during that time," Attes added, surprising me once again. "He will do well just to prove he is better than me, and I will be able to rest peacefully."

I smiled at that. "That's not the only reason I wanted to speak to you."

"Is that so?" He lifted a cup of likely cold coffee and drank. "Hopefully, it is a less depressing conversation."

"It is," I said. "We will not be using Sotoria's soul."

His head swung toward me so fast he probably gave himself whiplash. "What?"

"I can't do it. I can't force Sotoria to be reborn and used." As I told him what I'd said to Ash earlier, it was like witnessing a man finding a small slice of peace as disbelief gave way to relief. Attes's left hand dropped to his lap, and his right followed as I promised him that Sotoria would not be forced to live yet another life she didn't choose for herself. Tension eased out of his neck and shoulders when he understood that she would find rest. He slouched a little in his chair as I told him that Kolis would never see Sotoria again.

"He will remain entombed, and we will do everything to make sure of that. And Sotoria will have a choice."

"That is…" Attes's eyes closed as he tipped his head back, raising his arms. He dragged his palms down his face, then up and through his hair. Turning his head toward us, tears glimmered in his eyes. His voice was rough and thick when he spoke just three words. "That is everything."

I inhaled swiftly, fighting back a rush of my own freaking tears. Ash folded an arm around my waist from behind. He hauled me out of the chair and into his lap as he said, "You do love her."

Attes's laugh was shaky as he shook his head. "Sotoria could've killed two Primals if she had the chance."

Gods…

I squeezed Ash's arm, biting my lip.

"I've always known she would never be mine. I was okay with that. I could live with it. All I've ever wanted was for her to have peace." Clearing his throat, he smiled a little. "I guess that's the purest kind of love."

"Yeah," I whispered, blinking rapidly. "I believe so."

His eyes met mine and then Ash's. "Thank you."

"There is no need for thanks," Ash said. "None at all."

I swallowed the knot in my throat. "I was thinking it would be best to wait to release her until after Kolis is entombed."

"Agreed." He rubbed his palm over his chest. "I want to be there when we do it."

"Of course. You would be there even if you didn't have The Star," I told him.

He nodded again and cleared his throat once more, appearing to rein in his feelings. "You said something earlier, Sera. About the plans being brutal. You're wrong."

"I am?"

He was quiet for what felt like a small eternity. "When people think of war, they imagine endless, grand battles fought across many landscapes. They think it's nonstop violence stretching from one kingdom to the next the moment conflict erupts, leaving hallowed ground behind. In their minds, they see cities sacked and burned, left to rot along with the corpses of those who would've died for peace but perished for being in the way. One speaks of war, and mortals hear the pounding of warhorses' hooves, the clash of swords, the cries of the wounded and dying, and the whistle of arrows piercing the air. They picture men who were once loving fathers and sons, gentle husbands and tender lovers, becoming blood-hungry beasts, knowing that no one, neither King nor servant, will return without pieces of them forever lost. That's the kind of war mortals expect—that the young, in their naïvety, romanticize. Bloody, brutal, and unforgiving in its indiscriminate slaughter. That's not the kind of war Primals and gods were meant to engage in," he said, causing small bumps to rise along my arms. "However, that is the kind of war Kolis has started."

Attes's voice lowered, and he held my stare. "But what mortals and even some Primals don't realize is that there is rarely a distinct winner in that kind of war. The victor is simply the one who still stands. Not because of sheer willpower or even the greater strength in their values. The victor stands simply because of their brutality." One side of his lips curved up, hinting at a deep dimple in his scarred cheek. "But they never stand for long. Because despite every life they took, every city they burned, and every family that was simply in the way as they destroyed things to reach their target, twice that will inevitably rise to raise swords against the victor. That kind of war can never be won because it never ends. There are only reprieves." Eather streaked across his eyes. "But what you seek is how wars are won. Through cunning and precise actions before a single piece of armor is pierced on the battlefield. It is no less harsh, but it is not brutal. What is, is the morality of fools. The choice to make war instead of going after only those who have made the decisions that created the conflict. *That* is brutality."

48

Releasing my death grip on the porcelain sides of the toilet, I rocked back.

By some miracle, I'd made it—barely—to the bathing chamber before what felt like everything I'd eaten at breakfast made a reappearance.

Thankfully, Attes and Ash were at the Black Bay, speaking with Lailah. Ash hadn't wanted to leave my side since…well, since everything. But as soon as we'd finished speaking with Attes, my stomach had started churning. I was supposed to be downstairs with Rhain, but right now, my thoughts were on whatever the hell was going on with my body.

I'd felt fine one moment and not the very next second. Was it a lingering consequence of my fight with Kolis? Or did it have more to do with all the mental and emotional stuff? The grief? Like what I'd finally shared with Ash and the promise I'd made him make? Trauma did weird things to the body. Or was it seeing the raw emotion Attes struggled to control when speaking of both Sotoria and his brother?

Honestly, I didn't think it was any of those things. Or even my anxiety. I had been nauseous off and on since I Ascended, but I was past the point where I should be feeling any lasting effects.

Come to think of it, I had been nauseous while in Dalos. Granted, there was a realm of reasons to explain that, but…

Muscles in my sides aching and my throat stinging, I rose and went to the vanity. I rinsed my mouth and splashed cool water on my face. My temples throbbed, likely from the retching. It had been quite…vigorous. I winced, really regretting the extra helping of spiced sausage. Another wave of nausea swelled. Squeezing my eyes shut, I gripped the edges of the vanity. Skin clammy and stomach in knots, I focused on breathing through my nose until the sensation passed. I still didn't move for several minutes, half-afraid I would find myself on my knees once again. Though I wasn't sure what was left inside me at this point.

I pried my fingers from the vanity and stepped back gingerly. My reflection stared back at me. The bruises on my neck were faint, a gross bluish-green shade, but they were still there.

Shouldn't they have completely healed by now? The answer was yes, and I knew I wasn't the only one thinking that. I'd caught Ash staring at my throat several times this morning, his jaw clenched and ticking.

Pressing a palm to my unsettled stomach, I shuffled into the bedchamber and made a beeline for the bed. I lay down on my back and closed my eyes. Hopefully, whatever this was would pass in a few minutes. We had things to do today.

A war to start and end.

And our first move was summoning the Primals.

I swallowed, grateful the sour bitterness was gone and the pounding in my temples had begun to ease.

Gods, I felt like a mess.

A gross, tired mess.

Why was I still so damn tired? I had fallen back to sleep, and we'd slept in. Despite all that had led up to it, it had been a deep, restful sleep…

The corners of my lips turned down. The fatigue wasn't anything new. Before the attack on Lasania, I had been really tired in the evenings, and I'd slept deep and long. Even with the nightmares, that was something new for me. In the past, I'd rarely reach a level of sleep deep enough to dream. And if I did, I didn't remember them.

That sensation came again. Like I was forgetting something. But this time, I didn't. It had to do with dreams. Or *a* dream. Like the one I'd had while in stasis. The one where I'd been in my lake, and there had been a large feline on the bank, her coat the color of moonlight. She had been me. My *nota.* And she hadn't been alone, had she? She hadn't. In the shadows of the Dark Elms, there had been movement.

Two smaller…cubs.

I jerked upright so fast my stomach cramped. I started to stand, but the connection between my brain and limbs appeared to be severed as my thoughts raced, landing on one question.

When had I menstruated last?

I started to think back, week after week, before losing the ability to count joined my inability to move. All I knew was that it had been weeks. Like *a lot* of weeks. Enough that more than a month had passed. Enough for the on-again-off-again nausea to make sense—

Oh, gods.

"No," I stated, my voice hoarse but loud. "I'm freaking out for no reason."

And I was, because what I was thinking couldn't be possible. For the very shaky timeline to add up—for me to even feel some of the telltale signs of a…pregnancy—it would mean that I conceived *weeks* ago. A month.

Maybe even two. Perhaps even the first time Ash and I had sex. But that didn't make sense. A child could not be born of a Primal and a mortal—

But had I ever really been mortal?

"Oh, fuck," I whispered.

That was a damn good question because when exactly had those embers of life truly become a part of me, changing what I was on such a fundamental level that they couldn't be removed? The night I'd recklessly bitten Ash's thumb and tasted that tiny drop of blood? The very same night we'd first had sex? My heart started pounding. If that one drop of blood had irrevocably changed the biology of my body, making me a little bit more Primal than mortal, could that also mean that a child could be created?

Wait.

I'd seen more than one.

I'd seen two.

Twins.

I thought of the prophecy. A first daughter… And a second daughter. But that didn't sound like twins—

"But I saw *cubs*," I said out loud. "Cute, little, fluffy cave cats. I didn't see two toddlers frolicking in the fucking weeds. I'm not…"

My throat tightened, and my legs suddenly worked again. Shooting to my feet, I raced into the bathing chamber. Not to vomit. My stomach was settled. Mostly. I went to the mirror and yanked up the bottom of my tunic. I held the royal blue material beneath my breasts and stared at my lower abdomen. My head cocked to the side.

It looked the same. Soft. Concave at the naval and then slightly rounded. I turned sideways, seeing nothing—

"What am I doing?" I asked, a shrill giggle parting my lips. Would I even see a difference in my body at this point?

I didn't know a whole lot about pregnancy, but I'd been around enough pregnant maids at Wayfair. The answer was no. I wouldn't. My fingers tightened around the soft material. But could I really be far enough along that I would…what had Odetta called it when we'd happened upon the young, rosy-cheeked Emmeline, one of the chambermaids in the hall, clasping a bucket as she heaved?

"*Pay her no mind*," Odetta had warbled, urging me along when I stopped. "*She's just having a bit of the morning qualms*."

I hadn't any idea what that meant. I couldn't have been more than ten or so at the time. Curious child that I was, I'd asked. Odetta had said that she was with child, and as sure as the sun rose each morning in Lasania, roughly seven or so months later, she had given birth.

Emmeline hadn't looked pregnant, but she had also been of a willowy frame. However, there had been others with body types similar to mine who hadn't appeared as if they were with child for many months. So, that meant nothing.

Which wasn't exactly a relief because, in this situation, nothing could mean everything.

I couldn't be pregnant. Not after everything I'd gone through in Dalos. Not after being struck with eather, and the Fates only knew how many arrows. Not after the fight with Kolis. He'd broken bones. He'd tossed me around like I was that doll Jadis played with.

Not after what I'd done.

I stared down at my stomach, remembering how nearly every part of my body had been bruised…except for my lower abdomen, almost as if that part of me had been shielded. That sounded ridiculous.

"I can't be." I jerked my head to my reflection.

I didn't really see myself. I saw those *cubs*. I saw them as clearly as I had during stasis, except they changed in my mind now, becoming two mahogany-haired little boys with golden-bronze skin, one silver-eyed and the other…with eyes of silvery-gold—

What in the fuck?

I sucked in a shallow breath that went nowhere. Why in all the realms was I seeing *little boys*? It was official. I was losing my mind. Either way, I needed to know if I was…if I was pregnant, and I needed to know now. Right this fucking second. Or I would definitely go insane, and Ash would have to put me into stasis. But how could I find out? In Lasania, there were people, usually older women in Croft's Cross, to whom many went. Even the nobility. But I wasn't exactly sure how they could tell anyone anything. Then again, many went there for the teas that ensured there *wouldn't* be a fruitful union, too. Regardless, there was no way I was going to shadowstep my ass into Lasania.

I didn't think I could ever return there.

My mind raced. Those women people sought, wasn't it said they worshipped at Temples of the Primal Goddess of Love, Beauty, and *Fertility*? There was no way I would ask Maia, but could Aios somehow—?

"Sera?"

I was so caught up in my panic, I didn't feel Ash's approach. I squeaked, dropping my tunic and whirling toward the entrance.

A second later, he filled the doorway. His dark, reddish-brown hair—his *mahogany-hued* hair—was swept back in a knot at the nape of his neck. Several strands were loose and tousled, though.

"Are you all right?" he asked, concern filling his voice. "I felt your…panic."

"Uh…"

His gaze swept over me as if he were checking for injuries. The only one he'd find was to my brain. "It was so thick it nearly choked me," he continued.

I could only stare at him.

He walked in, eyeing the tub and then the space around us. "What happened?"

"Nothing." Clasping my hands together, I turned as he brushed past me, checking behind the short wall where the privy was. "No one is in here."

He faced me. "Then what caused you to feel this?"

"Why is your hair so messy?" I asked instead, willing my heart to slow.

"I was on the Rise near the Black Bay." He paused. "As you know."

I did know that.

Godsdamnit.

His eyes narrowed. "What's going on, Sera?"

A laugh crawled its way up my throat. One I knew would sound crazed if I allowed it any sort of freedom. I clamped my mouth shut.

"I'm starting to become worried." Ash crossed the distance between us, cupping my cheek. His forehead creased. "Why is your face damp and cold?"

"I just washed it." I forced my voice to be light, knowing I needed to calm down. There was no way I was telling him what I was thinking, causing him to—oh, gods, how would he even react? He'd likely be as panicked as me.

Maybe he'd vomit, too. I would if I were him.

"*Liessa*?" His thumb swept across my cheek. "I hoped we were beyond this."

"We are."

"Then talk to me."

Fuck. Shit. Damn.

None of that was helping. "I don't know why you felt that," I blurted out, thoughts racing. "I might have had a nightmare."

His brows shot up. "A nightmare?"

I nodded. I didn't want to lie, not after finally opening my dumb mouth and talking, but I also didn't want to say anything until I knew. And especially not right before I summoned the freaking Primals to basically tell them to join us or die.

What in the fuck kind of bad timing was this?

"Do you often have them while awake?" Ash asked.

"Not normally." Realizing that had been the stupidest excuse, I quickly added, "But I dozed off pretty quickly after you and Attes left. And before you ask, no, I don't know what I was dreaming about, but I do have a distinctive feeling I was having a nightmare."

His brow furrowed. A moment passed, and then another.

I shifted my weight from one foot to the other. "Are *you* okay?"

"I was," he stated, lowering his hand.

I started to ask what he meant, but then it occurred to me that he likely believed I'd had a nightmare about Kolis and that I was keeping it from him. Again.

Shit. Damn. Fuuuck.

"It wasn't that," I assured him. "I wasn't having a nightmare about

Kolis." My hands curled at my sides. "I swear, Ash. I'm fine, and I'm sorry I worried you."

"You don't have to apologize." He exhaled heavily. Some of the tension eased from his jaw.

"And you don't have to worry." I turned, making my way from the bathing chamber. "Did you speak to Lailah?"

He followed me. "Yes. She is a little shocked but on board."

"Good." I smoothed my hands down my thighs. I needed to pull it together. Even though it didn't feel like it at the moment, what we needed to discuss with the others was far more important. "Is it almost time?"

Ash eyed me closely and then nodded. "I need to change my shirt."

I glanced down at myself and figured I'd do the same. It took Ash two seconds to pull a dark gray tunic from a hanger. My gaze fell on the clothing hanging there, and for some reason, I reached for a black gown with silver ivy stitched along the waist and sides. I stared at it for a moment and then tugged it free. I didn't even know why. I'd blame the shocking possible revelation. Or maybe it was because, deep down, I didn't hate gowns.

I just hated being told to wear one.

"Can you help me?" I asked Ash.

He'd already donned the tunic, ready in less than a minute. It took me a little longer. Not because I had to undress and then shimmy my ass into the brocade gown—-thank the gods it wasn't skintight where I had to fight my possibly growing sto—

Nope.

Not thinking about that.

Nope. Nope. Nope.

Ash's calloused fingers lingered on the skin of my back as he clasped the row of hooks, sending tight shivers cascading down my spine. That was why it took longer. That and his insistence on being the one to secure the bone dagger beneath the skirt. His hands really lingered on the clasp of the thigh sheath he had replaced for me, causing my skin to flush and heat to pool low in my core.

Ash looked up at me through thick lashes as he fixed the gown. Then, he rose. "You look so beautiful."

"Thank you," I whispered. He ran a finger over the silver ivy encircling the waist of the gown that climbed the valley between my breasts.

"I really need to thank Erlina for her expert hand," he murmured, tracing the stitching that spread across the top of the bodice.

My skin tingled through the gown, and I looked up at him. "If you keep doing that, we will have to delay summoning the Primals."

A wolfish grin appeared as he ducked his head and kissed me so deeply that if I'd feared at all that his passion for me was diminished by everything that had happened and what I had shared with him, I had no doubts now.

But those doubts were gone anyway.

"Later," he promised, taking my hand.

We walked to the main floor, and I suspected that Ash had chosen to go this way to give me time instead of shadowstepping, just as he had before my public speech.

And I used every second of that to file the possibility of me being pregnant in the farthest recesses of my mind, tucking it in along with the thoughts of what I had done to the mortal realm. I had to do that so I could do this. If not, there was a good chance I would start running through the halls screaming.

Several guards lined the foyer—a new sight. They bowed their heads as we passed.

"Rhain is waiting for us in the crown room. He thinks you should definitely wear it now," Ash said, and I glanced at that damn empty pedestal. "Once you're ready, we'll summon the Primals."

I nodded, tightening my grip on his hand. There were guards everywhere I looked, even in the narrow hall that led to the chamber connected to the war room.

Rhain stood inside, between the empty pedestal that should've held Ash's crown and mine. When he saw me, his brows nearly climbed into his hair.

"You didn't have to change," he said, drawing a curious look from Ash.

"I know," I said. "I wanted to."

He swallowed, glancing at Ash. "You both look like the King and Queen you are."

Ash's hand slipped free of mine as he went to the crown and lifted it, the suns and diamonds glinting in the sunlight. He carefully placed it on my head and smiled as he lowered his hands.

I reached up, touching one of the spires. "I will never get over the fact that it doesn't weigh as much as it looks."

"Heavy is the head that wears the wrong crown," Ash said, smoothing a curl under the headpiece. "You now look even more beautiful."

"The most beautiful Queen who has ever lived," Kars said, entering the room with Saion and Rhahar.

Ash's gaze slid to the godling, and a low rumble of warning radiated from him.

I smacked his chest, and Kars fought a grin. "Thank you," I said, taking a deep breath and refusing to allow my thoughts to wander.

The door to the war room opened, revealing Nektas.

Ash took my hand, leading us to the interior door where the draken waited. As the others followed, my gaze swept over the numerous weapons lining the walls of the war room and the wooden table with far too many nicks and grooves in it to count as we entered.

Usually, I would love this space and all its stabby things, but this was the place where Ash had first learned of my betrayal. It was in the past and no longer mattered, but I still hated the room.

I looked over my shoulder at Nektas as we passed the oval table. "You're staying in this form?" I'd expected him to shift.

"I'm scarier in this form," he said.

Now that he'd mentioned it, he really was.

"Remember how to summon the Primals?" Ash asked, and I nodded. "Attes is here. You will not need to think of him."

"I know." Closing my eyes, I cleared my racing thoughts and first focused on Keella. Eather swelled inside. The sensation was strange, almost like a cord had formed and stretched across the realm. I could almost see it in my mind, and it reminded me of when Kolis had come out of stasis. I knew the moment I reached the Primal goddess, and as Ash had instructed before, I projected my summons to the throne room.

A moment later, I felt the throb of a Primal.

"That's my Queen," Ash murmured, his thumb stroking my side as I repeated it for Maia and then Penellaphe.

I felt them arrive and focused on Phanos. The appearance of another Primal throbbed through me. My breath caught a little, but I wasn't done.

I took another deep breath and closed my eyes once more. I felt the moment my compulsion reached the two Primals.

I compelled Veses and Kyn to appear before me.

The arrival of the remaining two Primals throbbed in the center of my chest, and I had to smirk, imagining their fury.

We stopped as we neared the final doorway—the one leading to the dais in the throne room. Doubts began creeping in. I had no idea where Maia and Phanos would stand. What if I said the wrong thing? What if I wasn't convincing? That was definitely possible. What if I walked right out there, took one look at Veses, and throat-punched her? Also, very likely. Or Kyn decided to breathe, and Ash would be forced to put me into stasis? Gods, that wasn't completely likely, but it wasn't impossible. And should we stand or sit? If I started pacing, would I walk right off the dais—?

Ash's fresh, citrusy scent enveloped me for a moment before his lips brushed my forehead, right below the crown. "You've got this."

Did I?

"You do," Ash whispered.

Had I asked that question out loud? My hands trembled slightly as my grip tightened on Ash's hand. Weight began settling on my chest, causing my shoulders and neck to tense.

I took a deep breath and held it for five seconds. Ash's gaze caught mine. He gave me a short, barely noticeable nod.

I reflexively sought that veil of nothingness where I could retreat into myself and become whatever was needed of me.

You've got this.

That was what he'd said to me before we met with the gods after I'd awakened, too. And while I hadn't been convinced, Ash *had* been sure. He had faith in me. He didn't believe my anxiety made me incapable. He didn't believe that me being born mortal made me weak. None of the gods here thought that.

I was *strong.*

My time in Dalos had proven that, and it had nothing to do with the essence pumping hotly through my veins. I didn't need to don the veil of nothingness to find strength. I just had to be myself. Though not the burn-it-all-down version. Maybe the fifty percent burn-it-all-down version—okay, more like seventy percent. But also who I was becoming.

"Ready?" Ash asked.

I nodded.

Ash held my gaze for a moment longer, and then Nektas opened the throne room door. Fresh, late-afternoon air washed over us as we walked across the dais, his hand remaining wrapped firmly around mine.

We passed the hauntingly beautiful thrones carved from blocks of shadowstone, their backs stretching into wings that touched at the tips. The only sound was our footsteps as Nektas veered to the right, and we reached the edge of the dais.

Thousands of candles jutted from the smooth, black walls, and hundreds more hovered above the main floor, scattered throughout and casting a soft fiery glow over the massive, circular chamber open to the shining stars. Guards lined the walls, two by two, standing together every four feet, dressed in black, their hands resting on the pommels of their swords. The main doors were closed, but I knew a small army's worth of guards was stationed outside the doors and all along the Rise.

Ash squeezed my hand, and I realized I was holding my breath for far longer than five seconds. Forcing my lungs to work, I looked past the empty shadowstone benches, my gaze momentarily snagging on Penellaphe. She…she looked well, dressed in a peach-hued tunic and pants. The bronze crown of olive branches and serpents looked better on her than on Embris. Though I could've done without the serpents. I started to look away, but a dark figure against the wall snagged my attention. Thierran. My lips twitched. He was leaning against the wall with one boot propped against the shadowstone. He stared straight ahead at no one in particular. It amused me that he had weaseled his way in. Then I saw who stood near him, and relief surged through me once more. I saw a familiar brown-haired god beside Attes: Elias. The guard I'd met in Dalos gave a short, quick nod. As Rhain moved to stand at the foot of the dais, my eyes locked with *hers*. I saw no one else.

Veses was toward the back, and it registered that she stood next to Kyn. Her blond hair fell in ringlets to her impossibly narrow waist, and the jade tree crown made from a stone matching the deep red of her gown sat upon her head. Her dress covered her from the neck down, yet every part of her body was still somehow revealed in the skintight crimson silk, from her ample breasts to the indent of her navel.

Her face had a strange pinch to it when she stared up at me, almost as if she couldn't believe either of us was standing there. Maybe it was the crown upon my head. Perhaps it was the fact that I dared.

Seconds ticked by with us staring at each other. I had no idea if she was thinking about the last time we'd seen one another in Dalos. Her shame? My pain? Was she reliving the moment Kolis had punished her by giving her to Kyn? Or how she'd ordered me not to intervene on her behalf? Saying that what Kolis had done was nothing, even though we both knew that wasn't true. Was she smug in the knowledge that she had tried to warn Nyktos, but I hadn't listened? Or did that knowledge make her uncomfortable?

I was thinking all those things, and as the seconds ticked by, I couldn't help but think about how Veses deserved all kinds of unimaginable pain for what she had done to Ash.

But my thoughts hadn't changed when it came to what Kolis had done to her. She didn't deserve that.

No one did.

I didn't have to like the bitch to acknowledge that.

A muscle twitched just above Veses' delicate brow, and then she looked away, her lip curling into a smirk. But I knew.

I knew she was unsettled by the sight of me. It made her *feel* something.

I looked at the Primal beside her. For some reason, the bastard was shirtless and barefoot. He, too, appeared stuck between shock and anger, his narrowed gaze darting between me and his brother, the reddish-black crown dull in the weakening sunlight pouring in from above.

As I stared at Kyn, a fierce storm of rage-fueled eather surged through me, threatening to consume every ounce of restraint I possessed. The air charged with it as I stared at the Primal who had played a role in my family's demise and the destruction of my home.

Everyone in the room felt the power pounding through me. I held Kyn's gaze, and Ash's hand tightened around mine.

One.

Two.

Three.

Four.

Five.

I counted between breaths as every fiber of my being screamed for vengeance. Yet I gritted my teeth and forced myself to hold back, knowing that succumbing to the rage would not only end with the Fates doing something messed up in return for violating the rules of balance but would also end with me causing more violence and suffering.

Reeling in my self-control, I forced my gaze from Kyn to the Primal of Rebirth. Keella wore a caped, golden gown, and upon her head sat the crown of pale-blue quartz with many limbs and leaves. I saw Bele then, but she, too, had changed her attire. Gone was her customary black. Now, she wore white pants and a fitted white tunic. A crown of ruby antlers sat upon her head. I thought it looked far better on her than on Hanan.

Another reddish-black helm caught my attention. My gaze locked with

Attes's. He winked. Beside me, Ash sighed. To his left stood the most beautiful Primal goddess I'd ever seen.

A crown of pearls, roses, and scalloped shells sat upon Maia's warm blond hair that fell in waves to her lush hips. The Primal Goddess of Love, Beauty, and Fertility wore a pale-pink gown similar to Keella's. She smiled as my gaze swept over her, and I felt relief at the response.

But it was the one who stood at the back of those before the dais, separate from everyone else, arms folded over his chest, that gave me hope. No crown sat upon the Primal God of the Sky, Sea, Earth, and Wind's burnt-umber head, but he didn't look shocked or angry. He looked…curious.

It really wasn't only about the sizes of Maia's or Phanos's armies anymore, even though we wanted as many soldiers on our side as against us. Though like Attes had said, we were going for more precision, targeted battles that didn't require grand landscapes. It was more about the fact that I didn't want to have to send them to Arcadia or worse.

But what was also huge was the silence in the throne room.

No one spoke.

Not even Kyn.

My mouth dried, and my gaze flickered over those before me. Anxiety threatened to rise like the three-headed serpent I'd faced in the cavern, poised to strike and deliver venomous self-doubt.

Tremors coursed through my hands, and I started to look at Ash but caught myself.

I was strong.

I'd *survived* being considered a failure to my family and a kingdom that never knew my name. I'd *survived* my mother's biting disappointment and Tavius's twisted cruelty. I'd *survived* the gods who had come to take me, and made it through Veses' attack. I'd *survived* an Ascension that should've killed me. I'd *survived* Kolis.

Most importantly, I'd survived *myself.*

I was strong.

I was worthy.

I could do this.

And I needed no one, not even Ash, to speak for me.

I had faith in myself.

Just as I'd had faith in Ezra when I told her to take the throne—

Something clicked into place in my head that had nothing to do with the ancient knowledge I'd gained during my Ascension. There had been a reason I'd asked that of Ezra. It was because she had *earned* it.

And I still had a chance to do that here before it became an ultimatum.

My heart slowed, and my hands ceased trembling. Tension eased from my muscles and chest. The warm hum of eather replaced it as I stepped forward. Ash's hand firmed around mine for a heartbeat and then slipped away. I stopped at the edge of the dais.

Below me, Rhain turned to the others. His chest rose with a deep breath. "Bow," he said, his voice booming. "Bow before—"

"I will not bow to *that*," Kyn spat, and my head jerked to him. "A common—"

"Finish that sentence," I said, my vision flashing between gold and silver, "and you will find yourself running from *that* common whore once again."

I heard a low, rough-sounding laugh from the direction of where Thierran stood in the alcove as Kyn glared at me. I arched a brow. His nostrils flared, but he kept his mouth shut, at least for now.

"Anyway," Rhain muttered, clearing his throat, "bow for the One who is born of—"

"No," I stopped him. His head swung toward me. I could feel Ash's stare boring into my back. My heart was thudding again, but this time, it was different. Manageable. "I do not expect any of you to bow before me."

Rhain looked like he wanted to run headfirst into a shadowstone wall. The others before me looked confused or, in Phanos's case, like he was thinking of nothing. However, I'd gotten Thierran's undivided attention.

"Yet," I added, catching the small smirk that brought out one dimple on Attes's cheek. "I don't want your loyalty simply because of the essence coursing through my veins or because of the crown upon my head. Come to think of it," I said, reaching for the crown. I lifted it, snagging a few hairs. The gold gleamed, and I glanced back at Ash. He watched me, curious but not concerned. His eyes were a molten silver, heated and bright. I looked back at those below. "I should not even be wearing this crown."

Rhain closed his eyes, and Bele exchanged nervous looks with Saion and Rhahar.

Veses was still smirking.

Half-tempted to toss the crown at her face, I resisted the urge and willed it…well, I willed it wherever the crown was supposed to go when I didn't want it. As it vanished from my hand, I hoped I hadn't sent it to the Abyss.

"I'm sure some of you were thinking that. Or have. I know I have," I admitted.

A throaty voice dug into every last nerve of mine. "Well," Veses drawled, "I'm glad we're on the same page."

My head snapped to her, but I didn't get a chance to respond.

"If you interrupt my wife again," Ash said, his voice a frigid warning that sent the flames above the candles flickering, "You will find yourself without the ability to do so."

Veses' mouth snapped shut. I didn't think it was only anger that stained her cheeks. Ash's threat had hurt her feelings, which was entirely fucked up.

But Veses was a mess.

I smiled at her. "I was saying that I have thought I shouldn't be wearing the crown. Not because I was born mortal or because there has never been a

Queen of the Gods."

"Or because the essence inside you comes from Eythos," Maia spoke up, her husky voice flat as she nodded in Ash's direction. "And from him?"

"Not even because of that," I said, keeping my hands at my sides and open. "However, I'm going to say what many have already thought, including me. Nyktos should be the true Primal of Life."

A gasp of surprise came from someone on the floor as I felt Ash move, stepping closer to me. Phanos's features sharpened, and his upper body leaned forward.

"Not because of who his father was or because of some birthright. As someone born mortal, I, more than most, know that birth doesn't make you worthy of loyalty. Nor does gender," I said, catching Phanos' stare. "Nyktos has *earned* any loyalty you may have felt toward him. He did so through blood and sacrifice. You know him. He's worthy of your loyalty whether you wish to admit it or not."

Candlelight glinted off the pearl crown as Maia tilted her head. "He has."

"But he is not the true Primal of Life," I said, holding her gaze for a moment. "And neither is Kolis." I took a small breath. "But you all already know that. Just like you know Kolis earned your loyalty through manipulation and fear. You all know him. And you know he is not worthy of your loyalty."

"That is blasphemous," Phanos stated blandly. "As is what you've done today."

"You think this is blasphemous?" We needed to lure Phanos to our side, but disbelief and anger seized my tongue. "Did you not think it was that when Kolis killed Eythos's wife simply because his brother refused to bring a mortal back to life for him?"

"A mortal he loved," he argued. "Sotoria—"

"Do not speak of Sotoria." Eather thrummed through me, and the corners of my vision turned silver-tinged gold once more. "You know nothing of her. And do not even dare defend his actions to me. What he feels for her is not love. It is a sick, twisted obsession."

From the sky above, the deep, rumbling call of a draken could be heard.

I exhaled slowly, pushing the anger back down. "Was it not blasphemous when Kolis struck out against others in his anger, killing women and men? Children?" I waited for anyone to answer. "No? How about when he stole the embers from your King and installed himself as such?" My gaze swept over those below. "Was it not blasphemous when he snapped the necks of my family for no reason other than to lash out?"

"How about when you killed Embris?" Veses challenged.

My back stiffened. "I shouldn't have done that. I lost control."

The throne room went completely silent. No one, not even Kyn, had expected me to say that.

"And I will forever bear the shame of my actions. Not because I killed him. I cannot bring myself to care about him," I said. "But I regret the consequences of my actions that were paid by the innocent."

A muscle ticked in Kyn's jaw when he folded his arms across his chest.

"I was told that Embris was a traditionalist," I continued. "He did not care about tradition when Kolis stole the embers or when he lashed out at the mortal realm."

"He did." Phanos's deep voice carried through the chamber. "But he was afraid."

"As if you weren't," Kyn mocked.

The Primal of Sky, Sea, Earth, and Wind ignored him. "At that time, Kolis had taken the embers, and he would have been able to Ascend another Primal in place of any he struck down. We all knew that."

I glanced at Attes. *None of us has had much of a choice.* That was what he'd said when it came to serving Kolis.

But once the embers faded in Kolis, the threat of death had passed for them, but not for the gods in their Courts, their draken, or anyone they may have cared for.

"Each of you did what was necessary to survive Kolis's reign. You did what was necessary," I repeated. The next words tasted of brimstone on my tongue. "I understand."

"Just as you did *whatever* was necessary to survive?" Veses asked, her silver eyes pulsing.

My skin prickled all over. *Breathe in.* The curve of Kyn's lips didn't help. "I did what I could to survive him. Just as far too many before me were made to do," I said, noticing Maia look at the floor. "And I hope each of you remembers all who didn't survive him, though I fear most of you don't."

Maia's eyes closed.

"Only because they have chosen to forget them," Bele stated.

"Not all of us," Maia whispered, lifting her head. Her eyes opened and glimmered. "Not all of us have forgotten. We couldn't…" She shook her head, then lifted her chin. "You are right. Our loyalty was one born of fear, first for ourselves and then for those we cared about." Her gaze moved from Ash to me. "That is not an excuse. It is just a truth. One that is the same for all of us."

"You do not speak for me, Maia," Veses snapped.

Maia's laugh was dry, and one side of her lips curled up. "Ah, yes, you have never experienced pain or fear at Kolis's hands."

"Would you like to experience that right now?" Veses asked, moving toward the other Primal goddess.

Ash stepped forward and looked at her. That was all he had to do. Veses halted.

"You say Kolis hasn't earned our loyalty," Phanos said. "But neither have you."

"You're right. I haven't." I turned at the waist to Ash. "But I have earned his loyalty. I did so through blood and sacrifice. He knows me. I am worthy of his loyalty." My gaze shifted to Rhain. His eyes were open. *Breathe out.* "I have earned the loyalty of those who've served him."

Rhain smiled slightly. "Seraphena has." He turned to the others. "She's earned it through blood and sacrifice." Rhain stomped his right boot.

I blinked, not expecting the clap of his heel against stone.

"We know her," Saion spoke from where he stood to our left, slamming his booted foot down.

"Seraphena is worthy of our loyalty," Rhahar said, ending with a stomp, and a thunderous sound of boots against stone echoed from the guards standing at the walls.

"Seraphena earned my loyalty," Nektas stated, and Phanos looked at him and *listened.* "She has earned the loyalty of my brethren. She has done so through blood and ash. She is worthy."

Emotion thickened my voice as my gaze moved to Maia, Keella, and then Phanos. "And I want to earn your loyalty."

"Sorry." Veses smiled. "But you're not my type."

I got what she was saying. I'd earned Ash's loyalty—and who knew who else—on my back.

And so had Ash.

His flesh thinned, and tendrils of dark Primal mist swirled around his legs.

"It's okay," I said, holding up a hand. "I find her attempts to insult me amusing. Soon, she'll call me freckled and fat, and everyone will be so impressed by her wittiness."

Phanos snorted, and Veses' head spun toward him. "What?" He shrugged. "You have always been terrible at insults."

Her red lips thinned as she shook her head. "Whatever."

"How will you earn the loyalty of those who may be in doubt?" Keella asked.

"All I have right now is my word that I will be a better choice, but I know that means little, if anything, to some of you." *Breathe in.* "But what you all need to know is that I don't want your fear. To be honest, I don't even want loyalty from some of you."

Veses stiffened. Out of the corner of my eye, I saw Elias elbow Thierran.

"Well, this has been an inspiring message," Kyn remarked, "but—"

"I wasn't done," I said.

"Of course, not," Veses muttered, widening her eyes at her blood-hued fingernails.

I took a breath and counted. "I can assure each of you that I do not plan to do what Kolis is planning." I looked at Phanos and then Maia. "Before Kolis believed me to be Sotoria, he only knew that the embers of life were in me. He planned to take them, and he would've. Do you know what would've happened if he had? He would've Ascended as the Primal of Life and Death."

Phanos cursed, and Maia pressed her hand to her chest, turning to Keella. Besides the Primal Goddess of Rebirth, Attes, and Bele, the only other two who didn't look surprised were Veses and Kyn.

They knew.

"That's impossible," Phanos argued.

"It's not," Keella said. "It would simply be joining the two Primal essences together, as it was when the Ancients ruled."

"As the Primal of Life and Death, he would not need any of you. Anger him, and he would simply kill you and Ascend another," I told them. "He still planned on doing it—taking the embers. He was only waiting until my Culling ended. But he was ready to end every one of you and every mortal ruler who did not swear absolute obedience and fealty to him."

"That is not the only concern." Penellaphe turned to face the others. "If Kolis had Ascended as the Primal of Life and Death, he would've awakened the ones who went to ground. The Ancients."

"You all know what will happen if those in the ground awaken," Keella warned. "It will not be just the mortal realm that burns."

Most had gone quiet then, left uneasy by the mere thought of the Ancients waking.

Veses stared straight ahead, her features pinched. "As long as the balance is maintained, which Kolis has done despite the fact that most of you would not give him credit for such, the Ancients will stay where they belong. In the ground." Her slim arms folded over her waist. "Him rising as such a Primal would not change that."

"But it would," I said. "No Primal of Life and Death should exist, for such a being would have the very powers the Ancients split from themselves to create the Primals." My brows knitted. "It would not wake them all, but the shift of power would disrupt the stasis of enough of them that the damage to the realm would be the same."

"Kolis wouldn't risk it then." Phanos's breath was ragged.

I looked at Kyn. "Would he risk it?"

Kyn only smirked.

"Fates," Maia whispered. Horror filled her beautiful features. "He could've doomed us all—more than he already has."

"If you feel that our King has doomed us, why have you not said anything, Maia?" Veses shot back. "You have had countless opportunities to speak your mind."

I hated to admit it, but Veses *almost* had a point. "Every single Primal in here could've said something—done something to stop Kolis." I could feel Attes's stare boring into me, and I knew he was thinking about the conversation we'd had while I was in Dalos. "But what would that have gained any of you but punishment and horror?"

"As we've said, each of us has had to survive," Ash spoke, his gaze sweeping over those below. "We are giving you the chance to do more than simply survive."

"And to do that," I said, "we have no intention of ruling as Kolis or even Eythos did."

That got everyone's attention.

Veses lowered her hand. "What's that supposed to mean?"

"I will not be the only one making decisions, deciding the future of the realms and the lives of everyone within them." My heart skipped a beat. "I will not rule with a Consort at my side. I will rule with a King at my side."

Phanos's arms unfolded, and Maia's mouth dropped open.

My eyes met Ash's. "We will rule together as King and Queen."

"Wow," Veses exclaimed, clapping her hands. "What a novel approach. So groundbreaking."

I tried counting again. I didn't even make it past one. "I swear to the Fates, Veses, I am doing everything in my power not to slam you face-first through a wall, but you are really testing me."

Veses' red-painted lips parted.

"I strongly advise you to rethink whatever is about to drip from your tongue." Shadows rose along Ash's legs as he stared down at Veses. "Seraphena likes you even less than I do. You piss her off, and I will not stop her until she nearly destroys you."

It took every ounce of maturity I had not to smile as Veses shut her wretched mouth.

"You say you're trying to be a better person," Phanos cut in. "Combined with what you've already done, that threat doesn't sound like you really mean it."

"Seraphena said *she* was trying to be a better person," Ash replied coolly. "I did not."

Phanos stiffened. "Then let me rephrase my question. How would ruling as a King or Queen be any different if only one of you shows restraint?"

"Both would show restraint if you all would shut the fuck up for five seconds," Attes retorted.

Kyn's head jerked in his brother's direction.

"However, unlike them, I have no need for restraint." Attes looked over his shoulder. "Think about that before you say something to me."

Kyn's jaw jutted, and he faced forward, crossing his arms.

Attes smirked.

Keella cleared her throat. "So, you two would rule equally?"

Taking a step back, Ash lifted my hand to his mouth. He pressed a kiss to the top as his eyes met mine. "Yes and no," he said, lowering my hand and letting go. My heart practically melted. "We would rule equally with the other Primals."

A hushed sound went through the throne room, and not a single Primal before me didn't look shocked. They hadn't been expecting that, and their stunned silence had to be a good thing. It had to be.

Phanos recovered first. "What exactly are you saying?"

"I don't think any one person should rule all, nor do I believe that two people should control everything," I said, keeping my hope in check. "There needs to be a…balance. And all of us need to have a vested interest and shared responsibility in all decisions. There needs to be fairness, and I think this is the only way."

"That is not the way the Courts were established." Phanos sounded incredulous.

"So?" I said. "Just because it hasn't been done doesn't mean it can't be."

"But it does," he insisted. "That's not what the Ancients intended."

"I hate to sound repetitive, but…so?" I replied. "There is no law prohibiting such a thing."

Phanos's eyes widened as if I had suggested we set fire to all the Temples in the mortal realm.

"Do any of you think Kolis would offer to share power with you?" Ash asked. "True power that comes without conditions?"

"Does serving you come without conditions?" Phanos asked.

I opened my mouth but stopped, shaking my head. "Siding with us isn't exactly free of conditions, but we would never ask you to sacrifice your people. And I"—I swallowed hard—"I am truly sorry for what you had to give."

Phanos lowered his gaze, his jaw hardening.

"Nyktos and I are not perfect. I have already made grave mistakes, and I am sure we will make more, but we will never ask you to kill someone who displeased us or punish someone you care for because we're unhappy with you," I continued. "We will not slaughter innocents to prove some irrelevant point or assuage some perceived insult. We will not strike out against you because of a difference of opinion." I glanced at Veses. "We will not seek to humiliate you to assert power or for amusement."

Veses' features sharpened until I saw shades of gray beneath her flesh.

"We will not imprison people for our twisted pleasure, and we will not play you against one another." My chin lifted. "We don't want a war that will spill over into the mortal realm. We don't want to leave Iliseeum soaked in the blood of gods and draken. All we ask is that you stand with us against Kolis."

Silence greeted my words.

"There is just one more thing each of you needs to be aware of before you choose," Ash said. "Two of you will not get the opportunity to make that choice."

"Oh, I wonder who those two are." Kyn barked out a laugh and moved forward a few feet. A smug smile twisted his handsome features. "I'd rather be fucked by one of my hounds," he said, making Veses' lip curl, "than swear allegiance to either of you."

My lips curved into a small smile as I met his glare. I didn't look away when Ash drifted to the edge of the dais.

"You can go ahead and leave, Veses," he said.

The Primal Goddess of Rites and Prosperity's brows flew up. "So, that's how this plays out? You're not even going to ask for my support?"

I rolled my eyes.

"No," he answered. "We already know where you stand, and even if you offered it, we don't want it."

She inhaled sharply. "Then why was I even summoned here? Other than you wanting to be graced by my presence?"

I rolled my eyes again.

"We wanted you to know what you could have had." Ash's smile sent chills down my spine. "Real freedom. No fear. True power. Now, you will have what you deserve. Nothing."

Her chin dipped as eather flared in her eyes. "That was unnecessarily rude. I remember a time when you wouldn't have—"

"You have no idea the effort it is taking for me not to fuck you up." Essence throbbed hotly, rising with my anger. "So, do not finish whatever disgusting, twisted thing was about to come out of your mouth."

Her arms unfolded, and her skin thinned again, showing a sheen of gray beneath. "And you have no idea what it's taking for me not to do the same."

"Are you out of your mind?" Attes whipped his head toward her. "You're really going to threaten her?"

"Don't try to reason with the dumb bitch," Bele tossed out. "I want to see what happens if she tries something."

Veses smirked, holding my stare. "I tried to talk some sense into you before. I warned you that you would regret not taking Kolis's deal. What happened to your family is your fault."

I stiffened.

"Leave," Ash ordered. "Now."

Veses huffed out a laugh and stepped back. Tendrils of mist gathered at her feet. "You all are making a mistake," she cast out with a sharp slice of her hand. "You'll see."

"Veses?" I called out to her. Her narrowed gaze swept to mine. I gave her a smile. "I'll be seeing you soon."

The Primal goddess vanished with a hiss.

"Fates, I hate that bitch," Bele muttered.

Maia laughed and smoothed her hands over her hips. "We are in perfect agreement there."

"Kyn?" Ash said.

The Primal lifted his stare to the dais, smirking. I waited until his arrogant gaze met mine before I said, "You will die."

The smile slipped from his face. It was so quiet you could hear a pin drop.

"You sound a lot like Kolis," Phanos remarked.

"I said I would not rule like Eythos or Kolis. I will not be unnecessarily cruel or brutal," I clarified. Remembering what Attes had said, I lifted my chin toward Kyn. "But I will not be forgiving to the point of foolishness. What you have done and the things you have aided in are abhorrent. We could never create real change with you at our side."

Kyn's eyes narrowed, and he swung his head toward Attes. "What do you have to say about that, brother?"

Attes didn't turn around, and I knew what he said next must have hurt him. "I have no brother."

"That's how you feel?" Kyn sneered.

"That's what *you* caused."

Kyn's flesh thinned, revealing swirling shades of silver underneath. Mist poured out of him as I held his glare. Some of the tension eased from Attes's shoulders once he was gone.

Phanos's gaze met mine and then shifted to Ash. "You're right. We have all just been surviving," he said. "But even on the off chance you can force Kolis to abandon his rule, he will not fall in line. You're a fool if you believe that. He will seek vengeance against everyone who stood against him and those who even considered it."

I tensed.

"I know you don't want to hear that, or maybe you don't like it, but even if Kolis is removed from Dalos, he will not simply go away. He will want retribution."

I wanted to tell him that simply forcing Kolis out wasn't our ultimate end goal, but instinct warned me to stay quiet.

"Kolis is too strong. He will fight back," Phanos stated, and I glanced at Rhahar and Saion. Neither looked happy as the Primal continued. "And he'll fight dirty." His gaze flicked to me. "You already know that." He exhaled heavily and lifted his chin. "I'm sorry, but I cannot swear fealty to either of you or lend my support."

Bitter disappointment swelled, its weight nearly crushing. We were offering him a chance to rule equally and live without fear. How could he reject that? But I already knew the answer. Fear. All the Primals who remained, and even the two who had left, had borne the brunt of Kolis's anger in the past.

"Then you will stand with Kolis?" Ash demanded, his voice a cold shadow that slipped over the floor and walls.

"I'd rather not stand with him either," he replied.

I frowned. "But you won't have a choice."

"Not unless he forces my hand. Until then, I will remain on my island and stay uninvolved," he confirmed, and Saion smirked. The Primal didn't miss that. "You don't like my answer?"

"I'm not surprised by your answer," Saion corrected. "You see, this is not your problem until it becomes your problem. You believe that staying uninvolved absolves you of responsibility for what will happen, but the thing is, Your Highness, doing nothing is doing something."

Phanos's jaw hardened as he stared at the god who'd once served him. A moment passed. "Then so be it." His silvery gaze fixed on Ash and me. "I'm hoping I have a choice and will be allowed to leave, unlike having *no* choice in coming here."

I looked at Ash, and he nodded. "You may leave," I said. "No one will stop you."

He hesitated, then nodded. "I wish you all the best."

I pushed down the disappointment. "Phanos?"

The mist rising from his legs slowed. "Yes?"

"You asked me to remember what you did for me when the time came," I said. "I will."

"Well." Attes cleared his throat, breaking the tense silence left in the wake of Phanos's departure. "I assume all those who remain have done so because we are of like minds?"

There were several nods.

"Then let's get this show on the road." Attes stepped forward and knelt, placing his left palm against the stone floor. "I will happily reaffirm that oath."

I jolted as essence crackled from his right hand. All thoughts of Phanos and the others vanished as raw energy licked over his palm before shifting into a pommel and then a hilt. The eather spun out, forming a long blade. He crossed the sword of eather over his chest.

"With my sword and my life," he said, his voice echoing throughout the chamber. "I swear to you, the One who is born of Blood and Ash, *the* Light and the Fire, and *the* Brightest Moon, the *true* Primal of Life and the *Queen* of the Gods and Common Man."

Gods, that was still such a long title.

I felt something in my chest. Something different than when he'd made the pledge before. This sensation was very similar to how the embers felt, as if a piece of Attes's essence now resided inside me.

His gaze shifted to Ash. "And I swear to you, the Asher, the One who is Blessed, the Guardian of Souls and the Primal God of Common Men and Endings, to honor your command with the full might of Vathi." Attes bowed his head.

The flames above the candles flickered wildly as a ripple of energy coursed through the chamber.

"Thank you," I whispered.

A dimple appeared on Attes's cheek.

"You may rise," Ash said. "And you also have my thanks."

Attes's head lifted, and the sword of eather collapsed. Both dimples were out in full force as he rose. I was happy to see them.

Bele stepped forward, her gaze locking with mine. "I know you're probably thinking that it's unnecessary for me to do this."

I was.

"But it's not. I'm proud to do it," Bele said, looking between Ash and me before following suit. A sword of eather appeared in her right hand. "With my sword and my life, I swear to you, the One who is born of Blood and Ash, *the* Light and the Fire, and *the* Brightest Moon, the *true* Primal of Life and the *Queen* of the Gods and Common Man. And I swear to you, the Asher, the One who is Blessed, the Guardian of Souls and the Primal God of Common Men and Endings, to honor your command with the full might," Bele paused, raising her eyebrow sardonically, "of Sirta."

My lips twitched as another wave of energy whipped the flames about, and I once more felt that strange sensation in my chest. "Thank you, Bele."

"No need to thank me." She lifted her head. "But can I rise now?"

"Yes," I said, wanting to laugh, but my throat felt too thick to allow it.

Penellaphe followed suit, summoning her sword of eather and speaking her vows. We thanked her, and then the beautiful Primal Goddess of Love, Beauty, and Fertility cleared her throat.

"I have stood aside for too long and for too many reasons." Her sandy-blond hair slipped over her shoulders as she knelt. "I will no longer do so."

A sword of eather took shape, its light glittering off her smooth, yellowish-brown cheeks. "I swear to you, the One who is born of Blood and Ash, *the* Light and the Fire, and *the* Brightest Moon, the *true* Primal of Life and the *Queen* of the Gods and Common Man." As the sensation of Penellaphe's oath faded, I felt a part of Maia take root in my chest. Her gaze shifted to Ash. "And I swear to you, the Asher, the One who is Blessed, the Guardian of Souls and the Primal God of Common Men and Endings, to honor your command with the full might of Kithreia." The candles' flames rose several inches as Maia bowed her head.

I thanked her. Ash told her we were honored, and when she rose, I saw determination etched into her features.

As she moved back, the Primal Goddess of Rebirth stepped from behind the group. Rich brown hair slipped over her shoulders as she tilted her head back to stare up at Ash and me.

Eather streaked across her eyes, filling them until they turned the shade of a polished diamond. "I think both of you know that I believe in you," she said, her lips curving into a smile, but there was something *off* about it. "But I cannot swear an oath to you—to either of you."

Shock whipped through me, and the entire chamber went silent. Clearly, no one else had been expecting that response either.

"Why?" Ash asked.

"When I assisted Eythos with Sotoria's soul, I upset the balance. My involvement shifted the future of the realms. Without it, Sotoria would've passed into the Vale," she said, and I saw Penellaphe fold a hand over her mouth. "And when the balance is unequal, it must be fixed."

"Kolis would've found her and brought her back." Anger was quickly replacing my shock. "How is that not an upset to the balance?"

"It is. And based on how things have turned out for Kolis, I believe he has paid that price, just as I have had to."

"What?" Ash demanded roughly. "What price were you forced to pay?"

Her chest rose with a weighted breath. "To right the balance, the Fates decided that I must swear a blood oath to Kolis, one that prevents me from ever using my Court against him."

My mouth dropped open.

"What the fuck?" Bele exploded. "How is that a suitable *fix*?"

"I cannot answer that," Keella stated. "But I can only assume that, in their minds, it ensures that I cannot be persuaded in—as the Fates presented it to me—'affairs that do not involve me.'"

I couldn't believe what I was hearing. "Which Fate made you do this?"

Penellaphe's head jerked in my direction.

"Kyros," she said.

Thank the gods it wasn't Holland because there was a good chance I would lose my shit.

"I know that one." Nektas's lip curled. "Never liked him."

"I wasn't too fond of him myself." The wan smile appeared once more on Keella's lips. "But it is not the Fates who decide such things. It is the essence of the realms."

Once more, I wasn't sure how much I believed that. Holland had intervened, as had Aydun in a way. I had a feeling that even this Kyros walked that fine line.

"You never should have been dragged into this," Ash spoke, the sorrow clear in his tone. "I am sorry that you were."

"I'm not. I don't regret my actions. Nor do I regret what must be done next." Her chin lifted. "The oath I made is between Kolis and me, not my Court."

"No," Ash gasped, sending a sense of dread through me.

"It's okay." Keella's smile deepened, and this time, it reached her eyes. "I am very old, Nyktos. Not much younger than Kolis. And with each passing year, it becomes harder to remember the small pleasantries in life and for those we should protect."

I sucked in a too-short breath as understanding flooded me. I pressed a hand to my chest when Maia's eyes closed.

Keella's gaze shifted to me. "We stood against the Ancients in defense of the mortals, each of us knowing the day would come when it would be us who lost the ability to care for them. To continue to see their beauty and appreciate them, flaws and all. I have passed that time."

"I don't believe that. You are not cold and cruel," I insisted.

"That is only because I still care enough to force myself to be warm and kind." She took another breath, then looked at Maia and Attes. "You two understand."

"I don't want to," Maia whispered. "But I do."

Attes nodded when Keella met his stare, his jaw clenched.

I racked my brain for an answer that didn't involve this. "Can't you go into stasis? Wouldn't that help?"

"It would if I'd been able to do so many years ago. And perhaps if Kolis hadn't done what he did, weakening all of us, infecting each and every one of us in some way. If so, sleep would help now. But even if I went into stasis, the Thyia Plains would still be my Court."

"Then we will fight without your Court," I decided. "We—"

"I am ready. I've been ready," Keella interrupted. "It's okay."

"No." Emotion thickened my voice. I didn't know Keella all that well, but I liked her, and this wasn't fair. "It's not okay."

"There is so much mortal left in you, Seraphena. I hope that does not fade," she said. Ash placed his hand against my lower back. "But you are thinking of me as if I am mortal and on the verge of death. I am not dying. I will pass on to Arcadia, transformed."

I had no idea what she meant by transformed, and my intuition was silent on that. It was not for those outside of Arcadia to fully understand, but what she spoke of was like death. And it would feel like that to those of us who remained.

"You understand, don't you, Nyktos?" she asked.

His hand moved in soothing circles on my back as he said, "I do."

Keella smiled. "I've spent the last couple of years preparing Ione for what I knew would come. She will be loyal to both of you and do all she can to stop Kolis."

I squeezed my eyes shut. Drawing in a shallow breath, I pulled myself together. Just as Ash and the others had done. I would have to mourn the loss of Keella. My lashes felt damp when I opened my eyes.

Ash's exhale was heavy. "When will this happen?"

"I must attend to some affairs first," Keella said. "But we will not want to wait long. Ione will need time to go through the Ascension."

"Okay," I said, my throat stinging. "When you're ready, I will do what needs to be done."

Tables and chairs had been brought into the throne room, along with drinks, as a good part of the evening was spent discussing our plans with our allies.

It felt strange to continue discussing plans after what Keella had shared, but here we were.

Moving on.

Maia had paled a little but said it needed to be done. Penellaphe had agreed, willing to do whatever was necessary to prevent further harm to the mortal realm.

Not gaining Phanos's support was a disappointment. If he attempted to protect Kolis from us, he had the soldiers and the ceeren to fight on land and at sea. Maia had suggested that it was possible he could change his mind. Neither Saion nor Rhahar was convinced of such. I allowed a little bit of hope to spark, but he still had a choice to make.

Each Primal knew that what we planned would come fast and hard. One would think the knowledge would've left a somber pall over the group, but there were smiles and warmth. Perhaps they were used to this.

I wasn't sure. But once we'd finished strategizing and Penellaphe shared that she had located Embris's stash of bones—it wasn't much, but it *would* help—what I had potentially discovered before the meeting surged to the surface.

My gaze fell on Maia. There was no way I was asking her.

I quietly excused myself. Ash wanted to step away with me, but I assured him that everything was fine, and I would return.

I made my way through the war room to the hall. I'd only gone a few steps before I heard Penellaphe calling my name. I turned, tangles twisting in my already knotted stomach. When I'd seen her last… I looked away, the back of my throat scalding with shame.

Penellaphe's steps slowed. She cleared her throat. "I wanted to see how you were but didn't want to ask in there."

"I'm…" I started to tell her I was okay but had a feeling she knew better. She'd seen me immediately after what I'd done. I took a deep breath, forcing myself to meet her gaze. It was strange seeing her with the silver eyes of a Primal. "I've been better."

A look of sympathy flickered across her features. Not pity. "I didn't get a chance to say this before. I'm sorry for your loss."

"Thank you." I exhaled long and slow. "How are you?"

"I'm okay." Her brow creased. "But I do feel a bit weird. Like I'm myself but…not."

A half-grin tugged at my lips. "I know the feeling."

She nodded. "Holland said it will eventually fade."

"It does." Mostly. But I figured I'd keep that part to myself. "I don't think I really gave you much of a choice when it came to the whole Ascension thing."

"It's okay," she was quick to say. "You knew me and weren't familiar with the other gods of Lotho. Your decision to Ascend me made sense."

"That wasn't the only reason. I trust you, and Holland clearly loves you.

That tells me you're…well, a good person."

"Holland does have good taste, if I do say so myself."

I smiled at that. "I hope you are truly okay with this. It puts you in danger."

"I have been in danger in one way or another for centuries, Sera," she said. "But now I can do something about it instead of Holland or another. I couldn't before."

That made me feel better about cornering her into this role. "Will you be staying longer? There's something I need to do really quick."

"Yes. I'll be around."

"Okay." I started to turn.

"Sera?" Penellaphe clasped her hands. "Holland mourns with you."

My breath caught, and I couldn't speak through the sudden burn in my throat.

Penellaphe's smile was sad. "See you in a bit."

I watched her turn and walk back to the throne room, then closed my eyes. *It'll get better*, I told myself. *I'll get better.* Opening my eyes, I began my search for Aios.

Luckily, I was able to find her in the kitchens, speaking with Valrie. They were talking about bringing in additional cooks—something Rhain had discussed with me. Gods, that felt like eons ago—but I suspected she also wanted to be close to the throne room.

"How did the meeting go?" she asked as I led her down the hall.

"As well as can be expected. Phanos is a no but claims he will not support Kolis either," I told her. "Maia is on board."

"Wow," she murmured.

I glanced over at her. "Surprised?"

"A little." Her brows pinched. "But I haven't spent much time with her in a very long time." She looked at me closely when I all but pulled her into the library. "Is everything okay?"

I closed the doors behind me and then faced her. Smiling, I did my best to act normal. "Yes."

"Are you sure?" She moved deeper into the cavernous space, her pale lavender gown swishing at her ankles. It didn't matter how many wall sconces were turned on, the light only ever cast a dull glow over the rows and rows of books and little else. But Aios was like a fiery torch in the dimness. "Besides the fact that I wouldn't expect you to be after…what happened, your smile says otherwise."

"What's wrong with my smile?"

"Nothing," she was quick to say. "It's just a bit large." A pause. "Unsettlingly so. Just like Bele's when she's faking it."

My lips flattened. "Everything is fine," I said for what felt like the hundredth time in the last twenty minutes. "I just wanted to ask you something in private that has nothing to do with the Primals or the meeting."

Curiosity etched into her features, and she sat on one of the long, crimson-hued couches. "I'm all ears."

I opened my mouth, but I wasn't sure how to ask the question without coming right out with it. "What I'm going to ask is going to sound really random," I began, passing the rolling ladder, my stomach twisting into knots. I glanced at the portraits of Ash's parents and then quickly averted my attention. Why had I chosen this space out of all the many, many empty chambers? Sadness dusted it and everything in it.

"Sera?" Aios's brow creased. "I think I prefer the unsettlingly large smile over this."

I frowned. "What is my face doing now?"

"You look rather…panic-stricken."

Well, I was starting to feel rather panic-stricken now that I didn't have the meeting to distract me.

I walked behind the couch across from Aios and willed my nerves to settle. I didn't need Ash picking up on my emotions. "In the mortal realm, there were these older women who worshipped at Maia's Temples and were often sought for specific reasons."

A lock of red hair cascaded down her arm as she cocked her head to the side. "I know of whom you speak. The Matrons."

"Yes. Them." I made another pass behind the couch. "They were able to answer certain questions. How? I don't know. But I assume they were taught by Maia or gods from her Court."

The crease between Aios's brows spread to her forehead. "You would be correct." She tipped forward, watching me. "Why are you asking questions about this?"

My heart thudded. "I'm not even sure—I mean, I am. What I want to know doesn't have anything to do with them." Pressure started to build in my chest, causing me to draw in a deeper breath. Stopping, I grasped the back of the couch. *Keep it together.* The last thing I needed was for Ash to run out of the throne room in search of me. "Are you able to tell if someone is with child?"

Aios's lips parted. They moved, but I didn't hear any sound. It could've been the blood pounding in my ears because, all of a sudden, sound came rushing back. "Surely, you don't mean…?" She hesitated as if saying the words aloud would make them real and she had to prepare herself. "Do you think you're with child?"

"What?" I laughed—or screeched like a large bird of prey. "No."

Aios stared at me. "Then why are you asking?"

"Because…" I dropped my forehead onto the back cushion and groaned. "Obviously, I'm asking for myself. And, honestly, I'm probably just overreacting. But you see, I've been nauseous lately, and I think I'm late." My fingers pressed into the cushion as something occurred to me. "I've been really emotional, too. I want to cry over everything and anything, and that isn't me. And I'm actually really late. That could simply be because of stress. A lot has happened." Forcing myself to lift my head, I looked over at Aios. "Are you able to tell me if I'm overreacting?"

Aios's mouth snapped shut, and she blinked rapidly. "I can."

My heart felt like it fell onto the floor. "Then you know?"

"Yes. No." She gave me a quick shake of her head. "I mean, I don't know simply by looking at you, but you were right when you said a lot has happened. You've been through a lot of stress, both physical and emotional. That can do all manner of things to the body."

Beneath my fingers, the backing of the couch creaked. "I know."

"And it's doubtful you would begin feeling symptoms so soon."

I wanted so badly to believe that. "But it isn't that soon."

"It's fairly difficult for Primals to conceive. Plus, you just Ascended into Primalhood, Sera. You were mortal before then. You would not have been able to conceive."

"Yeah, see, that's what I thought, but how mortal was I with Primal embers inside me? How mortal was I after taking Nyktos's blood?" I said. "Which I did more than once before the Ascension."

Aios's chest rose sharply against the delicate lacing of her bodice. "I…I didn't think about that. There's no one else like you. I suppose it could be possible, but…"

"I had this dream, or maybe it was a vision, while in stasis—" I closed my eyes for a heartbeat. "I saw two cubs."

"What?" she exclaimed.

"I saw my *nota* form, and then I saw two smaller versions of her," I said.

"Two?" Aios whispered.

"Two."

"Fates, Sera." Her throat worked on a swallow, and her shoulders squared. "I can tell you if you are. I would just need to place my hand on your stomach," she explained, her silver eyes wide. "You really think you're with child?"

A rather huge part of me screamed no. If I didn't know for sure, then I could continue on with, well, *everything* until I found out for myself one way or another. I wouldn't have to think about how I would accomplish *everything* while with child…or two. I wouldn't have to worry about how Ash would respond or—oh, gods—the fact that I could be responsible for another human being. Like really responsible, and not in some vague, Primal of Life and Queen of the Gods sort of way. I could have weeks, maybe even a month of not having to deal with what would be a fairly large complication. I could just pretend. I was really good at that.

But that was irresponsible. And while I was that on most days, I wasn't actively, idiotically irresponsible. Mostly. I cringed, thinking of what I'd done.

Aios opened her mouth and then closed it.

She rose. Her gown whispered over the stone as she quietly approached me. Coming to stand beside me, she smiled. "It will be easier if you straighten," she said. "You can still hold on to the couch if you'd like."

For a moment, I had utterly no idea what she was talking about. Then I realized I was still hunched over, clasping the back of the couch.

Gods.

Prying my fingers loose and straightening, I saw I'd left dents in the backing. "I'm not acting like a…a badass Primal right now."

Her smile softened. "You're acting like someone whose entire life may change in a matter of moments."

A whooshing motion swept through my chest, almost as if my heart decided it wanted nothing to do with this and had exited my body. "That didn't help."

"But that's the reality." Aios took my hand, and I jumped. I actually *jumped.* Her chin dipped. "Most people would be this nervous, Sera. Even if they were hoping for a yes."

Throat drying, I swallowed hard. "Okay."

"I need to touch your stomach—your bare stomach," she informed me.

"All right." Knees feeling weak, I grasped the skirt of the gown and lifted it above my waist. "Aios—" I stopped myself.

"What?"

Pressing my lips together, I shook my head. What I was thinking… "What if I am?" My voice cracked as those knots in my stomach doubled in size. "We have many fights ahead—"

"Let's cross that bridge when we get to it," she cut in.

"We're crossing that bridge right now," I countered. "Everything will change."

"It could." Her steady gaze held mine. "But it doesn't have to."

Air wheezed from my lungs. I knew what she meant.

"We just need to get to that point first," she continued, her voice gentle. "Okay?"

Unable to speak, I nodded.

"It will only take a few seconds." Her gaze lowered slightly.

The touch of her hand was surprisingly cool, and I jerked a little. She murmured an apology, her hand flattening just below my navel. I held my breath, counting as the glow of eather pulsed behind her pupils. Thin streaks radiated out, crisscrossing her irises. Her expression didn't change. There wasn't even a flicker of a muscle when she withdrew her hand.

The aura faded from behind her pupils, and she lifted her gaze to mine. What felt like a small eternity passed, but in reality, it could have only been a heartbeat or two.

She took a breath, and I could no longer breathe. "You're with child. Two of them."

I didn't remember walking around the couch and sitting, but I was. I was sitting with my hands limp in my lap and my heart beating slowly, steadily. There was a buzzing in my ears, but I wasn't running around screaming.

I was calm.

Aios sat beside me. She'd been quiet since she'd confirmed what I realized at some point I'd already known. At least, I think she had been. There was that buzzing.

"Sera?" she said tentatively.

"Yes?"

"Are you all right?"

I laughed. It was high-pitched. Strained.

"That was a silly question." She placed her hand on my arm. "You probably don't know what to feel."

"That…that is true." The breath I took was thin, but I was able to draw one in, which surprised me. This was one of those moments where having a complete meltdown would be understandable, but I was glad I wasn't. I so didn't need Ash picking up on any of my emotions right now.

I could feel the blood pounding in my temples. "Can you tell how far along I am?"

"Not to the exact date," she said, and for some reason, that made me want to laugh again. "But I would say you're at least ten or eleven weeks along. Perhaps even twelve."

Perhaps even…

That meant I could be three months along. That didn't seem like a long time, but it also felt like a lifetime. Either way, it definitely meant I'd conceived before I Ascended. Possibly the first time or two Ash and I had been together.

Gods.

"I don't even know if I want kids. How can I be having two of them?"

"I don't believe conception hinges on what one wants," she said gently. "But I get what you're saying."

The shelves of books blurred. "I don't even know if Nyktos wants children."

"It's not like you two have had much time to discuss such things."

"We…we haven't had any time." Eyes closing, I swallowed. "Not any real length of time to just be a…a couple, you know? We were in each other's way at first. Nyktos hadn't known he could love. And I was dying." The laugh I'd held back came then. "We didn't even know we had a future longer than the one we thought we had. There is still so much we need to learn about each other. I haven't even seen his paintings!"

Aios was quiet. She gently squeezed my arm, her eyes filled with sympathy.

And my mind was no longer empty. My thoughts raced. "We have so much to do."

"I know," she said, her voice soft as she squeezed my arm again.

"I can't sit out anything that must be done."

"If you decide to go through with this, it will change everything. You cannot go into battle—"

"Watch me," I replied, my voice hardening with a power that blazed as fierce as an inferno. "I won't let this stand in my way. I'm the Primal of Life. I'm needed to put Kolis in the ground. Besides that, I am a fighter, Aios. It's who I am. There is no way I could just stand by and do nothing."

"But think of the risks—"

"I know what the risks are."

"No, you don't. Not right at this moment," she corrected in that gentle way of hers. "Pregnancies are difficult in general. Even for a god or a Primal, and that's just when they're only carrying one child, not two." She twisted, pointing her knees toward me and lifting my hands from my lap. "Your loyalty and courage are admirable, Sera, but if this is what you decide, you must consider the fate of your unborn babes."

My hands trembled in her grasp. "How can I consider theirs but not the fate of the realms? We cannot allow Kolis to continue, and I need to be right beside Nyktos. If not, he could fall. And if he does…" Panic pierced my chest as I pulled my hands free. "I will be the ruin of realms."

Blood drained from her face. "Sera—"

"There cannot be a choice between the two," I shouted, my voice echoing through the chamber. The ferocity of my outburst left me breathless, and the silence hung heavily between us.

Aios nodded. "Okay." She cleared her throat, her eyes glistening. "There doesn't need to be a choice at all."

My breath snagged, and I recoiled. "I'm the Primal of *Life*, Aios."

"You are Seraphena first." The eather intensified behind her pupils. "A woman who has fought for her autonomy. This is your body."

My fingers dug into my knees. "You're a goddess of *fertility*, so hearing you speak of terminating a pregnancy to the Primal of *Life* is…kind of odd."

"What I am allows me to fully understand the complex nature of these things." She reached between us, tucking a stray curl behind my ear. "Sometimes, the time simply is not right. It happens. And if anyone faults you for that, that is on them. Not you. They do not live your life. It is their problem. Not yours." Her eyes met mine. "You don't need to make a decision right now. You have time."

"I know, and I agree with everything you've said." And I truly did. "But…"

"But what?" Her eyes searched mine. "Is that not an option?"

I opened my mouth, but I couldn't speak. Did I want to keep them? Be a mother?

I sucked in a sharp breath. It was almost as if the knowledge had finally made it past the shock. There was life inside me. *Lives.*

Acid gathered in the back of my throat. My gaze flickered to the portraits hung along the back wall, and I saw Ash in my mind's eye. He held a tiny, fragile life, cradled in his arms and against his chest.

Oh, gods.

My heart turned to mush at the same moment my stomach felt like it had dropped to the floor. Fear and even a bit of awe mingled with the weight of the reality.

"Thank you for confirming this and for reminding me I have options," I said. "But I can't make that choice without talking to Nyktos. I've…I've lied and hidden enough from him. I can't do that with this."

She held my stare and nodded. "Whatever path you choose, I will stand by your side. You are not alone in this, Sera. Just remember that."

Breathe in.

I sat on the edge of the underground pool, my feet in the warm water. I'd tucked the skirt of my gown under my knees, but the edges were still damp. My hands were clasped loosely in my lap as I watched the mills churn, keeping the water from going stagnant. My mother would be proud. I was the picture of serenity.

Hold.

I had to be, lest I wanted Ash to feel exactly how freaked out I was.

Or even possibly bring the entire palace down on my head, which would be bad. Really bad since the other Primals were still here.

Breathe out.

I had no idea how long I'd been down here. I'd need to make an appearance soon, but I wasn't sure how I could when there was a really good chance I would blurt out the news in front of the gods only knew who. It wasn't that I was hiding from Ash.

Okay, I kind of was.

I knew I needed to tell him that I…was pregnant. My stomach dipped and twisted, my gaze dropping to the churning, midnight-hued water. It was so clear it looked black due to the shadowstone floors. Just like my lake.

Breathe in.

This wasn't something I could keep from him or even wanted to. I needed to talk to him about this. I needed to know what he thought. How he would react.

But I also needed time to grasp the fact that I was…pregnant.

With two babes.

"Fuck," I whispered, then held my breath for a count of five.

What was I going to do? I barely knew how to take care of myself. How was I supposed to parent two children? Two *newborns* when I could barely handle Jadis when she was throwing a temper tantrum?

Granted, she could spit fire, and the babes wouldn't be able to do that, but I knew they could spew all manner of fluids.

Breathe out.

I didn't even know how to take care of a babe. I hadn't had the greatest role model when it came to parenting, but I didn't think I had to try all that hard to be better. More present. Loving. Caring—

I stopped myself. I'd have to get to the point where I worried about all of that.

My stomach dropped for the hundredth time, and I took another breath. And how would I do what was necessary while pregnant? I meant what I had said to Aios. There could be no choice between the two. My power was needed. There would be fights, and while it was harder to seriously injure me, the same couldn't be said for the lives I carried inside me.

Hold.

There doesn't need to be a choice at all.

Unclasping my hands, I placed one against my lower stomach. A year ago, I wouldn't have hesitated to seek the aid of one of the Matrons. Accidental conception happened even when every precaution in the realm was taken. I heard the maids whispering in Wayfair and knew teas could be consumed, and I didn't judge them. In fact, I was impressed by the fact that they could make that choice. Not a single conversation I'd overheard made it sound like it was an easy one. Many of them did so in tears, no matter the reason, whether it was because they didn't feel financially capable, their condition was a result of a brief dalliance, or from force. I imagined if their situations had been different, many of them would've opted to keep the babe.

Or maybe not. Either way, it never sounded like a flippant decision.

Breathe out.

But now? I didn't think I could do that because these were Ash's children. Ours. *Mine.*

My stomach turned over heavily, but for a different reason this time. Every couple of minutes, a tendril of *excitement* wove its way through the fear, panic, and disbelief, followed by something that felt damn powerful and *pure.* It was love.

How was that even possible? So quickly? It was the very last thing I'd ever thought to feel toward any babe, even mine. I wasn't the parental type. I never, not even as a little girl who still had the ability to have those sweet, foolish dreams, saw myself as a mother. But, gods, I felt love for them. And it was as fierce as what I felt for Ash. Protective. As if that motherly instinct I'd heard others speak about had snapped into place.

And, gods, it was the most unexpected emotion. A huge part of me was afraid to let those feelings grow, blossom, and spread because what if Ash wasn't happy about this? I felt like I couldn't allow myself to feel those emotions.

But that was…that was wrong.

Because I already knew I was keeping the lives growing inside me, even though it didn't seem fair. Unfair that I got to have this when I had stolen this very chance from others. And I had no idea how to be a parent, if I was capable, or even if I should. But they were ours. And if he couldn't accept this? Which was highly possible considering everything he'd faced—all we would *still* face… Damn, he hadn't even allowed people to stay in the palace and be close to him until recently because of Kolis. Still, his reluctance wouldn't change my mind.

But I knew it would change us, mates of the heart or not. It would change us in ways that would break my heart.

Feeling my chest tighten, I rose from where I sat and descended the steps. Water rose over my legs and quickly reached my hips as I walked forward. The hem of my gown lifted and floated when the water reached my waist. Once it lapped at my chest, I didn't go any farther. The deepest end of the pool would be well over my head, and I still hadn't learned how to swim.

And I was supposed to teach children? Things more important than swimming? Like how to be thoughtful and kind and how to stand up for themselves and others? How to be good, even though I wasn't entirely good?

The weight of it all bore down on my chest. I closed my eyes, letting myself slip underwater.

Sound ceased immediately.

My mind quickly followed.

There was just nothing as I floated. The tension all through my body began to ease. The mineral-rich water could have had something to do with that, but it was also the complete silence. The *nothingness.* The peace and the feeling of the water rushing over my face and—

Cold arms came around me, startling me as I was lifted from the water. My eyes flew open when my head broke the surface, and I dragged in a lungful of air.

"Sera," Ash gasped, scooping the wet hair back from my face. Strands of silvery eather whipped through his eyes. "What are you doing?"

"Sorry." My face warmed as I stared up at him. It had been so quiet underwater that I hadn't felt him approach. "I was just…doing my version of swimming."

"With your gown on?"

"Yeah?"

"While we had Primals in the throne room?"

Um…

"And I was waiting for you to return?"

"Sorry. It was a spur-of-the-moment thing." I clutched his shoulders. "And you're not dressed for swimming."

The eather in his eyes brightened until I almost couldn't see his pupils. "That's because I thought—" He stopped with a sharp inhale, his jaw clenching.

My eyes widened when I realized what he'd thought. "I wasn't trying to drown myself."

His arms tightened around me. "I wasn't thinking that."

"You sure about that?" My heart twisted. "I told you, Ash. I won't do that again."

Ash opened his mouth and then closed it. His eyes slammed shut. "I know. I just…I panicked, seeing you with your gown on and your arms outstretched. I don't think you realize how that looks to someone above water."

"I am sorry." My gaze dropped to where his white shirt was plastered to his chest.

Ash was quiet, drawing his hand up my back. "What drove you here?"

The reason, which I had somehow forgotten in those brief moments, came rushing back. My throat dried. I'd gone over all the different ways I could broach the subject with him while I sat at the pool's edge, and every single one of them vanished from my thoughts.

"I know something must be preying upon your mind," he continued, brushing his nose against mine. "For you to leave the throne room and seek the silence of water."

The fact that he remembered why I stayed underwater made my heart swell until it felt like it might burst, if not for the way it pounded wildly, threatening to bust through my rib cage.

I breathed in and counted to five. My throat suddenly felt like it was sealing.

He immediately picked up on my sharp spike of anxiety. "What is it?"

He paused, running his thumb across my cheek. The familiar cool caress did little to calm my nerves. "*Liessa*?"

Something beautiful.

Something powerful.

And I was powerful. Strong. Brave. I could fucking tell him that I was pregnant with his children.

The next breath I took lodged in my throat. "Maybe we should get out of the pool."

He frowned. "Why would we need to do that?"

"Because what I'm about to tell you will probably surprise you." I gripped the front of his shirt. "And you may faint or something."

He frowned. "I've never fainted."

"There's always a first time," I said. "Even for a Primal, I bet. And if that happens, you're really heavy, and I don't trust my ability to lift you from the water. I'd probably end up throwing you into a wall—"

"*Liessa*," he cut in, worry creeping into his features, mixing with bemusement. "What do you have to tell me?"

The words caught in my throat, choking me. I took a deep breath, trying to steady myself. "Ash," I said, my voice barely above a whisper. My stomach twisted into knots, and then the words tumbled out. "I'm…I'm pregnant."

52

The confession hung heavily in the air between us with a tangible weight that felt like it could collapse the walls of the pool. I waited for a reaction, but Ash, well, he had absolutely *none.*

He stood there, one arm around me and one hand against my cheek. His lips were parted. Worry was still etched into the striking lines of his face. He was as still as a statue. I didn't think he even breathed.

My concerns began to grow. Maybe he hadn't heard me. Or perhaps he hadn't understood what I'd said. That seemed silly, but he still hadn't moved.

"I'm pregnant," I repeated. "You see, I've been nauseous on and off for the last several, well, weeks to be honest—that doesn't matter right now. That's why I came down here. I needed to try to wrap my head around it before I told you." My heart still pounded. "So, yeah, I'm totally pregnant."

Ash's eyes widened, and a jolt ran through him. His arms fell to his sides and he jerked back. I breathed in and held my breath. He went completely still again, except for his chest. It rose and fell rapidly, and as the seconds ticked by, it felt like we were teetering on the edge of a precipice, where one wrong move could send us plummeting into the abyss.

"Pregnant?" he rasped, his voice wavering with surprise and disbelief.

"Yes." I nodded, feeling stupid tears crowding my eyes.

He went silent again, and I really began to think I should've made him get out of the pool.

The flames from the dozens of sconces on the rough walls suddenly flickered wildly as a pulse of energy left him, stroking the eather inside me.

Or maybe I should've kept this to myself until I figured out how to tell him without practically shouting it in his face.

His skin hadn't thinned, though, and he hadn't frozen the pool, so I thought perhaps that was a good sign.

But he stared at me, and I didn't think he saw me. He was focused on some distant point, and I could only imagine he was exactly where I'd been when Aios confirmed what I already knew.

I wanted to give him time. Gods knew I'd needed it, but my heart felt like it might come out of my chest. Each beat echoed with fear because everything would change if he didn't want them. I tried to say quiet, but for once in my godsforsaken life, I couldn't stop myself.

"I know this is a surprise. I was shocked, too. And we haven't even discussed something like this. I don't even know if you want children, and even if you do, the timing is so, so unbelievably bad." I folded my arms around me and began to tremble. "I'm so sorry—"

Another jolt ran through Ash, and then he was suddenly right in front of me, sending currents rippling through the pool. He clasped my cheeks. "Fates, Sera, don't apologize."

"I feel like I should," I whispered.

"Fates, no. I just…I wasn't expecting that." A tremor ran through his hands. His face was pale, his features stark. "You're sure?"

"Y-Yes. Aios confirmed it. That's what I was doing when I left the throne room."

A wisp of eather swirled through his eyes. "When I felt your anxiety spike today. I'd been feeling it on and off all day, but I thought it was about the Primal meeting…" He briefly closed his eyes. "That's why."

"I got sick, and it wasn't the first time."

"Why didn't you mention you were feeling unwell?"

"I thought it was because of the Ascension, like leftover effects. Or from…from everything else."

He shook his head. "I don't understand."

"Which part?"

"You said you've been feeling unwell for weeks."

"Yes. I was actually nauseous while I was in Dalos," I said, wrapping my hands around his wrists. "I just thought it was because of all of that. But—"

"That doesn't make sense, Sera," he said. "You are only recently not mortal. We would not have been able to conceive before then."

"Yeah, see, I thought that, too. But then I was like, how mortal was I really, with these embers in me since birth? And the first night we were together, I had your blood. Just a drop, but apparently, that one drop was super powerful." My fingers pressed into his hard skin. "But I also had your blood after that."

He opened his mouth but didn't speak.

My throat still felt dry and tight. "I started putting things together and realized I was late. Like really late. And with the nausea and everything…"

"How…how far along are we?" he asked, and my entire body shook. We. Not you. *We*. "Aios would've been able to see that."

"She…she did." My eyes stung even more now, but I wasn't sure if it was from relief or if I was about to have a breakdown. "She thinks I'm about three months along."

His lips parted again, and that uncomfortable silence fell once more.

I swallowed, unable to bear the quiet. "Earlier today, I remembered the dream I had in stasis—when I saw my *nota.* I'd been trying to remember it," I rushed on. "I didn't only see my *nota.* I saw two cubs on the bank of my lake. I don't know if it was a vision or something, but I didn't tell you when you checked on me before the meeting because I wasn't a hundred percent sure, and—"

"Two?" he croaked. "You saw two…*cubs*?"

The flames danced erratically once more. "You sure you don't want to get out of the pool?"

"Two?" he repeated.

"Yeah. Sorry. I hadn't gotten to that part yet. I probably should've just broken the news all at once." I wet my lips, and Ash went completely still yet again. "But, yes. Two. Aios also confirmed that. And I know this is overwhelming and will likely sound a little insane, but I think—no, I *know*—I love them already. I don't know how. I've never wanted children or honestly even liked being around them—fuck, I didn't really think about it, but I'm not getting rid of them because they are ours. They're—" My voice cracked again. "They're mine."

Ash was silent again. He stared down at me, his eyes still wide.

I wished I knew what he felt—what was going through his head. "What are you thinking?" I asked, my voice sounding entirely too small. "Feeling?"

"What am I…?" He laughed hoarsely. "I'm shocked as fuck. I don't know what to think. I…" He trailed off, slowly shaking his head. "With everything that has happened, I didn't want children, didn't want to expose them to what I experienced. So, I never really thought about the idea beyond that."

My fingers began to ache from how tightly I gripped him.

Another tremor ran through him. "But I could've…I could've lost you." His voice cracked, and another wave of power rippled out from him, stirring the waters. "I could've lost *them*."

Now, I went rigid. He sounded absolutely *destroyed* just thinking of the possibility.

Ash's eyes were glistening silver pools. "If I hadn't tried to Ascend you? Or if the Ascension hadn't worked…?" His hands shook as he slid one to the back of my head. "I would've lost everything and more."

I sucked in a thin breath, too afraid to even acknowledge what his words might signify.

"I'm going to be…" He blinked rapidly, and I didn't think the dampness on his cheeks was due to the pool water.

"Are…are you crying?" I whispered.

"I think so." His laugh was shaky, and gods, I didn't think anyone had ever seen Ash like this, wide-eyed and vulnerable. Wisps of eather whirled through his eyes. "I'm going to be a father?"

"Yes."

His eyes shut, and then my feet left the floor of the pool as he lifted me. My legs tangled in the wet gown, but I managed to wrap them around his waist. He held me so close I could feel his pounding heart.

I buried my face in the crook of his neck, breathing in his fresh scent. "Does this mean you're…happy about this?"

"Happy?" His hand ran up my back, tangling in my hair. "Fates, Sera, I…I don't think I've ever wanted something more."

What felt like a life-changing quake ran through me. "Really?"

"Yes. Really." Ash's hand closed around the nape of my neck. "How could I not?" His voice roughened. "When they will be a part of you. A part of us."

I opened my mouth, but whatever I'd been about to say came out as a ragged, muffled sound. Holding on to him with everything I had in me, I squeezed my eyes shut against the tide of emotion, but I still felt a few tears slip free.

"*Liessa*." Ash tilted his head, pressing his cheek against the side of my head. "Don't cry. Please. It kills me when you do."

"I don't mean to cry, and gods, I think they are why I've been so damn emotional, too." I struggled to rein in my emotions. "I just wasn't sure how you would feel about it. If you were unhappy…" I couldn't bring myself to say it.

He leaned his head back. "How could I ever be unhappy? You're having my child—my children." His chest rose swiftly as if the knowledge had hit him again. "That is a dream I never allowed myself to have," he said, and I shuddered at his words. He pressed a kiss to my damp cheek. "You said you already love them?"

My heart skipped a beat, and I lifted my head. Our eyes met. "I do, and that…that scares me. And then I'm even more scared because I'm scared. That makes me sound bizarre, doesn't it?"

"No, *liessa*, it doesn't." He chased the tears with a swipe of his thumb. "I'm scared, too, Sera. Neither of us planned for this, and our lives are about to change in ways I cannot even begin to imagine. But I know we will love them just as fiercely as we love each other. And I also know we'll figure everything out," he said, catching another tear. "We've got this, *liessa*."

Inhaling deeply, I nodded. "We do." Not just because we had to but because we *wanted* to, and I knew there was a world of difference between the two.

His forehead dropped to mine, and he tightened his arm around my waist. "Sera," he whispered, his lips brushing mine. He laughed, and it was a shaky but joyous sound. "We're going to be parents."

An unsteady laugh parted my lips as the new reality continued sinking in. Mates of the heart was a powerful thing, but this…this was different. The bond we now shared went far beyond just the two of us. We'd created two lives together. Not with eather or magic, but with just us—our love.

"Ash," I said, my voice barely audible above the soft sounds of the water. "I love you so much."

He pressed his lips to mine, the kiss slow and tender. It was like a balm to my soul, and I felt some of the panic and fear lifting, leaving urgent, feverish desire in its place. As the kiss took on a deeper, rougher, more urgent edge, I knew he was feeling every wild emotion I was.

"Make love to me." My fingers tangled in the wet strands of his hair. "Please."

"You never have to beg," he swore. "Ever."

Then his mouth covered mine again, and there was nothing slow about the way he kissed me. I felt the water churning around us, mirroring the ebb and flow of our rising passion. Our lips moved together, exploring and tasting until I was breathless with need.

Then, things became wonderfully chaotic.

His hands went to the clasps down the back of my gown, but he grew impatient before the first was undone. "I'm going to apologize ahead of time."

"Wha—?" I gasped as Ash gripped the back of the gown and tore the material straight down the middle. My eyes widened. "I really liked this gown."

"I'll have Erlina make you another," he promised, claiming my mouth once more.

The gown slipped down my hips and legs and then floated away in the water. I tugged at his shirt, hearing the soft cloth tear. He laughed roughly, ducking his head. His shirt joined the gown somewhere in the pool, his wet, cool hands slipping over my breasts. His tongue danced with mine, and I felt his hands slide to my hips. His fingers made their way under the band of the silky undergarments as mine slipped over his wet breeches. He shoved the scrap of lace down, helping me step free of it, continuing to kiss me.

His hands replaced mine, shoving his breeches down. He pulled me against him, and I gasped into his kiss as I felt him thick and hard against my belly.

"Ash," I moaned, his hand finding its way between my legs. His fingers traced delicate circles around my sensitive flesh, teasing and taunting me. My hips bucked against him instinctively, craving more of his touch. "I need you inside me." Heat surged between my thighs. "Now."

His answering groan sent a rush of hot pleasure through me. He lifted me, and I wrapped my legs around him once more. The arm at my waist shifted me until I felt the head of his cock at my entrance.

"I love you," he said, cradling the back of my head.

Ash thrust into me as he drew me down, filling me with one deep, startling thrust. My breath hitched at the feeling.

"Gods, *liessa*..." Ash panted, his eyes locked on mine. He began moving within me. "You feel perfect."

My nails dug into his shoulders, clinging to him as we picked up the pace. The water churned wildly around us, crashing against the sides of the pool. Waves of pleasure spun through my body, building and intensifying. Our moans and gasps echoed across the water, lost in the hum of the mills.

"This feels...it feels different." He groaned, and I tightened around him. "You. Us. Everything."

My mind raced, trying to process the myriad sensations—the pressure of Ash inside me, the water swirling around us, the sound of our mingled breathing and moans. It was overwhelming and intoxicating all at once.

"Hold on to me," he said against my lips.

"Always," I promised as he began walking us backward.

As we reached the steps, Ash lowered us so he was sitting and I was straddling him, my knees resting against the slick, smooth step. The change of position drew a ragged moan from me, and I let my forehead rest against his. Neither of us moved for several long moments. The water calmed, but our hearts didn't.

With one hand on my hip, Ash lifted me until only the tip of his cock remained inside me, and then he stilled.

I whimpered against his mouth, wiggling against him, but he held me in place. "*Ash*."

He chuckled, the sound husky and rough. "Fuck me, *liessa*."

The wicked demand ignited a fire. My blood burned, and my skin tingled. But his command did more. Gave more. He was freely handing over control.

And giving it to me.

Gods, I was so in love with him.

Muscles low in my stomach clenched. Our eyes locked. "Yes, my King."

His irises flashed silver when starlight filled them.

Pressing my hands against his chest, I slid down his length. The feel of him now was like a jolt of pure eather flooding my veins, making my heart race and my breathing shallow.

Our mouths came together once more, my body moving in a slow and sensuous dance. He held himself still, all but his hands. They roamed and explored, skating over the curves of my hips, the dip of my waist, and then the swells of my breasts as I rode him.

That deep, carnal sound came from him again. His hands slid to my bottom, his long fingers pressing into the flesh and squeezing. Every inch of my being ignited with pleasure, each stroke of his cock coaxing moans from my lips.

Moving up and down, I ran my hands over the muscles of his shoulders and traced my way down his chest, the coolness of his flesh under mine intensifying every ripple of sensation. I could feel power radiating off him as he restrained himself, and it caressed the same raw energy inside me, sending my desire soaring even higher.

His back bowed, and then his mouth replaced his fingers. I cried out when he sucked the hardened peak of my breast into his mouth. I gripped the back of his head, eyes closed and panting as I ground down on him, moving my hips in tight, almost frantic circles. I rocked against him, letting my head fall back and surrendering to the sensation—to the need. To him. Water whipped around us, splashing across the floor. I could feel myself tightening, rushing toward release, and in the back of my mind, it seemed almost impossible that the pleasure could feel this intense and stunning. What Ash had said moments ago had been correct. Everything did feel different. Every touch, every caress was heightened by the knowledge that our connection had grown deeper, somehow more profound. Maybe it was because our love for each other felt even more tangible now, taking shape inside me. Either way, the tension was like a rope being stretched too far.

"I could stay like this forever." Ash's parted lips touched mine. "Feeling myself deep inside you. Feeling you beginning to come. It's the perfect kind of peace."

With each word, each powerful thrust, the tension increased to new heights. "I love you."

Ash groaned, his arms encircling me as he pulled me down and against him, holding me tightly to his body. That rope broke, taking him with me. Waves of pleasure flooded me, and I cried out his name. I shook as the release continued spinning and pulsing through me, dragging me under its powerful embrace until I was limp in his arms, my cheek resting against his shoulder.

Ash's chest rose against mine in a ragged inhale. "Fates," he rasped.

My breath caught as I felt him jerk one last time inside me. "Same."

Silence fell between us, and he dragged his hand up under my hair in slow, soothing strokes. I couldn't help but think of all we'd had to overcome to get to this moment and the…the lives growing inside me. They felt like a testament to our love. A miracle.

Quite some time later, Ash and I lay in bed. I was on my back, my head resting on his chest. His head was propped up on the pillows, one hand in my hair and the other on my lower stomach. We were both naked, our bellies full of the dinner we'd shared, and our passions sated.

We'd made love again upon returning to the chamber, and then again after dinner. He'd offered his vein to me, and instinctually, I knew it was even more important for me to feed now. It wasn't just for me.

It was for the babes.

But…but what about him?

I sat up, facing him. Our eyes met. My heart began to race, but I wanted to do the same for him, even though my anxiety rose. I wanted to get over the fear. I needed to. "Ash, do you need—?"

"No. I fed from Rhain earlier." He guided my head back to his chest, and I fought to quell the rising disappointment. "I don't even know if I should be feeding from you now."

"Really?" The *vadentia* was quiet, and my stomach sank a little. "That could be a problem. If you can't take my blood, if nobody can, how will I Ascend others? That's the crux of our plan."

He was quiet for a moment. "We'll have to ask Kye."

I'd finally agreed to have the Healer come in the morning. Ash had wanted to summon him while we ate, but it was night, and nothing was going to change between now and tomorrow.

I thought about the whole process of exchanging blood—eather. "I Ascended Penellaphe, and it didn't cause any problems."

"We don't know that." His thumb moved in a slow circle under my navel. "It may explain why the last of the bruises haven't healed."

My chest clenched. Damn. That could explain it. I looked down at my stomach. The contrast of his golden-bronze hand against my paler skin was stark. "You know, I had bruises almost everywhere after fighting Kolis."

"I know," he growled.

Placing my hand over his, I tipped my head back to look up at him. "But I didn't have any on my stomach—on my lower stomach. It was almost like…"

"What?"

I lowered my gaze. "Like the essence was protecting that area—them." I let out a low laugh. "That sounds kind of ridiculous."

"I don't think it does," he said. "The essence is an extension of your will. Perhaps even on a subconscious level."

I nodded, falling quiet. He continued tracing circles over my belly, and I realized I had so many questions and thoughts.

"Do you want anything else to eat?" he asked.

I laughed and turned my head to the side. "If you have me eat anything else tonight, I think I'll burst."

He grinned at me. "We don't want that."

"No, it would be gross."

He chuckled, and for a little bit, a companionable silence descended between us as I watched his hand on my stomach. From the moment we'd lay down, his hand hadn't strayed far from that area, and that was…that was *sweet.*

Gods, we were going to have a babe. *Two* of them. My breath caught like it had every time that nugget of realization formed. What would Ezra—?

My heart twisted. I couldn't tell Ezra. Or my mother. Sorrow rose as I pressed my lips together. Ezra would've been happy—shocked but thrilled for me. My mother? I didn't know how she would've responded, but I would've liked to have the chance to learn.

I had to think of something else because I didn't think that kind of pain was good for the babes or me. Gods, a lot of things wouldn't be good.

It was quiet, but Ash knew my mind wasn't. "What are you thinking?"

I dragged my fangs over my lower lip. "Random stuff."

His thumb swept back and forth, just below my navel. "Like?"

"I was just wondering if shifting into my *nota* will affect them," I admitted. "I mean, I assume not since it hasn't yet, and instinct tells me no."

"But you're still worried?"

"Me? Never."

He laughed again, and gods, it was so rare to hear him laugh so deeply and freely. "Well, we're adding that to the list of things to ask Kye."

"It's going to be a long list," I murmured, thinking about tomorrow. I had no idea what would be involved when it came to that kind of checkup, and I wasn't even going to think about it because it would probably stress me out.

But the visit with Kye wasn't the only thing that had to happen tomorrow.

I'd told Veses I'd see her soon, and I would.

"Twins," Ash murmured, and I glanced up at him again. The hollows of his cheeks pinkened. Another laugh greeted me. "For some reason, it just hit me that we will have twins. I know. I should've figured that out hours ago."

I smiled. "Don't feel bad. I actually hadn't considered that either, to be honest. Twins do run in the family."

"I suppose." His finger trailed a circle around what I knew was a freckle. "My father and his brother were the first, but they weren't identical."

They had shockingly similar features, but they weren't exactly the same like Kyn and Attes. Their hair color was different, and Kolis's cheekbones were broader, but his mouth wasn't as full as Eythos's.

"I guess that means we could have something similar," I said, running my fingers back and forth over his forearm.

"Or they could be identical." He paused. "Or possibly a boy and a girl—fraternal twins." His hand stopped moving suddenly. "The first and second daughter…"

"The prophecy." I knew what he was thinking about. "I wondered the same thing myself, but I…don't think we're having daughters or even one of each."

His brows knitted. "Has your *vadentia* told you something?"

"No." I thought about the brief moment when I saw the two children who were the same but different in the smallest ways. Two mahogany-haired boys with rich, bronze skin. One with silver eyes and the other with golden-silver. "It's just a feeling."

He was quiet for a moment. "Either way, they will…they will want for nothing."

My lips curved up. "You're right."

He returned my smile. "I was thinking that, other than telling Nektas, we should probably keep the news of this quiet. This isn't information we want getting out."

"Yeah," I agreed. "Aios won't say anything until I tell her it's okay."

The quiet came again, and his fingers made those soothing circles and lines across my belly. Our children, be they sons or not, *would* want for nothing. Even though the idea of parenting still freaked me out, I would do *everything* in my power to be a good one. And I would do *everything* to become deserving of this…*blessing*.

Because it still seemed unfair that I got to have this. Like fate had messed up somehow, rewarding instead of punishing me.

"Ash," I said, my voice cracking under the weight of the emotions welling up inside me. "I'm so grateful for this, for us. For everything."

"Me, too, *liessa*." His head dipped, and he kissed me. "Me, too."

"Nyktos said you wanted to see me," Aios said as she crossed the fourth-floor antechamber, the hem of her sky-blue gown whispering over the stone floors.

She sat beside me on the couch while I sipped the juice Ash had insisted I finish. "You've made your choice?" she asked.

My heart fluttered. "*We've* made our choice. We're going to do…the parent thing."

Aios was quiet for a heartbeat and then squealed, causing me to jump. "I knew it!" She made another noise that sort of reminded me of a kitten, and then threw her arms around me. "Sorry! I'm so happy to hear this."

"I can tell." I only managed to hold on to my cup by sheer luck. "How did you know?"

"Nyktos sent Rhain to summon Kye," she explained, squeezing me until I was the one close to squeaking. "He told Rhain he wanted Kye to check you over to ensure you were healing, but…"

"But you knew better."

"I did." Sitting back, she clasped her hands and tucked them under her chin. "I would've supported you either way. Truly. But I am so excited and happy for you—for both of you. For all of us. Do you even know the last time a Primal had children?"

"When Nyktos was born?"

Aios laughed. "Of course, you know." She drew back. "When will you tell everyone? Please say soon because not telling Bele will drive me mad."

I laughed, setting my cup on the side table. "I'm not sure when, but with everything going on, we want to keep it quiet. Can you help with that?"

"Of course. I won't say a word, even though it *will* drive me mad." Her cheeks were flushed. "How did he take the news?"

"I think he almost passed out," I shared.

Aios giggled. "Fates, what I would have given to see that."

I grinned. "It was something else, but other than that, he was…he was perfect." Recalling his reaction once he got over his shock had my smile growing. "He's actually very excited."

Her smile faltered a bit as her gaze swept over my features. "Are you not excited? Now that you've talked to Nyktos?"

"I am," I was quick to say. "I'm also a little terrified."

"Understandable," she said, patting my knee. "Did you guys talk about how this does and doesn't affect things?"

"We talked about feeding and stuff," I told her. "That's something we have to ask Kye, but we haven't gotten to the part where I tell him that I won't be backing down from anything yet."

"How do you think he'll respond?"

I laughed. "Not at all well."

Aios nodded. "At least you're expecting him to put up a fight."

"I am. And I understand why he won't likely agree with me fighting. I get it. But if something happened to him and I wasn't there?" Pressing my lips together, I shook my head. "I can't even think about it." I blew out a breath. "Anyway, I know he will be an amazing father."

"And I believe you will make an incredible mother," she said, her voice unwavering.

I laughed. I couldn't help it. "I don't know."

Her delicate brows furrowed. "I do."

"I'm going to try. I want to because I…I love them already." A nervous laugh left me as Aios's features softened. My face warmed. "I do. And that makes me even more terrified," I admitted, my fears rising then. I couldn't put a lid on them. "I will do everything to be a good mother, even though I am possibly the worst and most undeserving person to have a child, let alone two of them." I frowned. "I don't even know how to swaddle one." I looked at her. "Do you?"

"Yes." Her lips twitched. "I can show you, but parenting is something you sort of learn along the way."

That sounded chaotic and unpredictable, especially when *I* was involved in learning along the way.

I swallowed hard. "Yeah, but it's more than that. I'm an anxious mess most days, and I can only imagine that will be, like, amplified, but…I guess being a nervous mess is normal when it comes to having children."

"It is. I can swear to that," she said. "I've known mothers on their sixth child still being incredibly anxious."

Sixth? My eyes widened, and I shook my head. I glanced at Aios, opened my mouth, and then closed it.

"What?" She nudged me with her shoulder.

"Nothing." I smiled. "I have no idea what Kye will do when he gets here."

"It won't be anything too invasive," she said. "Just a general exam.

Mostly, he will likely talk with you and Nyktos."

I exhaled slowly. "Okay."

Aios left so I could change into something other than a robe. I dressed not for the appointment with Kye but for what would come afterward, donning thick leggings and a white vest over a black linen blouse. I was finishing with the last of the hooks on the vest when I felt Nektas.

Leaving the top hook undone because it wasn't entirely comfortable, I returned to the antechamber.

The moment the draken walked in from the balcony and our eyes met, I knew Ash had told him. It was the softness in his features and gaze. I stopped halfway to the raised platform, a knot of emotion lodging in my throat.

In less than a breath, Nektas held me in his arms and lifted my bare feet off the floor. The hug surprised me, but I got over it quickly, throwing my arms around his neck. He smelled of wind and earth.

"Sera," he said in his gravelly voice, pressing his cheek to the side of my head.

I squeezed my eyes shut, soaking in his warmth. "Crazy, huh?"

He chuckled roughly. "It is, but in the best possible way." He lowered me to my feet and drew back, his hands moving to my shoulders as his thin pupils dilated. "I thought I scented something from you before but wasn't sure what it was."

My brows snapped together. "When you smelled death on me?"

"No." His laugh was low. "As I told you before, that was because I smelled Ash on you."

"Oh." My face warmed. "I probably could've lived without you bringing that up again."

"It was when you returned from the riders and we were on the balcony," he explained. "Your scent had changed."

"Do I even want to know what that means?"

One side of his lips curved up. "Your scent was richer and more of a mix of you and Ash than it ever was before. It has been so long since I've been around a Primal who was with child that it didn't even cross my mind." His hands slid to mine, and he held them gently. "I am so incredibly happy for you and Ash. This is..." He took a deep breath, his voice roughening even more. "This is something I never dared to dream for him."

"He said the same," I whispered, blinking back...what else? Tears. Gods, the crying thing was getting annoying. "How was he when he told you?"

"Eager," he said, letting go of my hands. My lips curved up. "As soon as we were alone, he blurted it out. I wasn't sure I had heard him correctly at first."

"Were you as still as a statue?" I asked. "Because he was when I told him."

"I'm sure I was." Strands of hair slid over his shoulder when he tilted his head. "What I saw in his eyes today…I've never seen before."

"What did you see?"

"It is hard to put into words." He took a moment. "But it was like seeing a man who suddenly realizes they have earned everything they could ever ask for."

"Oh." I clapped my hands over my mouth. "I think I'm going to cry."

That soft look filled his features once more. "It's okay if you do."

"No, it's not." I stepped back, waving my hands at my face as if that would actually help. "Okay. I need to talk about something other than Ash being perfect."

Nektas grinned at me. "We still on for today?"

I frowned. Nektas planned to travel with us to the Thyia Plains and then on to the Callasta Isles. "Why wouldn't we be?"

An indiscernible look flickered across his features. "Just checking." He quickly moved on. "How are you handling the news?"

"Oh, you know." Clearing my throat, I stopped flapping my hands at my face. "Alternating between being really happy, terrified, and excited while wondering what in the world I did to deserve this."

"I can name several reasons why you deserve this."

"And I can name one really big reason that nullifies all those reasons," I replied with a dry laugh.

The smile slipped from Nektas's face. "What do you mean?"

The same thing that happened with Aios repeated itself. My mouth opened but words sat defiantly on the tip of my tongue.

"Sera," he said, his vibrant gaze sweeping over my features.

Shaking my head, I plopped down on the sofa. "I…" This was hard to say out loud. "I just keep asking myself how this is possible. After all the lives I took, how did I end up carrying life inside me?"

A small frown pulled his brows down. "That's not how any of this works—"

"I know." I closed my eyes and then quickly reopened them. "What I mean is that there seems to be no balance in this. And yeah, I get that I conceived before I lost control, but I keep thinking it's not fair. It would have made more sense if fate had made me barren. Or if it took them from me after what I did…"

"I see what you're saying." Nektas came over and sat beside me. His large frame took up nearly two cushions. "Halayna felt something similar when she first learned she was pregnant with our daughter."

My head turned to him in surprise. This was only maybe the second time I'd ever heard him speak about his mate. "Why?"

"There used to be far more fighting among the draken, especially after Eythos was killed. We wanted justice but sought vengeance." His head tipped back on a heavy exhale. "My mate was extraordinarily kind and generous." He paused. "If she liked you."

I cracked a grin.

His lips followed suit. "But she was also as vicious as she was kind. When provoked, she was feared as much as I am. Possibly even more so because when she let loose on someone, she didn't hold back." He glanced at me sideways. "Sound like anyone we know?"

"Whatever," I murmured.

"After Eythos was killed, Halayna singlehandedly took out most of the draken that served in Veses' Court and wiped out the entirety of Hanan's."

My eyes widened. "Good gods."

"Like I said, she could be vicious. Fiercely so. It was one of the reasons I loved her." His chin lowered. "You may know a part of this story. It involves Reaver's parents."

"They were killed when Ash didn't respond to Kolis's summons in a timely manner."

Nektas nodded. "Kolis sent several of his draken. We lost Reaver's parents and two more in the battle, but Kolis lost twice that. His actions caused him to have fewer draken in his Court than Ash."

Anger grew within me. "Let me guess, he didn't believe himself responsible."

"You'd be correct," he replied. "We learned that Kolis was considering taking Reaver— demanding that Ash sever the bond with the youngling. Kolis felt as if he was owed."

My lips parted. "Oh, gods."

"When Halayna learned about it, she was enraged. Reaver had become a son to us. We knew what happened to the younglings in Kolis's Court. They never survived past their first full shift or adolescence. Neither Ash nor we would allow that to happen. Relations were tense in the years that followed." The ridges along his shoulders became more pronounced. "At that time, Kolis had three fully grown female draken. He sent them, likely believing they would be safe, along with Davon and two others," he said, speaking of the draken who shared his blood. "They were there to take Reaver, and it…it did not end well. In a way, we were sending a message back to Kolis. That he wasn't just fucking with his nephew. He was now fucking with us."

I had a feeling I knew where this was going. "He used the female draken almost like a shield."

"He did, and he was wrong for doing so. None of us cared who or what they were. Not when it came to Reaver. Halayna took out two of the females. The third—she was Davon's mate and the youngest of Kolis's draken—was Taliaya." Faint lines appeared at the corners of his eyes. "Davon created a path for her escape. My mate wasn't having that. Halayna went after her, catching up while they were over the Lassa Sea." Nektas was quiet for several moments. "If Halayna had time to cool down, if there weren't years of pain and loss at the hands of Kolis, she likely wouldn't have done what she did. She ripped Taliaya's throat out over the sea, sending her to a watery grave along with…"

I closed my eyes.

"Along with the child she carried within her," he said, his voice low. "We knew the moment Taliaya showed that she was pregnant. We could smell it. We couldn't believe Kolis sent her or that Davon allowed it, but then again, Davon, as much as he was a fucker, could do nothing but obey Kolis's orders." Nektas's gaze found mine. "Once Halayna returned and calmed, she was horrified by what she had done. Less than a year later, we learned she was with child."

I didn't know what to say, only because I knew how Halayna felt. Kolis had put everything into motion with his selfish, insane actions, but like me, Halayna had reacted in rage and pain, leaving devastation behind. I knew exactly how she felt.

"What she did to Taliaya and her unborn youngling haunted her. Stayed with her up until her death. The many nights that I held her as our daughter grew inside her and even after, telling her that she was worthy of our gift, were innumerable."

My heart was heavy. "Did she…?"

"Did she ever come to believe that?" he finished what I could not ask. "Halayna learned to separate the two. It wasn't easy, but she did come to realize that what she had done had nothing to do with our child, and I'm so…"

Hearing the rawness in his voice, I reached over and placed my hand on his arm.

"I'm so damn grateful she did." His eyes were like glittering blue diamonds. "Because she was able to enjoy what time she had with her daughter, and because of that, it has allowed me to do the same—to remain who I was, even after I lost her."

I leaned over, resting my head on his shoulder. "Is that why Davon was such an asshole?"

He chuckled roughly. "Davon was always one, but he worsened after his mate's death. Whatever good he had in him was gone."

I sat there for a few moments. "Was that really why Halayna was targeted by Kolis?"

"It was." He reached over with his other hand and cupped the back of my head. "Reaver doesn't know any of this."

I squeezed his arm. "He never needs to know."

"Halayna never stopped thinking about what she did. I'm sure it lessened as time passed, but it was with her every day. She still hungered for life and joy, and in the short time she had with Jadis, she was an amazing mother," he said quietly. "Just as you will be, Sera."

I pressed my lips together to stop their trembling.

"You will be as fierce and protective as she was," he said, his voice unwavering. "It doesn't matter what you have gone through in your past, nor does anything you have done to others or yourself. You will do just as my Halayna did. You will ensure you will be a good mother because *you* have control over that. Because you will love them that fiercely." He tipped my head back, and his eyes locked with mine. "And you will have both Ash and me to make sure you never forget that."

Kye, the Healer, was nervous when he first arrived, and I felt so incredibly bad for him as he went through a cursory exam.

Some of it was because he was handling the well-being of the true Primal of Life and the health of the children of a Primal of Death, but that wasn't the only reason.

There was also the oldest draken, who lingered on the balcony outside the bedchamber, a silent and watchful guardian who held the Healer's stare as he left the chamber. And then there was my husband, who for some reason, returned to the bedchamber as a man who really, *really* had a problem with another male being within two feet of me.

I was lying on my back, my hands resting on the bed beside me, my fingers thrumming idly. My vest had been removed, and my shirt was folded up to allow the Healer to push lightly on my lower stomach.

Ash watched the Healer's fingers as if he expected them to turn into daggers.

"I'm just checking the positioning of the uterus," Kye explained, his voice steady as he pressed around my pelvic bone. "Usually, this is done along with an internal exam—"

Ash's eyes narrowed, and a blast of cold air radiated off him. I scowled at him as Kye's light, yellowish-brown fingers trembled slightly.

"But that seems unnecessary at the moment," Kye said, his gaze moving to mine as he unfolded my shirt. "Let's talk about your breasts—"

A low growl came from where Ash stood to our left.

"*Nyktos*," I hissed.

"It's okay." Kye patted my hand and looked over his shoulder at Ash. "He's just being protective."

"More like a jerk," I muttered.

Ash raised a brow at me.

Kye chuckled. "I have read that when a Primal is expecting, it can stir their *nota* and cause, well, a primal response."

"To a Healer simply trying to do an exam to ensure that everything is fine?" I challenged, eyeing Ash.

"To anyone and anything that could be even remotely perceived as a threat, especially other males," Kye clarified, and I rolled my eyes. "The draken are the same, as are the ceeren. It is, one would say, a primitive instinct that is difficult to control."

"Perhaps you should go stand on the balcony with Nektas since you can't control your *primitive* instinct, then," I suggested.

"Not happening," Ash growled.

"Then stop snarling and making it feel ice-cold in here," I snapped back.

Crossing his arms, Ash said nothing. He would not make that promise.

I sighed, refocusing on the Healer. "I'm sorry. You were saying?"

A small grin appeared. "Have you experienced any breast tenderness?" he asked.

"A little bit today and on and off," I said. "Nothing too bad."

"Good," he replied, sitting down on the chair that had been moved close to the bed. "It's common, as well as seeing an increase in their size as the pregnancy continues."

Ash's brows rose slightly, and a half-grin appeared.

I shook my head. "What about the nausea?"

"Mortals tend to see a lessening in that toward the end of the first trimester. Gods aren't much different, though it tends to last a few weeks to a month longer." He glanced at the bound pad of paper he'd pulled from the satchel earlier and laid on the bed. "From what I have read, it is roughly the same for Primals."

"That is good news, then," I said.

Kye nodded. "You can sit up now if you'd like."

I sat up, crossing my legs at the ankles. Ash immediately sat behind me, looping an arm around my waist. I was irritated with how he was behaving, but I still leaned into him.

"From what I can tell, everything seems fine," he said. "Your heart rate is normal for a Primal, as is your blood pressure."

I still had no idea how he was able to figure out the pressure by pushing on my pulse and watching me closely, but I would have to take his word for that.

"Now, in terms of what to expect. I want to be upfront with both of you," he began. "It has been over two centuries since a Primal has been with child, and unfortunately, any who may have cared for your mother, Nyktos, are no longer with us. What I know is from notes found while serving in Kithreia and from what I found in the city athenaeum. I believe there is more to be found at Mount Lotho. I would like to go there as soon as possible."

"I…I'm not sure if that is wise right now," I said and felt Ash gearing up to argue.

"I'm aware of what is going on and understand the risks," Kye said. "Discovering what I can is worth it."

"You may leave whenever you wish to do so," Ash said, and my lips pursed. "We will make sure you are well guarded."

I relaxed a little upon hearing that.

"Thank you." Kye bowed his head at Ash.

"What can you tell us now?" he asked.

"From what I know, the first and second trimester of pregnancy for a Primal is not that much different than that of a god. It is different for a mortal, but that is neither here nor there," he said, resting his elbows on his bent knees. "It is the third trimester when things tend to get…tricky."

"What do you mean?" Ash stiffened behind me.

"As the babe—or in your case, babes—grow in size, they take more nutrition and blood from the mother, as well as eather. In fact, the essence will serve the needs of the babe first before the mother. That starts at conception but will become more so as the pregnancy progresses."

Ash's arm tightened around my waist. "Is that why her bruises still haven't healed completely?"

The Healer nodded. "With you having two to care for, it will take much more from you, leaving you weakened and unable to recover as quickly as you normally would. That is the biggest threat as you enter the third trimester, and I cannot stress more the dangers involved in that time. You will become, in a way, as close to a mortal as you will ever be again. I recommend not using the essence for anything unless absolutely necessary. You will need every bit of it to ensure the babes are growing and healthy and to keep yourself well enough to bring them into this realm."

I could feel Ash's heart pounding faster against my back as I pressed my lips together.

"Injuries you would normally heal from could put you into stasis, where your body would not be getting enough of what it needs." Kye took a deep breath. "You would lose the babes if that happened."

A dark, ominous sound rumbled from Ash, and my heart lurched. I reached down and placed my hand on his where it was flattened against my lower stomach. "But this is not something to really worry about until the third trimester, right?"

"It is something to be aware of now," he said carefully. "But again, it is more of a concern as the pregnancy progresses."

Okay. That was…good news. Kind of. I moved on. "What about feeding?"

"As long as you are receiving nourishment through your own feedings and eating well, it is okay until you enter the third trimester." He looked up at Ash. "At that point, I recommend finding a donor."

Well, we already had one of those.

I wiggled a little, uncomfortable with that, but there was still a huge sense of relief. This meant I could still Ascend the gods I needed to.

"The stronger the better," Kye continued. "Another Primal, if possible."

Uh…

"Consider it done," Ash stated, and I jerked my head back to look at him. He ignored my look. "What about taking on the *nota* form?" he asked. "She's done that twice since we've conceived, but before we knew she was pregnant."

"You shifted forms so soon? Remarkable," Kye murmured, smiling at me. "I have found nothing regarding that. I hope that is information I can find at Mount Lotho, but I would recommend not doing it again if at all possible, and absolutely not after the third trimester. That, logically, would present the largest risk of doing so."

"Makes sense," I murmured, imagining me attempting to shift forms with a stomach three times the size it was now. I glanced back at Ash. "Is it possible for the essence to protect them—the babes?"

"I have seen it happen with gods," he said. "Usually in severe cases. In a way, the eather seeks to protect and provide for the most vulnerable aspect of your being. It would be the same for a Primal."

I nodded and looked down to where Ash's and my hands rested. Knowing the eather would seek to protect them first brought forth a rush of relief.

"There is something I want to touch on," Kye said. "Since you were born mortal, I believe it would be wise if you gave birth as those who were once mortal do. Not all of them do this, but most choose to give birth in the mortal realm. It's a bit of a tradition."

"Is there a reason for that?" Ash asked with a frown.

"That's a complicated answer." A faint smile appeared. "It is believed that doing so pays respect to where they've come from by linking the next generation to the mortal realm. I have seen no…scientific evidence explaining *why* those born mortal have easier deliveries in the mortal realm, but they do. There must be something to it."

I glanced at Ash. "What do you think?"

"I think I want whatever is best for you and our babes," he responded. "If that means giving birth in the mortal realm, then so be it."

Plans were then made for Kye to travel to Lotho with one of the guards.

"There's just one last thing." Kye rose, picking up the pad of bound parchment. "If you are injured," he said, halting as a low growl came from Ash. The Healer swallowed, shoving the pad into his satchel. "I want to check you over, no matter how minor the injury is."

"She will not be injured," Ash stated, and I tensed. "But, in the unlikely event that it happens, we will contact you."

"Good." Kye drew the strap of his satchel over his head. "Now, if anything happens that concerns you—either of you," he said, glancing at Ash, "please summon me immediately."

"Is there anything we should be keeping an eye on?" I asked, unfolding my legs and turning so they hung off the bed. "Because I'm pretty sure everything will concern me."

The Healer smiled knowingly. "It's normal to be anxious when expecting, especially when it's your first go at this, but one thing to keep a watch for is bleeding. Light spotting is normal, but anything more than that, I want to know. Severe stomach pain is another thing, or if the nausea worsens to the point where you cannot keep food down. As the pregnancy progresses, there will be other things to keep an eye on, but right now, those are the things I want to know about immediately if they occur."

There were more things to potentially worry about? Great.

"If something like that occurs, does that mean the pregnancy is…?" Ash drew in a deep breath and shifted so he was sitting beside me. "Is in jeopardy?"

"Not always," Kye said. "It doesn't mean the babes will be lost, but it can be a cause for concern."

My heart dropped. "Could anything be done, or could I…?" I trailed off, instinct telling me that even as the true Primal of Life, there wouldn't be anything I could do.

The Primal Goddess of Love, Beauty, and Fertility was another story. However, the *vadentia* also warned me that a Primal intervention could incite the Fates' ire.

"Depending on the issue, there are things. Treatments. Certain action plans." His smile was kind and patient. "But do not stress yourselves over something that has yet to come and likely will not occur. You both have enough on your plates. You don't need unnecessary stress."

Ash slid me a sideways glance, and we both knew that unnecessary worry and me were like two peas in a pod.

After Kye said his goodbyes, Nektas stepped inside. "Everything okay?"

"For now." Ash reached over and tucked back a stray curl that had slipped free of the hair he'd braided this morning. "However, I do believe Sera is a bit irritated with me."

Nektas raised his brows.

"He kept growling and snarling at Kye," I explained, and Nektas grinned. "Which means the next several months are going to be *real* fun."

"Most definitely," remarked Nektas.

Ash frowned. "I just didn't like him touching you."

I looked at him.

"What?" he asked, sending a narrow-eyed look at the draken.

Nektas chuckled. "Nothing."

"Anyway." I drew out the word. "We should probably get a move on. We have things to do today—one I'm really not looking forward to. But the other?" I clapped my hands together. "I cannot wait."

Ash didn't stand when I did. He remained sitting, and I knew deep in my bones what was coming.

"Nektas," I said, realizing why he had asked if plans were still a go for today. "You should probably give us a couple of minutes."

He glanced between us. "I will wait for you both downstairs," he said, turning to the door.

"There is no need to wait for us." Ash leaned back on one elbow. To some, he was the picture of lazy indifference, but I could see the tension coiling inside him. "Plans have changed."

My mouth dropped open.

Nektas stopped.

"Since when have they changed?" I demanded.

His gaze flicked to where I stood. "Since roughly twelve hours ago."

I crossed my arms. "In other words, since you learned I was pregnant. And what exactly has changed?"

"*Everything*," he stated in a tone that would typically brook no argument.

54

I took a deep breath. "Ash," I began as, out of the corner of my eye, I saw Nektas quietly creeping toward the doors. "Me being pregnant cannot change what we've planned—what we've already discussed with the others. Everything is already in motion."

A muscle began ticking in his jaw as he stared up at me.

"Nor does it change that Kolis needs to be dealt with," I continued. "And we have very limited time before he comes out of stasis, which could happen at any minute. And the last thing we need is Kolis finding out…"

Gods, I couldn't finish that thought.

All the flesh visible on Ash's body briefly turned to midnight. "That will *never* happen," he snarled. "But you're right. Kolis still needs to be dealt with, and he will be. However, that doesn't and won't involve you."

I bristled. "Excuse me?"

"The last thing you need to be involved in, in your current condition—"

"My *condition*?" I interrupted softly.

"Oh, dear," murmured Nektas.

"Is to be anywhere near Kolis or any of his supporters." Ash continued like I hadn't spoken. "Nor should you even be thinking about leaving the Shadowlands. Kolis will not step foot here, and you're surrounded by guards and an army."

I drew in another breath, reminding myself that this was coming from a good place. Ash was being protective. "I understand why you feel this way—"

"Glad we're on the same page." A half-smile appeared.

"We are *so* not on the same page, Ash."

Wisps of eather swirled in his eyes. "You are carrying our children, Sera. You are in a vulnerable state, and I will not risk losing you or them."

"You are not going to lose me or them. I'm pregnant, Ash. Not unable to defend myself or fight," I argued.

"The Healer said you are in a weakened state and should avoid using the essence."

"Perhaps if you had spent the time listening to Kye instead of growling at him, you would've heard him say that was a concern for when I enter the third trimester," I pointed out. "And in case you're having difficulty with basic math, that's like many *weeks* from now."

The eather moved more wildly in his eyes. "I heard him perfectly clear. Things are more dangerous for you in the third trimester. That does not mean things are safe for you now." His head cut toward Nektas. "Where are you going?"

Nektas stopped with a hand on the doorknob. "Anywhere but here."

Ash's expression turned bland. "Before you do that, it would be great if you'd tell my lovely, far-too-brave wife that I'm right."

The draken opened his mouth.

"He is not going to agree with you," I insisted.

Ash arched a brow. "Considering that Nektas is intelligent, I am sure he will."

"And I'm sure that since he's so intelligent, he knows exactly what must be done and that it involves my participation."

"I think you're going to be disappointed."

I stepped toward the bed. "I think you're about to be kicked off that bed."

His lips curved up, revealing the tip of a fang. "Sounds like a good time."

"Oh, I can promise you it will *not* be a good time for you."

"If I may speak?" Nektas started.

"Yes," Ash said.

"No," I snapped.

Nektas sighed. "Ash, you're right."

Ash's smile was smug when I muttered, "You *were* my favorite draken."

"I'm going to ignore that," Nektas continued. "Because you are also right."

Ash's lips compressed into a thin line.

"And you two need to figure out what that means." Nektas opened the door. "I'll be waiting downstairs."

I watched the doors close, my foot tapping.

"*Liessa.*"

"Don't call me that."

Ash sat up. "You love it when I call you that."

"Not right now." I squared my shoulders. "Look, I get why you don't want me endangering the babes."

"It's not just them." Ash rose swiftly, stalking past me. "It is also you. We already know they are pulling on your essence. The evidence of that is still on your throat."

I turned as he went to the small table and picked up the water pitcher. "I can't deny that, but it doesn't change what needs to be done," I said.

"Not to sound repetitive, but it changes everything." He poured two glasses. "We can still Ascend Ione but have her come here. The other gods can also be Ascended."

"So, that's the plan?" I asked.

"Part of it."

"I'm sure I can guess the rest of this really well-thought-out plan full of problems." I tried to quell my anger. "Ione will be out of it after I Ascend her, which means she will be here, with no one in her Court."

He set the pitcher down. "We can send guards there."

"Guards that none of the gods in her Court are familiar with," I reasoned. "She needs to be in her Court with people both Keella and she trusts, which means I need to do what is expected of the true Primal of Life." I stared at his back. "And you need to be okay with that."

The hand at his side fisted. "Me being okay with you endangering yourself and our children is impossible."

"Then you need to not stand in my way and deal with it," I told him. "Because the only thing that is truly a danger to me is Kolis."

He faced me, the flesh along his jaw and cheekbones mottled with shadows. "I will handle him."

"You cannot handle him without me," I said. "And you know that. The fact that you know that is one of the many, many reasons I love you, so don't say you can."

He came forward and handed me a glass. The scent of strawberries reached me. "One of those reasons should be because I am willing to do anything to protect you and our children."

"It is," I insisted. "And, admittedly, you doing the growly thing was a little hot."

Ash smirked as he lifted his glass. "Knew it."

"But also annoying," I tacked on, taking a drink. "And yes, you wanting to protect us is one of those reasons, but your willingness to get yourself killed in the process is not."

Ash huffed. "I will not get myself killed."

"I know you will do everything possible to ensure that doesn't happen, but I also know Kolis will take the first chance he gets to kill you, and he can do it." My chest seized with real fear, and I didn't stop myself from feeling it. I wanted Ash to pick up on it, and I knew he did because he inhaled sharply, and the shadows deepened in his flesh. "You felt that?"

Ash said nothing.

"I know you did." My grip tightened on the glass. "The idea of you going after Kolis—going after any of the Primals without me—is terrifying. And yes, we can worry about the risks I'm taking, but what about the risks *you're* taking? What do you think you being injured or worse would do to me? To the lives I carry inside me? I cannot do any of this without you."

"You will not lose me." He clasped the back of my head with his free hand. "Never."

"Do you promise?"

"With every breath I take and every beat of my heart," he swore.

"Then to honor that, you know what must be done," I reasoned. "I need to fight beside you. And I need you to support that because you will not stop me from doing so."

The air around us dropped several degrees and charged, but I held his stare. "I don't want us to fight. Neither of us needs that. We need to stand together against Kolis. Not separate. I don't need you to want this. I need you to understand that this is how we ensure we have a future with our children."

Ash cursed and dropped his hand. He stepped back, the energy ramping up within him, stoking the eather inside me. "You know, I thought you asking me to take you to your lake was the hardest thing that would ever be asked of me." He turned fast and sharp, throwing his drink at the wall. The glass shattered, raining water and shards across the floor. "I was wrong."

My heart twisted and ached as I lifted my gaze from the mess to his rigid back. Wisps of eather drifted from his shoulders.

"You asking me to end your life was a nightmare made real," he said, his voice thin and icy. "But this…"

"This is not worse." I set my glass on the nightstand. "This is just reality." I walked toward him. "I'm sorry, Ash. I wish we didn't even need to have this conversation. I wish things were different. I want things to be different for us. I want to spend being pregnant worrying about being a good mother or how painful birth will be. I don't want to spend it worrying about what new horrific act Kolis will commit—and that is if I'm lucky. Because if we're not? It's over. It's all over. I will lose control. I will take Kolis out or die trying—"

"Don't speak of dying," Ash said, whipping toward me. His eyes were wide and full of pure, wild eather. "*Don't.*"

"Then don't make me fear that," I whispered. He started to turn from me, but I caught him before he could, curling my fingers into the hair at the nape of his neck. "Please."

A shudder went through Ash as he stepped into me, folding an arm around my waist. "Do you have any idea how hard this will be for me?" He pulled me to his chest. "When every instinct in me demands that I do everything possible to keep you safe?" He curled his other arm around my shoulders. "But I know you know how it feels. The only difference is that you are willing to face it head-on, and I'm trying to do everything to prevent it."

I held him even tighter than he embraced me. "I think we just show our love in different ways."

A rough chuckle stirred the hair on the top of my head. A moment passed. "Exactly how mad would you be if I locked you in this chamber?"

"I'm not even going to take that question seriously." I rubbed my nose and cheek against his chest. "We just need to be careful."

"You need to be careful, *liessa*," he corrected. "For both of us to do what needs to be done, it's going to be just as hard on you as it is on me. I have to allow you to fight, and you'll need to allow me to put myself in front of you. You're going to have to pull back and not rush into battles."

"I never rush into battles."

"Sera."

"What?"

"You're a terrible liar and that has not changed."

I pressed my forehead to his chest. "Whatever."

"I will do everything not to hold you back, but you also have to meet me halfway on this. It is the one time I will ask you to be less brave." His fingers delved into the hair above my braid. "And I can already feel how much you hate that."

I closed my eyes. He was right. I did hate the truth of what he said.

He tilted my head back so our eyes met. "But if we're both going to do this, you need to promise me you won't take any chances."

"I promise."

"I wasn't finished."

I frowned.

His lips quirked. "And you also have to promise me you will step out the first moment you're even remotely injured. Get to safety."

I opened my mouth.

"You're not just doing that for me. You're doing it for our children," he said, the eather retreating from his pupils. "But you also need to promise me one more thing."

"There's more?"

He ignored that. "You have to promise me you won't hold back when it comes to fighting Kolis—fighting anyone."

I frowned. "Didn't you just tell me to hold back?"

"That's not what I'm talking about," he said. "I asked you not to rush into battles. What we are talking about now is not holding back when there *is* a battle."

Getting what he meant, I nodded. "Holding back in battle has never been a real concern."

"Before? I would agree. But after what happened in Lasania…" His hand curved over my shoulder as I moved to step back. "You made me swear to you I would put you in the ground if you lost control."

My stomach hollowed. "That hasn't changed."

"I didn't say it had." His chest rose deeply. "You need to promise me that your fear of losing control will not stop you from using everything you have in you. That it won't stop you from being a little monstrous."

My lips parted as I stared up at him. All at once, I understood his concern and why he'd asked this.

"Do you trust me?" he inquired.

"Of course." Surprise swept through me.

"Then trust that I will always be by your side to pull you back from the brink," he said. "Okay?"

I nodded.

"Do we have a deal? One you agree to and won't secretly be angry about."

"Are *you* not going to be secretly angry about it?"

"Eventually," he muttered, brushing his lips over my forehead.

I exhaled heavily. "I agree as long as we both make another promise."

"I am forever wary of making you promises now," he said.

"This isn't a hard one," I assured him. "We promise that our children will grow with both of us by their sides. That we absolutely refuse to allow them to experience what we have."

The eather in Ash's eyes turned luminous. "I swear to you, *meyaah Liessa.* They will have two loving, *living* parents, and nothing—absolutely fucking nothing—will prevent us from ensuring that."

I believed him.

But my mind flashed to his promise to always be there to pull me back from the brink of disaster. I buried my face against his chest, breathing him in. A tiny part of me feared a time would come when not even he could stop me. My hand went to my lower stomach as I focused on my breathing. If they were ever threatened or harmed? Ash wouldn't be able to stop me.

He'd have to put me in the ground.

The Thyia Plains' guards were somber in their bows as Ash and I, followed by Nektas, walked the hall they lined.

Keella was waiting for us in the same room we had met her in the last time. She stood in a simple white sheath and smiled. "I was beginning to think you two may not be coming."

"Something came up," Ash answered, squeezing my hand. "We would've been here sooner."

"It's okay." She inclined her head regally toward Nektas, where he hung back. "I enjoyed these last minutes here. This is one of my favorite spots. I will miss it."

A pang of sorrow lanced my chest. "Are you sure you want to do this?"

"You could sit this out," Ash offered.

"That's what I told her," a steady voice came, drawing our attention to the veranda. A tall, slim figure with chin-length, reddish-brown hair came into view. The goddess Ione stopped just inside the chamber and bowed her head to us. "None of us is eager for her to pass on."

Seeing the goddess again brought forth mixed emotions—relief and also unease. The latter had nothing to do with her and everything to do with what had come after meeting her in Dalos.

"She has said this a time or a hundred," Keella said with a fond smile.

"Apparently, I haven't said it enough," Ione replied. "Because here we are."

"Yes," the Primal goddess said. "Here we are. Both more than ready to begin the next chapter of our stories, but only one willing to say it."

Ione crossed her arms over her fitted, light gray tunic, sighing heavily before her gaze met mine. "I am glad to see you again."

"The feeling is mutual." I slipped my hand free of Ash's and walked toward the goddess. "I didn't get a chance to thank you for the risk you took."

"No need to thank me." She clasped my wrist with a hand. "I couldn't have been happier to fuck with Kolis."

"Ione," sighed Keella.

"Sorry," Ione was quick to say. "I meant I was honored to fuck with Kolis on your behalf."

"Happier wasn't the word I had a problem with," murmured Keella.

A small grin appeared on Ione's face, and I had a feeling I was going to get along quite well with her. "You are still owed my thanks," I insisted. "You saved my life and did so at great risk to yours."

Ash spoke then. "You did. And you will forever have my gratitude."

Ione's gaze moved between us, and then she nodded. "I suppose I will graciously accept this unnecessary but understandable gratitude."

My lips twitched as I met her eyes. "Is this what you want for yourself?"

"*Want* is a strange word." The narrow bridge of her nose scrunched. "Feels kind of selfish to want this, but it *is* what I have been preparing for."

I nodded, turning back to Keella and Ash. I saw the Primal look at the goddess before saying, "I would like to do this on the veranda, under the skies."

"We can do this wherever you'd like," Ash assured her.

She smiled at him and came forward. "Come." She looped her arm around mine as Ione passed us. "Walk outside with me."

I went along, glancing back at Ash to see that Ione had stopped him with a question about what Keella had shared with her regarding our plans in dealing with Kolis. Nektas had come to the opening but did not follow Keella and me outside, giving us space while he kept a watchful eye.

Arching a brow, I said nothing until we were under the purple and violet clouds of the Thyia Plains. "I'm guessing you wanted to speak to me in private?"

"Whatever could have given you that impression?" she said with a laugh far lighter than someone who had come to the end of their…journey. "There is something I wanted to tell you that I wasn't sure if I could or should the last time we spoke."

"I think I know what it is." I followed her to the divan that I may have once laid upon, having a feeling I *did* know what she was about to mention. The lives I carried within me. After all, she was the Primal Goddess of Rebirth. "You know about my…?" What had Ash called it? "My condition?"

"If by condition, you mean that you're with child—two of them?" Keella laughed. "Yes, I know. Congratulations are in order. This is such a blessing," she said sincerely. "I didn't say anything before since I wasn't sure you were aware, but that's not what I wanted to discuss."

"Did you know when I was brought here before?" I asked, even though I was curious about what else she had to say.

"That's a complicated question to answer." She gazed up at the clouds. "Sensing the souls of unborn babes is not always easy and it varies from soul to soul, but with you, you were carrying Sotoria's soul. That acted almost as a shield. And afterward, well, there wasn't much time."

"No, there wasn't." I looked over at her. "I'm not going to make Sotoria be reborn again. Once Kolis is entombed, we want to give Sotoria a choice. Either to be reborn or to cross into the Vale. I'm hoping that will be something Ione will be able to assist us with."

"She will be able to." Keella was still looking at the sky. "I'm not surprised to hear you say that. I didn't think the idea of forcing her to be reborn with the sole purpose of destroying Kolis would sit well with you."

I nodded. "So, what was it you wanted to discuss?"

Her gaze lowered to mine. "It is Sotoria I actually wanted to speak with you about—her and the prophecy." She glanced back at the chamber. "It's something I didn't say when you two were here last—something Eythos told me, and my…my impressions of what he planned."

Curiosity rose. "What is it?"

Keella was silent for several moments. "Eythos spent a long time trying to decipher the prophecy and its true meaning. He even managed to speak to Delfai. I imagine the God of Divination didn't share that with you and Nyktos."

"No," I stated. "He did not."

A wry grin appeared. "When Eythos spoke with Delfai, it was when Etris Balfour—the last oracle—was still alive."

My brows shot up. I wasn't expecting her to say that.

"I don't know exactly what Etris or Delfai said to Eythos, but whatever was shared led Eythos to place the embers and Sotoria's soul into your bloodline. That was no random chance of opportunity."

I frowned. "But Roderick Mierel summoned him to save his people."

Keella nodded. "And Eythos was waiting for that moment. He knew Roderick would do so. You see, this prophecy had begun to fulfill itself before Sotoria was born. It started with the Silver Knight."

"The warrior Queen," I said, immediately thinking about what Ward had told me. "I'm named after her. Ward—the first *viktor*—saved who turned out to be my ancestor."

"She was, as one would say, *promised* by the Fates," she said. "Just like you."

Tiny bumps pimpled my skin. "So, you're basically saying Etris, or possibly even Delfai, told Eythos Roderick would summon him? It makes sense. The prophecy spoke of the desperation of golden crowns, but this really doesn't tell us anything new."

"No, but it does remind us how much needed to happen for us to be right here, right now," she said, pausing to inhale deeply. "What Eythos did was never just about stopping his brother. Yes, the prophecy spoke of Kolis, but also of greater dangers."

"The awakening of the Primal of Blood and Bone," I surmised.

"Yes, and what Eythos learned convinced him of who that Primal would be."

My fingers dug into my knees. "Do I even want to know?"

A wan smile appeared. "Sotoria."

"What?" I half-laughed. "How? She was mortal."

"So were you."

"Yeah, the moment that came out of my mouth, I realized how unwise it sounded," I admitted. "But this is different. I don't understand how that's possible."

"Neither do I. Eythos never said, but I do know that is why he put her soul in your bloodline," she said. "Eythos was trying to circumvent the prophecy, Sera. He hoped she would be reborn with the embers of life in her—allowing her to stop Kolis and make way for Nyktos to rise as the true Primal of Death. It would have also prevented her from rising as the Primal of Life and Death since he believed the prophecy referenced his son and Sotoria coming together in love."

A deep frown pulled at my lips at the idea of Sotoria being the one meant for Ash, even though that would've still technically been me. I rubbed my temples, thinking this was going to give me a headache.

"That is why he asked for the firstborn daughter of the Mierel bloodline," she continued. "And if he was right, then in his mind, there would be no threat of Sotoria rising as the Primal of Blood and Bone. To do so, it would've required her to kill Nyktos—something she would not do if she loved him."

"Okay," I said, following what she was saying. "But that didn't work. I'm not Sotoria, and her soul is in The Star."

"Correct. His plan worked, except for that." She looked at the pastel-colored clouds. "And his plan should've worked completely. My involvement ensured that. But something went impossibly wrong, and for that to have happened, there can only be one reason."

"The Fates got involved." My brows knitted. "They prevented Sotoria from being reborn in my bloodline. Why would they do that, though? They cannot want the Ancients to awaken."

"You must remember that prophecies are the dreams of the Ancients." Her eyes searched mine. "And you also know what that means."

I did. *Dreamt by the Ancients* meant dreamt by the Fates, and Keella was old enough to know exactly who the Fates were. I didn't speak any of that aloud, opting for a nod as the safest choice.

"And that means most of those Fates expect all that is said in the prophecy to happen," she said softly. "I don't know why they would want that, but their involvement ensured it is still possible."

My heart started pounding. "I don't understand how it *can* be possible. If Sotoria were reborn, she would be as she was before. A mortal."

"Unless the Fates intervene once more," she said. "It's imperative you follow through with what you plan regarding Sotoria. She needs to be freed as soon as it is safe to do so."

"Well, it's a good thing we already planned to do that," I said. "But what will stop the Fates from intervening even then—?" Then it struck me. "Because what is shown in the prophecy happens in the future. That is what Penellaphe said. If Sotoria were reborn now, she would live and die as a mortal long before what Penellaphe saw in the future could happen."

"Correct."

Something big still didn't make sense, and that came back to her. Sotoria. "Why Sotoria? Why would the Ancients dream of a mortal becoming such a powerful being? It's not because of what Kolis did to her. That dream happened long before that."

"That, I don't know," she said. "And if Eythos knew, he never said."

Closing my eyes again, I took a deep breath and exhaled slowly. I needed to release Sotoria's soul the moment Kolis was entombed and not a second after. If not?

Opening my eyes, I looked at her. "Do you believe the future is already written? That the threads that last cannot be unbroken?"

"I do not know," she said after a moment. "I hope to know the answer once I reach Arcadia."

Gods, I hoped so. Because if I failed now, and the threads of Fate kept stretching and expanding, Kolis wouldn't be the only problem Ash and I would one day face.

Lost in our thoughts, the Primal and I sat there briefly until Keella patted my arm. "It's time."

And it was.

Ash and Ione joined us while Nektas quietly crossed the veranda to walk the manicured lawn. I forced a smile when Ash sent me a curious look. As Ione moved to a divan across from Keella's, I pushed all I had learned to the farthest corners of my mind while Ione knelt, swearing her allegiance to us. Because as long as we didn't fail, I would not have to burden Ash with this.

I drank from Ione's wrist and took what I knew, building a wall of shadowstone and Ancient bone in my mind to place it behind. As my fangs pierced my skin and Ash let out a low growl at the sight, I built a shield. As Ione drank from me, I made myself forget what I had learned until I needed to remember it. And while I knelt at Keella's side and drank from the wound she had created herself, I prayed to the Fates—to the Ancients—that I would never have to remember.

When I felt Keella's last sluggish heartbeat, I lifted my head. Her breathing was shallow as she stared at the sky of her Court. Not once since we'd begun had she taken her gaze from it.

I still held on to her hand as I felt the warmth leave her. "Thank you," I said. I wasn't sure if I was thanking her for this sacrifice or for what she'd warned me about. Maybe both.

Ash knelt beside me, folding his arm around my waist. He placed his hand over mine and Keella's. "May the next journey bring you peace."

Tears blurred my vision as Keella's eyes fluttered and then closed. Her chest rose once more and did not fall, and then my chest flared with heat. I released the breath I held as a draken let out a mournful call in the distance.

"She looks so peaceful," I whispered. There was a smile on her lips and a tranquil ease to her features.

"She was ready," he said, catching a tear with the swipe of his thumb over my cheek.

I nodded, wanting that to make me feel better, but it really didn't. Letting go of her hand, I started to rise when it happened.

It started with one below her left eye. Then, two more on her chin. Ten along her throat. A dozen appeared on her forearm. They were like freckled stars, starting out as tiny pinpricks of light until eather seeped from her pores. The shimmery, silvery-white wave of light swept over her entire body, pulsing with a blinding intensity that forced both Ash and me to stand and move back.

Strands of eather unfurled, weaving delicate ribbons that stretched with an ethereal glow. I turned to where Ione sat, tears glimmering on her cheeks as she rose and stepped forward. Tendrils of eather illuminated the space between Keella and Ione as I stepped back into Ash's arms. I rested my cheek against his chest as the Primal energy threaded itself with Ione, and I felt the oath Ione had made lodge itself deeply within my chest.

In a loud clap of energy released, the radiant glow where Keella lay was gone.

And so was the Primal.

There wasn't much time to digest what had happened or what Keella had shared. Only seconds after the guards took Ione to her chambers to rest during her awakening, I felt that same sudden surge of restless, anxious energy I had experienced before.

At the veranda's edge, my grip tightened on Ash's hand, my other reflexively going to my stomach. "*Kolis.*"

A pulse of eather whipped through Ash's eyes, and Nektas quickly joined us. "You feel him?"

"Not as strongly as before," I told him. "But I think he's waking up."

Shadows appeared down his throat, swirling up the sides. "Then we must hurry." Mist seeped from the stone, churning around our legs as he pulled me to his side. "Remember what we talked about, *liessa.*"

"I remember," I said, leaning into his chest as he placed a hand on Nektas's shoulder. "You will take the lead."

"Let's see how long that lasts," Nektas remarked.

As the mist thickened and rose around us, Ash lowered his mouth to mine. His kiss was fierce and demanding in the seconds it took us to shadowstep to the Callasta Isles, causing my breath to hitch and heat to pool low in my stomach. I was smiling as the mist scattered.

Ash had shadowstepped us *inside* the Rise, near the main entrance of the sprawling one-level palace. I caught a quick glimpse of our surroundings. Red and white wildflowers bloomed among the knee-high grass. Heavy curtains of moss hung from tree branches that stretched like intertwined arms over wide pathways. Ivy covered the trunks of trees and spread along the walkway, cracking the stone beneath our booted feet and smothering the wall in the distance, revealing only glimpses of the dark red stone of the Rise. There was a surprising beauty in the untamed courtyard, and I couldn't help but wonder if Veses had intended for her land to remain like this or if it had become like this due to neglect.

A warning shout pierced the air, drawing my gaze to our right. A group of half a dozen guards adorned in red and gold jerked to a sudden stop as they walked along a path.

Ash spun, placing me between him and Nektas as absolute chaos erupted.

A fair-haired guard rushed forward, drawing a shadowstone dagger.

"Idiot," growled Nektas as Ash unsheathed a shadowstone sword.

Ash caught the guard's arm, cracking the bone. The man's yelp was silenced as Ash sliced the god's head from his shoulders. My chest throbbed with the echo of death, and I knew this was only the start.

There were only two less idiotic guards in the group of six. Their faces paled, and they spun on their heels, running off through the tall grass. The other three came right at us as horns blared from the Rise. The warning rumble of draken came from the sky.

Out of the corner of my eye, a wave of shimmery silver light swept over Nektas as he shifted. The sound of pounding boots echoed through the courtyard as Nektas's claws dug into the stone. His head snapped out, massive jaws opening. He caught the closest guard around the chest, his sharp teeth piercing armor and bone as he shook his head, tearing the guard in two.

My lip curled as my palms warmed. "Was that necessary?"

No. Nektas drew his horned head back. Blood seeped down his scales. *But it was fun.*

"Our ideas of fun couldn't be more different." I turned to the doors, willing them to open.

Metal ground together, then snapped as the locks broke. Ash whirled, his sword clashing with another as the heavy shadowstone doors swung open. He planted a boot in the guard's chest, caving in the bone as he threw out his left hand. Strands of shadowy eather laced with silver funneled from his palm, striking another guard. Thicker tendrils of essence snaked out, streaking through the trees. Warm pulses of death followed the cries of pain.

The urge to do something about that—to steal them from death's grip—was there, but I was able to fight the pull.

My gaze flickered over the interior of the palace, and I nearly tripped as I stalked toward the steps. I couldn't be seeing what I thought I was. I squinted, my upper lip curling as I stared at the watercolor paintings adorning the ceiling of the grand entryway.

They were paintings of Veses.

Naked Veses.

"What the fuck?" I muttered.

"I guess you're seeing her artwork," Ash said, snapping a guard's neck. "Interesting choice, eh?"

I snorted. "Interesting, indeed." Shaking my head, I stalked toward the wide steps just as guards rushed from the trees and poured out of the halls inside the palace.

"I would not run in this direction if I were you," I said as I started up the stairs.

They didn't.

One of Nektas's wings swept over my head as he swung around, slamming his tail into the guards. Several of them hit the trees with bone-sickening crunches. A few went *through* them.

Nektas stretched his neck out, a deep growl vibrating the frills around his neck. Smoke wafted from his nostrils as his jaws stretched open.

The air crackled as a funnel of silvery fire flowed into the opening, the flames hungry as they surged forward, rippling over the foyer's walls. Gauzy curtains ignited as the guards scattered. Even with their speed, they weren't fast enough. Their screams ended abruptly, their shadowstone armor melting, and their skin and bone turning to ash.

As the flames receded, the once-red-washed walls were painted with sooty fingers. I glanced up, smirking when I saw that the ceiling was a charred mess.

"Nice work," I told Nektas, stepping over the smoldering remnants of swords and shields.

Nektas made a low, chuffing sound, but a sudden roar of anger ended his amusement. I looked back to see him retreating from the entryway, his onyx and gray scales shimmering under the sunlight. A flash of gold scales blotted out the sun.

"Ash!" I shouted.

He whipped around, looking to the sky as shadowy tendrils swirled around him. A sudden burst of intense silvery fire poured from the sky, devouring the trees and guards belonging to the draken's own Court.

Moving with lightning speed, Ash crossed the distance between us as Nektas reared back, snarling. The golden draken descended through the smoke with the swiftness of a thunderclap. Nektas's massive body took to the air in a powerful leap. The two crashed above, a maelstrom of claws and silver fire.

Ash had started past me, but I hesitated, my eyes glued to the two draken. Nektas caught the other draken with claws as sharp as swords.

"He'll be okay," Ash assured me, touching my lower back. "I promise you."

His confidence calmed enough of my concern that I could turn away. My gaze briefly met his. His eyes were pools of resolve, mirroring what I felt inside.

"She could be anywhere," he said as we walked through the whirling smoke.

We didn't have time to search the whole damn palace. I closed my eyes for a fraction of a heartbeat. Where is Veses? The skin behind my left ear tingled as I saw… "A room of mirrors and glass."

"Her bedchamber," he growled.

My narrowed gaze cut to him. "I'm going to save my rage over you knowing what her bedchamber looks like so I can take it out on her."

"It's been decades since I crossed that threshold," he said as we entered a hall untouched by fire. There were more naked paintings of Veses engaged in all kinds of shenanigans with various men and women. "That was when I considered her a friend."

"You don't have to explain yourself. I'm just being irrationally jealous," I admitted, tensing as I heard more guards approaching.

Gripping the hilt of my dagger, I focused on the mouth of the hall, where it split. "Incoming."

Slipping past me, Ash swooped down and pressed a kiss to my forehead. Despite his lips being cool, my skin warmed and tingled from the brief, sweet touch.

"I can taste the bite of your fear," Ash said to the guards. His voice was somehow soft yet loud in the same breath and achingly cold as his head tilted slightly to the side. There was a shadowy half-smile on his lips as he scanned the dozens of guards. "Smell its bitter sweat."

I kept a close eye on them, fully prepared to unleash the eather ramping up inside me if I so much as thought I saw a finger twitch.

Ash tipped his head back more. "All of you have a choice to make. Step aside and live." His smile spread, as cold as the wind whipping through the hall. "Or refuse and die for the Primal who is too cowardly to show her face."

"Why," I said as the guards remained in front of us, "did I just find that so incredibly hot?"

"Naughty, *liessa*," he murmured, his gaze trained on the guards.

We gave them one more moment, not a second longer. I could still feel Veses. We wouldn't give her time to leave her Court, something I was surprised she hadn't done already.

Ash sighed. "So be it."

He became a blur as he shot forward, meeting the guards head-on. Distant roars shook the palace walls.

It took everything in me to hang back, watching Ash move with lethal grace. I should be right beside him, carving the path to Veses. But hand-to-hand combat was possibly the riskiest thing I could undertake while pregnant. Even if I deflected every blow, punches and kicks would slip by. My love for the babes was greater than my need to prove myself.

Arcs of pulsing energy extended from Ash's hands, striking down guards with terrifying and awe-inspiring precision. Chestplates and armor buckled. Bones snapped. Guards crumpled, their life force extinguished as swiftly as a snuffed candle.

The palace walls suddenly shook with a force like a mountain crashing into it. The lights overhead flickered wildly, and plumes of dust fell. A stream of fiery eather sliced through the hall we'd just come from, followed by a high-pitched shriek of pain.

"Careful!" Ash yelled in warning.

I gasped as the wind caught the fall of shimmery blood, spraying it in every direction. I shadowstepped back, knocking into Ash as a few drops splashed against the calves of my boots. Tiny holes immediately formed. I hissed, gritting my teeth as the blood burned my skin.

"Fuck." Ash snared me around the waist, lifting me off my feet. "You okay?"

"Yes." I gripped his arm with one hand. "It's not that bad—"

The golden draken crashed through the ceiling several feet away, sending large chunks of stone flying. Ash swore, darting to the side with me in his arms. And not a moment too soon. A chunk of red stone nearly the size of a draken's head slammed into the wall behind where we had just been standing. My chin jerked up to see Nektas veering back up into the air as another draken with honey-brown scales erupted from the clouds. I looked down to see a nude male lying in the rubble, his body bloody and broken. I knew he was dead. I'd felt it the moment the blood hit the air. I still winced.

"What a waste," I murmured.

Ash started to respond, but he felt it the same second I did—the sudden change in the air. It was as if energy were being sucked from it. We turned a second too late.

At the end of the hall, the Primal Goddess of Rites and Prosperity stood, draped in a gown of glittering diamonds. Behind her were at least a dozen guards.

Her red-painted lips curved as she threw out a hand, releasing a stream of eather that split into several smaller branches and moved through the air in a distinctively serpentine manner...because, *of course.*

Ash turned sharply, all but winging me backward. My stomach dropped as I yelled. Ash raised his arm, a wall of shadowy essence appearing seconds before the eather slammed into it. My feet skidded across the marble floor. A pillar stopped me as a bright flare of light erupted from the impact, and slivers of the eather pierced the shield, striking Ash. He staggered with a grunt.

Ash *staggered*, going down on one knee.

My heart stopped as he pitched forward, planting a hand on the floor. A sound like tinkling windchimes scratched at my nerves.

Veses was laughing.

For a moment, I stood frozen, barely hearing Ash as he said he was fine, that only the air had been knocked out of him. My entire being zeroed in on the Primal bitch.

Smirking, Veses stepped back, and the guards rushed forward.

A terrible sound came from me, a scream of rage as I pushed off the pillar. I flew past Ash as he rocked back. I knew he would be okay, but a part of my brain had simply clicked off. Veses had hurt Ash.

And that would be the last fucking time she did.

Essence roared through me, matching the terrifying sounds coming from above as Nektas fought in the sky. An orb of crackling power burst forth from my palm, and the guard who had been charging me slumped to the ground, an unspoken scream frozen on his lips. Another guard neared me, shadowstone sword raised high. Flipping my dagger, I ignored the scalding heat of the bone burning my fingers and slowed, sliding under his arm as I threw the weapon at the female guard. The blade slammed into her chest, piercing her armor. I popped to my feet and spun, grabbing the other guard by the hair. I jerked his head back and turned, shoving him into the path of a shadowstone sword. Death echoed in my chest as I prowled forward. Gold-and-silver eather powered down my right arm, streaking out and slamming into the stunned guard who had just taken out one of his comrades. I stopped at the female guard. Her skin was doing something strange, flaking off. Dipping, I tore the bone dagger free, then rose, the corners of my vision filling with eather. Two guards in front of me dropped their swords and ran. I started to pull on the eather but stopped myself at the last minute as words Holland had once spoken to me in training resurfaced. *There's no honor in striking those who run.* Air hissed between my clenched teeth, but I shifted my attention to those who'd decided to die today.

My dagger sliced through the air, meeting an attacker's flesh. It sang a quiet song of ending, one I had heard many times before. Maybe too many times. But it would continue singing as I snapped under the swing of a blade and slammed the dagger into a guard's back.

My gaze connected with Ash's as he stalked down the hall. His linen shirt was burned on his shoulder and stomach and stained with blood. It was all I could see as the palace shook once more.

"I'm going to destroy Veses," I promised, each word hissed with heat and vengeance. "I will lay waste to every guard." Power swelled inside me, pulsing through every vein. The floor trembled beneath me, cracking tile. "I will bring what remains of her draken to the ground." My left arm snapped out, catching a guard. I turned my head toward him. The hand I had around his throat shone the color of the sun. His eyes widened with fear. "And I will lay waste to her Court."

The sword slipped from his grip. "Please—"

A rumble came from the back of my throat, and I felt my nailbeds sting. My fingernails started to lengthen. I squeezed, tearing into his throat. Blood poured down his chest and splattered off the floor. His head rolled back and then fell as his body crumpled.

"Breathe." Ash was at my side. "Breathe through the anger."

I looked down at him—*wait*. Down at him?

"You're levitating again," he said, his silvery gaze full of heat. "And you're burning as brightly as the sun. It's fucking making my dick hard."

I blinked.

"But you're also close to shifting." He turned as shadowy eather rose, stabbing through the head of a guard. "You cannot shift, *liessa*."

The *babes*.

I dropped, landing on my feet. The quick reminder eased the rage pummeling through me just enough for me to pull in some semblance of control. I'd been this close to…

To fucking snapping.

I will not lay waste to her Court, I reminded myself. Kill her? Yes. Yes, I was going to do that for sure.

"You good?" Ash had a shadowstone sword in hand again, presumably taken from a fallen guard. He deflected a blow.

"Yes."

He struck the man down. "Then let's finish this."

We moved in unison like dancers swept up in a melody of violence. The winding hallways of the palace became our stage, every turn a potential ambush, every shadow a hiding place for death as guards kept coming at us. But Ash and I were two halves of a single deadly entity.

"Left," he called out, and I trusted the instruction implicitly. My turn was sharp, just in time to parry a wild swing aimed at my head. With a twist and a thrust, I reminded myself that hesitation was a luxury I could not afford.

Up ahead, guards waited in front of the double doors.

Ash tossed his sword aside as he moved forward. One of the guards got jerked up and away from the door, her body twisting and writhing. Another exploded into a fine shimmery dust. Ash threw out his arm, stopping me a second before draken fire burned through the ceiling and the remaining guards, leaving smoking piles of shadowstone and, well…stuff I wasn't going to look too closely at.

Ash lowered his arm, and I raised mine. My eyes narrowed on the doors. I blew them off their hinges. I caught a glimpse of Veses in her diamond dress just as one of the doors smacked into her.

Ash laughed.

Sheathing the dagger, I shot forward. The door lifted from Veses, smashing into the curtained bed. She rose, brushing dust off her glittering gown.

I was on her in a heartbeat, driving my knee into her stomach as I caught her arms, pinning them to the floor. I smiled down at her. "I told you I'd be seeing you again soon."

Her eather-soaked eyes stared daggers at me. "I thought you were trying to be a better person," she sneered.

"I was." I rose, grabbing a fistful of those ringlets as I dragged her to her feet. "As in the past tense."

"Or more like you were never better," she snarled.

"Yeah, maybe you're right."

Her eyes widened a fraction with surprise.

Smiling, I threw her to the side. Veses screamed as strands of her hair snapped. She crashed into the mirrors, shattering them.

Shaking the hair off my fingers, I walked to her as she stood. Eather poured into her veins, and her flesh thinned. She glanced at where Ash stood just inside the chamber, arms crossed and leaning casually against the wall. "Do you let her fight your battles now, *Ash*?"

My brows shot up. Did she just use that name?

"Only when I'd rather cut off my arms than have my skin touch yours," he replied.

Her lip curled. "There was a time—"

My fist slammed into her jaw, knocking her head back. She staggered, catching herself.

She slowly lifted her head. Blood poured from her mouth. "That wasn't necessary."

"Your lipstick is smeared," I said.

She frowned, lifting her hand to wipe at her cheek and mouth as she turned to look at herself in one of the still-intact mirrors. "My lipstick is fine—"

I grabbed her hair with both hands this time, pulling her down so fast and hard her feet kicked into the mirror.

Veses grunted. "I'm getting really tired of you touching my hair," she snapped, rising onto her elbows. Essence rippled over her. "You've made whatever point you're trying to make. Congratulations. You've killed some guards and draken and destroyed my palace. You're such a big, bad Primal now."

"You think we're here to just make a point?" I asked. "What do you think we'll do after we've made it?"

"Leave and gloat while I crawl back to Kolis to tell him how powerful you are?" She shrugged a shoulder. "Honestly, I don't give a fuck. You won't beat loyalty into me."

A laugh escaped me as understanding dawned.

The corners of her mouth turned down. "What is so funny, Seraphena?"

"Other than you?"

She rolled her eyes.

"You know, I expected you to run. I was surprised you didn't." I stared down at her. "I thought you were smarter than this."

"She's not," Ash remarked.

Veses started to turn her head toward Ash.

I snapped forward, straddling her. I grabbed her chin, forcing her attention back to me. "Don't look at him."

"You that insecure?" she spat.

I laughed at her. "You stayed because you really thought we were here to prove some kind of meaningless point?"

She raised her brows at me.

Then I truly understood. "That is why you haven't truly tried to defend yourself." Part of me couldn't believe it. "You think…"

"She does think you're better than her. Better than Kolis and his loyalists," Ash said. "And she's correct, but she came to the wrong conclusion on what that means for her."

He was right.

The way she went completely still beneath me said we were both correct. Her next words further confirmed it. "You're not going to kill me," she said, her lips twisted in a smug smile. "You had your chance before and you didn't. And you won't after what happened to Embris." She let her head fall back. "You haven't Ascended anyone to take my place. I would've felt it. I know you won't allow what happened after Embris to repeat."

I lowered my head until we were inches apart. "I didn't Ascend another to take your place because *I* will."

The smile slowly slipped from her face.

"I'm going to kill you, Veses."

Her lips parted. "No."

"No?"

"You wouldn't." Her gaze darted to Ash. "She won't."

Ash smiled. "She is."

Her wide gaze fixed on me. "Then I was wrong. You're no better. You're not just or fair—"

"Clearly, you have no idea who you're speaking to. He's the inherently just and fair one." I nodded in Ash's direction. "I'm the one who has to work at it."

"Work at it?"

"Yes. But you?" I tapped my fingers off her cheek as essence swelled in me—in her. "You're not worth the effort."

Pure, stark terror bled from her and choked the air.

I leaned in, my lips brushing the curve of her ear. "There is no room for forgiveness and fairness. I'm the reaction to your past actions. I am the consequence." Tendrils of eather rose from the floor. Strands of pure energy swirled around us. "You should be grateful, Veses."

"Really?" she gasped.

"A part of me wanted to make your death last for years—for the length of the deal you made with my husband. I wanted you to feel every painful, choking second of desperation and humiliation. I wanted to witness your pleas turning to silent screams of hopelessness. And gods…" I laughed again, the sound throaty and twisted. "That *does* sound like a good idea."

"*Liessa*," came the soft warning.

"But I am not cruel," I said. "That is the difference between you and me. I don't want to find pleasure in another's suffering."

She cried out as the eather lashed over her leg, stinging her skin.

"Okay. I lied. I do find a little bit of pleasure in your suffering," I said, tilting my head. "But I will not extend it. Because for whatever fucked-up reason, you did try to warn us. For that, I will not draw this out."

She inhaled sharply.

"I will take your Court, Veses, and I will make sure all knowledge and memory of you is stripped away. No generation going forward will know of you. You will not be forgotten, Veses. You will be *unknown*." The eather lashed out again, taking a strip of flesh. "You will die today."

Veses tensed, and I felt her summoning eather. It was too late for that. Jerking her head back, I struck, sinking my fangs into her throat. I drank deeply and hard, not allowing myself to taste her almost too-sweet blood.

She broke my hold on her arms, but Ash was there. He would touch her to protect me. He caught her wrists, holding them down as I pulled more and more of her life force into me. She bucked under me as another draken crashed into the palace. I drank and drank until I felt her heart stutter. I released my fangs then.

I lifted my head and, guided by instinct, placed my hand on her chest. Strangely, I didn't look her in the eye. I didn't want to as I willed the essence from her body. Her back bowed, lifting clear off the floor. I drew my hand back. Thin filaments of eather stretched from her chest to my palm. The essence soaked through my flesh, causing my breath to catch. Her eather pulsed and flowed, making light dance across the broken mirrors and walls. It poured out of her, and the floor began to tremble, the walls shuddering.

I didn't want to look at her.

But I did.

I made myself meet her gaze.

"Sera," Ash whispered. "Look at me."

I couldn't.

I shook my head, holding Veses' stare as the last of her essence left her body and entered mine—as the eather receded from her eyes and veins. I didn't know why I said what I did next. Maybe it was because I knew what Veses had gone through. At one point, she had been different but had become something cruel and sick due to Kolis's actions and influence. Perhaps she even willingly became what she was. But she wasn't always like this. Maybe I truly had no idea why I said what I did.

"I wish it could've been different for you," I said, my voice hoarse as the life flickered from her eyes. "I'm sorry it wasn't."

Midas, the capital of the Callasta Isles, was silent, and the air smelled of iron as I walked the center aisle of the City Hall while Nektas watched from his perch on the Hall's colonnade.

Bodies lined the aisle.

Hundreds of them.

"*Don't allow this to leave a mark*," Ash had said as we stood before the gods and godlings who'd refused our offer to start over with some semblance of civility. The majority had quickly accepted and pledged their loyalty to Ash and me, but it wasn't their loyalty we sought. We wanted their genuine promise to change the way they had lived under Veses' rule.

I had a feeling that, inevitably, more lives would join those we'd ended today. My suspicions of such were rooted in what lay just beyond the City Hall.

My gaze went to the patches of disturbed earth I saw through the colonnade. There were six of them, and they were as wide as Nektas was long.

A goddess who went by the name of Tindra had told us what they were. Mass graves. Both Ash and I were shocked. If anything was left of a god or mortal, it was generally burned. To leave them in the ground was to allow their bodies to rot. It was a sign of disrespect.

Tindra had said each gravesite likely contained hundreds of bodies. Which meant there were thousands of decaying corpses between the six sites. *Thousands*. When Ash had asked why they were not given a proper burial rite, Tindra explained that Veses never performed burial rites for those executed. And the crimes committed that were so deserving of capital punishment? It ranged from refusing to carry out an order to actual murder and everything in between. But it wasn't just the so-called criminals whose final resting place was so disgraceful. Victims who had lost their lives over a quarrel or at the hands of a jealous lover had been routinely tossed into these pits, as well.

My gaze shifted to the slender, dark-haired goddess. Her black robes rippled in the breeze as she stood silent and still, her brown-toned features somber as she stood before the fourth gravesite.

Tindra's husband had been one of the victims tossed so carelessly into the fourth site several decades ago.

"I think many were disgusted by what was happening," Tindra had said when asked why no one seemed to have an issue with this. "At least in the beginning. But this…this is how many have lived for so long. Die or survive by any means necessary. It's the only life we know."

I could see why Rhain had refused any claims to the Court. And what lay beyond the City Hall was why I feared that what remained of Veses' Court would shrink in the coming months and years.

I turned to where several gods of the Court were busy wrapping the bodies of the newly dead under the watchful eye of guards brought here when I summoned Attes to assist with locating whatever Ancient bones Veses had stashed away.

Don't let this leave a mark…

I motioned for Elias to join me. He'd come with Attes, and soon, a contingent of Attes's forces would join the Shadowlands in securing the Callasta Isles.

The brown-haired god approached, his hand resting on the hilt of his sword. He stopped a few feet from me and bowed.

"Elias." I sighed. "You do not need to bow."

"Sorry. It's a habit." He straightened, his gaze flickering briefly to the gravesites. "What can I do for you, *meyaah*—?"

"Sera," I corrected. Considering everything Elias had seen me go through while being held captive by Kolis, I believed we were well past formalities. "It's just Sera."

He nodded in acceptance after a moment.

I angled my body toward the gravesites. "There are thousands of bodies in those pits."

"Fates." Elias's gaze followed mine, his lips parting in disbelief.

"I know their souls have already passed on," I said, "but I would like for you to gather a team of gods from Midas to excavate the sites and give them proper burial rites. Kars will be able to assist you."

"I can do that." His gaze shifted. He was looking at Tindra. "She's still out there."

"Her husband is in that fourth gravesite," I told him. "She said he's been in there for decades."

"Fucking Fates," Elias muttered in disgust. "Some of them will be nothing but bones."

"I know." Chilled, I folded an arm over my lower stomach and looked at the god. "I have a feeling this isn't the only place like this we'll find. There may be similar ones in other Courts."

"You wouldn't be wrong." Elias ran a hand through his hair. "There are three times this many on the outskirts of Dalos."

Pressing my lips together, I closed my eyes. I wasn't surprised to hear that, yet I didn't know what to say.

Elias left to carry out my request. I saw him stop to speak with Tindra. Did they know each other? The answer started to come to me, but I stopped myself before I saw what was none of my business. Besides, I had already seen into the lives of enough people. It was how I knew that those we'd ended today weren't just being foolishly arrogant when they refused our offer. They'd had no intention of even attempting to live a different kind of life.

Ash arrived with Attes, the latter informing me they'd discovered one bone spear and some bone chains. It was only one set of chains, not nearly enough to keep Kolis secured, and that included what Penellaphe had managed to locate in Lotho. However, there were still more Courts to search.

My gaze shifted to the bodies filling the City Hall. And there would be more deaths.

Don't let this leave a mark…

Ash and I returned to the Shadowlands shortly after. We had our dinner in the antechamber after updating the others. I didn't think either of us was in the mood for company outside of each other.

I'd told him what Keella had shared with me. Parts of it were obviously no surprise since we had come to believe beforehand that part of what had happened had been Eythos's plan. He was disquieted by the idea of the Fates wanting to wake the Ancients as much as I was, though. In the end, it simply meant there was no room for error. Kolis had to be entombed, and Sotoria needed to be released immediately.

I watched Ash as he rooted through the bowl of sliced fruit, inspecting a strawberry before moving on to another until he found the plumpest one to offer me. He'd done the same with the melon, the chicken, and the vegetables.

"Why do you keep doing that?" I asked, biting into the sticky, sweet berry.

He glanced over at me with a raised brow as he chose a strawberry that looked deformed. "Doing what?"

"Inspecting each and every piece of food before you give it to me." I caught a drop of juice on my lip with the tip of my tongue.

I waited. Ash didn't answer. He was…staring at my lips.

"Ash?"

He blinked, lifting his gaze. There was no mistaking the heat in his eyes. "I'm sorry, what were you saying?"

I grinned and asked the question again.

"Oh." He shrugged as he sat back. "I just want to make sure you have the best there is to offer."

Now, it was my turn to blink repeatedly at him as I fought off a wave of emotion.

Ash eyed me closely. "You okay?"

I cleared my throat. "Yes." Leaning over, I wrapped my hand around the nape of his neck and drew his mouth to mine. His kiss tasted of strawberries. "I love you."

He returned the kiss, and for a little bit, the food was forgotten. So was everything else. It didn't stay that way, though. Now, I lay in bed beside him, my back nestled against his chest and his leg tucked between mine. His hand rested protectively over my stomach. I loved that. I loved sleeping this way, and I wanted to rest. I needed it. Tomorrow would be another…complicated day. But I stared at the shadowstone walls, my thoughts running from one to another. When I closed my eyes, I saw the bodies in the Callasta Isles City Hall and the disturbed soil outside the colonnade.

I saw Veses' face.

Gods, Kolis would be pissed when he woke.

"*Liessa*," Ash murmured. "What's on your mind?"

I frowned. "It boggles my mind that you can appear completely asleep and yet somehow know I'm not."

"It's another talent of mine," he remarked. "Talk to me."

Those three words still made me want to squirm a little, but they didn't incite as much unrest as they had before. "I'm just…I'm worried about the Callasta Isles—if our people are safe there," I said, placing my hand over his. "There's only one draken who didn't join the attack, but we can't even be sure he's trustworthy."

"Nektas seems to have taken Jarah at his word," he said, speaking of the younger draken with gold and black scales. "I'm sure things will be calm there, at least for a little while. If not, you will sense any great unrest."

I nodded, concentrating on the swoop of his thumb along the skin below my navel.

Ash was quiet for several minutes. "I don't think that's the only thing on your mind."

It wasn't.

"You're thinking about what we did today."

I was.

He pressed a kiss to my shoulder. "What did I tell you?"

"To not let it leave a mark."

His lips brushed over the skin he'd kissed, drawing a tight shiver from me. "But it is."

It was.

"Sera…"

"I want them to leave a mark," I blurted out. "I need them to."

He rose slightly, and even though I didn't look at him, I felt his questioning gaze on me.

"It's not like I regret what we did," I said, tracing the tendons on his hand. "It's what we should've done since the beginning. And I know it's neither right nor wrong. It's simply…necessary."

"But?" he asked quietly.

"But I…I keep seeing Veses' face," I admitted. "She really thought I wouldn't do it, and you wouldn't allow it."

"Her arrogance was only one of many self-destructive flaws."

Normally, I would've agreed with that or laughed. Possibly both. But I wasn't sure if that was why. "Deep down, Veses really did think we were…" The back of my eyes burned for some damn reason. "That we were better than that."

"She thought we would be like Eythos," he said, his arm tightening around me. "We are not."

"We aren't," I whispered.

Ash went still for a moment and then moved, guiding me onto my back. Our eyes locked. "You're upset."

"You're reading my emotions."

"You're projecting," he stated, shifting his weight onto his elbow. He cupped my cheek. "Do not spend a second being sad about Veses' fate."

"I'm not."

In the slivers of moonlight, I saw his eyebrow rise. "You're such a terrible liar."

"Whatever," I muttered.

Ash sighed. "I heard what you said to her, Sera. That you wished it could have been different for her and were sorry it wasn't."

I really should have kept that to myself.

"You meant that."

"I did." Frustration rose as my eyes continued to sting. "And I don't even know why. I hate Veses for what she did to you and for how she ran her Court. Still do, even though she's dead. And I don't regret ending her. It had to happen, but…" I closed my eyes, emotion lodging in my throat. "But she wasn't always like that. You said so yourself."

"Neither was Embris."

"Veses was different."

"Why is that?" he asked.

"I…" I breathed through my nose as words worked their way around the knot in my throat. "She said it was nothing."

Ash went still again.

"She said how Kolis treated her and the things he made her do was nothing." My voice came out hoarse. I opened my eyes. "It wasn't nothing. Gods know, I knew every time I said that what he did to me wasn't nothing. And I know—" My voice cracked, and I shook my head, not wanting to shed a godsdamn tear over Veses. "I know Veses knew that, too. But she loved him. And maybe that was what turned her into what she ended up being.

Always loving someone who loved someone else. I don't know. But I can see a—"

"You should never see yourself in her," he cut in, tipping my head back so my eyes met his. "Never."

"I can see a part of me in her," I continued, chest rising and falling fast. "Not the part that made her such a bitch, but the pain in her eyes. I saw it while in Dalos. She tried to hide it, but she…" A tear snuck free, and Ash immediately caught it with his finger. "But she did this—all of it—to herself. And if I…"

That was it.

If I had continued as if all that'd happened to me was nothing, I could've ended up like her. Maybe not as bad. Perhaps even worse, but in a different way. Because that kind of pain and shame, that kind of heartbreak, rotted you from the inside. It destroyed the glimpses of who you once were. And perhaps that was why her death bothered me. Because I could've done it to myself. Killing her was like killing that one part of me that had reluctantly connected to her.

I didn't have to say all of that, but Ash still understood. I knew he did as he kissed each tear that started off as grief and then became relief. When they stopped, and I eventually found myself nestled once more against his chest, I finally fell asleep.

And I slept deeply.

Until I woke before dawn, gasping for air as a shout of fury slammed around in my head. I felt that *cord*. The *connection* that signaled the balance being righted once more. Even with my eyes open, I could see the darkness descending—black streaked with crimson.

Kolis was awake.

"Whoa," Saion murmured as he leaned back in the settee.

I'd just finished the first stage of Ascension in case Phanos decided to either remain loyal to Kolis or refused to involve his Court. Only a tiny part of me held on to the hope that Phanos would choose us.

"You okay?" His cousin stood beside him, watching carefully as I closed the wound on my wrist.

"Yeah. Just a head rush." Saion looked dazed as he tried to focus on me. "Your blood is…" He trailed off as a low growl of displeasure echoed from behind me.

Beside me, Reaver lifted his scaled head. A few minutes ago, he had growled when Saion neared me, which forced the god to stay seated and me to go to him.

Saion cleared his throat, sitting straighter. "It's, um, something else."

I shot Ash a frown over my shoulder as Jadis turned in her father's lap, her brilliant blue eyes blinking. "You're being ridiculous again."

He ignored me, his glare fixed on Saion.

"Why is everyone growling at me today?" Saion asked.

The poor god was really having a rough morning.

I knew why Ash was growling. It was the whole keep-away-from-my-pregnant-wife thing, which made me so grateful that Kars was in the Callasta Isles because he'd surely get himself killed. But with Reaver, I had a feeling he was picking up on Ash's tension and responding to it.

"Did I do something?" Saion asked, bewildered.

"No," I was quick to answer, elbowing Ash in the stomach.

"Uh." Saion glanced at Rhahar and then Ash before raising his hands. "I feel the need to apologize."

"You don't need to apologize," I said. "He's just cranky."

"Cranky?" repeated Ash.

"Well," Nektas drawled, rising from his chair with Jadis in his arms. The little draken was still focused on Ash as she clutched her father's hair with her claws. "I think it's time we head to the Triton Isles."

"He's right." Saion shook his head, smothering a yawn. "Phanos would've felt this."

And with Kolis being awake, we needed to make it quick.

I ran my fingers over Reaver's head as Nektas handed Jadis off to Aios. The youngling immediately went for the goddess's hair. I turned to Ash and asked in a low voice, "You okay?"

The rigidness of his jaw was starting to fade. Nodding, he folded an arm around my waist, and I saw Reaver approaching Saion, cautiously nudging the god's leg with the top of his head. I guessed that was the draken's way of apologizing.

"Ready?" Nektas asked, approaching us.

"Yes." Ash looked at the others. "Remember, Kolis is awake. Everyone needs to be on high alert."

There were several nods of agreement, and as the mist began to swirl around us, I saw Aios stretch a hand toward Reaver. I didn't like leaving any of them while Kolis was awake, but I reminded myself that the younglings would soon return to Mount Rhee.

The smell of brine reached me before the bright light penetrated the fading mist. We were facing the sea. Sunlight glittered off the endless water, creating a stunning tapestry of sparkling diamonds. Squinting at the surface, I immediately thought of the ceeren who'd given their lives for me.

Gods, I really hoped Phanos made the right call—actually, speaking of Phanos… I started to step back—

Ash caught my arm as Nektas cursed. My gaze flew to his. "Careful," he said. "You're about to step on a *lamaea.*"

I spun around and looked down, quickly wishing I hadn't.

The pale gray creature wiggled and slid across the sand. The fleshy smack of its flopping fins and the slippery slide of its dragging tails could fill a bucket of nightmares. I was so shocked by the sight of it that I couldn't even concentrate enough to allow my *vadentia* to tell me what I was looking at. "What…what is that?"

"Another of my father's ill attempts at creating new life," he answered. "A *lamaea*."

The creature's almost mortal head and beady black eyes narrowed at Nektas. The draken gave the *lamaea* a wide berth.

"No offense," I murmured, "but your father really needed to stop trying."

"None taken." He stepped forward as if to walk in front of the creature.

My grip tightened on his hand, and I dug my boots into the sand. "Do you think that's wise?"

"They're harmless," he replied as the thing reared up on its fins, waving its tail arms. There was a distinctive fishy smell.

That was a whole lot of nope.

"Is it…waving at us?" I asked.

Ash grinned. "I believe so."

I gave a short, awkward wave back. The *lamaea* made a deep, chortling sound before flopping back to the sand. Somewhat dumbfounded, I watched it make its way to the shore and then disappear into the dazzling water.

"Damn it," Nektas growled, drawing my attention. He had one foot lifted, and the sole was covered in something thick and glossy. "I stepped in *lamaea* slime."

My lip curled as nausea rose so violently that I had to clap my hand over my mouth while Nektas charged up a short hill to where some leafy palm trees swayed in the breeze.

"Maybe you should wear shoes," Ash commented as he led me around the trail of…goo.

Nektas frowned as he dragged his foot over the grass. "Shoes are cumbersome."

Ash snorted, glancing back at me. Concern immediately filled his gaze. "You okay?"

Nektas looked up when I nodded and forced a swallow. "Yeah, I just don't need to be thinking of gooey stuff right now."

"You and me both," the draken muttered.

I trudged through the sand, a fine sheen of sweat breaking out across my forehead by the time we joined Nektas under the palms. I really should've worn one of those sleeveless tunics instead of the quarter-length-sleeve gray one. It was hot under the bright sun.

Wiping my forehead, I looked up and caught sight of the ivory-and-blue-painted limestone palace. The entire second- and third-floor walls were made of glass. "There's no Rise?"

"Phanos once said he didn't want his view of the ocean obstructed," Ash said as we crossed onto stone pavers carved into the shape of bivalve shells.

I could understand that desire as I scanned the silent palace grounds. "He isn't here."

"I don't think anyone is," Nektas said, eyeing the thicker foliage crowding the back of Phanos's palace. "Could they be on one of the other islands?"

"I don't know." Ash frowned as he released my hand and stalked toward the pillared veranda that appeared to circle the entire first level. Bright-red flowers lined the roof's edge, trailing long stems of blossoms. "There should still be guards present here."

As we followed Ash and stepped under the shade of the veranda, a sense of unease rose. A thin veneer of salt hung in the air as the wooden planks creaked under our steps. That gnawing sensation from deep within grew, sending a shiver of premonition down my spine.

"Something's not right," I murmured, almost to myself, but Ash caught the words and gave a curt nod, his jaw set in a way that told me he was on edge, too.

Beside me, Nektas's gaze darted around as he sniffed the air. "I don't like this. At all."

Neither did I.

We reached the back of the veranda, where the shade gave way to a glaring sunlit expanse. The bay unfolded before us, a canvas of vivid blue. Across the water, the silhouettes of other islands rose like slumbering giants. The quiet should have been calming, yet it only served to amplify the disquiet—the wrongness—that whispered through the sea breeze.

My eyes swept over the docks that jutted into the bay like bony fingers. Where ships should have been lashed securely to the moorings, there was only the slap of waves against empty wood. My stare fixed on the ghostly dance of loose ropes in the water.

When I spotted the ropes remaining on the docks, their edges frayed as if they had been hastily severed, my unease turned to dread. "How many ships does Phanos have?"

"Roughly two hundred," Ash stated grimly.

My heart sped up. Not all of Phanos's forty-some thousand soldiers were ceeren. Some were gods and godlings who wouldn't be able to take to the water themselves. My hands fisted as I lifted my gaze to the island, where I could see limestone buildings dotting the hills and valleys.

Eather throbbed intensely. "Phanos could be anywhere."

Ash turned to us. "Two hundred ships would be hard to miss, though," he stated, eather piercing his eyes like streaks of lightning. "Nektas, can you take to the air and see what you can find?"

"What about you two?" he asked as the breeze tossed long strands of hair across his broad shoulders. "I don't like the idea of you two staying here."

"We're not," Ash said. "We're going to return to the Shadowlands in case he's headed there."

"We also need to get word to Theon to be on the lookout," I said, and Ash nodded.

Nektas hesitated, clearly not wanting to leave us, but he nodded and turned, rushing toward the edge of the veranda. He leapt, a shimmery wave sweeping over his body as he shifted into his draken form. His massive wings cast foreboding shadows over the water as Ash came to my side. Dragging my gaze from Nektas, I reached for his hand—

I sucked in a sudden breath as an icy-cold sensation shot down my spine and spread throughout my limbs.

"What is it?" Ash demanded, clasping the nape of my neck.

"I…I don't know." Swallowing, I shook my head as a new awareness pressed down on me, heavy and dark, thudding in my chest and settling in the pit of my stomach. My hand went to my belly.

Ash's inhale was sharp. "Is it the babes?"

"No, it's something else." The skin beneath my ear erupted in tingles, and I said, "I need a minute to figure this out."

Ash went quiet but held on to me. I closed my eyes and concentrated. What I felt reminded me of the echo of death, but it was slightly different. "My stomach keeps dipping like…like something is gravely wrong. Not here, but—" My heart lurched, and my eyes flew open. "I think I'm sensing unrest in Iliseeum."

"Can you tell if it's in the Shadowlands?" His thumb swept over my fluttering pulse. "Or *where* it's coming from?"

"I don't know." My skin kept tingling. "But I think I can follow it. Like if I focus on it, I can take us to it."

A muscle flexed in his jaw. "I'd rather take you home first."

"We don't know if that's what I'm feeling," I argued. "We need to figure out what's happening, especially considering what we just found here."

Ash cursed, then nodded. His skin had already begun to thin as I stepped into him. Concentrating on the feeling of unrest, I summoned the eather and felt the Triton Isles slip away from us. The next breath I took filled my lungs with the scent of scorched earth and the metallic tang of blood as Ash and I shadowstepped smack-dab into the middle of a battle.

"Vathi," I gasped and knew immediately what we were seeing—what had happened.

Kyn had launched an attack against his brother.

I staggered back in shock as the ground quivered with the clash of shadowstone and pounding hoofbeats. My gaze darted across the long field that stretched into the horizon, where the sky bled with the silver of draken fire before the snowcapped mountains.

I spun, taking in the carnage. Everywhere I looked, gods dressed in black and others in crimson were locked in a fierce battle, striking down one another with an instinctual grace that almost hid their innate brutality. The shimmering waves of energy arced and crackled across the field as sword blows gave way to deadly streaks of eather. Charging fearlessly into battle, every swing of their swords and motion was a testament to the Primal gods they descended from.

The Primal God of War and Accord, and the Primal God of Peace and Vengeance.

Ash suddenly jerked me to his chest as a horse rushed past us, the rider—the *headless* rider—slumping to the side.

His eyes met mine. "Phanos is not here."

"I know. He's somewhere—*shit*." I shot to the side, eather responding at once as a massive, ugly-as-fuck *kynakos* launched itself into the air, snarling with a mouthful of blade-sharp fangs mere feet from Ash's back. I threw out my hand, releasing a stream of gold-tinged silver. I winced at the yelp as the essence smacked into the Dog of War, hitting it in the stomach.

Ash twisted at the waist, catching the arm of a soldier in a black uniform with crimson cloth stretched over shadowstone armor. The soldier shouted in pain as Ash broke the man's arm in one breath and then snapped his neck with brutal quickness in the next.

He spun toward me, eyes filling with eather. "Sera—"

"I'm not leaving," I cut in. "I'm fighting beside you." I sucked in a short breath as Ash suddenly lifted me and turned, shielding my body as eather erupted from his palm. A high-pitched shriek told me his aim had been deadly accurate. His gaze returned to mine. "I remember what I promised you," I said. "No unnecessary risks."

Ash froze for a heartbeat and then cursed. He clasped the back of my neck, drawing my head to his. "I'd better not see a single scratch on you, *liessa*. Not even one. So, be the badass Queen you are."

"Always," I swore.

He exhaled a ragged breath and glanced up. "Hold off on using the eather as much as you can," he said quickly, picking up the shadowstone sword the soldier had dropped. He pressed the hilt into my hand. Shadows blossomed over his cheeks. "We need to get to Attes. We cannot let him fall."

I nodded, stepping back. His hold on me firmed for a moment and then vanished. My gaze swept the field once more, easily picking out Kyn's soldiers. Crimson covered their armor, and the crests on their helmets were the same bloody shade.

I was really beginning to fucking hate that color.

Snapping forward, I went after the closest soldier, thrusting the sword through his back as a blast of frigid air suddenly rolled off Ash. He rose into the air, his skin hardening as it turned to the color of shadowstone. Dark shadows spilled out of him, spinning and churning as the hazy outline of wings swept out behind him.

"The bitch is on the field!" someone shouted.

My gaze jerked to the right. A soldier wheeled his horse around, his helmet with its tuft of red horsehair stained with blood. "Excuse me?"

The horse charged me, its nostrils flaring as its hooves kicked up soil.

A bolt of eather-laced shadows flowed past me, enveloping the soldier and his horse. In an instant, both were shimmery dust.

"Not the horse!" I cried out.

"*Liessa*..." Ash rose even higher, the churning eather spinning faster and faster. "Get ready."

I felt the essence surging within me as my hand instinctively tightened around the sword's hilt.

Before me, several soldiers whipped around. I held my breath and began to count. One. Two. The distraction cost them as their opponents from both sides struck them down. Three. Four—

Tendrils of shadowy eather snaked across the battlefield, sweeping over soldiers in red and weaving between those in black. The pounding echoes of death came so fast I couldn't even begin to count how many fell as the torrents of eather continued on their way, carving out a path that left only Attes's soldiers standing and...

Horses suddenly without riders.

My lips curved into a tight smile as I silently thanked Ash.

Then I saw them.

Attes and Kyn were on a hill, locked in a battle of swords and eather.

My chin dipped, and then I broke into a run, Attes's armies turning to follow as a roar shook the land.

A draken dove from the thick clouds, releasing a stream of fiery eather. I swallowed a shout as I slowed, throwing up my arm to ward off the heat as silver flames erupted before me. Fire swept over soldiers, indiscriminately lighting up everything on the field as the sound of pounding hooves jerked my head up. Through the receding flames, I saw a line of horses bearing down on me.

"Motherfucker," I spat, straightening as Aurelia arrived, her greenish-black scales bloody in some spots. She swooped down, digging her talons into the back of the other draken.

From the dying flames, a god lunged at me. *Don't take unnecessary risks,* I repeated to myself. With a deft sidestep, I swung the sword around, deflecting the blow and pushing him back. Another soldier drove her sword through his back.

"*Meyaah Liessa*," she said, wrenching her blade free.

"Hi!" I ran, leaping onto the ruins of a wall. I twisted, the sword arcing through the sky to pierce red armor, knocking a god off his horse. "Please don't bow!"

I took off toward the battling Primals as I summoned eather, releasing a wave of essence that swept adversaries off their feet, clearing a small space amid the chaos.

Above, the sky roared with the fire of a new draken. *Ehthawn.* His wings blotted out the sun intermittently, casting moving shadows over the battlefield. He unleashed his flames, turning patches of the field into infernos that consumed both soil and flesh. Even as I shoved the blade through a god's chest, I felt the heat on my face, the acrid smell of death and destruction lacing the air. I jumped from the wall as Ash landed, shadowy tendrils whipping out.

He and I surged forward, but it was different than before when I slipped away into battle. There was a pattern to how we moved, almost as if we were one. In the back of my mind, it made sense. We were two halves of the same whole, our movements nearly synchronized, punctuated by the thrust of my sword and the arc of his.

We wove through the combat with swift strikes and fluid defensive moves. Ash would maneuver a god to meet my sword, and I would kick another into his, each act a testament to our inherent understanding of each other.

But I knew there was a difference as I met fierce blows with the same strength and lashed out with the essence. When I fought before, I could always let go of my fear. I couldn't this time. Each swing and thrust was tinged with bitter emotion. I wasn't scared for myself or even Ash. I worried about the babes I carried inside me. My fear for them made each swing harder, every release of energy more violent. The fear didn't make me a worse fighter.

It made me a far deadlier one.

Overhead, Aurelia tore through a draken's throat, releasing him as he shifted into his mortal form and fell to the ground, only to be swallowed by the warring soldiers.

I drew in a stuttered breath as the pulse of death was a continuous throb in my chest. A wave of eather whipped out of Ash, slamming into the Dogs of War. The scent of burnt fur mingled with that of flesh as I shouted, swinging the blade down on a god's head. Blood spurted, spraying the front of my tunic and face.

The death…

There was so much.

A sudden wrenching sensation in the center of my chest caused me to stagger. I cried out, clutching at my breast, expecting to see a bone blade or blood, but there was nothing there. The pain wasn't really pain. It was more a dull ache but not a physical one. More like a loss…

Oh, gods.

I'd felt this when Keella died, and I knew who it was. I saw them in my mind, and my heart ached.

Ash was at my side at once, folding an arm around my waist. "What is it?" he demanded. "Where are you hurt?"

"It's not me." I rose with his help, the sudden knowledge of where Phanos had gone with his ships and armies weakening me. "It's Maia. She's fallen."

"Fuck," snarled Ash.

A blast of intense eather drew both our gazes to the hill. My heart clenched as I saw Kyn rise into the air ahead of us, driving Attes to the ground. Ash took to the air again, but one of Kyn's draken dove for him. Ash's cold laugh caused a sea of soldiers to look up at the gathering dark storm of energy.

A crack of power drew my attention to the hill. Attes was once more on his feet.

The field shook with the fury of the Primal brothers' clash as they came together, trading blows upon the hill that split the horizon like the spine of a slumbering draken. Dark clouds rolled above them, responding to the tempest of emotions inside them as their raw power beat the air. That kind of Primal energy kept the fighting gods from them, pushing the soldiers farther and farther back, but Ash and I pushed forward.

Kyn's and Attes's forms were blurs of motion, each strike a mirror image of the other. Their brutality was relentless, even as their swords shattered when they clashed. I pushed faster, picking up speed. I didn't want Attes to be the one to end his brother's life. I didn't want him to carry that with him. My wide eyes met Ash's. I could see that he felt the same.

Fuck.

I threw the sword at a soldier on horseback, hitting him in the chest. Then I shadowstepped, appearing several feet down the hill. Summoning eather, I started to rush up the remaining distance, Ash right beside me—

A wave of Primal power knocked both of us back as Attes yelled, slamming his fist into the center of Kyn's chest.

The impact shattered Kyn's armor. I stumbled, falling to my knees as fragments spun through the air, glinting like stars flung from the night sky. They fell to the ground below, merely discarded remnants.

No. No. No.

Kyn staggered, falling to his knees, his eyes widening with shock as Ash dragged me to my feet.

"Don't do it," I whispered—or maybe yelled. "Attes!"

He lurched forward, grabbing his brother by the throat. "Lailah," Attes shouted, my breath wilting in my chest as he turned toward us. Tears streamed down his face, mingling with blood. Eather pooled around his raised hand, crackling and spitting. "Ascend Lailah, Sera. Now!"

I was rooted to where I stood until Ash grabbed me by my shoulders. "You need to go," he said. "She's on the Rise by the Black Bay. Ascend Lailah. Do it now."

I sucked in air, gaze flying to Ash's. "Stay with him. Please."

"I will," he promised, letting go. "I love you."

"I love you, too," I whispered, stepping back as lightning erupted from the dark clouds overhead.

As gold-and-silver mist rose around me, Attes turned back to his brother. The last thing I heard before I appeared on the Rise was Attes screaming, and he sounded just as I had when I found my family impaled to the walls of Wayfair. His scream was that of a wild, broken animal full of sorrow and rage.

Only an hour or so past dawn, I'd woken to find Ash gone and suspected he had been at the Pillars since the fight in Vathi had fueled violent storms that swept through the mortal realm. The destruction and death weren't nearly as bad as they had been after Embris, but… Yeah, it was still bad.

And there was no guarantee that drawing Kolis out would prevent more destruction.

After eating a quick breakfast, I'd felt Ash's return and left to find him. On the way, I'd stopped by Aios's chambers and found Rhain there. I had a feeling he may have spent a decent part of the night watching over her.

"I didn't know what happened until Aios lit up with eather," Rhain said, standing on the other side of Aios's bed. "Then I knew." He sighed, thrusting a hand through his auburn strands. "We all knew."

"I didn't know Maia well." Heart heavy, my gaze flickered over Aios's peaceful features as I toyed with the button on my vest. I wanted Bele to be here for her when she woke. "But I wish…"

"There was nothing either you or Ash could've done," Rhain was quick to say. "It wasn't like preparing Saion triggered Phanos into making his choice. There was no way he could've readied his armies and left the Triton Isles in that little time."

"I know." But I also knew that Keella's and Veses' deaths, although for vastly different reasons, could've influenced what Phanos decided. It had been a risk, one we knew we were taking. I exhaled long and slow. "I didn't feel unrest in her Court. The attack must have been quick."

"Maia didn't have a large army," Rhain said. "Her forces would've been quickly overwhelmed."

I nodded, hoping that meant her death was as quick and painless as possible. We'd sent as many soldiers as we could spare to secure the Court, as did Ione, but from Nektas's quick flyover, we'd learned the capital was burning.

It felt like we were at war, even though it hadn't officially been declared. And maybe we were. Perhaps calling it a war didn't even matter. But I didn't know if we were winning or losing at this point. Yes, we'd taken Lotho, Sirta, the Callasta Isles, the entirety of Vathi, and once Kithreia was secure, it would be under our control, too. But we'd lost Maia and most of Veses' and Kyn's soldiers.

"How's Attes?" Rhain asked.

I shook my head. "I only saw him briefly when he returned with Nyktos late last night, but I imagine not good." I lifted my gaze to Rhain's. "I didn't want it to be him."

"I don't think Attes would've allowed it to be anyone *but* him."

My heart was even heavier because Rhain was right. Attes could've stepped back and allowed Ash to finish Kyn. He hadn't. To kill one's own brother? And a twin at that…

First, it was Kolis, and now Attes. Granted, it wasn't the same, but I knew this was something Attes may never truly get past, even if his twin was a grade-A asshole. In all honesty, Kolis hadn't. His grief and shame over killing Eythos had aided in him becoming what he had.

"Sera?" Concern tinged Rhain's voice. "Are you feeling unwell?"

His question pulled me from my thoughts. "Why do you ask?"

"You're holding your stomach."

I glanced down, and yep, my hand *was* pressed to my lower stomach. "Yeah." Dropping my arm, I cleared my throat and rose from the chair beside Aios's bed. "I'm going to check in with Nyktos. We should be meeting with the others soon."

"Sera," Rhain called. "Are you…?"

Stopping at the door, my stomach dipped as I met his stare. "What?"

He closed his mouth and shook his head. "Nothing." His attention turned once more to Aios. "I'll be down when we're ready."

I hesitated. Had he been about to ask if I was pregnant? I was probably jumping to conclusions, but we'd have to tell everyone sooner or later. I knew they would be happy, even Rhain, who I imagined would probably be more of a nervous wreck than me.

We would tell everyone once Kolis was dealt with, and it…it would be something to celebrate. We just had to get to that point.

I stopped on the second floor to check in on Lailah again. I had sat with her last night for a little while. I had no idea if she would be out longer than Aios since their Ascensions were different, and I hadn't been here when Bele rose as a Primal. As I neared the chamber, I felt a Primal nearby.

Cracking open the door, I saw that Lailah was still asleep. A chair was next to the bed that hadn't been there when I'd spent time with her last night. I leaned in a little farther, spotting a pair of dark boots tucked under the bed. I tilted my head, hearing the faint splash of water. Curiosity rose as I let my senses concentrate on the Primal presence.

Attes.

Nibbling on my lower lip, I stepped back and quietly closed the door. Normally, I wouldn't be too keen on the idea of him helping himself to the chambers Lailah was resting in, but I knew she was safe with him, and considering what he'd been through, I really couldn't make myself be angry at him.

I went downstairs, passing several guards in the foyer and main hall. They bowed in a wave along both sides as if their lives depended on it as Rhahar stepped out of the hall leading to Ash's office. "That's not necessary," I told them.

Rhahar's lips twitched as he pivoted on his heel and fell into step beside me. "It's charming how you keep telling them not to bow."

"At some point, I'm hoping they'll listen," I said, nearing the office.

"Or, at some point, you will accept how they choose to show you respect," he countered.

"It is unlikely either thing will happen," Ash's voice traveled from the office. He rose from where he was seated and stepped around his desk, the charcoal tunic he wore fitting the breadth of his shoulders to perfection. "Can you give us a moment, Rhahar?"

The god nodded, closing the door behind me. Ash extended his arm. I crossed the chamber and placed my hand in his. He pulled me to his chest, dipping his head to kiss me. It was such a soft and tender thing, but it still left me a little breathless when our lips parted.

"Sorry I wasn't with you when you woke this morning." Ash smoothed a stray curl back from my temple. "I was at the Pillars."

I rested my hands against his chest. "That's what I figured."

"Did you eat breakfast?" he asked.

"Yes, and I drank juice, too." I paused. "A full cup."

Ash grinned, running the tips of his fingers down my cheek. "How were you feeling this morning? Any nausea?"

"None today."

"That's three days in a row," he said. "Hopefully, you won't have any more spells."

"I hope so." I breathed in his fresh, citrusy scent and nuzzled his chest, rubbing my cheek against him like a cat seeking…wait. I blinked, wondering if I was somehow developing the tendencies of my *nota.*

Man, would I start clawing up the furniture?

"Have you had a chance to check in with Aios or Lailah?" he asked, drawing me from my bizarre thoughts.

"They're both still asleep," I said, keeping Attes's current whereabouts to myself as I stepped back, smoothing my hands over the hem of my blouse. "I should probably go ahead and try to summon a Fate so we can get the others here." Attempting to set up a meeting with Kolis was the only way we'd be able to lure him out of whatever hole he'd crawled into.

Ash nodded as he turned to his desk, reaching for a pitcher on a tray. "I'm ready whenever you are."

Ash poured two glasses of berry-infused water, and I took a deep breath and cleared my mind. Unlike last time, I didn't think of Holland as I summoned the eather. "Fates," I said as the essence pulsed through me, reverberating through my voice. "I request a meeting with one of you." I paused and then tacked on a surly, "Please."

Ash snorted. "The please was a nice touch."

I grinned as I took the water from him. "I guess we just wait now."

He nodded, leaning against his desk as he eyed me. "You started to turn golden when you summoned the Fate. It was hot."

I rolled my eyes, sitting down on a settee.

"I haven't seen you go full Primal yet," he noted, taking a sip. "You were close to doing so when we were in the Callasta Isles."

I thought about that. "I think I may have done it when I was in Lasania." My gaze fell to the violet-hued berries floating in my water. I cleared my throat. "But I really don't know what I looked like besides my skin kind of turning gold."

"I'm sure you were beautiful."

I smiled at that. Shortly after, Rhain, the cousins, and finally Attes joined us. There was no Fate among them, but the latter entered with wet hair and his features drawn into tight, somber lines. He dropped onto the settee across from me with a nod. I started to ask how he was but stopped myself as Rhain busied himself pouring drinks for everyone. I knew that I didn't like to be asked about my feelings, especially these kinds, particularly not in front of others.

I glanced around the office, growing impatient. Where was the Fate I'd summoned? Were they just taking their sweet time or ignoring me? I knew I hadn't done it wrong. Anxiety buzzed through me as I moved to the very edge of the settee.

"I think Aios will wake soon," Rhain stated as Ash moved to stand closer to me, picking up two of three glasses and handing them off to Saion and Rhahar before grabbing the third. "She was starting to move a little before I left."

"That's good," I said.

Ash nodded, his gaze straying to Attes. "Do you have any updates on the remainder of Kyn's army?"

He nodded, staring at the glass Rhain had given him. "When I went back early this morning, I was informed that about ten thousand surrendered," he shared stoically. "But their newfound loyalty to me isn't something I'm willing to trust in battle yet."

I hadn't known Attes had returned to Vathi. I must've been asleep when he left and returned.

"Understandable," Ash remarked.

"I assume we had defectors?" I said.

Attes nodded. "From what my generals could estimate, about ten thousand fell in battle."

"Good gods," I said.

His silvery gaze lifted to mine. "Yeah." His throat worked on a swallow. "That means roughly twenty thousand are likely fleeing to wherever Kolis is."

"That's disappointing to…" I stiffened, eather throbbing acutely in my chest. Awareness pressed down on me, alerting me to someone powerful.

Someone Ancient.

"What is it?" Ash asked.

"I think the Fate is here." I set the glass on the end table as everyone in the room went still. I rose, expecting a portal to rip open. When it didn't, my frown increased. "But I don't know where they are."

A second later, a knock sounded on the office doors. Six heads turned in that direction.

"Well, we know it's not Aydun since they actually knocked," I murmured.

Ash snickered at that, putting his glass on the table behind him. "Come in."

The door opened, and my mouth dropped open at who walked in. I almost couldn't believe that *he* had answered.

Holland stood near the pillars as the door swung closed behind him, dressed in white. We were all staring at him, but it was my gaze he held with those eyes full of stars and churning colors. I was in shock, unable to move or speak. He was the very last Fate I'd expected to show. Even though I had Ascended Penellaphe, something he had clearly appreciated, I figured I would likely never see him again. That he wouldn't want to see *me* again.

A fond, almost fatherly smile broke out across his handsome features, creating fine creases in his rich brown skin at the corners of his eyes. "Sera."

The sound of his deep voice—the familiarity of it and the kindness in that single word—did something to me.

Ash tensed as I jerked forward, almost as if he wished to stop me, but held himself back. I crossed the antechamber but stopped in front of Holland, a lump forming in my throat as we continued to stare at each other.

Without saying a word, Holland lifted his arms, and I might've thrown myself at him. A soft grunt turned into a surprised laugh as his strong arms wrapped around me, one hand folding over the back of my head.

A shudder went through me as I buried my face against his chest, my eyes squeezed shut.

"Well, that's not something you see every day," Attes drawled under his breath.

"I don't think you've ever greeted me in such a manner," Holland said, his voice low and rougher than normal. "Not since you were a child. I wasn't expecting that after…"

I inhaled deeply, soaking in the familiar scent of iron and earth. My thoughts felt a little bit messy. Even though I understood why, I was still angry with him for knowing that what happened in Lasania could've been possible and doing nothing, but I needed this hug from the man who was the closest thing to a father to me. I loved him, and gods, I was relieved to know that I still felt that way.

"I'm sorry," I whispered hoarsely. "I'm sorry for what I've done."

"I know, Sera." His embrace tightened, and I knew that he recognized what I was apologizing for. "I know."

Tears pricked my eyes as my fingers balled into the back of his tunic. "Do you…do you forgive me?" I asked, even though I knew I didn't deserve it.

"Oh, Sera." His chin lowered, and he spoke softly, "It is not my forgiveness you need, but you have it."

The breath I exhaled was ragged as I held on to him tightly. Slowly, I remembered that we weren't alone. Cheeks burning, I lifted my head.

Holland smiled and slid his hands to mine. He gently squeezed my fingers, and his stare lifted to where Ash stood, now only a foot behind me. "It is good to see you, too."

"Same," Ash replied with the level of enthusiasm Reaver had shown when speaking of practicing his letters.

"Ash," I hissed.

Holland chuckled, unbothered. "It's okay." With one last squeeze, he released my hands. "He has a right to be wary of my presence." Holland's swirling, odd but beautiful gaze moved over the others, who all remained transfixed where they stood. "Hello."

"Hi." Saion drew out the word while a pale-faced Rhain raised a hand in acknowledgment.

Attes lifted his glass in greeting. "I don't believe we've met."

"We have not," Holland replied. "But that is a good thing, is it not?"

My brows snapped together as Attes snorted.

Ash snaked an arm around my waist, guiding me back so he stood a hairsbreadth behind me once more.

I rolled my eyes, caught between being charmed and annoyed by him clearly stepping into his fierce protective mode.

Holland turned his attention back to me, his gaze briefly dropping to Ash's arm. The smile widened again as he refocused on me. "How are you feeling?"

"Good. I mean, I feel stronger than I ever have." I stared up at him, still somewhat shocked to see him and unsure how to answer. The last time we'd seen each other, well, it hadn't been the time to exchange pleasantries. "I'm still getting used to the whole foresight thing."

"It takes a while to grow accustomed to it, but you will soon truly be a know-it-all."

My laugh was shaky. "And here I thought I already was."

"So, I'm going to hazard a guess here and say you two know each other?" Attes stated.

I started to respond but stopped myself, unsure how much I could share.

"I've known Seraphena since she was a child." Holland clasped his hands behind his back. "I trained her."

"You…acted as her *viktor*, then." Attes studied Holland from over the rim of his glass. "Didn't know the Arae were allowed to get so hands-on."

"There is much we're able to do," Holland replied. "As you are well aware."

My gaze shot to Attes. The Primal had lowered his glass. Did he know what Holland truly was? Nektas hadn't said none of the other Primals knew, only that he remembered the Ancients more clearly than some of the oldest Primals.

"I wish I could linger, but doing so would likely draw the ire of the others." Holland cleared his throat, angling his body toward Ash and me. "You summoned a Fate?"

"That would be correct," Ash replied.

I shot him a sharp look of warning over my shoulder.

Ash ignored it. "We appreciate the fact that you knocked. The last one didn't."

"That would be Aydun you speak of," he replied. "He is not known for his decorum."

"I can't argue with that," I said. "We wanted to set up a meeting with Kolis."

Holland didn't even bat an eyelash. "When and where?"

"In the Bonelands," Ash said, naming the one place closest to Oak Ambler without being an inhabited place in the mortal realm. "And as soon as possible."

Holland nodded as he clasped his hands together. "And the reason," he said, catching my gaze, "you *want* to give for the meeting?"

I caught on to what he was asking. He wanted to know what we wanted Kolis to believe. He asked for the lie. "We would like to make a truce."

One of the stars in his eyes brightened. "Is that so?"

I nodded. "If he agrees to meet with us, I'm willing to give him what he wants in exchange for coming to an agreement."

Holland's head tilted. "And do you request a Fate to moderate such a meeting?"

"No," Ash answered.

"Without a Fate present, there is no guarantee of nonviolence."

"We know," I said. Without a Fate present, we also wouldn't be obligated to make any deals that we would be held accountable for, which was the main reason we didn't want a Fate there. We had no plans to offer shit to Kolis. Besides, even if we were truly attempting to enter into a new *eirini*, I already knew Kolis would no longer just accept Sotoria's soul. He wanted our suffering. But I also knew he would do and risk anything to get his hands on Sotoria again. So, we were playing this game as dirty as he had because he would never see her again.

The way Holland's eyes glimmered told me he either suspected what we were up to or had already seen it all in one of those many threads. "That is all?"

I nodded.

"I will go to him immediately," he said. "I can't say how long it will take before he agrees."

"He'll agree," I stated.

Holland's gaze lowered with a sigh. "If you are speaking of Sotoria's soul, he will."

From the settee, Attes's lip curled. I stepped out of Ash's hold before the other Primal could say something that would add to his troubles. "I know you can't stay, but I…I wish you could."

That softness returned to Holland's features. "As do I."

"Before you leave," Ash said, "I do have a question about Aydun. He knew we had entered an *eirini* before but made no mention of that. Seems odd that he wouldn't have reminded Sera, especially considering she just rose as the Primal of Life."

Holland grimaced. "I wish I could say for certain why Aydun failed to mention it." Holland's gaze searched mine. "But he should have. I am sorry he didn't."

"It's not your fault." Something crossed my mind. He had mentioned inciting the ire of the other Ancients. My stomach pitched. "Will you get in trouble for answering the summons considering our history?"

The colors slowed in his eyes. "Some of the others were not pleased with my intention to do so, but if I were in the wrong, the realms would have prevented me from doing so. The others know this."

"I am never going to get used to the idea of the essence as some sort of living entity capable of critical thinking," I admitted.

"Interesting," Ash remarked, kicking off tiny warning bells. "If the others are aware of this, why would they still be unhappy with you answering the summons? It can't just be your history with Sera."

"That is…a complicated question." For the first time since I'd learned of Holland's true identity, he looked uncertain how to answer as he stared at Ash. "One that may have crossed your mind."

I turned to Ash, frowning. "What has crossed your mind?"

He folded his arms over his chest and eyed the Fate. "We have both questioned the methods of how the Fates right the balance."

"We have."

"As have I," Attes remarked. "If anyone cares to know."

"Well, I'm not sure I believe that it is always the essence itself intervening," Ash continued. "And I'm sure that is something you've thought."

I had, and it immediately made me think of that damn prophecy and what Keella had shared.

Ash smiled tightly. "We also know the only way Kolis ever had knowledge of The Star was because a Fate told him about it. Of course, it could have been done as it was suggested."

Delfai had mentioned that Kolis might have used someone the Fate loved to manipulate them into giving him what he wanted. That would be on par with Kolis's past behavior, but Ash was right. How the Fates—the *Ancients*—intervened often made no sense. Tension crept into my muscles. There were times when actions to right the balance almost seemed to be in Kolis's favor, creating another situation that would tip the scales again. Until recently, we didn't know why they would do that. Now, we knew they wanted to wake the Ancients—clearly, not all of them wanted that, but why would *any* of them want to do that? That was what Ash was getting at by his question to Holland.

I met the Ancient's stare. "We know why some of the Fates have been intervening. They want the Ancients to wake up."

As Saion let out a low whistle, Rhain looked like he might fall over.

"That is a question I cannot answer." Sighing heavily, Holland sat on the edge of the settee. "And not because I know the answer and cannot say, but because I don't."

"It wasn't a question," Ash pointed out.

Holland looked up. "You're right."

When that was all he said, I drew a hand over my face and briefly squeezed my eyes shut. I knew there were things Holland couldn't say, and I really had no idea how Penellaphe dealt with the vague non-answers. "So, theoretically, let's say someone out there wants the Ancients to wake. Why? Because they want to see the realms destroyed?"

"I don't think anyone wants complete and utter destruction—"

"Even if the destruction isn't complete, it will be damn near close to that," I cut in. I mean, look at what I did as a baby Primal.

"I know, but theoretically, some could view the Awakening as inevitable and seek to control it," he said, then shrugged. "Some could believe it is the only way to save the realms."

"Why would anyone theoretically think that?" Ash demanded.

"Perhaps those who have been in a deep sleep have lost some of their bitterness. It's hard to tell if that would be the case, but it's not impossible." Holland rested his hands on his knees. "And if not, theoretically, there could be a few who would see the Awakening as a restart."

"You mean a purge," Ash corrected.

"One where the numbers of mortals and even the gods are greatly reduced and far more manageable to be controlled," Holland finished.

"By the Ancients themselves," Ash surmised. "So, it's possible that some of the Fates want to return to the way it first was."

What Ash didn't know was that the Fates *were* the Ancients, which made his theory all the more plausible.

"Theoretically speaking, yes," Holland corrected, and I rolled my eyes. "And the way it first was, wasn't bad. Your draken can tell you that."

"Yeah, but look how it ended," Attes reminded him.

"I can't even fathom how any of the Fates would want this—would want to take this risk," I began.

"A theoretical risk," Holland tacked on.

I ignored that. "It's…" My eyes shot to Holland's. "It's Kolis, isn't it? All he has done, has caused. That is what they want to restart."

"Kolis's actions have cost the realms much," Holland stated quietly. "And it would take twice as long to undo what he has done."

"How would the Ancients' Awakening cost the realms less?" Rhain demanded. "They're beings of absolute power."

"And absolute power corrupts," I tacked on. "Just as it did before."

Holland nodded. "But those who do not seek power remain uncorrupted by it."

Ash huffed. "It's really that simple?"

"Yes." Holland looked at him. "Even though Primals are not absolute, the power you wield is enough to taint and infect. You both know that, but I do not fear that kind of power ever corrupting Sera."

I stiffened. "You know that's not true. It has."

Ash looked at me sharply, but Holland spoke before he could. "What you did in Lasania was not due to any corruption of power. It was pain, pure and simple. I do not fear corruption from you because you do not want power. You never have."

I shifted from one foot to the other. "That's true. It doesn't mean I won't be a…a *more* responsible Primal of Life," I quickly added as I glanced at Attes and the others. "But I am better suited to be in battles than I am to decide them."

"It's not a question of you being better suited," Holland said. "It's only what you have experience in. That will change." He paused. "But you will never hunger for power. Even though those who came before you ruled, none hungered for it. It is not in your bloodline."

Tiny bumps erupted over my skin as I held Holland's stare. My bloodline. It started with the Silver Knight. "Is my…bloodline special?"

"Your bloodline was chosen."

I knew that from what Keella had shared, but it made me think of *future* bloodlines. Our children. Their children.

Suddenly cold, I shook those thoughts from my head. "What do you think, Holland? Would you theoretically risk waking the Ancients to fix everything Kolis has wrought upon the realms?"

Holland leaned back, running his hands over the thighs of his loose white pants. "I think you know the answer to that, Sera."

I did.

Or at least I hoped I did and that he believed it was too much of a risk, but I didn't tell him about our plan for Sotoria. I also hadn't told him I was pregnant. Of course, he could already be very aware of that, but a tiny part of me doubted I understood what Holland truly wanted. Because he, too, had intervened in ways.

"I know talk of the Ancients is concerning," Holland began.

Ash laughed harshly. "Yes. It's *concerning*."

"But it is not your problem. Not yet," he said.

My frown deepened. "That's real reassuring."

"Kolis is your problem. Left unchecked, he will continue to shift the balance. Then, what some of the Fates may or may not want won't matter."

"Yeah, but if any of them are actively working against us, it is our problem," Ash argued.

"Currently, there is only so much they can do." Holland's gaze moved between the two of us. "Like me, they must walk a fine line of interference because the essence has and will react on its own."

I thought about Aydun. He had failed to mention the *eirini*, but he had also seemed to push me toward preventing war. "And what exactly happens if a Fate crosses that line, and the essence decides to react?"

Holland's eyes met mine. "It would use the eather inside us to destroy us, and yes, that has happened before."

My heart plummeted, along with any idea of asking Holland if he knew how to keep Kolis weakened and entombed for any real length of time.

Fear rose. "I know you say you walk a fine line when it comes to interfering, but I don't want you anywhere near that line." My heart kicked up. "You shouldn't even be here."

"I'm fine. As I said, the realms would've let me know if I was crossing a line." His smile caused the stars in his eyes to brighten. "But I shouldn't linger much longer."

Another wave of disappointment rose, and I couldn't stop myself from asking, "We won't ever be able to spend time together, will we? Like share a meal or just catch up?"

Holland's smile dimmed, as did the brightness of the silver bursts in his eyes. He shook his head.

I inhaled sharply, closing my eyes. Sorrow swelled in my chest, the weight heavy and aching. When I exhaled, I felt Ash's arm come around my waist again. "I get it. I do," I said as Ash pulled me close to his side. I opened my eyes. "It's just not fair."

"It does feel that way," Holland said quietly. "But this unfairness ensures there can be fairness."

Taking another deep breath, I pushed the sadness aside. I had to, but it was hard.

"I should be on my way to speak with Kolis." Rising, he approached me and clasped my arms. "I *am* very proud of you, Sera. Truly." He looked at Ash, who had become my shadow as Holland let go. "And you. Your father is proud of you."

"Is?" I felt Ash stiffen behind me.

"You released Eythos's soul, allowing him to enter Arcadia, and Fates can travel into Arcadia," Holland explained as Attes sat straighter in his chair. "Eythos has returned to be at Mycella's side."

"Oh," I whispered, smacking a hand over my mouth as I twisted toward Ash.

The line of his shoulders went rigid. "How is that possible? Kolis destroyed her soul, ushering in her final death."

"He attempted to, and in a way, he succeeded," Holland shared. "But a Fate intervened."

"Oh, my gods," I whispered, pressing my other hand to Ash's chest.

Ash's eyes glistened as he stared at the Fate, and gods, if any of his tears broke free, I would sob. Like ugly sob on the floor.

"I don't understand," Ash said hoarsely. He folded his hand over mine.

"Neither do I." Attes sounded as shaken as Ash.

"It is rare for a Fate to intervene in such a way, but your father was well-liked by many of them. Your mother even more." Holland smiled, but there was a hint of sadness to it. "Perhaps one day I will be able to tell you more about how it was made possible."

As I felt Ash's heart pound against my palm, I thought I knew what such an act had brought upon the unknown Fate.

Their own destruction.

The hem of the velvety robe swished around my slippered feet as I paced the bedroom. Holland hadn't returned by late evening, and I kept telling myself that I didn't need to be worried about that. Kolis was the type to purposely delay agreeing to meet with us just to convince himself he had the upper hand. I was nervous about how things would go down, but it wasn't the only thing that eventually drove me from the bedchamber.

Ash had left after dinner to check in with Theon. I'd felt him return a bit ago, but he hadn't come back to our rooms.

I was worried about him.

Learning that your mother's soul wasn't completely destroyed was good news—happy news—but it was also a lot to take in. To process. And he'd been quiet ever since Holland left.

I willed my heart to slow as I went down the staircase. It had been pounding on and off all evening, and I didn't think that was good for the babes.

As I neared the second floor, I decided to check in on Lailah really quick. Aios had awakened this afternoon and immediately wanted to go to Kithreia to inspect its current state, but it wasn't safe for her to do so yet. Phanos's ships had moved toward Dalos, but that was still too close, and our forces wouldn't have arrived yet. Instead, she had left for Sirta, and despite knowing that Bele would keep her safe while she was in a vulnerable state, I hadn't wanted her to go. Bele's Court was also at risk if Phanos went after *her*.

Our armies were rapidly thinning as we attempted to protect the Courts. Which meant we would have a battle on our hands if Kolis brought Phanos's armies to the Bonelands, along with those who'd fled to Dalos—which he most likely would. We could lose more people.

No wonder my heart kept racing.

Exhaling roughly, I walked the second-floor hall, picking up on Attes's presence. I stopped for a moment and then forged on. Quietly, I cracked open the door.

Lailah rested on the bed, her mass of tight braids lying on a chest that rose and fell steadily. My gaze shifted to the Primal sitting at her side.

Attes sat with his feet resting on the edge of the bed, slumped a little in the armchair, sandy-brown waves tumbling over his forehead and cheeks. He looked asleep. I started to close the door.

"You're not going to say hello?" Attes said without looking up, the tone of his voice flatter than it had been when I saw him earlier.

I stopped. "I thought you were sleeping."

"Nah." Attes lifted his head then. His scar stood out starkly against his paler-than-normal skin. "I'm just meditating. Never tried it before. Thought now was as good a time as ever."

I arched a brow. "How's that working out for you?"

"Not particularly well." One side of his lips curved up. There was no hint of a dimple. The grin was empty. "The whiskey I tried to take from your husband's office would've probably helped, but instead, I was lectured by a Primal significantly younger than me that the last thing I needed was to drink myself into a stupor."

I probably wouldn't have stopped Attes, but then again, I had a history of not making the greatest life choices. "Have you slept at all?"

He shifted in the chair, draping an arm over the back. "Yeah."

I had a feeling he was lying. "Have you eaten? Fed?"

A soft laugh rumbled from him. "I'm fine, Sera."

"No, you're not," I said, and his gaze finally met mine. "I don't expect you to be. No one would."

He stared at me for a long moment. "You sound like Nyktos."

"If he said something like that, he was speaking the truth." I leaned against the doorframe. "I'm sorry, Attes."

Thick lashes lowered. "So am I."

Neither of us said anything for several moments. We both just watched Lailah, which I doubted she would be too happy to discover if she woke up. It was Attes who ended the silence.

"It's not like I didn't know what he had become." There was a roughness to his voice now, and as much as hearing that made my chest ache, it was better than the flatness. "Or that I held on to any hope that he could be saved. I accepted he couldn't. Knew the Kyn I grew up with and loved was long gone. But you know what I saw in the seconds before I…before I ended him?"

"What?" I whispered.

"I saw the Kyn who sat beside me after my children were killed. Who was there for me when I felt like my world had been destroyed." His head tipped back, and his gaze went to the ceiling. "That's the Kyn I keep seeing."

"Maybe…maybe that's the Kyn you should remember and mourn," I said.

"But is that right? Considering everything he's done?"

"He was still your brother, and you still had good times with him." I lifted a shoulder, searching for something that felt like the right thing to say. "How he turned out doesn't erase who he once was."

Now, it was Attes who raised a brow as he looked at me. "You really believe the shit you're saying?"

"Well, not for me. I only knew him as the asshole he was," I admitted, and a wry grin tugged at his lips. "But regarding you and what you know? Yeah, I believe it."

Attes seemed to consider that, then nodded. "I guess I should be thankful for his attack. Because of him, we now have enough Ancient bones."

Ash, Nektas, Aurelia, and apparently Attes, had raided Kyn's palace last night with success. "We do."

"I'm guessing your Fate hasn't returned yet?"

"No." I straightened, feeling the ball of anxiety growing.

"Phanos will try to talk Kolis out of it. So will Varus," Attes said, referencing the once-entombed god I had yet to see. A muscle ticked in his jaw. "But Kolis won't listen to them. He will agree. Sotoria is his weakness. He'll risk anything while ignoring common sense and every red flag to get her."

"That's what we're counting on." I thought of something as my gaze moved from him to Lailah. "If Sotoria chooses to be reborn, will you still go into stasis?"

"Yes," he said without hesitation. "I have to, Sera. If I don't, I wouldn't be in a good headspace to even be around her. If she retains her memories, I wouldn't be the Attes she remembers. And that's..." He sighed heavily. "That's the last thing she'd need. And if she chooses to be reborn, I want her life to be happy. To be good. She deserves that."

"But you love her," I whispered.

Attes nodded. "And that is why I will be in stasis."

Heart twisting, I drew in a breath that stung. To give up the possibility of being with someone just to make sure there was no chance you would disappoint or cause them harm? And he would be giving up that opportunity. I doubted a mortal's lifespan was enough time in stasis for it to be of any real help. That was true love.

My gaze shifted back to the sleeping Primal goddess. "Do you love Lailah?"

Attes was quiet for so long, I didn't think he'd answer. When he did, he did so with a question. "Do you think it's possible to love two people at the same time?"

I thought about it. "I think it depends on the person. Not everyone would be able to, but some could. And probably do."

His gaze flickered to mine before returning to Lailah. "I agree with that."

That wasn't an answer.

But it also was.

Saying goodnight, I closed the door. As I started down the hall, I wished I could've said something to help Attes with his grief, but I knew there really wasn't anything I *could* say that would heal those deep wounds. They were like mine. Only time would mend them, I supposed. At least, I hoped.

My heart was even heavier, those emotions mixing with the agitation as my pace quickened in my search for Ash, my slippers whispering over the stone. I could've just waited for him to return to our chambers. Or, at the very least, put on something other than a robe since I wore nothing but a thin nightgown underneath. But I wanted to make sure he was okay, and, well, I was feeling rather…needy.

I hoped he was alone. I wanted some time with him before we barreled forward with our plans. A few moments where I could be Sera and not a Queen. Or the Primal of Life. Or even a fighter. Where we weren't on the verge of coming face-to-face with Kolis. I wanted time where I didn't have to be strong.

Luckily, the foyer was empty. I let my instincts guide me past the hall leading to his office and to the guarded doors of the throne room. What was he doing in there? The guards bowed as they opened the door for me.

"Thank you," I said, stepping into the dimly lit space.

Only a few of the candles on the walls burned, and it was too overcast for much starlight to come in through the open ceiling, but I immediately saw Ash. He stood on the dais near the thrones. A flutter erupted in my chest, easing the heaviness there as his gaze locked with mine.

"What are you doing in here?" I asked, starting toward him.

"Thinking," he said, crossing his arms. "Has Lailah awakened yet?"

"No." I passed the empty benches. "But I imagine she will soon."

His gaze tracked my approach with a predatory glint that brought a flush to my skin.

"I saw Attes," I told him. "Since he wasn't allowed to have whiskey, he's with her."

Ash snorted. "If he had the whiskey, the only difference would be that he'd be drunk off his ass while in her chambers."

I climbed the steps. "Probably."

"It will do him some good," he said after a moment. "Being near her, that is."

I raised a brow, thinking that was the first time he didn't have something caustic to say about Attes's interest in Lailah. "Hopefully Theon feels the same."

A half-grin pulled at his lips. "I think he will, just this once."

"So, what were you thinking about?" I asked as he opened his arms to me. I stepped into his embrace, resting my hands on his dark-gray tunic. The moment one of his arms came around me, the racing of my heart slowed, and that anxious knot of energy loosened. The effect he had on me was nothing short of magical.

He buried his hand in the hair above my braid. "Our children."

My brows flew up. I had thought he'd say something about his mother. "I wasn't expecting that answer."

Another grin appeared, but this one was almost…*shy*. "I wasn't really expecting to be thinking about that myself. It didn't start off that way. When I wandered in here, I was thinking about my mother and how she is now with my father. I still can't believe it."

"It's hard to believe," I said, rubbing his chest.

"I didn't know the Fates could do something like that." He gave a short laugh. "Obviously, I forgot how powerful they are."

If he only knew…

"Learning about your mom is a lot to process," I told him.

"It is," he said. "Don't get me wrong. I'm so godsdamn relieved. It's just that I spent my entire life believing she was really gone, and that I wouldn't even get to see her when I finally entered Arcadia. It's like having to rework my brain. It will take a while."

His gaze moved around the empty space. "And while I was in here, I started to think about how I never got to witness both of them in here. See them sit on the thrones. I only saw my father."

I quieted, waiting for him to continue.

"When I was old enough, I was allowed to watch any meetings he had with other gods or people who came from Lethe," he said after a couple of moments. "As we waited for those meetings to begin, I would crawl all over the benches. Run from one to the other. Crawl under them. Only the Fates know why. Ehthawn was younger then, too. Not as young as Reaver, but small enough that he could easily move through the room with me."

Gods, my heart squeezed as I pictured Ash as a little boy, playing with a draken. And it wasn't hard to imagine it because I had a feeling our sons would be the spitting image of him as a child.

Our sons?

Look at me, thinking as if I knew for sure they would be boys. But I kind of felt like I *did* know for sure. I grinned as I pressed my cheek to his chest.

"Anyway, I got to thinking about our children and how they will one day be doing the same thing. Maybe in this throne room or perhaps wherever we decide to stay when this is over," he said, and my breath caught. "Except there will be two of them, and Jadis and Reaver to chase after them. And…" His voice thickened with emotion, drawing my gaze to his. His eyes shone brightly. "And there will be us. We will be sitting in those thrones, watching them."

Oh, gods, I didn't know what to say to that. What he had been thinking about was so unexpected, so perfect, that emotion swelled fiercely.

"Ash," I whispered, my fingers curling into his stiff tunic.

He smiled, a small upward tilt of his lips. "I love what I feel from you right now." His hand swept down my back. "It is...*everything*."

"*You* are everything." I rose onto my tiptoes, shuddering as his cool breath fanned across my cheek.

The touch of his mouth against mine had the same reaction it always did. As our lips met, the realms condensed to just us. There was no one else. No other expectations or duties. No looming battles where one mistake could cause us to lose it all. It would always be like that, and that was a fact I would never be uncertain of.

One hand slipped under my braid to curl around the nape of my neck. He tilted my head, deepening the kiss. A crescendo of need quickly swelled between us as his other hand traced the curve of my spine, charting a path over the velvet of my robe. It ignited a fire as he pressed his hand against my lower back, drawing me closer and leaving no room between our bodies. I could feel him, hard and insistent against my belly, a pressure that sent a cascade of desire pooling at my core.

A certain type of madness urged me on. We were nowhere near anywhere private. Anyone could walk in on us. A draken could fly over and get an eyeful. But I was breathless with desire—with want—for him and only him.

I guided him backward until the backs of his legs met the throne. He sat without protest, looking up at me with heavy-lidded eyes and parted lips. Holding his gaze, I positioned myself atop him, straddling the man who was and would always be my entire world.

The coolness of the stone beneath my bare knees caused my breath to catch as our lips came together once more. It was as fierce as the hold he had on my heart and soul. He kissed me with a hunger that mirrored my own, sipping from my lips as his fingers made quick work of the buttons on my robe. The sides parted, and then, I felt his cold fingers through the thin silk of my nightgown. I moaned into his mouth, and before I could even take another breath, the bodice of the nightgown gave way beneath his touch, tugged down to bare me to his gaze. A shiver ran through me as the cooler air of the room met my heated flesh.

"Beautiful," he murmured roughly, cupping my breasts in his hands. He dragged a thumb over one rosy peek, groaning as the nipple puckered. "These are so fucking beautiful."

Ash lowered his head, taking the nipple into his mouth. His fangs scraped my skin, and the sensation was sharp, a wicked sting that spiraled throughout my entire body. His tongue swirled, drawing a gasp from my lips, the sound lost in the vastness of the throne room. He drew the sensitive flesh into his mouth, and my hips jerked, rubbing at the hard ridge of him.

With my heart racing, my hands moved to the flap of his breeches. I wasn't nearly as nimble as him, and what he was doing with his fingers as he took my other breast into his mouth didn't help. Still, I managed to free him.

His mouth left my breast, and his head fell back. My fingers brushed the cool hardness, tracing the line of his desire before I closed my hand around him.

His hips punched up, and his hands slipped beneath the robe and gown to close around mine. "I need in you," he rasped. "Now."

Dropping my forehead to his, I guided his cock with an urgency that bordered on desperation. The feeling of his cool tip against my heated dampness nearly undid both of us.

He pulled me down hard as he thrust up. The moment he entered me, I cried out, a riot of raw sensations pounding through me.

Neither of us moved for several seconds, our breaths coming in short, shallow pants. I felt him trembling, the same need building in me. I began to rock slowly, wanting to savor the small bite of pain as I stretched to accommodate every thick inch. The fullness was addictive.

Ash's lips danced across my collarbone, each kiss igniting trails of fire on my skin as his grip tightened even more on my hips, fingers digging in with a possessiveness that sent tingles racing all over my skin. We moved in sync on the throne, thrusting and grinding, our mouths coming together.

The throne room echoed with the sounds of our breaths mingling in the charged air. I rode him, clutching at his shoulder with one hand, the fingers of my other tugging on his silken strands. Every rise and fall of my hips drew me closer to the precipice. One of his hands slid to my ass, his fingers pressing into the softness there with an intensity that matched the mounting pressure within me. The other slipped free of the robe to find my braid. He gripped it hard, tugging my head back so he could see me.

Heat spiraled, coiling tighter, an invisible force pulling at the very core of my being. The striking lines of Ash's face were etched with concentration. His eyes were locked on mine, witnessing the moment my body tensed. And then, with his name a cry on my lips that filled the vastness of the chamber, pleasure shattered me. It was a starburst, radiating out from the place we were joined, sending shockwaves through every nerve ending.

I shuddered, waves of ecstasy rolling over me as his release swiftly followed. His hold on me became a vise, holding me still as he found his escape. Ash's head tipped back against the throne, a low groan reverberating off the cold stone walls, filling the room with the echoes of his pleasure.

As the last tremors of our passion ebbed, I collapsed against him. We remained entwined upon the throne as our breathing and hearts slowed.

"I don't think I will ever think of this throne the same way again," he said.

I laughed against his neck. "Me, neither."

His hand smoothed over the braid. "I assume all of that was a pretty good indicator that you liked what I was thinking about?"

"That would be a safe assumption."

Ash's chuckle brought a wide smile to my lips. I loved that sound.

Tugging on the braid, he guided me back so there was some space between our bodies. "Are you nervous about facing Kolis?"

"I'm surprised you haven't sensed my anxiety."

"You must be getting better at shielding," he said. "I guess that's a yes?"

I nodded, biting my lip. His cool fingers grazed my breasts.

One side of his lips curled up as he tugged the nightgown's bodice into place. "It's okay to be nervous."

"I know."

His gaze met mine when he pulled the two halves of the robe together. "And scared."

"I'm not scared. I mean, I'm not scared of seeing Kolis. I don't fear him anymore," I said, holding still as he buttoned the robe. "I fear losing people we care about. I…I fear failing."

"I wish I could promise that we won't lose anyone else, but I can't." Eather pierced his eyes. "I can promise we will not fail. We will trap and entomb that bastard. We will give Sotoria her choice. We will ensure that Iliseeum and the mortal realm are taken care of." Dipping his head, he pressed a kiss to my temple. "And we will have a near eternity of moments like this. You and me. Our children chasing each other around the throne room. We will get to watch them grow and find love. We will become grandparents, and then we will watch *them* grow." He cupped my cheek. "All the while, Kolis will be where we put him, and he will stay there."

I fought back tears. "That sounds…beautiful and perfect."

"It will be a beautiful and perfect reality, *liessa*."

But would it be a reality?

My heart skipped, but I shut those thoughts down and tipped forward, kissing Ash. We would make this our reality.

We *had* to.

Holland arrived as dawn painted a canvas of wispy pink and orange that blended into the blue expanse. He did not linger at all this time.

He took my hand before he left but didn't say anything; just held my gaze silently. I knew him well enough to recognize that the crease between his brows was one of concern, and his faint smile before it disappeared was full of conviction.

He was worried.

But he also had faith in me—in Ash and the others. And I chose to keep reminding everybody of that as we gathered in the war room.

The Ancient had faith in us, and that had to mean something.

Kolis had agreed to meet us in the Bonelands tomorrow when the sun was at its peak over the ruins of a Sun Temple. While I had no idea which one he spoke of, having only seen the bare bones of one during my brief time in the Shadowlands, Ash knew exactly which one.

"Kolis will not honor his word to come alone," Ash stated. "We know he will bring his forces."

"Good thing we don't plan to honor that either," Bele said from where she sat cross-legged at the other end of the table.

Ash's smile was frigid. "Sera and I will be near the Temple but not in it. That thing is barely standing, and I don't want either of us in it if it goes off the cliff."

"I support that statement," I said, earning a snort from Thierran, who sat by Penellaphe, the cowl of his hood up. "Where is this Temple, by the way?" I asked.

"It's by the southern cove." Standing, Theon pointed at a map of the Bonelands he'd drawn. It was spread across the table and pinned down by a dagger. "The Temple Kolis is talking about is here." He dragged his finger up. "It sits on the bluffs overlooking the shore and faces the bay, but you will not have a clear view of the water from there with all the trees that have grown along the cliffs. The bay is the safest and quickest way to make landfall."

Attes's eyes narrowed on the map. "That shoreline is still rocky outside the bay, and the waters are rough."

"That won't stop the ceeren from coming ashore," Saion stated. "They'll have no problems traveling in that water. And once it gets shallow enough, they'll shift forms."

"And will come with weapons," Rhahar added, glancing at Attes and Kars. "Everyone needs to remember they have a nasty bite."

My head jerked up in surprise.

"The ceeren's teeth are sharp as daggers and can take out chunks of flesh, scaled or not," Saion explained, catching my stare before the *vadentia* could answer. "And I do mean *all* their teeth. They can also partially shift. So, even in their mortal forms, you'll want to keep all body parts away from their mouths."

My lip curled. I didn't remember seeing anything like that when I was with them.

"Kolis has to know we have been in the Bonelands, but I want you to move our ships farther out either way, where the Primal mist will cloak them," Ash said to Theon, eyeing the map with a thoughtful expression. "Aren't there caves along that shore?"

"There are," Theon answered. "And beneath the Temple, too."

"Perfect," Ash mused. He, Attes, and the twins had been doing most of the strategizing. I was doing a lot of listening. This wasn't my wheelhouse, and I wasn't familiar with the landscape. "Kolis will expect us to have backup, but I want our numbers hidden as much as possible."

"He'll either attack before he arrives or…" Attes said. "He may hold off if he thinks attacking will jeopardize him getting The Star." His lashes lifted. "But the moment he realizes you don't have it, he will come hard."

My stomach dipped, but I wasn't worried about that nugget of fear or embarrassed by it. Anyone with a head on their shoulders would feel that upon hearing that the true Primal of Death would go all out. And fear wasn't necessarily bad as long as one harnessed it wisely.

"We need an archery regiment in those caves." Ash brushed a shorter strand of his hair back from his face. "I want them there, knowing the moment the ceeren shift, they should let loose with the arrows, whether Kolis has arrived, attacked, or not."

"Phanos's ships will be carrying gods who don't have fins," Lailah pointed out. She had awakened sometime in the middle of the night, looking the same except for the brand-new Primal eyes. "That's why he'll come into the bay."

Attes glanced at Ash. A moment passed, and Ash nodded for him to go ahead. "We want to stop as many of his forces from getting on land as possible." His gaze found Nektas. "You'll be staying close to your Queen."

I rolled my eyes.

"And King," he continued. "But we want a quadrant of draken on those cliffs."

"Can do." Nektas drew his thumb over his chin. "When the ships are sighted, you want them lit up?"

"Yes," Ash answered without hesitation.

I shifted in my seat, uneasy with the knowledge that those ships would be packed like sardines and also that I wasn't all that uncomfortable with the plan. Considering what I was, I kind of felt like I should be.

Oh, well.

I removed my hand from my stomach and propped my elbows on the table. "I doubt Kolis will put all his forces on those ships or in any one area."

"It would be really nice of him if he did." Lailah sat back, twisting a braid between her fingers.

Attes smirked. "The Bonelands' eastern mountains border Dalos," he said, referencing the mountains that'd once been the prisons. "And I know damn well that…Kyn would've put regiments there." He cleared his throat. "We've had eyes on the Bonelands' side, but there was no way to monitor movement into the mountains without being seen."

"So, you think Kolis has regiments there already?" I asked.

"It's what I would've instructed him to do." He picked up his glass. "So, Kyn would have told him the same if discussions of the Bonelands arose."

"They did while I was there," I said. "With that in mind, I think it's safe to assume he may have shared strategy plans with him."

Attes took a drink. "Kyn would've moved them through the mountains and into the Bonelands when the decision was made to meet there. And he would've done so on foot. It will be faster than attempting it on horseback."

My gaze shot to Ash's. "That means Kolis can be doing that right now."

"We have forces closer," Ash reminded me. "Theon has been stationed not too far from there."

"Below the Temple is an open area, bordered by the cliffs on one side and the forest on the other." Theon circled his finger over an area of the map near the Temple. "I would suggest," he said with a heavy sigh, "creating a first line of defense by moving the forces already there to the eastern forest. They can be there in an hour. It's dense and dark. Enough that our soldiers would be hidden. A second line could be in the caves. The third line, near you and Sera. The trees are thickest there, so the strongest should be up there."

Ash's jaw tightened. "And because of how dense the eastern woods are, Kolis's regiments will also be well hidden as they move westward. Those in that first line will get hit the hardest and suffer the most casualties."

Theon inhaled deeply. "I know, but they are the closest, and we need to secure that open field to limit access to the Temple."

Ash didn't like it. Neither did I. But Theon was right. "Thierran, you'll be up with us, nice and hidden. You need to stay out of all the fighting until

Sera summons you, or you don't have a choice."

"That's not much fun," the God of Dreams remarked.

"Bele, you will be up with us." Ash's gaze flicked to Attes. "So will you."

"I need to be on the second line," Attes argued. "That's where the fighting will be the heaviest. If our line breaks, the Temple will be overrun."

"Good point." Ash let out an aggravated breath.

"I'll take Kars and you two." Attes nodded at the cousins. "Rhain should be with you all."

My gaze darted from Kars to Rhahar and Saion. While the latter had been Ascended, none of them were Primals. They were gods, which meant they could be killed with shadowstone and eather. Thinking that made my heart race, even though none of them looked nervous. Kars was actually smiling.

"I don't think Saion should be on the second line," I said. "Or in the Bonelands."

Saion stiffened. "What do you mean?"

"We need Phanos taken out, and when that happens, you will finish your Ascension," I reminded him—and everyone. "You'll be vulnerable in those moments, and we may be unable to get you out."

"Fuck," he muttered, rubbing his brow. "I didn't even think of that."

"Good call." Ash smiled at me, and I felt like clapping myself on the back. Somehow, I managed to refrain from doing so. "The Shadowlands still need to be guarded in case Kolis attacks here to draw our attention. You will be needed here."

Saion wasn't happy, but he nodded.

"I am ready," Penellaphe said, drawing our attention. "I know I haven't been Ascended for long, but I am ready to join the fight."

"As am I," Ione joined in. "I have trained as a guard and can wield a sword."

"Penellaphe," Ash began.

"I know I may not appear to have had any training." Penellaphe's chin lifted, sending long, honey-hued strands cascading over her back. "But I, too, once trained as a guard."

"It has nothing to do with that," I said. "Eventually, you will have to use the eather despite your training, which will impact the mortal realm."

"And it will already be severe with just Sera and Kolis on the field," Ash said. "Add in Attes? Bele and me? Phanos? We must do whatever we can to prevent a full-scale war and lessen the impact on the mortal realm."

Penellaphe relented first, then Ione reluctantly submitted.

"I assume this part of the conversation doesn't apply to me." Lailah looked over the table between Ash and me.

"You just woke up," Rhain said. "You can't be out there."

Lailah's brows shot up. "You cannot be serious."

"He is," Theon stated, crossing his arms. "Look, Aios isn't arguing—"

"That's because Aios isn't a trained warrior!" Lailah's head shot toward the redheaded Primal goddess. "No offense."

"None taken." Aios lifted a hand. "But even if I were, I understand why I cannot be on the field."

Theon smirked at his sister.

Lailah's eyes narrowed. "I am one of the most trained guards in all of Iliseeum—without using eather."

"No one is denying that," Attes said. "But you are vulnerable."

"That's bullshit." Her nostrils flared.

"I would target you in battle," I said. "If I knew someone on Kolis's side had *just* Ascended into Primalhood, I would go after them. Not only because they would be vulnerable but because it would make others vulnerable. We would seek to protect you. That's why Saion cannot be on the battlefield."

Lailah's mouth opened, but after a moment, it closed.

"I know it's hard not to be out there when your brother and those you care about are." I held her gaze. "Just as it is hard for Aios, Ione, and Penellaphe. And if you hadn't just Ascended, we would have you out there instead of Bele."

Bele scowled. "Rude."

"However, as Nyktos said, we need to do everything we can to lessen the impact on the mortal realm," I told her. "That is why we seized the other Courts. Not just to gain more numbers but also to prevent the Primals from fighting and adding to the harm that we—that *I*—have already caused."

I could feel Ash's gaze on me as I watched Lailah. Seconds ticked by, and then she finally exhaled heavily and nodded.

The meeting continued. Further plans were established. Draken blood had been drawn and sealed in the basalt vials. The bone chains were already deep underground in Oak Ambler, and once we were done with our discussions, I spent the better part of the day with Reaver and Jadis, soaking in as much time as I could with them while practicing finding Nektas's imprint and communicating with him.

I was sure after about fifteen minutes he wanted to throw me out a window.

Then we all had dinner together, a fine current of unease humming under each laugh and smile. Ash and I made love, and each kiss, every sigh carried with it the hum of dread fueled by the knowledge that if we failed tomorrow, we would lose…

Our children.

Each other.

Our future.

Those we cared for.

Everything.

Ash and I stood in silence among the thick, gnarled roots of the sweeping trees that jutted out from the sides of the rocky bluffs overlooking the coast of the sun-speckled Bonelands. The absence of birds singing or even the rustle of the smallest critters moving through the heavy foliage left only the sound of the salty breeze rattling the leaves.

My gaze swept over the land below surrounded by the bluffs and the dense forests bordering the fields. The wind whispered over the rocky hills and flowed through the valley, but the tall, thin, purple-and-red wildflowers that bloomed from the soil that cradled the bones of gods and mortals were still. So was the knee-high grass. It was almost as if the wind didn't dare disturb the final resting place of the long-forgotten warriors that had fallen like leaves in an unforgiving autumn during the battle with the Ancients.

Under the sword strapped to my back, a chill tiptoed down my spine. "I don't remember this place being so…"

Ash's hand tightened around mine, and he tore his gaze from the horizon. "What?"

"Creepy," I murmured.

"It only feels that way because you know what took place here," he said, a strand of hair that had escaped the knot at his nape blowing across his cheek.

"That and all the dead bodies in the ground," I pointed out. "How many do you think are buried here?"

"Tens of thousands."

Gods.

I swallowed. "Maybe I shouldn't have asked that."

Ash's chuckle tugged at my lips as I eyed the forest. To the untrained or unsuspecting eye, it appeared as if Ash and I stood alone on the bluffs.

That was not the case.

The trees were so thick that only the thinnest rays of sunlight penetrated the depths, but every so often, I caught a brief reflection bouncing off our regiment's sharpened shadowstone swords where they waited to the east. Just as we'd discussed, our ships lay shrouded in the heavy mists bordering the Skotos Mountains. Tucked within the embrace of the jagged cliffs and within the caves beneath us, Attes stood with the bulk of our armies, their discipline ensuring no clank of armor nor murmur betrayed them. Seven of our draken were nestled among the crags of the cliffs, their scales blurring the line between rock and beast. Bele and Rhain, along with Thierran and a smaller regiment, were hidden in the trees along the bluff we stood upon.

I took a deep breath and held it for the count of five as I turned my attention to the ancient, sprawling Temple on the bluff to our right. The thing was massive, the length the same as the House of Haides.

"It was one of the first Temples erected," Ash said, following my gaze. "Where Ancients once greeted mortals."

The Temple must have been a sight to behold. It was impressive even now, with its fractured walls and half-crumbling pillars bearing the scars of war and time. The defiant roof remained, as well as several halls and some inner walls of chambers.

Exhaling for the count of five, I looked past the ruins. "I hate waiting."

"Never would've guessed that," Ash remarked, his gaze piercing the horizon.

Time stretched thin and taut as we waited for the serpent to lift his head from his lair. I wasn't sure how long we'd been here, but I knew it had to be past the time when Kolis agreed to meet.

Eather pulsed. "What if I was wrong?" I whispered in a voice barely louder than the rattle of leaves.

"You're not." Ash's thumb swept over my marriage imprint. "You know that. He's just trying to assert control." His silvery gaze met mine. "But he has no control. Not over us. Not over what will happen."

I nodded, forcing myself to inhale again. "I know. I'm sorry. I'm just—"

"You have nothing to apologize for," he interrupted, squeezing my hand as he lowered his head to kiss me. "Being anxious is normal."

My lips tingled when he returned his attention to the sea. I found myself staring at the ruins once more. The Temple was on the brink of collapse, sustained only by deeply rooted desperation and deception but very close to completely collapsing under one strong wind. It sort of mirrored Kolis's reign, didn't it? And Ash and me? We were the storm that would topple the false King's dominion.

Tension charged the atmosphere as I cast my gaze to the horizon, where the seas disappeared into the sky.

"There they are," murmured Ash.

My eyes narrowed as white-tipped waves formed and were replaced by quick bursts of color—vivid blues, glittering pinks, and intense greens. Line after line formed, their fins silently slicing through the water. They were fast, giving only seconds-long glimpses of their muscular arms and sleek bodies undulating in the water as sunlight filtered through the waves and glinted off shadowstone swords secured firmly to their backs. As they drew closer, I could make out cloth the color of the sea, partially covering their chests and tails.

Well, at least our forces would not have to fight against nude regiments. That seemed like it would be rather distracting.

A sudden pulse of thought, urgent and clear, reached me. *Meyaah Liessa*, Nektas called. *We have spotted Phanos's fleet.*

My free hand fisted. "Phanos's ships have been seen."

Ash's lip peeled back in a quiet snarl as he released my hand and stepped forward. Anger and bitter disappointment rose, stoking the eather. The corners of my vision turned white as I stepped up on the rock beside Ash.

I'd known that Kolis would not honor his word and come alone. We hadn't. And I'd also known Phanos would show. None of that was surprising. Still, I couldn't get past the fact that he stood with Kolis. That his fear of the Primal god was that great. Or maybe it wasn't fear. Perhaps Saion and Rhahar were correct, and Phanos simply preferred that things not change. Static danced over my skin. It didn't matter either way.

Ash turned, placing his hand on my cheek. Where I stood on the rock, put us at eye level. "Phanos made his choice," he said, the timbre of his steady voice contrasting with the storm brewing within my very being. "And he will die today for it."

He would.

Concentrating, I followed Nektas's imprint. *The moment they near the bay, let me know.*

Will do.

Ash's fingers found mine once more. Our hands clasped, entwined like the roots of the ancient trees surrounding us. I looked at him. His gaze met mine. There was so much love and strength there that I felt the eather rippling inside me. But there was also a pinch of concern to the line of his mouth as his other hand clasped the back of my head.

"There are no more lines to be crossed, *liessa.* If you need to use the essence, do not hold back," he said, drawing his thumb over my pulse. "Unleash everything you have in you to protect yourself and our children. That will not make you the kind of monster you fear." His eyes searched mine. "It will only make you a mother defending our babes' lives, and that is all that matters. Understood?"

Drawing in a staggered breath, I nodded. "I will not hold back."

"And you will not let any of it leave a mark," he commanded, eyes lighting with eather.

"I won't," I swore.

"That's my girl."

Ash's lips crashed into mine. The kiss was deep and fierce, an urgent clash of tongues and fangs that sent a jolt of raw energy coursing through him to me. It was a proclamation that became a promise as he spoke. "The next time we kiss, it will be over Kolis's body."

A savage smile spread across my lips. "I can't wait."

Letting go of my neck, he held on to my hand until I jumped from the rock. Ash and I stood vigilant, like a pair of sentinels.

"The ceeren have slowed," Ash noted.

Every muscle in my body tensed. Time seemed to slow to an infinite crawl, and then I heard Nektas's voice once more. *Phanos's ships are nearing the bay*. There was a pause. *Ehthawn can see soldiers on the gangways. Some are beginning to lower boats.*

My hands fisted as I repeated the update to Ash.

"I know we want Kolis out in the open before striking, but we can't let those ships get close," Ash reminded me. "They get on shore, we'll be swamped."

Holding his gaze, I nodded. Concentrating on Nektas's imprint, I exhaled slowly. *Burn the ships coming toward the bay. All of them.*

There was silence once more as I turned my gaze back to the sky. Theon had been right. From where we stood, we couldn't see the bay or where Ehthawn and Crolee were hidden in the eastern mountain coastline. I didn't even see or hear them take flight, but I didn't take my eyes off the sky over the bay. The clouds were scattered and wispy but still provided some level of coverage. I held my breath and counted to five.

Suddenly, the two dark shapes belonging to Ehthawn and his cousin appeared above the clouds. In the next heartbeat, they broke free, diving toward the bay. Twin streams of flames erupted from them. I sucked in a short breath as the entire landscape suddenly lit up with the silvery glow of draken fire.

We couldn't see the ships, but we heard the exact moment the fire struck them. It was a boom of splintering wood and a rage of crackling embers that muffled shouts of pain. The feeling of death followed and kept coming, pressing down on my chest as Crolee and Ehthawn flew over each other, raining down fiery destruction as they continued farther out.

A piercing whistle came from the sea by the bluffs, jerking our attention from the silvery glow. The ceeren were moving once more, racing toward the shore.

"Fire!" Theon called from below.

The sharp whistle of arrows taking to the air quickly answered. I wanted to look away but forced myself to watch as the projectiles plummeted at neck-breaking speed. Lean bodies suddenly jerked while others swam past. Fins disappeared under water rapidly turning a reddish hue.

Another volley of arrows was released as the sea churned with raw, primal ferocity when the ceeren breached the surf. They didn't even miss a step. Saltwater coursed off their lithe forms, and they shed their iridescent scales in a shimmery wave of eather as they withdrew their swords. Within a few heartbeats, the shore was filled with ceeren. Our soldiers rushed from the caves. Swords met as arrows ripped through the sky above them, aiming for those in the water.

My nails dug into my palms when I saw one of ours fall. Eather pressed against my skin as I caught sight of Theon driving his blade through a ceeren's chest. I stepped toward the bluff's edge—

Clashing of swords from the eastern forests rang out, whipping our heads around. Branches rattled and snapped as bursts of eather lit up the shadows.

The echo of death was continuous now.

Our first line in the forest fell with shocking swiftness, causing my heart to stutter. Essence poured into my veins.

"*Breathe.*" Ash captured my hand. The feeling of his flesh against mine was grounding. "You need to conserve your energy for when Kolis gets here."

It took everything in me to hold back as Kolis's soldiers burst from the shadows of the forest hugging the field's edges, a sea of crimson sweeping across the land.

A crackling bolt of eather echoed from below, slamming into the center of the soldiers as Attes led the second line out onto the field in a clash of shadowstone and eather. It was hard to make sense of what I was seeing for a moment. The fighting was chaotic and brutal, drenching the tall grass in shimmering red.

A shout from behind us caused my heart to drop. I turned to the trees, fingers splaying wide as blades streaked against blades and armor echoed.

"They got behind us somehow." Ash cursed. "That division must've split off at some point, skirting the area to come up the bluffs."

I reached behind me and unsheathed my sword, catching quick, darting glimpses of crimson among the trees.

"Here they come," Ash said, unhooking the short swords from his chest.

The air thrummed with tension as the ground beneath us vibrated with pounding footfalls. I couldn't think of Bele, Rhain, or anyone flanking us. I had to focus.

Without warning, a figure leapt from one of the jagged cliffs above, his silhouette outlined against the sky for half a second. There was a glint of something dull and white.

He landed before me with a thud and rose as several more figures came over the cliff. My gaze locked with the one before me. His eyes were a pale, milky blue, framed by wings painted in crimson.

Revenants.

I had to give it to Kolis. Sending the ones who couldn't easily be killed to the Temple was clever.

Darting to the left, I dipped under the Revenant's swing and popped up. My sword cut through the air, cleaving the Revenant's neck. Blood spewed as he fell forward.

"Not the head." Ash kicked a Revenant back into the rocky wall. "We need their mouths or, at the very least, their throats intact."

"Whoops." My gaze went to the shard of bone the Rev had dropped. It was more like a spike. I saw then that the Revenant wore gloves.

Damn, we should've thought of that.

"They have Ancient bones," I shouted as Ash withdrew his sword from a Revenant's chest.

"I see that." Ash grunted, sending a Revenant over his shoulder.

I picked up the fallen bone, wincing as it burned my left hand. I didn't hold it for long. Without hesitation, I thrust it into the Revenant's back, hoping it would keep the fucker dead until it was removed—like it incapacitated a Primal.

Ash snapped the bone of a Revenant's arm. Its Ancient-bone spike hit the rocky soil as Ash grasped him by the throat. "Where is Kolis?"

The Revenant said nothing, and energy suddenly ramped up, causing the hairs on the back of my neck to rise.

"I will only ask you one more time." Ash lifted the Revenant into the air. "Where the fuck is Kolis?"

Slowly, I turned toward the eastern mountains. White, puffy clouds thickened, darkening into steely gray before turning a deep charcoal. They rolled over the peaks and the forests of the Bonelands, casting an ominous shadow. The temperature started to drop, and I knew Ash was only partially responsible for it.

My heart slowed. My breathing evened out.

Awareness throbbed in my chest as eather pulsed hotly through me.

Kolis was here.

A loud rumble echoed through the skies like heavy thunder, muffling the sharp clang of blades striking against one another.

"Finally," Ash muttered, dropping the Revenant.

Off the cliff.

Well, that was one way to get rid of a Revenant.

A dark shadow glided through the churning clouds over the field. My grip on the sword firmed. The pulse of death continued to flare from the battlefield below.

A large draken broke through the clouds, casting a foreboding shadow over the valley. I knew this draken, recognized the onyx scales that looked as if they'd been dipped in crimson.

Naberius.

I felt Nektas draw near as the draken's battle-worn wings swept out, slowing his descent over the cliffs above. His hind legs touched down on the ridge above us, shaking the land when his forelegs lowered. Talons dug into the rocky ledge, sending soil and rock tumbling. The draken, with his crown of immense horns arching back, turned his head toward us. Snarling, his lips peeled back over sword-sharp teeth. Nab snarled and lowered himself, revealing the—*wait*. My mouth dropped open. There was no way, but unless I was hallucinating, the figure in crimson astride his colossal back was Kolis.

I couldn't believe what I was seeing as I sheathed the short sword. Glancing at Ash, I saw that he didn't look surprised to see Kolis riding the draken.

A rush of powerful air flowed up the side of the bluffs behind us as Nektas made his presence known. His wings swept over Ash's and my heads as he landed beside us, shaking the ground and the Temple ruins. He prowled forward, wisps of smoke wafting from his nostrils when he lifted his head toward Nab, releasing a long, low rumble of warning.

Nab huffed, his eyes narrowing—his crimson eyes. I stiffened as I stared. The irises encircling the thin, vertical pupils were still red. That didn't make any sense. All the draken—

Then it struck me, filling me with another wave of disbelief. What Ash had said about Naberius being as old as Kolis now made sense. Nab wasn't a normal draken.

Naberius was the bastard's version of Ash's Odin.

The true Primal of Death and the true Primal of Life didn't ride upon horses. I should've known that, but the information had been buried with all the other stuff I'd learned during my Ascension.

My eyes widened again as another realization slammed into me. That meant that when I was ready, and that cuff magically appeared, it wouldn't be a horse I summoned—

I stopped those thoughts. Now was so not the time to focus on that.

"Nice of you to finally join us," Ash spoke, his voice calm but each word laced with hatred.

Kolis leaned back, letting go of one of the spikes protruding from Nab's back. His golden hair fell over his forehead, obscuring a part of the crimson wings he'd painted on his face. How cute. Now, he matched his minions. "You burned my ships."

I snapped out of my stupor, stepping forward. "We burned Phanos's ships."

Eyes streaked with crimson slid to me.

"Do not look at her," Ash growled, his flesh thinning and shadows appearing underneath.

Kolis smirked and continued staring down at me.

The shadows in Ash's flesh darkened as tendrils of eather spilled out of him.

He's about to lose it, Nektas warned me.

I reached over, fingers gliding through the icy eather gathering around him. Placing my hand on his arm, I squeezed gently.

Ash's eyes flashed pure silver. I feared he would launch himself at Kolis for a moment, but then the mist around him slowed.

"Charming," Kolis remarked. "That Fate claimed it would just be a meeting among us three."

"And you agreed to that. But, unsurprisingly, you did not honor it," I retorted, letting go of Ash's arm.

He gestured idly to the fighting on the field below. "It appears to me that neither did you."

"Of course, not," Ash replied. I saw Bele creeping closer through the trees to our right. "We knew you wouldn't be brave enough to show alone."

Nab snarled at Ash as Kolis leaned forward. The curve of the Primal's lips immediately set off warning bells.

"Do not say whatever it is you're thinking," I warned, eather crackling in my veins as the field below us lit up with streaks of eather. I felt Phanos's arrival.

I wanted to turn to the fighting but didn't dare take my eyes off Kolis.

His grin grew into a twisted smile, causing the wings painted on his face to lift. "Nephew," he purred, and my skin crawled. "I can still taste her blood in my mouth and feel her on my fingers."

There was no time to feel anything in response to his words. Not disgust or shame. Not even anger. Ash shifted instantly, his flesh hardening and turning as dark as the night. Eather swept out from his back in twin arcs. I grabbed his arm again.

"Don't." I held on. "Don't give him what he wants."

Frigid air poured across the bluffs, a thin layer of ice forming on the compacted soil and rock. The sound that came from Ash rumbled over the area, and I knew I needed to act quickly. Nektas drew his head back, his frills beginning to vibrate. We'd gotten what we needed. Kolis had been lured out. Now, we just needed him off Naberius and preferably not on a damn cliff above us before I summoned Thierran.

Ash was beginning to rise beside me. "You came here for The Star," I shouted, my grip on Ash's arm slipping. "Being disgusting won't help you get what you've always wanted."

Kolis didn't look away from Ash as he said, "I'm curious. What exactly made you change your mind, Seraphena?"

"I want this to end," I answered, hearing Ash's growl grow louder. "Too much blood has been spilled."

"You've spilled far more than I," he replied. "You've cost me Embris, Veses, and Kyn."

"I have, but that is nothing compared to what you have done in all your years or what we will both do if we continue fighting." I was relieved to see that Ash had regained some control over himself. He returned to the ground beside me, but his skin was still the hue of shadowstone. "I want to end this. Right now."

Kolis's chuckle turned my stomach. "What did I tell you, Seraphena? The last time we had the pleasure of being in each other's presence?"

"I don't know," I gritted out. "You talk a lot and yet speak only bullshit, so it's kind of hard to remember everything."

His upper lip curled, and blotches of crimson appeared on his skin. "You had your chance to accept the deal I offered. That is no longer on the table. You will give me The Star, and I will have both of you in chains."

Kolis lifted his hand. I heard them before I saw them, the rasp of their claws against rock.

They came from behind Kolis, as large as warhorses, their slick, obsidian skin as hard as shadowstone, and their heads featureless except for the thin slits above their gaping maws.

Dakkais.

Dozens of them.

Naberius rocked back, pushing off the cliff with a powerful sweep of his wings as the dakkais leaped into the air.

"Fuck," Ash growled, pulling his swords free once more.

There was no way to keep track of Kolis as the nightmarish beasts rushed us.

I unsheathed the sword as Nektas's head snapped forward. He caught one of the dakkais in his mouth. Turning his head sharply, he split the creature in two as one leapt toward Ash, but he was quick, plunging his sword into the creature's chest.

I spun as a dakkai charged, saliva dripping from its teeth. I cleaved off its head as I caught sight of Bele leaping over a fissure. She landed on a boulder, effortlessly switching to a bow and shadowstone arrows to avoid the eather drawing the dakkais. Rhain raced out of the trees, followed by several soldiers.

Ash swore, kicking a dakkai back as sudden screams of pain tore through the air. I whirled toward the field, my breath catching in horror when I saw dozens more dakkais joining the fray.

"Sera!" Ash shouted, spinning me around.

Hot breath that smelled of sulfur and stale lilacs swamped me. I thrust out with the sword, but the creature yelped before I made contact, falling to the ground. One of Ash's blades jutted from its back.

Nektas's tail swept across the ground, edging me back and releasing a stream of fire. Silver flames engulfed the dakkais, but more came over the cliff's edge, snarling and spitting. I braced myself, but they veered to my right.

They were heading straight for Nektas.

"Nektas!" Ash yelled, bringing his sword down as Rhain drove his into a dakkai's back.

I screamed when the dakkais swarmed the draken, digging into his scales with their claws. They climbed him as he slammed his tail down and twisted, trying to shake them off. Blood sprayed the ground, and Nektas reared back, emitting a deep cry.

The sight of his blood and the sound of his pain undid whatever restraint I had left in me. The air around me charged, reacting to the eather erupting from my pores.

"Don't!" Ash shouted. "It will draw them to you."

"I know," I growled. That's what I wanted. The moment eather sparked, the dakkais clawing at Nektas froze, then lifted their heads in unison.

The clouds above us deepened in color as rage poured into me. I thrust out my left hand, silvery strands of eather tinged in gold erupting from my palm and mirroring my will. The tendrils lifted and arced, slamming into the dakkais, throwing them off Nektas and to the ground, where they lay smoldering.

A shadow rushed over us, and I looked up to see Aurelia. She landed near Nektas, tucking a wing over his side, fire spilling from her mouth. She turned her head, enveloping the dakkais that remained on the bluffs.

I rushed to Nektas's side, careful of the dripping blood. My heart twisted as I saw the deep gouges in his sides. He'd be okay. He had to be. Fear dripped through me. "Nektas?"

I'll heal, came his raspy voice. *I just need a few minutes.*

"I want you out of here," I demanded.

That's not going to happen.

"Where did he go?" Ash seethed, stalking forward. He jerked to a stop and then rushed past me, heading toward the edge overlooking the battlefield.

Bele jumped off the rock, driving her knee into a fallen Revenant's chest, knocking it back. She slammed her blade into its chest as it started to come back to life.

"Rhain!" she shouted. "We need to put them down."

The god rushed to Bele's side, and I turned to Aurelia. "Keep him safe until he's healed."

She answered by shielding his head with her much smaller one.

"Not again," Bele groaned, rising as Revenants swarmed the bluff. "Oh, great. And we've got even more visitors."

Ash's head cut toward the bluff overlooking the sea. Ceeren pulled themselves over the edge, their beautiful faces streaked with blood. I took a deep breath, holding it.

I knew Kolis was still nearby. He was hiding somewhere. But when my gaze met Ash's, I knew he was thinking the same thing I was. We couldn't leave everyone to deal with this.

I stalked toward the nearest Revenant, deflecting a blow. Then another. I glanced up, seeing red scales high above the clouds. It was Naberius, but that wasn't good news.

"Kolis's draken," I hissed, driving the sword through a Revenant's chest.

"Focus on the Revenants," Ash commanded, his voice laced with authority. "Our draken will meet his in the sky."

I nodded, steeling myself for the carnage to come as the air came alive with bloodshed. Shoving a Revenant back, Ash sliced into its chest.

Aurelia caught a ceeren in her jaws, and Nektas threw at least three into the trees with a punishing sweep of his tail. The wounds in his side didn't seem as deep as before.

I drove my sword down and saw blood dotting Rhain's face. "You okay?"

"Not my blood." He knelt by a fallen Rev, pulling a vial from his satchel. He pried the mouth open, pouring two second's worth of draken blood into the Revenant's mouth. "At least, not all of it."

I glanced at the Revenant Rhain knelt by. It was still out, but its body began convulsing as its flesh flushed and then bubbled—

"You're probably not going to want to watch that," Rhain called.

Too late.

The bubbles along the Revenant's flesh exploded, and the skin melted. I lowered my sword as muscles and tendons caught fire as if they were nothing but paper. Holes appeared in bones and ignited, burning even those. There was nothing left but a mess of pink and scraps of charred flesh.

"That is…disgusting," I muttered.

"Sera!" Ash shouted. "Behind you!"

I spun, coming face-to-face with a shadowstone blade wielded by a dark-haired goddess. A wave of fiery pain went down my arm as I lurched to the side.

Ash's growl tore through the air a second before a stream of shadowy eather smacked into her.

"Are you okay?" Ash was at my side in a heartbeat.

"Yes." I breathed through the pain. "Just a scratch."

He stared at me for a moment, then snapped forward. Pinching my chin in a gentle grip, he thrust his sword, catching either a ceeren or a Revenant as he kissed me.

He lifted his head and pulled his sword free. His hand dropped to my hip, and he nudged me to the side, gripping the hair of what turned out to be a ceeren. It snapped at him, and he dragged his sword up, disemboweling it.

Above, roars shattered the skies when our draken met Kolis's. Flames of eather licked from their jaws as they descended upon his draken. Talons dug in, ripping through hard scales.

I dragged my attention away, scanning for any sign of Kolis. A ceeren came at me, the cloth she wore dripping pinkish water. Her full lips peeled back over bloody teeth. I parried a blow aimed at my heart.

Another charged, and I threw out my hand. Eather powered down my arm. The burst of Primal energy slammed into the ceeren. He stumbled back, looking down at the charred hole in his chest. His knees buckled, and I clenched my jaw against the throb of death.

The female ceeren screamed, drawing her sword back—

A shadowstone blade sliced through her neck. Her body went in one direction and her head in the other.

Ash stood there, more fresh blood dripping from his sword.

"Thanks."

"Don't mention it." His gaze turned to the sky as a red-and-black draken dug its talons into the back of a smaller, brown one. "Fucking Diaval."

I inhaled sharply as Diaval tore into the draken's throat, ripping through scales and bone. Aurelia let out a staggering, mournful call when the brown draken fell, shifting into his mortal form.

Ehthawn crashed into Diaval with a thunderous clap. They were a spiral of wings and talons, tearing into each other. Behind them, another draken plunged into the ocean, sending a geyser of water shooting into the sky.

I staggered at the haunting sight, forcing my gaze away. I couldn't let it get to me right now.

Ash prowled toward the cliff's edge. Scanning the sky for Naberius, I joined him.

Down below, I saw Phanos take a hit of Primal essence, throwing him back as Attes stalked forward, eather dripping from his fingers.

"Kolis is still here," I said, my chest rising and falling sharply. Rhahar leapt over a dakkai, slamming his sword through a crimson god's head.

"And so are the rest of his armies." Ash lifted his blood-soaked sword, pointing at the forest line.

My gaze lifted, and the air fled my lungs.

A wave of crimson flowed out of the trees like an unforgiving tide. Thousands swarmed the field, just like the dakkais on the bluff had. And they kept coming.

"The bulk of their armies wasn't on the ships," I whispered.

"No," Ash growled.

The sea of crimson swept over the field, causing my heart to stutter. There were too many, especially with Theon's forces still battling the ceeren. I flinched as Phanos struck Attes, knocking him into a dakkai's path—

A fair-haired soldier snapped forward, blocking the dakkai from reaching Attes. Kars. It was Kars who jabbed out with his blade. He was quick but…

The dakkai clamped down on his throat.

"No!" I shouted, lurching forward. A shudder went through me, warming my palms.

Ash caught my arm, but I barely felt his grip as both the dakkai and Kars went down.

Attes stumbled and grabbed the dagger, tossing it aside. He was frozen for a second, almost like he was thinking the same thing I was. What had Kars been thinking? He was a godling. Attes would've likely handled the dakkai, but it didn't matter. It was too late. Attes stepped back. His free hand fisted, and he turned his head toward Phanos. A scream of rage erupted from him, and he flew toward the other Primal just as two draken spiraled to the ground below, locked in a deadly embrace, blood and fiery eather pouring out of them both.

"Crolee," Ash rasped. They hit the rocky shore, the impact an echo of finality that caused my body to flash cold and then hot.

A buzzing started in my ears, muting Nektas's call of sorrow. I pulled my arm free of Ash's, the sword I held slipping from my fingers and clanging off the ground.

More crimson soldiers surged forward from the mouth of the forest, their armor and swords not yet bloodied by battle. I could barely see our people among the crimson gods—could barely hear Ash's voice as he grabbed a ceeren, snapping its neck. I looked down the bluff's rocky hill, seeing gods in crimson scale the peak. I thought Ash was calling my name as an eather arrow struck the first god who crested the rise.

I wasn't breathing.

We were failing. My hand went to my stomach. Our future was slipping between our fingers. They would all die while Kolis hid. Rhahar. Our soldiers. Possibly even Attes. Then Rhain and Bele, once they swarmed the bluff. Their bodies would fall, just as Kars and Crolee had. Their bones would join…

They're called the Bonelands.

I looked down, the blood dripping from my fingers darkening the soil and rock.

The land was littered with those who'd fallen in the war with the Ancients, the remains of gods, long-since-forgotten mortal warriors, Primals, and…

And dragons.

Suddenly, I saw the Shade in the Dying Woods—the one I'd touched. How it had started to come back to life.

There was a reason I'd suggested the Bonelands to Ash. Why I had stood on the Rise looking at the Shades after I'd brought life back to the Shadowlands.

Death couldn't break the bonds of Life's touch.

I looked at Ash. "I'll be right back."

He shoved a god from his sword, and his head jerked toward me. Eather swelled in me as I stepped toward the edge. He shouted my name, and it carried on the wind when I shadowstepped to the field below, near Kars' body.

Locked in their own fights, no one noticed me as I stalked forward. Dropping to my knees beside the godling, I slammed my hands onto the bloodied grass, eather swelling inside me and combining with all the yawning hopelessness and bitter desperation I'd felt moments ago. But I channeled everything in me—the suffocating fear and soul-destroying shame for what had been done to me, for what I'd done to the mortal realm—and all of it built inside me.

Then, I let go.

Because no more would die. We would not fail. Our future *wasn't* lost.

The edges of my vision turned silver and gold, snapping my head back. "I am done with this!" A scream of rage erupted from deep within me, releasing the Primal essence—unleashing my will as I summoned the fallen gods and dragons. "All of this."

All across the field, heads turned to me. Soldiers in crimson and dark gray froze as my hands sank through the grass and into the soil, and eather whirled down my arms. Attes turned, and Phanos staggered back, his bloody mouth dropping open when the eather receded from his veins. Silvery-white light drenched the ground, rippling out from my hands.

Beneath me and all around, the ground trembled and then roared. Deep fissures appeared across the sacred land, spreading like veins, opening and spewing soil and rocks into the air.

A heartbeat passed.

Then two.

Thin, bleached-white fingers appeared in the clouds of dust radiating from the fissures. They dug into the disturbed soil, clawing their way free. Fleshless arms appeared from the darkness. Hairless skulls. And they kept coming, a wave of bone and tattered tunics, bearing the sigils of forgotten kingdoms, their bony hands lifting ancient, rusted swords. The great hills deep within the forests shuddered, uprooting trees and shedding centuries of sediment until foot-long, serrated teeth became visible. Wings of cartilage and delicate bones lifted into the air. The wind answered in a whisper, two words that echoed over and over as an army rose.

Meyaah Liessa.

62

The army of bones held still as soil continued falling. They waited for orders.

They waited for me.

Their Queen.

"Protect what is mine. Destroy the crimson soldiers," I hissed, eather pounding into each word as my will poured into my army. "Destroy the crimson draken and those who came from the sea, then return to your rest."

All across the field and into the forest, the army swept forward, and dragons rose into the air, their bones creaking and grinding together. Their roars were deeper, more guttural, sending a wounded Diaval fleeing toward the eastern mountains.

The screams that came brought a smile to my face as I rose, essence crackling from my fingertips. Across the field, a wave of red was falling into the grass, littering the ground.

A flash of crimson-and-gold snagged my attention. My gaze shot to the ruins of the Temple. I caught a fleeting glimpse of Kolis's silhouette right before he slipped through the half-crumbling archway of the old Temple.

I walked forward, a burst of eather rushing through me as Diaval dove through the thick clouds, releasing a stream of fire that pounded the field, igniting everything in its path, killing both crimson and black soldiers alike.

Rage exploded in my gut. My vision narrowed on the draken, the realm fading into a red haze of fury. Instinct took over, and I inhaled, pulling eather from the realm. All across the field, tiny silvery dots appeared and pulsed. They raced toward me in a flash, joining the crackling essence gathering around my palm as I stepped forward. Thrusting out my hand, a spinning, crackling stream of silver-and-gold eather erupted from my palm. The raw Primal power slammed into the pretty-haired fucker's underside.

The funnel of fire evaporated, and Diaval let out a whine of pain. His wings flapped wildly, and the eather swept over his body before fading out.

He veered sharply, his horned head swinging toward me. An outline appeared through the clouds, twice the size of Nektas, beginning to swirl and thin.

Diaval hovered in the air, letting out a roar that shook the trees.

Smirking, I lifted an arm and extended my middle finger. The wings of a bone dragon scattered the dark clouds.

Diaval twisted in midair, but the bone dragon was fast, tearing its claws into the draken's back. I only winced a little at his scream of pain. My attention shifted back to the Temple. I shadowstepped to the archway.

In the shadowy interior, a crimson god stood before me. He was tall and slender, with hair as blond as mine and eyes the color of citrine. He smiled at me, and it was like Kolis's. Fake. Cold.

"Who are you?" I asked.

The god bowed slightly. "Varus."

"Oh. You."

He straightened, the smile turning smug. "You've heard of me?"

"Barely."

Varus frowned.

I shot forward and gripped the god by the throat, then turned, throwing him through an opening between the pillars. His shout of surprise faded as he plummeted to the field below. The army of bones would take care of him.

Footsteps echoed through the entire Temple. Within seconds, the decaying halls were filled with Kolis's soldiers.

One smirked, withdrawing a dull white sword. "You shouldn't have come alone."

"She didn't," came a deep voice behind me, his fresh citrus scent sweeping over me.

I smiled, and the god's grin faded.

"Was that just Varus?" Ash asked, handing me one of his swords. "Being thrown out of here?"

"It was."

He chuckled, his hand grazing my hip as he stepped forward. I thought I smelled the faint scent of his blood, but it was passing. "I assume there's a reason you're here."

"Kolis." I looked to my right when the gods charged. "He's playing hide and seek. Are you injured?"

"Of course, the coward is. And no, I'm not injured," he said. "By the way, there are a whole lot of dead people doing a whole lot of killing out there."

"Good."

The soldiers surrounded us, and my grip tightened around my sword, the blade an extension of my will. *Breathe in.* They attacked at once. There was no time to think or feel fear in the chaos of blades. *Hold.* Blood sprayed the failing walls as I sliced through one god and then another. I fell into the madness, barely feeling the bone-shaking blows, my sword clashing with others. I no longer felt the echoes of death, or maybe it was just so constant that I had finally tuned it out. *Breathe out.* Back-to-back with me, Ash fought with deadly precision, his movements lethal. *Hold.* I cut down a god, cleaving his body in two, and stepped over the mess—

A blow connected with my jaw, knocking my head back. Stunned, I stumbled into one of the pillars. Tiny fissures appeared in the stone, and a metallic wetness filled my mouth.

Ash spun with a snarl, shooting forward. He caught the fist and shattered each bone with one squeeze. The god howled, dropping to his knees.

"That wasn't nice." I pushed forward, spitting out a mouthful of blood as I drove the sword through the god's throat.

Ash released him, letting him fall back, then turned toward me, his features hard.

"I'm okay," I said at once, stretching out my jaw to ease the throbbing there. When I turned to kick a god back into the sword Ash held, I saw that the side of his tunic was torn, and the ragged edges were soaked, darkening the material. Two gods raced at us, weapons raised, and concern immediately flooded me. "You lied! You are injured."

"I didn't lie, *liessa.*" With a swift turn, he struck with both swords, cutting down the gods simultaneously. "I was injured. Briefly."

"You bled," I growled, spinning toward a goddess in crimson. I ducked beneath her swinging blade, feeling the rush of air signaling the narrow miss. Rising behind her, I caught her loose, dark hair and jerked her head back, plunging my sword through her back. Shimmery blood sprayed the faded walls. "How did it happen?"

"I was distracted." His sword sliced through leather and bone as I dropped to my hands and knees to avoid the sweep of a sword. "By a certain wife who decided to go onto the battlefield."

Pressing my lips together, I rocked back on my knees and kicked out, sweeping the god's legs out from under him. "Sorry."

"Uh-huh." He bowed, driving his sword down through the chest of the god I'd knocked down. Thick lashes lifted. Eyes streaked with silver met mine. "The next time you do something like that,"—he yanked the blade free—"I'm going to spank you."

My skin flushing hotly, I spun, shoving the sword back. A strangled grunt told me my aim was on point. "Was that supposed to be a threat of punishment?" I darted to the side, slamming my elbow into a crimson god's stomach. "If so,"—my blade pierced armor and tissue—"it's getting the absolute opposite response."

"I know." His voice was a sensual growl as he turned, throwing a shadowstone sword. It caught a god in the head. "I can taste your arousal, *liessa.*"

I started to respond when I spotted Kolis at the end of the hall, ducking under another archway. Another dozen crimson-garbed gods poured out.

"This is getting really annoying," I muttered. I had no idea what game he was playing, but I was also so very done with him.

As I slid under a wild swing, I pictured Thierran in my mind and summoned him. I trusted that he would keep a low profile until we had Kolis cornered.

Ash and I carved a path through the Temple hall, leaving a grotesque carpet of bodies behind. More soldiers loomed ahead, just another wave crashing toward us. But we were the rock that would break them apart.

As we neared the archway, the air crackled around us. I spun, letting out a shout of warning.

Kolis materialized directly behind Ash, descending on him in a heartbeat.

Ash spun, pulling his sword back and plunging it deep into Kolis's chest. The impact knocked the Primal of Death back several feet before he caught himself.

Looking down at the sword's hilt, he laughed and grasped it.

I pushed forward, and Ash flew toward him, slamming his fist into Kolis's jaw. I didn't make it very far. An arm snagged me around the waist as Kolis staggered and then steadied himself. He pulled the sword free. The blade shattered, and he vanished again. Suddenly, I was moving through the air—

I smacked into a wall with enough force that my spine would've broken if I'd been mortal. Still, my immediate concern was the lives I carried within me as I fell forward. Primal or not, the impact had rattled every part of me and stunned me for several seconds.

Ash's head cut toward me when I landed on one hand and my knees. I looked up through several loose curls to see Ash coming for me.

The air behind him warped, and Kolis appeared again.

"Behind you!" I screamed.

Kolis's lips curved up, and Ash turned. The true Primal of Death was on him in a heartbeat, gripping the front of Ash's tunic and baring his fangs. I shoved up off my hand, desperate to intervene.

"Oh, look," Kolis spat. "The bitch is already on her knees."

A roar left Ash, shaking the ruins as he jerked forward, bashing his head into Kolis's. I started to rise, but a boot connected with my jaw, knocking my head back sharply. Pain shot down my spine, and the muscles along my neck protested. The sound of fists connecting with flesh echoed through the Temple.

A hand clamped down on my throat, lifting me roughly to my feet and then off them.

Varus stared up at me, his once smooth complexion torn open across his cheeks. "Payback's a bitch," he snarled.

There were only a few seconds to consider how strong the once-entombed god was before I was suddenly flying into the darkness.

In those brief seconds of weightlessness, I wasn't thinking about myself or Ash. I was thinking about our children. I managed to twist my body so my upper back and shoulders took the brunt of the impact, a heartbeat before I crashed into the floor with enough force to knock the air from my lungs and crack the stone beneath me.

Fuck.

That hurt.

A lot.

A wall suddenly exploded, and Ash and Kolis came through it, sending chunks of stone flying in every direction. By the grace of the Fates, only the smallest pelted me as Ash and Kolis rose toward the pitched ceiling.

They were both in their Primal forms, a blur of shadows and crimson, clashing with the force of colliding stars and exchanging blows with their fists and eather.

An uncomfortable sense of déjà vu swept through me as they fought, and pain swept up and down the length of my body in waves.

"You still think you can defeat me, nephew?" Kolis's laugh carried the scent of stale lilacs when he threw Ash to the floor. "I am true Death."

Ash landed in a crouch, his pure silver gaze briefly meeting mine. I willed my stupid legs and arms to move. The pain was quickly fading, but all I managed to do was the lamest thing ever. I gave Ash a thumbs-up.

"There is no Primal more infinite than true Death," Kolis boasted, crimson-streaked darkness spinning around him. "Nothing more certain and inevitable than I. There is no bond I cannot break, no magic I cannot undo, or life I cannot take."

A low growl came from Ash. He rose, nearly solid wings appearing from the mist gathering around him. "You are and have always been nothing."

Kolis looked down. "I was going to keep you alive, chained at the foot of my throne until I released her from her misery. Oh, how I looked so forward to it. Seeing every pain I inflicted on her mirrored in your features." Crimson throbbed in the air, and the scent of death filled the chamber. "But I see now that I will just have to settle for your death and her endless suffering."

Ash sneered. "Are you done talking, for fuck's sake?"

A hiss slithered from Kolis, and the mist around him whipped out, spreading across the length of the chamber and billowing against the ceiling. "It is you who will become nothing," Kolis seethed, his gaze shooting to me. "And so shall…" He trailed off as his head cocked. "I see your soul. I see…" He inhaled sharply with a shout of rage. "I see their souls!"

Oh, fuck.

Ash flew off the floor, sending a blast of eather into Kolis.

The true Primal of Death flew back, stopping in midair. "She's pregnant!" His laugh was coarse—and crazed. "She will get to have children?"

Panic threatened to explode through me, but I fought it back. The pain finally retracted, giving me control over my body. I sat up. My hands were empty. I had no idea where I'd dropped the sword.

"I will carve them from her womb and feed them to my dakkais," he swore.

"The fuck you will." Ash crashed into Kolis with the force of a tempest.

"No. Better yet, she will birth them." He grabbed Ash's cheeks, his voice filling with a sinister glee. "And I will raise them as mine. They will be my gift to Sotoria—"

Ash's head snapped forward, and he tore into Kolis's throat.

Kolis laughed, grabbed Ash by the hair, and tossed him aside.

I gathered my legs under me just as Varus hopped over the half-standing wall. Eather tinged in red sparked from his fingertips. He smirked.

"Kolis says I cannot kill you." Varus raised his hands. "But he did say I could hurt—"

The pillars behind Varus exploded under the strength of a black-and-gray-spiked tail.

Nektas.

His tail rushed across the floor, ramming into Varus. The god shrieked—actually *shrieked*—going airborne. My gaze tracked him as he flew across the Temple and out another opening.

I laughed.

Pushing through any lingering pain, I leapt to my feet, watching Ash and Kolis crash into the floor toward the back of the Temple, causing the entire structure to tremble. I started toward them, beginning to summon Thierran again—

I sucked in a sharp breath and felt a wrenching motion deep in my chest.

I froze. It was the same as I'd felt before, but not quite so intense. The sensation flowed through me, and the sky beyond the Temple lit up with silvery fireworks.

A Primal had fallen.

From the back of the chamber, Kolis roared in anger. It hadn't been one of ours.

Phanos.

High-pitched, mournful calls split the air in a song of death. It was the ceeren, crying out in anguish.

As wrong as it was, a smile crossed my lips. I lifted my head—

The space around me stirred as Ash's roar thundered. I spun, catching a brief glimpse of Kolis skidding across the ruined floor before my gaze locked with the pale blue eyes of a Revenant.

Callum smiled. "Miss me?"

I stepped to the side, fast but not fast enough. Air punched from my lungs in a fiery burst of pain.

Shadows peeled away from the sides of the Temple, rippling and racing across the floor. I looked down.

A bone dagger jutted out of me, the hilt reverberating from the impact of the thrust. The ungodly heat of the bone blade started to burn my flesh. I staggered back. "Were you aiming for my heart?"

"I was."

I lifted my gaze, and a metallic taste filled my mouth again. "Guess what?" I gritted out, grabbing the hilt. "You missed."

Callum sighed, shoulders slumping. "Shit."

Behind him, a violent, churning mass of shadows pulsed and throbbed. In the center, two silvery eyes glowed with feral rage.

"And you've really pissed off my husband." I smiled through the burn of pain. "Fucker."

Callum started to turn, but the shadows snaked out, slamming into him. Twin streams of smoky eather burst through his shoulders, throwing him back several feet behind me and into a hall. Another sliced through his stomach. Screaming, he flailed wildly as he was sucked into the air.

Jaw clenched, I yanked the bone dagger free. It hadn't been in there long. I would heal. At some point. "Gods," I hissed, taking a deep breath, then looked… I could no longer see Callum—well, I saw pieces of him falling and splattering off the floor, but I didn't think that counted.

He'd come back.

I started to turn but stopped. My eyes narrowed on the air distorting around Callum's remains. "What the—?"

But right now, that wasn't the biggest problem, nor was the pain in my chest.

Kolis had released Naberius.

The draken formed from crimson-and-black mist in a wave of scales and bared teeth. A meaty foreleg swept out, his talons as sharp as daggers.

"Watch out!" I screamed, but it was too late.

Naberius raked his talons across Ash's back, cutting through his wings. He stumbled, pain flashing across his features for the briefest moment when his wings evaporated in a shower of sparks. The scent of his blood ignited a fury in my chest, hotter and brighter than the flames of a thousand suns. The ceiling overhead suddenly shook. Something large and heavy had landed on the roof. A crack immediately appeared.

The ceiling peeled back, and Nektas descended into the chamber, sinking his forelegs into Naberius's back.

The other draken roared in agony as Nektas lifted, carrying Nab upward.

"Return to me!" Kolis shouted, brushing his hand over the cuff on his upper arm. "Now."

Naberius shuddered, turning into a shimmery red-and-silver mist as Kolis landed on the floor. Stone and debris slid across the floor when he stalked toward Ash.

"I will strip the flesh from your bones, nephew." Eather spun from his hands. "She will be cloaked in your skin—" His words ended in a shout of anger as Thierran appeared behind him like a hooded wraith, clasping the sides of Kolis's head.

Kolis's body bowed, and his arms went rigid. A low murmur came, like a whisper of wind rolling through the chamber. Thierran reached deep into Kolis's mind and took his worst fears, amplifying them. Behind the painted red wings, his eyes went wide. The mist around Kolis evaporated as Ash straightened, exhaling heavily and shaking off the pain. The eather slowed, and Kolis's mouth dropped open. His pupils dilated as the murmurs increased, feeding the waking nightmare.

"No," rasped Kolis. He began to tremble. Streaks of dampness cut through the red paint under his eyes. "No. I love you. I've always loved you."

"Sick fuck," Ash growled.

Thierran's gaze met mine. "You need to knock him out. Now."

"Gladly," I spat.

I extended my hand, palm upturned toward the sky, and drew upon the ancient power coursing through my veins. The air crackled with energy, every particle vibrating with the force of my will.

"Sotoria—no," Kolis begged—*sobbed*. "Please."

Eather crackled across my palm. I unleashed the bolt of pure power, a torrent of light so intense it seemed to tear the very fabric of the realm.

The bolt struck true, hitting Kolis in the chest. He let out an ear-splitting scream when the energy coursed through him, throwing Thierran back. The eather seared Kolis's flesh and bones, making him convulse. Blood poured from his mouth as he dropped to his knees and fell forward.

"He shut the fuck up." Ash kicked the Primal onto his back. "Finally."

"Does the wound still burn?" Ash asked, he and Attes carefully lifting a section of bone chain.

"Barely," I admitted, eyeing the back of Ash's shredded tunic. The jagged tears Naberius had delivered had stopped bleeding by the time we arrived in Oak Ambler.

"Get ready," Attes said with a hiss of pain. He looked as ragged as we did. His clothing was torn and bloodied, and it looked like a dakkai or draken had gotten ahold of his arm. The deep gouge in his flesh had closed but was still a bright pink. "He's starting to twitch."

My gaze went back to Kolis. Attes had stripped his chest bare. The trapped arm jerked.

Ash dropped his side of the chains over a very sensitive part of Kolis, drawing a snort from me. Both of them stepped back. Faint smoke had begun rising from the chains resting against flesh. Attes handed Ash a sharpened bone with one end wrapped in a thick cloth.

Really should've considered wearing gloves.

Kolis came awake all at once. The name he bellowed rattled over the cavernous walls. *Sotoria.*

Gods.

I unsheathed the bone dagger from my thigh.

His wild gaze darted around, landing on Ash and then me, his chest rising fast beneath the chains. "What in the…?" His head fell back against the slab of mineral and stone. A look of relief skittered across his face. "Sotoria wasn't… It wasn't real."

He smiled.

The fucker *smiled*, and it was real, transforming his too-perfect features beneath the streaked wings painted on his face.

Gods.

I snapped forward, dragging the bone over Kolis's left wrist as Ash sliced into his right. Blue-tinted blood spilled over his flesh, spreading down his wide-stretched arms. The relief quickly vanished when Kolis's surroundings finally sank in.

He cursed, hurling various insults in both the mortal tongue and the ancient Primal language. We ignored him, slashing the arteries running up both legs. Blood was quickly pooling on the floor under him—

"I will fuck your corpses," Kolis raged.

The blood wasn't draining from Kolis quickly enough, in my opinion.

Ash raised a brow and moved away, reaching for the bone chains. "I'm not sure what is more perverse," Ash remarked, moving toward the bone chains. "The necrophilia or the incest."

"Do we have to pick one?" I asked.

Ash laughed.

"You aren't doing shit," I said to Kolis, kneeling over him. He glared at Ash as if he could will him into nonexistence. "You will be right here. If you *do* wake up at some point, I imagine you will fall into madness before you lose consciousness again."

"Fall into madness." Attes huffed. "I think that's already water under the bridge."

I smiled. "Years will pass. Centuries. You will be forgotten." I leaned to the side so my face was in front of his. He still stared at Ash. "And Sotoria?"

His eyes finally shot to mine, burning with unholy hatred.

"She will be free of you," I said. "She will never have to fear you again."

"*So'lis* will be reborn," he seethed, blood and spit trailing down his chin. The sheen of red bone beneath his flesh was visible. "Mark my words. The Fates will decree it. They will reset the balance, and nothing—absolutely nothing—in this realm or beyond will stop me from having her. I will rise again as the Bringer of Death and Destruction."

I stilled.

Ash yanked the bone chains tighter, pinning Kolis onto his back. "If that day comes, we'll be waiting."

I shook my head, rising so I stood over his legs.

Kolis snarled, his fangs snapping at the air, his gaze dropping to the bone dagger and then lifting to mine. "Do it. I dare you, Seraphena."

I laughed, and high above us, thunder rolled. "You don't have to dare me."

Attes tossed another section of chain over Kolis's groin, drawing out a hiss of pain. "My bad," he said. "They slipped."

Kicking his head back against the stone, Kolis laughed. "I'm going to beat those babes from your stomach and dine on—"

Ash moved fast. He slammed his fist *through* Kolis's throat, tearing tendons and shattering bones in one wet, crunchy-sounding punch. "As my wife just said, you aren't doing shit."

Eather flared weakly around Kolis's form as his mouth moved wordlessly.

"What?" I leaned over, curving a hand around my ear. "I can't hear you."

His eyes turned, becoming black pools. My body immediately went cold, and the nape of my neck tingled. The nothingness of his eyes swirled around a pinprick of *red*. Blood not yet spilled. And in that burning crimson, I saw…

Sucking in a breath, I jerked back. Ash's gaze flew to mine as he shook the gore from his hand. "*Liessa*?"

I blinked, my heart pounding. "It's okay." I swallowed hard, glancing at the second dagger Ash had gifted me that I clutched tightly, and then I looked over my shoulder to where Attes stood, his hand tight around the shaft of a bone spear. "You partial to that spear?"

Attes's head cocked, his eyebrows furrowing. "Not exactly."

"Good, because I'm going to need this dagger," I said, turning back to Kolis. "I'm not going to waste it on you. It's too pretty." I held it between us, wanting him to see it—wanting him to remember it. "Besides, if you do come back? And she is reborn?"

Kolis went still.

"I will place this dagger in her hand myself," I whispered. "And it will be she who drives it through your heart."

Leaning back, I held his gaze as I sheathed the dagger. Without taking my eyes from Kolis, I extended my hand.

Attes walked the spear to me. I took it and rose, adjusting my grip on the leather band down the center. My muscles trembled with the need to drive it through Kolis's heart and into the blood-soaked stone below him, but…

I raised my eyes to where Ash stood on Kolis's other side.

But the pain Kolis had caused me was nothing compared to what he had done to Ash.

Taking a deep, cleansing breath, I handed the spear to Ash.

His gaze dropped to the weapon and then returned to mine. "You sure?"

I nodded.

He froze for a moment, his chest still, and then he reached across Kolis's prone body and clasped the nape of my neck. His fingers curled into the braid there to guide my mouth to his. The kiss was fierce and hard, an expression of both savage gratitude and a promise that he would show me just how thankful he was later as he took the weapon from me.

He slowly lifted his mouth and pressed his forehead to mine. "I love you, *liessa.*"

"I love you," I whispered.

His hand slipped from my braid, and I stepped back. I could feel Kolis's unwavering stare on me now, full of hatred. I didn't look at him. He wasn't worth it. When Ash turned back to Kolis, he didn't speak. Again, he wasn't worth it. Ash folded his left hand under his right and lifted the spear. A heartbeat passed. That was all.

Ash sank to one knee and plunged the spear into Kolis's chest. Ribs cracked and gave way. I exhaled roughly as the spear struck true. Kolis jerked, his fingers clawing into the stone beneath him.

I looked at Kolis's face, and hairs rose all over my body. Our eyes met. His mouth stretched wide in a silent roar. A bright, ruby glow rippled over his body, sparking and sputtering against the floor and then quickly retracting. His skin thinned and vanished, revealing the churning, crimson-streaked black vines etched into the bones beneath.

The air stilled.

The realm went silent.

Kolis's…presence eased away from me.

"Here we go," Attes murmured.

Ash's head bowed as the spear hit stone and then sank into it. The impact was a shockwave, shaking the floor and rattling the damp-looking walls. A stale-lilac-smelling wind blew the wisps of hair back from my face. Dust and dirt fell from the ceiling, and red-and-black eather erupted from where the spear had been plunged deep into Kolis's chest. Streams of essence snaked out, filling the air with a thousand screams. The twisted mass of energy streaked to the north and south, then to the east and west, slamming into the walls and crawling up them. I tensed, realizing his energy was…was seeking a way out. If that happened, the city would be leveled.

The eather rolled over the ceiling, and cracks appeared in the walls, the floor, and above us. The screams continued as the celastite in the walls held firm, serving two purposes: to keep the essence of the realms out and the Primal essence inside.

Eather pulsed, washing the space in a crimson glow. My boots sent loosened dirt and small stones scattering when I stepped back, watching the light fade into the fissures that had formed shapes. Circles with a vertical line through them.

The symbol of Death.

Nearly the same as the Mierel Crest.

Ash rose as the last of the eather seeped into the walls. He turned to me, but my gaze returned to Kolis.

The true Primal of Death was nothing but bone and empty flesh, already turning gray.

Ash returned to my side, taking my hand as I breathed in, and it felt like the first real breath I'd ever taken.

We walked from the underground chamber onto one of the many cliffs overlooking the Stroud Sea, the salty breeze washing over us. Bright sunlight reflected off the white-tipped waves crashing against the rocky shore below.

Behind us, the earth shuddered. Stone tumbled, and dirt fell in sheets as Attes collapsed the tunnel that led to Kolis's tomb.

It was done.

As Ash's arm draped over my shoulders, I closed my eyes and breathed deeply, leaning into Ash. I was so damn tired, exhausted to the bone, but my lips split into a wide smile.

Kolis was entombed, and he would remain that way forevermore.

We'd won.

"It's over," Ash said, tipping his chin to the sky.

My smile froze and then faded. I should be celebrating. I wanted to continue smiling. *We'd won.* I should be cheering. It *was* over.

For now.

But Kolis's promise haunted every step I took as I left the tunnel. So did the damn prophecy.

Keella's warning whispered through my thoughts, the image of the air warping around Callum's remains forming in my mind. I'd forgotten about that as the old Temple was destroyed. And something about that caused a great sense of unease to rise.

Ash's arm tightened around me. "Let's go home," he said, brushing his lips over my temple. "I want you checked before we take care of Sotoria."

That wasn't the only thing we needed to do. I had to make sure the bone army returned to their slumber. We needed to check on the state of things in the Bonelands. Help our wounded. Count our dead. But…

A chill crawled across my neck and then slithered down my spine. Tiny hairs all over my body began to rise when I looked up at Ash.

His hand slid over my upper back, and he turned to me. "Sera?" Concern darkened his eyes. "What is it?"

I wasn't sure, but the unease intensified, causing my pulse to speed up.

Ash turned me so I was facing him. He clasped my cheeks. "Sera?"

"What's going on?" Attes asked, joining us at the cliff's edge, the blood spotting his face turning pink in the sunlight.

"I don't know." Ash's gaze searched mine. "Talk to us, *liessa*."

My heart pounded. "We need to take care of Sotoria now."

Ash's jaw immediately hardened. "I think that can wait until Kye—"

"It really can't." I swallowed. "We need to do it now."

His eyes narrowed. "Is your *vadentia* telling you something?"

"I don't know, but remember what Keella said about the prophecy?" I reminded him, and Ash swore. He knew how important it was to free Sotoria before the Fates did something idiotic, but he was battling with his need to make sure the babes and I were okay. I twisted toward Attes. "I need you to take us to The Star."

Attes frowned. "I can do that, but I'd prefer if we backed up a second first because you are acting—"

"No," I interrupted. "We need to go there," I insisted. "*Now*."

Attes led us through the maze of halls forged from shadowstone deep beneath his palace in Essaly. His armor had vanished, and he'd dropped his swords upon entering. We were all tired, and the wound in my shoulder had faded to a dull ache, but our steps were fast.

Flames ignited from the torches lining the hall as we passed, casting an amber glow that beat back the darkness.

I walked beside Ash, my hand held tightly in his while he continuously smoothed his thumb over the top of it. The whole time, I kept telling myself we still had a chance to truly stop the prophecy from coming true. We'd entombed Kolis. All we needed to do now was release Sotoria. If so, Kolis would remain where we'd put him, the Ancients would stay in the ground, and Sotoria would be given a choice—something she hadn't had in far too many years.

Then everything would be perfect. We could relax. Iliseeum would change. So would the mortal realm. Ash and I could have the future he'd spoken of the night in the throne room.

Attes stopped before a door carved from a smooth, glossy shadowstone slab. He placed his hand on the surface, and the door swung open in a silent glide across the floor. Candles along the walls lit the small, circular chamber, casting a soft, flickering glow over jeweled chests of various sizes.

Attes entered first, but he'd only taken two steps before jerking to a stop. The sudden rush of eather inside him charged the air. "No."

Upon hearing that single word, my skin flashed hot and then cold. And I knew. I fucking knew.

"What?" Ash asked.

"The Star..." Attes staggered past the chests toward a pedestal surrounded by thick candles raised in iron candelabras.

A pedestal as bare as the one in the House of Haides.

"It's gone." He threw out an arm in an angry sweep, sending several chests slamming against the walls. "It was here this morning. I check it every day, in the morning and at night. This is impossible."

Ash's hand slipped free of mine as he scanned the chamber. "I doubt this is something you would've misplaced. So, who else knows about this room?"

"No one," Attes gritted out, thrusting his hand through his hair. He tugged at the strands. "Absolutely fucking no one. That is why I kept it here."

"That's not true," I said, and they both turned to me. "The Fates know. They see all. It wouldn't matter where you hid The Star. They would always be able to find it."

Attes's eyes widened. "Sure, but why would they take it?"

"Remember what Holland said about some of the Fates wanting to wake the Ancients in a way they believed could be controlled?" I said. "They would need her soul to do that."

Ash's gaze swung back to mine, and he cursed.

"Why would they need her soul for that?" Attes demanded, chest rising and falling rapidly as his eather began churning along the flesh of his throat. He stepped toward me, his tone hardening. "What do you know that you haven't told me?"

Ash was immediately in front of me. "Speak to my wife in that tone again, and you will find yourself unable to speak another word."

"It's okay." I touched Ash's back. "He's not angry with me."

"I don't give a fuck who he's angry at," Ash growled, glaring at Attes. "You're telling me that you knew just about every damn thing my father was planning, but you didn't know the actual reason he put Sotoria's soul into her bloodline?"

Attes's gaze was locked on the Primal before him. "He put her soul there so she could stop Kolis once and for all."

"It was never just about him," I said. "It's the prophecy. Eythos was trying to circumvent it, hoping Sotoria would be reborn now and marry his son long before the time period Penellaphe saw in her vision."

"Yeah, I'm really confused since that *is* what Eythos planned." Attes took a step back, drawing in a deep breath. "Didn't work out that way."

"No shit," Ash bit out.

Attes ignored him. "You know what? It doesn't matter." Jaw flexing, he looked between us. "We need to get that diamond back."

"And I have a good idea who has it." Fury rose swiftly in me, and I latched onto it. Essence throbbed heavily in me. "I want a Fate here right now," I demanded, the power in my voice causing the chests to tremble and the candles to flicker as my will filled the chamber. "I don't care which of you answers, but you'd better answer right now."

Shockingly, they answered at once. The air around us filled with energy, causing the flames on the candles to shoot toward the ceiling. Before the empty pedestal, the air distorted.

Just as I had seen it do in the old Temple.

A tear in the realm appeared, and none other than the nipple-pierced Aydun stepped out, his swirling eyes landing directly on me. "You're summons was grossly impolite. You're lucky it was I—"

"I don't give a fuck about how impolite it was," I hissed, and Ash shifted so he stood in front of me once more. I sidestepped him. "Give me The Star. Now."

Aydun's brows rose, and the colors of his eyes stilled, the stars brightening until they cast a silvery glow over his cheeks. "I see that you're in a highly emotional state. Therefore, I will forgive your impudence this time."

I opened my mouth.

"Do you have The Star?" Ash jumped in before I could say something way ruder.

The Ancient glanced at Ash. "Do I have The Star? As in, is it in my possession?"

A low growl rumbled from my chest.

Brown hair fell against his sculpted cheek when Aydun turned his head toward me. "I see you're going to be the reckless one this time," he noted. "Your anger is misplaced, Seraphena. It was not I who took The Star."

My hands fisted at my sides. "I don't care which of you took it. I want it back."

"It's too late for that."

I inhaled sharply. "No, it is not."

Aydun held my stare. "Yes, it is, and you know it. A part of you has always known that," he said, and my heart skipped. His voice lowered. "Fate always finds a way, Seraphena."

A harsh, biting laugh escaped me. "Yeah, because fate keeps fucking things up."

Aydun arched a brow.

"Okay. I'm missing some vital information," Attes began. "And honestly, I don't give a fuck at this point. Eythos had his plans. They didn't turn out exactly as he'd planned, but Kolis was entombed. He has been dealt with. Sotoria is Sotoria. Sera is Sera. That is old news, and all I want is for Sotoria to be free." His voice cracked a little on the last word. "For her to either choose peace or live a normal life." He moved toward the Ancient. "And don't you dare fucking deny her that."

"A normal life?" Aydun repeated. "Sotoria has never lived a normal life."

"Yeah, thanks to Kolis," I snapped. "And you all messing with her life."

"You misunderstand, Seraphena." He eyed me curiously. "Have you never wondered why Sotoria?"

"Of course, I've wondered that," I said, struggling to keep the essence down.

"There was a reason Kolis was so drawn to her. Her bloodline is old and managed to carry just enough essence no matter how many generations passed." Aydun gave Attes a tight smile. "It's the same reason you found yourself drawn to her."

"What the fuck?" rasped Attes.

"Sotoria is a direct descendant of the first mortal created by the blood of Eythos and the first draken," Aydun said. "And I don't mean in the way all mortals are descended from the first. Eythos created more than one mortal."

"Obviously," Ash drawled.

"He created several, but she descended from the *first*, who also happened to give birth to the first mortal children—a son, a daughter, and then a second."

I tensed.

"Sotoria descends directly from that second daughter, born in a shroud. Chosen even before Kolis first saw her picking flowers for her sister's wedding, just like every single second daughter of her bloodline afterward." Aydun cocked his head. "Until you."

My mouth dropped open, and Ash's head jerked toward me. "You cannot be saying what I think you are."

"That you and Sotoria are of the same bloodline? Yes. That is what I'm saying. Sotoria was never randomly reborn into anyone. She was always reborn in the Mierel bloodline," he told us as if it was something we should've always known.

And granted, now hearing it, it *was* something we should've figured out, especially after Keella told me that Eythos answering Roderick Mierel's summons was no random opportunity.

"And that is where your father"—he paused to look at Ash—"made his mistake."

"He asked for the first daughter," Ash murmured, his arms unfolding and falling to his sides.

"Eythos was brilliant. He knew what Sotoria descended from. He'd figured out what she would one day become, but for some absolutely mind-numbing reason, he and Keella believed that having her soul reborn in a first daughter was the key to everything." Aydun rolled his eyes, and, oh boy, that was a weird sight to witness, given those kaleidoscope eyes. "That was why she was not reborn. To be honest, I'm surprised Eythos didn't damn the realms with that one act of stupidity. You were a first daughter, never meant to carry much essence in you, let alone embers of life. You should've died."

A growl ripped out of Ash's throat. "What did you just say?"

"It was no threat," Aydun replied calmly. "Just a statement of fact. First sons and daughters are never meant to be, well, of much importance in the grand scheme of things. Which is why it always amuses me that mortals place so much emphasis on firstborns." He shrugged. "But somehow, your tenacious little self survived, and here we are."

The three of us stared at him, and for some idiotic reason, I blurted out the very next thing that entered my mind. "I'm actually related to that fucker Callum?"

Aydun frowned. "Distantly related, but yes."

My upper lip curled. "Ew."

"As disturbing as that realization may be," Ash said after a moment, pulling his gaze from me to focus on the Fate, "and as interesting as this little history lesson has been, it doesn't change why we summoned you. We want The Star."

"Thank you for finding my history lesson interesting," Aydun replied. "But as I said, it is too late."

"No, it's not," I snarled. "All you have to do is go and get it from wherever one of your fellow assholes stashed it."

Aydun blinked at me. "Look, you succeeded in preventing a full-scale war between the Primals. Barely," he tacked on. "Many gods and Primals were lost, but a true war would've lasted years, if not decades or longer. So, congratulations."

Attes snorted at that.

"You managed to stop the Ancients from being too disturbed," Aydun went on. "But Eythos failed to stop the prophecy, as did you."

"She did not fail shit," Ash warned.

"Okay. Both of you failed, then. Does sharing the responsibility make it easier to swallow?" Aydun challenged. "You could've released Sotoria the moment her soul was placed in The Star. You didn't."

"It was too risky," I argued.

"True. Kolis would've felt her. He's had enough of her blood that every time she is reborn, he senses her," he said, and disgust swept through me. "And now that he's also had your blood, he would've *definitely* felt her because a tiny part of you has mingled with her and vice versa."

I stepped back and then snapped forward when Ash moved toward the Ancient. I grabbed his arm, holding him back.

Aydun sighed. "Why are you mad at me for once again stating a simple fact?"

"It doesn't matter." I wrapped my arms around Ash's. "What does, is that you also know it was too risky to release Sotoria until Kolis was entombed. He would've burned through the realms to get to her and then disappeared into some hole with her."

"Yes, he would have," Aydun stated, glancing at one of the nearby chests. "What's in these?"

"That's not important," Attes bit out. "We didn't know that him having her blood from her prior lives was something he could've picked up on." His gaze found mine. "That means if we had released Sotoria now and she chose to live a mortal life, Kolis would've felt her, even while entombed. It may have taken him a while to get his ass free, but he would have had one big motivation to do so."

Meaning he wouldn't have remained entombed for thousands of years. Not even hundreds. Or decades. "Gods."

Attes dragged a hand over his face. "So, what does this mean?"

The Fate nudged a chest with his foot. "It's pretty obvious if you would all give yourself five seconds to think about it."

I opened my mouth, but Ash spoke. "She will be reborn from the Mierel bloodline."

"She will be reborn as the second daughter of the Mierel bloodline," Aydun corrected. "Whenever that happens."

Ash looked down at me. So did Attes. My entire body was tingling, and not necessarily in a good way. I placed a hand on my stomach. Attes's gaze followed my motion with a frown.

"Don't worry." Aydun tipped the chest, and something metal clanged around inside it. "You do not carry daughters."

Ash's head snapped to the Fate.

"Male twins tend to run in your bloodline," he remarked. "Hopefully, they will turn out better than their predecessors and current company."

I gaped at him.

"Sotoria's soul is beyond your reach now. You all need to accept that. Now, we are left with only one way to prevent her from being reborn from *the giver of blood and the bringer of bone, the Primal of Blood and Ash.*"

Muscles up and down Ash's arm tensed. "If you're about to suggest what I think you are—"

"You will do what?" Aydun challenged, finally ceasing messing with the chests. "Attack me? Curse at me? Go ahead. It won't change what will come. It won't change that you will both continue to risk the safety of the realms out of selfishness to bring two babes into the realm that will eventually have babes of their own until one of them is the cause of millions of deaths—"

Ash broke my hold, lurching at the Ancient. My shout was lost in a rush of air that pushed Ash back to where I stood.

"For the third time, your anger is misplaced." Aydun's chin lowered as he fully faced us. "She will be reborn of your bloodline—*the giver of blood and the bringer of bone*—and she will carry within her the embers of life and death. Touched by life and death."

I stood there, rooted to the floor, the spot on my shoulder where the crescent-shaped birthmark rested beginning to tingle.

"Her shroud will be that of crimson-and-gold and will bear a royal mark," he said, sparks flying from his fingers as he moved his hand through the air. Faint silvery flames followed, forming a painfully familiar symbol.

The crown of elm and the sword—the slightly slanted sword.

The crown of life.

The sword of death.

But the flames changed, taking on more characteristics of the symbol of death. The crown became a circle, and the sword an arrow drenched in gold and surrounded by crimson.

Wrapped in the shroud of death.

My nostrils flared, and I gritted my teeth.

"She will be a Queen of Flesh and Fire, and she will usher in the end with the name of the true Primal of Life on her lips," Aydun said as the flaming symbol faded. "Death and destruction will follow her."

Silence fell then, settling over the chamber. Seconds ticked by.

"This isn't fair to her," I whispered hoarsely. "I didn't want this for her, not after all her suffering."

"She'll likely have no knowledge of her past," Aydun said, causing the three of us to look at him sharply.

"I don't understand," Attes said.

"Those who are reborn may have memories of their previous lives, but they often show as dreams or instances of déjà vu," he explained. "But they almost always fade as who that person has become in their new life begins to take shape." He paused. "They may be the same soul and look identical to who they were before, but they are not entirely the same person."

"Well," Attes sighed. "I guess that is a relief."

"Doesn't make it any better," I said.

"No," Aydun agreed. "I suppose it doesn't."

"Nothing is written in stone." Ash curved his arm around my shoulders. "Prophecy or not. This may never come to pass."

Aydun's head tilted again. "You're right. Nothing is predestined. There is hope. You may still be able to prevent the rise of the Primal of Blood and Bone—a being who will not only awaken Death and those in the ground but also carry within her absolute power." His eyes met mine. "And you know what they say about absolute power."

I did.

I'd said it myself.

"But she will have nowhere near the strength she will grow into when Death comes for her. She, like you, would be a..." He smiled. "A baby Primal."

I glared at him.

"So, she will likely fall to Death whilst in the process of waking the Ancients," he said. "And even if she somehow manages to defeat Death, she would be corrupted just as those in the ground were—and at a much faster rate." Aydun straightened to his full, towering height. "And if that happens, it will take every single god and even those in the ground to bring her down. For she will destroy all of us."

Aydun was wrong, though.

He was *wrong*.

The corners of my lips curved up.

He frowned, and Ash sent me a questioning look.

"I'm not sure why you're smiling," Attes muttered.

"Is that all?" I asked.

For a moment, the Ancient looked uncertain, and then he, too, smiled faintly. "It is."

"Why is it now just hitting me that you are with child?" Attes murmured from where he sat across from Ash and me. We'd come upstairs and ended up in what appeared to be Attes's office.

There were no empty shelves on his walls. Just a shit ton of weapons.

I kind of liked it.

"With two," Attes corrected, blinking rapidly. "Congratulations—" He sat up straight, his head swinging toward Ash. "You let her fight while pregnant?"

"While I wasn't entirely thrilled with her doing so," Ash replied, taking a drink of the whiskey Attes had poured for him, "I do not control what she does."

I raised my brows at Attes.

"Fates," the Primal muttered, rubbing his hand over his face. "Neither of you is thinking about listening to that fuck of a Fate and…" He swallowed the whiskey, lips peeling back. "Ending their lives before they begin, are you?"

"No," Ash said.

"Good. You two deserve the joy of parenthood and its horrors." A brief dimple appeared in a flash of a grin, and I thought about his children. Would he ever have more? "Besides, there are other ways to prevent…fuck, to prevent Sotoria from being reborn."

"I'm sorry." I leaned forward, resting my elbows on my knees. "Maybe we should've risked releasing her sooner."

"You know what would've happened if we had." He lowered his glass.

"At least she is safe for now." Ash rubbed my back. "She's not really conscious while in The Star, right?"

I steepled my fingers under my chin. "Not always."

"Then, to her, it will be as if she is sleeping," he said.

"Yeah." I closed my eyes, absolutely hating that Sotoria was trapped in The Star, aware or not. It wasn't fair. "We should still try to find it."

"The Fates could've hidden it anywhere," Attes said.

"Or given it to someone." I thought about what I'd seen around Callum's remains. "We need to find Callum."

Ash's eyes narrowed. "You think the Fates gave it to him? The last I saw of him, he was in pieces."

"He's her brother." And my…well, whatever. I told them what I'd seen before the Temple collapsed.

Ash cursed. "Fucking Fates."

"Ditto," I murmured, looking across at Attes. "You were right about there being other ways to prevent her from being reborn. We're having sons."

Attes nodded.

Beside me, Ash sighed heavily and tilted his head back, the glass of whiskey resting on his knee. "I know what you are thinking."

I pressed my lips together. Ash had envisioned our sons scrambling over benches in the throne room, playing with Reaver and Jadis, and then our grandchildren doing the same.

There would be no grandchildren.

I closed my eyes. We would have to ensure our sons never had children. Maybe they would be lucky and would never want them, nor whomever they ended up falling in love with. Not everyone did, and it would be for the best if they felt that way. But if they *did* want children? I shook my head. It wasn't right or fair. Neither was what had been done to Sotoria.

"We shouldn't rely on them never procreating," Attes said quietly.

"I know." Ash finished off his whiskey and set the glass aside. "We need to look for Callum. In the meantime, plan for the day that either fate or nature finds a way." A muscle ticked in his jaw. "She will not be born all-powerful. No god or Primal is. She will be vulnerable until Ascension," he said, each word filled with distaste. "Fuck."

I stared at him, understanding what he was suggesting. That would be a mark neither of us would bear because I didn't think we would survive it.

"No," I said, eather flooding my veins. I had to rein it back in. "If she manages to be born, she deserves to live."

Ash's eyes met mine. "I agree. I do."

"Stop there." I rose, beginning to pace. "I understand what it means if she's born. But I also know that doesn't mean the Ancients will awaken here. And yeah, I am damning the lands beyond the Primal Veil."

Attes's brow furrowed, and he looked up at me.

"And if they do awaken here, then we will do everything we can to lessen the damage. And like those before us, put them back in the ground," I said. "Because I will not be a part of murdering a child or an adult of my blood," I said. "And I know you would not be able to live after doing something like that, Ash, no matter if it was carried out by our words or hands."

"No," he said quietly. "I would not."

"Neither of us would." I idly rubbed my lower stomach.

"I'm not going to disagree with you two on this," Attes said, leaning back. "But there is also the fact that Kolis will wake."

"And if that happens, I will put the dagger in her hand myself," I swore, repeating what I had told Kolis. "One thing I'm not worried about is her being corrupted."

"Is that why you were smiling before Aydun left?" Attes asked.

"Power and consequence come from the will of the beholder, right?" I stopped behind Ash, placing my hands on his shoulders. "Both of you were there when Holland said it. None born from my bloodline hungered for power. None will."

"Well, at least we don't have to worry about that," Attes remarked.

"No. That's one good thing." I squeezed Ash's shoulders. "There is something else Aydun said. She will be born in a shroud. That means she'll be born mortal."

Ash's head tilted back. "You're right." His eyes searched mine. "But our sons will be born in the mortal realm."

Damn it, I'd forgotten what Kye had said, but that wasn't what I was thinking about. "If the prophecy holds true, she won't be born until a long time from now, and the whole *born of the same misdeeds* thing? I have a feeling she will believe herself to be mortal. That she will be surrounded by them." Letting go of Ash's shoulders, I walked around the couch and sat beside him. "Maybe I'm completely wrong about that, but Aydun said she would call the name of the true Primal of Life."

The skin between Ash's brows creased. "He did."

"Then we need to make sure no mortals know who the true Primal of Life is."

He stiffened. "Sera—"

"They can believe it is you. I will be known as the Consort or whatever," I said in a rush. "If my name isn't known, she cannot speak it."

"We don't even know what speaking your name will do, but it sure didn't sound like it would stop the prophecy if she didn't say it," he argued.

"For Aydun to mention it, it has to mean something."

"Yeah, the same Fate who failed to mention the *eirini*," Attes commented. "But she has a point. It could be something small, but it is something."

Ash was shaking his head.

"The mortals don't need to know about me. We can have other gods answer their summonses and have Rhain or Rhahar be known as the—"

"It will mean you are never known," he interrupted, eather piercing his eyes. "And you have lived long enough without being known."

"I know—"

"I cannot allow that." His hand cut furiously through the air. "Your name will be known, as well as all you have accomplished and sacrificed. There will be stories and songs written about you. People will celebrate your name. The name that brings others joy. You will not be unknown—"

"Ash," I whispered, cupping his cheek and blinking back tears. I knew why he wanted to deny this. And gods, it made me love him even more.

"You cannot tell me you will not be hurt by this, Sera." His cold fingers curled around my wrist. "You won't only be unknown. You will eventually be forgotten."

Hearing that did make my stomach drop. I couldn't deny it. Being forgotten was almost the same as never existing, and Ash understood how much it had hurt not to be known by anyone. How it had made me feel like a specter among the living. But something struck me in that moment. That was then. It wasn't me now.

"You know me," I said. "My children will know me. Attes will, and everyone else I care about will know me."

The muscle in his jaw clenched against my palm. "That isn't enough."

"But it is." I leaned over and kissed him softly, then rested my forehead against his. "You are enough."

64

Two months later…

Ash stared down at me, his eyes never leaving my face as he entered me with one hard thrust of his hips that shook the glasses and dishware on the antechamber table.

We had just finished breakfast and should be getting ready. The other Primals and gods wanted a celebration, and Ash and I not only thought it was a good idea but also figured it was time. The last several weeks had been for mourning those we'd lost, and this event was to celebrate their memories as much as it was to mark our victory. The event would be at the City Hall, and Rhain was running around like a madman. He would probably have a breakdown if he knew what we were doing.

We hadn't planned to end up this way. It just sort of happened. I'd stood to ready myself and mentioned that Erlina had made adjustments to the gown I wanted to wear. It had become too tight around both breasts and my lower stomach. The growing bump wasn't entirely noticeable to the eye, depending on what I wore, but Ash had such a voracious reaction. He'd kissed me, and that single kiss had turned into one that ended with me splayed across the table, my robe unbuttoned, and Ash between my thighs.

"If we're late," I said, biting my lower lip as pleasure darted through my veins, "Rhain will be so mad."

Ash moved slowly inside me, clearly in no hurry. The hand on my hip tightened. "We'll just tell him we took our time with dessert."

A giggle snuck free. "Dessert with breakfast?"

"Mm-hmm." His gaze left mine and traveled downward. He cupped a breast with his other hand. The sweep of his thumb over my nipple had my back arching off the table. A smoky grin appeared. "They are so much more sensitive."

They definitely were. Sometimes, even clothing irritated or aroused them.

Right now, it was the latter.

Ash's head dipped. His lips found mine once more, and I tasted cream on his tongue. He sipped from my lips and kept up that slow, torturous tempo with his hips. His mouth left mine, blazing a path over my jaw and then down my throat. He lingered there, kissing and licking until he reached where my pulse beat wildly. I tensed around him in sweet, heady anticipation. After a heartbeat, I felt the graze of his sharp fangs. My fingers pressed into the skin of his chest as the scrape sent a burst of desire through me with only a hint of unease. That was progress.

A lot of progress.

Over the last two months, we'd been slowly working together to overcome my trauma related to feeding. Maybe *overcome* wasn't the right word. I'd come to believe that trauma wasn't always something you could overcome and no longer be affected by. The mind didn't work that way, be you mortal, god, or Primal. Trauma stayed with you, sometimes returning at night or during the quieter parts of the day. Other times, it disappeared for days or weeks. But I was beginning to live with it. To acknowledge it and then handle it, just like I had when it came to my anxiety. Neither were the sum of who I was. It was just a *part* of who I was.

Either way, Ash hadn't wanted to push it at first, telling me we could wait until our sons were born, but it wasn't something I was willing to put off until then. We still had time before I was too far along in my pregnancy for Ash to be able to feed, and I wanted to share that with him again before the babes came. I wasn't exactly sure why, but it was important to me. So, Ash had relented. And to be honest, I think he started to enjoy the process after a while. The teasing drags of his fangs, the brief, shallow bites that only drew a drop of blood, had gone from causing me to lock up in dread and shame to something that had my blood pounding with lust and need.

He gave me one of those tiny bites that drew just a hint of blood, then chased it away with his tongue, making me moan. He stilled for a few seconds afterward, like he always did. I knew what he was doing in those brief heartbeats. He was tasting my emotions, making sure I was okay.

And right then, I was more than okay.

I was *ready*.

"More," I whispered.

Ash chuckled against my pulse, and then his tongue slid over my skin, causing my breath to hitch. He drew the flesh of my throat into his mouth, wringing a gasp from me, but he moved on.

A hint of disappointment rose. "Ash?"

"Hmm?" His lips danced over my collarbone.

I slid my hands to his shoulders. "I'm ready."

Ash froze for just a second and then shuddered. "I know you are." He pushed into me, grinding against my clit. "You're soaking wet."

Warmth hit my cheeks. "I wasn't talking about *that.*"

"I know."

"Then—"

Ash moved with lightning speed, closing his mouth over mine. His deep kiss was like a match striking flint, kicking off a shower of sparks. It was possessive. Almost feral in its neediness, and I fucking loved it.

I lifted my legs, curling them around his waist, and pushing up to meet the plunge of his hips. He groaned against my mouth, and a full-body tremor swept through him. My lips felt swollen when his mouth left mine.

"I want you to watch me," he ordered in a voice wrapped in silk and shadows. He kissed my chin and then the crook of my neck. "I don't want you to take your eyes off me. Understand?"

I nodded, watching him as the edges of his hair teased the side of my breast.

He halted, his breath cool against my nipple, and his gaze flicking to mine. "I want to hear you say it, *liessa.*"

My eyes narrowed slightly. "Yes."

That shadowy smile returned. "That's my Queen."

His head lowered once more, but his gaze remained locked onto mine as he took the peak of my breast into his mouth. The graze of his fangs against my soft flesh sent desire streaking through me. He drew the turgid peak into his mouth, and even if he hadn't ordered me, I wouldn't have been able to look away. His tongue swirled over the hardened bud, and my eyes started to flutter shut as I rocked against him. Acute wisps of pleasure spread through me. I was aching by the time he let go.

"Keep watching."

"I am," I panted.

"Good." His hair teased my skin as he moved to my left breast. His tongue traveled up the swell. "Whose mouth is on you?"

I blinked. "Yours."

He nipped at the skin.

"My King?"

Ash caught my nipple between his thumb and forefinger. I cried out, back bowing, and his grin was downright wicked. "I want you to say my name."

My legs tightened around him, and our eyes locked once more. An aching pressure settled in my chest and between my thighs. "Nyktos."

His growl rumbled through me.

I grinned. "*Ash.*"

He showed his approval with a flick of his tongue. "And whose cock is inside you?"

My heart was pounding so fast. "Ash—" He struck before I could even finish saying his name.

Ash pierced the skin of my breast right above my nipple. His gaze still holding mine, I cried out. My hands flew to his hair as the sharp burst of pain momentarily overwhelmed my senses, stroking that fear I fought so hard to deal with, but…

But it was his quicksilver eyes that held mine.

It was Ash's fangs that had pierced my vein. It was Ash's lips and mouth that moved hungrily. It was Ash's throat that swallowed greedily. It was Ash who drank from me. His cock still deep inside me. It was his name that I had called out when his fangs sank into me.

And it was his name I shouted again as the pain quickly gave way to pleasure, but it…it felt different, causing my thoughts to run together chaotically. It had been so long since I'd felt his bite, but even then, I knew this was different. Stronger. He groaned, continuing to drink from me. Eather whirled through his eyes, and his pupils dilated. It had also been too long since he'd tasted more than a drop of my blood.

The steady drag and pull of Ash taking my blood into himself was the kind of ecstasy that was as fierce as a current of eather coursing through me, consuming every sense with searing intensity and leaving no room to think of anything, let alone feel anything but his mouth and the decadent agony he unleashed. I came apart without warning, my back arching. I held his mouth to my breast.

The sound that came from him was animalistic. My grip loosened. His hips moved faster, each thrust deeper and harder as he drank from me. And his gaze—his beautiful silver eyes—remained locked on mine, keeping me grounded. He didn't look away, not even to blink, until he closed the wound with a sweep of his tongue.

"Sera," he said, stretching up to take my mouth in his. I tasted my blood on his lips. His chest was harder against mine, and when I ran my hands from his hair over his shoulders, I felt his flesh becoming smoother. "I'm going to fuck you now."

Ash pulled free of me and lifted me from the table. I caught a glimpse of his shadowstone-hued skin. The moment my feet touched the stone floor, he turned me with one hand on my hip. The other pressed me down until my chest was flush against the table. His hand left my hip, sliding between my cheek and the table so I rested on his forearm. He thrust deeply, all the way to the hilt.

He held himself completely still, his length and hardness filling me as his rough, short breaths stirred the hair at my temple. "You okay?"

"Yes," I breathed.

Then he moved again, and things…things sort of spun out of control.

Ash reached down, hooking his arm around my thigh. He lifted my leg so my knee was on the table. The angle sent him deeper. He moved behind me, fast and hard, each thrust shaking the dishware even more than before. The way he placed me on the table and his dominating presence held me in place. There was no escaping the plunge of his hips, nowhere to hide from the fire he was building inside me. Not that I wanted to. I reveled in every hard, raw pump of his hips and the slick feel of him. I clutched the fingers of his hand beside my head, the contrast of my skin against the now-midnight hue of his startling. Oh, gods. I could feel him growing thicker, larger as he shifted completely into his Primal form. The sounds that came from me as he fucked me scorched the air. My body started to stiffen, and tension coiled tighter and tighter inside me. He thrust in, his hips rolling and grinding—

My head kicked back, and that tension erupted, shattering into a thousand silken shards. Ash pressed in, holding still as wisps of shadowy eather whipped out, flowing across the table when he roared his release. Something cracked somewhere. I wasn't sure what it was. The pleasure swept us both up in a storm that rose and fell in crashing waves until we were both spent.

I slowly became aware of something cool and damp slipping over our joined hands. My eyes fluttered open to see a puddle. I followed the streams of water to the shattered glasses.

My eyebrows rose. "Ash?"

"Mmm?"

"You broke the glasses."

"I did?" He lifted his head from my shoulder. "Fuck."

I grinned. "I think that is what broke them."

He laughed roughly. "You okay?"

"Perfect."

"You are."

My grin grew as he leaned over me, kissing my cheek. He eased himself from me and lifted me from the table, then turned me again. But this time, he sat.

Ash didn't just jerk me onto his lap. He slowly lowered me and brought my gaze to his. Once he didn't detect anything off, he folded his arms around me, holding me close to his chest.

"I think," he said, his chest rising and falling against my hand, "we need to end breakfast this way every day."

"Then we will really be out of glasses."

He chuckled, smoothing several curls back from my face. "Worth it."

We sat there for a little bit, letting our hearts slow. We needed to start getting ready. My hand slid over his chest as I started sitting up—

I jolted, my gaze going to where my hand rested on his chest. I could feel his heart beneath my palm, beating in a steady rhythm that…

Gasping, my head jerked up. "Do you feel that?"

His half-hooded gaze swept over me. "Your come on my dick? I do."

My eyes widened. "Oh, my gods, I'm not talking about that!"

"Look at you." He toyed with my hair. "Blushing."

I felt like my face was on fire. "I'm talking about our hearts." I stopped the hand that was wandering from my stomach and brought it to my chest. "Focus."

His lazy grin froze, and then the haze disappeared from his eyes. He sat straighter.

"They…they're beating in sync, aren't they?" I said.

"I think they are." He swallowed thickly, his voice filling with wonder. "I think it's because we're mates of the heart, but…" He trailed off with a frown and then blinked. "This is the first time I've fed from you since you awakened."

Nodding, I bit my lower lip and felt the twinge in my breast as if his bite mark responded to his words.

"It's like a bond, right?" he said. "I think having your blood is like a final connection, which means…"

"What?"

His eyes held mine, and a slow grin started to stretch across his lips. "I think we'll find out soon enough."

"What do—?"

Ash kissed me, parting my lips with a sweep of his tongue. The moment my heart sped up, I felt his doing the same under my palm. The sensation was…it was *wild*.

"We'll talk more after the celebration," he said once the kiss ended. "We need to get ready now since you made us late."

I drew back. "*I* made us late?"

"That's what I'm telling Rhain," he said, catching my wrist as I went to smack his chest. He laughed. "Be good."

"I'm choosing to ignore both of those statements so *you* won't make us any more late," I said. "I need to put actual, real clothing on."

"Please, do." His fingers tightened around my hair. "I would hate to start the celebration by carving out the eyes of anyone who looks at you."

I laughed as our eyes met. And gods, what I saw in his stare made my heart skip. It was utter devotion. I clasped his cool cheeks. "How did I get so lucky to have your love?"

"You weren't lucky, *liessa*." Ash's lips brushed mine. "I was."

I held Reaver's hand and cradled Jadis against my hip as we walked under the twinkling lights strung across the City Hall.

I considered it practice for the future as I smiled at those we passed.

The little girl I carried was in her draken form, which meant her claws were buried in my hair, and I was pretty sure some of it was in her mouth based on how Reaver looked up at her with narrowed eyes.

Both draken had insisted on coming with me, although I had a feeling Jadis only wanted to go because Reaver had taken my hand.

The whole time I'd spoken with Erlina, I'd felt Ash's gaze. He wasn't the only one who watched my every move. So did Rhain and Nektas. Ash and I had shared with Rhain a month ago that we were expecting so he could assist Kye and Aios in gathering information. Of course, I wanted the others to know, but things hadn't been entirely peaceful over the last two months. There were outbursts of violence in several of the Courts once ruled by those loyal to Kolis. The ceeren numbers had been severely depleted, but they were still out there, with only a few swearing allegiance to Saion. We knew we hadn't rounded up all the Revenants, but we would. Then there were the draken loyal to Kolis. Not all of them had perished, and it wasn't until a few days after entombing Kolis that I thought of Sax, the draken who'd once served Eythos. When I asked Nektas if he had sensed Sax in the Bonelands, he'd shared that he hadn't. He hadn't joined the fight, and we didn't know if that meant he was dead or not. We were looking for him.

But once we were sure the last of those loyal to Kolis were dealt with—or, at the very least, no longer posed a great risk—we would share the news with everyone.

I could feel their eyes on me even now as I made my way back to our table placed before the dais. We hadn't eaten on the dais like two supreme rulers looking over everyone. Only Ehthawn was stretched out before the thrones, watching over everything. My heart panged for the loss of Crolee and the other draken—for Kars and all those we'd lost.

Well, not everyone.

While I was still conflicted over Veses, I wasn't exactly sad. My gaze swept over the smiling faces and moved to the colonnade's torchlit alcove. As joyful music echoed through the coliseum, a lone figure stood in the shadows, leaning against the wall, nursing a bottle of liquor.

Attes.

I'd seen him often these last two months. When he wasn't in Vathi assisting Lailah with establishing her rule and preparing Theon, he was in the Shadowlands. Ash had said it was because being in Vathi reminded him too much of his brother.

Reaver squeezed my hand. "Sera?"

"Yes?"

"Why are you sad?" he asked, and Jadis stopped tugging on my hair.

That damn *notam*.

"I'm just thinking about those we miss," I told him.

He nodded, his small lips pinched. "I think about my parents sometimes," he said after a moment. "I don't remember much about them, but I miss them."

"Does thinking about them make you sad?" I asked as I led them past a group of young godlings with wide eyes.

One of his shoulders lifted. "Yes, but Nek told me once that it's a good kind of sadness to have because it means you remember them, and memories will keep them alive with you."

I thought about that. Nektas was right. Ezra, Marisol, and my mother lived on in my memories, even if it hurt right now. And someday, I would visit them and my father. "That is very true." I glanced over at Jadis, who most definitely had my hair in her mouth. "Your father is very wise."

She chirped but I heard her soft voice say *daddy*.

My lips curved up as we neared the group of Primal goddesses. I'd never heard her call him that before. It was adorable.

The drumbeat rose, and the tempo of the music picked up. When I reached the Primals, I saw partners separating, forming two lines that faced each other.

"You all aren't dancing?" I asked.

Bele snorted. "I'd rather not have broken toes by the evening."

Aios rolled her eyes and folded her arms over her emerald gown. "I'm not that bad of a dancer."

"There are many reasons I love you, *so'vit*," Bele said as Ione grinned from where she stood behind them. "But your dancing skills are not one of them."

"I'm sure the same can be said about your tact," Ione commented.

"I can agree with that." Aios laughed and leaned over to kiss Bele.

Grinning, I met Ione's stare. She stepped around them so she could hear me when I spoke in a low voice. "Any luck?"

Ione had been attempting to catch what she called an impression of Sotoria's soul. We weren't even sure if it was possible since it was held in The Star.

She shook her head. "Not yet," she said, clasping her hands. "I was thinking of entering the mortal realm and seeing if that helped."

Instinct told me that Callum was likely in possession of her soul, and it would be wise of him to stay far away from Iliseeum. But how long could he get by in the mortal realm? Thierran had also been traveling through dreams to see if he could pick up on anything, which was highly disturbing to think about, but we weren't even sure if whatever Callum was *could* dream. That was something I hadn't considered until Thierran mentioned it.

"Let me know what you find out," I said.

"Of course." Ione watched the couples loop arms as they met in the middle.

"I'm not sure if you're aware of this or not," Bele said from behind the rim of her glass, "but Jadis is currently eating your hair."

Ione did such a quick double-take that strands of dark hair smacked her chin. "Oh, dear."

"I think she's mostly nibbling on it," I said.

"As if that is better," Reaver said under his breath.

"I agree with that, little man." Bele winked at him.

Reaver beamed up at her.

"Are you still hungry, honey?" Aios asked, reaching up and gently tugging my hair free from Jadis's mouth. Her silver eyes were still a shock for me to see.

Eyes big and wide, Jadis nodded her little diamond-shaped head.

I wasn't sure how she was still hungry since she had eaten at least two platefuls. "Then let us get you back to your father."

Jadis gave my hair a tug of happy agreement, nearly jerking my head off my shoulders.

"Wow," Bele murmured.

I would have a sore neck by the time this night was over.

Avoiding the dancing, I skirted the edges of the Hall's floor. As I rounded the table, Ash's gaze followed me. I had to bite the inside of my lip to keep myself from smiling.

I came up behind Nektas. "I have something for you."

He shifted back and lifted his hands. Jadis reached for her father with one arm. "You need to let go of her hair."

For a second, I didn't think she would. Several strands were stretched across the space between me and where she was nestled against Nektas's chest.

"I fear you will have little hair left on your head," Rhain commented from the other side of Nektas. Beside him, Rhahar hid his snort behind his glass.

Nektas sighed, gently prying his daughter's claws free. "Sorry about that."

"It's okay." Catching sight of Attes as I smoothed the strands, I smiled down at Reaver. "Will you do me a favor?"

He nodded eagerly.

"Can you keep Ash company for me while I speak to Attes?"

Ash raised a brow but remained silent, sipping from his cup.

"I can." He drew out the word, looking over his shoulder at Ash while Nektas chuckled under his breath. "But he'd probably enjoy your company more."

One side of Ash's lips curved up.

"Not true. He always enjoys your company." Cradling the back of his head, I kissed his blond hair and met Ash's gaze.

He gave me a subtle nod.

The moment I let go of Reaver, he darted past Nektas and scrambled into the chair I had occupied. I watched a smile break out across Ash's face as he shifted his attention to the youngling. When I turned, Nektas caught my arm.

"He's not doing great," Nektas noted in a low voice, nodding toward the colonnade's alcove as he rubbed the spot between Jadis's wings. "Aurelia is worried."

I glanced up to see the female draken perched on the pillars above where Attes stood in the shadows. "I know."

I quickly passed the long table, spotting Saion with a deck of cards. I had no idea what was going on there, but the devious glint in the Primal's eyes and the way Theon sat across from him, shaking his head, told me Saion would likely gain some coin before the night ended.

Picking up the lacy skirt of my black gown, I climbed the short set of steps and crossed into the alcove. Attes didn't look at me as I approached, but he gave me an elaborate bow.

I shook my head at the gesture. "Surprised to see you standing in the shadows."

"I know. It does seem like something your husband would do." A quick grin appeared. There was no dimple. "There's really no reason."

I knew that was a lie as I studied his profile. In the last two months, there had been moments when Attes seemed more like his old self. He'd do his level best to annoy Ash. He'd laugh. He'd smile. But I only saw the dimples appear when he was driving Lailah mad about something. Then, there were all the other moments where he looked like he hadn't slept in several days. What concerned me the most was that, more and more, his features were utterly impassive, like he felt absolutely nothing.

"Please, don't," he said, his eyes meeting mine.

"Don't what?"

"Ask if I'm okay." He sighed, his gaze leaving mine again. "I am."

"I won't ask it," I said. "But I also know you're not."

He took a swig of what was likely whiskey. I followed his gaze, realizing he was watching Lailah dance with a man I didn't recognize. Her braids were down and flowed around her shoulders bared by her white gown.

"She looks beautiful tonight," I commented.

"She does."

My gaze roamed over the tall, dark-haired male as he lifted her and spun, sending the hem of her gown billowing. I sensed the man was a god, but I stopped myself from seeing more. "Who is she dancing with?"

"Some jackass."

I looked at him. "Then why aren't you dancing with her?"

"Because I'm a worse jackass." He grinned, and the dimple on his right cheek winked into existence. "I've been thinking."

"Oh, no," I teased lightly, even though I had a good idea exactly what he had been thinking about.

Attes's smirk was halfhearted. "I think it's time."

I drew in a breath that stung my throat. "When?"

"Tomorrow."

My eyes fell shut. *Tomorrow*?

"I've stayed longer than I planned," he continued. "Lailah is ready. So is Theon. Vathi will be in good hands."

"Until you return," I added, my voice hoarse as I opened my eyes.

His stare met mine. "Until I return."

This time, I breathed through my nose. I wanted to tell him they weren't ready, but that wouldn't be fair to the twins, and it would also be a lie.

"Don't."

I blinked rapidly. "What am I not to do now?"

"Be sad."

A shaky laugh left me.

He lowered the bottle. "I'm not dying, Sera. I'm just going into stasis. I will be resting."

"I know, but…" My chest rose as I forced in a deep breath. "But I was hoping you wouldn't be ready."

Attes said nothing to that.

I lifted my gaze to his. "I will miss you."

He smiled and looked away. We stood in silence for several minutes, each watching Lailah and the others dancing.

"Attes?"

"Yes, my Queen?"

"You'd better not take too long. I feel as if we will need your aid when it comes to keeping track of these two," I said, patting my stomach.

"Not sure if you really want my influence."

"And I'm pretty sure I do." I stretched up and kissed his cheek. "You're a good man, Attes."

His cheeks pinkened, and I could've sworn I heard a low growl coming from the floor. "And I think you're trying to get me murdered before I can even go *into* stasis."

"He would never." I patted Attes's arm, reluctant to leave his side. "If you need anything between tonight and tomorrow…"

He nodded. I knew he wouldn't need anything. This would be the last time I spoke to him until…until he was ready.

I looked away from him, catching sight of someone who sent a bolt of surprise through me.

Ward stood beside Penellaphe, where she spoke with Ione. I had no idea where Bele and Aios had disappeared to. I hadn't expected to see Ward here. I'd figured the likelihood of him attending was about the same as Holland showing up. Ward looked over to where I stood, a faint smile on his handsome face.

"I'm going to go annoy your husband by complimenting how lovely you look in your gown." Attes pushed off the wall, drawing my attention back to him.

I arched a brow. "And here you were, just worried about being murdered by him."

"I decided watching him struggle not to throttle me is worth the risk," he said with a wink.

Laughing, I watched him make his way to Ash, knowing this was for the best. He was tired. He needed rest. He needed to heal so he didn't become his brother.

And when he was ready to return to us, we would be waiting.

I stayed where I was as Ward excused himself to join me in the alcove.

"I hear many congratulations are in order," he said, the skin at the corners of his eyes creasing with his smile.

I glanced down in surprise. I'd thought the style of gown, how it gathered under my breasts and with its loose waist, had hidden the small bump.

"It's not noticeable," he assured me.

"Then…" My head jerked up, and I sighed. "Holland?"

Ward nodded. "He wanted you to know that he's absolutely thrilled," he said. "He would've given the message to Penellaphe, but he hasn't told her."

"Really?"

"He knows it is wise for only a few to know at this time," He paused. "And he also knows that Penellaphe will be too excited not to blurt it out."

I looked over at Penellaphe, resisting the urge to cradle my stomach, something I found myself doing often for no reason at all. "You really think she will be excited?"

"Of course." A slight frown appeared. "Why wouldn't she be?"

"The prophecy." Since Penellaphe hadn't been there either time when we spoke with Keella, I had filled her in on what we had learned and what Aydun said. "You're aware of what we discovered?"

Ward nodded.

Something occurred to me then. "If we are somehow unable to prevent Sotoria from being reborn? A *viktor* will likely be involved."

The breeze ruffled his sandy-brown hair as he tilted his head. "I can't say for sure, but she would usher in great change."

"She will do more than just that."

His gaze lifted to mine.

"Holland said that none in my bloodline has ever hungered for power," I said after a moment. "Even those who held power. I imagine that will hold true, be they mortal, god, or Primal."

Ward was silent.

"If she is reborn and given a *viktor*, I want it to be you. I plan to get a message to Holland to let him know that I have requested this. I don't think he'll refuse. I feel like he owes me."

Ward's sea-blue eyes shot to mine. "I—"

"If not for you, I would not be standing here today. You saved my namesake and likely my life in Lotho," I said quickly. "I trust you."

"You barely know me."

"I know that you would not kill a child," I replied.

He closed his mouth, but I swore I saw relief in his eyes.

I looked closely at him. "What did you think I was going to ask?"

Ward didn't answer immediately. "What my last Queen asked of me."

My brows flew up. "I would never ask you to kill a child."

"I do not mean to insult you with such a suggestion," he said. "But she will not be just a child, whether she hungers for power or not. She will wake the Ancients."

"I know." My fingernails pressed into my palms. "But until then, she will be a child. One day, she may become a great and powerful being, but she…" Pressure clamped down on my chest, and I had to count to five. "Kolis will be aware of her from the moment she's reborn. It may take him years after to free himself, but he will do so, and he will come for her. I doubt we will get lucky and have him only find her after she rises as this Primal." I absolutely hated what I said next because it made me feel like I was aiding in history repeating itself. That I was taking part in what I wanted to prevent Sotoria from ever experiencing again. "She will have no real memory of herself—or of Kolis and what he will do to her. And I assume the Fates will demand that nobody warn her in order to keep the balance." I spat the last word. "She needs to be trained to defend herself."

I held my breath for five more seconds. "Just as you trained the Silver Knight. Just as Holland trained me."

Ward was silent for several moments. "Okay." He nodded. "I will do as you ask. I will serve as her *viktor* with honor, and I will not fail you." His chin lifted. "I will not fail her."

Ash held my hand, running his thumb over the golden swirl as cups at the table were continuously refilled, and laughter mingled with the music.

I threaded the fingers of my free hand through Reaver's soft hair. He was half-lying on Attes with his head in my lap. Jadis had left her father to wind herself around Ash's shoulders. Why she liked that so much was beyond me.

My gaze flickered over those before us. I smiled at seeing Bele and Aios finally dancing, holding each other as they slowly swayed completely off-beat with the lively music. Lailah had joined Theon, both moving to sit opposite Attes. For once, Theon wasn't looking at Attes like he wished to punch him. They were actually having a conversation. I think that had a lot to do with the god sitting next to Lailah. It turned out he wasn't an asshole. He was one of Attes's generals. Farther down the table, Thierran had joined Ione and Penellaphe. Ward was with them, and they were watching a card game between Saion and Rhahar that had grown to include Rhain.

I glanced up at the colonnade. Aurelia was gone. Now, she sat on the other side of Nektas, having donned a linen gown that reminded me of what Jadis often wore.

It was the first time I'd seen her in her mortal form.

Aurelia had an earthy beauty to her and a husky, infectious laugh. I caught Nektas's lips curving up at the sound of it more than once as we all…as we all simply enjoyed one another's company.

Family.

That was what all of them were to me. To Ash. Family. With them, I would always be seen. Accepted. With them, I knew it would one day be easier to accept and live with the terrible things I'd done and experienced. That's what family did.

And I would do everything in my power to protect them. Just like we would do everything we could to ensure that a powerful being like a Primal of Blood and Bone wasn't created from our union. Our sons would, too. They had to.

But that sense of knowing filled me even as I sat there with my hand wrapped firmly in Ash's. The future wasn't completely written in stone. There were choices. Free will. There were things that not even the Fates could predict. There was *love.* What had not yet come to pass could be altered. I knew that. I *believed* in that.

But the two daughters had been promised eons ago. The rise of a great Primal of Life and Death had been seen. The remaking of the realms and the end had been foretold. When I looked down at Reaver, I knew in my heart and felt it written in my bones that she would return.

The true focus of the prophecy. The harbinger that would set Kolis free, unleashing death and destruction. She who would awaken the Ancients and leave the realms in ruin.

It had all started with her, and it would end with her. The one who was the beginning and the end.

The Queen of Flesh and Fire.

Sotoria reborn.

The Primal of Blood and Ash.

So, when that day came, we would be ready.

Until then?

Ash squeezed my hand. I looked over at him. Nyktos. My King. My husband.

My everything.

His lips moved in a silent *I love you.*

Until then?

We wouldn't waste a fucking second.

The One Who is Blessed

As Nyktos looked over the new building plans for housing in Vathi that both Lailah and Theon had signed off on, he sensed that his wife was nearby.

Without moving his head, he glanced up to find her standing just beyond the pillared alcove of his office. Or should he say, he saw her attempting to hide behind the pillared alcove. Her swollen stomach made that impossible. It was also the source of the emotions assaulting him all at once.

Love was first and foremost, causing the essence to thrum intensely in his veins. He'd never thought it would be possible to feel such love for her and his babes—their sons—he'd yet to look upon. Unsurprisingly, the second emotion was desire, and it was just as intense as the sweeter, softer ones, striking him hard in the gut. Most days, he just had to look at her for his dick to get hard, but as their babes grew in her, he found it incredibly difficult not to walk around with a raging arousal. As her stomach grew, she became even more beautiful and sexier to him. Perhaps it was the glow to her skin that reminded him of the late-summer sun—an actual golden glow—that had been seen the last two months. It could also be the visual reminder of what their love and passion had created that fueled his lust. The only thing that cooled his desire was the final set of emotions.

Concern.

Anxiety.

Fear.

Sera was nearing the end of her term, likely only days away from giving birth, and the last several weeks had been hard. She tired more easily. Sleep was more difficult. And she needed to feed almost daily. They had expected this. Bringing a child of two Primals into the world wasn't easy. *Two* of them, even less so.

But his wife was strong. He knew that. She would bring their sons into this world, likely cursing and attempting to strangle him in the process.

However, she was supposed to be resting. That was what Kye had ordered when she experienced some light bleeding. The Healer and Aios had assured them that Sera was fine and the babes were not at risk, but said they needed to keep an eye on it. So far, there hadn't been any more spotting, but when she'd awoken three days ago to find herself bleeding, he'd been terrified that something was wrong.

Fates, he hadn't been that afraid since she'd been taken from him.

But he wasn't surprised to find her lingering outside his office now. His wife didn't handle *resting* all that well.

He turned his gaze back to the plans. "*Liessa*."

Silence greeted him, but when he looked up through his lashes, he saw her take a small step back.

His lips twitched. "I know you're hiding there."

"I'm not hiding."

"*Liessa*," he purred.

A heavy sigh echoed softly from the hall, and he couldn't hold back the grin any longer. "You're supposed to be resting."

"I've rested," she moaned, her footsteps soft against the stone. "I'm so rested that if I have to spend another minute resting, I may start doing so with my fists."

"That doesn't sound very restful," he said, chuckling as he looked up. His gaze swept over her, and fuck, his dick was immediately as hard as the shadowstone walls. Her fingers danced over the pale, silvery hair he'd braided that morning where it lay over one shoulder. She wore a linen gown, a color somewhere between blue and green, and even though it was loose, the lightweight material stretched taut across breasts that had also swelled with her pregnancy.

They were absolutely…mouthwatering.

His dick throbbed, so he pulled his gaze from her chest and got his libido under control. Since the incident a few days ago, sex was out of the question. So was finding release. Sure, he could use his hand, but he didn't want to feel that without her right there with him, feeling the same. So, he chose to wait until it was safe. And he was fine, even if that meant waiting weeks or months.

He would always wait for her.

Sliding the plans aside, he leaned back and watched her approach him, cradling her stomach, her toes peeking out from under the hem of her gown with every step. Bele had teased her the night before that she waddled now, but he thought each of her steps was as graceful and elegant as always.

"And when I'm forcing myself to rest, my mind doesn't. It wanders," she added, stopping at the edge of his desk. She smoothed a thumb over the glossy leaves of some sort of plant with trailing stems.

He was pretty sure Rhain was responsible for it. And the last five. They kept dying. "Where did it wander to this time?"

"Where did it not?" She rubbed her belly. "But what really occupied my thoughts was our living situation."

Ash knew immediately what she meant. They'd discussed whether to stay in the Shadowlands or take up residency in Dalos. A new palace was being built there—one that would not reek of Kolis's stench.

A lot was being done in the Court to erase Kolis's rule and show everyone who the true Primal of Life was. The statues being erected revealed it was a Queen who truly ruled, despite what the mortals believed.

At first, neither of them had any desire to leave the Shadowlands. Even with the changes being made, Dalos was still a place of bad memories for them. It would take a very long time—if ever—for that to change. But as time passed, a glow had started up in her eyes when she spoke about Dalos. A bone-deep need to be there tied to the essence pumping through her veins. It was her seat of power, after all.

But that was the thing. Sera had no thirst for power.

"I was thinking over what you suggested before." She leaned her hip against the desk, letting go of the plant. He immediately saw that the leaf was a brighter green. "That we don't have to choose between the two. We could live in both places."

"We can," he agreed.

She nodded. This wasn't a decision they needed to make now, especially with the babes on the way, but he knew his wife. It didn't matter if the move was months if not years away and wasn't something she needed to spend her time on. It was just how her mind worked.

He loved that part of her.

Except for when it kept her awake or stopped her from resting.

Pushing his chair back, he extended his hand to her, and she came to him with a small grin.

Threading his fingers around her much warmer ones, he carefully tugged her onto his lap and wrapped an arm around her, letting his hand rest on her belly. The way she immediately relaxed into him was nothing short of a fucking miracle. There had been no brief seconds of hesitation, nor did he pick up on any faint traces of unease. Every day wasn't like this. There were still moments when she fought her thoughts to stop them from taking her back to when she was in Dalos. He hated them because he loathed that the bastard still plagued her. Would likely always do so in some shape or form. But he was never prouder of her than in *these* moments when there was no hesitation.

Because she was strong enough to not let the memories take hold. Because she was able to beat them back when they did.

Tilting his head to the side, he caught a wild curl and tucked it behind her ear. It was always the same one, refusing to be tamed into a braid. "How are you feeling?"

"Other than bored?" She rested a hand on his arm. "I feel fine."

He exhaled quietly and soaked in her features, counting each freckle on her face. Thirty-six. There were shadows under her eyes he would do anything to remove, but she'd had a restless night, waking more than once.

The last time, she didn't go back to sleep. There had been other nights like that, where it had nothing to do with the babes she carried.

Nightmares found her.

Not of her time being held by Kolis. He knew because the aftermath of those nightmares tasted of the sourness of shame. These were nightmares birthed of what she had done after the bastard struck out at Lasania.

He kissed her temple, wishing he could make the nightmares and guilt go away while knowing he couldn't. And shouldn't. She needed to carry those marks to help ensure new ones weren't carved into her flesh.

But the truth was, even knowing that, if he had a way to take it away from her, he would.

"Are those the new housing plans?" she asked, peering at the papers on the desk.

"They are."

"You think that will be enough?"

"For now, yes." He moved his thumb in a slow circle over her stomach. "But since Kyn did very little with much of his portion of Vathi, there is more than enough land to build new housing without encroaching upon the areas used for crops."

She nodded, her gaze taking on a distant quality.

He had a feeling he knew where her mind had gone. "Attes will return."

"I know." She gave him a small smile. "I just miss him."

A low growl rumbled out of him instinctually. It had nothing to do with her or her friendship with the often-irritating-as-fuck Primal.

Sera's eyes rolled. "You're ridiculous."

"You're beautiful," he replied, brushing his lips over her brow.

"Flattery will get you every—"

His groan interrupted her as she shifted in his lap midsentence, inadvertently rubbing her ass against the hard ridge of his arousal.

A pretty flush crept over her face. Gods, he wanted to capture that blush with paint and commit it to canvas. He wanted to know which colors he'd have to mix to find that lovely shade. The urge reminded him of something as he said, "You were saying?"

"I can't remember what I was saying," she said.

"You are so easily distracted."

"In my defense, the hard cock pressing into my ass *is* really distracting."

Another rough sound came from him.

A sly grin started to tip up her lips, and the scent of her arousal flooded him.

"Stop," he said, "thinking about my dick."

"Perhaps you should stop thinking about it and my ass," she retorted.

He shot her a playful glare. "What you ask is impossible."

Her laugh was soft, and then her lashes swept down, fanning her cheeks. "You know," she began, pressing the swell of her breasts against his chest.

"There are…other things I can do." She wiggled in his lap like the little vixen she was. "I could give you examples."

"I'm fully aware of those examples, *liessa*." His hand dropped to her braid. "You could use your hand. You could even use these." The backs of his fingers brushed the swell of her breasts, and the scent of her arousal increased, spicy and heavy. His voice dropped when his lips coasted over hers. "Your mouth."

Sera's breath caught.

He dragged his fingers farther down her braid. "But I think there is something else we can do instead."

"Hmm?" she murmured.

He could tell her thoughts were still lingering on using her mouth to please him. "Well, more like somewhere we can go."

Sera immediately sat straighter. She would've toppled right out of his lap if he hadn't tightened his arm around her. She didn't even notice as her eyes widened with excitement. "Is it *finally* what I think it is?"

He grinned. "Come." Taking her hand once more, he helped her stand.

Sera was a ball of anticipation where she walked beside him, their progress slow as they made their way to the chamber in the east wing of the third floor. It had slipped both of their minds over the last several months with all that had come after entombing Kolis. He'd meant to show her before this. Something always came up, though.

But not today.

Nothing would stop Nyktos from showing his wife his paintings.

And perhaps, if his Queen was not too tired afterward, he would have her sit for him, and he would know exactly which paints it took to capture the pink in her cheeks and the green and silver in her eyes.

After all, getting her to blush was easy.

Nyktos knew just how.

The Star

The one we watched was neither alive nor dead. Neither god nor mortal, yet risen from Primal blood.

He was something else.

An abomination.

And yet, it was a miracle of creation that even the most jaded had to admire.

There were no others like him, but the realms had whispered that another would come—neither dead nor alive, god nor mortal. An abomination. A miracle. A cruel twist of fate.

The first daughter, with blood full of fire, fated for the once-promised King.

The first Chosen who would fail. Who would be forgotten, just like the ancestor she would so closely resemble. Her failure would signal the eventual arrival of the second daughter, the one born with blood full of ash and ice, the other half of the future King.

So, we did what we always did. We *watched.*

And he walked for days, weeks, and years, his face no longer painted in gold.

He always came back to the same place—where it all began.

The Cliffs of Sorrow.

He never stayed long while sitting on the edge, arms wrapped tightly around the brown leather satchel he always carried with him. The one he didn't open.

He walked as kingdoms fell and new ones rose in their places. He traveled as all the old Primals faded into history, as the one who had created him was forgotten. He continued as new gods rose and their offspring inhabited the mortal realm. He walked the lands east of the Skotos then, staying hidden as the son of Primals helped build the new world. He didn't return to the east after wolves were given dual lives by the true Primal of Life to guide the offspring of mates of the heart. Like with the draken, he was clever enough to suspect that they would sense something off about him. He walked as the pestilence of the most *craven* spread across the mortal realm. He traveled as the War of Two Kings ignited, forcing the great kingdom to the east to near ruin. He continued as Nyktos honored the oath he'd made to the true Primal of Life, and, one by one, the gods went to sleep to prevent vengeance against those who had harmed her child.

The one who walked only stopped when he saw *her*, his hand protectively cradling the leather satchel that had faded from brown to yellow in the centuries that had passed.

We waited.

We waited and watched as he whispered in the new Queen's ear, told her more than what the son of Primals had even spoken of. We watched as heroes became villains and entire histories were rewritten. We wept when the forgotten symbol of true Death was raised throughout the mortal realm, etched in gold and surrounded by crimson. And we saw the day he brought the Crimson Queen to the cliffs and, for the first time, opened the satchel, now a shade of tan, pulling out The Star. We watched as he gave it to the Queen, and she took possession of it with great care.

And we knew that what the realms had first whispered thousands of years ago, even before a Queen ruled Iliseeum, would not be stopped.

And we saw.

Her birth stirred Death from his slumber. Each year that passed, he grew stronger, and those buried even deeper than him in lands across all the realms began to grow restless. We could not look away when her Ascension, at the hands of her fated mate, released Death and woke our brethren in lands beyond the Primal Veil. We wept again as the tallest mountains erupted, spewing forth flames and clouds that consumed all in their path, boiling the rivers and turning seas into deserts as they clawed their way from the ground. We didn't look away when they saw what man had done to their precious land and blessed forests. We mourned as they laid waste to sprawling stone kingdoms and toppled great steel cities in their rage, ending the lives of billions of mortals in one cruel sweep of retribution.

For as told by the last oracle, they had risen as the ruin and wrath of the once-great beginning.

And she, the second daughter, with blood full of ash and ice, fated for the future King, summoned the true Primal of Life and then rose as Blood and Bone.

And what we saw then, as old gods rose and the Primal Veils weakened, shocked even the eldest of us. We saw the future that would come, but this end was different.

It would be a beginning soaked in blood. For every choice—from the moment the first *viktor* sacrificed himself to save the Silver Queen to when Sotoria fell from the cliffs; when Nyktos screamed at the realms and Ascended a mortal to become the Queen of the Gods; the failure of the first daughter and the birth of the second; the desperate love of a mate, to that of a mother's desperation—and every action had been birthed from the same emotion.

Whether it was unrequited or welcomed. Whether it was felt between siblings who never moved past the loss of the other or for one's children before they were even born into the realm. Whether it was forged from unending grief, between true mates of the heart, or drove a mother to plunge a dagger into the heart of her true mate instead of her daughter. It was all the same. Some great. Some terrible. And it had driven the realms to the brink of what was to come.

It was the most selfish and altruistic thing in all the realms, more powerful than the Ancients, and the only thing that could snap the threads of fate. It was the only hope the realms had now.

Love.

DISCOVER MORE JENNIFER L. ARMENTROUT

From Blood and Ash
Blood and Ash Series, Book One
Available in hardcover, e-book, and trade paperback.

Captivating and action-packed, From Blood and Ash is a sexy, addictive, and unexpected fantasy perfect for fans of Sarah J. Maas and Laura Thalassa.

A Maiden…

Chosen from birth to usher in a new era, Poppy's life has never been her own. The life of the Maiden is solitary. Never to be touched. Never to be looked upon. Never to be spoken to. Never to experience pleasure. Waiting for the day of her Ascension, she would rather be with the guards, fighting back the evil that took her family, than preparing to be found worthy by the gods. But the choice has never been hers.

A Duty…

The entire kingdom's future rests on Poppy's shoulders, something she's not even quite sure she wants for herself. Because a Maiden has a heart. And a soul. And longing. And when Hawke, a golden-eyed guard honor bound to ensure her Ascension, enters her life, destiny and duty become tangled with desire and need. He incites her anger, makes her question everything she believes in, and tempts her with the forbidden.

A Kingdom…

Forsaken by the gods and feared by mortals, a fallen kingdom is rising once more, determined to take back what they believe is theirs through violence and vengeance. And as the shadow of those cursed draws closer, the line between what is forbidden and what is right becomes blurred. Poppy is not only on the verge of losing her heart and being found unworthy by the gods, but also her life when every blood-soaked thread that holds her world together begins to unravel.

A Kingdom of Flesh and Fire

Blood and Ash Series, Book Two

Available in hardcover, e-book, and trade paperback.

Is Love Stronger Than Vengeance?

A Betrayal…

Everything Poppy has ever believed in is a lie, including the man she was falling in love with. Thrust among those who see her as a symbol of a monstrous kingdom, she barely knows who she is without the veil of the Maiden. But what she *does* know is that nothing is as dangerous to her as *him.* The Dark One. The Prince of Atlantia. He wants her to fight him, and that's one order she's more than happy to obey. *He may have taken her, but he will never have her.*

A Choice…

Casteel Da'Neer is known by many names and many faces. His lies are as seductive as his touch. His truths as sensual as his bite. Poppy knows better than to trust him. He needs her alive, healthy, and whole to achieve his goals. But he's the only way for her to get what she wants—to find her brother Ian and see for herself if he has become a soulless Ascended. Working with Casteel instead of against him presents its own risks. He still tempts her with every breath, offering up all she's ever wanted. Casteel has plans for her. Ones that could expose her to unimaginable pleasure and unfathomable pain. Plans that will force her to look beyond everything she thought she knew about herself—about him. Plans that could bind their lives together in unexpected ways that neither kingdom is prepared for. And she's far too reckless, too hungry, to resist the temptation.

A Secret…

But unrest has grown in Atlantia as they await the return of their Prince. Whispers of war have become stronger, and Poppy is at the very heart of it all. The King wants to use her to send a message. The Descenters want her dead. The wolven are growing more unpredictable. And as her abilities to feel pain and emotion begin to grow and strengthen, the Atlantians start to fear her. Dark secrets are at play, ones steeped in the blood-drenched sins of two kingdoms that would do anything to keep the truth hidden. But when the earth begins to shake, and the skies start to bleed, it may already be too late.

The Crown of Gilded Bones
Blood and Ash Series, Book Three
Available in hardcover, e-book, and trade paperback.

Bow Before Your Queen Or Bleed Before Her…

She's been the victim and the survivor…

Poppy never dreamed she would find the love she's found with Prince Casteel. She wants to revel in her happiness but first they must free his brother and find hers. It's a dangerous mission and one with far-reaching consequences neither dreamed of. Because Poppy is the Chosen, the Blessed. The true ruler of Atlantia. She carries the blood of the King of Gods within her. By right the crown and the kingdom are hers.

The enemy and the warrior…

Poppy has only ever wanted to control her own life, not the lives of others, but now she must choose to either forsake her birthright or seize the gilded crown and become the Queen of Flesh and Fire. But as the kingdoms' dark sins and blood-drenched secrets finally unravel, a long-forgotten power rises to pose a genuine threat. And they will stop at nothing to ensure that the crown never sits upon Poppy's head.

A lover and heartmate…

But the greatest threat to them and to Atlantia is what awaits in the far west, where the Queen of Blood and Ash has her own plans, ones she has waited hundreds of years to carry out. Poppy and Casteel must consider the impossible—travel to the Lands of the Gods and wake the King himself. And as shocking secrets and the harshest betrayals come to light, and enemies emerge to threaten everything Poppy and Casteel have fought for, they will discover just how far they are willing to go for their people—and each other.

And now she will become Queen…

The War of Two Queens
Blood and Ash Series, Book Four
Available in hardcover, e-book, and trade paperback.

War is only the beginning…

From the desperation of golden crowns…

Casteel Da'Neer knows all too well that very few are as cunning or vicious as the Blood Queen, but no one, not even him, could've prepared for the staggering revelations. The magnitude of what the Blood Queen has done is almost unthinkable.

And born of mortal flesh…

Nothing will stop Poppy from freeing her King and destroying everything the Blood Crown stands for. With the strength of the Primal of Life's guards behind her, and the support of the wolven, Poppy must convince the Atlantian generals to make war her way—because there can be no retreat this time. Not if she has any hope of building a future where both kingdoms can reside in peace.

A great primal power rises…

Together, Poppy and Casteel must embrace traditions old and new to safeguard those they hold dear—to protect those who cannot defend themselves. But war is only the beginning. Ancient primal powers have already stirred, revealing the horror of what began eons ago. To end what the Blood Queen has begun, Poppy might have to become what she has been prophesied to be—what she fears the most.

As the Harbinger of Death and Destruction.

A Soul of Ash and Blood

Blood and Ash Series, Book Five

Available in hardcover, e-book, and trade paperback.

Only his memories can save her…

A great primal power has risen. The Queen of Flesh and Fire has become the Primal of Blood and Bone—the true Primal of Life and Death. And the battle Casteel, Poppy, and their allies have been fighting has only just begun. Gods are awakening across Iliseeum and the mortal realm, readying for the war to come.

But when Poppy falls into stasis, Cas faces the very real possibility that the dire, unexpected consequences of what she is becoming could take her away from him. Cas is given some advice, though—something he plans to cling to as he waits to see her beautiful eyes open once more: Talk to her.

And so, he does. He reminds Poppy how their journey began, revealing things about himself that only Kieran knows in the process. But it's anybody's guess what she'll wake to or exactly how much of the realm and Cas will have changed when she does.

#1 New York Times bestselling author Jennifer L. Armentrout revisits Poppy and Casteel's epic love story in the next installment of the Blood and Ash series. But this time, Hawke gets to tell the tale.

VISIONS OF FLESH AND BLOOD

A Blood and Ash/Flesh and Fire Compendium
Available in hardcover, e-book, and trade paperback.

VISIONS OF FLESH AND BLOOD: a Blood and Ash/Flesh and Fire Compendium is a comprehensive companion guide for background, history, reader-favorite information, art, and reference materials. Combined with original short stories and scenes from some of the world's most beloved characters, as well as never-before-seen visual enticements, it's a treat for the senses.

Told from the point of view of Miss Willa herself, the compendium acts like research material but reads like a journal and cache of personal notes, allowing the reader to revisit the characters and history they so love yet view things in a different way.

VISIONS OF FLESH AND BLOOD by Jennifer L. Armentrout with Rayvn Salvador is a must-add addition to the series that any Blood and Ash/Flesh and Fire fan will enjoy.

ON BEHALF OF BLUE BOX PRESS,

Liz Berry, M.J. Rose, and Jillian Stein would like to thank ~

Steve Berry
Doug Scofield
Benjamin Stein
Kim Guidroz
Chelle Olson
Hang Le
Chris Graham
Tanaka Kangara
Jessica Saunders
Malissa Coy
Jen Fisher
Stacey Tardif
Suzy Baldwin
Grace Wenk
Laura Helseth
Jessica Mobbs
Mona Awad
Vonetta Young
Dylan Stockton
Kate Boggs
Richard Blake
and Simon Lipskar